THE BLADE MUST  ELSE IT WILL BREAK . . .

"Here, pupil. You might as well see this for yourself."

Now that the scroll was in his hands, Raistlin wondered if he had the courage to read it. He hesitated a moment to insure that his hands did not tremble and betray him, then, with outward nonchalance masking inward apprehension, he unrolled the scroll.

He tried to read it, but his nervousness impaired his eye sight. The words would not come into focus. When they did, he did not comprehend them.

The aspiring magus, Raistlin Majere, is hereby summoned to the Tower of High Sorcery at Wayreth to appear before the Conclave of Wizards on the seventh day of the seventh month at the seventh minute of the seventh hour. At this time, in this place, you will be tested by your superiors for inclusion into the ranks of those gifted by the three gods, Solinari, Lunitari, Nuitari.

To be invited to take the Test is a great honor, an honor accorded to few, and should be taken seriously. You may impart knowledge of this honor to members of your immediate family, but to no others. Failure to accede to this injunction could mean the forfeiture of the right to take the Test.

In the unfortunate event of your demise during the Test, all personal effects will be returned to your family.

Amazed and aghast, he stared at his master. "This . . . this can't be right. I am too young."

"That is what I said," Theobald stated in nasty tones. "But I was overruled."

Raistlin read the words again, words that, though they were not in the least magical, began to glow with the radiance of a thousand suns.

RAISTLIN MAJERE WILL BE FORGED BY MAGIC AND BATTLE, INTO MAGE AND MASTER. BUT WHAT WILL SURVIVE OF HIM BEYOND HIS OVERWHELMING AMBITION?

OMNIBUSES

RAISTLIN CHRONICLES

MARGARET WEIS & DON PERRIN

An ambitious young man sacrifices all he has to gain the powers of a wizard.
What happens will change him in ways he never expected.

The Soulforge
Brothers at Arms

DRAGONLANCE CHRONICLES

(July 2010)

MARGARET WEIS & TRACY HICKMAN

A group of friends reunites to save their homeland from the forces of the
Queen of Darkness. But can these disparate men and women come
together to become heroes?

Dragons of Autumn Twilight
Dragons of Winter Night
Dragons of Spring Dawning

THE ELVEN NATIONS

PAUL B. THOMPSON, TONYA C. COOK, AND DOUGLAS NILES

When the proud leader of the Silvanesti elves dies, his twin sons find
themselves locked in a bitter battle for the future of the elves.

Firstborn
The Kinslayer Wars
The Qualinesti

MARGARET WEIS
& DON PERRIN

RAISTLIN
CHRONICLES

THE SOULFORGE
BROTHERS AT ARMS

Raistlin Chronicles Omnibus

©2010 Wizards of the Coast LLC

Published by Wizards of the Coast LLC

DRAGONLANCE, WIZARDS OF THE COAST, and their respective logos are trademarks of Wizards of the Coast LLC in the U.S.A. and other countries.

Printed in the U.S.A.

Cover art by Daniel Horne

The Soulforge originally published April 1998
Brothers at Arms originally published September 1999

This Edition First Printing: March 2010
9 8 7 6 5 4 3 2 1

ISBN: 978-0-7869-5394-3
620-25149000-001-EN

U.S., CANADA,
ASIA, PACIFIC, & LATIN AMERICA
Wizards of the Coast LLC
P.O. Box 707
Renton, WA 98057-0707
+1-800-324-6496

EUROPEAN HEADQUARTERS
Hasbro UK Ltd
Caswell Way
Newport, Gwent NP9 0YH
GREAT BRITAIN
Save this address for your records.

Visit our web site at www.wizards.com

Dedicated with love and friendship to
Tracy Raye Hickman.

ACKNOWLEDGMENTS

This is to gratefully acknowledge the help of the friends of Krynn on the alt.fan.dragonlance newsgroup. They have walked that magic land more recently than I and were able to supply me with invaluable information.

I would like to acknowledge the work of Terry Phillips, whose original Adventure Gamebook, *The Soulforge*, was the inspiration for my story.

THE SOULFORGE

RAISTLIN

CHRONICLES

MARGARET WEIS

FOREWORD

IT'S BEEN OVER TEN YEARS SINCE WE GATHERED IN MY LITTLE APARTMENT for a game session. DRAGONLANCE was known only to a handful of us then, an infant full of promise not yet realized. We were playing the first adventure of what would eventually prove to be a wonderful experience for millions—but on that night, as I recall, we mostly didn't know what we were doing. I was running the game from my own hastily assembled design notes. Both my wife and Margaret were there among a host of others who were struggling to find their characters from the thin shadowy outlines we had given them. Who were these Heroes of the Lance? What were they really like?

We were just settling in to the game when I turned to my good friend Terry Phillips and asked what his character was doing. Terry spoke . . . and the world of Krynn was forever changed. His rasping voice, his sarcasm and bitterness all masking an arrogance and power that never needed to be stated suddenly were real. Everyone in the room was both transfixed and terrified. To this day Margaret swears that Terry wore the black robes to the party that night.

Terry Phillips happened to choose Raistlin for his character and in that fated choice gave birth to one of DRAGONLANCE's most enduring characters. Terry even wrote an Adventure Gamebook on Raistlin's tests which bore the same title as the book you hold in your hands. Krynn—not to mention Margaret and myself—owe no small debt of gratitude to Terry for bringing us Raistlin.

Other characters in DRAGONLANCE may belong to various creators, but Margaret, from the very outset, made it clear to all concerned that Raistlin was hers and hers alone. We never begrudged her the dark mage—she seemed to be the only one who could comfort his character and soothe his troubled mind. The truth is that Raistlin frightened the rest of us into distance. Only Margaret knew how to bridge that abyssal gulf.

Now you hold the story of Raistlin as told by Margaret—the one person who knows him best of all. The journey may not always be comfortable but it will be a worthy one. Margaret has always been a master storyteller. Here, now, is the story that she has longed to tell.

And if Terry is reading this now—wherever he is—I wish him peace.

—Tracy Hickman
October 10, 1997

THE CREATION OF RAISTLIN MAJERE

Margaret Weis

I'M OFTEN ASKED, "WHO'S YOUR FAVORITE CHARACTER?" THIS IS tantamount to asking a mother to name her favorite child! We love our children for themselves, a love individual as each child.

It is true, however, that a writer comes to know and like some characters better than others. Some I know better than I know my own friends and family! The innermost recesses we hide from the world are clearly visible to our Creator. Playing God with my characters, I see their weaknesses, their strengths, their inner doubts and turmoil, and their dark and secret parts. Raistlin Majere was such a character.

When I first met Raistlin, he was a name on a Character Sheet. I knew his "stats," developed for the DRAGONLANCE roleplaying game. I knew he was a third-level mage in his early twenties. I knew he was slight in build, wore red robes, and that he was known among his friends as "The Sly One." I knew he had a strong, well-built, powerful twin brother named Caramon. But he was just one of a number of characters—Tanis, Sturm, Flint, Tasslehoff—until I read the passage that said Raistlin had "golden skin and hourglass eyes."

"Why does he have golden skin and hourglass eyes?" I asked, puzzled.

"Because the artists think he would look cool!" was the reply.

This intrigued me. I had to know the reason Raistlin had golden skin and hourglass eyes. In trying to solve this mystery, I was led to an understanding of the true nature of Raistlin's character.

That he would be jealous of his good-looking, stronger twin brother was a natural feeling to which every person who has ever grown up with a sibling could relate. That he was not generally trusted or well liked by his peers was obvious. If his friends called him "The Sly One," what would his enemies term him? Naturally he would be the target of bullies, which would lead his brother to protect him. It seemed to me that Raistlin would grow dependent on his brother for such protection, but that he would, at the same time, resent Caramon for it. Thus Raistlin would constantly struggle against a love as smothering as it was nurturing.

The fact that Raistlin was of slight build and physically weaker than his brother seemed to indicate a sickly youth, which might also be indicative of an introspective nature, particularly if he was forced to spend time cooped up in a sickbed. Such a childhood would have contributed to his feeling of alienation from his peers but would later give him empathy for others in like circumstances.

That Raistlin would turn to the study of magic was again obvious. Of course, it would be his elder half-sister, the restless and ambitious Kitiara, who would lead his thoughts in that direction. In a rough and dangerous world her younger brother lacked physical strength to wield a weapon. He needed some way to defend himself. Magic was the answer, especially since he already showed some talent in that area. Raistlin soon came to realize that magic was also the means by which he could gain power and ascendancy over others.

All very intriguing, but it didn't explain the golden skin and hourglass eyes. Certainly he wasn't born with them. His twin brother and his elder half-sister were perfectly normal-looking humans. Perhaps his study of magic had caused this transformation. He must have had to take a test to prove his abilities to the wizards who lived in the Towers of High Sorcery.

What sort of magical test would they give young wizards? A difficult test, probably extremely difficult. Otherwise anyone with a bit of talent could declare himself a wizard. What if the Test required that a mage stake his or her very life on the outcome? And what if something happened during the Test that caused Raistlin's skin to acquire a golden tinge and to give him eyes that would see the ravages of time upon all living things? Thus the Test in the Tower of High Sorcery came into existence. It was during that Test that Raistlin had the fateful meeting with the lich, Fistandantilus.

I became so fascinated with Raistlin that I wrote a short story about his journey to the Tower to take the Test. I also came to know a lot about Caramon on that trip. I saw Caramon's great inner goodness that to his friends would seem a weakness but that in the end would be the rock on which he would build a successful and happy life.

I'm still learning about Raistlin. With every book I write about him and his twin and their adventures in the world, I discover something new. Raistlin is, and continues to be, a favorite of all the many different characters it has been my privilege and my joy to know.

—Margaret Weis
August 1998

4

THE ALLOYS PRODUCED BY EARLY IRON WORKERS . . . were made by heating a mass of iron ore and charcoal in a forge or furnace having a forced draft. Under this treatment, the ore was reduced to the sponge of metallic iron filled with a slag composed of metallic impurities and charcoal ash. This sponge of iron was removed from the furnace while still incandescent and beaten with heavy sledges to drive out the slag and to weld and consolidate the iron. . . . Occasionally this technique of iron making produced, by accident, a true steel . . .[1]

---

1 "Steel Production" Microsoft® Encarta® Encyclopedia, 1993-1995.

BOOK 1

A mage's soul is forged in the crucible of the magic.

—Antimodes of the White Robes

1

HE NEVER WORE HIS WHITE ROBES WHILE TRAVELING. Few mages did, in those days, the days before the great and terrible War of the Lance spilled out of its cauldron like boiling oil and scalded the countryside. In those days, just fifteen or so years before the war, the fire beneath the pot had been lit, the Dark Queen and her minions had struck the sparks that would start the blaze. The oil was cool, black, and sluggish in the cauldron. But at the bottom, the oil was beginning to simmer.

Most people on Ansalon would never see the cauldron, much less the bubbling oil inside, until it was poured on their heads, along with dragonfire and the countless other horrors of war. At this time of relative peace, the majority of people living on Ansalon never looked up, never looked from side to side to see what was going on in the world around them. Instead, they gazed at their own feet, plodding through the dusty day, and if they ever lifted their heads, it was usually to see if it was likely to rain and spoil their picnic.

A few felt the heat of the newly kindled fire. A few had been watching closely the turgid black liquid in the cauldron. Now they could see that it was starting to simmer. These few were uneasy. These few began to make plans.

The wizard's name was Antimodes. He was human, of good middle-class merchant stock, hailing from Port Balifor. The youngest of three, he had been raised in the family business, which was tailoring. To this day, he still displayed with pride the scars of the pinpricks on the middle finger of his right hand. His early experience left him with a canny business sense and a taste for, and knowledge of, fine clothing, one reason he rarely wore his white robes.

Some mages were afraid to wear their robes, which were a symbol of their calling, because that calling was not well loved in Ansalon. Antimodes was not afraid. He did not wear his white robes because white showed the dirt. He detested arriving at his destination mud-splattered, the stains of the road upon him.

He traveled alone, which in those uneasy days meant that he was either a fool, a kender, or an extremely powerful person. Antimodes was not a fool, nor was he a kender. He traveled alone because he preferred his own company and that of his donkey, Jenny, to that of almost all others of his acquaintance. Hired bodyguards were generally loutish and dull, not to mention expensive. Antimodes could adequately and handily defend himself, should need arise.

The need had rarely arisen, in all his fifty-plus years. Thieves look for prey that is timid, cowering, drunk, or heedless. Though his finely made dark blue woolen cloak with its silver clasps showed him to be a man of wealth, Antimodes wore that cloak with an air of confidence, riding with his back straight on his daintily stepping donkey, his head held high, his sharp-eyed gaze taking notice of every squirrel in the trees, every toad in the ruts.

He displayed no weapon, but his long sleeves and tall leather boots could easily conceal a poignard; the bags that dangled from his hand-tooled leather belt almost certainly contained spell components. Every thief worth his lock-picking tools recognized that the ivory case Antimodes wore on a leather thong looped around his chest contained magical scrolls. Shadowy figures lurking in the hedgerows slunk out of his way and waited for likelier victims.

Antimodes was journeying to the Tower of High Sorcery in Wayreth. He was taking the long way around, for he could have easily walked the corridors of magic in order to reach the tower from his home in Port Balifor. He had been requested to make the journey overland. The request had come from Par-Salian, head of the Order of White Robes and head of the Wizards' Conclave, and therefore, strictly speaking, Antimodes's master. The two were fast friends, however, their friendship dating back to the day when both were young and had arrived at the Tower at the same time to take the exacting, grueling, and occasionally lethal test. Both had been kept waiting in the same antechamber in the tower, each had shared his trepidation and fear with the other, each had found much-needed comfort, consolation, and support. The two White Robes had been friends ever since.

Thus Par-Salian "requested" that Antimodes take this long and tiresome journey. The head of the conclave did not order it, as he might have done with another.

Antimodes was to accomplish two goals during his journey. First, he was to peer into every dark corner, eavesdrop on every whispered conversation, peep through the shutters of every window that was locked and bolted. Second, he was to look for new talent. The first was a bit dangerous; people do not take kindly to snoops, especially if said people have something to hide. The second was tedious and boring, for it generally meant dealing with children, and Antimodes had an aversion to children. All in all, Antimodes preferred the spying.

He had written his report in his neat and precise tailor's handwriting in a journal, which he would turn over to Par-Salian. Antimodes reread in his mind every word in that journal as he trotted along on his white donkey, a present from his eldest brother, who had taken over the family business and was now a prosperous tailor in Port Balifor. Antimodes spent his time on the road pondering all he had seen and heard—nothing significant, everything portentous.

"Par-Salian will find this interesting reading," Antimodes told Jenny, who gave her head a shake and pricked her ears to indicate her agreement. "I look forward to handing the journal over," her master continued. "He will read it and ask questions, and I will explain what I have seen and heard, all the while drinking his most excellent elven wine. And you, my dear, will have oats for dinner."

Jenny gave her hearty approval. In some places in which they'd stayed, she'd been forced to eat damp, moldy hay or worse. Once she'd actually been offered potato peelings.

The two had nearly reached their journey's end. Within the month, Antimodes would arrive at the Tower of High Sorcery in Wayreth. Or, rather, the tower would arrive at Antimodes. One never found the magical Tower of Wayreth. It found you, or not, as its master chose.

This night Antimodes would spend in the town of Solace. He might have pushed on, for the season was late spring, and it was only noon, with plenty of daylight left for travel. But he was fond of Solace, fond of its famous inn, the Inn of the Last Home, fond of Otik Sandath, the inn's owner, and especially fond of the inn's ale. Antimodes had been tasting that chilled dark ale with its creamy head in his imagination ever since he had swallowed his first mouthful of road dust.

His arrival in Solace went unnoticed, unlike his arrival in other towns in Ansalon, where every stranger was taken to be a thief or plague-carrier, a murderer or kidnapper of children. Solace was a different town than most on Ansalon. It was a town of refugees, who had fled for their lives during the Cataclysm and had only stopped running when they came to this location. Having once been strangers on the road themselves, the founders of Solace took a kindly view toward other strangers, and this attitude had been passed down to their descendants. Solace had become known as a haven for outcasts, loners, the restless, the adventuresome.

The inhabitants were friendly and tolerant—up to a point. Lawlessness was known to be bad for business, and Solace was a town with a sharp eye for business.

Being located on a bustling road that was the major route from northern Ansalon to all points south, Solace was accustomed to entertaining travelers, but that was not the reason few noticed the arrival of Antimodes. The main reason was that most of the people of Solace never saw him, due to the fact that they were high above him. The major portion of the town of Solace was built in the vast, spreading, gigantic branches of the immense and wondrous vallenwood trees.

The early inhabitants of Solace had literally taken to the trees to escape their enemies. Having found living among the treetops to be safe and secure, they had built their homes among the leaves, and their descendants and those who came after them had continued the tradition.

Craning his neck, Antimodes looked up from the donkey's back to the wooden plank bridges that extended from tree to tree, watching the bridges swing and sway as the villagers hastened across on various errands. Antimodes was a dapper man, with an eye for the ladies, and though the women of Solace kept their flowing skirts firmly in hand when crossing the bridges, there was always the possibility of catching a glimpse of a shapely ankle or a well-turned leg.

Antimodes's attention to this pleasant occupation was interrupted when he heard sounds of shrill yelling. He lowered his gaze to find that he and Jenny had been overtaken by a brigade of bare-legged, sunburned boys armed with wooden swords and tree-branch spears and giving battle to an army of imaginary foes.

The boys had not meant to run down Antimodes. The swirl of battle had carried them in his direction; the invisible goblins or ogres or whatever enemy the boys chased were in full retreat toward Crystalmir Lake. Caught up in the shouting, yelling, sword-thwacking melee, Antimodes's donkey, Jenny, shied and danced, wild-eyed with fright.

A mage's mount is not a war-horse. A mage's mount is not trained to gallop into the noise and blood and confusion of battle or to face spears without flinching. At most, a mage's mount must accustom herself to a few foul-smelling spell components and an occasional lightning show. Jenny was a placid donkey, strong and hale, with an uncanny knack for avoiding ruts and loose stones, providing her rider with a smooth and comfortable journey. Jenny considered that she'd put up with a great deal on this trip: bad food, leaky accommodations, dubious stablemates. An army of stick-wielding boys was simply too much to bear.

By the twitch of her long ears and the baring of her yellow teeth, Jenny was obviously prepared to strike back by bucking and kicking at the boys, which would have probably not damaged the boys much but would certainly dislodge her rider. Antimodes endeavored to control the donkey, but he was not having any luck. The younger boys, maddened with battle lust, did not see the man's distress. They swirled about him, lashing out with their swords, shrieking and crowing in shrill triumph. Antimodes might well have entered Solace on his posterior, when, out of the dust and noise, an older boy—perhaps about eight or nine—appeared, caught hold of Jenny's reins, and, with a gentle touch and forceful presence, calmed the terrified donkey.

"Go around!" the youth ordered, waving his sword, which he had shifted to his left hand. "Clear out, fellows! You're frightening the donkey."

The younger boys, ranging in age from six upward, good-naturedly obeyed the youth and continued on their rowdy way. Their shouts and laughter echoed among the enormous trunks of the vallenwood trees.

The older boy paused and, with an accent that was definitely not of this part of Ansalon, spoke his apology as he soothingly stroked the donkey's soft nose. "Forgive us, good sir. We were caught up in our play and did not notice your arrival. I trust you have taken no harm."

The young man had straight, thick blond hair, which he wore bowl-cropped around his ears in a style that was popular in Solamnia, but nowhere else on Krynn. His eyes were gray-blue, and he had a stem and serious demeanor that belied his years, a noble bearing of which he was extremely conscious. His speech was polished and educated. This was no country bumpkin, no laborer's son.

"Thank you, young sir," Antimodes replied. He carefully took stock of his spell components, checking to make certain that the buffeting he had taken had not loosened any of his pouches he wore on his belt. He was about to ask the young man's name, for he found himself interested in this youth, but, on looking up, he found the young man's blue eyes fixed upon the pouches. The expression on the youthful face was one of disdain, disapproval.

"If you are certain you are well, Sir Mage, and have taken no harm from our play, I will take my leave." The youth made a stiff and rigid bow and, letting loose the donkey's halter, turned to run after the other boys. "Coming, Kit?" he called brusquely to another older boy, who had halted to study the stranger with interest.

"In a minute, Sturm," said the other youth, and it was only when she spoke that Antimodes realized this curly-haired boy, wearing pants and a leather vest, was actually a girl.

She was an attractive girl—now that he studied her closely—or perhaps he should say "young lady," for though only in her early teens, her figure was well defined, her movements were graceful, and her gaze was bold and unwavering. She studied Antimodes in her turn, regarding him with an intense, thoughtful interest that he found difficult to understand. He was accustomed to meeting with disdain and dislike, but the young woman's interest was not idle curiosity. Her gaze held no antipathy. It seemed as if she were making up her mind about something.

Antimodes was old-fashioned in his attitude toward women. He liked them soft and perfumed, loving and gentle, with blushing cheeks and properly downcast eyes. He realized that in this day of powerful female wizards and strong female warriors his attitude was backward, but he was comfortable with it. He frowned slightly to indicate his own disapproval of this young hoyden and clucked at Jenny, urging her in the direction of the public stables, located near the blacksmith's shop. The stables, the blacksmith's, and the baker's shop, with its immense ovens, were three of the few buildings in Solace situated on the ground.

Even as Antimodes passed by the young woman, he could feel her brown-eyed gaze focused on him, wondering, considering.

2

NTIMODES SAW TO IT THAT JENNY WAS COMFORTABLY ESTABLISHED, WITH an extra measure of feed and a promise from the stableboy to provide the donkey with extra attention, all paid for, of course, in good Krynn steel, which he laid out with a lavish hand.

This done, the archmage took the nearest staircase leading up to the bridge walks. The stairs were many, and he was hot and out of breath by the time he finished the climb. The shadows of the vallenwoods' thick foliage cooled him, however, providing a shady canopy under which to walk. After a moment's pause to catch his breath, Antimodes followed the suspended walkway that led toward the Inn of the Last Home.

On his way, he passed numerous small houses perched high in the tree branches. House designs varied in Solace, for each had to conform to the tree in which it stood. By law, no part of the living vallenwood could be cut or burned or in any other way molested. Every house used the broad trunk for at least one wall, while the branches formed the ceiling beams. The floors were not level, and there was a noticeable rocking motion to the houses during windstorms. Such irregularities were considered charming by the inhabitants of Solace. They would have driven Antimodes crazy.

The Inn of the Last Home was the largest structure in Solace. Standing some forty feet above ground level, it was built around the bole of a massive vallenwood, which formed part of the Inn's interior. A veritable thicket of timbers supported the inn from beneath. The common room and the kitchen were on the lowest level. Sleeping rooms were perched above and could be reached by a separate entrance; those requiring privacy were not forced to traipse through the common room.

The inn's windows were made of multicolored stained glass, which, according to local legend, had been shipped all the way from Palanthas. The stained glass was an excellent advertisement for the business; the colors glinting in the shadows of the leaves caused the eye to turn in that direction, when otherwise the inn might have been hidden among the foliage.

Antimodes had eaten a light breakfast, and he was therefore hungry enough to do full justice to the proprietor's renowned cooking. The climb up the stairs had further sharpened Antimodes's appetite, as did the smells wafting from the kitchen. Upon entering, the archmage was greeted by Otik himself, a rotund, cheerful middle-aged man, who immediately remembered Antimodes, though the mage had not been a guest in perhaps two years or more.

"Welcome, friend, welcome," Otik said, bowing and bobbing his head as he did to all customers, gentry or peasant. His apron was snow-white, not grease-stained as with some innkeepers. The inn itself was as clean as Otik's apron. When the barmaids weren't serving customers, they were sweeping or scouring or polishing the lovely wooden bar, which was actually part of the living vallenwood.

Antimodes expressed his pleasure in returning to the inn. Otik proved he remembered his guest by taking Antimodes to his favorite table near one of the windows, a table that provided an excellent view, through green-colored glass, of Crystalmir Lake. Without being asked, Otik brought a mug of chilled dark ale and placed it before Antimodes.

"I recall how you said you enjoyed my dark ale last time you were here, sir," Otik remarked.

"Indeed, Innkeep, I have never tasted its like," Antimodes replied. He also noted the way Otik carefully kept from making any reference to the fact that Antimodes was a user of magic, a delicacy Antimodes appreciated, though he himself scorned to hide who or what he was from anyone.

"I will take a room for the night, with luncheon and dinner," said Antimodes, bringing out his purse, which was well stocked but not indecently full.

Otik replied that rooms were available, Antimodes should have his pick, they would be honored by his presence. Luncheon today was a casserole of thirteen different types of beans simmered with herbs and ham. Dinner was pounded beef and the spiced potatoes for which the inn was famous.

Otik waited anxiously to hear his guest say that the bill of fare was perfectly satisfactory. Then, beaming, the barkeep bustled fussily off to deal with the myriad chores involved in running the inn.

Antimodes relaxed and glanced about at the other customers. It being rather past the usual luncheon hour, the inn was relatively empty. Travelers were upstairs in their rooms, sleeping off the good meal. Laborers had returned to their jobs, business owners were drowsing over their account books, mothers were putting children down for afternoon naps. A dwarf—a hill dwarf, by the looks of him—was the inn's only other customer.

A hill dwarf who was no longer living in the hills, a hill dwarf living among humans in Solace. Doing quite well, to judge by his clothes, which consisted of a fine homespun shirt, good leather breeches, and the leather apron of his trade. He was not more than middle-aged; there were only a few streaks of gray in his nut-brown beard. The lines on his face were uncommonly deep and dark for a dwarf of his years. His life had been a hard one and had left its mark. His brown eyes were warmer than the eyes of those of his brethren who did not live among humans and who seemed to constantly be peering out from behind high barricades.

Catching the dwarf's bright eye, Antimodes raised his ale mug. "I note by your tools that you are a metal worker. May Reorx guide your hammer, sir," he said, speaking in dwarven.

The dwarf gave a nod of gratification and, raising his own mug, said, speaking in Common, "A straight road and a dry one, traveler," in gruff return.

Antimodes did not offer to share his table with the dwarf, nor did the dwarf seem inclined to have company. Antimodes looked out the window, admiring the view and enjoying the pleasant warmth seeping through his body, a refreshing contrast to the cool ale that was soothing his dust-parched throat. Antimodes's assigned duty was to eavesdrop on any and all conversation, and so he listened idly to the conversations of the dwarf and the barmaid, though it did not appear to him that they were discussing anything sinister or out of the ordinary.

"Here you go, Flint," said the barmaid, plunking down a steaming bowl of beans. "Extra portion, and the bread's included. We have to get you fattened up. I take it you'll be leaving us soon?"

"Aye, lass. The roads are opening up. I'm behind time as it is, but I am waiting for Tanis to return from visiting his kin in Qualinesti. He was supposed to be back a fortnight ago, but still no sign of his ugly face."

"I hope he's all right," the barmaid said fondly. "I don't trust them elves, and that's a fact. I hear he doesn't get on with his kin."

"He's like a man with a bad tooth," the dwarf grumbled, though Antimodes could detect a note of anxiety in the dwarf's gruff tone. "He has to keep wiggling it to make sure it still hurts. Tanis goes home knowing that his fine elf relatives can't stand the sight of him, but he keeps hoping maybe this time matters will be different. But no. The blasted tooth's just as rotten as it was the first time he touched it, and it's not going to get better till he yanks it out and has done with it."

The dwarf had worked himself up into red-faced indignation by this time, topping off his harangue with the somewhat incongruous statement of, "And us with customers waiting." He took a swig of ale.

"You've no call to call him ugly," said the barmaid with a simper. "Tanis looks like a human. You can't hardly see any elf in him at all. I'll be glad to see him again. Let him know I asked about him, will you, Flint?"

"Yes, yes. You and every other female in town," the dwarf returned, but he muttered the words into his beard, and the barmaid, who was heading back to the kitchen, did not hear him.

A dwarf and a half-elf who were business partners, Antimodes noted, making deductions about what he'd heard. A half-elf who had been banished from Qualinesti. No, that wasn't right. A banished half-elf could not go back home. This one had done so. He'd left his elven homeland voluntarily, then. Not surprising. The Qualinesti were more liberal-minded about racial purity than their cousins, the Silvanesti, but a half-elf was half-human in their eyes and, as such, tainted goods.

So the half-elf had left his home, come to Solace, and joined up with a hill dwarf, who had himself probably either left his thane and his clan or had been cast out. Antimodes wondered how the two had met, guessed it must be an interesting story.

It was a story he was not likely to hear. The dwarf had settled down to shoveling beans into his mouth. Antimodes's own plate arrived, and he gave the meal his full attention, which it well deserved.

He had just finished and was sopping up the last bit of gravy with his last bite of bread when the door to the inn opened. Otik was there to greet the new guest. The innkeeper appeared nonplussed to find a young woman, the same curly-haired young woman Antimodes had met earlier on the road. "Kitiara!" Otik exclaimed. "Whatever are you doing here, child? Running an errand for your mother?"

The young woman cast him a glance from her dark eyes that might have sizzled his flesh. "Your potatoes have more brains than you do, Otik. I run errands for no one."

She shoved past him. Her glance swept the common room and fixed on Antimodes, much to his astonishment and annoyance.

"I've come to speak to one of your guests," the young woman announced.

She ignored Otik's fluttering, "Now, now, Kitiara. I'm not sure you should be bothering the gentleman." Kit strode up to Antimodes, stood beside his table, gazed down on him.

"You're a wizard, aren't you?" she asked.

Antimodes indicated his displeasure by not rising to greet her as he would have done to any other female. Expecting either to be made sport of or perhaps propositioned by this ill-mannered hoyden, he set his face in stern lines of disapproval.

"What I am is my own affair, young lady," he said with sardonic emphasis on the last word. He shifted his gaze deliberately out the window, indicating that the conversation was ended.

"Kitiara . . ." Otik hovered anxiously. "This gentleman is my guest. And this is really not the time or the place to . . ."

The young woman put her brown hands on the table and leaned over it. Antimodes was now starting to be truly angered by this intrusion. He shifted his attention back to her, noting as he did so—he would have been less than human if he had not noticed—the curve of her full breasts beneath the leather vest.

"I know someone who wants to become a wizard," she said. Her voice was serious and intense. "I want to help him, but I don't know how. I don't know what to do." Her hand lifted in a gesture of frustration. "Where do I go? Who do I talk to? You can tell me."

If the inn had suddenly shifted in its branches and dumped Antimodes out the window, he could not have been more astonished. This was highly irregular! This simply wasn't done! There were proper channels. . . .

"My dear young woman," he began.

"Please." Kitiara leaned nearer.

Her eyes were liquid brown, framed by long, black, thick lashes. Her eyebrows were dark and delicately arched to frame the eyes. Her skin was tanned by the sun; she'd led an outdoor life. She was well muscled, lithe, and had grown through the awkwardness of girlhood to attain the grace, not of a woman, but of a stalking cat. She drew him to her, and he went willingly, though he was old enough and experienced enough to know that she would not permit him to come too close. She would allow few men to warm themselves at her inner fire, and the gods help those who did.

"Kitiara, leave the gentleman to his dinner." Otik touched the girl's arm.

Kitiara rounded on him. She did not speak, she merely looked at him. Otik shrank back.

"It is all right, Master Sandath." Antimodes was quick to intervene. He was fond of Otik and did not want to cause the innkeeper trouble. The dwarf, who had finished his dinner, was now taking an interest, as were two of the barmaids. "The young . . . um . . . lady and I have some business to transact. Please, be seated, mistress."

He rose slightly and made a bow. The young woman slid into the chair opposite. The barmaid whisked over to clear the plates—and to try to satisfy her curiosity.

"Will there be anything else?" she asked Antimodes.

He looked politely at his young guest. "Will you have something?"

"No, thanks," said Kitiara shortly. "Be about your business, Rita. If we need anything, we'll call."

The barmaid, offended, flounced off. Otik cast Antimodes a helpless, apologizing glance. Antimodes smiled, to indicate he wasn't the least concerned, and Otik, with a shrug of his fat shoulders and, wringing his pudgy hands, walked distractedly away. Fortunately the arrival of additional guests gave the innkeeper something to do.

Kitiara settled down to business with a serious intensity that drew Antimodes's approval.

"Who is this person?" he asked.

"My little brother. Half-brother," she amended as an afterthought.

Antimodes recalled the scathing look she'd given Otik when he mentioned her mother. No love lost there, the archmage guessed.

"How old is the child?"

"Six."

"And how do you know he wants to study magic?" Antimodes asked. He thought he knew the answer. He'd heard it often.

He loves to dress up and play wizard. He's so cute. You should see him toss dust into the air and pretend he's casting a spell. Of course, we assume it's a stage he's going through. We don't really approve. No offense, sir, but it's not the sort of life we had in mind for our boy. Now, if you could talk to him and tell him how difficult . . .

"He does tricks," said the girl.

"Tricks?" Antimodes frowned. "What sort of tricks?"

"You know. Tricks. He can pull a coin out of your nose. He can throw a rock into the air and make it disappear. He can cut a scarf in two with a knife and give it back good as new."

"Sleight-of-hand," said Antimodes. "You realize, of course, that this is not magic."

"Of course!" Kitiara scoffed. "What do you think I am? Some yokel? My father—my real father—took me to see a battle once, and there was a wizard who did some true magic. War magic. My father's a Solamnic knight," she added with naive pride that made her suddenly seem a little girl.

Antimodes didn't believe her, at least the part about her father being a Solamnic knight. What would the daughter of a Solamnic knight be doing running around like a street urchin in Solace? He could well believe that this tomboy was interested in military matters. More than once, her right hand had rested on her left hip, as if she were either accustomed to wearing a sword or accustomed to pretending that she wore one.

Her gaze went past Antimodes, out the window, and kept going. In that gaze was yearning, longing for distant lands, for adventure, for an end to the boredom that was probably about to stifle her. He was not surprised when she said, "Look, sir, I'm going to be leaving here sometime soon, and my little brothers will have to fend for themselves when I'm gone."

"Caramon will be all right," Kitiara continued, still gazing out at the smoky hills and the distant blue water. "He's got the makings of a true warrior. I've taught him all I know, and the rest he'll pick up as he goes along."

She might have been a grizzled veteran, speaking of a new recruit, rather than a thirteen-year-old girl talking of a little snot-nosed kid. Antimodes almost laughed, but she was so serious, so earnest, that instead he found himself watching and listening to her with fascination.

"But I worry about Raistlin," Kitiara said, her brows drawing together in puzzlement. "He's not like the others. He's not like me. I don't understand him. I've tried to teach him to fight, but he's sickly. He can't keep up with the other children. He gets tired easily and he runs out of breath."

Her gaze shifted to Antimodes. "I have to leave," she said for the second time. "But before I go, I want to know that Raistlin is going to be able to take care of himself, that he'll have some way to earn his living. I've been thinking that if he could study to be a wizard, then I wouldn't have to worry."

"How old . . . how old did you say this boy was?" Antimodes asked.

"Six," said Kitiara.

"But . . . what about his parents? Your parents? Surely they . . ."

He stopped because the young woman was no longer listening to him. She was wearing that look of extreme patience young people put on when their elders are being particularly tedious and boring. Before Antimodes could finish, she had twisted to her feet.

"I'll go find him. You should meet him."

"My dear . . ." Antimodes started to protest. He had enjoyed his conversation with this interesting and attractive young person, but the thought of entertaining a six-year-old was extremely unwelcome.

The girl ignored his protests. She was out the door of the inn before he could stop her. He saw her running lightly down the stairs, rudely shoving or bumping into anyone who stood in her way.

Antimodes was in a quandary. He didn't want to have this child thrust upon him. Now that she was gone, he didn't want to have anything more to do with the young woman. She had unsettled him, given him an uneasy feeling, like the aftereffects of too much wine. It had been fine going down, but now he had a headache.

Antimodes called for his bill. He would beat a hasty retreat to his room, though he realized with annoyance that he would be held a virtual prisoner there during the rest of his stay. Looking up, he saw the dwarf, whose name he recalled was Flint, looking back.

The dwarf had a smile on his face.

Most likely Flint was not thinking at all about Antimodes. The dwarf may have been smiling to himself over the delicious meal he had just enjoyed, or he may have been smiling at the taste of the ale, or just smiling over the pleasantness of the world in general. But Antimodes, with his customary self-importance, decided that Flint was smirking at him and the fact that he, a powerful wizard, was going to run away from two children.

Antimodes determined then and there that he would not give the dwarf any such satisfaction. The archmage would not be driven out of this pleasant common room. He would remain, rid himself of the girl, deal quickly with the child, and that would be an end of it.

"Perhaps you would care to join me, sir," Antimodes said to the dwarf.

Flint glowered and flushed red and ducked his head into his ale. He muttered something about rather having his beard boiled before he'd share a table with a wizard.

Antimodes smiled coldly to himself. Dwarves were notorious for their distrust and dislike of wielders of magic. The archmage was now certain that the dwarf would leave him alone. Indeed, Flint quaffed his ale in a hurry and, tossing a coin on the table, gave Antimodes a curt nod and stumped out of the inn.

And here, on the dwarf's heels, came the girl, hauling along not one child but two.

Antimodes sighed and ordered a glass of Otik's finest two-year old mead. He had a feeling he was going to need something potent.

3

THE ENCOUNTER WAS LIKELY TO PROVE MORE UNPLEASANT THAN Antimodes had feared. One of the boys, the one Antimodes assumed was the elder, was an attractive child, or would have been had he not been so extremely dirty. He was sturdily built, with thick arms and legs, had a genial, open face and a gap-toothed smile, and he regarded Antimodes with friendly interest and curiosity, not in the least intimidated by the well-dressed stranger.

"Hullo, sir. Are you a wizard? Kit says you're a wizard. Could you do some sort of trick? My twin can do tricks. Would you like to see him? Raist, do the one where you take the coin out of your nose and—"

"Shut up, Caramon," said the other child in a soft voice, adding, with a frowning glance, "You're being foolish."

The boy took this good-naturedly. He chuckled and shrugged, but he kept quiet. Antimodes was startled to hear the two were twins. He examined the other boy, the one who did tricks. This child was not in the least attractive, being thin as a wraith, grubby, and shabbily dressed, with bare legs and bare feet and the peculiar and distasteful odor that only small and sweaty children emit. His brown hair was long, matted, and needed washing.

Antimodes regarded both children intently, and made a few deductions.

No loving mother doted over these boys. No loving hands combed that tangled hair, no loving tongue scolded them to wash behind their ears. They did not have the whipped and hangdog air of beaten children, but they were certainly neglected.

"What is your name?" Antimodes asked.

"Raistlin," replied the boy.

He had one mark in his favor. He looked directly at Antimodes while speaking. The one thing Antimodes detested most about small children was their habit of staring down at their feet or the floor or looking anywhere except at him, as though they expected him to pounce on them and eat them. This boy kept his pale blue eyes level with those of the adult, held them fixed and unwavering on the archmage.

These blue eyes gave nothing, expected nothing. They held too much knowledge. They had seen too much in their six years—too much sorrow, too much pain. They had looked beneath the bed and discovered that there really were monsters lurking in the shadows.

So, young man, I bet you'd like to be a mage when you grow up!

That was Antimodes's standard, banal line in these circumstances. He had just sense enough *not* to say it. Not to say it to those knowing eyes.

The archmage felt a tingling at the back of his neck. He recognized it—the touch of the fingers of the god.

Tamping down his excitement, Antimodes spoke to the older sister. "I'd like to talk to your brother alone. Perhaps you and his twin could—"

"Sure," said Kitiara immediately. "C'mon, Caramon."

"Not without Raistlin," Caramon said promptly.

"Come on, Caramon!" Kitiara repeated impatiently. Grasping him by the arm, she gave him a yank.

Even then, the boy held back from his sister's strong and impatient tug. Caramon was a solid child. It seemed unlikely that his sister would be able to budge him without resorting to a block and tackle. He looked at Antimodes.

"We're twins, sir. We do everything together."

Antimodes glanced at the weaker twin to see how he was taking this. Raistlin's cheeks were faintly flushed; he was embarrassed, but he seemed also smugly pleased. Antimodes felt a slight chill. The boy's pleasure in his brother's show of loyalty and affection was not that of one sibling's pleasure in the love of another. It was more like the pleasure a man takes in exhibiting the talents of a well-loved dog.

"Go on, Caramon," Raistlin said. "Perhaps he'll teach me some new tricks. I'll show them to you after supper tonight."

Caramon looked uncertain. Raistlin cast his brother a glance from beneath the thatch of lank, uncombed hair. That glance was an order. Caramon lowered his eyes, then, suddenly cheerful again, he grabbed hold of his sister's hand.

"I hear Sturm's found a badger hole. He's going to try to whistle the badger out. Do you think he can do it, Kit?"

"What do I care?" she asked crossly, Walking off, she smacked Caramon a blow on the back of his head. "Next time do as I tell you. Do you hear me? What kind of soldier are you going to make if you don't know how to obey my orders?"

"I'll obey orders, Kit," said Caramon, wincing and rubbing his scalp. "But you told me to leave Raistlin. You know I've got to watch out for him."

Antimodes heard their voices arguing all the way down the stairs.

He looked back at the boy. "Please sit down," he said.

Silently Raistlin slid into the chair opposite the mage. He was small for his age, his feet did not reach the floor. He sat perfectly still. He didn't fidget or jitter. He didn't swing his legs or kick at the legs of the chair. He clasped his hands together on the table and stared at Antimodes.

"Would you like something to eat or drink? As my guest, of course," Antimodes added.

Raistlin shook his head. Though the child was filthy and dressed like a beggar, he wasn't starving, Certainly his twin appeared well fed. Someone saw to it that they had food on the table. As for the boy's excessive thinness, Antimodes guessed that it was the result of a fire burning deep down in the inner recesses of the child's being, a fire that consumed food before it could nourish the body, a fire that left the child with a perpetual hunger he did not yet understand.

Again Antimodes felt the sanctifying touch of the god.

"Your sister tells me, Raistlin, that you would like to go to school to study to be a mage," Antimodes began, by way of introducing the topic.

Raistlin hesitated a moment, then said, "Yes, I suppose so."

"You suppose so?" Antimodes repeated sharply, disappointed. "Don't you know what you want?"

"I never thought about it," Raistlin replied, shrugging his thin shoulders in a gesture remarkably similar to that of his more robust twin. "About going to school, I mean. I didn't even know there were schools to study magic. I just thought magic was a . . . a"— he searched for the phrase—"a part of you. Like eyes or toes."

The fingers of the god hammered on Antimodes's soul. But he needed more information. He had to be sure.

"Tell me, Raistlin, is anyone in your family a mage? I'm not prying," Antimodes explained, seeing a pained expression contort the child's face. "It's just that we've found that the art is most often transmitted through the blood."

Raistlin licked his lips. His gaze dropped, fixed on his hands. The fingers, slender and agile for one so young, curled inward, "My mother," he said in a flat voice. "She sees things. Things far away. She sees other parts of the world. She watches what the elves are doing and the dwarves beneath the mountain."

"She's a seer," said Antimodes.

Raistlin shrugged again. "Most people think she's crazy." He lifted his gaze in defiance, ready to defend his mother. When he found Antimodes regarding him with sympathy, the boy relaxed and the words flowed out, as if a vein were cut open.

"She forgets to eat sometimes. Well, not forgets exactly. It's like she's eating somewhere else. And she doesn't do work around the house, but that's because she's not really in the house. She's visiting wonderful places, seeing wonderful, beautiful things. I know," Raistlin continued, "because when she comes back, she's sad. As if she didn't want to come back. She looks at us like she doesn't know us sometimes."

"Does she talk about what she's seen?" Antimodes asked gently.

"To me, a little," the boy answered. "But not much. It makes my father unhappy, and my sister . . . well, you've seen Kit. She doesn't have any patience with what she calls Mother's 'fits.' So I can't blame Mother for leaving us," Raistlin continued, his voice so soft that Antimodes had to lean forward to hear the child. "I'd go with her if I could. And we'd never come back here. Never."

Antimodes sipped his drink, using the mead as an excuse to keep silent until he had regained control of his anger. It was an old story. one he'd seen time and again. This poor woman was no different from countless others. She had been born with the art, but her talent was denied, probably ridiculed, certainly discouraged by family members who thought all magic-users were demon spawn. Instead of receiving the training and discipline that would have taught her how to use the art to her benefit and that of others, she was stifled, smothered. What had been a gift had become a curse. If she were not already insane, she soon would be.

There was no longer a chance to save her. There was yet a chance to save her son. "What work does your father do?" Antimodes asked.

"He's a woodcutter," Raistlin answered. Now that they had shifted topics, he was more at ease. His hands flattened on the table. "He's big, like Caramon. My father works really hard. We don't see him much." The child didn't appear overly distressed by this fact.

He was silent a moment, then said, his brow furrowed with the seriousness of his thought process, "This school. It isn't far away, is it? I mean, I wouldn't like to leave Mother for very long. And then there's Caramon. Like he said, we're twins. We take care of each other."

I'm going to be leaving sometime soon, the sister had said. *My little brothers will have to fend for themselves when I'm gone.*

Antimodes clasped hands with the god, gave Solinari's hand a deal-clinching shake. "There is a school quite close by. It is located about five miles to the west in a secluded wood. Most people have no idea it is even there. Five miles is not a long walk for a grown man, but it is quite a hike for a small boy, back and forth every day. Many students board there, especially those who come from distant parts of Ansalon. It would be my suggestion that you do the same. The school is only in session eight months out of the year. The master takes the summer months off to spend at the Tower of Wayreth. You could be with your family during that time. I would have to talk to your father, though. He is the one who must enroll you. Do you think he will approve?"

"Father won't care," Raistlin said. "He'll be relieved, I think. He's afraid that I'll end up like Mother." The child's pale cheeks were suddenly stained red. "Unless it costs a lot of money. Then I couldn't do it."

"As to the money."—Antimodes had already made up his mind on that point—"we wizards take care of our own."

The child didn't quite understand this. "It couldn't be charity," Raistlin said. "Father wouldn't like that at all."

"It's not charity," Antimodes said briskly. "We have funds set aside for deserving students. We help pay their tuition and other expenses. Can I meet with your father tonight? I could explain this to him then."

"Yes, he should be home tonight. The job's almost finished. I'll bring him here. It's hard for people to find our house sometimes after dark," Raistlin said apologetically.

Of course it is, Antimodes said silently, his heart wrenched with pity. A sad, unhappy, slovenly kept house, a lonely house. It hides among the shadows and guards its dark secret.

The child was so thin, so weak. A good strong gust of wind would flatten his frail frame. Magic might well be the shield that would protect this fragile person, become the staff upon which he could lean when he was weak or weary. Or the magic might become a monster, sucking the life from the thin body, leaving a dry, desiccated husk. Antimodes might well be starting this boy on the path that would lead to an early death.

"Why do you stare at me?" the child asked curiously.

Antimodes gestured for Raistlin to leave his chair and come stand directly in front of him. Reaching out, Antimodes took hold of the boy's hands. The youngster flinched and started to squirm away.

He doesn't like to be touched, Antimodes realized, but he maintained his hold on the boy. He wanted to emphasize his words with his flesh, his muscle, his bone. He wanted the boy to feel the words as well as hear them.

"Listen to me, Raistlin," Antimodes said, and the boy quieted and held still. He realized that this conversation was not that of an adult talking down to a child. It was one equal speaking to another. "The magic will not solve your problems. It will only add to them. The magic will not make people like you. It will increase their distrust. The magic will not ease your pain. It will twist and burn inside you until sometimes you think that even death would be preferable."

Antimodes paused, holding fast to the child's hands that were hot and dry, as if he were running a fever. The archmage was ranging about mentally for a means of explanation this young boy might understand. The distant ringing tap of the blacksmith's shop, rising up from the street below, provided the metaphor.

"A mage's soul is forged in the crucible of the magic," Antimodes said. "You choose to go voluntarily into the fire. The blaze might well destroy you. But if you survive, every blow of the hammer will serve to shape your being. Every drop of water wrung from you will temper and strengthen your soul. Do you understand?"

"I understand," said the boy.

"Do you have any question for me, Raistlin?" Antimodes asked, tightening his grip. "Any question at all?"

The boy hesitated, considering. He was not reluctant to speak. He was wondering how to phrase his need.

"My father says that before mages can work their magic, they are taken to a dark and horrible place where they must fight terrible monsters. My father says that sometimes the mages die in that place. Is that true?"

"The Tower is really quite a lovely place, once you become accustomed to it," said Antimodes. He paused, choosing his words carefully. He would not lie to the child, but some things were beyond the understanding of even this precocious six-year-old. "When a mage is older, much older than you are now, Raistlin, he or she goes to the Tower of High Sorcery and there takes a test. And, yes, sometimes the mage dies. The power a mage wields is very great. Any who are not able to control it or to commit their very lives to it would not be wanted in our order."

The boy looked very solemn, his eyes wide and pale. Antimodes gave the hands a squeeze, the boy a reassuring smile. "But that will be a long, long time from now, Raistlin. A long, long time. I don't want to frighten you. I just want you to know what you face."

"Yes, sir," said Raistlin quietly. "I understand."

Antimodes released the boy's hands. Raistlin took an involuntary step backward and, probably unconsciously, put his hands behind his back.

"And now, Raistlin," said Antimodes, "I have a question for you. Why do you want to become a mage?"

Raistlin's blue eyes flared. "I like the feeling of the magic inside me. And"—he glanced at Otik, bustling about the counter; Raistlin's thin lips parted in a pallid smile—"and someday fat innkeepers will bow to me."

Antimodes, taken aback, looked at the child to see if he were joking. Raistlin was not.

The hand of the god on Antimodes's shoulder suddenly trembled.

4

A MONTH LATER TO THE NIGHT, ANTIMODES WAS COMFORTABLY ensconced in the elegant chambers of Par-Salian of the White Robes, head of the Conclave of Wizards.

The two men were very different and probably would not have been friends under ordinary circumstances. Both were about the same age, in their fifties. Antimodes was a man of the world, however. Par-Salian was a man of books. Antimodes liked to travel, he had a head for business, he was fond of good ale, pretty women, comfortable inns. He was nosy and inquisitive, fussy in his dress and his habits.

Par-Salian was a scholar, whose knowledge of the art of magic was undeniably the most extensive of any wizard then living upon Krynn. He abhorred travel, had little use for other people, and was known to have loved only one woman, a misguided affair that he regretted to this day. He took little care of his personal appearance or physical comfort. If absorbed in his studies, he often forgot to come to meals.

It was the responsibility of some of the apprentice magic-users to see to it that their master took sustenance, which they did by surreptitiously sliding a loaf of bread beneath his arm as he read. He would then absentmindedly munch on it. The apprentices often joked among themselves that they could have substituted a loaf of sawdust for the bread and Par-Salian would have never known the difference. They held him in such awe and reverence, however, that none dared try the experiment.

This night, Par-Salian was entertaining his old friend, and therefore he had left poring over his books, though not without a pang of regret. Antimodes had brought as a gift several scrolls of dark magic, which the archmage had acquired by chance on his travels. One of their black-robed sisters, an evil wizardess, had been slain by a mob. Antimodes had arrived too late to save the wizardess, which he would have at least made a halfhearted attempt to do, all mages being bound together by their magic, no matter to which god or goddess they pledged their allegiance.

He was, however, able to persuade the townspeople, a set of superstitious louts, to allow him to remove the wizardess's personal effects before the mob set fire to her house. Antimodes had brought the scrolls to his friend, Par-Salian. Antimodes had kept for himself an amulet of summoning undead spirits. He could not and would not have used the amulet—the undead were a smelly, disgusting lot, as far as he was concerned. But he intended to offer it in trade to some of his black-robed brethren in the tower.

Despite the fact that Par-Salian was of the White Robes, completely dedicated to the god Solinari, he was able to read and understand the scrolls of the evil wizardess, though at some pain to himself. He was one of the very few wizards ever who had the power to cross allegiances. He would never make use of them, but he could take note of the words used to perform the spell, the effects of the spell, the components needed to cast it, the spell's duration, and any other interesting information he came across. His research would be recorded in the annals of the Tower of Wayreth. The scrolls themselves would then be deposited in the tower's library, with an assigned valuation.

"A terrible way to die," said Par-Salian, pouring his guest a glass of elven wine, nicely chilled and sweet, with just a hint of woodbine, which reminded the drinker of green forests and sunlit glens. "Did you know her?"

"Esmilla? No." Antimodes shook his head. "And you could say that she asked for it. The mundane will overlook the snatching of a child or two, but start passing bad coins and they—"

"Oh, come now, my dear Antimodes!" Par-Salian looked shocked. He was not noted for his sense of humor. "You're joking, I think."

"Well, perhaps I am." Antimodes grinned and sipped his wine.

"Yet I see what you mean." Par-Salian struck the arm of his high-backed wooden chair in impatience. "Why do these fool mages insist on wasting their skills and talents in order to produce a few poor quality coins, which every shopkeeper between here and the minotaur islands can tell are magicked? It just doesn't make any sense to me."

Antimodes agreed. "Considering the effort one expends on producing only two or three steel coins, a mage could do manual labor for less effort and make far more. If our late sister had continued to sell her services to rid the town of rats, as she had been doing for years, she would no doubt have been left in peace. As it was, the magically created coins threw everyone into a panic. First, most people believed that they were cursed and were terrified to touch them. Those who didn't think the money was cursed feared that she was about to start minting coins at a rate to rival the Lord of Palanthas and would soon own the town and everything in it."

"It is precisely for this reason that we have established rules about the reproduction of coins of the realm," said Par-Salian. "Every young mage tries it once. I did and I'm sure you probably did yourself."

Antimodes nodded and shrugged.

"But most of us learn that it simply isn't worth the time and effort, not to mention the serious impact we could have on Ansalon's various economies. This woman was certainly old enough to know better. What was she thinking?"

"Who knows? Gone a bit daft, maybe. Or just greedy. She angered her god, however. Nuitari abandoned her to her fate. Whatever defensive spells she tried to cast fizzled."

"He is not one to permit the frivolous use of his gifts," said Par-Salian in stern and solemn tones.

Antimodes shifted his chair a bit nearer the fire that crackled on the hearth. He always felt extremely close to the gods of magic when visiting the Tower of High Sorcery—close to all the gods of magic, the light, the gray, and the dark. This closeness was uncomfortable, as if someone was always breathing down the back of his neck, and was the main reason Antimodes did not live in the tower but chose to reside in the outside world, no matter how dangerous it might be for magic-users. He was glad to change the subject.

"Speaking of children . . ." Antimodes began.

"Were we?" Par-Salian asked, smiling.

"Of course. I said something about snatching children."

"Ah, yes. I remember. Very well, then, we were speaking of children. What have you to say about them? I thought you didn't like them."

"I don't, as a rule, but I met a rather interesting youngster on my trip here. He's one to take note of, I think. In fact, I believe three already have." Antimodes glanced outside the window toward the night sky, where shone two of the three moons sacred to the gods of magic. He nodded his head knowingly.

Par-Salian appeared interested. "The child has innate gifts? Did you test him? How old is he?"

"About six. And, no. I was staying at the inn in Solace. It wasn't the time or the place, and I've never put much stock in those silly tests anyway. Any clever child could pass them. No, it was what the boy had to say and how he said it that impressed me. Scared me, too, I don't mind telling you. There's more than a bit of cold-blooded ambition in that boy. Frightening in one so young. Of course, that could come from his background. The family is not well off."

"What did you do with him?"

"Enrolled him with Master Theobald. Yes, I know. Theobald is not the Conclave's greatest teacher. He's plodding and unimaginative, prejudiced and old-fashioned, but the boy will get a good, solid grounding in the basics and strict discipline, which won't hurt him. He's been running wild, I gather. Raised by an older half-sister, who is something special in her own right."

"Theobald is expensive," said Par-Salian. "You implied the boy's family was poor."

"I paid for his first semester." Antimodes waved away any acknowledgment that he'd done something laudable. "The family must never know, mind you. I made up some tale about the tower having established funds for deserving students."

"Not a bad idea," said Par-Salian thoughtfully. "And one we might well put into practice, especially now that we're seeing some of the unreasoning prejudice against our kind starting to die off. Unfortunately, fools like Esmilla keep putting us in a bad light. Still, I believe that people are in general more tolerant. They're starting to appreciate what we do for them. You travel abroad openly and safely, my friend. You could not have done so forty years ago."

"True," Antimodes admitted, "although I believe that in general the world is altogether a darker place these days. I ran into a new religious order in Haven. They worship a god known as Belzor, and it sounds very much to me as if they're planning on cooking and serving up that same old tripe we heard from the Kingpriest of Istar before the gods—bless their hearts—dropped a mountain on him."

"Indeed? You must tell me about it." Par-Salian settled back more comfortably in his chair. Taking a leather-bound book from the table at his side, he opened it to a blank page, dated it, and prepared to write. They were about to get down to the important business of the evening.

The main part of Antimodes's job was to report on the political situation of the continent of Ansalon, which, as was nearly always the case, was done up in a confused and tangled knot. This included the new religious order, which was discussed and summarily dismissed.

"A charismatic leader out of Haven," Antimodes reported. "He has only a few followers and promises the usual assortment of miracles, including healing. I didn't get a chance to see him, but from what I heard he is probably a rather highly skilled illusionist with some practical knowledge of herb lore. He's not doing anything in the way of healing that the Druids haven't been practicing for years, but it's all new to the people of Abanasinia. Someday we may have to expose him, but he's not doing any harm at the moment and is, in fact, doing some good. I'd recommend that we not start trouble. It would look very bad for us. Public sympathy would be all on his side."

"I quite agree." Par-Salian nodded and made a brief note in his book. "What about the elves? Did you go through Qualinesti?"

"Only the outskirts. They were polite, but they wouldn't permit me to go farther. Nothing's changed with them in the last five hundred years, and provided the rest of the world leaves them alone, nothing will change. As for the Silvanesti, they are, as far as we know, hiding out in their magical woods under the leadership of Lorac. I'm not telling you anything you don't already know, however," Antimodes added, pouring himself another glass of elven wine. The topic had reminded him of the excellence of its taste. "You must have had a chance to talk to some of their mages."

Par-Salian shook his head. "They came to the Tower this winter, but only on business, and then they were close-lipped and spoke to us humans only when absolutely necessary. They would not share their magic with us, though they were quite happy to use ours."

"Do they have anything we would want?" Antimodes asked with a faintly amused smile.

"So far as scrollwork, no," Par-Salian replied. "It is shocking how stagnant the Silvanesti have become. Not surprising, considering their terrible distrust and fear of change of any sort. The only creative mind they have among them belongs to a young mage known as Dalamar, and I'm certain that as soon as they discover what he's been dabbling in, they'll throw him out on his pointed ear. As to their top White Robes, they were quite eager to obtain some of the new work being done on evocation spells, particularly those of a defensive nature."

"They wanted to pay in gold, which is worthless these days. I had to be quite firm and insist on either hard steel, which, of course, they don't have, or barter. Then they wanted to palm off on me some moldy magical spells that were considered old-fashioned in my father's day. In the end, I agreed to trade for spell components; they grow some quite lovely and unusual plants in Silvanesti, and their jewelry is exquisite. They traded and left, and I haven't seen them since. I wonder if they're not facing some threat in Silvanesti or if they've divined that some threat is approaching. Their king, Lorac, is a powerful mage and something of a seer."

"If they are, we'll never know about it," Antimodes said. "They would rather see their people wiped out before they would lower themselves to ask any of us for help."

He sniffed. He hadn't any use at all for the Silvanesti, whose white-robed wizards were part of the Conclave of Wizards, but who made it clear that they considered this a tremendous condescension on their part. They did not like humans and indicated their dislike in various ways, such as pretending they could not speak Common, the language of all races on Krynn, or turning away in contempt when any human dared to desecrate the elven language by speaking it. Incredibly long-lived, the elves saw change as something to be feared. The humans, with their shorter life spans, more frenetic lives, and constant need to "improve," represented everything the elves abhorred. The Silvanesti elves hadn't had a creative idea in their heads in the last two thousand years.

"The Qualinesti elves, on the other hand, keep a close watch on their borders, but they do permit people of other races to enter, provided they have permission from the Speaker of the Sun and Stars," Antimodes went on. "Dwarven and human metalsmiths are highly regarded and encouraged to visit—though not to stay—and their own elven artisans do occasion-ally travel to other lands. Unfortunately, they frequently meet with much prejudice and hatred."

Antimodes knew and liked many of the Qualinesti and was sorry to see them misused. "Several of their young people, particularly the eldest son of the speaker—what's his name?"

"The speaker? Solostaran."

"No, the eldest son."

"Ah, you must mean Porthios."

"Yes, Porthios. He's said to be thinking that the Silvanesti have the right idea and that no human should enter Qualinesti land."

"You can't really blame him, considering the terrible things that happened when the humans entered Qualinesti land after the Cataclysm. But I don't think we need worry. They'll bicker over this for the next century unless something pushes them one way or the other."

"Indeed." Antimodes had noted a subtle change in Par-Salian's voice. "You think something is likely to push them?"

"I've heard rumblings," said Par-Salian. "Distant thunder."

"I haven't heard thunder," Antimodes said. "The few Black Robes I meet these days are a little too smooth. They act as if bat guano wouldn't ignite in their hands."

"A few of the more powerful have quietly dropped out of sight," said Par-Salian.

"Who's that?"

"Well, Dracart, for one. He used to stop by on a regular basis to see what new artifacts had come in and to check on possible apprentices. But the only wizards of the Black who have come by lately have been those of low ranking, who wouldn't be invited to share the secrets of their elders. And even they seem a bit edgy."

"I take it, then, you have not seen the fair Ladonna," Antimodes said with a sly wink.

Par-Salian smiled faintly and shrugged. That fire had died years ago, and he was too old and too absorbed in his work to be either pleased or annoyed by his friend's teasing.

"No, I have not spoken to Ladonna this past year, and what is more, I believe that whatever she is doing she is deliberately hiding from me. She refused to attend a meeting of the heads of the orders, something which she's never done before. She sent a representative in her name—a man who said exactly three words the entire time and those were 'pass the salt.' " Par-Salian shook his head. "Queen Takhisis has been quiet too long. Something's up."

"All we can do is watch and wait, my friend, and be prepared to act when necessary." Antimodes paused, sipped his elven wine. "One bit of good news I have is that the Solamnic knights are finally beginning to pull themselves together. Many have reclaimed their family estates and are rebuilding their holdings. Their new leader, Lord Gunthar, is a keen politician who has the ability to think with his head, not his helmet. He's endeared himself to the local populace by cleaning out a few goblin strongholds, mopping up some bandits, and sponsoring jousts and tourneys in various parts of Solamnia. Nothing the rabble likes more than to see grown men hammer on each other."

Par-Salian looked grave, even alarmed. "I don't consider this good news, Antimodes. The knights have no love for us. If they stop at hunting goblins, that is one thing, but you can be certain that it will be only a matter of time before they add sorcerers to their list of enemies, as they did in the old days. Such is even written into the Measure."

"You should meet with Lord Gunthar," Antimodes suggested, and he was amused to see Par-Salian's white eyebrows nearly shoot off his head. "No, I'm quite in earnest. I'm not suggesting you should invite him here, but—"

"I should think not," Par-Salian said stiffly.

"But you should make a trip to Solamnia. Visit him. Assure him that we have only the good of Solamnia in mind."

"How can I assure him of that when he could point out, with considerable justification, that many in our order do not have the good of Solamnia in mind? The knights distrust magic, they distrust us, all of us, and I must tell you that I'm not particularly inclined to trust them. It seems to me wise and prudent to keep out of their way, to do nothing to draw attention to ourselves."

"Magius was the friend of Huma," prodded Antimodes.

"And if I recall the legend correctly, Huma was not greatly respected by his fellow knights for that very reason," Par-Salian returned dryly. "What news of Thorbardin?" He changed subject abruptly, indicating that the matter was closed.

Antimodes was diplomatic enough not to continue to press the issue, but he decided privately that he would visit Solamnia, perhaps on the way back, though that would mean going a considerable distance out of his way to the north. He was as curious as a kender about the Solamnic knights, who had long been held in disrespect and even antipathy by people who had once looked upon the knighthood as law-givers and protectors. Now it appeared as if the knighthood was regaining something of its old standing.

Antimodes was eager to see this for himself, eager to see if somehow he might be able to profit from it. He would not mention this junket to Par-Salian, of course. The Black Robes were not the only members of the conclave to keep their doings secret.

"The dwarves of Thorbardin are still in Thorbardin, we presume, mainly because no one has seen them leave. They are completely self-sufficient, with no reason to take any interest in the rest of the world, and I really don't see why they should. The hill dwarves are expanding their territory, and many are starting to travel to other lands. Some are even taking up residence outside their mountain homelands." Antimodes thought of the dwarf he'd met in Solace.

"As to the gnomes, they are like the dwarves of Thorbardin, with one exception—we assume the gnomes still reside in Mount Nevermind because no one has seen it explode yet. The kender appear to be more prolific than ever; they go everywhere, see everything, steal most of it, misplace the rest, and are of no use whatsoever."

"Oh, I think they are of use," said Par-Salian earnestly. He was known to be fond of kender, mainly so (Antimodes always said sourly) because he remained isolated in his tower and never had dealings with them. "Kender are the true innocents of this world. They remind us that we spend a great deal of time and energy worrying about things that are really not very important."

Antimodes grunted. "And so when may we expect to see you abandon your books, grab a hoopak, and take off down the road?"

Par-Salian smiled back. "Don't think I haven't considered it, my friend.

I believe I would be a deft hand at hoopak flinging, if it came to that. I was quite skilled with a slingshot when I was a child. Ah, well, the evening grows long." This was his signal to end the meeting. "Will I see you in the morning?" he asked with a faint anxiety, which Antimodes understood.

"I would not dream of interfering in your work, my friend," he answered. "I will have a look through the artifacts and scrolls and the spell components, especially if you have some elven merchandise. There's one or two things I want to pick up. Then I'll be on my way."

"You are the one who would make a good kender," said Par-Salian, rising in his turn. "You never stay in one place long enough for the dust to settle on your shoes. Where do you go from here?"

"Oh, round and about," Antimodes said lightly. "I'm in no hurry to return home. My brother is capable of running the business quite well without me, and I've made arrangements for my earnings to be invested, so that I make money even when I'm not there. Much easier and far more profitable than chanting spells over a lump of iron are. Good night, my friend."

"Good night and safe journeying," Par-Salian said, taking his friend by the hand and giving it a hearty shake. He paused a moment, tightened his grasp.

"Be careful, Antimodes. I don't like the signs. I don't like the portents. The sun shines on us now, but I see the tips of dark wings casting long shadows. Continue sending me your reports. I value them highly."

"I will be careful," said Antimodes, a little troubled by his friend's earnest appeal.

Antimodes was well aware that Par-Salian had not told all he knew. The head of the conclave was not only adept at seeing into the future, he was also known to be a favorite of Solinari, the god of white magic. Dark wings. What could he possibly mean by that? The Queen of Darkness, dear old Takhisis? Gone but not forgotten. Not dare forgotten by those who studied the past, by those who knew of what evil she was capable.

Dark wings. Vultures? Eagles? Symbols of war? Griffins, pegasi? Magical beasts, not seen much these days. Dragons?

Paladine help us!

All the more reason, Antimodes determined, why I should find out what's happening in Solarnnia. He was heading out the door when Par-Salian again stopped him. "That young pupil . . . the one of whom you spoke. What was his name?" It took Antimodes a moment to shift his thoughts to this different tack, another moment to try to remember.

"Raistlin. Raistlin Majere."

Par-Salian made a note of it in his book.

5

I T WAS EARLY MORNING IN SOLACE, VERY EARLY. The sun had not yet dawned
when the twins awoke in their small home that lurked in the shadows of
a vallenwood. With its ill-fitting shutters, shabby curtains, and straggling,
half-dead plants, the house looked nearly as forlorn and neglected as the
children who inhabited it.

Their father—Gilon Majere, a big man with a broad and cheerful face,
a face whose natural placidity was marred by a worry line between his
brows—had not come home that night. He had traveled far from Solace
on a job for a lord with an estate on Crystalmir Lake. Their mother was
awake, but she had been awake since midnight.

Rosamun sat in her rocking chair, a skein of wool in her thin hands. She
would wind the wool into a tight ball, tear it apart, and then rewind it. All
the while she worked, she sang to herself in an eerie low-pitched voice or
sometimes paused to hold conversations with people who were not visible
to anyone except her.

If her husband—a gentle, caring man—had been at home, he would
have persuaded her to leave off her "knitting" and go to bed. Once in bed,
she would continue to sing, would be up again in an hour.

Rosamun had her good days, her lucid periods, when she was cognizant
of much of what was going on around her, if not particularly interested
in participating in it. The daughter of a wealthy merchant, she had
always relied on servants to do her bidding. Now they could not afford
servants, and Rosamun was inept at running a household herself. If she
was hungry, she might cook something. There might be enough left
over for the rest of the family, provided she didn't forget about the food

completely and leave it to burn in the kettle.

When she fancied she was doing the mending, she would sit in her chair with a basket of torn clothes in her lap and stare out the window. Or she might put her worn cloak about her shoulders and go "visiting," wandering the shaded walkways to call on one of their neighbors, who generally kept an eye out for her and managed to be gone when Rosamun rang the bell. She had been known to forget where she was and would stay in someone's house for hours until her sons found her and fetched her home.

Sometimes she would recall stories about her first husband, Gregor uth Matar, a rogue and a rake, of whom she was stupidly proud and still loved, though he had abandoned her years before.

"Gregor was a Solamnic knight," she was saying, talking to her unseen listeners. "And he did so love me. He was the most handsome man in Palanthas, and all the girls were mad about him. But he chose me. He brought me roses, and he sang songs beneath my window and took me riding on his black horse. He is dead now. I know it. He is dead now, or he would have come back to me. He died a hero, you know."

Gregor uth Matar had been declared dead, at any rate. No one had seen or heard from him in seven years, and most believed that if he wasn't decently dead he should have been. His loss was not generally mourned. He might well have been a knight of Solamnia, but if so he had been banished from that strict order years ago. It was known that he, his new wife, and their baby daughter had left Palanthas by night and in a hurry. Rumor followed him from Solamnia to Solace, whispering that he had committed murder and had escaped the hangman only by means of money and a fast horse.

He was darkly handsome. Wit and charm made him a welcome companion in any tavern, as did his courage—not even his enemies could fault him on that—and his willingness to drink, gamble, and fight. Rosamun spoke truly about one of his traits. Women adored him.

An avowed fragile beauty, with auburn hair, eyes the color of a summer forest, and silken white skin, Rosamun had been the one to conquer him. He had fallen in love with her with all of his passionate nature, had remained in love with her longer than might have been expected. But when love died, it could never, for him, be rekindled.

They had lived well in Solace. Gregor made periodic journeys back to Solamnia, whenever money was running low. His highly placed family apparently paid him well to keep out of their lives. Then came the year he returned empty-handed. Rumor held it that Gregor's family had finally cut him off. His creditors pressing him hard, he traveled north to Sanction to sell his sword to whoever would have him. He continued to do so, coming back home at intervals but never staying long. Rosamun was wildly jealous, accused him of leaving her for other women. Their quarrels could be heard throughout most of Solace.

And then one day Gregor left and never returned. Rumor agreed that he was probably dead, either from a sword thrust in front or, more likely, a knife in the back.

One person did not believe him to be dead. Kitiara lived for the day when she would be able to leave Solace and set out in search of her father.

She talked of this as she did what she could, in her impatient way, to ready her little brother for his journey to his new school. Raistlin's few clothes—a couple of shirts, some trousers, and some oft-mended stockings—were done up in a bundle, along with a thick cloak for the winter.

"I'll be gone by spring," Kit was saying. "This place is too stupid for words." She lined her brothers up for inspection. "What do you think you're doing? You can't go to school dressed like that!"

Grabbing Raistlin, she pointed at his bare and dusty feet. "You have to wear shoes."

"In the summer?" Caramon was stunned.

"Mine don't fit me," Raistlin said. He'd had a small growth spurt that spring. He was now as tall as his twin, if only about half his weight and a quarter of his girth.

"Here. Wear these." Kit hunted out a pair of Caramon's old shoes from last winter and tossed them at Raistlin.

"They'll pinch my toes," he protested, regarding them glumly.

"Wear them," Kit ordered. "All the other boys in the school wear shoes, don't they? Only peasants go barefoot. That's what my father says."

Raistlin made no reply. He slid his feet into the worn shoes.

Picking up a dirty dishcloth, Kit dipped it in the water bucket and scrubbed Raistlin's face and ears so vigorously that he was certain at least half his skin must be missing.

Squirming free of his sister's grasp, Raistlin saw that Rosamun dropped her ball of wool on the floor. Her beauty had faded, like a rainbow fades when the storm clouds overtake the sun. Her hair was drab and lusterless, her eyes had too bright a luster, the luster of fever or madness. Her pale skin had a gray cast to it. She stared vaguely at her empty hands, as if she were wondering what to do with them. Caramon picked up the wool, handed it to her.

"Here, Mother."

"Thank you, child." She turned her vacant gaze to him. "Gregor's dead, do you know that, child?"

"Yes, Mother," Caramon said, not really hearing her.

Rosamun would often make incongruous statements like this. Her children were used to them and generally ignored them. But this morning Kitiara rounded on her mother in sudden fury. "He's *not* dead! What do you know? He never cared for you! Don't say things like that, you crazy old witch!"

Rosamun smiled and twined her wool and sang to herself. Her boys stood nearby, quiet, unhappy. Kit's words hurt them far more than they hurt Rosamun, who wasn't paying the slightest attention to her daughter.

"He's *not* dead! I know it and I'm going to find him!" Kitiara declared, her vow low and fervent.

"How do you know he's alive?" Caramon asked. "And if he is, how will you find him? I've heard there are lots of people in Solamnia. Even more than here in Solace."

"I'll find him," Kit replied confidently. "He told me how." She gazed at them speculatively. "Look, this is probably the last time you'll see me for a long while. Come here. I'll show you something if you promise not to tell."

Leading them into the small room where she slept, she produced from her mattress a crudely crafted, handmade leather pouch. "In here. This is my fortune."

"Money?" Caramon asked, brightening.

"No!" Kitiara scoffed at the notion. "Something better than money. My birthright."

"Let me see!" Caramon begged.

Kitiara refused. "I promised my father I would never show it to anyone. At least not yet. Someday, though, you will see it. When I come back rich and powerful and riding at the head of my armies, then you will see it."

"We'll be part of your army, won't we, Kit?" Caramon said. "Raist and me."

"You'll be captains, both of you. I'll be your commander, of course," Kit said matter-of-factly.

"I'd like being a captain." Caramon was enthusiastic. "What about you, Raist?"

Raistlin shrugged. "I don't care." After another lingering glance at the pouch, he said quietly, "We should leave now. I'll be late."

Kit eyed them, her hands on her hips. "You'll do, I suppose. You come straight back home, Caramon, after you drop Raistlin off. No hanging about the school. You two have to get used to being separated."

"Sure, Kit." It was now Caramon's turn to be glum.

Raistlin went to his mother, took her by the hand. "Good-bye, Mother," he said with a catch in his voice.

"Good-bye, dear," she said. "Don't forget to cover your head when it's damp."

And that was his blessing. Raistlin had endeavored to explain to his mother where he was going, but she had been completely unable to comprehend. "Studying magic? Whatever for? Don't be silly, child."

Raistlin had given up. He and Caramon left the house just as the sun was gilding the tips of the vallenwood leaves.

"I'm glad Kit didn't want to come with us. I have something to tell you," Caramon said in a loud whisper. He glanced back fearfully to see if his sister was watching them. The door slammed shut. Her duty for the morning done, Kitiara was going back to bed.

The children took the tree walkways as far as they could. Then, when the rope bridges came to an end, the twins ran down a long staircase to reach the forest floor. A narrow road, little more than two wheel ruts and a hard-baked footpath, led in the direction they were going.

The boys ate hunks of stale bread, which they had torn off a loaf that had been left out on the table.

"Look, there's blue stuff on this bread," Caramon noted, pausing between bites.

"It's mold," said Raistlin.

"Oh." Caramon ate the bread, mold and all, observing that it "wasn't bad, just sort of bitter."

Raistlin carefully removed the part of the bread with the mold. He studied the mold intently, then slipped the piece inside a pouch he carried with him everywhere. By the end of the day, that pouch would be filled with various specimens of plant and animal life. He spent his evenings studying them.

"It's a long walk to the school," Caramon stated, his bare feet scuffing up the dirt on the road. "Almost five miles, Father says. And once you get there, you have to sit at a desk all day and not move, and they don't let you go outside or nothing. Are you sure you're going to like that, Raist?"

Raistlin had seen the interior of the school only once. It consisted of a large room, with no windows, so that there were no outside distractions. The floor was stone. The desks stood high off the stone floor, so that the winter cold would not chill their feet. The students sat on tall stools. Shelves containing jars with various herbs and other things in them that ranged from the horrible and disgusting to the pleasant or mysterious lined the walls. These jars held the spell components. Other shelves held scroll cases.

Most of the scrolls were blank, meant for the students to write upon. But some were not.

Raistlin thought of this quiet, dark room, the peaceful hours spent in study with no distractions from unruly brothers, and he smiled. "I won't mind it," he said.

Caramon had picked up a stick, was slashing about with it, pretending it was a sword. "I wouldn't want to go there. I know that. And that teacher. He has a face like a frog. He looks mean. Do you think he'll whip you?"

The teacher, Master Theobald, had indeed looked mean. Not only that, but their first meeting proved him to be haughty, self-important, and probably less intelligent than the majority of his pupils. Unable to gain their respect, he would almost certainly resort to physical intimidation. Raistlin had seen the long willow branch standing in a prominent place beside the master's desk.

"If he does," Raistlin said, thinking of what Antimodes had told him, "it will be just another blow of the hammer."

"You think he'll hit you with a hammer?" Caramon demanded, horrified. He halted in the middle of the road. "You shouldn't go to that place, Raist."

"No, that's not what I meant, Caramon," Raistlin said, trying to be patient with his twin's ignorance. After all, the statement had been somewhat bizarre. "I'll try to explain. You fight with a stick now, but someday you'll own a sword, a real sword, won't you?"

"You bet. Kit's going to bring me one. She'll bring you one, too, if you ask her."

"I already have a sword, Caramon," Raistlin said. "Not a sword like yours. Not one made of metal. This sword is inside me. It's not a very good weapon right now. It needs to be hammered into shape. That's why I'm going to this school."

"To learn to make swords?" Caramon asked, frowning with the mental effort. "Is it a blacksmith school, then?"

Raistlin sighed. "Not real swords, Caramon. Mental swords. Magic will be my sword."

"If you say so. But anyhow, if that teacher does whip you, just tell me." Caramon clenched his fists. "I'll take care of him. This sure is a long walk," he repeated.

"It is a long walk," Raistlin agreed. They'd gone only about a quarter of the distance, and he was already tired, although he didn't admit it. "But you don't have to come with me, you know."

"Well, of course I do!" Caramon said, looking astonished at the idea. "What if you get attacked by goblins? You'd need me to defend you."

"With a wooden sword," Raistlin observed dryly.

"Like you said, someday I'll have a real one," Caramon answered, his enthusiasm undaunted by logic. "Kitiara promised. Hey, that reminds me of what I was going to tell you. I think Kit's getting ready to go somewhere. Yesterday I ran into her coming down the stairs from that tavern at the edge of town. The Trough."

"What was she doing there?" Raistlin asked, interested. "For that matter, what were you doing there? That place is rough."

"I'll say!" Caramon agreed. "Sturm Brightblade says it's a place where thieves and cutthroats hang out. That's one reason I was there. I wanted to see a cutthroat."

"Well," said Raistlin with a half-smile, "did you see one?"

"Naw!" Caramon was disgusted. "At least, I don't think so. All the men were pretty ordinary. Most didn't look any different from Father, only not as big."

"Which is exactly what a good assassin would look like," Raistlin pointed out.

"Like Father?"

"Certainly. That way, he can sneak up on his victim without the victim noticing him. What did you think an assassin would look like? Dressed all in black with a long black cape and a black mask over his face?" Raistlin asked mockingly.

Caramon pondered. "Well . . . yes."

"What an idiot you are, Caramon," Raistlin said.

"I guess so," Caramon replied, subdued. He stared down at his feet, kicked at the dirt for a few moments. But it wasn't in Caramon's nature to be depressed for long. "Say," he said cheerfully, "if they really are ordinary, maybe I did see a cutthroat after all!"

Raistlin snorted. "What you did see was our sister. What was she doing there? Father wouldn't like her going into places like that."

"That's what I told her," Caramon said, self-righteous. "She smacked me and said that what Father didn't know wouldn't hurt him, and I was to keep my mouth shut. She was talking to two grown-up men, but they left when I came. She was holding something in her hand that looked like a map. I asked her what it was, but she just pinched my arm real hard"—Caramon exhibited a blue and red bruise—"and took me away and made me swear on a grave in the graveyard that I'd never say a word to anyone. Otherwise a ghoul would come and get me one night."

"You told me," Raistlin pointed out. "You broke your promise."

"She didn't mean you!" Caramon returned. "You're my twin. Telling you is like telling myself. 'Sides, she knows I'll tell you. I swore for both of us, anyway. So if the ghoul comes and gets me, it'll get you, too. Hey, I wouldn't mind seeing a ghoul, would you, Raist?"

Raistlin rolled his eyes but said nothing. He saved his breath. He hadn't covered half the distance to the school yet and already he was exhausted. He loathed his frail body that seemed determined to thwart every plan he made, to ruin every hope, to wreck every desire. Raistlin cast a jealous glance at his well-built, stout, and healthy twin.

People said there had once been gods who ruled over mankind, but the gods had grown angry at man and had gone away. Before they left, the gods had cast down a fiery mountain on Krynn, shattering the world. Then they had abandoned man to his fate. Raistlin could well believe that this was so. No just and honorable god would have played such a cruel joke as had been played on him-splitting a single person in two, giving one twin a mind without a body, the other a body without a mind.

Yet it would be comforting to think that there was an intelligent reason behind the decision, a purpose; comforting to know that he and his twin were not just some freak of nature. It would be comforting to know that there were gods, if only so that one could blame them!

Kitiara often told Raistlin the story of how he had nearly died, how she had saved his life when the midwife had told her the baby was good as dead and to leave it alone to gasp out its pitiful life. Kit was always a little miffed that Raistlin was not properly grateful to her. She was never to know, being strong herself, that sometimes, when Raistlin's body burned with fever and his muscles ached beyond endurance, when his mouth was parched with a thirst he could never quench, he cursed her in the night.

But Kitiara had been responsible for his entry into the school of magic. She had made amends.

If only he could manage to reach that school without collapsing first.

A farm cart, trundling past, proved Raistlin's salvation. The farmer stopped and asked the boys where they were going. And although he frowned when Raistlin told him of their destination, he agreed to give them a lift. He gazed pityingly at the frail child, coughing in the dust and the wheat chaff blowing off the fields.

"You plan on making this walk this every day, lad?"

"No, sir," Caramon answered for his brother, who couldn't speak. "He's going to magic school to learn to make swords. And he's got to stay there by himself, and they won't let me stay with him."

The farmer was a kindly man who had small children of his own. "Look, boys, I come this way every day. If you met me at the crossroads of a morning,

I could give you a lift. I'll meet you in the afternoon coming back. That way, you could at least be home with your family in the evenings."

"That'd be great!" Caramon cried.

"We can't pay you," Raistlin said at the same time, his face flushed with shame.

"Pshaw! I don't expect pay!" the farmer shot back, looking quite fierce. He glanced sidelong at the boys, especially the sturdy Caramon. "What I could use is help in the fields. My own young'uns are too little to be of much good to me yet."

"I could work for you," said Caramon promptly. "I could help you while Raist is in school."

"It's agreed, then."

Caramon and the farmer each spat on their palms, clasped hands on the bargain.

"Why did you agree to work for him?" Raistlin demanded after they had settled themselves at the back of the empty wagon, their feet dangling over the edge.

"So you could ride back and forth to school," Caramon said. "Why? What's wrong with that?" Raistlin bit his tongue. He should thank his brother, but the words stuck in his throat like a bad-tasting physic.

"It's just . . . I don't like you working for me. . . ."

"Oh, heck, Raist, we're twins," Caramon said, and grinning happily, he nudged his brother in the ribs. "You'd do the same for me."

Thinking about it, as the cart rolled toward Master Theobald's School for Mages, Raistlin wasn't all that certain he would.

❷

The farmer's cart was there to pick them up in the afternoon. Raistlin returned home to find that his mother had never missed him. Kitiara was surprised to see him back and demanded to know the reason. She was always angry when her plans were thwarted. She had made up her mind that Raistlin was to board at the school, and she was displeased to hear that he had decided to do otherwise.

She had to hear the story of the farmer twice, and even then was certain he was up to no good. The idea of Caramon working for the farmer further angered her. Caramon would grow up to be a farmer, she said in disgust. With manure instead of blood on his boots.

Caramon protested that he would not. They argued for a while; Raistlin went to bed with a headache. He awoke to find the argument settled. Kit appeared to have other things on her mind. She was preoccupied, more irritable than usual, and the boys were careful to keep out of the way of the flat of her hand. She did see to it that they were fed, however, frying up some dubious bacon and serving the remainder of the moldy bread.

Late that night, as Kitiara slept, small, deft hands lifted the pouch from her belt. Fingers, whose touch was delicate as the legs of a butterfly, removed the pouch's contents—a torn leaf of paper and a thick, folded piece of leather. Raistlin took them both to the kitchen, studied them by the light of the banked cooking fire.

Traced on the paper was a family crest picturing a fox standing victorious over a dead lion. The motto was "None too mighty" and beneath that was written "Matar." On the soft leather was a crudely drawn map of the route between Solace and Solamnia.

Swiftly Raistlin folded the paper, tucked it back into the pouch, and reattached the pouch onto Kit's belt.

Raistlin did not mention his find to anyone. He had learned early on that knowledge is power, especially knowledge of other people's secrets.

The next morning Kitiara was gone.

6

IT WAS HOT IN THE MAGE SCHOOL. A fire roaring on the hearth heated the windowless classroom to an almost unbearable degree. Master Theobald's voice droned through the heat, whose currents could be seen radiating from the fireplace. A fire spell was the one spell the master was truly adept at casting. He was pleased to show off his talent whenever he could.

Raistlin didn't mind the heat nearly as much as the other boys. He would have enjoyed it if it weren't for the fact that he would soon have to go out into the cold and the snow. Moving from one extreme to the other, venturing out into the chill in sweat-damp robes, took its toll on Raistlin's frail body. He was just now recovering from a sore throat and high fever that had robbed him of his voice for several days, forcing him to remain at home in bed.

He detested missing school. He was more intelligent than the master. And Raistlin knew in his soul that he was a better wizard than Master Theobald. Still, there were things he could learn from the master, things he must learn. The magic burned inside Raistlin like the fever, more pleasant yet just as painful. What Master Theobald knew and Raistlin did not was how to control the burning, how to make the magic serve the spellcaster, how to transmit the fever to words that could be written and spoken, how to use the fever to create.

Master Theobald was such an inept teacher, however, that Raistlin often felt as if he were lying in ambush, waiting to pounce upon the first bit of useful information that might accidentally wander in his direction.

The pupils of Master Theobald sat on their tall stools and tried desperately to stay awake, not easy to do in the heat after the heavy midday meal.

Anyone caught dozing off would be awakened by the whip-snap of the lithe willow branch across his shoulders. Master Theobald was a big, flabby man, but he could move quickly and quietly when he wanted to. He liked nothing better than to catch a pupil napping.

Raistlin had spoken quite glibly to his brother about being whipped that first day of school. Since then his thin shoulders had felt the snap of the willow branch, a pain that cut more deeply into the soul than into the flesh. He had never before been struck, except for the occasional smack from his sister, slaps which were delivered in a spirit of sibling affection. If Kitiara sometimes hit harder than she'd meant, her brothers knew that it was the thought that counted.

Master Theobald hit with a gleam in his eye and a smile on his fat face that left no doubt he enjoyed meting out punishment.

"The letter *a* in the language of magic," Master Theobald was saying in his somnambulistic monotone, "is not pronounced 'aa' as it is in the Common vernacular, nor is it pronounced 'ah' as you will hear it in the elven, nor yet 'ach' as we find it spoken among the dwarves."

Yes, yes, thought Raistlin drearily. Get on with it. Quit showing off. You've probably never spoken to an elf in your life, you fat old dundering idiot.

"The letter *a* in the language of magic is spoken as 'ai.' "

Raistlin snapped to alertness. Here was information he needed. He listened attentively. Master Theobald repeated the pronunciation.

" 'Ai.' Now, you young gentlemen, say this after me."

A drowsy chorus of *ais* sighed through the stifling room, punctuated by one strong *ai* spoken firmly by Raistlin. Generally his voice was the quietest among them, for he disliked drawing attention to himself, mainly because such attention was usually painful. His excitement at actually learning something useful and the fact that he was one of the few awake and listening had prompted him to speak more loudly than he'd intended.

He immediately regretted having done so. Master Theobald regarded Raistlin with an approving eye, at least what could be seen of that eye through the pouches of fat surrounding it, and gently tapped the willow branch upon the desk.

"Very good, Master Raistlin," he said.

Raistlin's neighbors cast him covert, malignant glances, and he knew he'd be made to pay for this compliment. The boy to his right, an older boy, almost thirteen, who had been sent to the school because his parents could not stand to have him around the house, leaned over to whisper.

"I hear you kiss his arse every morning, 'Master Raistlin.' "

The boy, known as Gordo, made vulgar smacking sounds with his lips. Those sitting nearby responded with smothered giggles.

Master Theobald heard and turned his eye on them. He rose to his feet and the boys immediately hushed. He headed for them, the willow branch in his hand, when he was distracted by the sight of a small pupil actually slumbering soundly, his head on his arms, his eyes closed.

Master Theobald smiled. Down came the willow branch across the small shoulders. The pupil sat bolt upright with a pained and startled cry.

"What do you mean, sir, sleeping in my class?" Master Theobald thundered at the young malefactor, who shrank before his rage and surreptitiously wiped away his tears.

During this commotion, Raistlin heard a flurry of activity behind him, a sort of scuffling, but he didn't bother to look around. The antics of the other boys seemed petty and stupid to him. Why did they waste their time, such precious time, in nonsense?

He said "ai" quietly to himself until he was sure he had it right, and even wrote down the vowel combination upon his slate in order to practice it later. Absorbed in his work, he ignored the muffled giggles and sniggers going on around him. Master Theobald, having completely demoralized one small urchin, returned to his desk well satisfied. Seating himself ponderously, he continued with the lesson.

"The next vowel in the language of the arcane is *o*. This is not pronounced 'oo,' nor yet 'och,' but 'oa.' Pronunciation is most important, young gentlemen, and therefore I suggest you pay attention. Pronounce a spell incorrectly and it will not work. I am reminded of the time when I was a pupil of the great wizard—"

Raistlin fidgeted in irritation. Master Theobald was off on one of his tales, stories that were dull and boring and served invariably to laud the mediocre talents of Master Theobald. Raistlin was copying down carefully the letter *o* with the phonetic pronunciation "oa" next to it when suddenly his stool shot out from underneath him.

Raistlin tumbled to the floor. The fall, completely unexpected, was a hard one. Stinging pain shot through his wrist, which he'd instinctively used to try to catch himself. The stool toppled to the floor with a loud clatter. His neighbors broke into guffaws, immediately silenced.

Master Theobald, his face purple against his white robes, sprang to his feet and stood quivering in rage like a mound of vanilla pudding.

"Master Raistlin! What is the meaning of this disruption to my lecture?"

"He went to sleep, sir, and fell off his stool," Gordo offered helpfully.

Crouched on the floor, nursing his injured wrist, Raistlin located the string that had been tied to the leg of his stool. As he reached to grab it, the string slithered across the floor to disappear up the sleeve of Devon, one of the Gordo's minions, who sat behind him.

"Sleeping! Interrupting me!" Master Theobald snatched up the willow branch and bore down upon Raistlin. Seeing the blow coming, he hunched his shoulders, and raised his arm to make himself as small a target as possible.

One cut of the willow sliced the flesh of Raistlin's upraised arm, narrowly missing his face. The master lifted his hand to strike again.

Rage, hot as a forge fire, burned through Raistlin. His anger consumed his fear, consumed his pain. His first wild impulse was to leap to his feet and attack his teacher. A trickle of common sense, icy cold, ran through Raistlin's body. He felt the idea as a physical sensation, a chill that tingled his nerve endings and set him shivering, even in the white heat of his fury. He saw himself attacking the master, saw himself looking the fool—a puny weakling with spindly arms shrieking in a high-pitched voice, flailing away impotently with his tiny fists. Worse, he would be the one in the wrong. Master Theobald would triumph over him. The other boys—Raistlin's tormentors—would laugh and gloat.

Raistlin gave a strangled gasp and went limp, lying on his back, his legs twisted at an angle, knees together. One hand slid nervelessly to the floor, the other lay flaccid across his thin chest. His eyelids closed. He made his breathing as quiet as he could manage, quiet and shallow.

Raistlin had been sick many times during his short life. He knew how to be sick, he knew how to feign illness. He lay, pale and shattered and apparently lifeless, on the floor at the master's feet.

"Cripes!" said Devon, the boy who had tied the string to the stool. "You've killed him!"

"Nonsense," said Master Theobald, though his voice cracked on the word. He lowered the willow stick. "He's just . . . just fainted. That's all. Fainted. Gordo"—he coughed, was forced to clear his throat—"Gordo, go fetch some water."

The boy ran off to do as he was told. His feet pounded on the stone floor; Raistlin could hear him fumbling at the water bucket. Raistlin continued to lie where he had fallen, his eyes closed, not stirring or making a sound. He was enjoying this, he discovered—enjoying the attention, enjoying their fear, their discomfiture.

Gordo ran back with the water dipper, slopping most of the water over the floor and the skirts of the master's robes.

"You clumsy oaf! Give me that!" Master Theobald cuffed Gordo, snatched the dipper from him. The master knelt down beside Raistlin, very gently dabbed the child's lips with water.

"Raistlin," he said in a soft, whining whisper. "Raistlin, can you hear me?"

Laughter bubbled up inside Raistlin. He was forced to exert an extraordinary amount of self-control to contain it. He lay still one more minute. Then, just as he could feel the master's hand starting to tremble in anxiety; Raistlin moved his head from side to side and made a small moaning sound.

"Good!" said Master Theobald, sighing in relief. "He's coming around. You boys back off. Give him air. I'll take him to my private quarters."

The master's flabby arms lifted Raistlin, who let his head loll, his legs dangle. He kept his eyes closed, moaning now and then as he was carried in state to the master's quarters, all the boys traipsing along after them, though Theobald ordered them angrily several times to remain in the schoolroom.

The master laid Raistlin down upon a couch. He drove the other boys back to the classroom with threats, not the willow branch, Raistlin noted, peering through a slit in his closed eyelids. Theobald shouted for one of the servants.

Raistlin allowed his eyes to flicker open. He kept them deliberately unfocused for a moment, then permitted his eyes to find Master Theobald.

"What . . . what happened?" Raistlin asked weakly. He glanced vaguely around, tried to lift himself. "Where am I?"

The exertion proved too much. He fell back upon the couch, gasping for breath.

Master Theobald hovered over him. "You . . . um . . . had a bad fall," he said, not looking directly at Raistlin, but darting nervous glances at him from the corner of his eyes. "You fell off your stool."

Raistlin glanced down at his arm, where an ugly red welt was visible against his pale skin. He looked back at Master Theobald. "My arm stings," he said softly.

The master lowered his gaze, sought the floor, looked up gladly when the servant, a middle-aged woman who did the cooking and cleaning and took care of the boys, entered the room. She was extremely ugly, with a scarred face, missing the hair on one side of her head. It had been burned off, purportedly because she'd been struck by lightning. This perhaps accounted for the fact that she was quite slow mentally.

Marm, as she was known, kept the place clean, and she'd never yet poisoned anyone with her cooking. That was about all that could be said of her. The boys whispered that she was the result of one of Master Theobald's spells gone awry, and that he kept her in his household out of guilt.

"The boy had a bad fall, Marm," said Master Theobald. "See to him, will you? I must return to my class."

He cast a final anxious glance backward at Raistlin, then swept out of the room, inflating himself with what was left of his pride.

Marm brought a cold, wet cloth that she slapped over Raistlin's forehead and a cookie. The cloth was too wet and dripped greasy water into Raistlin's eyes, the cookie was burnt on the bottom and tasted like charcoal. Grunting, Marm left him to recover on his own and went back to whatever it was she had been doing. Judging from the greasy water, she was washing dishes.

When she was gone, Raistlin removed the cloth and cast it aside in disgust. He threw the cookie into the fireplace with its ever-present fire. Then he lay back comfortably on the couch, snuggled into the soft cushions, and listened to the master's voice, which could be heard droning, in a somewhat subdued tone, through the open door.

"The letter *u* is pronounced 'uh.' Repeat after me."

" 'Uh,' " said Raistlin complacently to himself. He watched the flames consume the log and he smiled. Master Theobald would never strike him again.

7

THE LESSON ANOTHER DAY WAS PENMANSHIP. Not only did a mage have to be able to pronounce the words of magic correctly, but the mage must also be able to write them down, form each letter into its proper shape. Words of the arcane must be penned with precision, exactness, neatness, and care on the scroll, else they would not work. Write the spell word *shirak,* for example, with a wobble in the *a* and a scrunch in the *k,* and the mage who wants light will be left in the dark.

Most of Master Theobald's students, true to the naturally clumsy characteristics of small boys, were fumble-fisted. Their quill pens, on which they had to carve the points themselves, either split or sputtered, bent or broke or leapt out of their clutching fingers. The boys invariably ended up with more ink on themselves than on the scrolls, unless they happened to upset the ink bottle, which accident occurred on a regular basis.

Any visitor entering the school on the afternoon of penmanship classes to find himself confronted by the inky faces and hands of innumerable small demons, might well have imagined that he'd wandered into the Abyss by mistake.

This thought crossed the mind of Antimodes the moment he walked through the door. This and a sudden swift memory of his own days in the schoolroom, a memory brought on mostly by the smell—small bodies overly warmed by the fire, the cabbage soup they'd choked down for lunch, ink and warm sheepskins—caused him to smile.

"The Archmagus Antimodes," announced the servant, or something approximating that, for she completely mangled his name.

Antimodes paused in the doorway. The flushed, inky, frustrated faces of twelve boys lifted from their work to stare at him with hope in their eyes. A savior, perhaps. One who would free them from their toil. A thirteenth face looked up, but not as quickly as the others. That face appeared to have been intent upon its work, and only when that work was completed did it lift to stare at the visitor.

Antimodes was pleased—quite pleased—to see that this face was almost completely devoid of ink, with the exception of a smudge along the left eyebrow, and that there was not an expression of relief on the face, but rather one of irritation, as if it resented being interrupted in its work.

The irritation passed swiftly, however, once the face recognized Antimodes, as Antimodes had recognized the face.

Master Theobald rose hastily from his chair, officious and ponderous, jealous and insecure. He did not like Antimodes, because the master suspected—and rightly so—that Antimodes had been opposed to Theobald's appointment as schoolmaster and had voted against him in the conclave. Antimodes had been outvoted, Par-Salian himself having presented very strong arguments in Theobald's favor: He was the only candidate. What else were they to do with the man?

Even his friends agreed that Theobald would never make more than a mediocre mage. There were some, Antimodes among them, who questioned how he had managed to pass the Test in the first place. Par-Salian was always evasive whenever Antimodes brought up the subject, and Antimodes was left to believe that Theobald had been passed on the condition that he accept a teaching assignment, a job no one else wanted.

Antimodes could offer no better suggestion. He himself, given the choice, would have preferred going to Mount Nevermind to instruct the gnomes in pyrotechnics to teaching snot-faced human children magic. He had grudgingly gone along with the majority.

Antimodes was forced to admit that Par-Salian and the others had been right. Theobald was not a particularly good teacher, but he saw to it that his boys—the girls had their own school in Palanthas, taught by a slightly more competent wizardess—learned the basics, and that was all that was necessary. He would never light any fires in the average student, but where the fire of greatness already burned, Master Theobald would stoke it.

The two mages met with a show of amicability in front of the children.

"How do you do, sir?"

"How do you do, my dear sir?"

Antimodes was gracious in his greeting and lavish in his praise of the classroom, which to himself he thought was unbearably hot, stuffy, and dirty.

Master Theobald was profuse in his welcome, all the time certain that

Antimodes had been sent by Par-Salian to check up on him and bitterly resenting the fact that the archmage was carelessly wearing a luxuriant cape made of fine lamb's wool that would have cost the teacher a year's salary.

"Well, well, Archmagus. Are the roads still snow-covered?"

"No, no, Master. Quite passable. Even up north."

"Ah, you've come from the north, have you, Archmagus?"

"Lemish," Antimodes said smoothly. He'd actually been much farther north than that quaint and woodsy little town, but he had no intention of discussing his travels with Theobald.

Theobald had no use for travel of any sort. He raised his eyebrows in an expression of disapproval, manifested his disapproval by turning away and ending their conversation. "Boys, it is my great honor to introduce to you Archmagus Antimodes, a wizard of the White Robes."

The boys sang out an enthusiastic greeting.

"We have been practicing our writing," said Theobald. "We were just about to conclude for the day. Perhaps you would like to see some of our work, Archmagus?"

Actually there was only one pupil in whom Antimodes was interested, but he solemnly walked up and down the aisles and regarded with feigned interest letters that were every shape except the correct shape, and one game of *x*'s and *o*'s, which the player made a vain attempt to cover up by overturning his ink bottle on top of it.

"Not bad," said Antimodes, "not bad. Quite . . . creative . . . some of these." He came to Raistlin's desk—his true goal. Here he paused and said with sincerity, "Well done."

A boy behind Raistlin made a noise, a rude noise.

Antimodes turned.

"Pardon, sir," the boy said, with apparent contriteness. "It was the cabbage for lunch."

Antimodes knew that noise hadn't been caused by cabbage. He also knew what it implied, and he immediately realized his mistake. He remembered the ways of small boys—he had been a bit of a troublemaker himself as a youth. He should not have praised Raistlin. The other boys were jealous and vindictive, and Raistlin would be made to suffer.

Trying to think of some way to rectify his mistake, prepared to point out a flaw—no one was perfect, after all—Antimodes looked back at Raistlin.

On Raistlin's thin lips was a pleased smile. One could almost call it a smirk.

Antimodes swallowed his words, with the result that he very nearly choked on them. Coughing, he cleared his throat and walked on. He saw nothing after that. His thoughts were turned inward, and it wasn't until he came face-to-face with Master Theobald that Antimodes realized he was still in the classroom.

He stopped short, looked up with a start. "Oh . . . er . . . very nice work from your pupils, Master Theobald. Very nice. If you wouldn't mind, I should like to speak to you privately."

"I really should not leave the class . . . ."

"Only for a moment. I'm certain these fine young gentlemen"—Antimodes gave them a smile—"will be content to study on their own in your absence."

He was fully aware that the fine young gentlemen would probably take advantage of the opportunity to play marbles, draw obscene pictures on their practice scrolls, and splatter each other with ink.

"Only a moment of your time, Master Theobald," Antimodes said with the utmost respect.

Scowling, Master Theobald stomped out of the classroom, leading his way into his private quarters. Here he shut the door and faced Antimodes.

"Well, sir. Please make haste."

Antimodes could already hear the uproar break out in the classroom.

"I should like to talk to each pupil individually, if you please, Master Theobald. Ask them each a few questions."

At this, Master Theobald's eyebrows nearly took wing and flew off his head. Then they came together over the puffy eyelids in a suspicious frown. Never before in all his years of teaching had any archmagus ever bothered to visit his classroom, much less demand a private chat with the students. Master Theobald could only jump to one conclusion, and he did, landing on it squarely with both feet.

"If the conclave does not find my work to be satisfactory . . ." he began in huffy tones.

"They do. Quite the contrary," Antimodes said, hastening to reassure him. "It's just some research I'm conducting." He waved his hand. "Investigating the philosophical reasoning that prompts young men to choose to spend their time in this particular course of study."

Master Theobald snorted.

"Please send them in to see me one by one," said Antimodes.

Master Theobald snorted again, turned on his heel, and waddled back into the classroom.

Antimodes settled himself in a chair and wondered what in the name of Lunitari he was going to say to these urchins. In reality, he wanted only to talk to one pupil, but he dare not single out Raistlin again. The Archmagus was still pondering things when the first, the eldest boy in the school, entered the room, abashed and embarrassed.

"Gordo, sir." The boy made an awkward bow.

"And so, Gordo, my boy" said Antimodes, embarrassed himself but attempting to conceal it, "how do you plan to incorporate the use of magic into your everyday life?"

"Well, s-sir," Gordo stammered, obviously baffled, "I don't rightly know." Antimodes frowned.

The boy grew defensive. "I'm only here, sir, 'cause my ma makes me come. I don't want to have nothing to do with magic."

"What do you want to do?" Antimodes asked, surprised.

"I want to be a butcher," Gordo said promptly.

Antimodes sighed. "Perhaps you should have a talk with your mother. Explain to her how you feel."

The boy shook his head, shrugged. "I've tried. It's all right, sir. I'll stay here until I'm old enough to be apprenticed, then I'll cut and run."

"Thank you," Antimodes said dryly. "We'll all appreciate that. Please tell the next boy to come in."

By the end of five interviews, Antimodes's antipathy for Master Theobald had changed to the most profound pity. He also felt alarmed and dismayed. He had learned more in fifteen minutes talking to these five boys than he had in five months of traveling throughout Ansalon.

He was well aware—he and Par-Salian had often discussed it—that mages were viewed with suspicion and distrust by the general populace. That was as it should be. Wizards should be surrounded with an aura of mystery. Their spellcasting should inspire awe and a proper amount of fear.

He found no awe among these boys. No fear. Not even much respect. Antimodes might blame Master Theobald and did blame the master for some of the problem. Certainly he did nothing to inspire his students, to lift them from the common everyday muck of ignorance in which they were wallowing. But there was more to it than that.

There were no children of nobles in this school. Insofar as Antimodes knew, there were few children of nobles in any of the schools of magic in Ansalon. Only among the elves was the study of the arcane considered suitable for the upper class, and even they were discouraged from devoting their lives to it. King Lorac of Silvanesti had been one of the last elves of royal blood known to have taken the Test. Most were like Gilthanas, youngest son of the Speaker of the Sun and Stars of Qualinesti. Gilthanas could have been an excellent mage, had he taken the time to study the art. But he merely dabbled in magic, refused to take the Test, refused to commit himself.

As to humans, these children were sons of middle-class merchants, most of them. That wasn't bad—Antimodes himself had come from such a background. He at least had known what he wanted and had been willing to fight for it, his parents having been completely opposed to the very idea of his studying magic. But these children had been sent here because their parents had no idea what else to do with them. They were sent to study magic because they weren't considered good enough to do anything else.

Were wizards truly held in such low regard?

Depressed, Antimodes huddled down in the overstuffed chair, as far from the fire as he could drag it, and mulled this over in his mind. The depression had been growing on him ever since his trip to Solamnia.

The knights and their families had been polite, but then they would always be polite to any well-to-do, fair-spoken traveling human stranger. They had invited Antimodes to stay in their dwellings, they had fed him roast meats, fine wines, and entertained him with minstrels. They had not ever once discussed magic, had never asked him to assist them with his spellcasting, or made reference to the fact that he was a wizard. If he brought it up, they smiled at him vaguely and then quickly changed the subject. It was as if he had some type of deformity or disease. They were too polite, too well bred to shun him or openly revile him for it. But he was well aware that they averted their glances when they thought he wasn't looking. In truth, he disgusted them.

And he disgusted himself. He saw himself for the first time through the eyes of these children. He had tamely gone along with the knights' cold-shouldered treatment, had even curried their favor in a most undignified manner. He had suppressed who and what he was. He had not unpacked his white robes once during the trip. He had removed his pouches of spell components and hidden the scroll cases under the bed.

"At my age, you'd think I would know better," he said to himself sourly. "What a fool I made of myself. They must have rolled their eyes and breathed sighs of relief when I left. It is a good thing Par-Salian doesn't know of this. I'm thankful I never mentioned my intention of traveling to Solamnia to him."

"Greetings again, Archmagus," said a child's voice.

Antimodes blinked, returned to the present. Raistlin had entered the room. The archmage had been looking forward to this meeting. He had taken a keen interest in the boy since the first time they'd met. The conversations with the other children had been merely a ruse, contrived in order to have the chance to talk privately with this one extraordinary child. But his recent discoveries had so devastated Antimodes that he found no pleasure in talking with the one student who showed any aptitude at all for magic.

What future lay ahead for this boy? A future in which wizards were stoned to death? At least, Antimodes thought bitterly, the populace had feared Esmilla, the black-robed wizardess, and fear implies a certain amount of respect. How much worse if they had merely laughed at her! But wasn't that where they were heading? Would magic end up in the hands of disappointed butchers?

Raistlin coughed slightly and shifted nervously on his feet. Antimodes realized that he'd been staring at the child in silence, long enough to make Raistlin feel uncomfortable.

"Forgive me, Raistlin," Antimodes said, motioning the boy to come forward. "I have traveled far and I am weary. And my trip was not entirely satisfactory."

"I'm sorry to hear that, sir," Raistlin said, regarding Antimodes with those blue eyes that were much too old and wise.

"And I am sorry that I praised your work in the schoolroom." Antimodes smiled ruefully. "I should have known better."

"Why, sir?" Raistlin was puzzled. "Wasn't it good, as you said?"

"Well, yes, but your classmates . . . I should not have singled you out. I know boys your age, you see. I was a bit of a rascal myself, I'm sorry to say. I'm afraid they'll be hard on you."

Raistlin shrugged his thin shoulders. "They're ignorant."

"Ahem. Well, now." Antimodes frowned, disapproving. It was all very proper for him, an adult, to think this, but it seemed wrong in the child to say it. Disloyal.

"They can't rise to my level," Raistlin continued, "and so they want to drag me down to theirs. Sometimes"—the blue eyes staring at Antimodes were as clear and brilliant as glare ice—"they hurt me."

"I . . . I'm sorry," Antimodes said, a lame statement, but then he was so completely taken aback by this child, by his coolness and astute observations, that he could think of nothing more intelligent.

"Don't be sorry for me!" Raistlin flared, and there was the flash of fire on the ice. "I don't mind," he added more calmly and shrugged again. "It's a compliment, really. They're afraid of me."

The populace had feared Esmilla, the black-robed wizardess, and fear implies a certain amount of respect. How much worse if they had merely laughed at her! Antimodes recalled his own thoughts. Hearing them repeated in this childish treble sent a shiver up his spine. A child should not be this wise, should not be forced to bear the burden of such cynical wisdom this young.

Raistlin smiled then, an ingenuous smile. "It's a hammer blow. I think about what you told me, sir. How the hammer blows forge the soul. And the water cools them. Except I don't cry. Or if I do," he added, his voice hardening, "it's when they can't see me."

Antimodes stared, amazed and confused. Part of him wanted to hug close this precocious child, while another part warned him to snatch the child up and toss him into the fire, crush him as one crushes the egg of a viper. This dichotomy of emotion so unsettled him that he was forced to rise to his feet and take a turn about the room before he felt capable of continuing the conversation.

Raistlin stood silently, waiting patiently for the adult to finish indulging himself in the strange and inexplicable behavior adults often exhibited. The boy's gaze left Antimodes and strayed to the book shelves, where the gaze focused and sharpened with a hungry edge.

That reminded Antimodes of something he'd meant to tell the boy and had, in the ensuing disturbing conversation, almost forgotten. He returned to his chair, sat forward in the seat.

"I meant to tell you, young man. I saw your sister when I was in . . . on my travels."

Raistlin's gaze darted back to the archmage, was alight with interest. "Kitiara? You saw her, sir?"

"Yes. I was quite astonished, I may tell you. One doesn't expect . . . a girl that age . . ." He paused, not quite certain where, under the light of the lad's blue eyes, to go from here.

Raistlin understood. "She left home shortly after I was enrolled in the school, Archmagus. I think she'd wanted to leave before that, but she was worried about Caramon and me. Me especially. She figures that now I can take care of myself."

"You're still only a child," Antimodes said sternly, deciding precocious-ness had gone far enough.

"But I can take care of myself," Raistlin said, and the smile—the smirk Antimodes had seen earlier—touched his lips. The smile widened when Master Theobald's loud, haranguing voice was heard booming through the door.

"Kitiara came home a couple of months after she left, before winter set in," Raistlin continued. "She gave Father some money to pay for her room and board. He said it wasn't necessary but she said it was; she wouldn't take anything from him ever again. She wore a sword, a real one. It had dried blood on it. She gave Caramon a sword, but Father was angry and took it away from him. She didn't stay long. Where did you see her?"

"I can't quite recall the name of the place," Antimodes said, carefully evasive. "These small towns. They all look alike after a while. She was in a tavern with some . . . companions."

Disreputable companions, he almost said, but he didn't, not wanting to upset the child, who seemed genuinely fond of his half-sister. He had seen her among mercenary soldiers of the very worst sort, the kind who sell their swords for money and are willing to sell their souls, too, if anyone happened to want the wretched things.

"She told me a story about you," Antimodes went on quickly, not giving the child time to ask more questions. "She said that when your father first brought you here, to Master Theobald's, you came into his library—this very room—sat down and began to read one of the books of magic."

At first Raistlin looked startled, then he smiled. Not the smirk, but a mischievous grin that reminded Antimodes that this boy really was only six years old.

"That wouldn't be possible," Raistlin said, with a sidelong glance at Antimodes. "I'm only now learning to read and write magic."

"I know it's not possible," Antimodes replied, smiling himself. The boy could be quite charming when he chose. "Where would she have come by such a story, then?"

"My brother," Raistlin answered. "We were in the classroom, and my father and the master were talking about letting me enter the school. The master didn't want to admit me."

Antimodes raised his eyebrows, shocked. "How do you know? Did he say so?"

"Not in so many words. But he said I wasn't properly brought up. I should speak only when I was addressed, and I should keep my eyes down and not 'stare him out of countenance.' That's what he said. I was 'pert' and 'glib' and 'disrespectful.' "

"So you are, Raistlin," admonished Antimodes, thinking he should. "You should show your master and your classmates more respect."

Raistlin shrugged, dismissed them all with that shrug, and continued with his story. "I got bored listening to Father apologize for me, and so Caramon and I went exploring. We came in here. I pulled a book off the shelf. One of the spellbooks. Only a practice one. The master keeps the real spellbooks locked up in his cellar. I know."

The child's voice was cool, serious; the eyes glistened with longing. Antimodes was suitably alarmed and made a mental note to warn Theobald that his precious spellbooks may not be as safe as the master imagined.

Then suddenly the boy was a boy again. "I may have told Caramon the spellbook was real," Raistlin said, the mischievous grin returning. "I don't remember. Anyway, Master Theobald came dashing in, all huffing and puffing and mad. He scolded me for wandering off and 'invading his privacy,' and when he saw me with the book, he got madder still. I wasn't reading a spell. I couldn't read any of it.

"But"—Raistlin gave Antimodes a sly glance—"there's an illusionist in town. His name is Waylan, and I've heard him use magic and I memorized some of the words. I know the spells won't work, but I use them for fun when the other boys are playing at war. I said some of the words. Caramon was all excited and told Father that I was going to summon a demon from the Abyss. Master Theobald got really red in the face and grabbed the book away from me. He knew I wasn't really reading the words," Raistlin added coolly. "He just wanted a chance to get rid of me."

"Master Theobald accepted you into his school," said Antimodes sternly. "He didn't 'get rid of you,' as you put it. And what you did was wrong. You should not have taken the book without his permission."

"He had to take me," Raistlin said flatly. "My schooling was bought and paid for." He stared very hard at Antimodes, who, having expected this, was prepared for it and returned the stare with bland innocence.

The child had met his match. He lowered his gaze, shifted it to the bookcase. One corner of his mouth twitched. "Caramon must have told Kitiara. He really did think I was going to summon a demon, you know. Caramon's like a kender. He'll believe anything you tell him."

"Do you love your brother?" Antimodes asked impulsively.

"Of course," Raistlin responded blandly, smoothly. "He's my twin."

"Yes, you are twins, aren't you?" Antimodes said reflectively. "I wonder if your brother has a talent for magic? It would seem logic—"

He stopped, confounded, struck dumb by the look Raistlin gave him. It was a blow, as if the child had struck out with his fists. No, not with fists. With a dagger.

Antimodes recoiled, startled unpleasantly by the malevolence in the child's expression. The question had been idle, harmless. He had certainly not expected such a reaction.

"May I return to class now, sir?" Raistlin asked politely. His face was smooth, if somewhat pale.

"Uh, yes. I . . . uh . . . enjoyed our visit," said Antimodes.

Raistlin made no comment. He bowed politely, as all the boys were taught to bow, then went to the door, opened it.

A wave of noise and heat, bringing with it the smell of small boys and boiled cabbage and ink, surged into the library, reminding Antimodes of the tide coming in on the dirty beaches at Flotsam. The door shut behind the boy.

Antimodes sat quite still for long moments, recovering. This was difficult to do at first, because he kept seeing those blue poignard eyes, glittering with anger, sliding through his flesh. Finally, realizing that the day was winding on and that he wanted to reach the Inn of the Last Home before dark, Antimodes shook off the aftereffects of the unfortunate scene and returned to the schoolroom to make his farewells to Master Theobald.

Raistlin, Antimodes noted, did not look up as he entered.

The ride along the road on his placid donkey Jenny, past fields green with the early summer's first blooms, soothed Antimodes's soul. By the time he reached the inn, he could even laugh at himself ruefully, admit that he'd been in the wrong for asking such a personal question, and shrug off the incident. Putting Jenny up in the public stables, Antimodes wended his way to the inn, where he coated his troubles with Otik's honey mead and slept soundly.

☻

That meeting was the last time Antimodes would see Raistlin for many years. The archmage maintained his interest in Raistlin and kept current on his advancement through his studies. Whenever a wizards' conclave was called, Antimodes made it a point to seek out Master Theobald and interrogate him. Antimodes continued paying for Raistlin's education as well. Hearing of the progress of the pupil, Antimodes considered it money well spent.

But he would not forget his question about the twin brother.

Nor would he forget Raistlin's answer.

BOOK 2

I will do this. *Nothing in my life matters except this. No moment in my life exists except this moment. I am born in this moment, and if I fail, I will die in this moment.*

—Raistlin Majere

1

"RAIST! OVER HERE!" CARAMON WAVED FROM THE FRONT OF THE FARMER'S cart, which he was driving. At the age of thirteen, so tall and broad and muscular that he often passed for much older, Caramon had become Farmer Sedge's top field hand.

Caramon's hair curled on his brow in soft auburn rings, his eyes were cheerful, friendly, and guileless: gullible. The children adored him, and so did every shyster, beggar, and con artist that passed through Solace. He was unusually strong for his age, also unusually gentle. He had a formidable temper when riled, but the fuse was buried so deep and took so long to burn that Caramon usually realized he was angry only when the quarrel had long since ended.

The only time his anger exploded was when someone threatened his twin. Raistlin lifted his hand to acknowledge his brother's shout. He was glad to see Caramon, glad to see a friendly face.

Seven winters ago, Raistlin had decided that he must board at Master Theobald's school during the coldest months of the year, an arrangement that meant for the first time in their lives the twin brothers were separated.

Seven winters passed, with Raistlin absent from his home. In springtime, like this spring, when the sun melted the frozen roads and brought the first green and golden buds to the vallenwoods, the twins were reunited.

Long ago, Raistlin had given up secretly hoping that someday he would look into a mirror and see in himself the image of his handsome twin. Raistlin, with his fine-boned features and large eyes, his soft-to-the-touch reddish hair that brushed his shoulders, would have been the more hand-some of the two but for his eyes. They held the gaze too long, stared too deeply, saw too much, and there was always the faint hint of scorn in them, for he saw clearly the shams and artifices and absurdities of people and was both amused and disgusted with them.

Jumping down from the cart, Caramon gave his brother a boisterous hug, which Raistlin did not return. He used the bundle of clothes he held in both arms as an excuse to avoid an overt show of affection, a show Raistlin found undignified and annoying. His body stiffened in his brother's embrace, but Caramon was too excited to notice. He grabbed the bundle, flung it in the back of the cart.

"C'mon, I'll help you up," Caramon offered.

Raistlin was beginning to think he wasn't as glad to see his twin as he'd first imagined. He had forgotten how irritating Caramon could be.

"I'm perfectly capable of climbing onto a farm cart without assistance," Raistlin returned.

"Oh, sure, Raist." Caramon grinned, not the least offended.

He was too stupid to be offended.

Raistlin pulled himself up onto the cart. Caramon bounded up into the driver's seat. Grasping the reins, he made clucking sounds with his tongue at the horse, turned the beast around, and started back up the road toward Solace.

"What's that?" Caramon jerked his head around, looked behind him at the school.

"Pay no attention to them, my brother," Raistlin said quietly.

Classes were over. The master usually took advantage of this time of day to "meditate," which meant that he could be found in the library with a closed book and an open bottle of the port wine for which Northern Ergoth was famous. He would remain in his meditative state until dinner, when the housekeeper would awaken him. The boys were supposed to use this time for study, but Master Theobald never checked on them, and so they were left to their own devices. Today a group had gathered at the back of the school to bid farewell to Raistlin.

"'Bye, Sly!" they were yelling in unison, the cry being led by their instigator, a tall boy with carrot-orange hair and freckles, who was new to the school.

"Sly!" Caramon looked at his brother. "They mean you, don't they?" His brows came together in an angry scowl. "Whoa, there!" He brought the cart to a halt.

"Caramon, let it pass," Raistlin said, placing his hand on his brother's muscular arm.

"I won't, Raist," Caramon returned. "They shouldn't call you names like that!" His hands clenched into fists that, for a thirteen-year-old, were formidable.

"Caramon, no!" Raistlin ordered sharply. "I will deal with them in my own time, in my own way."

"Are you sure, Raist?" Caramon was glaring back at the taunting boys. "They won't call you names like that if their lips are split open."

"Not today, perhaps," Raistlin said. "But I have to go back to them tomorrow. Now, drive on. I want to reach home before dark."

Caramon obeyed. He always obeyed when his twin commanded. Raistlin was the acknowledged thinker of the two, a fact that Caramon cheerfully admitted. Caramon had come to depend on Raistlin's guidance in most areas of life, including the games they played with the other boys, games such as Goblin Ball, Kender Keep Away, and Thane Beneath the Mountain. Due to his frail health, Raistlin could not participate in such exuberant sports, but he watched intently. His quick mind developed strategies for winning, which he passed on to his brother.

Minus Raistlin's tutelage, Caramon would mistakenly score goals for his opponents in Goblin Ball. He nearly always ended up being the kender in Kender Keep Away, and he constantly fell victim to the military tactics of the older Sturm Brightblade in Thane Beneath the Mountain. When Raistlin was there to remind him which end of the field was which, and to offer cunning ploys to outwit his opponents, Caramon was the winner more often than not.

Once again he clucked at the horse. The cart rolled down the rutted road. The catcalls ended. The boys grew bored and turned to other sport.

"I don't understand why you didn't let me pound them," Caramon complained.

Because, Raistlin answered silently, I know what would happen, how it would end. You would "pound them," as you so elegantly put it, my brother. Then you would help them to their feet, slap them on their backs, tell them you know they didn't mean it, and in the end you would all be the best of friends.

Except for me. Except for the "Sly One."

No, the lesson will be mine to teach. They will learn what it means to be sly.

He might have continued to sit, brooding and plotting and mulling over such wrongs, but for his brother, who was rattling on about their parents, their friends, and the fine day. Caramon's cheerful gossip teased his brother out of his ill humor. The air was soft and warm and smelled of growing things, compounded with horse and newly mown grass, much better smells than that of cooked cabbage and boys who bathed only once a week.

Raistlin breathed deeply of the soft, fragrant air and didn't cough. The sunshine warmed him pleasantly. and he found himself listening with keen enjoyment to his brother's conversation.

"Father's been gone these last three weeks and likely won't be back until the end of the month. Mother remembered that you were coming home today. She's been a lot better lately, Raist. You'll notice the change. Ever since the Widow Judith started coming to stay with her when she has her bad days."

"Widow Judith?" said Raistlin sharply. "Who's Judith? And what do you mean, stay with Mother when she has her bad days? What about you and Father?"

Caramon shifted uncomfortably on his seat. "It was a hard winter, Raist. You were gone. Father had to work. He couldn't take off or we would have starved. When Farmer Sedge was snowed in and didn't need me, I got a job in the stables, feeding the horses and mucking out. We tried leaving Mother alone, but—well, it wasn't working. One day she tipped over a candle and didn't notice. It nearly burned down the house. We did the best we could, Raist."

Raistlin said nothing. He sat on the cart, grimly silent, angry at his father and brother. They should not have left his mother in the care of strangers. He was angry at himself. He should not have left her.

"The Widow Judith's real nice, Raist," Caramon went on defensively. "Mother likes her a lot. Judith comes every morning, and she helps Mother dress and fixes her hair. She makes her eat something, and then they do sewing and stuff like that. Judith talks to Mother a lot and keeps her from going into her fits." He glanced uneasily at his brother. "Sorry, I mean trances."

"What do they talk about?" Raistlin asked.

Caramon looked startled. "I dunno. Female stuff, I guess. I never listened."

"And how can we afford to pay this woman?"

Caramon grinned. "We don't pay her. That's what's great about this, Raist! She does it for nothing."

"Since when have we lived off charity?" Raistlin demanded.

"It's not charity. Raist. We offered to pay her, but she wouldn't take it. She helps others as part of her religion—that new order we heard about in Haven. The Belzorites or some such thing. She's one of them."

"I don't like this," Raistlin said, frowning. "No one does something for nothing. What is she after?"

"After? What could she be after? It's not like we have a house crammed with jewels. The Widow Judith's just a nice person, Raist. Can't you believe that?"

Apparently Raistlin could not, for he continued to ask questions. "How did you come across such a 'nice person,' my brother?"

"Actually, she came to us," Caramon said after taking a moment to recollect. "She came to the door one day and said that she'd heard Mother wasn't feeling well. She knew we men-folk"—Caramon spoke the plural with a touch of pride—"needed to be out working and said that she'd be glad to sit with Mother while we were gone. She told us she was a widow lady, her own man was dead, her children grown and moved on. She was lonely herself. And the High Priest of Belzor had commanded her to help others."

"Who is Belzor?" Raistlin asked suspiciously.

By this time, even Caramon's patience was exhausted.

"Name of the Abyss, I don't know, Raistlin," he said. "Ask her yourself. Only be nice to the Widow Judith, all right? She's been real nice to us." Raistlin did not bother to respond. He fell into another brooding silence.

He did not himself know why this should upset him. Perhaps it was nothing more than his own feelings of guilt for having abandoned his mother to the care of strangers. Yet something about this wasn't quite right. Caramon and his father were too trusting, too ready to believe in the goodness of people. They could both be easily taken in. No one devoted hours of her day to caring for another without expecting to gain something by it. No one.

Caramon was casting his brother worried, anxious glances. "You're not mad at me, Raist, are you? I'm sorry I snapped at you. It's just . . . well, you haven't met the widow yet, and—"

"You seem to be faring well, my brother," Raistlin interrupted. He did not want to hear any more about Judith.

Caramon straightened his back proudly. "I've grown four inches since fall. Father measured me on the doorframe. I'm taller than all our friends now, even Sturm."

Raistlin had noticed. He could not help but notice that Caramon was no longer a child. He had grown that winter into a comely young man— sturdy, tall for his age, with a mass of curly hair and wide-open, almost unbearably honest brown eyes. He was cheerful and easygoing, polite to his elders, fun-loving and companionable. He would laugh heartily at any joke, even if it was against himself. He was considered a friend by every young person in town, from the stern and generally morose Sturm Brightblade to the toddlers of Farmer Sedge, who clamored for rides on Caramon's broad shoulders.

As for the adults, their neighbors, especially the women, felt sorry for the lonely boy and were always inviting him to share a meal with the family. Due to the fact that he never turned down a free meal, even if he'd already just eaten, Caramon was probably the best-fed youngster in Solace.

"Any word from Kitiara?" Raistlin asked.

Caramon shook his head. "Nothing all winter. It's been over a year now since we heard from her. Do you think . . . I mean . . . Maybe she's dead. . . ."

The brothers exchanged glances, and in that exchange, the resemblance between the two, not usually noticeable, was quite apparent. Both shook their heads. Caramon laughed.

"All right, so she's not dead. Where is she, then?"

"Solamnia," said Raistlin.

"What?" Caramon was astonished. "How do you know that?"

"Where else would she go? She went to search for her father, or at least for his people, her kin."

"Why would she need them?" Caramon wondered. "She's got us."

Raistlin snorted and said nothing.

"She'll be back for us, at any rate," Caramon said confidently. "Will you go with her, Raist?"

"Perhaps," Raistlin said. "After I've passed the Test."

"Test? Is that like the tests Father gives?" Caramon looked indignant. "Miss one lousy sum and get sent to bed without any supper. A guy could starve to death! And what good is arithmetic to a warrior, anyway? Whack! Whack!"

Caramon slashed an imaginary sword through the air, startling the horse. "Hey! Oops. Sorry, there, Bess. I suppose I might need to know numbers for counting the heads of all the goblins I'm going to kill or how many pieces of pie to cut, but that's it. I certainly don't need twice-times and divisors and all that."

"Then you will grow up ignorant," said Raistlin coldly. "Like a gully dwarf."

Caramon clapped his brother on the shoulder. "I don't care. You can do all the twice-times for me."

"There might be a time when I am not there, Caramon," Raistlin said.

"We'll always be together, Raist," Caramon returned complacently. "We're twins. I need you for twice-times. You need me to look after you."

Raistlin sighed inwardly, conceding this to be true. And it wouldn't be so bad, he thought. Caramon's brawn combined with my brain . . .

"Stop the cart!" Raistlin ordered.

Startled, Caramon yanked on the reins, brought the horse to a halt. "What is it? You got to go pee? Should I come with you? What?"

Raistlin slid off the seat. "Stay there. Wait for me. I won't be long."

Landing on the hard-baked dirt, he left the road and plunged into the thick weeds and underbrush. Beyond him, a stand of wheat rippled like a golden lake, washed up against a shoreline of dark green pines. Pawing through the weeds, shoving them aside impatiently, Raistlin searched for the glint of white he'd seen from the cart.

There it was. White flowers with waxy petals, set against large, dark green leaves with saw-toothed edges. Tiny filaments hung from the leaves. Raistlin paused, inspected the plant. He identified it easily. The problem was how to gather it. He ran back to the cart.

"What is it?" Caramon craned his neck to see. "A snake? Did you find a snake?"

"A plant," Raistlin said. Reaching into the cart, he grabbed hold of his bundle of clothes, pulled out a shirt. He returned to his find.

"A plant . . ." Caramon repeated, his face wrinkling in puzzlement. He brightened. "Can you eat it?"

Raistlin did not reply. He knelt beside the plant, the shirt wrapped around his hand. With his left hand, he unclasped a small knife from his belt, and, moving cautiously, careful to keep his bare hand from brushing against the filaments, he snipped several of the leaves from the stem. He picked up the leaves with the hand protected by the shirt and, carrying them gingerly, returned to the wagon.

Caramon stared. "All that for a bunch of leaves?"

"Don't touch it!" Raistlin warned.

Caramon snatched his hand back. "Why not?"

"You see those little filaments on the leaves?"

"Fill-a-whats?"

"Hairs. The tiny hairs on the leaves? This plant is called 'stinging nettle.' Touch the leaves and they'll sting you enough to raise red welts on your skin. It's very painful. Sometimes people even die from it, if they react badly to it."

"Ugh!" Caramon peered down at the nettle leaves lying in the bottom of the wagon. "What do you want a plant like that for?"

Raistlin settled himself back onto the wagon's seat. "I study them."

"But they could hurt you!" Caramon protested. "Why do you want to study something that could hurt you?"

"You practice with the sword Kitiara brought you. Remember the first time you swung it? You nearly cut your foot off!"

"I still have the scar," Caramon said sheepishly. "Yeah, I guess that's true." He clucked at the horse and the cart lurched forward.

The brothers spoke of other matters after that. Caramon did most of the talking, relating the news of Solace—those who had newly moved into town, those who had left, those who had been born, and those who had died. He told of the small adventures of their group of friends, children with whom they'd grown up. And the truly remarkable news: A kender had taken up residency. The one who'd caused such a stir at the fair. He'd moved in with that grumpy dwarf metalsmith; much to the dwarf's ire, but what could you do about it, short of drowning the kender, whose untimely demise was expected daily. Raistlin listened in silence, letting his brother's voice flow over him, warming him like the spring sunshine.

Caramon's cheerful, mindless prattle removed some of the dread Raistlin felt, dread about going home and seeing his mother again. Her health had always been failing, it seemed to him. The winters drained her, sapped her strength. Every spring he returned to find her a little paler, a little thinner, a little farther removed into her dream world. As for this Widow Judith helping her, he would believe that when he saw it.

"I can drop you off at the crossroads, Raist," Caramon offered. "I have to work in the fields until sundown. Or you can come with me if you want. You can rest in the wagon until it's time go home. That way we can walk back together."

"I'll go with you, my brother," Raistlin said placidly.

Caramon flushed with pleasure. He started telling Raistlin all about the family life of Farmer Sedge and the little Sedges.

Raistlin cared nothing about any of them. He had staved off the hour when he must return home, he had insured that he would not be alone when he first encountered Rosamun. And he had made Caramon happy. It took so little to make Caramon happy.

Raistlin glanced back at the stinging nettle leaves he'd gathered. Noticing that they were starting to wilt in the sunshine, he tenderly wrapped the shirt more closely around them.

✛

"Jon Farnish," said Master Theobald, sitting at his desk at the front of the class. "The assignment was to gather six herbs that may be used for spell components. Come forward and show us what you found."

Jon Farnish, red hair gleaming, his freckled face carefully arranged to appear solemn and studious—at least while it was in view of the master—slid off the high stool and made his way to the front of the classroom. Jon Farnish bowed to Master Theobald, who smiled and nodded. Master Theobald had taken a liking to Jon Farnish, who never failed to be immensely impressed whenever Master Theobald cast the most minor of spells.

Turning his back on Master Theobald, facing his classmates, Jon Farnish rolled his eyes, puffed out his cheeks, and pulled his mouth down at the corners, making a ludicrous caricature of his teacher. His classmates covered their mouths to hide their mirth or looked down hurriedly at their desks. One actually began to laugh, then tried to change it to a cough, with the result that he nearly choked himself.

Master Theobald frowned.

"Silence, please. Jon Farnish, do not let these rowdy individuals upset you."

"I'll try not to, Master," said Jon Farnish.

"Continue, please."

"Yes, Master." Jon Farnish thrust his hand into his pouch. "The first plant I gathered—"

He halted, sucked in a breath, gasped, and screeched in pain. Flinging the pouch to the floor, he wrung his right hand.

"Something . . . something stung me!" he babbled. "Ow! It hurts like fire! Ow!"

Tears streamed down his cheeks. He thrust his hand beneath his armpit and did a little dance of agony in the front of the room.

Only one of his classmates was smiling now.

Master Theobald rose to his feet, hastened forward. Prying loose Jon's hand, the mage examined it, gave a grunt. "Go into the kitchen and ask cook for some butter to put on it."

"What is it?" Jon Farnish gasped between moans. "A wasp? A snake?"

Picking up the pouch, Master Theobald peered inside. "You silly boy. You've picked stinging nettle leaves. Perhaps from now on, you'll pay more attention in class. Go along with you and stop sniveling. Raistlin Majere, come forward."

Raistlin walked to the front of the class, made a polite bow to the master. Turning, he faced his classmates. His gaze swept the room. They stared back at him in sullen silence, their lips compressed, eyes shifting away from his triumphant gaze.

They knew. They understood.

Raistlin thrust his hand into his pouch, drew forth some fragrant leaves. "The first plant I am going to talk about today is marjoram. Marjoram is a spice, named for one of the old gods, Majere. . . ."

2

THE FIRST FEW DAYS OF THE SUMMER OF RAISTLIN'S THIRTEENTH YEAR were unusually hot. The leaves of the vallenwoods hung limp and lifeless in the breathless air. The sun bronzed Caramon's skin, burned Raistlin's as the two made the daily trek back and forth from school to home in the farmer's cart.

In school, the pupils were dull and stupid from the heat, spent the days swatting at flies, dozing off, waking to the sting of Master Theobald's willow branch. Finally even Master Theobald conceded that they were accomplishing nothing. Besides, there was the Wizards' Conclave he wanted to attend. He gave his students a holiday for eight weeks. School would recommence in autumn, after the harvest.

Raistlin was thankful for the holiday; at least it was a break in the dull routine. Yet he hadn't been home for more than a day before he wished he was back in school. Reminded of the teasing, the cabbage, and Master Theobald, he wondered why he wasn't happy at home. And then he realized he wouldn't be happy anywhere. He felt restless, dissatisfied.

"You need a girl," Caramon advised.

"I hardly think so," Raistlin answered acerbically. He glanced over to a group of three sisters, pretending to be wholly absorbed in hanging the laundry over the vallenwood limbs to dry. But their attention was not on shirts and petticoats. Their eyes darted daring, smiling glances at Caramon. "Do you realize how silly you look, my brother? You and the others? Puffing up your chests and flexing your muscles, throwing axes at trees or flailing away at each other with your fists. All for what? To gain the attention of some giggling girl!"

"I get more than giggles, Raist," Caramon said, with a lewd wink. "Come on over. I'll introduce you. Lucy said she thought you were cute."

"I have ears, Caramon," Raistlin returned coldly. "What she said was that your baby brother was cute."

Caramon flushed, uncomfortable. "She didn't mean it, Raist. She didn't know. I explained to her that we were the same age, and—"

Raistlin turned and walked away. The girl's heedless words had hurt him deeply, and his pain angered him, for he wanted to be above caring what anyone thought of him. It was this traitorous body of his, first sickly and frail, now teasing him with vague longings and half-understood desires. He considered it all disgusting anyway. Caramon was behaving like a stag during rutting season.

Girls, or the lack of them, were not his problem, at least not all of it. He wondered uneasily what was.

The heat broke suddenly that night in a violent thunderstorm. Raistlin lay awake to watch the bolts of light streak the roiling clouds with eerie pinks and oranges. He reveled in the booms of thunder that shook the vallenwoods and vibrated through the floorboards. A blinding flash, a deafening explosion, the smell of sulfur, and the sound of shattering wood told of a lightning strike nearby. Shouts of "Fire!" were partially lost in the crashing thunder. Caramon and Gilon braved the torrential rain to go out to help battle the blaze. Fire was their worst enemy. Though the vallenwood trees were more resistant to fire than most others, a blaze out of control could destroy their entire tree town. Raistlin stayed with his mother, who wept and trembled and wondered why her husband hadn't remained home to comfort her. Raistlin watched the progress of the flames, his spellbooks clasped fast in his hand in case he and his mother had to run for it.

The storm ended at dawn. Only one tree had been hit, three houses burned. No one had been injured; the families had escaped in time. The ground was littered with leaves and blasted limbs, the air was tainted with the sickening smell of smoke and wet wood. All around Solace, small streams and creeks were out of their banks. Fields that had been parched were now flooded.

Raistlin left his home to view the damage, along with almost every other person in Solace. He then walked to the edge of the tree line to see the rising water. He stared at the churning waters of the creek. Normally placid, it was now foam-flecked, swirling angrily, gnawing away at the banks that had long held it confined.

Raistlin felt complete sympathy.

Autumn came, bringing cool, crisp days and fat, swollen moons; brilliant colors, reds and golds. The rustle and swirl of the falling leaves did not cheer Raistlin's mood. The change of the season, the bittersweet melancholy that belongs to autumn, which brings both the harvest and the withering frost, served only to exacerbate his ill humor.

This day, he would return to school, resume boarding with Master Theobald. Raistlin looked forward to going back to school as he had looked forward to leaving—it was a change, at least. And at least his brain would have something to do besides torment him with images of golden curls, sweet smiles, swelling breasts, and fluttering eyelashes.

The late autumn morning was chill; frost glistened on the red and golden leaves of the vallenwood and rimed the wooden walkways, making them slippery and treacherous before the sun came out to dry them. Clouds hung gray and lowering over the Sentinel Peaks. The smell of snow was in the air. There would be snow on the mountaintop by the end of the week.

Raistlin thrust his clothes into a bag: two homespun shirts, underclothes, an extra pair of slops, woolen stockings. Most of his clothes were new, made by his mother. He needed the new clothes. He had gained in height that summer, keeping up with Caramon, though he lacked the bulk of his sturdy brother. The added height only served to emphasize Raistlin's excessive thinness.

Rosamun came out of her bedroom. Pausing, she stared at him with her faded blue eyes. "Whatever are you doing, child?"

Raistlin glanced up warily from his work. His mother's soft brown hair was brushed and combed and neatly arranged beneath a cap. She was wearing a clean skirt and bodice over a new blouse, a blouse she had sewn herself under the Widow Judith's tutelage.

Raistlin had tensed instinctively at the sound of her voice. Now, seeing her, he relaxed. His mother was having another good day. She had not had a bad day during his stay at home that summer, and Raistlin supposed they had the Widow Judith to thank for it.

He did not know what to make of the Widow Judith. He had been prepared to distrust her, prepared to discover something nefarious about her, some hidden motive for her selflessness. Thus far his suspicions had proven unfounded. She was what she appeared—a widow in her forties, with a pleasant face, smooth hands with long, graceful fingers, a melodious voice, a way with words, and an engaging laugh that always brought a smile to Rosamun's pale, thin face.

The Majere house was now clean and well organized, something it had never been before the Widow Judith's arrival. Rosamun ate meals at regular hours. She slept through the night, went to market, went visiting—always accompanied by the Widow Judith.

The Widow Judith was friendly to Raistlin, though she was not as free and easy with him as she was with Caramon. She was more reserved around Raistlin, and, he realized, she always seemed to be watching him. He could not do anything around the house without feeling her eyes on him.

"She knows you don't like her, Raist," Caramon said to him accusingly.

Raistlin shrugged. That was true, though he couldn't quite explain why. He did not like her and was quite certain she didn't like him.

One of the reasons may have been that Rosamun, Gilon, Caramon, and the Widow Judith were a family. and Raistlin was not part of it. This was not because he hadn't been invited, but because he willfully chose to remain on the outside. During the evenings when Gilon was home, the four would sit outdoors, joking and telling stories. Raistlin would remain indoors, poring over his school notes.

Gilon was a changed man now that his wife had been rescued from her storm-tossed mind, and was apparently resting comfortably in safer waters. The worry lines smoothed from his brow, he laughed more often. He and his wife could actually carry on a relatively normal conversation.

Summer work was closer to home; Gilon was able to be with his family more often. Everyone was pleased about this except Raistlin, who had grown accustomed to his father being gone, felt constrained when the big man was around. He didn't particularly like the change in his mother, either. He rather missed her odd fancies and flights, missed the times she had been his alone. He didn't like the new warmth between her and Gilon; their closeness made him feel further isolated.

Caramon was obviously Gilon's favorite, and Caramon adored his father. Gilon tried to take an interest in the other twin, but the big woodsman was very like the trees he cut—slow growing, slow moving, slow thinking. Gilon could not understand Raistlin's love of magic and though he had approved sending his son to the mage school, Gilon had secretly hoped the child would find it tedious and leave. He continued to nurture the same hope and always looked disappointed on the day when school recommenced and Raistlin began packing. But amidst the disappointment, there was now a relief. Raistlin this summer had been like a stranger boarding with the family, an irritable, unfriendly stranger.

Gilon would never admit this, even to himself, but he was going to be glad to see one of his sons depart.

The feeling was mutual. Raistlin sometimes felt sorry he couldn't love his father more, and he was vaguely aware that Gilon was sorry he couldn't love his strange, unchancy son.

No matter, Raistlin thought, rolling up his stockings into a ball. Tomorrow I will be gone. He found it difficult to believe, but he was actually looking forward to the smell of cooked cabbage.

"What are you doing with your clothes, Raistlin?" Rosamun asked.

"I am packing, Mother. I return to Master Theobald's tomorrow to board there over the winter." He tried a smile at her. "Had you forgotten?"

"No," Rosamun said in tones colder than the frost. "I was hoping that you would not be going back there."

Raistlin halted his packing to regard his mother with astonishment. He had expected such words from his father.

"What? Not go back to my studies? Why would you think such a thing, Mother?"

"It is wicked, Raistlin!" Rosamun cried vehemently; with a passion frightening in its intensity. "Wicked, I tell you!" She stomped her foot, drew herself up. "'r forbid you to go back there. Ever!"

"Mother . . ." Raistlin was shocked, alarmed, perplexed. He had no idea what to say. She had never before protested his chosen field of study. He had wondered, at times, if she even knew he was studying magic, much less cared. "Mother, some people think ill of mages, but I assure you that they are wrong."

"Gods of evil!" she intoned in a hollow voice. "You worship gods of evil, and at their behest, you perform unnatural acts and unholy rites!"

"The most unnatural thing I've done so far, Mother, is to fall off my stool and nearly split my skull open," said Raistlin dryly. Her accusations were so ludicrous, he found it difficult to take this conversation seriously.

"Mother, I spend my days droning away after my master, learning to say 'ah' and 'oo' and 'uh.' I cover myself with ink and occasionally manage to write something that is almost legible on a bit of parchment or scroll. I tramp about in fields picking flowers. That is what I do, Mother. That is all I do," he said bitterly. "And I assure you that Caramon's job mucking out stables and picking corn is far more interesting and far more exciting than magic."

He stopped talking, astonished at himself, astonished at his own feelings. Now he understood. Now he knew what had been chafing at him all summer. He understood the anger and frustration that bubbled like molten steel inside him. Anger and frustration, tempered by fear and self-doubt.

Ink and flowers. Reciting meaningless words day after day. Where was the magic? When would it come to him?

Would it come to him?

He shook with a sudden chill.

Rosamun put her arm around his waist, rested her cheek against his. "You see? Your skin—it's hot to the touch. I think you must have a fever. Don't go back to that dreadful school! You only make yourself sick. Stay here with me. I will teach you all you need to know. We will read books together and work out sums like we used to do when you were little. You will keep me company."

Raistlin found the idea surprisingly tempting. No more of the inanities of Master Theobald. No more silent, lonely nights in the dormitory, nights made all the more lonely because he was not alone. No more of this inner torment, this constant questioning.

What had happened to the magic? Where had it gone? Why did his blood burn more at the sight of some silly giggling girl than it did when he copied down his *oas* and *ais*?

He had lost the magic. Either that, or the magic had never been there. He had been fooling himself. It was time to admit defeat. Admit that he had failed. Return home. Shut himself away in this cozy, snug room, warm, safe, surrounded by his mother's love. He would take care of her. He would send the Widow Judith packing.

Raistlin bowed his head, unwilling she should see his bitter unhappiness. Rosamun never noticed, however. She caressed his cheek and playfully turned his face to the looking glass. The mirror had come with her from Palanthas. It was her prized possession, one of the few relics of her girlhood.

"We will have such splendid times together, you and I. Look!" she said coaxingly, regarding the two faces in the reflection with complacent pride. "Look how alike we are!"

Raistlin was not superstitious. But her words, spoken in all innocence, were so very ill-omened that he couldn't help but shudder.

"You're shivering," Rosamun said, concerned. "There! I said you had a fever! Come and lie down!"

"No, Mother. I am fine. Mother, please . . ."

He tried to edge away. Her touch, which had seemed so comforting, was now something loathsome. Raistlin was ashamed and appalled that he felt this way about his mother, but he couldn't help himself.

She only clasped him more tightly, rested her cheek against his arm. He was taller than she was by at least a head.

"You are so thin," she said. "Far too thin. Food doesn't stick to your bones.

You fret it away. And that school. I'm sure it's making you ill. Sickness is a punishment for those who do not walk the paths of righteousness, so the Widow Judith says."

Raistlin didn't hear his mother, he wasn't listening to her. He was suffocating, felt as if someone were pressing a pillow over his nose and mouth. He longed to break free of his mother's grasp and rush outside, where he could gulp down huge drafts of fresh air. He longed to run and to keep on running, run into the sweet-scented night, journey along a road that would take him anywhere but here.

At that moment, Raistlin knew a kinship with his half-sister, Kitiara. He understood then why she had left, knew how she must have felt. He envied her the freedom of her life, cursed the frail body that kept him chained to home's hearth, kept him fettered in his schoolroom.

He had always assumed the magic would free him, as Kitiara's sword had freed her. But what if the magic did not free him? What if the magic would not come to him? What if he had indeed lost the gift? He looked into the mirror, looked into his mother's dream-ravaged face, and closed his eyes against the fear.

3

SNOW WAS FALLING. The boys were dismissed early, told to go play outdoors until dinner. Exercising in the cold was healthful, expanded the lungs. The boys knew the real reason they were being sent outside. Master Theobald wanted to get rid of them.

He had been strangely preoccupied all that day, his mind—what there was of it—somewhere else. He taught class absent-mindedly, not seeming to care whether they learned anything or not. He had not had recourse to the willow branch once, although one of the boys had drifted off to sleep shortly after lunch and slept soundly and noisily through the remainder of the afternoon.

Most of the boys considered such inattention on their master's part a welcome change. Three found it extremely uncomfortable, however, due to the fact that he would occasionally lapse into long, vacant silences, his gaze roving among these three eldest in his class.

Raistlin was among the three.

Outside, the other boys took advantage of the heavy snowfall to build a fort, form armies, and pelt each other with snowballs. Raistlin wrapped himself in a warm, thick cloak—a parting gift, oddly enough, from the Widow Judith—and left the others to their stupid games. He went for a walk among a stand of pines on the north side of the school.

No wind blew. The snow brought a hush to the land, muffling all sound, even the shrill shouting of the boys. He was wrapped in silence. The trees stood unmoving. Animals were tucked away in nest or lair or den, sleeping their winter sleep. All color was obliterated, leaving in its absence the white of the falling snow, the black of the wet tree trunks, the slate gray of the lowering sky.

Raistlin stood on the edge of the forest. He had intended to walk among the trees, to follow a snow-choked path that led to a little clearing. In the clearing was a fallen log, which served well as a seat. This was Raistlin's refuge, his sanctuary. No one knew about it. Pines shielded the clearing from the school and the play yard. Here Raistlin came to brood, to think, to sort through his collection of herbs and plants, to mull over his notes, reciting to himself the letters of the alphabet of the language of the arcane.

He had been certain, when he'd first marked the clearing as his own, that the other boys would find it and try to spoil it—drag off the log, perhaps; dump their kitchen scraps here; empty their chamber pots in it. The boys had left the clearing alone. They knew he went off somewhere by himself, but they made no attempt to follow him. Raistlin had been pleased at first. They respected him at last.

The pleasure had soon faded. He came to realize that other boys left him alone because, after the nettle incident, they detested him. They had always disliked him, but now they distrusted him so much that they derived no pleasure from teasing him. They left him severely alone.

I should welcome this change, he said to himself.

But he didn't. He found that he had secretly enjoyed the attention of the others, even if such attention had annoyed, hurt, or angered him. At least by teasing him they had acknowledged him as one of them. Now he was an outcast.

He had meant to walk to the clearing this day, but, standing on the outskirts, looking at the trackless snow flowing in smooth, frozen ripples around the boles of the trees, he did not enter.

The snow was perfect, so perfect that he could not bring himself to walk through it, leaving a floundering trail behind, marring the perfection.

The school bell rang. He lowered his head against the icy flakes that a slight, rising breeze was blowing into his eyes. Turning, he slogged his way back through the silence and the white and the black and the gray, back to the heat and the torpor and loneliness of the schoolroom.

❂

The boys changed their wet clothes and filed down to supper, which they ate under the watchful, if somewhat vacant, eye of Marm. Master Theobald entered the room only if necessary to prevent the floor from being awash in soup.

Marm reported any misdeeds to the master, and so the bread-tossing and soup-spitting had to be kept to a minimum. The boys were tired and hungry after their hard-fought snow battles, and there was less horseplay than usual. The large common room was relatively quiet except for a few smothered giggles here and there, and thus the boys were extremely surprised when Master Theobald entered.

Hastily the boys clamored to their feet, wiping grease from their chins with the backs of their hands. They regarded his arrival with indignation. Dinner was their own personal time, into which the master had no right or reason to intrude.

Theobald either didn't see or decided to ignore the restless feet shuffling, the frowns, the sullen looks. His gaze picked out the three eldest: Jon Farnish; Gordo, the hapless butcher; and Raistlin Majere.

Raistlin knew immediately why the master had come. He knew what the master was going to say, what was going to happen. He didn't know how he knew: premonition, some hereditary offshoot of his mother's talent, or simple logical deduction. He didn't know and he didn't care. He couldn't think clearly. He went cold, colder than the snow, fear and exultation vying within him. The bread he had been holding fell from his nerveless hand. The room seemed to tilt beneath him. He was forced to lean against the table to remain standing.

Master Theobald called off the names of the three, names that Raistlin heard only dimly through a roaring in his ears, the roaring as of flames shooting up a chimney.

"Walk forward," said the master.

Raistlin could not move. He was terrified that he would collapse. He was too weak. Was he falling sick? The sight of Jon Farnish, tromping across the floor of the common room with a hangdog air, certain that he was in trouble, brought a derisive smile to Raistlin's lips. His head cleared, the chimney fire had burnt itself out. He strode forward, conscious of his dignity.

He stood before Theobald, heard the master's words in his bones, had no conscious recollection of hearing them in his ears.

"I have, after long and careful consideration, decided that you three, by virtue of your age and your past performance, will be tested this night to determine your ability to put to use the skills you have learned. Now, don't be alarmed."

This to Gordo, whose eyes, white-rimmed and huge with consternation, seemed likely to roll from their sockets.

"This test is not the least bit dangerous," the master continued soothingly. "If you fail it, nothing untoward will happen to you. The test will tell me if you have made the wrong choice in wanting to study magic. If so, I will inform your parents and anyone else interested in your welfare"—here he looked very sharply at Raistlin—"that, in my opinion, your remaining here is a waste of time and money."

"I never wanted to be here!" Gordo blurted out, sweating. "Never! I want to be a butcher!"

Somebody laughed. Frowning in anger, the master sought the culprit, who immediately hushed and ducked behind one of his fellows. The others were silent. Certain that peace was restored, Theobald looked back at his pupils.

"I trust you two do not feel the same way?"

Jon Farnish smiled. "I look forward to this test, Master."

Raistlin hated Jon Farnish, could have slain him in that instant. He wanted to have spoken those words! Spoken them with that casual tone and careless confidence. Instead, Raistlin could only fumble and stammer, "I . . . I am . . . am ready. . . ."

Master Theobald sniffed as if he very much doubted this statement. "We will see. Come along."

He shepherded them out of the common room, the wretched Gordo sniveling and protesting, Jon Farnish eager and grinning, as if this were playtime, and Raistlin so wobbly in the knees that he could barely walk.

He saw his life balanced on this moment, like the dagger Caramon stood on its point on the kitchen table. Raistlin imagined being turned out of the school tomorrow morning, sent home with his small bundle of clothes in disgrace. He pictured the boys lining the walkway, laughing and hooting, celebrating his downfall. Returning home to Caramon's bluff and bumbling attempts to be sympathetic, his mother's relief, his father's pity.

And what would be his future without the magic?

Again Raistlin went cold, cold all over, cold and ice-hard with the terrible knowledge of himself.

Without the magic, there could be no future.

Master Theobald led them through the library, down a hallway to a spell-locked door leading to the master's private quarters. All the boys knew where the door led, and it was postulated among them that the master's laboratory—of which he often spoke—could be reached through this door. One night a group of the boys, led by Jon Farnish, had made a futile attempt to dispel the magic of the lock. Jon had been forced to explain the next day how he had burned his fingers.

The three boys in tow behind him, the master came to a halt in front of the door. He mumbled in a low voice several words of magic, words which Raistlin, despite the turmoil in his soul, made an automatic, concentrated effort to overhear.

He was not successful. The words made no sense, he could not think or concentrate, and they left his brain almost the moment they entered. He had nothing in his brain, nothing at all. He could not call to mind how to spell his own name, must less the complicated language of magic.

The door swung open. Master Theobald caught hold of Gordo, who was taking advantage of the spell being cast to do a disappearing act of his own. Master Theobald dug his pudgy fingers into Gordo's shoulder, thrust him, blubbering and whimpering, into a sitting room. Jon Farnish and Raistlin followed after. The door swung shut behind them.

"I don't want to do it! Please don't make me! A demon'll grab me sure!" Gordo howled.

"A demon! What nonsense! Stop this sniveling at once, you stupid boy!" Master Theobald's hand, from force of habit, reached for the willow branch, but he'd left that in the schoolroom. His voice hardened. "I shall slap you if you don't control yourself this instant."

The master's hand, though empty, was broad and large. Gordo glanced at it and fell silent, except for a snivel now and then.

"Won't do no good, me going down there," he said sullenly. "I'm rotten at this here magic."

"Yes, you are," the master agreed. "But your parents have paid for this, and they have a right to expect you to at least make the attempt."

He moved a fancifully braided rug aside with his foot, revealing a trapdoor. This, too, was wizard-locked. Again the master mumbled arcane words. He passed his hand three times over the lock, reached down, clasped hold of an iron ring, and lifted.

The trapdoor opened silently. A set of stone stairs led down into warm, scented darkness.

"Gordo and I will go first," Master Theobald said, adding caustically, "to clear the place of demons."

Grasping the unfortunate Gordo by the scruff of his neck, Theobald dragged him down the stairs. Jon Farnish clattered eagerly after him. Raistlin started to follow. His foot was on the top stair when he froze.

He was about to set foot into an open grave.

He blinked his eyes, and the image vanished. Before him were nothing more sinister than cellar stairs. Still, Raistlin wavered there on the threshold. He had learned from his mother to be sensitive to dreams and portents. He had seen the grave quite clearly and he wondered what it meant, or if it meant anything at all. Probably it was nothing more than his cursed fancy, his overactive imagination. Yet, still, he hovered on the stairs.

Jon Farnish was down there, except it wasn't Jon Farnish. It was Caramon, standing over Raistlin's grave, gazing down at his twin in pitying sorrow.

Raistlin shut his eyes. He was far from this place, in his clearing, seated on the log, the snow falling on him, filling his world, leaving it cold, pure, trackless.

When he opened his eyes, Caramon was gone and so was the grave.

His step quick and firm, Raistlin walked down the stairs.

4

THE LABORATORY WAS NOT AS RAISTLIN—OR ANY OF THE OTHER BOYS IN the class—had imagined. Much speculation had been given to this hidden chamber during clandestine midnight sessions in the dormitory room. The master's laboratory was generally conceded to be pitch dark, knee-deep in cobwebs and bats' eyeballs, with a captured demon imprisoned in a cage in a corner.

The elder boys would whisper to the new boys at the start of the year that the strange sounds they could hear at night were made by the demon rattling his chains, trying to break free. From then on, whenever there was a creak or a bump, the new boys would lie in bed and tremble in fear, believing that the demon had freed itself at last. One night the cat, mousing among the pots and kettles, knocked an iron skillet off the wall caused a general outbreak of panic, with the result that the master, having been wakened by the heartrending cries of terror, heard the story and banned all conversation after the candles had been removed.

Gordo had been one of the most inventive when it came to giving life to the demon in the laboratory, effectively frightening the wits out of the three six-year-olds currently boarding at the school. But it was now apparent that Gordo had scared no one quite as much as himself. When he turned around and actually beheld a cage in the corner, its bars shining in the soft white light cast by a globe suspended from the ceiling, the boy's knees gave way and he sank to the floor.

"Drat the boy, whatever is the matter with you? Stand on your own two feet!" Master Theobald gave Gordo a prod and a shake. "Good evening, my beauties," the master added, peering into the cage. "Here's dinner."

The wretched Gordo turned quite pale, evidently seeing himself as the next course. The master was not referring to the boys, however, but to a hunk of bread that he dredged up from his pocket. He deposited the bread in the cage, where it was immediately set upon by four lively field mice.

Gordo put his hand on his stomach and said he didn't feel so good.

Under other circumstances, Raistlin might have been amused by the discomfiture of one of his most inveterate tormentors. Tonight he was far too pent up, anxious, eager, and nervous to enjoy the whimperings of the chastened bully.

The master made Gordo sit down on the floor with his head between his legs, and then went to a distant part of the laboratory to putter about among papers and inkpots. Bored, Jon Farnish began teasing the mice.

Raistlin moved out of the glare of the light, moved back into the shadows, where he could see without being seen. He made a methodical sweep of the laboratory, committing every detail to his excellent memory. Long years after he left Master Theobald's school, Raistlin could still shut his eyes and see every item in that laboratory, and he was only in it once.

The lab was neat, orderly, and clean. No dust, no cobwebs; even the mice were sleek and well groomed. A few magical spellbooks, bound in noncommittal colors of gray and tan, stood upon a shelf. Six scroll cases reposed in a bin designed to hold many more. There was an assortment of jars intended for storing spell components, but only a few had anything in them. The stone table, on which the master was supposed to perform experiments in the arcane, was as clean as the table on which he ate his dinner.

Raistlin felt a sadness seep into him. Here was the workshop of a man with no ambition, of a man in whom the creative spark had flickered out, presuming that spark had ever once been kindled. Theobald came to his lab not to create, but because he wanted to be alone, to read a book, throw crumbs to the mice in their cage, crush some oregano leaves for the luncheon stew, perhaps draw up a scroll now and then—a scroll whose magic might or might not work. Whether it did or it didn't was all the same to him.

"Feeling better, Gordo?" Master Theobald bustled about importantly, doing very little with a great deal of fuss. "Fine, I knew you would. Too much excitement, that's all. Take your place at the far end of the table. Jon Farnish, you take your place there in the center. Raistlin? Where the devil—oh! There you are!" Master Theobald glared at him crossly. "What are you doing skulking about there in the darkness? Come stand in the light like a civilized human being. You will take your place at the far end. Yes, right there."

Raistlin moved to his assigned seat in silence. Gordo stood

hunch-shouldered and glum. The laboratory was a sad disappointment, and this was starting to look far too much like schoolwork. Gordo was bitter over the lack of a demon.

Jon Farnish took his seat, smiling and confident, his hands folded calmly on the table in front of him. Raistlin had never hated anyone in his life as much as he hated Jon Farnish at that moment.

Every organ in Raistlin's body was tangled up with every other organ. His bowels squirmed and wrapped around his stomach, his heart lurched and pressed painfully against his lungs. His mouth was dry, so dry his throat closed and set him coughing. His palms were wet. He wiped his hands surreptitiously on his shirt.

Master Theobald sat at the head of the table. He was grave and solemn and appeared to take exception to the grinning Jon Farnish. He frowned and tapped his finger on the table. Jon Farnish, realizing his mistake, swallowed his grin and was immediately as grave and solemn as a cemetery owl.

"That's better," said the master. "This test you are about to take is quite a serious matter, as serious as the Test you will take when you are grown and prepared to advance through the various ranks of magical knowledge and power. I repeat, this test is every bit as serious, for if you do not pass the one, you will never have a chance to take the other."

Gordo gave a great, gaping yawn.

Master Theobald cast him a reproving glance, then continued. "It would be advisable if we could give this test to every child who enrolls in one of the mage schools prior to his or her entrance. Unfortunately, that is not possible. In order to take this test, you must possess a considerable amount of arcane knowledge. Thus the conclave has deemed that a student should have at least six years of study before taking the elementary test. Those who have completed six years will be given the elementary test even if they have previously shown neither talent nor inclination."

Theobald knew, but did not say, that the failed student would then be placed under surveillance, watched throughout the rest of his life. It was improbable, but such a failure might become a renegade wizard, one who refused to follow the laws of magic as handed down and adjudicated by the conclave. Renegade wizards were considered extremely dangerous—rightly so—and were hunted by the members of the conclave. The boys knew nothing about renegade wizards, and Master Theobald wisely refrained from mentioning it. Gordo would have been a nervous wreck the remainder of his existence.

"The test is simple for one who possesses the talent, extremely difficult for one who does not. Every person wanting to advance in the study of magic takes the same elementary test. You are not casting a spell, not even a cantrip. It will take many more years of study and hard work before you have the discipline and control necessary to cast the most rudimentary of magical spells. This test merely determines whether or not you have what was called in the old days 'the god's gift.' "

He was referring to the old gods of magic, three cousins: Solinari, Lunitari, Nuitari. Their names were all that was left of them, according to most people on Ansalon. Their names clung to their moons, to the silver moon, the red, and the supposed black moon.

Wary of public opinion, aware that they were not universally liked or trusted, the wizards took care not to become involved in religious arguments. They taught their pupils that the moons influenced magic much the way they influenced the tides. It was a physical phenomenon, nothing spiritual or mystical about it.

Yet Raistlin wondered. Had the gods truly gone from the world, leaving only their lights burning in night's window? Or were those lights glints from immortal, ever-watchful eyes? . . .

Master Theobald turned to the wooden shelves behind him, opened a drawer. He drew out three strips of lamb's skin, placed a strip in front of each boy. Jon Farnish was taking this quite seriously now, after the master's speech. Gordo was resigned, sullen, wanting to end this and return to his mates. He was probably already concocting the lies he would tell about the master's laboratory.

Raistlin examined the small strip of lamb's skin, no longer than his forearm. The skin was soft, it had never been used, was smooth to the touch.

The master placed a quill pen and an inkpot in front of each of the three boys. Standing back, he folded his hands over his stomach and said, in solemn, sonorous tones, "You will write down on this lamb's skin the words *I, Magus.*"

"Nothing else, Master?" asked Jon Farnish.

"Nothing else."

Gordo squirmed and bit the end of his quill. "How do you spell *Magus?*"

Master Theobald fixed him with a reproving stare. "That is part of the test!"

"What . . . what will happen if we do it right, Master?" Raistlin asked in a voice that he could not recognize as his own.

"If you have the gift, something will happen. If not, nothing," replied Master Theobald. He did not look at Raistlin as he spoke.

He wants me to fail, Raistlin understood, without quite knowing why. The master did not like him, but that wasn't the reason. Raistlin guessed that it had something to do with jealousy of his sponsor, Antimodes. The knowledge strengthened his resolve.

He picked up the quill, which was black, had come from the wing of a crow. Various types of quills were used to write various scrolls: an eagle's feather was extremely powerful, as was that of the swan. A goose quill was for everyday, ordinary writing, only to be used for magical penning in an emergency. A crow quill was useful for almost any type of magic, though some of the more fanatic White Robes objected to its color.

Raistlin touched the feather with his finger. He was extraordinarily conscious of the feather's feel, its crispness contrasting oddly with its softness. Rainbows, cast by the globe light, shimmered on the feather's glistening black surface. The point was newly cut, sharp. No cracked and sputtering pen for this important event.

The smell of the ink reminded him of Antimodes and the time he had praised Raistlin's work. Raistlin had long ago discovered, through eavesdropping on a conversation between the master and Gilon, that Antimodes was paying the bill for this school, not the conclave, as the archmagus had intimated. This test would prove if his investment had been sound.

Raistlin prepared to dip the quill in the ink, then hesitated, feeling a qualm of near panic. Everything he had been taught seemed to slide from his mind, like butter melting in a hot skillet. He could not remember how to spell Magus! The quill shook in his sweaty fingers. He glanced sidelong, through lowered lashes, at the other two.

"I'm done," said Gordo.

Ink covered his fingers; he'd managed to splash it on his face, where the black splotches overlapped the brown freckles. He held up the scroll, on which he'd first printed the word *Magos*. Having sneaked a peak at Jon Farnish's scroll, Gordo had hastily crossed out *Magos* and written *Magus* in next to it.

"I'm done," Gordo repeated loudly. "What happens now?"

"For you, nothing," said Theobald with a severe look.

"But I wrote the word just as good as him," Gordo protested, sulking.

"Have you learned nothing, you stupid boy?" Theobald demanded angrily. "A word of magic must be written perfectly, spelled correctly, the first time. You are writing not only with the lamb's blood but with your own blood. The magic flows through you and into the pen and from thence onto the scroll."

"Oh, bugger it," said Gordo, and he shoved the scroll off the table.

Jon Farnish was writing with ease, seemingly, the pen gliding over the sheepskin, a spot of ink on his right forefinger. His handwriting was readable, but tended to be cramped and small.

Raistlin dipped the quill in the ink and began to write, in sharply angled, bold, large letters, the words *I, Magus.*

Jon Farnish sat back, a look of satisfaction on his face. Raistlin, just finishing, heard the boy catch his breath. Raistlin looked up.

The letters on the sheepskin in front of Jon Farnish had begun to glow. The glow was faint, a dim red-orange, a spark newly struck, struggling for life.

"Garn!" said Gordo, impressed. This almost made up for the demon.

"Well done, Jon," said Master Theobald expansively.

Flushed with pleasure, Jon Farnish gazed in awe at the parchment and then he laughed. "I have it!" he cried.

Master Theobald turned his gaze to Raistlin. Though the master attempted to appear concerned, one corner of his lip curled.

The black letters on the sheepskin in front of Raistlin remained black.

Raistlin clutched the quill so violently he snapped off the top. He looked away from the exultant Jon Farnish, he paid no attention to the scornful Gordo, he blotted from his mind the leering triumph of the master. He concentrated on the letters in *I, Magus* and he said a prayer.

"Gods of magic, if you are gods and not just moons, don't let me fail, don't let me falter."

Raistlin turned inward, to the very core of his being, and he vowed, I will do this. Nothing in my life matters except this. No moment of my life exists except this moment. I am born in this moment, and if I fail, I will die in this moment.

Gods of magic, help me! I will dedicate my life to you. I will serve you always. I will bring glory to your name. Help me, please, help me!

He wanted this so much. He had worked so hard for it, for so long. He focused on the magic, concentrated all his energy. His frail body began to wilt beneath the strain. He felt faint and giddy. The globe of light expanded in his dazed vision to three globes. The floor was unsteady beneath him. He lowered his head in despair to the stone table.

The stone was cool and firm beneath his fevered cheek. He shut his eyes, hot tears burned the lids. He could still see, imprinted on his eyelids, the three globes of magical light.

To his astonishment, he saw that inside each globe was a person.

One was a fine, handsome young man, dressed all in white robes that shimmered with a silver light. He was strong and well muscled, with the physique of a warrior. He carried in his hand a staff of wood, topped by a golden dragon's claw holding a diamond.

Another was also a young man, but he was not handsome. He was grotesque. His face was round as a moon, his eyes were dry, dark and empty wells. He was dressed in black robes, and he held in his hands a crystal orb, inside which swirled the heads of five dragons: red, green, blue, white, and black.

Standing between the two was a beautiful young woman. Her hair was as black as the crow's wing, streaked with white. Her robes were as red as blood. She held, in her arms, a large leather-bound book.

The three were vastly different, strangely alike.

"Do you know who we are?" asked the man in white.

Raistlin nodded hesitantly. He knew them. He wasn't quite sure he understood why or how.

"You pray to us, yet many speak our names with their lips only, not their hearts. Do you truly believe in us?" asked the woman in red.

Raistlin considered this question. "You came to me, didn't you?" he answered. The glib answer displeased the god of light and the god of darkness. The man with the moon face grew colder, and the man in white looked grim. The woman in red was pleased with him, however. She smiled.

Solinari spoke sternly. "You are very young. Do you understand the promise you have made to us? The promise to worship us and glorify our names? To do so will go against the beliefs of many, may put you into mortal danger."

"I understand," Raistlin answered without hesitation.

Nuitari spoke next, his voice like splinters of ice. "Are you prepared to make the sacrifices we will require of you?"

"I am prepared," Raistlin answered steadily, adding, but only to himself, after all, what more can you demand of me that I have not already given?

The three heard his unspoken response. Solinari shook his head. Nuitari wore a most sinister grin.

Lunitari's laughter danced through Raistlin, exhilarating, disturbing. "You do not understand. And if you could foresee what will be asked of you in the future, you would run from this place and never come back. Still, we have watched you and we have been impressed with you. We grant your request on one condition. Remember always that you have seen us and spoken to us. Never deny your faith in us, or we will deny you."

The three globes of light coalesced into one, looking very much like an eye, with a white rim, a red iris, a black pupil. The eye blinked once and then remained wide open, staring.

The words *I, Magus* were all he could see, black on white lamb's skin.

"Are you ill, Raistlin?" The master's voice, as through a dank fog.

"Shut up!" Raistlin breathed. *Doesn't the fool know they are here? Doesn't he know they are watching, waiting?*

"*I, Magus.*" Raistlin whispered the words aloud. Black on white, he imbued them with his heart's blood.

The black letters began to glow red, like the sword resting in the blacksmith's forge fire. The letters burned hotter and brighter until *I, Magus* was traced in letters of flame. The lamb's skin blackened, curled in upon itself, was consumed. The fire died.

Raistlin, exhausted, sagged on his stool. On the stone table before him was nothing but a charred spot and bits of greasy ash. Inside him burned a fire that would never be quenched, perhaps not even in death.

He heard a noise, a sort of strangled croak. Master Theobald, Gordo, and Jon Farnish were all staring at him, wide-eyed and openmouthed.

Raistlin slid off his stool, made a polite bow to the master. "May I be excused now, sir?"

Theobald nodded silently, unable to speak. He would later tell the story at the conclave, tell of the remarkable test performed by one of his young pupils, relate how the lamb's skin had been devoured by the flames. Theobald added, with due modesty, that it was his skill as a teacher that had undoubtedly inspired his young pupil, wrought such a miracle.

Antimodes would make a special point to inform Par-Salian, who noted the incident with an asterisk next to Raistlin's name in the book where he kept a list of every student of magic in Ansalon.

That night, when the others were asleep, Raistlin wrapped himself in his thick cloak and slipped outside.

The snow had stopped falling. The stars and moons were scattered like a rich lady's jewels across the black sky. Solinari was a shining diamond. Lunitari a bright ruby. Nuitari, ebony and onyx, could not be seen, but he was there. He was there.

The snow glistened white and pure and untouched in the lambent light of stars and moons. The trees cast double shadows that streaked the white with black, black tinged with blood-red.

Raistlin looked up at the moons and he laughed, ringing laughter that echoed among the trees, laughter that could be heard all the way to heaven. He dashed headlong into the woods, trampling the white unbroken snow banks, leaving his tracks, his mark.

BOOK 3

The magic is in the blood, it flows from the heart. Every time you use it, part of yourself goes with it. Only when you are prepared to give of yourself and receive nothing back will the magic work for you.

—Theobald Beckman, Master

1

RAISTLIN SAT ON HIS STOOL IN THE CLASSROOM, HUNCHED OVER HIS desk, laboriously copying a spell. It was a sleep spell, simple for an experienced wizard, but still far beyond the reach of a sixteen-year-old, no matter how precocious. Raistlin knew this because, though he had been forbidden to do so, he had attempted to cast the spell.

Armed with his elementary spellbook, smuggled out of school beneath his shirt, and the requisite spell component, Raistlin had tried to cast the sleep spell on his uneasy but stead-fastly loyal brother. He had spoken the words, flung the sand into Caramon's face, and waited.

"Stop that, Caramon! Put your hands down."

"But, Raist! I got sand in my eyes!"

"You're supposed to be asleep!"

"I'm sorry, Raist. I guess I'm just not tired. It's almost suppertime."

With a deep sigh, Raistlin had returned the spellbook to its place at his desk, the sand to its jar in the laboratory. He had been forced to acknowledge that perhaps Master Theobald knew what he was talking about—on this occasion, at least. Casting a magic spell required something more than words and sand. If that was all it took, Gordo would have been a mage and not slaughtering sheep, as he was now.

"The magic comes from within," Master Theobald had lectured. "It begins at the center of your being, flows outward. The words pick up the magic as it surges from your heart up into your brain and from thence into your mouth. Speaking the words, you give the magic form and substance, and thus you cast the spell. Words spoken from an empty mouth do nothing but move the lips."

And though Raistlin more than suspected Master Theobald of having copied this lecture from someone else (in fact, Raistlin was to find it several years later, in a book written by Par-Salian), the young student had been impressed by the words and had noted them down carefully in the front of his spellbook.

That speech was in his thoughts as he copied—for the hundredth time—the spell onto scrap paper, preparatory to copying the spell into his primer. A leather-bound book, the primer was given to each novice mage who had passed his initial test. The novitiate would copy into his primer every spell committed to memory. In addition, he must also know how to pronounce correctly the words of the spell and how to write it onto a scroll, and he must know and have collected any components that the spell required.

Every quarter Master Theobald tested the novitiates—there were two in his school, Raistlin and Jon Farnish—on the spells they had learned. If the students performed to the master's satisfaction, they were permitted to write the spell into their primers. Only yesterday, at the end of the spring quarter, Raistlin had taken the test on his new spell and had passed it easily. Jon Farnish, by contrast, had failed, having transposed two letters in the third word. Master Theobald had given Raistlin permission to copy down the spell—the very sleep spell he had attempted to cast—into his primer. The master had sent Jon Farnish to copy the spell out two hundred times, until he could write it correctly.

Raistlin knew the sleep spell backward and forward and inside out. He could have written it upside down while standing on his head. Yet he could not make it work. He had even prayed to the gods of magic, asking for their help, as they had given him help during his elementary test. The gods were not forthcoming.

He did not doubt the gods. He doubted himself. It was some fault within him, something he was doing wrong. And so, instead of copying the spell into his primer, Raistlin was doing much the same as Jon Farnish, going over and over the words, meticulously writing down every letter until he could convince himself that he had not made a single mistake.

A shadow—a broad shadow—fell across his page.

He looked up. "Yes, Master?" he said, trying to hide his irritation at the interruption and not quite succeeding.

Raistlin had long ago realized that he was smarter than Master Theobald and more gifted in magic. He stayed in the school because there was nowhere else to go, and, as this proved, he still had much to learn. Master Theobald could cast a sleep spell.

"Do you know what time it is?" Master Theobald asked. "It is dinnertime.

You should be in the common room with the other boys."

"Thank you, but I'm not hungry, Master," Raistlin said ungraciously and went back to his work.

Master Theobald frowned. A well-fed man himself, one who enjoyed his meat and ale, he could not understand someone like Raistlin, to whom food was fuel to keep his body going and nothing more.

"Nonsense, you have to eat. What are you doing that is so important it causes you to skip a meal?" Master Theobald could see perfectly well what Raistlin was doing.

"I am working at copying this spell, Master," Raistlin said, gritting his teeth at the man's idiocy. "I do not feel ready yet to write in my primer."

Master Theobald looked down at the scraps of paper littering the desk. He picked up one, then another. "But these are adequate. Quite good, in fact."

"No, there must be something wrong!" Raistlin said impatiently. "Otherwise I could have been able to cast—"

He had not meant to say that. He bit his tongue and fell silent, glowering down at his ink-stained fingers.

"Ah," said Master Theobald, with the ghost of a smile, which, since Raistlin was not looking, he did not see. "So you have been attempting a little spellcasting, have you?"

Raistlin did not reply. If he could have cast a spell now, he would have summoned demons from the Abyss and ordered them to haul off Master Theobald.

The master leaned back and laced his fingers over his stomach, which meant that he was about to launch into one of his lectures.

"It didn't work, I take it. I'm not surprised. You are far too proud, young man. Far too self-absorbed and self-satisfied. You are a taker, not a giver. Everything flows into you. Nothing flows out. The magic is in the blood, it flows from the heart. Every time you use it, part of yourself goes with it. Only when you are prepared to give of yourself and receive nothing back will the magic work for you."

Raistlin lifted his head, shook his long, straight brown hair out of his face. He stared straight ahead. "Yes, Master," he said coldly, impassively. "Thank you, Master."

Master Theobald's tongue clicked against the roof of his mouth. "You are seated on a very high horse right now, young man. Someday you will fall off. If the fall doesn't kill you, you might learn something from it." The master grunted. I'm going to dinner now. I'm hungry."

Raistlin returned to his work, a scornful smile curling his lips.

2

T HAT SUMMER, THE SUMMER OF THE TWINS' SIXTEENTH YEAR, LIFE FOR the Majere family continued to improve. Gilon had been hired to help cut a stand of pines on the slopes of Prayer's Eye Peak. The property belonged to an absentee lord, who was having the wood hauled north to build a stockade. The job paid well and looked as if it would last a long time, for the stockade was going to be a large one.

Caramon worked full time for the prospering Farmer Sedge, who had extended his land holdings and was now shipping grain, fruits, and vegetables to the markets of Haven. Caramon worked long hours for a portion of the crops, some of which he sold, the rest he brought home.

The Widow Judith was considered a member of the family. She maintained her own small house, but for all practical purposes, she lived at the Majeres'. Rosamun could not manage without her. Rosamun herself was much improved. She had not fallen into one of her trancelike states in several years. She and the widow performed the chores around the house and spent much of their time visiting the neighbors.

Had Gilon known exactly what such visits entailed, he might have been worried about his wife. But he assumed Rosamun and the widow were doing nothing more than sharing the latest gossip. He could not know, nor would he have believed, the truth of the matter.

Gilon and Caramon both liked the Widow Judith. Raistlin grew to dislike her more than ever, perhaps because during the summer he was home with her, whereas the other two were not. He saw the influence the widow wielded over his mother, and he disliked and distrusted it. More than once, he came in on their whispered conversations, conversations that would end abruptly upon his arrival.

He tried to eavesdrop, hoping to hear what the two were saying. The Widow Judith had excellent hearing, however, and he was usually discovered. One day, however, the two women happened to be sitting at the kitchen table beneath a window where several pies were cooling. Walking up on them from outside, his footsteps lost among the rustling of the leaves of the vallenwood tree, Raistlin heard their voices. He halted in the shadows.

"The High Priest is not pleased with you, Rosamun Majere. I have had a letter from him this day. He wonders why you have not brought your husband and children into the arms of Belzor."

Rosamun's response was meek and defensive. She had tried. She had spoken to Gilon of Belzor several times, but her husband had only laughed at her. He did not need to have faith in any god. He had faith in himself and his good right arm and that was that. Caramon said he was quite willing to attend the meetings of the Belzorites, especially if they served food. As for Raistlin . . . Rosamun's voice trailed off.

As for Raistlin, he was eager to hear more, but at that moment the Widow Judith rose to see to the pies and saw him standing at the corner of the house. He and Judith looked intently at each other. Neither gave anything away to the other, however, except a shared enmity. The Widow Judith brought in the pies and closed the shutters. Raistlin continued on to his garden.

Who in the Abyss is this Belzor, he wondered, and why does he want to embrace us?

"It's some sort of thing of mother's," said Caramon, upon questioning. "You know. One of those woman things. They all meet together and talk about stuff. What kind of stuff? I don't know. I went once but I fell asleep."

Rosamun never said anything to Raistlin about Belzor, rather to Raistlin's disappointment. He considered bringing up the matter himself, but he feared this would involve talking to the Widow Judith, and he avoided contact with her as much as possible. The master was off on his visit to the conclave. School was out for the summer. Raistlin spent his days planting, cultivating, and adding to his collection of herbs. He was gaining some small reputation among the neighbors for his knowledge of herbs, sold what he himself did not need and thus was able to contribute to the family's income. He forgot about Belzor.

The Majere family was happy and prosperous that summer, a summer that would stand out in the twins' minds as golden, a gold that shone all the more brightly in contrast to the coming darkness.

❽

Raistlin and Caramon were walking along the road leading to Solace, returning from Farmer Sedge's. Caramon was coming back from work. Raistlin had gone to the farmer's to deliver a bundle of dried lavender. His clothes still smelled of the fragrant flower. From that time, he would never be able to abide the scent of lavender.

As they neared Solace, a small boy sighted them, began waving his arms, and broke into a run. He came pounding along the dusty track to meet them.

"Hullo, young Ned," said Caramon, who knew every child in town. "I can't play Goblin Ball with you right now, but maybe after dinner we—"

"Hush, Caramon," Raistlin ordered tersely. The child was wide-eyed and solemn as an owlet. "Can't you see? Something's wrong. What is it? What has happened?"

"There's been an accident," the boy managed to gasp, out of breath. "Your . . . your father."

He might have said more, but he'd lost his audience. The twins were racing for home. Raistlin ran as fast as he could for a short distance, but not even fear and adrenaline could keep his frail body going for long. His strength gave out and he was forced to slow down. Caramon kept going but, after a few moments, realized he was alone. He paused to look behind for his brother. Raistlin waved his brother on ahead.

Are you sure? Caramon's worried look asked.

I am sure, Raistlin's look answered.

Caramon nodded once, turned, and kept running. Raistlin made what haste he could, anxiety knotting his stomach and chilling him, causing him to shiver in the summer sunshine. Raistlin was surprised at his reaction. He had not supposed he cared this much for his father.

They had driven Gilon in a wagon from Prayer's Eye Peak back to Solace. Raistlin arrived to find his father still in the wagon with a crowd gathered around. At the news of the accident, almost everyone in town who could leave his work had come running, come to stare at the unfortunate man in mingled horror, concern, and curiosity.

Rosamun stood at the side of the wagon, holding fast to her husband's bloodstained hand and weeping. The Widow Judith was at her side.

"Have faith in Belzor," the widow was saying, "and he will be healed. Have faith."

"I do," Rosamun was saying over and over through pale lips. "I do have faith. Oh, my poor husband. You will be well. I have faith. . . ."

People standing nearby glanced at each other and shook their heads. Someone went to fetch the stable owner, who was supposed to know all about setting broken bones. Otik arrived from the inn, his chubby face drawn and grieved. He had brought along a jug of his finest brandy, his customary offering in any medical emergency.

"Tie Gilon to a stretcher," the Widow Judith said. "We'll carry him up the stairs. He will mend better in his own home."

A dwarf, a fellow townsman whom Raistlin knew by sight, glowered at her. "Are you daft, woman! Jouncing him around like that will kill him!"

"He shall not die!" said the Widow Judith loudly. "Belzor will save him!"

The townspeople standing around exchanged glances. Some rolled their eyes, but others looked interested and attentive.

"He better do it fast, then," muttered the dwarf, standing on tiptoe to peer into the wagon. Beside him, a kender was jumping up and down, clamoring, "Let me see, Flint! Let me see!"

Caramon had climbed into the wagon. Almost as pale as his father, Caramon crouched beside Gilon, anxious and helpless. At the sight of the terrible injuries—Gilon's cracked rib bones protruded through his flesh, and one leg was little more than a sodden mass of blood and bone—a low, animal-like moan escaped Caramon's lips.

Rosamun paid no attention to her stricken son. She stood at the side of the wagon, clutching Gilon's hand and whispering frantically about having faith.

"Raist!" Caramon cried in a hollow voice, looking around in panic.

"I am here, my brother," Raistlin said quietly. He climbed into the wagon beside Caramon.

Caramon grasped hold of his twin's hand thankfully, gave a shuddering sigh. "Raist! What can we do? We have to do something. Think of something to do, Raist!"

"There's nothing to do, son," said the dwarf kindly. "Nothing except wish your father well on his next journey."

Raistlin examined the injured man and knew immediately that the dwarf was right. How Gilon had managed to live this long was a mystery.

"Belzor is here!" the Widow Judith intoned shrilly. "Belzor will heal this man!"

Belzor, Raistlin thought bitterly, is taking his own sweet time.

"Father!" Caramon cried out.

At the sound of his son's voice, Gilon shifted his eyes—he could not move his head—and searched for his sons.

His gaze found them, rested on them. "Take care . . . your mother," he managed to whisper. A froth of blood coated his lips.

Caramon sobbed and covered his face with his hand.

"We will, Father," Raistlin promised.

Gilon's gaze encompassed both his sons. He managed a fleeting smile, then looked over at Rosamun. He started to say something, but a tremor of pain shook him. He closed his eyes in agony, gave a great groan, and lay still.

The dwarf removed his hat, held it to his chest. "Reorx walk with him," he said softly.

"The poor man's dead. Oh, how sad!" said the kender, and a tear trickled down his cheek.

It was the first time death had come so close to Raistlin. He felt it as a physical presence, passing among them, dark wings spreading over them. He felt small and insignificant, naked and vulnerable.

So sudden. An hour ago Gilon had walked among the trees, thinking of nothing more important than what he might enjoy for dinner that night.

So dark. Endless darkness, eternal. It was not the absence of light that was as frightening as the absence of thought, of knowledge, of comprehension. Our lives, the lives of the living, will go on. The sun shines, the moons rise, we will laugh and talk, and he will know nothing, feel nothing. Nothing.

So final. It will come to us all. It will come to me.

Raistlin thought he should be grieved or sorrowful for his father, but all he felt was sorrow for himself, grief for his own mortality. He turned away from the broken corpse, only to find his mother still clinging to the lifeless hand, stroking the cooling flesh, urging Gilon to speak to her.

"Caramon, we have to see to Mother," Raistlin said urgently. "We must take her home."

But on turning, he found that Caramon was in need of assistance himself. He had collapsed near the body of his father. Painful, choking sobs wrenched him. Raistlin rested his hand comfortingly on Caramon's arm.

Caramon's big hand closed convulsively around his twin's. Raistlin could not free himself, nor did he want to. He found comfort in his brother's touch. But he didn't like the fey look on his mother's face.

"Come, Mother. Let the Widow Judith take you home."

"No, no!" cried Rosamun frantically. "I must not leave your father. He needs me."

"Mother," Raistlin said, now starting to be frightened. "Father is dead. There is nothing more—"

"Dead!" Rosamun looked bewildered. "Dead! No! He can't be! I have faith."

Rosamun flung herself on her husband. Her hands grasped his blood-soaked shirt. "Gilon! Wake up!"

Gilon's head lolled. A trickle of blood flowed from his mouth.

"I have faith," Rosamun repeated with a heartbroken whimper. Her hands were bloody, she clung to the blood-soaked shirt.

"Mother, please, go home!" Raistlin pleaded helplessly.

Otik took hold of Rosamun's hands and gently freed her grip. Another neighbor hurriedly covered the body with a blanket.

"So much for Belzor," said the dwarf in a grating undertone.

He had not meant his words to be overheard, but his voice was deep and had a good carrying quality to it. Everyone standing around heard him. A few looked shocked. Several shook their heads. One or two smiled grimly when they thought no one was watching.

The Widow Judith had done a good deal of proselytizing since her arrival in town, and she'd gained more than a few converts to her new faith. Some of those converts were regarding the dead man with dismay.

"Who's Belzor?" the kender asked eagerly in shrill tones. "Flint, do you know Belzor? Was he supposed to heal this poor man? Why didn't he, do you suppose?"

"Hush your mouth, Tas, you doorknob!" the dwarf said in a harsh whisper.

But this was a question many of the faithful newcomers were asking themselves. They looked to the Widow Judith for an answer.

The Widow Judith had not lost her faith. Her face hardened. She glared at the dwarf, glared even more fiercely at the kender, who was now lifting the corner of the blanket for a curious peep at the corpse.

"Perhaps he's been healed and we just haven't noticed," the kender offered helpfully.

"He has not been healed!" The Widow Judith cried out in dolorous tones. "Gilon Majere has not been healed, nor will he be healed. Why not, do you ask? Because of the sinfulness of this woman!" The Widow Judith pointed at Rosamun. "Her daughter is a whore! Her son is a witch! It is her fault and the fault of her children that Gilon Majere died!"

The pointing finger might have been a spear ripping through Rosamun's body. She stared at Judith in shock, then screamed and sank to her knees, moaning.

Raistlin was on his feet, climbing over the body of his father. "How dare you?" he said softly, menacingly to the widow. Reaching the side of the wagon, he vaulted out. "Get out of here!" He came face-to-face with the widow. "Leave us alone!"

"You see!" The Widow Judith backed up precipitously. The pointing finger shifted to Raistlin. "He is evil! He does the bidding of evil gods!"

A fire blazed up within Raistlin, blazed up white hot, consumed sense, consumed reason. He could see nothing in the glare of the blaze. He didn't care if the fire destroyed him, just so long as it destroyed Judith.

"Raist!" A hand grabbed him. A hand, strong and firm, reached into the midst of the blaze and grasped hold of him. "Raist! Stop!"

The hand, his brother's hand, dragged Raistlin out of the fire. The terrible white-hot glare that had blinded him died, the fire died, leaving him cold and shivering, with a taste of ashes in his mouth. Caramon's strong arms wrapped around Raistlin's thin shoulders.

"Don't harm her, Raist," Caramon was saying. His voice came out a croak, his throat was raw from weeping. "Don't prove her right!"

The widow, white-faced and blenching, had backed up against a tree. She glanced about at her neighbors. "You saw, good people of Solace! He tried to kill me. He's a fiend in human clothing, I tell you! Send this mother and her demon spawn away! Cast them out of Solace! Show Belzor that you will not tolerate such evil!"

The crowd was silent, their faces dark and impassive. Moving slowly, they came together to form a circle—a protective circle with the Majere family in the center. Rosamun crouched on the ground, her head bowed. Raistlin and Caramon stood close together, near their mother. Although Kitiara was not there—she had not been with the family in years—her spirit had been invoked, and she was also present, if only in the minds of her siblings. Gilon lay dead in the wagon, his body covered by a blanket. His blood was starting to seep through the wool. The Widow Judith stood outside the circle, and still no one spoke.

A man shoved his way through from the back of the crowd. Raistlin had only an indistinct impression of him; the still-smoldering fire within clouded his vision. But he would remember him as tall, clean-shaven, with long hair that covered his ears, fell to his shoulders. He was clad in leather, trimmed with fringe, and wore a bow over one shoulder.

He walked up to the widow.

"I think you are the one who had better leave Solace," he said. His voice was quiet, he wasn't threatening her, merely stating a fact.

The widow scowled at him and flashed a glance around at the people in the crowd behind him. "Are you going to let this half-breed talk to me like this?" she demanded.

"Tanis is right," said Otik, waddling forward to lend his support. He waved a pudgy hand, in which he still held his brandy jug. "You just go along back to Haven, my good woman. And take Belzor with you. He's not needed around here. We care for our own."

"Take your mother home, lads," said the dwarf. "Don't fret about your pa. We'll see to the burial. You'll want to be there, of course. We'll let you know when it's time."

Raistlin nodded, unable to speak. He bent down, grasped hold of his mother. She was limp in his hands, limp and shredded, like a rag doll that has been worried and torn by savage dogs. She gazed about her with a vacuous expression that Raistlin remembered well; his heart shriveled within him.

"Mother," he said in a choked voice. "We're going to go home now."

Rosamun did not respond. She did not seem to have heard him. She sagged, dead weight, in his arms.

"Caramon?" Raistlin looked to his brother.

Caramon nodded, his eyes filled with tears.

Between them, they carried their mother home.

3

THE FOLLOWING MORNING, GILON MAJERE WAS BURIED BENEATH THE vallenwoods, a seedling planted on his grave as was customary among the inhabitants of Solace. His sons came to the ceremony. His wife did not.

"She's sleeping," said Caramon with a blush for his lie. "We didn't want to wake her."

The truth was, they couldn't wake her.

By afternoon, everyone in Solace knew that Rosamun Majere had fallen into one of her trances. She had fallen deep this time, so deep that she could hear no voice—however loved—that called to her.

The neighbors came, offering condolences and suggestions to aid in her recovery, some of which—the use of spirits of hartshorn, for instance, which she was to inhale—Raistlin tried. Others, such as jabbing her repeatedly with a pin, he did not.

At least not at first. Not before the terrible fear set in.

The neighbors brought food to tempt her appetite, for the word spread among their friends that Rosamun would not eat. Otik himself brought an immense basket of delicacies from the Inn of the Last Home, including a steaming pot of his famous spiced potatoes, Otik being firm in the belief that no living being and very few of the unliving could hold out long against that wonderful garlic-scented aroma.

Caramon took the food with a wan smile and a quiet thank you. He did not let Otik into the house but stood blocking the door with his big body.

"Is she any better?" Otik asked, craning to see over Caramon's shoulder.

Otik was a good man, one of the best in Solace. He would have given away his beloved inn if he had thought that would have helped the sick woman. But he did enjoy gossip, and Gilon's tragic death and his wife's strange illness were the talk of the common room.

Caramon finally managed to close the door. He stood listening a moment to Otik's heavy footsteps tromping across the boardwalk, heard him stop to talk to several of the ladies of the town. Caramon heard his mother's name mentioned frequently. Sighing, he took the food into the kitchen and stacked it up with all the rest of the provisions.

He ladled spiced potatoes into a bowl, added a tempting slab of ham fresh baked in cider, and poured a glass of elven wine. He intended to take them to his mother, but he paused on the threshold of her bedroom.

Caramon loved his mother. A good son was supposed to love his mother, and Caramon had been as good a son as he knew how to be. He was not close to his mother. He felt closer to Kitiara, who had done more to raise both him and Raistlin than had Rosamun. Caramon pitied his mother with all his heart. He was extremely sad and worried for her, but he had to steel himself to enter that room as he imagined he would one day have to steel himself to enter battle.

The sickroom was dark and hot, the air fetid and unpleasant to breathe and to smell. Rosamun lay on her back on the bed, staring up at nothing. Yet she saw something, apparently, for her eyes moved and changed expression. Sometimes the eyes were wide, the pupils dilated, as if what she saw terrified her. At these times, her breathing grew rapid and shallow. At other times, she was calm. Sometimes she would even smile, a ghastly smile that was heartbreaking to see.

She never spoke, at least that they could understand. She made sounds, but these were guttural, incoherent. She never closed her eyes. She never slept. Nothing roused her or caused her to look away from whatever visions she saw, visions that held her enthralled.

Her bodily functions continued. Raistlin cleaned up after her, bathed her. It had been three days since Gilon's burial, and Raistlin had not left his mother's side. He slept on a pallet on the floor, waking at the least sound she made. He talked to her constantly, telling her funny stories about the pranks the boys played at school, telling her about his own hopes and dreams, telling her about his herb garden and the plants he grew there.

He forced her to take liquid by dipping a cloth in water, then holding it to her lips and squeezing it into her mouth, only a trickle at a time lest she choke on it. He had tried feeding her, too, but she had been unable to swallow the food, and he had been forced to give this up. He handled her gently, with infinite tenderness and unflagging patience.

Caramon stood in the doorway, watching the two of them. Raistlin sat beside his mother's bed, brushing out her long hair and reciting to her stories of her own girlhood in Palanthas.

You think you know my brother, Caramon said, talking silently to a line of faces. You, Master Theobald, and you, Jon Farnish, and you, Sturm Brightblade, and all the rest of you. You call him "Sly" and "Sneak." You say he's cold and calculating and unfeeling. You think you know him. I know him. Caramon's eyes filled with tears. I know him. I'm the only one.

He waited another moment until he could see again, wiping his eyes and his nose on the sleeve of his shirt, slopping the wine over himself in the process. This done, he drew in a last, deep breath of fresh air and then entered the dark and dismal sickroom.

"I brought some food, Raist," said Caramon.

Raistlin glanced at his brother, then turned back to Rosamun. "She won't eat it."

"I . . . uh . . . meant it for you, Raist. You got to eat something. You'll get sick if you don't," Caramon added, seeing his brother's head start to move in negation. "And if you get sick, what will I do? I'm not a very good nurse, Raist."

Raistlin looked up at his brother. "You don't give yourself enough credit, my brother. I remember times when I was ill. You would make shadow pictures on the wall for me. Rabbits . . ." His voice died away.

Caramon's throat closed, choked by tears. He blinked them away quickly and held out the plate. "C'mon, Raist. Eat. Just a little. It's Otik's potatoes."

"His panacea for all the ills of the world," Raistlin said, his mouth twisting. "Very well."

He replaced the brush on a small nightstand. Taking the plate, he ate some of the potatoes and nibbled a little on the ham. Caramon watched anxiously. His face fell in disappointment when Raistlin handed back the plate, still more than half filled with food.

"Is that all you want? Are you sure? Can I get you something else? We've got lots."

Raistlin shook his head.

Rosamun made a sound, a pitiful murmur. Raistlin moved swiftly to attend her, bending over her, talking to her soothingly, helping her to lie more comfortably. He moistened her lips with water, chaffed the thin hands.

"Is . . . is she any better?" Caramon asked helplessly.

He could tell at a glance she wasn't. But he hoped he might be wrong. Besides, he felt the need to say something, to hear his own voice. He didn't like it when the house was so strangely quiet. He didn't like being cooped up in this dark, unhappy room. He wondered how his brother could stand it.

"No," Raistlin said. "If anything, she is worse." He paused a moment, and when he spoke next, his voice was hushed, awed. "It's as if she's running down a road, Caramon, running away from me. I follow after her, I call to her to stop, but she doesn't hear me. She doesn't pay any attention to me. She is running very fast, Caramon. . . ."

Raistlin stopped talking, turned away. He pretended to busy himself with the blankets.

"Take that plate back to the kitchen," he ordered, his voice harsh. "It will draw nice."

"I'll . . . I'll take the plate back to the kitchen," Caramon mumbled and hurried off.

Once in the kitchen, he flung the plate toward what he assumed was the table; he couldn't see very well for the blur in his eyes. Someone knocked on the door, but he ignored it, and after a while whoever it was went away. Caramon leaned against the fireplace, gulping in deep breaths, blinking very hard and fast, willing himself not to cry anymore.

Regaining his composure, he returned to the sickroom. He had news that would, he hoped, bring a small amount of cheer to his twin.

He found Raistlin seated once more by the bed. Rosamun lay in the same position, her staring eyes sunken in her head. Her wasted hands lay limp on the counterpane. Her wrist bones seemed unnaturally large. Her flesh seemed to be slipping away with her spirit. She appeared to have deteriorated in just the few moments Caramon was gone. He shifted his gaze hurriedly away from her, kept it focused on his twin.

"Otik was here," Caramon said unnecessarily, for his brother had surely deduced this from the arrival of the potatoes. "He said that the Widow Judith left Solace this morning."

"Did she," Raistlin said, a statement, not a question. He looked around. A flicker of flame lit his red-rimmed eyes. "Where did she go?"

"Back to Haven." Caramon managed a grin. "She's gone to report us to Belzor. She left claiming he was going to come here and make us sorry we were ever born."

An unfortunate choice of phrase. Raistlin winced and looked quickly at their mother. Caramon took two swift steps, laid his hand on his brother's shoulder, gripped it hard.

"You can't think that, Raist!" he admonished. "You can't think that this is your fault!"

"Isn't it?" Raistlin returned bitterly. "If it hadn't been for me, Judith would have let mother alone. That woman came because of me, Caramon. I was the one she was after. Mother asked me to quit my magic once. I wondered why she should say such a thing. It was Judith, hounding her. If I had only known at the—"

"What would you have done, Raistlin?" Caramon interrupted. He crouched down beside his brother's chair, looked up at him earnestly. "What would you have done? Quit your school? Given up the magic? Would you have done that?"

Raistlin sat silent a moment, his hands absently plucking the folds of his worn shirt. "No," he said finally. "But I would have talked to mother. I would have explained to her."

He glanced at his mother. Reaching out, he took hold of the pitifully thin hand, squeezed it, not very gently, willing to see some response, even a grimace of pain.

He could have crushed that hand in his hand, crushed it like an empty eggshell, and Rosamun would have never so much as blinked. Sighing, he looked back at Caramon.

"It wouldn't have made any difference, would it, my brother?" Raistlin asked softly.

"None in the world," Caramon said. "None at all."

Raistlin released his mother's hand. The marks of his fingers were red on her pallid flesh. He took hold of his brother's hand and held it tightly. They sat together in silence for long moments, finding comfort in each other, then Raistlin looked quizzically at his brother.

"You are wise, Caramon. Did you know that?"

Caramon laughed, a great guffaw that broke like thunder in the dark room, alarmed him. He clapped his hand over his mouth, flushed red.

"No, I'm not, Raist," he said in a smothered whisper. "You know me. Stupid as a gully dwarf. Everyone says so. You got all the brains. But that's all right. You need them. I don't. Not so long as we're together."

Raistlin abruptly released his grip. He drew his hand away and averted his face. "There is a difference between wisdom and intelligence, my brother." His voice was cold. "A person may have one without the other. Why don't you go for a walk? Or go back to work for your farmer?"

"But, Raist—"

"It's not necessary for both of us to remain here. I can manage."

Caramon rose slowly to his feet. "Raist, I don't—"

"Please, Caramon!" Raistlin said. "If you must know the truth, you fidget and fuss, and that drives me to distraction. You will feel better for the fresh air and exercise, and I will be better for the solitude."

"Sure, Raist," Caramon said. "If that's what you want. I'll . . . I guess I'll go see Sturm. His mother came to call and brought some fresh-baked bread. I'll just go and say thank you."

"You do that," Raistlin said dryly.

Caramon never knew what brought on these sudden dark and bitter moods, never knew what he'd said or done that quenched the light in his brother as surely as if he'd doused him with cold water. He waited a moment to see if his brother might relent, say something more, ask him to stay and keep him company. But Raistlin was dipping a bit of cloth into a pitcher of water. He held the cloth to Rosamun's lips.

"You must drink a little of this, Mother," he said softly.

Caramon sighed, turned, and left.

A day later, Rosamun was dead.

4

THE TWINS BURIED THEIR MOTHER IN THE GRAVE NEXT TO THEIR FATHER. Only a few people stood with them at the burial. The day was wet and chill, with a touch of early autumn in the air. Rain poured down steadily, soaking to the skin those who gathered around the grave. The rain drummed on the wooden coffin, formed a small pool in the grave. The vallenwood sprig they planted drooped, sad and forlorn, half-drowned.

Raistlin stood bareheaded in the rain, though Caramon had several times anxiously urged him to cover his head with the hood of his cloak. Raistlin did not hear his brother's pleas. He heard nothing but the fall of the drops on the wooden coffin, a small coffin, almost that of a child. Rosamun had shrunk to skin and bones in those last terrible days. It was as if whatever she was seeing held her fast in its claws, gnawed her flesh, fed off her, devoured her.

Raistlin knew he himself was going to fall ill. He recognized the symptoms. The fever already burned in his blood. He was alternately sweating and shivering. His muscles ached. He wanted so much to sleep, but every time he tried, he heard his mother's voice calling to him, and he would be instantly awake.

Awake to the silence, the dreadful silence.

He wanted to cry at the burial, but he did not. He forced the tears back down his throat. It wasn't that he was ashamed of them. He did not know for certain for whom he wept—for his dead mother or for himself.

He was not aware of the ceremony, was not aware of the passage of time. He might have been standing on the edge of that grave all his life. He knew it was over only when Caramon plucked at his sleeve. At that, it wasn't

Caramon who convinced his twin to leave but the sound of the dirt clods striking the coffin, a hollow sound that sent a shudder through Raistlin.

He took a step, stumbled, and nearly fell into the grave. Caramon caught him, steadied him.

"Raist! You're burning up!" Caramon exclaimed in concern.

"Did you hear her, Caramon?" Raistlin asked anxiously, peering down at the coffin. "Did you hear her calling for me?"

Caramon put his arm around his twin. "We have to get you home," he said firmly.

"We must hurry!" Raistlin gasped, shoving aside his brother's hand. He seemed intent on leaping into the grave. "She's calling me."

But he couldn't walk properly. Something was wrong with the ground. It rolled like the back of a leviathan, rolled and pitched him off.

He was sinking, sinking into the grave. The dirt was falling on him, and still he could hear her voice. . . .

Raistlin collapsed, fell to the ground at the graveside. His eyes closed. He lay unmoving in the mud and fallen leaves. Caramon bent over him. "Raist!" he called, giving him a little shake.

His twin did not respond. Caramon glanced around. He was alone with his brother, except for the gravedigger, who was shoveling as rapidly as he could to get in out of the wet. The other mourners had left as soon as decently possible, heading for the warmth of their homes or the crackling fire in the Inn of the Last Home. They had spoken their final condolences hurriedly, not really knowing what to say. No one had known Rosamun very well, no one had liked her.

There was no one to help Caramon, no one to advise him. He was on his own. He bent down, prepared to lift his brother in his arms and carry him home.

A pair of shining black boots and the hem of a brown cloak came into his view.

"Hello, Caramon."

He looked up, thrust back his hood to see better. The rain poured down, streamed from his hair into his eyes.

A woman stood in front of him. A woman around twenty years of age, maybe older. She was attractive, though not beautiful. Her hair, beneath her hood, was black and curled damply around her face. Her eyes were dark and bright, perhaps a little too bright, shining with a diamond's hardness. She wore brown leather armor, molded to fit over her curvaceous figure, a green loose-fitting blouse, green woolen hose, and the shining black boots that came to her knees. A sword hung from her hip.

She seemed familiar. Caramon knew he knew her, but he didn't have time to sort through the lumberyard that was his memory. He mumbled something about having to help his brother, but the woman was now down beside him, kneeling over Raistlin.

"He's my brother, too, you know," she said, and her mouth twisted in a crooked smile. "Kit!" Caramon gasped, recognizing her at last. "What are you—Where did you—How did—"

"Here, we better get him somewhere warm and dry," Kitiara interrupted, taking charge of the situation, much to Caramon's relief.

She was strong, as strong as a man. Between the two of them, they lifted Raistlin to his feet. He roused briefly, stared around with unfocused eyes, muttered something. His eyes rolled back, his head lolled. He lost consciousness again.

"He's . . . he's never been this sick!" Caramon said, his fear something real and alive inside him, squeezing his heart. "I've never seen him this bad!"

"Bah! I've seen worse," said Kitiara confidently. "Lots worse. I've treated worse, too. Arrow wounds in the gut, legs cut off. Don't worry," she added, her smile softening in sympathy for Caramon's anguish. "I fought Death before over my baby brother and I won. I can do it again if need be."

They carried Raistlin up the long flight of stairs to the boardwalk, made their way beneath the dripping tree branches to the Majeres' small house. Once inside, Caramon built up the fire. Kit stripped off Raistlin's wet clothes with swift, unblushing efficiency. When Caramon ventured a mild, embarrassed protest, Kitiara laughed.

"What's the matter, baby brother? Afraid this will shock my delicate feminine sensibilities? Don't worry," she added with a grin and a wink, "I've seen men naked before."

His face extremely red, Caramon helped his sister lay Raistlin down in his bed. He was shivering so that it seemed he might fall out. He spoke, but he made no sense and would occasionally cry out and stare at them with wide, fever dilated eyes. Kit rummaged through the house, found every blanket, and piled them over him. She placed her hand on his neck to feel his pulse beat, pursed her lips in a thoughtful frown, and shook her head. Caramon stood by, watching anxiously.

"Is that crone still around?" Kit asked abruptly. "You know, the one who talked to trees and whistled like a bird and kept a wolf for a pet?"

"Weird Meggin? Yeah, she's still around. I guess." Caramon was doubtful. "I don't go to that part of town much. Father doesn't—" He paused, swallowed, and began over. "Father didn't want us to go there."

"Father isn't around anymore. You're on your own now, Caramon," Kitiara returned with brutal frankness. "Go to Weird Meggin's and tell her you need elixir of willow bark. And hurry up. We've got to bring down this fever."

"Elixir of willow bark," Caramon repeated to himself several times. He put on his cloak. "Anything else?"

"Not right now. Oh, and Caramon"—Kitiara halted him as he stood in the open doorway—"don't tell anyone I'm back in town, will you?"

"Sure, Kit," Caramon answered. "Why not?"

"I don't want to be bothered by a lot of tittle-tattlers snooping around and asking questions. Now, go along. Wait! Do you have any money?"

Caramon shook his head.

Kitiara reached into a leather purse she wore on her belt, fished out a couple of steel coins, and tossed them to him. "On your way back from the old crone's, stop by Otik's and buy a jug of brandy. Is there anything in the house to eat?"

Caramon nodded. "The neighbors brought lots of stuff."

"Ah, I forgot. The funeral meats. All right. Go on. Remember what I said: tell no one I'm here."

Caramon departed, a little curious about his sister's injunction. After several moments of long and considered thought, he at last decided that Kitiara knew what she was doing. If word got out that she was in town, every gossip from here to the Plains of Dust would be snooping around. Raistlin needed rest and he needed quiet, not a stream of visitors. Yes, Kit knew what she was doing. She would help Raistlin. She would.

Caramon generally took a positive view of things. He was not one to fret over what had happened in the past or worry about what might come in the future. He was honest and trusting, and like many honest, trusting people, he believed that everyone else was honest and trustworthy. He put his faith in his sister.

He hastened through the pouring rain to Weird Meggin's, who lived in a tumbledown shack that sat on the ground beneath the vallenwood trees, not far from the disreputable bar known as The Trough. Concentrating on his errand, muttering "willow bark, willow bark," to himself over and over, Caramon almost tripped over an ancient gray wolf lying across the threshold.

The wolf growled. Caramon backed up precipitously.

"Nice doggie," Caramon said to the wolf.

The wolf rose to its feet, the fur on its back bristling. Its lips parted in a snarl, showing extremely yellow but very sharp teeth.

The rain beat down on Caramon. His cloak was wet through. He stood ankle-deep in mud. He could see candlelight in the window and a figure moving around inside. He made another attempt to pass the wolf.

"There's a good dog," he said and started to pat the wolf on the head.

A snap of the yellow teeth nearly took off Caramon's hand.

Abandoning the door, Caramon thought he might tap on the window-pane. The wolf thought he wouldn't. The wolf was right.

Caramon couldn't leave. Not without the elixir. Shouting at the door wasn't very polite, but in these circumstances, it was all the desperate Caramon had left to try.

"Weird—I mean—"Caramon flushed, started over."Mistress Meggin! Mistress Meggin!"

A face appeared in the window, the face of a middle-aged woman with gray hair pulled back tight. Her eyes were bright and clear. She didn't look crazy. She gazed intently at the sopping wet Caramon, then left the window. Caramon's heart sank into the mud, which seemed to be up around his knees now. Then he heard a grating sound, as of a bar being lifted. The door swung open. She spoke a word to the wolf, a word Caramon couldn't understand.

The wolf rolled over, all four paws in the air, and the crone scratched its belly.

"Well, boy" she said, looking up, "what do you want? The weather's a bit inclement for you to be throwing rocks at my house, isn't it?"

Caramon went red as a pickled beet. The rock-throwing incident had happened a long time ago, he'd been a small boy at the time, and he had assumed she wouldn't recognize him.

"Well, what do you want?" she repeated.

"Bark," he said in a low voice, ashamed, flustered, and embarrassed. "Some sort of bark. I . . . I forget what."

"What's it for?" Meggin asked sharply.

"Uh . . . Kit . . . No, I don't mean that. It's my brother. He has a fever."

"Willow bark elixir. I'll fetch it." The crone eyed him. "I'd ask you to come in out of the rain, but I'll wager you wouldn't."

Caramon peered past her into the shack. A warm fire looked inviting, but then he saw the skull on the table—a human skull, with various other bones lying about. He saw what looked like a rib cage, attached to a spine. If it had not been too horrible to even imagine, Caramon might have thought the woman was attempting to build a person, starting from the bones and working outward.

He took a step backward. "No, ma'am. Thank you, ma'am, but I'm quite comfortable where I am."

The crone grinned and chuckled. She shut the door. The wolf curled up on the threshold, keeping one yellow eye on Caramon.

He stood miserably in the rain, worried over his brother, hoping the crone wouldn't be long and wondering uneasily if he dared trust her. Perhaps she might need more bones for her collection. Perhaps she'd gone to get an ax. . . .

The door opened with a suddenness that made Caramon jump.

Meggin held out a small glass vial. "Here you go, boy. Tell your sister to have Raistlin swallow a large spoonful morning and night until the fever breaks. Understand?"

"Yes, ma'am. Thank you, ma'am." Caramon fumbled for the coins in his pocket. Realizing suddenly what she'd said, he stammered, "It's not . . . um . . . for my sister. She's not here . . . exactly. She's away. I don't—" Caramon shut his mouth. He was a hopeless liar.

Meggin chuckled again. "Of course she is. I won't say anything to anyone. Never fear. I hope your brother gets well. When he does, tell him to come visit me. I miss seeing him."

"My brother comes here?" Caramon asked, astonished.

"All the time. Who do you think taught him his herb lore? Not that dundering idiot Theobald. He wouldn't know a dandelion from a crab apple if it bit him on the ass. You remember the dose, or do you want me to write it down?"

"I . . . I remember," said Caramon. He held out a coin.

Meggin waved it away. "I don't charge my friends. I was sorry to hear about your parents. Come visit me yourself some time, Caramon Majere. I'd enjoy talking to you. I'll wager you're smarter than you think you are."

"Yes, ma' am," said Caramon politely, having no idea what she meant and no intention of ever taking her up on her offer.

He made an awkward bow and, holding the vial of willow bark elixir as tenderly as a mother holds her newborn child, he slogged through the mud to the staircase leading back up into the trees. His thoughts were extremely confused. Raistlin visiting that old crone. Learning things from her. Maybe he'd touched that skull! Caramon grimaced. It was all extremely baffling.

He was so flustered that he completely forgot he was supposed to stop at the inn for the brandy. He received a severe scolding from Kit when he reached home, and had to go back out in the rain after it.

5

RAISTLIN WAS VERY ILL FOR SEVERAL DAYS. The fever would subside somewhat after a dose of the willow bark, but it would always go back up again, and each time it seemed to go higher. Kitiara made light of his twin's illness whenever Caramon asked, but he could tell she was worried. Sometimes in the night, when she thought he was asleep, he'd hear Kit give a sharp sigh, see her drum her fingers on the arm of their mother's rocking chair, which Kit had dragged into the small room the twins shared.

Kitiara was not a gentle nurse. She had no patience with weakness. She had determined that Raistlin would live. She was doing everything in her power to force him to get better, and she was irritated and even a little angry when he did not respond. At that point, she decided to take the fight personally. The expression on her face was so grim and hard and determined that Caramon wondered if even Death might not be a little daunted to face her.

Death must have been, because that grim presence backed down.

On the morning of the fourth day of his twin's illness, Caramon woke after a troubled night. He found Kit slumped over the bed, her head resting on her arms, her eyes closed in slumber. Raistlin slept as well. Not the heavy, dream-tortured sleep of his sickness, but a healing sleep, a restful sleep. Caramon reached out his hand to feel his brother's pulse and, in doing so, brushed against Kitiara's shoulder.

She bolted to her feet, caught hold of the collar of his shirt with one hand, twisted the cloth tight around his neck. In her other hand, a knife flashed in the morning sunlight.

"Kit! It's me!" Caramon croaked, half-strangled.

Kit stared at him without recognition. Then her mouth parted in a crooked grin. She let loose of him, smoothed the wrinkles from his shirt. The knife disappeared rapidly, so rapidly that Caramon could not see where it had gone.

"You startled me," she said.

"No kidding!" Caramon replied feelingly. His neck stung from where the fabric had cut into his flesh. He rubbed his neck, gazed warily at his sister.

She was shorter than he was, lighter in build, but he would have been a dead man if he hadn't spoken up when he did. He could still feel her hand tightening the fabric around his throat, cutting off his breathing.

An awkward silence fell between them. Caramon had seen something disquieting in his sister, something chilling. Not the attack itself. What he'd seen that bothered him was the fierce, eager joy in her eyes when she made the attack.

"I'm sorry, kid," she said at length. "I didn't mean to scare you." She gave him a playful little slap on his cheek. "But don't ever sneak up on me in my sleep like that. All right?"

"Sure, Kit," Caramon said, still uneasy but willing to admit that the incident had been his fault. "I'm sorry I woke you. I just wanted to see how Raistlin was doing."

"He's past the crisis," Kitiara said with a weary, triumphant smile. "He's going to be fine." She gazed down on him proudly, as she might have gazed down on a vanquished foe. "The fever broke last night and it's stayed down. We should leave him now and let him sleep."

She pushed the reluctant Caramon out the door. "Come along. Listen to big sister. By way of repaying me for that fright you gave me, you can fix my breakfast."

"Fright!" Caramon snorted. "You weren't frightened."

"A soldier's always frightened," Kit corrected him. Sitting down at the table, she hungrily devoured an apple, still green, one of this season's first fruits. "It's what you do with the fright that counts."

"Huh?" Caramon looked up from his bread slicing.

"Fear can turn you inside out," Kit said, tearing the apple with strong white teeth. "Or you can make fear work for you. Use it like another weapon. Fear's a funny thing. It can make you weak-kneed, make you pee your pants, make you whimper like a baby. Or fear can make you run faster, hit harder."

"Yeah? Really?" Caramon put a slice of bread on the toasting fork, held it over the kitchen fire.

"I was in a fight once," Kit related, leaning back in her chair and propping her booted feet on another nearby chair. "A bunch of goblins jumped us. One of my comrades—a guy we called Bart Blue-nose 'cause his nose had a kind of strange bluish tint to it—anyway, he was fighting a goblin and his sword snapped, right in two. The goblin howled with delight, figuring he had his kill. Bart was furious. He had to have a weapon; the goblin was attacking him from six directions at once, and Bart was dancing around like a fiend from the Abyss trying to keep clear. Bart takes it into his head that he needs a club, and he grabs the first thing he can lay his hand on, which was a tree. Not a branch, a whole god-damned tree. He dragged that tree right out of the ground—you could hear the roots pop and snap—and he bashed the goblin over the head, killed it on the spot."

"C'mon!" Caramon protested. "I don't believe it. He pulled a tree out of the ground?"

"It was a young tree," Kit said with a shrug. "But he couldn't do it again. He tried it on another, about the same size, after the fight was over, and he couldn't even make the tree's branches wiggle. That's what fear can do for you."

"I see," said Caramon, deeply thoughtful.

"You're burning the toast," Kit pointed out.

"Oh, yeah! Sorry. I'll eat that piece." Caramon snatched the blackened toast from the fork, put another in its place. A question had been nagging at him for the last day or so. He tried to think of some subtle way of asking, but he couldn't. Raistlin was good at subtleties; Caramon just blundered on ahead. He decided he may as well ask it and have done with it, especially since Kitiara appeared to be in a good mood.

"Why'd you come back?" he asked, not looking at her. Carefully he rotated the toast on the fork to brown the other side. "Was it because of Mother? You were at her burial, weren't you?"

He heard Kit's boots hit the floor and glanced up nervously, thinking he'd offended her. She stood with her back turned, staring out the small window. The rain had stopped finally. The vallenwood leaves, just starting to turn color, were tipped with gold in the morning sun.

"I heard about Gilon's death," Kitiara said. "From some woodsmen I met in a tavern up north. I also heard about Rosamun's . . . sickness." Her mouth twisted, she glanced side-long at Caramon. "To be honest, I came back because of you, you and Raistlin. But I'll get to that in a moment. I arrived here the night Rosamun died. I . . . um . . . was staying with friends. And, yes, I went to the burial. Like it or not, she was my mother. I guess her death was pretty awful for you and Raist, huh?"

Caramon nodded silently. He didn't like to think about it. Morosely he munched on the burnt toast.

"Do you want some eggs? I can fry 'em," he said.

"Yes, I'm starved. Put in some of Otik's potatoes, too, if you've got any left." Kit remained standing by the window. "It's not that Rosamun meant anything to me. She didn't." Her voice hardened. "But it would have been bad luck if I hadn't gone."

"What do you mean, 'bad luck'?"

"Oh, I know it's all superstitious nonsense," Kit said with a rueful grin. "But she was my mother and she's dead. I should show respect. Otherwise, well"—Kit looked uncomfortable—"I might be punished. Something bad might happen to me."

"That sounds like the Widow Judith," Caramon said, cracking eggshells, making a clumsy and ineffectual attempt at extricating the egg from the shell. His scrambled eggs were noted for their crunchy texture. "She talked about some god called Belzor punishing us. Is that what you mean?"

"Belzor! What a crock. There are gods, Caramon. Powerful gods. Gods who will punish you if you do something they don't like. But they'll reward you, too, if you serve them."

"Are you serious?" Caramon asked, staring at his sister. "No offense, but I've never heard you talk like that before."

Kitiara turned from the window. Walking over, her strides long and purposeful, she planted her hands on the table and looked into Caramon's face.

"Come with me!" she said, not answering his question. "There's a city up north called Sanction. Big things are happening there, Caramon. Important things. I plan to be part of them, and you can, too. I came back on purpose to get you."

Caramon was tempted. Traveling with Kitiara, seeing the vast world outside of Solace. No more backbreaking farm work, no more hoeing and plowing, no more forking hay until his arms ached. He'd use his arm for sword work, fighting goblins and ogres. Spending his nights with his comrades around a fire, or snug in a tavern with a girl on his knee.

"What about Raistlin?" he asked.

Kit shook her head. "I had hoped to find him stronger. Can he work magic yet?"

"I . . . I don't think so," said Caramon.

"Odds are he won't ever be able to use it, then. Why, the mages I've heard of are practicing their skills at the age of twelve! Still, I'm sure I could get a job for him. He's well schooled, isn't he? There's a temple I know about. They're looking for scribes. Easy work and fat living. What do you say? We could leave as soon as Raistlin is well enough to travel."

Caramon allowed himself one more glimpse of walking around this town called Sanction, armor clanking, sword rattling on his hip, the women admiring him. He put the vision away with a sigh.

"I can't, Kit. Raist would never leave that school of his. Not until he's ready to take some sort of test that they give in a big tower somewhere."

"Well, then, let him stay," Kitiara said, irritated. "You come alone."

She eyed Caramon, giving him almost the same look he'd imagined from the women in Sanction. But not quite. Kit was sizing him up as a warrior. Self-conscious, he stood straighter. He was taller than the boys his age, taller than most men in Solace. The heavy farm labor had built up his muscles.

"How old are you?" Kit asked.

"Sixteen."

"You'd pass for eighteen, sure. I could teach you what you'd need to know on our way north. Raistlin will be fine here on his own. He's got the house. Your father left it to you two, didn't he? Well, then! There's nothing stopping you."

Caramon might be gullible, he might be thickheaded—as his brother often told him he was—and slow of thought. But once he had made up his mind about something, he was as immovable as Prayer's Eye Peak.

"I can't leave Raistlin, Kit."

Kitiara frowned, angry, not accustomed to having her will thwarted. Folding her arms across her chest, she glared at Caramon. Her booted foot tapped irritably on the floor. Caramon, uncomfortable beneath her piercing gaze, ducked his head and whipped the eggs right out of the bowl.

"You could talk to Raistlin," Caramon said, his voice muffled by his shirt collar, into which he was speaking. "Maybe I spoke out of turn. Maybe he'll want to go."

"I'll do that," Kitiara said, her tone sharp. She was pacing the length of the small room.

Caramon said nothing more. He dumped what remained of the eggs into a skillet and placed it over the fire. He heard Kit's booted footfalls sound hollowly on the wood, winced at a particularly loud and angry stomp. When the eggs were cooked, the two sat down to breakfast in silence.

Caramon risked a glance at his sister, saw her regarding him with an affable air, a charming smile.

"These eggs are really good," said Kit, spitting out small bits of shell. "Did I ever tell you about the time the bandit tried to stab me in my sleep? What you did reminded me of the story. We'd had a hard fight that day, and I was dead tired. Well, this bandit . . ."

Caramon listened to this story and to many other exciting adventures during the day. He listened and enjoyed what he heard—Kit was an excellent storyteller. Every so often, Caramon would go to the bedroom to check on Raistlin and find him slumbering peacefully. When Caramon returned, he would hear yet another tale of valor, daring, battles fought, victory, and wealth won. He listened and laughed and gasped in all the right places. Caramon knew very well what his sister was trying to do. There could be only one answer. If Raistlin went, Caramon would go. If Raistlin stayed, so did Caramon.

That evening, Raistlin woke. He was weak, so weak that he couldn't lift his head from the pillow without help. But he was lucid and very much aware of his surroundings. He didn't appear all that surprised to see Kitiara.

"I had dreams about you," he said.

"Most men do," Kit returned with a grin and a wink. She sat down on the edge of the bed, and while Caramon fed his brother chicken broth, Kitiara made Raistlin the same proposition she'd made Caramon.

She wasn't quite as glib, talking to those keen blue, unblinking eyes that looked right through her and out the other side. "Who is it you work for?" Raistlin asked when Kit had finished.

Kitiara shrugged. "People," she said.

"And what temple is this where you would have me work? Dedicated to what god?"

"It's not Belzor, that's for sure!" Kitiara said with a laugh.

When Caramon, spooning broth, tried to say something, Raistlin coldly shushed him.

"Thank you, Sister," Raistlin said at last, "but I am not ready."

"Ready?" Kit couldn't figure out what he was talking about. "What do you mean, 'ready'? Ready for what? You can read, can't you? You can write, can't you? So you don't have any talent for magic. You gave it a good try. It's not important. There are other ways to gain power. I know. I've found them."

"That's enough, Caramon!" Raistlin pushed away the spoon. Wearily he lay back down on the pillows. "I need to rest."

Kit stood up. Hands on her hips, she glared at him. "That addle-pated mother of ours had you wrapped in cotton, for fear you'd break. It's time you got out, saw something of the world."

"I am not ready," Raistlin said again and closed his eyes.

Kitiara left Solace that night.

"I'm only making a short trip," she told Caramon, drawing on her leather gloves. "To Qualinesti. Do you know anything about that place?" she asked offhandedly. "Its defenses? How many people live there? That sort of thing?"

"I know elves live there," Caramon offered after a moment's profound thought.

"Everyone knows that!" Kit scoffed.

Putting on her cloak, she drew her hood over her head.

"When will you be back?" Caramon asked.

Kit shrugged. "I can't say. Maybe a year. Maybe a month. Maybe never. It depends on how things go."

"You're not mad at me, are you, Kit?" Caramon asked wistfully. "I wouldn't want you to be mad."

"No, I'm not mad. Just disappointed. You'd have been a great warrior, Caramon. The people I know would have really made something of you. As for Raistlin, he's made a big mistake. He wants power, and I know where he could get it. If you both hang around here, you'll never be anything but a farmer, and he'll be—like that fellow Waylan—a coin-puking, rabbit-pulling conjurer who's the joke of half of Solace. It's such a waste."

She gave Caramon a slap on the cheek that was meant to be friendly but which left the red mark of her hand. Opening the door, Kit peered outside, looking in both directions. Caramon couldn't imagine what she was looking for. It was well past midnight. Most of Solace was in bed.

"Good-bye, Kit," he said.

"Good-bye, Baby Brother."

He massaged his stinging cheek and watched her walk off through the moonlit branches of the vallenwood, a black shadow against silver.

6

RAISTLIN WOKE TO THE SOUND OF RAIN PELTING THE ROOF. Thunder rumbled from sky to ground, the vallenwoods shuddered. The dawn was gray, tinged with pink lightning. Rain was falling on the newly dug graves, forming drowning pools around the vallenwood saplings planted at the head of each.

He lay on his bed and watched the gray gradually lighten as the storm passed. All was quiet now, except for the incessant drip of water falling on sodden leaves. He lay without moving. Movement took an effort, and he was too tired. His grief had emptied him. If he moved, the dull, aching pain of his loss would flood in on him, and though the emptiness was bad, it wasn't as bad as the pain.

He could not feel the bedclothes under him. He could not feel the blanket that covered him. He had no weight or substance. Was this what it was like in that coffin? In that grave? To feel nothing, ever again? To know nothing? Life, the world, the people in the world go on, and you know nothing, forever surrounded by a cold and empty, silent darkness?

Pain burst the levee, surged in to fill the void. Pain and fear, hot, burning, welled up inside him. Tears stung his eyelids. He closed his eyes, squeezed them shut and wept, wept for himself and for his mother and father, for all those who are born of the darkness, who lift their wondering eyes to the light, feel its warmth on their skin, and who must return again to darkness.

He wept silently, so as not to wake Caramon. He did this not so much out of consideration for his brother's weariness as for his own shame at his weakness.

The tears ended, leaving him with a bad taste of salt and iron in his mouth, a clogged nose, and a tightness in his throat, which came from muffling his sobs. The bedclothes were damp; his fever must have broken during the night. He had only the vaguest recollection of being sick, a recollection tinged with horror—in his fevered dreams, he had become entwined with Rosamun. He was his mother, a shrunken corpse. People stood around the bed, staring down at him.

Antimodes, Master Theobald, the Widow Judith, Caramon, the dwarf and the kender, Kitiara. He begged and pleaded with them to give him food and water, but they said he was dead and he didn't need it. He was in constant terror that they would dump him in a coffin and lower him into the ground, into a grave that was Master Theobald's laboratory.

Remembering the terrible dreams robbed them of some of their power. The horror lingered, but it was not overwhelming. The wool blanket covering him was rough and chafed his skin; beneath it, he was wearing nothing.

He tossed the blanket aside. Weak and tottering from his illness, he stood up. The air was chill and he shivered, groped hastily for his shirt, which had been flung over the back of a chair. Dragging the shirt on over his head, he thrust his arms into the sleeves, then stood in the middle of the small room and wondered bleakly, What now?

There were two wooden beds in the room, each bed built into a wall. Raistlin crossed the room to look down on the slumbering form of his twin. Caramon was a late sleeper, a heavy sleeper. Usually he lay easily and comfortably on his back, his big body spread all akimbo, arms flung wide, one leg hanging off the bed, the other bent at the knee, leaning against the wall. Raistlin, by contrast, slept in a tight, huddled ball, his knees drawn up to his chin, his arms hugging his chest.

But Caramon's sleep this day was as restless and uneasy as his twin's. Fatigue kept him manacled to his bed, he was so exhausted that not even the most terrifying dreams could jolt his body from sleep. He rolled and tossed, his head jerked back and forth. His pillow lay on the floor, along with the blankets. He had twisted the sheet so that it straggled around him like a winding cloth.

He muttered and mumbled and panted, tugged at the collar of his nightshirt. His skin was clammy, his hair damp with sweat. He looked so ill that Raistlin, concerned, placed his hand on his brother's forehead to feel if he were running a fever.

Caramon's skin was cool. Whatever troubled him was of the mind, not the body. He shuddered at Raistlin's touch and begged, "Don't make me go there, Raist! Don't make me go there!"

Raistlin brushed aside a lock of the curly, tousled hair that was falling into his brother's eyes and wondered if he should wake him. His brother must have been awake many long nights and he needed his rest, but this was more like torture than sleep. Raistlin put his hand on his twin's broad shoulder, shook it.

"Caramon!" he called peremptorily.

Caramon's eyes flared wide. He stared at Raistlin and cringed. "Don't leave me! Don't! Don't leave me! Please!" He whimpered and flung himself about on the bed with such violence that he nearly fell on the floor.

This was not dreaming. It was vaguely familiar to Raistlin, then suddenly frighteningly familiar.

Rosamun. She had been much like this.

Perhaps this wasn't sleep. Perhaps this was a trance, similar to the trances into which Rosamun had stumbled, never to find her way back out.

Caramon had not previously evinced any signs that he had inherited his mother's fey talent. He was her son, however, and her blood—with all its strange fancies—ran in his veins. His body was weakened by nights of wakeful watching, tending his sick brother. His mind was upset by the tragic loss of his beloved father, then he had been forced to stand by helplessly and watch his mother dwindle away. With the body's defenses lowered, the mind's defenses confused and overwhelmed, his soul was laid bare and vulnerable. It might well retreat into dark regions never known to exist, there to find refuge from the battering armies of life.

What if I lose Caramon?

I would be alone. Alone without family or friend, for Raistlin could not count on Kitiara as family, nor did he want to. Her crudeness and her untamed animal nature disgusted him. That's what he told himself. In reality, he feared her. He foresaw that someday there would be a power struggle between them, and, alone, he was not certain that he was strong enough to withstand her. As for friends, on this point he could not delude himself. He had none. His friends were not his friends at all, they were Caramon's.

Caramon was often irritating, often annoying. His slow thought processes frustrated his quicker thinking twin, who was at times tempted to grab hold of Caramon and shake him on the faint hope that a sensible thought might accidentally tumble out. But now, faced with the possibility of losing his brother, Raistlin looked into the void where Caramon had been and realized how much he would miss him, and not for just companionship, or to have someone strong on which to lean. Mentally speaking, Caramon was not a brilliant swordsman, but he made a good fencing partner.

Besides, Caramon was the only person Raistlin had ever known who could come close to making him laugh. Shadow puppets on the wall, ridiculous rabbits . . .

"Caramon!" Raistlin shook his brother again.

Caramon only moaned and raised his hands, as if warding off some blow. "No, Raist! I don't have it! I swear I don't have it!"

Frightened, Raistlin wondered what to do. He left the bedroom, went in search of his sister, with some idea of sending Kit out to fetch Weird Meggin.

But Kitiara was gone. Her pack was gone; she must have left during the night.

Raistlin stood in the parlor of the silent house, the too-silent house. Kitiara had packed all Rosamun's clothes and possessions away in a wooden chest, stowed it under the bed. His mother's rocking chair remained, however, the only one of her possessions that Kit had not removed, mainly because there was a shortage of chairs in the house as it was. Rosamun's presence lingered like the fragrance of faded rose petals. The very emptiness, the lack of her, recalled his mother vividly to his mind.

Too vividly. Rosamun sat in the chair, rocking. She rocked leisurely back and forth, her dress rustling. The toes of her small feet, encased in soft leather shoes, lightly touched the floor and then slid beneath her dress when the chair rocked backward. Her head and her gaze remained level, her lips smiling at Raistlin.

He stared, willing with an aching heart for this to be true, even as a part of him knew it wasn't.

Rosamun ceased rocking, rose from the chair with grace and ease. He was conscious of sweet fragrance as she passed near him, a fragrance of roses. . . .

In the next room, his brother gave a fearful yell, a horrible scream, as though he were being burned alive.

The scent of roses in his nostrils, Raistlin searched the room, found what he sought. A dish of dried and withered rose petals had been placed on a table to sweeten the sickness-tainted air. He dipped his hand into the dish, and carried the rose petals into the bedroom.

Caramon clutched the sides of the bed, his hands white-knuckled. The bed shook beneath him. His eyes were wide open, staring at some horror visible only to himself.

Raistlin had no need to refer to his primer for the wording of the spell. The words were etched into his brain with fire, and like a wildfire racing across parched grass, so the magic raced from his brain down his spine, burned through every nerve, enflamed him.

He crushed the rose petals, strewed them over his brother's tormented form.

"Ast tasarak sinuralan kyrnawi."

Caramon's eyelids fluttered. He gave a great sigh, shuddered, then his eyes closed. He lay for a moment, flattened on the bed, not breathing, and Raistlin knew a fear unlike any he'd ever previously experienced. He thought his twin was dead.

"Caramon!" Raistlin whispered. "Don't leave me, Caramon! Don't!" His hands gently brushed the rose petals from Caramon's still face.

Caramon drew a breath, long, deep, and easy. He let that breath go and then drew another, his chest rising and falling. His face smoothed, the dreams had not cut too deep, had not left their chisel mark upon him. The lines of weariness, grief, and sorrow would soon fade away, ripples on the surface of his customary genial tranquility.

Weak with relief, Raistlin sank down beside his brother's bed, rested his head in his hands. It was only then, his eyes closed, seeing nothing but darkness, that Raistlin realized what he had done.

Caramon was asleep.

I cast the spell, Raistlin said inwardly. The magic worked for me.

The fire of the spellcasting flickered and died out, leaving him weak and shaking so that he could not stand, yet Raistlin knew such joy as he had never known in his life.

"Thank you!" Raistlin whispered, his fists clenched, his nails digging into his flesh. He saw again the eye, white, red, black, regarding him with satisfaction. "I won't fail you!" he repeated over and over. "I won't fail!"

The eye blinked.

A tiny pinprick of concern, of jealous doubt, jabbed him.

Had Caramon fallen into a trance? Was it possible that he had likewise inherited the magic?

Raistlin opened his eyes, stared hard and long at his slumbering brother. Caramon lay on his back, one arm flopped over the edge of the bed, the other across his forehead. His mouth was open, he gave a prodigious snore. He had never looked more foolish.

"I was mistaken," Raistlin said, and he pushed himself to his feet. "It was a bad dream, nothing more." He smiled scornfully at himself. "How could I have ever imagined that this great oaf would inherit the magic?"

Raistlin left the room on tiptoe, moving quietly so as not to disturb his brother, and shut the door to their room softly behind him. Entering the parlor, Raistlin sat down in his mother's rocking chair, and, rocking gently back and forth, he reveled fully in his triumph.

7

CARAMON SLEPT THAT DAY THROUGH AND ON INTO THE NIGHT. The next day he woke, recalled nothing of his dreams, was amused and even skeptical to hear his twin describe them.

"Pooh, Raist!" Caramon said. "You know I never dream."

Raistlin did not argue. He himself was gaining strength rapidly, was strong enough to sit at the kitchen table that morning with his brother. The day was warm; a soft breeze carried sounds of women's voices, calling and laughing. It was laundry day, and the women were hanging their wet clothes among the leaves to dry. The early autumn sunshine filtered through the changing leaves, casting shadows that flitted around the kitchen like birds. The twins ate breakfast in silence. There was much they had to talk about, much they needed to discuss and settle, but that could wait.

Raistlin touched each moment that passed, held each moment cupped in his mind until it slipped away through his fingers, to be replaced by another. The past and all its sorrow was behind him; he would never turn around to look back. The future, with its promise and its fears, lay ahead of him, shone warm on his face like the sunshine, darkened his face like the shadows. At this moment, he was suspended between past and future, floating free.

Outside, a bird whistled, another answered. Two young women let fall a wet sheet onto one of the town's guardsmen, who was walking his beat on the ground below. The sheet enveloped him, to judge by his muffled, good-natured cursing. The young women giggled and protested that it was an accident. They ran down the stairs to reclaim their linen and spend a few pleasant moments flirting with the handsome guard.

"Raistlin," said Caramon, speaking reluctantly, as if he, too, were under the spell of the sun, the breeze, the laughter, and loath to break it. "We have to decide what to do."

Raistlin couldn't see his brother's face for the sunshine. He was sensible of Caramon's presence, sitting in the chair opposite. Strong and solid and reassuring. Raistlin remembered the fear he'd experienced when he had thought Caramon was dead. Affection for his brother welled up inside him, stung his eyelids. Raistlin drew back out of the sun, blinking rapidly to clear his vision. The moments had begun to slide by faster and faster, no longer his to touch.

"What are our options?" Raistlin asked.

Caramon shifted his bulk in his chair. "Well, we turned down going with Kit. . . ." He let that hang a moment, silently asking if his twin might reconsider.

"Yes," Raistlin said, a note of finality.

Caramon cleared his throat, went on. "Lady Brightblade offered to take us in, give us a home."

"Lady Brightblade," said Raistlin with a snicker.

"She is the wife of a Solamnic knight," Caramon pointed out defensively.

"So she claims."

"C'mon, Raist!" Caramon was fond of Anna Brightblade, who had always been very kind to him. "She showed me a book with their family coat-of-arms. And she acts like a noble lady, Raist."

"How would you know how a noble lady acts, my brother?"

Caramon thought this over. "Well, she acts like what I imagine a noble lady would act like. Like the noble ladies in those stories . . ."

He fell silent, left his sentence unfinished, except in the minds of both twins. Like those stories Mother used to tell us. To speak of her aloud was to invoke her ghost, which remained inside the house.

Gilon, on the other hand, had departed. He had never been there much in the first place, and all he left behind was a vague, pleasant memory. Caramon missed his father, but already Raistlin was having to work to remember that Gilon was gone.

"I do care to have Sturm Brightblade as a brother," Raistlin commented. "Master My-Honor-Is-My-Life. He's so smug and arrogant, parading his virtue up and down the streets, making a show of righteousness. It's enough to make one puke."

"Ah, Sturm's not so bad," Caramon said. "He's had a rough time of it. At least we know how our father died," he added somberly. "Sturm doesn't even know if his father's dead or alive."

"If he's that worried, why doesn't he go back and find out the truth?" Raistlin said impatiently. "He's certainly old enough."

"He can't leave his mother. He promised his father, the night they fled, that he'd take care of his mother, and he's bound by that promise."

"When the mob attacked their castle—"

"Castle!" Raistlin snorted.

"—they barely escaped with their lives. Sturm's father sent him and his mother out into the night with an escort of retainers. He told them to travel to Solace, where he would join them when he could. That was the last they heard of him."

"The knights must have done something to provoke the attack. People just don't suddenly take it into their heads to storm a well-fortified keep."

"Sturm says that there are strange people moving into the north, into Solamnia. Evil people, who want only to foment trouble for the knights, drive them out so that they can move in and seize control."

"And who are these unknown evil-doers?" Raistlin asked caustically.

"He doesn't know, but he thinks they have something to do with the old gods," Caramon replied, shrugging.

"Indeed?" Raistlin was suddenly thoughtful, recalling Kitiara's offer, her talk of powerful gods. He was also thinking back to his own experience with the gods, an experience he had wondered about since. Had it really happened? Or had it happened because he wanted it so much?

Caramon had spilled some water on the table, and now he was damming it up with his knife and fork, trying to divert the course of the tiny river so that it wouldn't drip onto the floor. He was busy with this as he spoke and did not look at his brother. "I said no. She wouldn't have let you go on with your schooling."

"What are you talking about?" Raistlin asked sharply, looking up. "Who wouldn't let me go on with my schooling?"

"Lady Brightblade."

"She said that, did she?"

"Yeah," Caramon answered. He added a spoon to the dam. "It's nothing against you, Raist," he added, looking up to see his brother's thin face grow hard and cold. "The Solamnic knights think that magic-users are outside the natural order of things. They never use wizards in battle, according to what Sturm says. Wizards lack discipline and they're too independent."

"We like to think for ourselves," said Raistlin, "and not blindly obey some fool commander who may or not have a brain in his head. Yet they say," he added, "that Magius fought at the side of Huma and that he was Huma's dearest friend."

"I know about Huma," Caramon said, glad to change the subject. "Sturm told me stories about him and how, long ago, he fought the Queen of Darkness and banished all the dragons. But I never heard of this Magius."

"No doubt the knights would like to forget that part of the tale. Just as Huma was one of the greatest warriors of all time, so Magius was one of the greatest wizards. During a battle fought against the forces of Takhisis, Magius was separated from Huma's side. The wizard fought on alone, surrounded by the enemy, until, wounded and exhausted, he could no longer summon the strength to cast his magic. That was in the days when wizards were not allowed to carry any weapon other than their magic. Magius was captured alive and dragged back to the Dark Queen's camp.

"They tortured him for three days and three nights, trying to force him to reveal the location of Huma's encampment so they could send assassins to kill the knight. Magius died, never revealing the truth. It was said that when Huma received the news of Magius's death and learned how he had died, he grieved so for his friend that his men thought they might lose him as well.

"Huma ordered that, from then on, wizards would be permitted to carry one small, bladed weapon, to be used as a last defense if their magic failed them. This we do in the name of Magius to this day."

"That's a great story," Caramon said, so impressed he let his river overflow. He went to fetch a cloth to wipe up the water. "I'll have to tell that to Sturm."

"You do that," Raistlin said wryly. "I'll be interested to hear what he has to say." He watched Caramon clean the floor, then said, "We have chosen not to join forces with our sister. We have decided that we do not want to be taken under the wing of a noble Solamnic lady. What do you suggest we do?"

"I say we live here, Raist," Caramon answered steadily. He stood up from his mopping. Hands on his hips, he surveyed the house as if he were a potential buyer. "The house is ours free and clear. Father built it himself. He didn't leave any debts. We don't owe anybody anything. Your school's paid for. We don't have to worry about that. I earn enough working for Farmer Sedge to keep us in food and clothes."

"It will be lonely for you when I am gone in the winter," Raistlin observed.

Caramon shrugged. "I can always stay with the Sedges. I do sometimes anyway if the snow blocks the road. Or I can stay with Sturm or some of our other friends."

Raistlin sat silent, brooding, frowning.

"What's the matter, Raist?" Caramon asked uneasily. "Don't you think it's a good plan"

"I think it's an excellent plan, my brother. I don't feel right about you supporting me, however."

Caramon's worried expression eased. "What does it matter? What's mine is yours, Raist, you know that."

"It does matter to me," Raistlin returned. "Very much. I must do something to pay my share."

Caramon gave the matter serious thought for about three minutes, but apparently that process hurt, for he began rubbing his head and said that he thought it must be about time for lunch.

He left to go rummage in the larder while Raistlin considered what he might do to add to their upkeep. He was not strong enough for farm labor, nor did he have the time for any other job, with his studies. His schooling now meant more than anything, was doubly important. Every spell he learned added to his knowledge . . . and to his power.

Power over others. He remembered Caramon, strong and muscular, falling into a deep slumber, lying comatose at the command of his weaker brother. Raistlin smiled.

Returning with a loaf of bread and a crock of honey, Caramon placed an empty vial down in front of his brother. "This belongs to that old crone, Weird Meggin. It had some sort of tree juice in it. Kit gave it to you to bring your fever down. I should probably return that to her," he said reluctantly, adding in an awed tone, "Do you know, Raist? She's got a wolf that sleeps on her door stoop and a human head sitting right smack on her kitchen table!"

Weird Meggin. An idea stirred in Raistlin's mind. He lifted the vial, opened it, sniffed. Elixir of willow bark. He could make that easily enough. Other herbs in his garden could be used for cures as well. He now had the power to cast minor magicks. People would pay good steel if he could ease a colicky baby into sleep, bring down a man's fever, or cause an itchy rash to disappear.

Raistlin fingered the vial. "I'll return this myself. You needn't come if you don't want to."

"I'm coming," Caramon said firmly. "Where did she get that skull, huh? Just ask yourself that. I wouldn't want to walk in and see your head in her dining room. You and me, Raist. From now on, we stick together. We're all each other's got."

"Not quite all, my dear brother," Raistlin said softly. His hand went to the small leather bag he wore at his waist, a bag containing his spell components. It held only dried rose petals now, but soon it would hold more. Much more.

"Not quite all."

BOOK 4

Who wants or needs any gods at all? I certainly don't. No divine force controls my life, and that's the way I like it. I choose my own destiny. I am slave to no man. Why should I be a slave to a god and let some priest or cleric tell me how to live?

—Kitiara uth Matar

RAISTLIN CHRONICLES

1

TWO YEARS PASSED. Spring's gentle rains and summer's sunshine caused the vallenwood saplings on the grave sites to straighten, sending forth green shoots. Raistlin spent winters at the school. He added another elementary spell—a spell he could use to determine if an object might be magical—to his spellbook. Caramon spent the winters working in the stables, the summers working at Farmer Sedge's. Caramon wasn't home much during the winter. The house was lonely without his brother and "gave him the creeps." When Raistlin returned, however, the two lived there almost contentedly.

That spring brought the customary May Day festival, one of Solace's largest celebrations. A huge fair was set up in a large area of cleared land on the town's southern borders.

Free at last to travel, now that the winter thaw had cleared the roads, merchants came from all parts of Ansalon, eager to sell the wares they had spent all winter making.

The taciturn, savage-looking Plainsmen traders were first to arrive, coming from villages with outlandish, barbaric names, such as Que-teh and Que-kiri. Clad in animal skins decorated with uncouth ornaments said to honor their ancestors, whom they worshiped, the Plainsmen held themselves aloof from the other inhabitants of the region, though they took their steel readily enough. Their clay pots were much prized; their hand-woven blankets were extraordinarily beautiful. Some of their other goods, such as the bead-decorated skulls of small animals, were coveted by the children, to the shock and dismay of their parents.

Dwarves, well dressed, wearing gold chains around their necks, traveled from their underground realm of Thorbardin, bringing with them the metalwork for which they were famous, displaying everything from pots and pans to axes, bracers, and daggers.

These Thorbardin dwarves sparked the first incident of the fair season. The Thorbardin dwarves were in the Inn of the Last Home, partaking of Otik's ale, when they began to make disparaging comments regarding that ale, which they maintained was far below their own high standards. A local hill dwarf took exception to these comments on Otik's behalf, added a few of his own relevant to the fact that a mountain dwarf wouldn't know a good glass of ale if it was poured over his head, which it subsequently was.

Several elves from Qualinesti, who had brought with them some exquisite gold and silver jewelry, maintained that the dwarves were all a pack of brutes, worse than humans, who were bad enough.

A brawl ensued. The guards were summoned.

The Solace residents took the side of the hill dwarf. The flustered Otik, not wanting to lose customers, was on both sides at the same time. He thought that perhaps the ale might not up to his usual high standards, was forced to admit that the Thorbardin gentlemen might be right on that point. On the other hand, Flint Fireforge was an exceptional judge of ale, having tasted a great deal of it in his time, and Otik felt called upon to bow to his expertise.

Eventually it was determined that if the hill dwarf would apologize to the mountain dwarves and the mountain dwarves would apologize to Otik, the entire incident would be forgotten. The leader of the Thorbardin dwarves, wiping blood from his nose, stated in surly tones that the ale was "drinkable." The hill dwarf, massaging a bruised jaw, mumbled that a mountain dwarf might indeed know something of ale, having spent enough nights on the barroom floor lying face first in it. The Thorbardin dwarf didn't like the sound of that, thought it might be another insult. At this juncture, Otik hastily offered a free round to everyone in the bar to celebrate their newfound friendship.

No dwarf alive has ever turned down free ale. Both sides went back to their seats, each group convinced that their side had won. Otik gathered up the broken chairs, the barmaids picked up the broken crockery, the guards drank a glass in honor of the innkeeper, the elves looked down their long noses at the lot of them, and the incident ended.

Raistlin and Caramon heard about the fight the next day as they shoved their way through the crowds milling among the booths and tents.

"I wished I'd been there." Caramon gave a gusty sigh and clenched his large fist.

Raistlin said nothing, he hadn't been paying attention. He was studying the flow of the crowds, trying to determine where would be the most advantageous place to establish himself. At length he settled on a spot located at the convergence of two aisles. A lace-maker from Haven was across from him on one side and a wine merchant from Pax Tharkas on the other.

Placing a large wooden bowl in front of a nearby stump, Raistlin gave Caramon his instructions.

"Walk to the end of this row, turn around, and stroll back. You're a farmer's son in town for the day, remember. When you come to me, stop and stare and point and create a commotion. Once the crowd begins to form around me, move to the outside of the circle and catch people as they walk past, urge them to take a look. Got that?"

"You bet!" said Caramon, grinning. He was enjoying himself immensely.

"And when I ask for a volunteer from the crowd, you know what you must do."

Caramon nodded. "Say I've never seen you before in my life and that there's nothing at all inside that box."

"Don't overact," Raistlin cautioned.

"No, no. I won't. You can count on me," Caramon promised.

Raistlin had his doubts, but there was nothing more he could do to alleviate them. He had rehearsed Caramon the night before, and he could only hope his twin would remember his lines.

Caramon departed, heading for the end of the row as he'd been directed. He was almost immediately waylaid by a stout little man in a garish red waistcoat, who drew Caramon toward a tent, promising that inside the tent Caramon could see the epitome of female beauty, a woman renowned from here to the Blood Sea, who was going to perform the ritual mating dance of the Northern Ergothians, a dance that was said to drive men into a frenzy. Caramon could witness this fabulous sight for only two steel pieces.

"Really?" Caramon craned his neck, trying to sneak a peek through the tent flap.

"Caramon!" His brother's voice snapped across the back of his neck.

Caramon jumped guiltily and veered off, much to the chagrin of the stout little man, who cast Raistlin a baleful look before catching hold of another yokel and resuming his spiel.

Raistlin positioned the wooden bowl so that it showed to best advantage, dropped a steel piece inside to "prime the pump," then laid out his equipment at his feet. He had balls for juggling, coins that would appear inside people's ears, a remarkable length of rope that could be cut and made perfectly whole again in an instant, silken scarves that would flow wondrously from his mouth, and a brightly painted box from which would emerge a peeved and disheveled rabbit.

He wore white robes, which he had laboriously sewn himself out of an old bed sheet. The worn spots were covered with stars and moon faces: red and black. No true wizard would have been caught dead wearing such an outlandish getup, but the general public didn't know any better and the bright colors attracted attention.

The juggling balls in his hands, Raistlin mounted the stump and began to perform. The multicolored balls—toys from his and Caramon's childhood—spun in his deft fingers, flashed through the air. Immediately several children ran over to watch, dragging their parents with them.

Caramon arrived, to loudly exclaim over the wonders he was witnessing. More people came to watch and to marvel. Coins clinked in the wooden bowl.

Raistlin began to enjoy himself. Although he was not performing real magic, he was casting a spell over these people. The enchantment was helped by the fact that they wanted to believe in him, were ready to believe in him. He liked the admiration of the children especially, perhaps because he remembered himself at that age, remembered his own awe and wonder, remembered where that awe and wonder had led.

"Wow! Would you look at that!" cried a shrill voice from the crowd. "Did you really swallow all those scarves? Doesn't it tickle when they come out?"

At first Raistlin thought the voice belonged to a child, then he noticed the kender. Dressed in bright green pants, a yellow shirt, and an orange vest, with an extremely long topknot of hair, the kender surged forward to the front of the crowd, which parted nervously at his coming, everyone clutching his purse. The kender stood in front of Raistlin, regarding him with openmouthed admiration.

Raistlin cast an alarmed glance at Caramon, who hurried over to stand protectively beside the wooden bowl that held their money.

The kender seemed familiar to Raistlin, but then kender are so appallingly different from normal people that they all look alike to the untrained eye.

Raistlin thought it wise to distract the kender from the wooden bowl. He did this by first extracting one of his juggling balls from the kender's pouch, then causing a shower of coins to fall from the kender's nose, much to the diminutive spectator's wild delight and mystification. The audience—quite a large audience now—applauded. Coins clinked into the bowl.

Raistlin was taking a bow when, "For shame!" a voice cried.

Raistlin rose from his bow to look directly into the face—the blotchy, vein-popping, infuriated face—of his schoolmaster.

"For shame!" Master Theobald cried again. He leveled a quivering, accusing finger at his pupil. "Making an exhibition of yourself before the masses!"

Conscious of the watching crowd, Raistlin tried to maintain his composure, though hot blood rushed to his face. "I know that you disapprove, Master, but I must earn my living the best way I know how."

"Excuse me, Master sir, but you're blocking my view," said the kender politely, and he reached up to tug at the sleeve of the man's white robe to gain his attention.

The kender was short and Master Theobald was shouting and waving his arms, which undoubtedly explains how the kender missed the sleeve and ended up tugging on the pouch of spell components hanging from the master's belt.

"I've heard how you've been earning your living!" Master Theobald countered. "Consorting with that witch woman! Using weeds to fool the gullible into thinking they've been healed. I came here on purpose to see for myself because I could not believe the stories were true!"

"Do you really know a witch?" asked the kender eagerly, looking up from the pouch of spell components.

"Would you have me starve, Master?" Raistlin demanded.

"You should beg in the streets before you prostitute your art and make a mockery of me and my school!" Master Theobald cried.

He reached out his hand to drag Raistlin down from the stump.

"Touch me, sir"—Raistlin spoke with quiet menace—"and you will regret it."

Theobald glowered. "Do you dare to threaten—"

"Hey, Little Fella!" Caramon cried, lumbering in between the two. "Toss that pouch over here!"

"Goblin Ball!" shouted the kender. "You're the goblin," he informed Master Theobald and sent the pouch whizzing over the mage's head.

"This yours, huh, wizard?" Caramon teased, capering and waving the pouch in front of Theobald's face. "Is it?"

Master Theobald recognized the pouch, clapped his hand to his belt where the pouch should be hanging. Blue veins popped out on his forehead, his face flushed a deeper red.

"Give that to me, you hooligan!" he cried.

"Down the middle!" yelled the kender, making an end sweep around the Master.

Caramon tossed the pouch. The kender caught it, amidst laughter and cheers from the crowd, who were finding the game even more entertaining than the magic. Raistlin stood on the stump, coolly watching the proceedings, a half-smile on his lips.

The kender reached up to throw a long pass back to Caramon when suddenly the pouch was plucked out of the kender's hand.

"What the—" The kender looked up in astonishment.

"I'll take that," said a stem voice.

A tall man in his early twenties, with eyes as blue as Solamnic skies, long hair worn in an old-fashioned single braid down his back, took hold of the pouch. His face was serious and stem, for he was raised to believe that life was serious and stern, bound with rules whose rigid iron bars could never be bent or dislodged. Sturm Brightblade closed the pouch's drawstrings, dusted off the pouch, and handed it, with a formal bow, to the furious mage.

"Thank you," said Master Theobald stiffly. Snatching back the pouch, he thrust it safely up his long, flowing sleeve. He cast a baleful gaze at the kender, and then, turning, he coldly regarded Raistlin.

"You will either leave this place or you will leave my school. Which is it to be, young man?"

Raistlin glanced at the wooden bowl. They had quite enough money for the time being, anyway. And in the future, what the master did not know would not hurt him. Raistlin would simply have to be circumspect.

With an appearance of humility, Raistlin stepped down from the stump.

"I am sorry, Master," said Raistlin contritely. "It won't happen again."

"I should hope not," said Master Theobald stiffly. He departed in a state of high dudgeon that would only increase upon his return home to find that most of his spell components, to say nothing of his steel pieces, had disappeared—and not by magic.

The crowd began to drift away, most of them quite satisfied, having seen a show well worth a steel coin or two. Soon the only people remaining around the stump were Sturm, Caramon, Raistlin, and the kender.

"Ah, Sturm!" Caramon sighed. "You spoiled the fun."

"Fun?" Sturm frowned. "That was Raistlin's schoolmaster you were tormenting, wasn't it?"

"Yes, but—"

"Excuse me," said the kender, shoving his way forward to talk to Raistlin. "Could you pull the rabbit out of the box again?"

"Raistlin should treat his master with more respect," Sturm was saying.

"Or make the coins come out of my nose?" the kender persisted. "I didn't know I had coins up my nose. You think I would have sneezed or something. Here, I'll shove this one up there, and—"

Raistlin removed the coin from the kender's hand. "Don't do that. You'll hurt yourself. Besides, this is our money."

"Is it? You must have dropped it." The kender held out his hand. "How do you do? My name is Tasslehoff Burrfoot. What's yours?"

Raistlin was prepared to coldly rebuff the kinder—no human in full possession of his sanity, who wanted to keep firm hold on such sanity, would ever willingly associate with a kender. Raistlin recalled the stupefied look on Master Theobald's face when he had seen his precious spell components in the hands of a kender. Smiling at the memory, feeling that he was in the kender's debt, Raistlin gravely accepted the proffered hand. Not only that, but he introduced the kender to the others.

"This is my brother, Caramon, and his friend, Sturm Brightblade. "

Sturm appeared extremely reluctant to shake hands with a kender, but they had been formally introduced and he could not avoid the handshake without appearing impolite.

"Hi, there, Little Fella," Caramon said, good-naturedly shaking hands, his own large hand completely engulfing the kender's and causing Tasslehoff to wince slightly.

"I don't like to mention this, Caramon," said the kender solemnly, "since we've only just been introduced, but it is very rude to keep commenting on a person's size. For instance, you wouldn't like it very much if I called you Beer Barrel Belly, would you?"

The name was so funny and the scene was so ludicrous—a mosquito scolding a bear—that Raistlin began to laugh. He laughed until he was weak from the exertion and was forced to sit down on the stump. Pleased and amazed to see his brother in such a good humor, Caramon burst out in a loud guffaw and clapped the kender on the back, kindly picked him up afterward.

"Come, my brother," said Raistlin, "we should gather our belongings and start for home. The fairgrounds will be closing soon. It was very good meeting you, Tasslehoff Burrfoot," he added with sincerity.

"I'll help," offered Tasslehoff, darting eager glances at the many colored balls, the brightly painted box.

"Thanks, but we can manage," Caramon said hurriedly, retrieving the rabbit just as it was disappearing into one of the kender's pouches. Sturm removed several of the silk scarves from the kender's pocket.

"You should be more careful of your possessions," Tasslehoff felt called upon to point out. "It's a good thing I was here to find them. I'm glad I was. You really are a wonderful magician, Raistlin. May I call you Raistlin? Thanks. And I'll call you Caramon, if you'll call me Tasslehoff, which is my name, only my friends call me Tas, which you can, too, if you like. And I'll call you Sturm. Are you a knight? I was in Solamnia once and saw lots of knights. They all had mustaches like yours, only more of it—the mustache, I mean. Yours is a bit scrawny right now, but I can see you're working on it."

"Thank you," Sturm said, stroking his new mustache self-consciously.

The brothers started moving through the crowd, heading toward the exit. Saying that he'd seen all he cared to see for the day, Tasslehoff accompanied them. Not caring to be seen in public in company with a kender, Sturm had been about to take his leave of them when the kender mentioned Solamnia.

"Have you truly been there?" he asked.

"I've been all over Ansalon," said Tas proudly. "Solamnia's a very nice place. I'll tell you about it if you'd like. Say, I have an idea. Why don't you come home with me for supper? All of you. Flint won't mind."

"Who's Flint? Your wife?" Caramon asked.

Tasslehoff hooted. "My wife! Wait till I tell him! No, Flint's a dwarf and my very best friend in all the world, and I'm his best friend, no matter what he says, except for maybe Tanis Half-Elven, who is another friend of mine, only he's not here right now, he's gone to Qualinesti where the elves live." Tas stopped talking at this juncture, but only because he'd run out of breath.

"I remember now!" exclaimed Raistlin, coming to a halt. "I knew you looked familiar. You were there when Gilon died. You and the dwarf and the half-elf." He paused a moment, eyeing the kender thoughtfully, then said, "Thank you, Tasslehoff. We accept your invitation to supper."

"We do?" Caramon looked startled.

"Yes, my brother," said Raistlin.

"You'll come, too, won't you?" Tasslehoff asked Sturm eagerly.

Sturm was stroking his mustache. "My mother's expecting me at home, but I don't believe she'll mind if I join my friends. I'll stop by and tell her where I'm going. What part of Solamnia did you visit?"

"I'll show you." Tasslehoff reached around to a pouch he wore on his back—the kender was festooned with pouches and bags. He pulled out a map. "I do love maps, don't you? Would you mind holding that corner? There's Tarsis by the Sea. I've never been there, but I hope to go someday, when Flint doesn't need my help so much, which he does dreadfully right now. You wouldn't believe the trouble he gets into if I'm not there to keep an eye on things. Yes, that's Solamnia. They have awfully fine jails there . . . ."

The two continued walking, the tall Sturm bent to study the map, Tasslehoff pointing out various places of interest.

"Sturm's taken leave of his senses," said Caramon. "That kender's probably never been anywhere near Solamnia. They all lie like . . . well, like kender.

And now you've got us eating supper with one of them and a dwarf! It's . . . it's not proper. We should stick to our own kind. Father says—"

"Not anymore he doesn't," Raistlin interrupted.

Caramon paled and lapsed into an unhappy silence.

Raistlin laid his hand on his brother's arm in silent apology. "We cannot stay cooped up forever in our home, wrapped in a safe little cocoon," he said gently. "We finally have a chance to break free of our bindings, Caramon, and we should take it! We'll need a little time for our wings to dry in the sun, but soon we'll be strong enough to fly. Do you understand?"

"Yes, I think so. I'm not sure I want to fly, Raist. I get dizzy when I'm up too high." Caramon, added thoughtfully, "But if you're wet, you should definitely go home and dry off."

Raistlin sighed, patted his brother's arm. "Yes, Caramon. I'll change my clothes. And then we'll have dinner with the dwarf. And the kender."

2

THE HOUSE OF FLINT FIREFORGE WAS CONSIDERED AN ODDITY AND ONE of the wonders of Solace. Not only was it built on the ground, but it was also made entirely of stone, which the dwarf had hauled all the way from Prayer's Eye Peak. Flint didn't care what people said about him or his house. In the long and proud history of dwarfdom, no dwarf had ever lived in a tree.

Birds lived in trees. Squirrels lived in trees. Elves lived in trees. Flint was neither bird, nor squirrel, nor elf, thanks be to Reorx the Forger. Flint did not have wings, nor a bushy tail, nor pointed ears—all of which, as everyone knows, are indigenous to tree-dwelling species. He considered living in trees unnatural as well as dangerous.

"Fall out of bed and that'll be the last fall you ever take," the dwarf was wont to say in dire tones.

It was useless to point out to him, as did his friend and business partner, Tanis Half-Elven, that even in a tree house one fell out of bed and landed on the floor, likely suffering nothing worse than a bruised backside.

Tree house floors were made of wood, Flint maintained, and wood was known to be an untrustworthy building material, subject to rot, mice, and termites, likely to catch fire at any moment, leaky in the rain, drafty in the cold. A good, stiff puff of wind would carry it away.

Stone, now. Nothing could beat good, solid stone. Cool in the summer, warm in the winter. Not a drop of rain could penetrate stone walls. The wind might blow as hard as it liked, blow until it was red in the face, and your stone blocks would never so much as quiver. It was well known that stone houses were the only houses to have survived the Cataclysm.

"Except in Istar," Tanis Half-Elven would tease.

"Not even stone houses can be expected to survive having a great bloody mountain dropped down on top of them," Flint would return, always adding, "Besides, I have no doubt that way down in the Blood Sea, where all know the city of Istar was cast, certain lucky fish are living quite comfortably."

On this particular day, Flint was inside his stone house attempting to make some sense of the disorder in which he lived. Disorder was a constant state of affairs ever since the kender had moved in.

The two unlikely roommates had met on market day. Flint was showing his wares, and Tasslehoff, passing through town on his way to anywhere interesting, had stopped at the dwarf's stall to admire a very fine bracelet.

What happened next is subject to who tells the story. According to Tas, he picked up the bracelet to try it on, discovered it fit perfectly, and was going off in search of someone to ask the price.

According to Flint, he came out of the back of the booth, after a refreshing nip of ale, to find Tasslehoff and the bracelet both disappearing rapidly into the crowd. Flint nabbed the kender, who loudly and shrilly proclaimed his innocence. People stopped to watch. Not to buy. Just to watch.

Tanis Half-Elven, arriving on the scene, broke up the altercation, dispersed the crowd. Reminding the dwarf in low tones that such scenes were bad for business, Tanis persuaded Flint that he didn't really want to see the kender hung from the nearest vallenwood by his thumbs. Tasslehoff magnanimously accepted the dwarf's apology, which Flint couldn't recall ever having made.

That evening, the kender had showed up on Flint's doorstep, along with a jug of excellent brandy, which Tasslehoff claimed to have purchased at the Inn of the Last Home and which he had brought the dwarf by way of a peace offering. The next afternoon, Flint had awakened with a hammer-pounding headache to find the kender firmly ensconced in the guest bedroom.

Nothing Flint did or said could induce Tasslehoff to leave.

"I've heard tell that kender are afflicted with—what do they call it?— wanderlust. That's it. Wanderlust. I suppose you'll be coming down with that soon," the dwarf had hinted.

"Nope. Not me." Tas had been emphatic. "I've gone through that already. Outgrown it, you might say. I'm ready to settle down. Isn't that lucky? You really do need someone to look after you, Flint, and I'm here to fill the bill. We'll share this nice house all through the winter. I'll travel with you during the summer. I have the most excellent maps, by the way. And I know all the really fine jails . . . ."

Thoroughly alarmed at this prospect, more frightened than he'd ever been in his life, even when held captive by ogres, Flint had sought out his friend, Tanis Half-Elven, and had asked him to help him either evict the kender or murder him. To Flint's amazement, the half-elf had laughed heartily and refused. According to Tanis, life shared with Tasslehoff would be good for Flint, who was much too reclusive and set in his ways.

"The kender will keep you young," Tanis had said.

"Aye, and likely I'll die young," Flint had grumbled.

Living with the kender had introduced Flint to a great many people in Solace, most notably the town guardsmen, who now made the dwarf's house their first stop when searching for missing valuables. The sheriff soon grew tired of arresting Tas, who ate more than his share of prison food, walked off with their keys, and persisted in making helpful suggestions about how they could improve their jail. Finally, at the suggestion of Tanis Half-Elven, the sheriff had decided to quit incarcerating the kender, on the condition that Tas be remanded into Flint's custody. The dwarf had protested vehemently, but no one listened.

Now, every day after Flint's morning housecleaning, he would place any strange new objects he'd happened to find out on the door stoop. Either the town guard came to collect them or their neighbors would stop by and rummage through the pile, searching for items they had "dropped," items that the kender had thoughtfully "found."

Life with the kender also kept Flint active. He had spent half of this morning searching for his tools, which were never in their proper place. He'd discovered his most valuable and highly prized silver hammer lying in a pile of nutshells, having apparently been used as a nutcracker. His best tongs were nowhere to be found. (They would turn up three days later in the creek that ran behind the house, Tasslehoff having attempted to use them to catch fish.) Calling down a whole cartload of curses on the kender's topknotted head, Flint was searching for the tea kettle when Tasslehoff flung open the door with a heart-stopping bang.

"Hi, Flint! Guess what? I'm home. Oh, did you hit your head? What were you doing under there in the first place? I don't see why you should be looking for the tea kettle under the bed. What kind of doorknob would put a tea kettle under the—Oh, you did? Well, isn't that odd. I wonder how it got there. Perhaps it's magic! A magic tea kettle.

"Speaking of magic, Flint, these are some new friends of mine. Mind your head, Caramon. You're much too tall for our door. This is Raistlin and his brother Caramon. They're twins, Flint, isn't that interesting? They look sort of alike, especially if you turn them sideways. Turn sideways, Caramon, and you, too, Raistlin, so that Flint can see. And that's my new friend Sturm

Brightblade. He's a knight of Solamnia! They're staying to dinner, Flint. I hope we've got enough to eat."

Tas concluded at this point, swelling with pride and the two lungfuls of air required for such a long speech.

Flint eyed the size of Caramon and hoped they had enough to eat as well. The dwarf was in a bit of a quandary. The moment they stepped across his threshold, the young men were guests in his house, and by dwarven custom that meant they were to be treated with the same hospitality he would have given the thanes of his clan, had those gentlemen ever happened to pay Flint a visit, an occurrence which was highly unlikely. Flint was not particularly fond of humans, however, especially young ones. Humans were changeable and impetuous, prone to acting rashly and impulsively and, in the dwarf's mind, dangerously. Some dwarven scholars attributed these characteristics to the human's short life span, but Flint held that was only an excuse. Humans, to his way of thinking, were simply addled.

The dwarf fell back on an old ploy, one that always worked well for him when confronted by human visitors.

"I would be very pleased if you could stay to dinner," said the dwarf, "but as you can see, we don't have a single chair that will fit you."

"I'll go borrow some," offered Tasslehoff, heading for the door, only to be stopped short by the tremendous cry of "No!" that burst simultaneously from four throats.

Flint mopped his face with his beard. A vision of the suddenly chairless people of Solace descending on him in droves caused him to break out in a cold sweat.

"Please do not trouble yourself," said Sturm, with that cursed formal politeness typical of Solamnic knights. "I do not mind sitting on the floor."

"I can sit here," Caramon offered, dragging over a wooden chest and plopping down on it. His weight caused the hand-carved chest to creak alarmingly.

"You have a chair that would fit Raistlin," Tasslehoff reminded him. "It's in your bedroom. You know, the one we always use whenever Tanis comes over to—Why are you making those faces at me? Do you have something in your eye? Let me look. . . ."

"Get away from me!" Flint roared.

His face flushed red, the dwarf fumbled in his pocket for the key to the bedroom. He always kept the door locked, changed the lock at least once a week. This didn't stop the kender from entering, but at least it slowed him down some. Stomping into the bedroom, Flint dragged out the chair that he saved for the use of his friend and kept hidden the rest of the time.

Positioning the chair, the dwarf took a good hard look at his visitors. The young man called Raistlin was thin, much too thin, as far as the dwarf was concerned, and the cloak he was wearing was threadbare and not at all suited to keep out the autumn chill. He was shivering, his lips were pale with the cold. The dwarf felt a bit ashamed for his lack of hospitality.

"Here you go," he said. Positioning the chair near the fire, he added gruffly, "You seem a bit cold, lad. Sit down and warm yourself. And you"—he glowered at the kender—"if you want to make yourself useful, go to Otik's and buy—buy, mind you!—a jug of his apple cider."

"I'll be back in two shakes of a lamb's tail," Tas promised. "But why two shakes? Why not three? And do lambs even have tails? I don't see how—"

Flint slammed the door on him.

Raistlin had taken his seat, edged the chair even closer to the fire. Blue eyes, of a startling clarity, regarded the dwarf with an intense gravity that made Flint feel extremely uncomfortable.

"It is not really necessary for you to give us dinner—" Raistlin began.

"It isn't?" exclaimed Caramon, dismayed. "What'd we come here for, then?"

His twin flashed him a look that caused the bigger youth to squirm uncomfortably and duck his head. Raistlin turned back to Flint.

"The reason we came is this: My brother and I wanted to thank you in person for speaking up for us against that woman"—he refused to dignify her with a name—"at our father's funeral."

Now Flint recalled how he knew these youngsters. Oh, he'd seen them around town since they were old enough to be underfoot, but he had forgotten this particular connection.

"It was nothing special," protested the dwarf, embarrassed at being thanked. "The woman was daft! Belzor!" Flint snorted. "What god worth his beard would go around calling himself by the name of Belzor? I was sorry to hear about your mother, lads," he added, more kindly.

Raistlin made no response to that, dismissed it with a flicker of his eyelids. "You mentioned the name 'Reorx.' I have been doing some studying, and I find that Reorx is the name for a god that your people once worshiped."

"Maybe it is," said Flint, smoothing his beard and eyeing the young man mistrustfully. "Though I don't know why a human book should be taking an interest in a god of the dwarves."

"It was an old book," Raistlin explained. "A very old book, and it spoke not only of Reorx, but of all the old gods. Do you and your people still worship Reorx, sir? I don't ask this idly," Raistlin added, a tinge of color staining his pale cheeks. "Nor do I ask to be impertinent. I am in earnest. I truly wish to know what you think."

"I do as well, sir," said Sturm Brightblade. Though he sat on the floor, his back was as straight as a pike staff.

Flint was astonished. No human had ever, in all the dwarf's hundred and thirty-some years, wanted to know anything at all about dwarven religious practices. He was suspicious. What were these young men after? Were they spies, trying to trick him, get him into trouble? Flint had heard rumors that some of the followers of Belzor were preaching that elves and dwarves were heretics and should be burned.

So be it, Flint decided. If these young men are out to get me, I'll teach them a thing or two. Even that big one there. Bash him in the kneecaps and he'll be cut down to about my size.

"We do," said Flint stoutly. "We believe in Reorx. I don't care who knows it."

"Are there dwarven clerics, then?" Sturm asked, leaning forward in his interest. "Clerics who perform miracles in the name of Reorx?"

"No, young man, there aren't," Flint said. "And there haven't been since the Cataclysm."

"If you've had no sign that Reorx still concerns himself over your fate, how can you still believe in him?" Raistlin argued.

"It is a poor faith that demands constant reassurance, young human," Flint countered. "Reorx is a god, and we're not supposed to understand the gods. That's where the Kingpriest of Istar got into trouble. He thought he understood the minds of the gods, reckoned he was a god himself, or so I've heard. That's why they threw the fiery mountain down on top of him.

"Even when Reorx walked among us, he did a lot that we don't understand. He created kender, for one," Flint added in gloomy tones. "And gully dwarves, for another. To my mind, I think Reorx is like myself—a traveling man. He has other worlds he tends to, and off he goes. Like him, I leave my house during the summer, but I always come back in the fall. My house is still here, waiting for me. We dwarves just have to wait for Reorx to come back from his journeys."

"I never thought of that," said Sturm, struck with the notion. "Perhaps that is why Paladine left our people. He had other worlds to settle."

"I'm not sure." Raistlin was thoughtful. "I know this seems unlikely, but what if, instead of you leaving the house, you woke up one morning to find that the house had left you?"

"This house will be here long after I'm gone," Flint growled, thinking the young man was making a disparaging remark about his handiwork. "Why look at the carving and joining of the stone! You'll not see the like between here and Pax Tharkas."

"That wasn't what I meant, sir," Raistlin said with a half-smile. "I was wondering . . . It seems to me . . ." He paused, making an effort to say exactly what he did mean. "What if the gods had never left? What if they are here, simply waiting for us to come back to them?"

"Bah! Reorx wouldn't hang about, lollygagging his time away, without giving us dwarves some sort of sign. We're his favorites, you know," Flint said proudly.

"How do you know he hasn't given the dwarves a sign, sir?" Raistlin asked coolly.

Flint was hard put to answer that one. He didn't know, not for sure. He hadn't been back to the hills, back to his homeland in years. And despite the fact that he traveled throughout this region, he hadn't really had that much contact with any other dwarves. Perhaps Reorx had come back and the Thorbardin dwarves were keeping the god a secret!

"It would be like them, damn their beards and bellies," Flint muttered.

"Speaking of bellies, isn't anybody else hungry?" Caramon asked plaintively. "I'm starved."

"Such a thing is not possible," said Sturm flatly.

"It is, too," Caramon protested. "I haven't had anything to eat since breakfast."

"I was referring to what your brother said," Sturm returned. "Paladine could not be in the world, witnessing the hardships my people have been forced to endure, and do nothing to intercede."

"From what I've heard, your people witnessed the hardships suffered by those under their rule calmly enough," Raistlin returned. "Perhaps because they were responsible for most of it."

"That's a lie!" Sturm cried, jumping to his feet, his fists clenched.

"Here, now, Sturm, Raist didn't mean that—" Caramon began.

"Are you telling me that the Solamnic knights did not actively persecute magic-users?" Raistlin feigned astonishment. "I suppose the mages simply grew weary of living in the Tower of High Sorcery in Palanthas, and that's why they fled from it in fear for their lives!"

"Raist, I'm sure Sturm didn't intend to—"

"Some call it persecution. Others call it rooting out evil!" Sturm said darkly.

"So you equate magic with evil?" Raistlin asked with dangerous calm.

"Don't most people with any sense?" Sturm returned.

Caramon rose to his feet, his own fists clenched. "I don't think you really meant that, did you, Sturm?"

"We have a saying in Solamnia. 'If the boot fits—' "

Caramon took a clumsy swing at Sturm, who ducked and lunged at his opponent, catching him in his broad midsection. Caramon went over backward with a "woof," Sturm on top of him, pummeling him. The two crashed into the wooden chest, breaking it into its component parts and smashing the crockery that was being stored inside. The two continued their scuffling on the floor, rolling and punching and flailing away at each other.

Raistlin remained sitting by the fire, watching calmly, a slight smile on his thin lips. Flint was disturbed by such coolness, so disturbed that he lost the moment when he might have stopped the fight. Raistlin did not appear worried, concerned, or shocked. Flint might have suspected him of having provoked this battle for his own amusement, except that he did not appear to be enjoying the show. His smile was not one of pleasure. It was faintly derisive, his look disdainful.

"Those eyes of his shivered my skin," Flint was later to tell Tanis. "There is something cold-blooded about him, if you take my meaning."

"I'm not sure I do. Are you saying that this young man deliberately provoked his brother and his friend into a fistfight?"

"Well, no, not exactly." Flint considered. "His question to me was sincere. I've no doubt of that. But then, he must have known how the talk of gods and all that hoo-hah about magic would affect a Solamnic knight. And if there was ever a Solamnic knight walking around without his armor, that is young Sturm for you. Born with a sword up his back, as we used to say.

"But that Raistlin." The dwarf shook his head. "I think he just liked knowing that he could make them fight, best friends and all."

"Hey, now!" Flint shouted, suddenly realizing that he wasn't going to have any furniture left if he didn't put an end to the brawl. "What do you think you're doing? You've broken my dishes! Stop that! Stop it, I say!"

The two paid no heed to the dwarf. Flint waded into the fray. A swift and expert kick to the outside of the kneecap sent Sturm rolling. He rocked in agony on top of the bits of broken crockery, clutching his knee and biting his lip to keep from crying out in pain.

Flint grabbed hold of a handful of Caramon's long, curly hair and gave it a swift, sharp tug. Caramon yelped and tried unsuccessfully to prize loose the dwarf's hold. Flint had a grip of iron.

"Look at you both!" the dwarf stated in disgust, giving Caramon's head a shake and Sturm another kick. "Acting like a couple of drunken goblins. And who taught you to fight? Your great-aunt Minnie? Both of you taller than me by a foot at least, maybe two feet for the young giant, and here you are. Flat on your back with the foot of a dwarf on your chest. Get up. Both of you."

Shamefaced and teary-eyed from the pain, the two young men slowly picked themselves up off the floor. Sturm stood balancing on one leg, not daring to trust his full weight to his injured knee. Caramon winced and massaged his stinging scalp, wondering if he had a bald spot.

"Sorry about the dishes," Caramon mumbled.

"Yes, sir, I am truly sorry," Sturm said earnestly. "I will make recompense for the damage, of course."

"I'll do better than that. I'll pay for it," Caramon offered.

Raistlin said nothing. He was already counting out money from their take at the fair.

"Darn right you'll pay for it," the dwarf said. "How old are you?"

"Twenty," answered Sturm.

"Eighteen," said Caramon. "Raist is eighteen, too."

"Since he knows we are twins, I'm certain Master Fireforge has figured that out," Raistlin said caustically.

Flint eyed Sturm. "And you plan to be a knight." The dwarf's shrewd gaze shifted to Caramon. "And you, big fellow. You figure on being a great warrior, I suppose? Sell your sword to some lord."

"That's right!" Caramon gaped. "How did you know?"

"I've seen you around town, carrying that great sword of yours—handling it all wrong, I might add. Well I'm here to tell both of you right now that the knights'll take one look at you and the way you fight, Sturm Brightblade, and they'll laugh themselves right out of their armor. And you, Caramon Majere, you couldn't sell your fighting skills to my old grannie."

"I know I have a lot to learn, sir," Sturm replied stiffly. "If I were living in Solamnia, I would be squire to a noble knight and learn my craft from him. But I am not. I am exiled here." His tone was bitter.

"There's no one in Solace to teach us," Caramon complained. "This town is way too quiet. Nothing ever happens here. You'd think we'd at least have a goblin raid or something to liven things up."

"Bite your tongue, lad. You don't know when you're well off. As for a teacher, you're looking at him." Flint tapped himself on the breast.

"You?" Both young men appeared dubious.

Flint stroked his beard complacently. "I had my foot on both of you, didn't I? Besides"—reaching out, he gave Raistlin a poke in the ribs that caused him to jump—"I want to talk to the book reader here about his views on a good many matters. No need to talk of money," the dwarf added, seeing the twins exchanging doubtful glances and guessing what they were thinking. "You can pay me in chores. And you can start by going to the inn and seeing what's become of that dratted kender."

As if the words had conjured him, the door was thrown open by the "dratted" kender.

"I've got the cider and a kidney pie that someone didn't want, and—Ah, there! I knew it!"

Tasslehoff gazed sadly at the remains of the chest and the broken dishes. "You see what happens, Flint, when I'm not around?" he said, solemnly shaking his topknot.

3

THE UNLIKELY FRIENDSHIP BETWEEN THE YOUNG HUMANS, THE DWARF, and the kender flourished like weeds in the rainy season, according to Tasslehoff. Flint took exception to being called a "weed," but he conceded that Tas was right. Flint had always had a soft spot in his gruff heart for young people, particularly those who were friendless and alone. He had first become acquainted with Tanis Half-Elven when he met that young man living in Qualinesti, an orphan that neither race would claim. Tanis was too human for the elves, too elven for humans.

Tanis had been raised in the household of the Speaker of the Sun and Stars, the leader of the Qualinesti, growing up with the Speaker's own children. One of those children, Porthios, hated Tanis for what he was. Another cousin, Laurana, loved Tanis too much. In that is another tale, however.

Suffice it to say that Tanis had left the elven kingdom some years ago. He'd gone for help to the first person—the only person—he knew outside of Qualinesti: Flint Fireforge. Tanis had no skill at all in working metal, but he did have a head for figures and a keen business sense. He soon discovered that Flint was selling his wares far below their true worth. He was cheating himself.

"People will be happy to pay more for quality workmanship," Tanis had pointed out to the dwarf, who was terrified that he would lose his clientele. "You'll see."

Tanis proved to be right, and Flint prospered, much to the dwarf's astonishment. The two became partners. Tanis began accompanying the dwarf on his summer travels. Tanis hired the wagon and the horses, put up the booths at the local fairs, made appointments to show Flint's wares privately to the well-to-do.

The two developed a friendship that was deep and abiding. Flint asked Tanis to move in with him, but Tanis pointed out that the dwarf's house was a bit cramped for the tall half-elf. Tanis's dwelling place was nearby, however, built up in the tree branches. The only quarrel the two ever had—and it wasn't really a quarrel, more of a grumbling argument—was over Tanis's trips back to Qualinesti.

"You're not fit for anything when you come back from that place," Flint said bluntly. "You're in a dark mood for a week. They don't want you around; they've made that plain enough. You upset their lives and they upset yours. The best thing for you to do is wash the mud of Qualinesti off your boots and never go back."

"You're right, of course," said Tanis reflectively. "And every time I leave, I swear I will never return. But something draws me back. When I hear the music of the aspen trees in my dreams, I know it is time for me to return home. And Qualinesti is my home. They can't deny it to me, no matter how they'd like to try."

"Bah! That's the elf in you!" Flint scoffed. " 'Music of the aspen trees!' Horse droppings! I haven't been home in one hundred years. You don't hear me carrying on about the music of the walnuts, do you?"

"No, but I have heard you express a longing for proper dwarf spirits," Tanis teased.

"That's completely different," Flint returned sagaciously. "We're talking life's blood here. I do wonder that Otik can't seem to get the recipe right. I've given it to him often enough. It's these local mushrooms, or what humans think pass for mushrooms."

Despite Flint's urgings, Tanis left that fall for Qualinesti. He was gone during Yule. The heavy snows set in, and it began to look as if he wouldn't be back before spring.

Flint had always been a bit lonely when Tanis was gone, though the dwarf would have cut off his beard before he admitted it. The inadvertent addition of Tasslehoff eased the dwarf's loneliness some, though Flint would have cut off his head before he admitted that. The kender's lively chatter filled in the silence, though the dwarf always irritably put a stop to it when he found himself becoming too interested.

Teaching the young humans how to handle themselves in a fight gave Flint a true feeling of accomplishment. He showed them the little tricks and skillful maneuvers he had learned from a lifetime of encounters with ogres and goblins, thieves and footpads, and other hazards faced by those who travel the unchancy roads of Abanasinia. He likened this feeling of satisfaction to that of turning out an exceptional piece of metalwork.

In essence, he was doing much the same: shaping and crafting young lives as he shaped and crafted his metal. One of them, however, was not particularly malleable.

Raistlin continued to "shiver" Flint's skin.

The twins were nineteen that winter, and they were spending the winter together.

Early in the fall, a fire had burned down Master Theobald's mage school, forcing him to relocate. By this time, Theobald was well known and trusted in Solace. The authorities—once assured that the fire had been from natural causes and not supernatural—gave him permission to open his new school within the town limits.

Raistlin no longer needed to board at the school. He could spend the winters at home with Caramon. But neither he nor Caramon were home much of the time.

Raistlin enjoyed the company of the dwarf and the kender. He required knowledge of the world beyond the vallenwoods, knowledge of a world in which he would soon be taking his place. Since acquiring the ability to cast his magic, he had dared to dream of his future.

Raistlin was now an assistant teacher at the school. Master Theobald hoped that by providing some honorable way for the young man to earn money, Raistlin would quit performing in public. Raistlin was not a particularly good teacher; he had no patience for ignorance and tended to be extremely sarcastic. But he kept the boys quiet during Master Theobald's afternoon nap, which was all the master required. Master Theobald had once mentioned that Raistlin might like to open a mage school himself. Raistlin had laughed in the master's face.

Raistlin wanted power. Not power over a bunch of mewling brats, dully reciting their *aas* and *ais*. He wanted the power he held over people when they watched him cast even minor cantrips. Their expressions of awe, their wide-eyed respect were deeply gratifying. He saw himself gaining increasing power over others.

Power for good, of course.

He would give money to the impoverished, health to the sickly, justice to evildoers. He would be loved, admired, feared, and envied. If he was going to hold sway over vast numbers of people (such are the ambitious dreams of youth!), he would need to know as much as possible about those people—all of them, not just humans. The dwarf and the kender proved to be excellent character studies.

The first thing Raistlin learned was that a kender's fingers are into everything, and a kender's hands will carry it off. He had been enraged the first time Tasslehoff appropriated the small bag in which the young mage proudly kept his one and only spell component.

"Look what I found!" Tasslehoff announced. "A leather pouch with the letter *R* on it. Let's see what's inside."

Raistlin recognized the pouch, which only moments earlier had been hanging from his belt. "No! Wait! Don't—"

Too late. Tas had opened the pouch. "There's a bunch of dried-up flowers in here. I'll just empty those out." He dumped the rose petals on the floor, looked back inside. "Nope, nothing else. That's odd. Why would anyone—"

"Give me that!" Raistlin snatched the pouch. He was literally trembling with rage.

"Oh, is that yours?" Tas looked up at him, eyes bright. "I cleaned it out for you. Someone had stuck a bunch of dead flowers inside it."

Raistlin opened his mouth, but words were not only inadequate, they were nonexistent. He could only glare, make incoherent sounds, and at least satisfy some of his anger by casting a furious glance at his laughing brother.

After losing the pouch and the rose petals twice more, Raistlin realized that outrage, threats of violence and/or legal action did not work with kender. He could never catch the deft fingers that could untie any knot, no matter how tight and slide the bag away with the lightness of touch of a spider. Coping with Tasslehoff required subtlety.

Raistlin conducted an experiment. He placed a rounded lump of brightly colored glass, acquired from leavings at the glassblowers, inside his pouch. The next time Tas "found" the pouch, he discovered the glass inside. Enchanted, he drew out the glass, dropped the pouch to the floor. Raistlin retrieved the pouch and his spell components intact. After that, he took to putting some trinket or interesting object (a bird's egg, a petrified beetle, a sparkling rock) in the pouch. Whenever he missed it, he knew where to look.

As Raistlin learned more about kender, Caramon was learning the fine and not-so-fine points of dwarven combat.

Due to the short stature of dwarves and the fact that they generally fight opponents much taller than themselves, dwarven fighting techniques are not elegant. Flint used a number of moves—groin kicks and rabbit punches, for example—that were not chivalrous, according to Sturm.

"I will not fight like a common street brawler," he protested.

The time of year was the deepest part of midwinter. Crystalmir Lake was frozen and snow-covered. Most people kept indoors where it was warm, toasting their feet and drinking hot punch. Flint had Sturm and Caramon outside, working them into a lather, "toughening them up."

"Is that so?" Flint walked over to stand beneath the tall young man. Drops of water from his panting breath coated Sturm's mustaches, making him look like walrus, according to Tasslehoff.

"And what will you do when you are attacked by a common street brawler, laddie?" Flint demanded. "Raise your sword to him in some fool salute while he kicks you in your privates?"

Caramon guffawed. Sturm frowned at the vulgarity, but conceded that the dwarf had a point. He should at least know how to counter such an attack.

"Goblins, now," Flint continued his lecture. "They're basically cowards, unless they're fired up with liquor, and then they're just plain crazed. A goblin will always try to jump you from behind, slit your throat before you know what's hit you. Like this . . . He'll use his hairy hand to muffle your scream, and with his other, draw the blade right across here. You'll bleed to death almost before your body hits the ground.

"Now, here's what you do. You use the goblin's own weight and forward movement against him. He comes at you, jumps on you like this . . . ."

"Let me be the goblin!" Tasslehoff begged, waving his hand. "Please, Flint! Let me!"

"All right. Now, the kender—"

"Goblin!" Tas corrected and leapt onto Flint's broad back.

"—jumps on you. What do you do? Just this."

Flint grabbed hold of the kender's two hands that were clutching for his throat and, bending double, flipped the kender over his head.

Tas landed hard on the frozen, snow-covered ground. He lay there a moment, gasping and gulping.

"Knocked the air clean out me!" he said when he could talk. He scrambled to his feet. I've never not been able to breathe before, have you, Caramon? It's an interesting feeling. And I saw the stars and it's not even night. Do you want me to do it to you, Caramon?"

"Hah! You couldn't flip me!" Caramon scoffed.

"Maybe not," Tas admitted. "But I can do this."

Clenching his fist, he drove it right into Caramon's broad midriff.

Caramon groaned and doubled over, clutching his gut and sucking air.

"Well struck, kender," came an approving voice that rang out over the laughter of the others.

"Not bad, Tasslehoff. Not bad," said another.

Two people, heavily muffled in furs, were walking through the snow.

"Tanis!" Flint roared in welcome.

"Kitiara!" Caramon cried out in surprise.

"Tanis and Kitiara!" Tasslehoff yelled, though he'd never seen or met Kitiara before in his life.

"Here, now. Do you all know each other?" Tanis demanded. He looked from Caramon and Raistlin to Kitiara in astonishment.

"I should," answered Kitiara with her crooked grin. "These two are my brothers. The twins I was telling you about. And as for Brightblade, here, he and I used to play together." Her crooked smile gave the words a salacious meaning.

Caramon whistled and poked Sturm in the ribs. Sturm flushed in embarrassment and anger. Saying stiffly that he was needed at home, he bowed coldly to the newcomers, turned on his heel, and stalked off.

"What'd I say?" Kit asked. Then she laughed and, holding out her arms, invited her brothers to her embrace.

Caramon gave her a bear hug. Showing off his strength, he lifted her from the ground.

"Very good, little brother," she said, eyeing him approvingly when he set her down. "You've grown since I saw you last."

"Two whole inches," Caramon said proudly.

Raistlin turned his cheek to his sister, avoided her embrace. Kitiara, with a laugh and a shrug, kissed him, an obliging peck. He stood motionless beneath her scrutinizing gaze, his hands folded in front of him. He was wearing the robes of a mage now, white robes, a gift from his mentor, Antimodes.

"You've grown, too, baby brother," Kit observed.

"Raistlin's grown a whole inch," said Caramon. "It's my cooking that's done it."

"That wasn't what I meant," said Kit.

"I know. Thank you, Sister," Raistlin replied. The two exchanged glances, in perfect accord.

"Well, well," said Kit, turning back to Tanis. "Who would have thought it? I leave my brothers babes in arms and come back to find them grown men. And this"—she turned to the dwarf—"this must be Flint Fireforge."

She held out her gloved hand. "Kitiara uth Matar."

"Your servant, ma'am," said Flint, accepting her hand.

The two shook hands with every mark of mutual pleasure in the meeting.

"And I'm Tasslehoff Burrfoot," said Tas, offering one hand to be shaken while the other was gliding toward the young woman's belt.

"How do you do, Tasslehoff," Kit said. "Touch that dagger and I'll use it to slice off your ears," she added good-naturedly.

Something in her voice convinced Tasslehoff that she meant what she said. Being rather fond of his ears, which served to prop up his topknot, Tasslehoff began to rummage through a pouch Tanis obviously didn't want.

Flint deemed that the lessons were over, invited his guests inside for a sip and a bite.

Tanis and Kit shed their cloaks. Kitiara was dressed in a long leather tunic that came to midthigh. She wore a man's shirt, open at the neck, and a finely tooled leather belt of elven make and design. She was unlike any woman the others had ever known, and none of them, including her brothers, seemed to know quite what to make of her.

Her gaze was that of a man, bold and straightforward, not the simpering, blushing modesty of a well-bred woman. Her movements were graceful—the grace of a trained swordsman—and she had the confidence and coolness of a blooded warrior. If she was a bit cocky, that only enhanced her exotic appeal.

"You've noticed my belt," she said, proudly exhibiting the hand-tooled leather girdle that encircled her slender waist. "It's a gift from an admirer."

None of those present had to look far to find the gift giver. Tanis Half-Elven watched Kit's every movement with open admiration.

"I've heard a lot about you, Flint," Kit added. "All good, of course."

"I haven't heard a thing about you," Flint returned, with his customary bluntness. "But I'll wager I will." He looked at Tanis, and mingled with his affection for his friend was a hint of concern. "Where did you two meet?"

"Outside of Qualinesti," said Tanis. "I was on my way back to Solace when I heard screams coming out of the woods. I went to investigate and found what I thought was this young woman being attacked by a goblin. I ran to her aid, only to discover that I'd been mistaken. The screams I'd heard were coming from the goblin."

"Qualinesti," Flint said, eyeing Kit. "What were you—a human—doing in Qualinesti?"

"I wasn't in Qualinesti," Kit said. "I was just near there. I've been in those parts several times. I pass through them on my way here."

"Way through from where?" Flint wondered.

Kit either didn't hear his question or she ignored it. He was about to repeat himself when she motioned her brothers to step forward for introductions.

"I'm Tanis Half-Elven," said Tanis, offering his hand.

Caramon, in his enthusiasm, almost shook the half-elf's hand off. Raistlin brushed his fingers across the half-elf's palm.

"I'm Caramon Majere, and this is my twin brother, Raistlin. We're Kit's half-brothers, really," Caramon explained.

Raistlin said nothing. He curiously examined the half-elf, about whom he'd heard much, for Flint talked about his friend daily. Tanis was dressed like a hunter, in a brown leather jerkin of elven make, green shirt and brown hose, brown traveling boots. He wore a sword at his waist, carried a bow and a quiver of arrows. His elven heritage was not readily apparent, except perhaps in the finely chiseled bones of his face. If his ears were pointed, it was impossible to tell, for they were covered over by his long, thick brown hair. He had the height of an elf, the broader girth of a human.

He was a handsome man, young looking, but possessing the gravity and maturity of a much older man. Small wonder he had attracted Kit's attention.

Tanis regarded the brothers in his turn, marveling at the coincidence. "Kit and I meet by chance on the road. We become friends, and then I arrive home to find her brothers and my best friends have become friends! This meeting was fated, that's all there is to it."

"For a meeting to be fated implies that something significant must come of it in the future. Do you foresee such an occurrence, sir?" Raistlin asked.

"I . . . I guess it could," Tanis stammered, taken aback. He wasn't quite certain how to respond. "In truth, I meant it as a joke. I didn't intend—"

"Don't mind Raistlin, Tanis," Kitiara interrupted. "He's a deep thinker. The only one in the family, by the way. Stop being so serious, will you?" she said to her younger brother in an undertone. "I like this man and I don't want you scaring him off."

She grinned at Tanis, who smiled back at her. Raistlin knew then that the half-elf and his sister were more than friends. They were lovers. The knowledge and the sudden image in his mind made him feel uncomfortable and embarrassed. He suddenly disliked the half-elf intensely.

"I'm glad to see you've been keeping my old friend Flint out of trouble, at least," Tanis continued. Embarrassed himself, he hoped to change to subject.

"Hah! Out of trouble!" Flint glowered. "Darn near drowned me, they did. It's lucky I survived."

The story of an ill-fated boat trip had to be told then and there, with everyone talking at once.

"I found the boat—" Tasslehoff began.

"Caramon, the big lummox, stood up in it—"

"I was only trying to catch a fish, Flint—"

"Upset the whole blasted boat. Gave us all a good soaking—"

"Caramon sank like a stone. I know, because I threw a whole lot of stones in the water, and they all went down just like Caramon, without even a bubble—"

"I was worried about Raist—"

"I was quite capable of taking care of myself, my brother. There was an air pocket underneath the overturned boat, and I was in no danger whatsoever, except of having an imbecile for a brother. Trying to catch a fish with your bare hands—"

"—jumped in after Caramon. I pulled him out of the water—"

"You did not, Flint! Caramon pulled himself out of the water. I pulled you out of the water. Don't you remember? You see what trouble you get into without me—"

"I do remember, and that wasn't the way it was at all, you dratted kender, and I'll tell you one thing," Flint stated emphatically, bringing the confused tale to a close. "I'm never setting foot in a boat again so long as I live. That was the first time, and it will be the last, so help me, Reorx."

"I trust Reorx will honor that vow," said Tanis. He clapped the dwarf affectionately on the shoulder and rose to leave. "I'm going to go see if my house is still standing. You want to come along?"

Tanis asked the question of Flint, but his eyes went to Kitiara.

"I'll go!" Tas signed on eagerly.

"No, you won't," Flint said, collaring the kender and hauling him backward.

"You're coming home with us, aren't you, Kit?" Caramon asked teasingly.

"Maybe later," said Kitiara. Reaching out, she took hold of Tanis's hand. "Much later."

"Oh, shut up," Raistlin said crossly when Caramon wanted to talk about it.

4

Spring came to Solace, bringing with it budding flowers, baby lambs, nesting birds. Blood that had grown cold and sluggish in the winter warmed and thinned. Young men panted and girls giggled. Of all the seasons of the year, Raistlin detested springtime most.

"Kit didn't come home again last night," Caramon said with a wink over breakfast.

Raistlin ate bread and cheese, made no comment. He had no intention of encouraging this line of discussion.

Caramon needed no encouragement, however. "Her bed wasn't slept in. I'll bet I know whose bed was slept in, though. Not that they probably did much sleeping."

"Caramon," said Raistlin coldly, rising to his feet, leaving his breakfast mostly untouched. "You are a pig."

He carried the scraps of his meal to the two field mice he had captured and now kept in a cage, along with the tame rabbit. He had developed certain theories concerning the use of his herbs, and it seemed wiser to test out these theories on animals rather than his patients. Mice were easy to catch and cheap to maintain.

Raistlin's first experiment had not worked out, having fallen victim to the neighbor's cat. He had chastised Caramon quite severely for permitting the cat to enter the house. Caramon, who was fond of cats, promised to entertain the animal out-of-doors from then on. The mice were safe, and Raistlin was quite pleased with the results of his latest experiment. He poked the crumbs through the bars.

"It is bad enough our sister whoring herself, without you making dirty remarks about it," Raistlin continued, giving the rabbit fresh water.

"Aw, c'mon, Raist!" Caramon protested. "Kit isn't . . . what you said. She's in love with the guy. You can see that from the way she looks at him. And he's crazy about her. I like Tanis. Flint's told me a lot about him. Flint says that this summer Tanis'll teach me to use my sword and the bow and arrow. Flint says Tanis is the greatest archer who ever lived. Flint says—"

Raistlin ignored the rest of the conversation. Brushing the crumbs from his hands, he gathered up his books. "I must leave now," he said, rudely cutting his brother off in midsentence. "I am late for school. I will see you this evening, I suppose? Or perhaps you are going to move in with Tanis Half-Elven?"

"Well, no, Raist. Why should I move in with him?"

Sarcasm was lost on Caramon.

"You know, Raist, being with a girl is lots of fun," Caramon continued. "You never talk to any of them, and there's more than one who thinks you're pretty special. Because of the magic and so forth. And how you cured the Greenleaf baby of croup. They say that baby would have died if you hadn't helped her, Raist. Girls like that sort of thing."

Raistlin paused in the doorway. his cheeks faintly burning with pleasure. "It was only a mixture of tea and a root I read about called ipecacuanha. The baby had to throw up the phlegm, you see, and the root mixture caused the child to vomit. Do girls . . . do they truly talk about . . . about such things?"

Girls were, to Raistlin's mind, strange creatures, as unreadable as a magic spell from the tome of some high-ranking archmagus, and just as unattainable. Yet Caramon, who in some matters was as dense as a fallen log, talked to girls, danced the round dances popular at festivals with them, did other things with them, things that Raistlin dreamed about in the dark hours of the night, dreams that left him feeling ashamed and unclean. But then Caramon, with his brawny build, his curly hair, his big brown eyes and handsome features, was attractive to women. Raistlin was not.

The frequent illnesses that still afflicted him left him thin and bony. with no appetite for food. He had the same well-formed nose and chin as Caramon, but on Raistlin the features were more finely planed and pointed, giving him the sly, crafty appearance of a fox. He disliked round dancing, considered it a waste of time and energy, besides which it left him breathless, with a pain in his chest. He didn't know how to talk to girls, what to say. He had the feeling that, although they listened to him politely enough, behind those sparkling eyes, they were secretly laughing at him.

"I don't think they talk about ipe—ipe—ipecaca—whatever that long-tailed word was," Caramon admitted. "But one of them, Miranda, said it was wonderful the way you saved that baby's life. It was her little niece, you see. She wanted me to tell you."

"Did she?" Raistlin murmured.

"Yeah. Miranda's wonderful, isn't she?" Caramon gave a gusty sigh. "I've never seen anyone so beautiful. Oops"—he glanced outdoors, to see the sun starting to rise—"I've got to get going myself. We're planting today. I won't be home until after dark."

Whistling a merry tune, Caramon grabbed his pack and hastened off.

"Yes, my brother, you are right. She is very beautiful!" Raistlin said to the empty house.

Miranda was the daughter of a wealthy clothier, recently arrived to set up business in Solace. Her father's best advertisement, Miranda dressed in the finest clothes, cut and sewn in the very latest style. Long strawberry blond hair fell in lazy ringlets to her waist. Graceful and demure, fragile and winsome, innocent and good, she was utterly captivating, and Raistlin was not the only young man to admire her immensely.

Raistlin had sometimes fancied that Miranda would occasionally glance his way and that her look was inviting. But he always told himself that this was just wishful thinking. How could she possibly care about him? Whenever he saw her, his heart raced, nearly suffocating him. His blood burned, his skin grew cold and clammy. His tongue, normally so glib, could speak only inanities, his brain turned to oatmeal. He could not even look her in the face. Whenever he came close to her, he had difficulty keeping his hand from reaching out to caress one of those flame-colored curls.

There was another factor. Would I be as interested in this young woman if she had not won Caramon's admiration as well? Raistlin asked himself.

The top of Raistlin's mind answered immediately "Yes!" The depths pondered the question uneasily. What demon in Raistlin led to this constant competition with his own twin? A one-sided competition, at that, for Caramon was serenely unaware of it.

Raistlin recalled a story Tasslehoff had told them about a dwarf coming upon a slumbering red dragon. The dwarf attacked the sleeping dragon with ax and sword, hammered at it for hours until he was exhausted. The dragon never even woke up. Yawning, the dragon rolled over in its sleep and squashed the dwarf flat.

Raistlin empathized with that dwarf. He felt as if he were constantly battling his twin, only to have Caramon roll over on him and crush him. Caramon was the better-looking, the better liked, the better trusted. Raistlin was "deep," as Kit described him, or "subtle," as Tanis had once said of him, or "sly," as his classmates termed him. Most people tolerated his presence only because they liked his brother.

At least I am gaining some small reputation as a healer, Raistlin thought as he walked along the boardwalk, trying to avoid breathing in the fragrant spring air, which always made him sneeze.

But the glow of satisfaction no sooner was kindled in him, giving him some small share of warmth, when that infernal demon of his whispered bitterly, Yes, and perhaps that is all you will ever be—a minor mage, a weed-chopping healer—while your warrior brother does great deeds, wins great reward, and covers himself in glory.

"Oh, dear! Oh, my goodness!"

Startled, Raistlin came up short, with the realization that he'd just bumped into someone. He had been concentrating on his thoughts, hurrying along so that he wouldn't be late, and not watching where he was going.

Lifting his head, about to mutter some apology and push his way past, he saw Miranda.

"Oh, dear," she said again and peered over the edge of the railing. Several bolts of fabric lay scattered on the ground beneath them.

"I'm so terribly sorry!" Raistlin gasped. He must have plowed straight into her, causing her to drop the bolts of cloth. They had fallen off the boardwalk, tumbled in a spiral of bright color to the ground.

That was his first thought. His second—and one that caused him even more confusion—was that the boardwalk was wide enough for four people to walk on it abreast and there were only two of them on it at present. One of them, at least, must have been watching where she was going.

"Wait . . . wait here," Raistlin stammered. "I'll . . . I'll go pick them up."

"No, no, it was my fault," the girl returned. Her green eyes glowed like the new budding leaves of the trees that spread their limbs over them. "I was watching a pair of nesting sparrows. . . ." She blushed, which made her even prettier. "I wasn't looking. . . ."

"I insist," Raistlin said firmly.

"We'll go together, shall we?" Miranda forestalled him. "It's a lot to carry, for just one."

She shyly slid her hand into his.

Her touch sent flame through him, flame similar to that of his magic, only hotter. This flame consumed, the other refined.

The two walked side by side down the long stairs to the ground below. The area was still in shadow, the early morning sun was only just filtering through the shiny new leaves. Miranda and Raistlin gathered up the bolts of cloth slowly, taking their time. Raistlin said he hoped the dew would not harm the fabric. Miranda said that there had been no dew at all that morning, nothing to speak of, and that a good brushing would set them right.

He helped her fold up the long lengths of cloth, taking one end while she took the other. Every time they came together, their hands touched.

"I wanted to thank you personally," Miranda said, looking up at him during one of these moments as they stood there, the cloth held between them. Her eyes, glimmering through a veil of reddish blond eyelashes, were entrancing. "You saved my sister's baby. We're all so very grateful."

"It was nothing," Raistlin protested. "I'm sorry. I didn't mean that the way it sounded! The baby is everything, of course. What I meant was that what I did was nothing. Well, not that either. What I meant was—"

"I know what you meant," said Miranda and closed both of her hands over his. They dropped the cloth. She lifted her lips, closed her eyes. He bent over her. "Miranda! There you are! Stop dawdling, girl, and bring along that cloth. I need it for Mistress Wells's bodice."

"Yes, Mother." Miranda stooped, hastily gathered up the cloth in a bundle, not bothering to fold it. Holding the fabric in her arms, she whispered softly and breathlessly, "You will come to visit me some evening, won't you, Raistlin?"

"Miranda!"

"Coming, Mother!"

Miranda was gone, departing in a flutter of skirts and trailing fabric.

Raistlin remained standing where she'd left him, as if he'd been struck by lightning and his feet had melted to the spot. Dazed and dazzled, he considered her invitation and what it meant. She liked him. Him! She had chosen him over Caramon, over all the other men in town who were vying for her affection.

Happiness, pure and untainted, happiness such as he had rarely experienced, poured over him. He basked in it, as in a hot summer sun, and felt himself grow like the newly planted seeds. He built castles in the air so rapidly that within seconds they were ready for him to take up residence.

He saw himself her acknowledged favorite. Caramon would envy him for a change. Not that what Caramon thought mattered, because Miranda loved him, and she was everything good and sweet and wonderful. She would bring out what was good in Raistlin, drive away those perverse demons—jealousy, ambition, pride—who were always plaguing him. He and Miranda would live above the clothier shop. He didn't know anything at all about running a business, but he would learn, for her sake.

For her sake, he would even give up his magic, if she asked him.

The laughter of children jolted Raistlin from his sweet reverie. He was now very late for school and would receive a severe scolding from Master Theobald.

A scolding which Raistlin accepted so meekly, gazing at Theobald with what might almost be termed an affectionate smile, that the master was more than half convinced his strangest and most difficult pupil had, at long last, gone quite mad.

☹

That night—for the first time since he had started school, not counting those times when he was ill—Raistlin did not study his spellcasting. He forgot to water his herbs, left the mice and the rabbit to scrabble frantically in their cages, hungry for the food he neglected to give them. He tried to eat but couldn't swallow a mouthful. He dined on love, a dish far sweeter and more succulent than any served at the feast of an emperor.

Raistlin's one fear was that his brother would return before nightfall, for then he would have to waste time answering all sorts of stupid questions. Raistlin had his lie prepared, a lie brought to mind by Miranda herself. He had been called out to tend to a sick child. No, he did not need Caramon as an escort.

Fortunately Caramon did not return home. This was not unusual during planting season, when he and Farmer Sedge would stay out working in the fields by the light of the bright moon.

Raistlin left their house, walking the boardwalks. In his fancy, he walked on moonlit clouds.

He went to Miranda's house, but he was not going to visit her. Visiting a young unmarried woman after dark would not have been proper. He would speak to her father first, obtain his permission to court his daughter. Raistlin went only to gaze at the place where she lived, hoping perhaps to catch a glimpse of her through the window. He imagined her sitting before the fire, bent over her evening's sewing. She was dreaming of him, perhaps, as he was dreaming of her.

The clothier's business was on the lower level of his house, one of the largest in Solace. The lower level was dark, for the business was shut up for the night. Lights gleamed in the upper level, though, shining through gabled windows. Raistlin stood quietly on the boardwalk in the soft spring evening gazing up at the windows, waiting, hoping for nothing more than the sight of the light shining on her red-gold curls. He was standing thus when he heard a noise.

The sound came from down below, from a shed on the ground beneath the clothier's. Probably a storage shed. The thought came immediately to Raistlin's mind that some thief had broken into the shed. If he could catch the thief, or at least halt the robbery, he would, in his fevered, impossibly romantic condition, have a chance to prove himself worthy of Miranda's love.

Not stopping to think that what he was doing was extremely dangerous, that he had no means of protecting himself if he did come upon a thief, Raistlin ran down the stairs. He could see his way easily enough. Lunitari, the red moon, was full this night and cast a lurid glow along his path.

Reaching the ground, he glided forward silently, stealthily toward the shed. The lock on the door hung loose, the door was shut. The shed had no windows, but a soft light, just barely visible, gleamed out of a knothole on one side. Someone was definitely inside. Raistlin had been about to burst in the door, but common sense prevailed, even over love. He first would look through the knothole, see what was going on. He would be witness to the thief's activities. This done, he would raise the alarm, prevent the thief's escape.

Raistlin put his eye to the knothole.

Bundles of cloth had been stacked on one side of the shed, leaving a cleared place in the center. A blanket was spread on that cleared place. A candle stood on a box in a corner. On the blanket, indistinct in the shadows cast by the candle's wavering flame, two people writhed and panted and squirmed.

They rolled into the candle's light. Red curls fell across a bare white breast. A man's hand squeezed the breast and groaned. Miranda giggled and gasped. Her white hand raked across the man's naked back.

A broad, muscular back. Brown hair, brown curly hair, shone in the candlelight. Caramon's naked back, Caramon's sweat-damp hair.

Caramon nuzzled Miranda's neck and straddled her. The two rolled out of the light. Pants and heaves and smothered giggles whispered in the darkness, giggles that dissolved into moans and gasps of pleasure.

Raistlin thrust his hands into the sleeves of his robe. Shivering uncontrollably in the warm spring air, he walked silently and rapidly back to the stairs that were blood red in Lunitari's smugly smiling light.

5

RAISTLIN FLED ALONG THE BOARDWALKS, WITH NO IDEA WHERE HE WAS or where he was going. He knew only that he could not go home. Caramon would be returning later, when his pleasure was sated, and Raistlin could not bear to see his brother, to see that self-satisfied grin and smell her scent and his lust still clinging to him. Jealousy and revulsion clenched Raistlin's stomach, sent bitter bile surging up his throat. Half blind, weak, and nauseous, he walked and walked, blind and uncaring, until he walked straight into a tree limb in the darkness.

The blow to his forehead stunned him. Dazed, he clung to the railing. Alone on the moonlit stairs, his hands dappled with the blood-red light, shaking and trembling with the fury of his emotions, he wished Caramon and Miranda both dead. If he had known a magical spell in that moment that would have seared the lovers' flesh, burned them to ashes, Raistlin would have cast it.

He could see quite clearly in his mind the fire engulfing the clothier's shed, see the flames—crackling red and orange and white-hot—consuming the wood and the flesh inside, burning, purifying . . .

A dull aching pain in his hands and wrists jolted him back to conscious awareness. He looked down to see his hands white-knuckled in the moonlight. He had been sick, he realized from the stench and a puddle of puke at his feet. He had no recollection of vomiting. The purging had done him some good apparently. He was no longer dizzy or nauseated. The rage and jealousy no longer surged inside him, no longer poisoned him.

He could look around now, take his bearings. At first, he recognized nothing. Then slowly he found a familiar landmark, then another. He knew where he was. He had traversed nearly the length of Solace, yet he had no memory of having done so. Looking back, it was as if he looked into the heart of a conflagration. All was red fire and black smoke and drifting white ash. He gave a deep sigh, a shuddering sigh, and slowly let go his stranglehold on the railing.

A public water barrel stood nearby. He dared not yet put anything into his shriveled stomach, but he moistened his lips and splashed water on the boards where he'd been sick. He was thankful no one had seen him, thankful no one else was around. He could not have borne with pity.

As Raistlin came to figure out where he was, he came to the realization that he shouldn't be here. This part of Solace was not considered safe. One of the first to be built, its dwellings were little more than tumbledown shacks, long since abandoned, the early residents having either prospered and moved up in Solace society or foundered and moved out of town altogether. Weird Meggin lived not far from here, and this was also the location of The Trough, which must have been very close by.

Drunken laughter drifted up through the leaves, but it was sporadic and muffled. Most people, even drunkards, were long abed. The night had crossed its midpoint, was in the small hours.

Caramon would be home by now, home and probably frantic with worry at the absence of his twin.

Good, Raistlin said sourly to himself. Let him worry. He would have to think up some excuse for his absence, which shouldn't be too difficult. Caramon would swallow anything.

Raistlin was chilled, exhausted, and shivering; he'd come out without a cloak, and he would have a long walk home. But still he lingered by the railing, looked back with uneasiness on the moment when he'd wished his brother and Miranda dead. He was relieved to be able to tell himself that he had not meant it, and he was suddenly able to appreciate the strict rules and laws that governed the use of magic. Impatient to gain power, he had never understood so clearly the importance of the Test, which stood like a steel gate across his future, barring his entry to the higher ranks of wizardry.

Only those with the discipline to handle such vast power were granted the right to use it. Looking back on the savagery of his emotions, his desire, his lust, his jealousy, his rage, Raistlin was appalled. The fact that his body—the yearnings and desires of his body—could have so completely overthrown the discipline of his mind disgusted him. He resolved to guard against such destructive emotions in the future.

Pondering this, he was just about to set out for home when he heard booted footsteps approaching. Probably the town guard, walking their nightly patrol. He foresaw annoying questions, stern lectures, perhaps even an enforced escort home. He sidled near the bole of the tree, crept into its shadow, out of Lunitari's light. He wanted to be alone, he wanted to talk to no one.

The person continued walking, moved out of the shadows cast by the tree leaves, and entered a red pool of moonlight. The person was cloaked and hooded, but Raistlin knew Kitiara immediately, knew her by her walk—her long, quick, impatient stride that never seemed to carry her to her destination fast enough.

She passed close by Raistlin. He could have reached out to brush her dark cloak, but he only shrank still deeper into the shadows. Of all the people he did not want to see this night, Kitiara was foremost. He hoped she would remove herself from his vicinity quickly, so that he could return home, and he was extremely frustrated to see her halt at the water barrel.

He waited for her to take her drink and go on, but, though she did drink from the gourd cup attached to the barrel by a rope, she didn't move on. She dumped the gourd back into the water; it fell with a splash. Crossing her arms, Kit leaned back against the barrel and took up a position of waiting.

Raistlin was stranded. He could not leave his tree. He could not step out into the moonlight without her noticing him. But by now he would not have left if he could have. He was intrigued and curious. What was Kitiara doing? Why was she out walking the streets of Solace at this time of night, walking alone, her half-elf lover nowhere to be seen?

She was meeting someone; that much was obvious. Kit was never good at waiting for anything, and this was no exception. She had not been standing two minutes before she stirred restlessly. She crossed her feet, uncrossed her feet, rattled the sword at her waist, slapped her leather gloved hands together, took another drink of water, and more than once leaned forward to peer impatiently down the walkway.

"I will give him five more minutes," she muttered. The night air was still, and Raistlin could hear her words quite clearly.

Footsteps sounded, coming from the direction in which Kit had been looking. She straightened, her hand going reflexively to the hilt of her sword.

The other figure was that of a man, also cloaked and hooded and reeking of ale. Even from where he stood, no more than ten paces from them, Raistlin could smell the liquor on the man. Kit wrinkled her nose in disgust.

"You sot!" Kit sneered. "Keep me waiting in the cold for hours while you suck down rotgut, will you! I've half a mind to slit your ale-swilling belly!"

"I am not past our meeting time," said the man, and his voice was cold and, surprisingly, sober. "If anything, I am early. And one cannot sit in a tavern, even in a tavern as wretched as The Trough, without drinking. Though I am thankful to say that more of that foul liquid the barkeep has the temerity to call ale is on me than is inside me. The barmaid helps herself to her own wares apparently. She managed to spill nearly a full flagon on me. . . . Did you hear that?"

Raistlin had shifted his position ever so slightly in order to relieve a sudden painful cramp in his left leg. He had made hardly any noise at all, yet the man had heard him, for the hooded face turned in Raistlin's direction. Steel flashed in the moonlight.

Raistlin held perfectly still, not even breathing. He did not want to be caught spying on his sister. Kit would be furious, and she had never had any qualms about relieving her anger with the flat of her hand. She might do worse now. And even if she didn't, even if she were inclined to be at all tenderhearted with her baby brother, then the man with the voice like frost-rimed iron would not.

Yet even as fear clenched his already shriveled belly, Raistlin realized that he did not dread being caught because he feared punishment, but because he would miss a chance to discover one of Kit's secrets. Kit had already tried to draw him into her world, place him under her influence. Raistlin was certain she would try again, and he had no intention of playing a subservient role to anyone. Someday he would have to oppose the wishes of his willful sister. He would need every weapon at his disposal for the combat.

"Your ears are playing tricks on you," Kit said after a moment's pause, during which both had listened intently.

"I heard something, I tell you," the man insisted.

"It must have been a cat, then. No one comes here this time of night. Let's get down to business."

Raistlin could see the flash of moonlight off the hilt of Kit's sword; she had drawn aside her cloak to remove a leather scroll case she carried tucked into her belt.

"Maps?" the man asked, looking down at the case.

"See for yourself," she said.

The man unscrewed the end and drew out several sheaves of paper. He spread these out, partially unrolled, on the lid of the water barrel, studied them in the moonlight.

"It's all there," Kit said complacently, pointing with a gloved finger. "Plus more than your lord asked for. The defenses of Qualinesti are delineated on the main map: number of guard posts, number of guards posted, how often the guards are changed, what type of weapons they carry, and so forth. I walked the entire border of Qualinesti myself twice. I've marked on a different map weak spots in their defense, possible areas of penetration, and I've indicated the easiest access routes from the north."

"This is excellent," the man said. He rolled up the sheaves of paper, slid them carefully back into the scroll case, and tucked the scroll case into the top of his boot. "My lord will be pleased. What else have you learned about Qualinesti? I hear you've taken a half-elf lover who was born in—ulp!"

Kit had grabbed hold of the ties of the drawstring on the man's hood. Giving them an expert twist, she jerked him, half strangled, toward her.

"You leave him out of this!" she told him, her voice soft and lethal. "If you think I would demean myself by sleeping with any man in order to gain information, you're wrong, my friend. And you could be dead wrong if you say or do anything to make him the least suspicious."

Steel glinted in the moonlight; Kit held a knife in her other hand. The man glanced down at it, glanced again at Kit's eyes, flashing brighter than the steel, and he raised his hands in deprecating agreement.

"Sorry, Kit. I didn't mean anything by it."

Kitiara released him. He rubbed his neck where the drawstring had cut into it. "How did you get away tonight?"

"I told him I was spending the evening with my brothers. I'll have my money now."

The man reached beneath his cloak, brought out a purse, and handed it over.

Kitiara opened the bag, held it to the light, and estimated the amount of the money quickly by eye. She held up a large coin, studied it, then tucked the coin into the palm of her glove. Pleased, she tied the purse to her belt.

"There's more where that came from if you happen to pick up any additional information about Qualinesti and the elves. Information that you just happen to find 'lying around.'"

Kitiara chuckled. The money had put her in a good mood. "How do I contact you?"

"Leave a message at The Trough. I'll stop by whenever I'm passing this way. But won't you be traveling north soon?" he asked.

Kit shrugged. "I don't think so. I'm happy enough where I am for the time being. There's my little brothers to think of."

"Uh-huh," the man grunted.

"They're getting to the age where they could be of some use to us," Kit continued, ignoring him.

"I've seen them around town. The big one we could use as a soldier maybe, though he's clumsy as a kobold and looks about as bright. The other, though—the magic-user. Rumor has it that he's quite talented. My lord would be pleased to have him join his ranks."

"Rumor has it wrong! Raistlin can pull a coin out of his nose. That's about it. But I'll see what I can do." Kit held out her hand.

The man took hold of her hand, shook it, but didn't immediately let go. "Lord Ariakas would be pleased to have you join us as well, Kit. On a permanent basis. You'd make a fine commander. He said so."

Kit removed her hand from the man's grasp, placed it on the hilt of her sword. "I didn't know His Lordship and I were on such familiar terms," she said archly. "I've never met the man."

"He knows you, Kit. By sight and by reputation. He's impressed, and this"—the man indicated the map case—"will impress him further. He's prepared to offer you a place in his new army. It's a great opportunity. One day he will rule all of Ansalon, and after that all of Krynn."

"Indeed?" Kit lifted her eyebrow. She appeared impressed. "He doesn't think small, does he?"

"Why should he? He has powerful allies. Which reminds me. How do you feel about dragons?"

"Dragons!" Kit was amused. "I think they are fine for scaring the wits out of little children, but that's about all. What do you mean?"

"Nothing in particular. You wouldn't be fearful of them, would you?"

"I fear nothing in this world or the next," Kit said, a dangerous edge to her voice. "Does any man say different?"

"No one says different, Kit," the man responded. "My lord has heard us all speak of your courage. That's why he wants you to join us."

"I'm happy here," Kit said, shrugging off the offer. "For the time being, at least."

"Suit yourself. The offer—By Takhisis, I heard that!"

Uncomfortable prickling sensations had been shooting up the backs of Raistlin's legs. He had tried to shift his foot, wiggle his toes, and he'd tried to do it silently. Unfortunately the board on which he stood was loose and creaked loudly when his foot moved.

"Spy!" the man said in his cold voice.

A flutter of black cloak, a leap, and a bound, and he was standing in front of Raistlin, his strong hand gripping Raistlin's cloak. Words of magic flew out of the young mage's head on wings of terror.

The man dragged Raistlin out from behind the tree. Forcing him to his knees, the man yanked off the hood of Raistlin's cloak. He grabbed a handful of Raistlin's hair, jerked his head back. Steel flashed red in the moonlight.

"This is what we do to spies in Neraka."

"You fool! Stop!" Kitiara's arm slammed into the man's hand, knocking the arm backward and the knife to the boardwalk.

The man turned on her in fury, his lust for blood hot. The point of her sword at his throat cooled him.

"Why did you stop me? I wasn't going to kill him. Not yet, anyhow. He'll talk first. I need to know who's paying him to spy on me."

"No one's paying him to spy on you," said Kitiara scornfully. "If he's spying on anyone, he's spying on me."

"You?" The man was skeptical.

"He's my brother," said Kitiara.

Raistlin crouched on his knees, his head bowed. Shame and embarrassment overwhelmed him. He could have wished to die rather than face his sister's wrath and, worse, her disdain.

"He's always been a little snoop," said Kitiara. "We call him the Sly One. Get up!"

She cuffed Raistlin across the face hard. He tasted blood.

To his astonishment, after she'd struck him, Kitiara put her arm around his neck, hugged him close.

"There, that was for being bad," she said to him playfully. "Now that you're here, Raist, let me introduce you to a friend of mine. Balif is his name. He's sorry he scared you like that. He thought you were a thief. Aren't you, sorry, Balif?"

"Yeah, I'm sorry," said the man, eyeing Raistlin.

"And you were acting like a thief, skulking around in the night. What are you doing out this late, anyway? Where were you?"

"I was with Weird Meggin," said Raistlin, wiping blood from his split lip. "She had found a dead fox. We were dissecting it."

Kit wrinkled her nose and frowned. "That woman's a witch. You should stay away from her. So, little brother," Kit said offhandedly, "what did you think about what Balif and I were discussing?"

Raistlin looked stupid, copying his twin's blank stare and dumbfounded expression. "Nothing." He shrugged. "I didn't hear that much of it. I was just walking by, and—"

"Liar," growled the man. "I heard a noise when we first started talking, Kit. He's been there the whole time."

"No, I haven't, sir." Raistlin spoke in conciliatory tones. "I was going to walk past, but I heard you mention dragons. I stopped to listen. I couldn't help myself. I have always been interested in stories of the old days. Particularly dragons."

"That's true," said Kitiara. "He's always got his nose in a book. He's harmless, Balif. Quit worrying. Run along home, Raist. I won't mention the fact that you've been with that witch woman to anyone."

His gaze met hers.

And I won't mention to Tanis the fact that you've been out in the night with another man, Raistlin promised her silently.

She smiled. They understood each other perfectly sometimes.

"Go along!" She gave him a shove.

Muscles stiff and aching, fear and blood leaving a bitter taste in his mouth, a taste that sickened him, he made his way across the boardwalk. Hearing sounds of footsteps and afraid that Balif was coming after him, Raistlin glanced back.

Balif was leaving by the stairs, his cloak swirling around him.

Kitiara had fished the coin out of her glove. She flipped it into the air, caught it. Leaning over the rail, she called after him, "I'll keep in touch!"

Raistlin heard the man's brief, cold laughter. Footsteps continued on the stairs and then died away as the man reached ground level.

Kitiara remained standing by the water barrel, her head lowered, her arms crossed over her chest. She was deep in thought. After a moment, she shook herself all over, as if shaking off all doubt and questions. Drawing her hood close to conceal her face, she set off at a brisk pace.

Raistlin took a circuitous route home, one that was longer but would insure he did not cross his sister's path. He mulled over Kit's conversation, trying to ferret out a meaning, but he was too stupid with fatigue to make any sense of it. His body was drained. It was all he could do to force himself to place one foot in front of the other, trudge the weary way back home.

Caramon would be awake, worried sick, asking questions.

Raistlin smiled grimly. He wouldn't have to lie. He would simply say that he'd spent the evening with their sister.

6

THE TWINS TURNED TWENTY THAT SUMMER.

Their Day of Life Gift was supposed to have been a joyous celebration. Kitiara gave them a party, inviting their friends to the Inn of the Last Home, treating them to supper and all the ale they could drink, which, in the dwarf's case, was an alarming amount. Everyone was having a good time, with the exception of the guests of honor.

Raistlin had been in a foul mood since spring, more than usually sarcastic and bitter, especially with his brother. Their mutual birthday, with its necessary reminders of their dead parents, only appeared to sharpen the edge of his bad humor.

Caramon was glum, having just heard the news that Miranda, the girl he currently adored, had suddenly up and married the miller's son. The unseemly haste with which the wedding was held gave rise to speculations of the most scandalous nature. Caramon's disappointment in the matter was lightened somewhat when he noticed that news of Miranda's nuptials actually brought a smile to Raistlin's face. The smile was dark and unpleasant, not the sort of smile that warms the heart, but it was a smile. Caramon took this as a good sign and hoped fervently that his currently unhappy home life would improve.

The Day of Life Gift party lasted well into the night, and the warmth and good spirits of everyone else soon thawed Raistlin's chill. This was the first celebration Kitiara had attended for her brothers since they were small, almost too small to remember. These past months were the longest period of time she had spent in Solace since her girlhood.

"For a backwater town, it isn't nearly as boring as I remember," she replied in answer to Raistlin's caustic query. "I don't have to be anywhere, not for a while, at least. I'm having fun, baby brother."

She was in wonderful spirits that night, and so was Tanis Half-Elven. The two sat next to each other and their mutual admiration was obvious. Each watched the other with warm, bright eyes. Each urged the other to tell favorite stories. With secret smiles and sidelong glances, each reminded the other of some joke known only to the two of them.

"Tonight's celebration is on me," said Kit, when it came time to settle the reckoning. "I'm paying for everything."

She tossed three large coins onto the table. Otik, his broad face beaming, reached out for them. Raistlin deftly slid his hand under Otik's, snatched up one of the coins, and held it to the light.

"Steel. Minted in Sanction," Raistlin observed, studying them. "Newly minted, I would say."

"Sanction," Tanis repeated, frowning. "That city has the reputation of an evil place. How did you come by coins from Sanction, Kit?"

"Yes, where did you find such an interesting coin, Sister?" Raistlin asked. "Look at this—it has a five-headed dragon stamped on it."

"An evil image," said Tanis, looking grave. "The ancient sign of the Dark Queen."

"Don't be silly! It's a coin, not some evil artifact! I won it playing at bones with a sailor," Kit said, her crooked smile limpid. "Lucky at bones, unlucky at love, so they say. But I proved them wrong. The very next day, I met you, lover." She leaned over to Tanis, kissed him on the cheek.

Her tone was easy, casual, her smile genuine. Raistlin would never have had reason to doubt her if he had not seen that coin, or one like it, sparkle in Lunitari's light only a month ago.

The half-elf believed her; that much was certain. But then Tanis was so besotted with Kitiara that she could have told him she'd sailed to the moon and back on a gnome ship and he would have asked her for details of the voyage.

None of the others questioned her either. Flint regarded all his friends with a patronizing, grandfatherly air, which was degenerating rapidly with every ale the dwarf drank. Tasslehoff roamed happily around the inn, much to the dismay of the other customers. The members of the party took turns rescuing people from the kender, who, after two pints of ale, was wont to regale them with his favorite Uncle Trapspringer stories. Flint and Tanis returned the customers' belongings or made restitution if the "borrowed, strayed or otherwise abandoned" personal possessions were irretrievably lost in the kender's many pouches.

As for Caramon, he was watching his twin with almost pitiful anxiety, willing desperately that Raistlin should have a good time. Caramon was elated when his morose brother actually looked up from the single glass of wine he had not even touched to ask, "Speaking of dragons, I am currently pursuing a course of study on beasts from antiquity. Does anyone know any stories about dragons?"

"I know one," offered Sturm, who, having imbibed two mugs of mead in honor of the occasion, was unusually loquacious.

He told the company a story about the Solamnic knight Huma and how he had fallen in love with a silver dragon, who had taken the disguise of a human female. The tale was well received and raised speculation. Dragons, good and evil, had once lived on Krynn; the old tales were filled with stories of them. Were such tales true? Did dragons really exist, and if so, what had happened to them?

"I've lived in this world a long time," said Tanis, "and I've never seen any sign of dragons. It's my belief that they exist only in the lays of the minstrels."

"If you deny the existence of dragons, you deny the existence of Huma Dragonbane," said Sturm. "He was the one who drove the dragons from the world, the good dragons agreeing to leave with the evil in order not to upset the balance. That is why you see no dragons."

"Uncle Trapspringer met a dragon once—" Tasslehoff began excitedly, but the party was slated to hear no more. Flint kicked the stool out from under Tas, depositing the kender and his ale on the floor.

"Dragons are kender tales," said Flint with a disgusted snort. "Nothing more."

"Dwarves tell dragon stories, too," Tas said, not at all disconcerted. He picked himself up, looked sadly into his empty ale mug, and traipsed off to ask Otik for a refill.

"Dwarves tell the best dragon stories," Flint stated. "Which is only natural, considering that we once competed with the great beasts for living space. Dragons, being quite sensible creatures, preferred to live underground. Oftentimes a dwarven thane would pick out a snug, dry mountain for his people, only to find that a dragon had entertained the same idea."

Tanis laughed. "You can't have it both ways, old friend. Dragons can't be false in kender tales and true in dwarf tales."

"And why not?" Flint demanded angrily. "Have you ever known a kender to speak a true word? And have you ever known a dwarf to lie?"

He was quite pleased with his argument, which made sense when viewed through the bottom of an ale mug.

"What do you say, Raist?" Caramon asked. His brother appeared to be taking an interest in this subject, unlike many subjects previous.

"As I said, I have read of dragons in my books," Raistlin replied. "They mention magical spells and artifacts related to dragons. The books are old, admittedly, but why would such spells and artifacts have been created if the beasts were only mythological?"

"Exactly!" cried Sturm, tapping his mug on the table and bestowing a rare look of approbation on Raistlin. "What you say is quite logical."

"Raist knows a story about Huma." Caramon was pleased to see the two almost friendly. "Tell it, Raist."

When he heard that the story dealt with magic-users, Sturm frowned again and pulled at his mustaches, but the frown gradually lessened as the story went along. He gave it grudging approval at the end, stating with a brusque nod, "The wizard showed great courage—for a magic-user."

Caramon flinched, fearing his brother would take offense at this remark and launch an attack. But Raistlin, his tale concluded, was watching Kitiara, did not even appear to have heard Sturm's comment. Relaxing, Caramon gulped down his ale, called for another, and yelped in pain as a small girl with fiery red curls leapt on him from behind, crawled like a squirrel up his back.

"Ouch! Confound it, Tika!" Caramon endeavored to rid himself of the child. "Aren't you supposed to be in bed?" he demanded, glaring around at the little girl with a mock ferocity that made her giggle. "Where's Waylan, your good-for-nothing father?"

"I don't know," the youngster replied with equanimity. "He went off somewhere. He's always going off somewhere. I'm staying with Otik until he comes back."

Otik bustled over, apologizing and scolding in the same breath. "I'm sorry, Caramon. Here, you young imp, what are you doing bothering the customers?" He grasped the child firmly, led her off. "You know better than that!"

"'Bye, Caramon!" Tika called, waving her hand delightedly.

"What an ugly little kid," Caramon muttered, turning back to his drink. "Did you ever see so many freckles?"

Raistlin had taken advantage of the distraction to lean over to his sister. "What do you think, Kit?" he asked with a slight smile.

"About what?" she asked nonchalantly. Her gaze was fixed on Tanis, who had gone to the bar for two more ales.

"Dragons," he said.

Kit cast him a sharp glance.

Raistlin met her scrutinizing gaze with bland innocence.

Kit shrugged, gave an affected laugh. "I don't think about dragons at all. Why should I?"

"It's just that I saw your expression change when I first brought up the subject. As if you were going to say something, then didn't. You've traveled so much. I'd be interested to hear what you had to say," he concluded respectfully.

"Pah!" Kit was brusque, appeared displeased. "The expression on my face was pain. My stomach's churning. I think that venison Otik fed us tonight was tainted. You were wise not to eat it. I've heard enough about Solamnic knights and about dragons," she added when Tanis returned. "It's silly arguing about something no one can prove. Let's change the subject."

"Very well," said Raistlin. "Let's talk about the gods, then."

"Gods! That's even worse!" Kit said, groaning. "I suppose you've become a convert of Belzor now, little brother, and that you're going to proselytize. Let's leave, Tanis, before he starts his harangue."

"I am not speaking of Belzor," Raistlin returned with a touch of asperity. "I am speaking of the old gods, those who were worshiped before the Cataclysm. The old gods were equated with dragons, and it is said that some of them existed in dragon form. Queen Takhisis, for example. Like her image on the coin. It seems to me that a belief in dragons must of necessity argue a belief in these gods. Or the other way round."

Everyone—with the exception of Kit, who rolled her eyes and kicked Tanis underneath the table—had an opinion. Sturm stated that he'd done some thinking about this since their last conversation, had spoken to his mother about Paladine. His mother stated that the knights still believed in the god of light. They were waiting for Paladine to return home with an apology for being gone so long. If so, the knights might be willing to forgive and forget the god's past misdeeds.

The elves, according to Tanis, were convinced that the gods—all the gods—had left the world due to the wickedness of humans. When humans were finally eradicated from the world—which must surely happen, since they were notoriously combative-then the true gods would return.

After giving the matter considerable thought, Flint was inclined to believe that Reorx, having been fed lies by the mountain dwarves, was holed up inside Thorbardin, with no knowledge that the hill dwarves were in need of his divine help.

"Trust a mountain dwarf to pretend that we don't exist. They wish we'd fall off the face of Krynn, that's what. We're a shame and an embarrassment to them," Flint concluded.

"Could you fall off the face of Krynn?" Tas asked eagerly. "How would you do it? My feet seem to be pretty firmly planted on the ground. I don't think I could drop off. What if I stood on my head?"

"If there was a true god in this world, the kender would have all dropped off it by now," Flint grumbled. "Would you look at that doorknob? Standing on his head!"

It might be more accurate to say that Tasslehoff was attempting to stand on his head. He had his head planted on the floor and was kicking his legs, trying to get his feet into the air, but not having much success. Finally he did manage to stand on his head, with the result that he almost immediately toppled over. Nothing daunted, he tried again, this time taking the precaution of placing himself next to a wall. Fortunately for the party and the rest of the customers, this endeavor absorbed the kender's attention and energies for a considerable length of time.

"If the ancient gods are still around somewhere," said Tanis, resting his hand on Kit's, urging her to be patient, to stay awhile longer, "then there should be some sign of their presence. In the old days, it was said that the clerics of the gods had the power to heal sickness and injuries, that they could even restore life to the dead. The clerics disappeared right before the Cataclysm and have not been seen since, at least that the elves have heard."

"Clerics of Reorx live," Flint maintained, his tone bitter. "I'm convinced of it. They're inside Thorbardin. All sorts of miracles are performed in the halls of our ancestors, halls where by rights we hill dwarves should be now!" He thumped the table with his fist.

"Come, old friend," Tanis admonished mildly. "You remember that time we met the mountain dwarf at the fair in Haven last fall. He claimed that it was the hill dwarves who had clerical powers and refused to share them with their cousins in the mountain."

"Of course he would say that!" Flint bellowed. "To ease his guilty conscience!"

"Tell us a story about Reorx," suggested Caramon, the peacemaker, but the dwarf was angry and wouldn't talk.

"Some of these followers of the new gods claim to have that power," Tanis stated, giving Flint time to cool off. "The clerics of Belzor, for, one. The last time I was in Haven, they made a big show of it. Caused cripples to get up and walk and dumb people to speak. What do you say, Kit?"

He'd caught her in a prodigious yawn, which she didn't bother to hide. Raking back her curly hair, she laughed carelessly. "Who wants or needs any gods at all? I certainly don't. No divine force controls my life, and that's the way I like it. I choose my own destiny. I am slave to no man. Why should I be a slave to a god and let some priest or cleric tell me how to live?"

Tanis applauded her when she finished and saluted her with a raised glass. Flint was frowning and thoughtful. When his glance fell on Tanis, the frown deepened into concern. Sturm stared raptly into the fire, his dark eyes unusually bright, as if he saw Paladine's knights once more riding into battle in the name of their god. Caramon had long since dozed off. He lay with his head on the table, his hand still wrapped around his ale mug, softly snoring. Tasslehoff, to the wonder and amazement of all, had managed to stand on his head and was shrilly demanding that everyone look at him—quickly, before he fell off the face of Krynn.

"We've stayed long enough," Kit whispered to Tanis. "I can think of lots more interesting things to do than hang around here." Taking hold of his hand, she brought it to her lips, kissed his knuckles.

Tanis's heart was in his eyes, as the saying goes. His love and longing for her was apparent to everyone watching him. Everyone except Kit, who was now playfully nibbling on the knuckles she had previously been kissing.

"I'm going to have to leave Solace soon, Kit," he said to her softly. "Flint will be taking to the road any day now."

Kitiara rose to her feet. "All the more reason not to waste what time we have left. Good-bye, little brothers," she said, not looking at them. "Happy Day of Life Gift."

"Yes, best wishes," Tanis said, turning to Raistlin with a warm smile. He patted the snoring Caramon on the shoulder.

Kitiara put her arm around the half-elf's waist, leaned into him. He placed his arm affectionately on her shoulder. Walking side by side, so closely that they almost tripped over each other's feet, the two left the inn.

Flint sighed and shook his head. "More ale," he called gruffly.

"Did you see me, Flint? Did you see me?" Tasslehoff, his face bright red, skipped back to the table. "I stood on my head! And I didn't fall off the face of Krynn. My head stuck to the floor just like my feet do. I guess you'd have to not have any part of you touching. Do you suppose if I jumped off the roof of the inn? . . ."

"Yes, yes, go ahead," Flint muttered, preoccupied.

The kender dashed away.

"I'll go stop him," Sturm offered and left in hasty pursuit.

Raistlin poked his brother, prodded him awake.

"Uh? What?" Caramon grunted, sitting up and peering around, bleary-eyed. He'd been dreaming of Miranda.

Raistlin raised his half-empty wineglass. "A toast, my brother. To love."

"To love," Caramon mumbled, sloshing ale on the table.

7

As it turned out, Tanis and Flint did not leave Solace that summer. Caramon had already departed for work in the early morning dawn and Raistlin was putting his books together, preparatory to going to his school, when there was a knock on the door. Simultaneous with the knock, the door flew open and Tasslehoff Burrfoot jumped in.

Flint had been trying to teach the kender that a knock on the door was generally conceded among civilized peoples as an announcement of one's presence and a request to be admitted. One waited patiently at the door until the knock was answered and the door was opened by the person residing in the household.

Tasslehoff simply could not grasp the concept. Knocking on doors was not much practiced in the kender homelands. It wasn't necessary. Kender doors usually stood wide open. The only reason to shut them was during inclement weather.

If a visiting kender walked in on his hosts and found that they were engaged in some pursuit in which he was not particularly welcome, the visitor could either sit in the parlor and wait until his hosts showed themselves or he was free to leave—after ransacking the dwelling for anything interesting, of course.

Some uninformed people on Ansalon maintained that this custom was followed because kender had no locks on their doors. This was not true. All doors to kender dwellings had locks, generally a great many locks of differing types. The locks were only used when a party was in progress. There was no door knocking at these times. The guests were expected to pick the locks to obtain entry, this being the major form of entertainment for the evening.

Thus far, Flint had trained Tasslehoff to at least knock on the door, which he did, generally knocking on the door as he opened it, or else opening it and then knocking on it, as a way to loudly announce his presence in case no one noticed him.

Raistlin was prepared for Tasslehoff's arrival, having heard the kender shouting his name breathlessly six doors down and having heard the neighbors shout back to ask if he knew what time of the morning it was. He also heard Tas stop to inform them of the correct time.

"Well, they were the ones who asked," Tasslehoff said indignantly, swinging inside with the door. "If they didn't want to know, why were they shouting like that? I tell you"—he fetched a sigh as he settled himself down at the kitchen table—"I don't understand humans sometime."

"Good morning," said Raistlin, removing the teapot from the kender's hand. "I will be late for my classes. Was there something you wanted?" he asked severely as Tasslehoff was reaching for the bread and the toasting fork.

"Oh, yes!" The kender dropped the fork with a clatter and jumped to his feet. "I almost forgot! It's a good thing you reminded me, Raistlin. I'm extremely worried. No, thank you, I couldn't eat a thing. I'm too upset. Well, maybe a biscuit. Do you have any jam? I—"

"What do you want?" Raistlin demanded.

"It's Flint," said the kender, eating the jam out of the crock with a spoon. "He can't stand up. He can't lie down either, or sit down for that matter. He's in extremely bad shape, and I'm really worried about him. Truly worried."

The kender was obviously upset, because he shoved the jam pot away even though it still had some jam inside. He did put the spoon in his pocket, but that was only to be expected.

Raistlin retrieved the spoon and asked more about the dwarf's symptoms.

"It happened this morning. Flint got out of bed, and I heard him give a yell, which sometimes he does in the morning, but that's usually after I've gone into his room to say good morning when he wasn't exactly ready for it to be morning yet. But I wasn't in his room at all, and he still yelled. So I went into his room to see what was the matter, and there he was, bent double like an elf in a high wind. I thought he was looking at something on the floor, so I went over to look at whatever he was looking at, but then I found out he wasn't, or if he was he wasn't meaning to. He was looking at the floor because he couldn't do anything else.

" 'I'm stuck this way, you miserable kender!' That's what he said. I was miserable for him, so that was pretty accurate. I asked him what happened."

" 'I bent down to lace my boots and my back gave out.' I said I'd help him straighten up, but he threatened to hit me with the poker if I came near him, so—while it might have been interesting, being hit with a poker, something that's never happened to me before—I decided that hitting me wasn't going to help Flint much, so I better come to you and see if you could suggest anything."

Tasslehoff regarded Raistlin with anxious expectancy. The young man had put his books down and was searching among jars containing unguents and potions that he'd concocted from his herb garden.

"Do you know what's wrong?" Tas asked.

"Has he been troubled with back pain before?"

"Oh, yes," said Tas cheerfully. "He said that his back has been hurting him ever since Caramon tried to drown him in the boat. His back and his left leg."

"I see. That's what I thought. It sounds to me as if Flint is suffering from a defluxion of rheum," Raistlin replied.

"A defluxion of rheum," Tas repeated the words slowly, savoring them. He was awed. "How wonderful! Is it catching?" he asked hopefully.

"No, it is not catching. It is an inflammation of the joints. It can also be known as lumbago. Although," Raistlin said, frowning, "the pain in the left leg might mean something more serious. I was going to send some oil of wintergreen home with you to rub into the afflicted area, but now I think I had better come take a look myself."

❂

"Flint, you have an influx of runes!" Tasslehoff cried excitedly, racing through the door, which he had neglected to shut on his way out and which the dwarf, in his misery, could not manage to reach.

Flint had scarcely moved from the place where the kender had left him. He was bent almost double, his beard brushing the floor. Any attempt to straighten brought beads of sweat to his forehead and gasps of agony to his lips. His boots remained unlaced. He stood hunched over, alternately swearing and groaning.

"Runes?" the dwarf yelled. "What has this got to do with runes?"

"Rheum," Raistlin clarified. "An inflammation of the joints caused by prolonged exposure to cold or dampness."

"I knew it! That damn boat!" Flint said with bitter triumph. "I say it again: I'll never set foot in one of those foul contraptions again so long as I live, I swear it, Reorx." He would have stamped his foot upon the vow, this being considered proper among dwarves, but the movement caused him to cry out in pain and clutch the back of his left leg.

"I've got my wares to sell this summer. How am I supposed to travel like this?" he demanded irritably.

"You're not traveling," said Raistlin. "You are going back to bed, and you're going to stay there until the muscles relax. You're all knotted up. This oil will ease the pain. I'll need your help, Tas. Lift his shirt."

"No! Stay away from me! Don't touch me!"

"We're only trying to help you to—"

"What's that smell? Oil of what? Pine tree! You're not going to feed me any tree juice!"

"I'm going to rub it on you."

"I won't have it, I tell you! Ouch! Ouch! Get away! I have the poker!"

"Tas, go fetch Tanis," Raistlin ordered, seeing that his patient was going to be difficult.

Although he was extremely sorry to leave in the midst of such excitement, the kender ran off to deliver his message. Tanis returned in haste, alarmed by Tasslehoff's somewhat confused account that Flint had been attacked by runes, which Raistlin was trying to cure by making him swallow pine needles.

Raistlin explained the situation in more detailed and coherent terms. Tanis concurred in both the diagnosis and the treatment. Overriding the dwarf's vehement protests (first forcibly removing the poker from his hand), they rubbed the oil into his skin, massaged the muscles of his legs and arms until he was finally able to straighten his back enough to lie down.

Flint maintained the entire time that he was not going to bed. He was setting out on his summer travels to sell his wares. There was nothing any of them could do to stop him. He kept this up as Tanis helped him hobble to the bed, kept it up though he had to compress his lips against the pain that he said was like a goblin's poison dagger stuck in the back of his leg. He kept it up until Raistlin told Tas to run to the inn and ask Otik for a jug of brandy.

"What's that for?" Flint asked suspiciously. "You going to rub that on me now?"

"You're to swallow a dram every hour," Raistlin replied. "For the pain. So long as you stay in bed."

"Every hour?" The dwarf brightened. He settled himself more comfortably among the pillows. "Well, perhaps I'll just take today off. We can always start tomorrow. Make certain Otik sends the good stuff!" he bellowed after Tas.

"He won't be going anywhere tomorrow," Raistlin told Tanis. "Or the day after, or any time in the near future. He must stay in bed until the pain goes away and he can walk freely. If he doesn't, he could be crippled for life."

"Are you sure?" Tanis looked skeptical. "Flint's complained of aches and pains as long as I've known him."

"This is different. This is quite serious. It has something to do with the spine and the nerves that run up the leg. Weird Meggin treated a person who was suffering symptoms similar to this once, and I helped her. She explained it to me using a human skeleton she had dissected. If you would accompany me to her house, I could show you."

"No, no! That won't be necessary," Tanis said hurriedly. "I'll take your word for it." He rubbed his chin and shook his head. "But how in the name of the Forger of the World we're going to keep that ornery old dwarf in bed, short of tying him to the bedposts, is beyond me."

The brandy aided them in this endeavor, rendering the patient calm, though not quiet, and in a relatively good humor. He actually did what he was told and remained in bed voluntarily. They were all pleasantly surprised. Tanis praised Flint highly for being such a model patient.

What none of them knew was that Flint had actually made an attempt to get out of bed the first night he was incapacitated. The pain was excruciating, his leg had collapsed under him. This incident scared the dwarf badly. He began to think that perhaps Raistlin knew what he was talking about. Crawling back into bed, Flint determined secretly to stay there as long as it took to heal. Meanwhile, he had a good time ordering everyone about and making Caramon feel wretchedly guilty for having been the cause of it all.

Tanis certainly did not mind staying in Solace instead of traveling around Abanasinia. Kitiara remained in Solace as well, much to the astonishment of her brothers.

"I never thought I'd see Kit fall in love with any man," Caramon said to his twin one evening over supper. "She just doesn't seem the affectionate type."

Raistlin sneered. " 'Love' is not the word, my brother. Love involves caring, respect, fondness. I would term our sister's attachment for the half-elf as one of 'passion,' or perhaps 'lust' might be a better word. I would guess, from the stories our mother told us, that Kitiara is much like her father in that regard."

"I suppose," Caramon responded, looking uncomfortable. He never liked to talk about their mother if he could help it. His memories of her were not pleasant ones.

"Gregor's love for Rosamun was extremely passionate—while it lasted," Raistlin said, with ironic emphasis on the latter part of his sentence. "He found her different from other women, she amused him. I'm sure there is a certain amusement factor involved with Kitiara's relationship with the half-elf. He is undoubtedly very different from other men she has known."

"I like Tanis," Caramon said defensively, thinking that his brother's words disparaged his friend. "He's a great guy. He's giving me sword fighting lessons. I'm getting really good at it. He said so. I'll have to show you sometime."

"Of course you like Tanis. We all like Tanis," Raistlin said with a shrug. "He is honorable, honest, trustworthy, loyal. As I said, he is far different from any other man our sister has loved."

"You can't know that for sure," Caramon protested.

"Oh, I can, my brother. I can," Raistlin said.

Caramon wanted to know how, but Raistlin refused to elaborate. The twins were silent, finishing their meal. Caramon ate voraciously, devouring everything on his plate and then looking around for more. He had only to wait. Raistlin picked at his food, eating only the choicest morsels, shoving aside any bit of meat with the least amount of gristle or any piece that happened to be even slightly underdone. Caramon was always willing to finish the scraps.

He carried away the wooden bowls to be washed. Raistlin fed his mice and cleaned their cage, then went into the kitchen to help his brother.

"I wouldn't want anything bad to happen to Tanis, Raist," Caramon said, not looking up from his work.

"My dear brother, you have more water on the floor than you do in the bucket. No! Finish what you are doing. I will mop it up." Grabbing the rag, Raistlin bent down, wiped it over the stone flagon floor. "As for Tanis, he is quite old enough to take care of himself, Caramon. He is, I believe, well over one hundred."

"Maybe he's old in years, Raist, but he's not as old as you and I in some ways," Caramon said. He stacked up the wet bowls and utensils, wrung out the cloth, and shook the water from his hands, which he then wiped on his shirtfront.

Raistlin snorted, clearly disbelieving.

Caramon tried to make himself clear. "Because he's honest, he thinks everyone else is honest, too. And loyal and honorable. But you and I—we know that's not true. Especially it's not true with Kit."

Raistlin looked up swiftly. "What do you mean?"

Caramon flushed, ashamed for his sister. "She lied to Tanis about that money, Raist. The steel coins from Sanction. She told Tanis that she won the money playing at bones with a sailor. Well, I was with her a few days earlier when she came over here to see if I wanted to practice my sword fighting with her. When she was ready to leave, she sent me to fetch her cloak from the chest in the bedroom. When I picked up the cloak, the purse with the coins fell out and the coins spilled. I looked at one, because I'd never seen a coin like it. I asked her where they came from."

"What did she say?"

"She said that it was pay she'd earned for work she'd done up north. She said that there was lots more money where that came from and that I could earn my share and so could you, if you'd give up this foolery about magic and come with us. She said she wasn't ready to go north yet, that she was having too much fun here, and anyway I needed more training and you had to be convinced that you were . . ." Caramon hesitated.

"I was what?" Raistlin prodded him.

"A failure in magic. That's what she said, Raist. Not me, so don't get mad."

"I'm not mad. Why would she say such a thing?"

"It's because she's never seen you do any magic, Raist. I told her that you were real good, but she only laughed and said I was so gullible I'd swallow any bit of hocus-pocus. I'm not. You've taught me better than that," Caramon stated emphatically.

"I believe that I have taught you better than even I realized," Raistlin said, regarding his brother with a certain amount of admiration. "You knew all this and still kept quiet about it?"

"She told me not to say anything, not even to you, and I wasn't going to, but I don't like it that she lied about the money, Raist. Who knows where it came from? And I didn't like that money either." Caramon shivered. "It had a strange feel to it."

"She didn't lie to you," Raistlin said, thoughtful.

"Huh?" Caramon was amazed. "How do you know that?"

"Just a hunch," Raistlin said evasively. "She's talked about working for people in the north before now."

"I don't want to go up there, Raist," Caramon said. "I've made up my mind. I'd rather be a knight, like Sturm. Maybe they'd let you be a war wizard, like Magius."

"I would like to train as a warrior mage," Raistlin said. "The knights would not have me, nor do I think they would take you either. But we could work together, perhaps in the mercenary line, combining sorcery and steel. Warrior mages are not common, and people would pay well for such skills."

Caramon was radiant with pleasure. "That's a great idea, Raist! When do you think we should start?" He looked prepared to rush out the door at that very moment.

"Not for some time yet," Raistlin returned, controlling his brother's impatience. "I would have to leave the school. Master Theobald would have apoplexy if I even mentioned such a thing. In his mind, magic is to be used only in such dire situations as starting campfires if the wood is wet. But we must not rush into this, Brother," he admonished, seeing Caramon already starting to polish his sword. "We need money. You need experience. And I need more spells in my spellbook."

"Sure, Raist. I think it's a great idea, and I plan to be ready." Caramon ceased his work, looked up, his expression solemn and troubled. "What do we say to Kit?"

"Nothing. Not until the time comes," Raistlin said. He paused a moment, then added with a grim smile, "And let her keep thinking I have no talent for magic."

"Sure, Raist, if that's what you want." Caramon couldn't quite figure that one out, but, figuring that Raistlin knew best, he always obeyed his brother's wishes. "What do we do about Tanis?"

"Nothing," Raistlin said quietly. "There is nothing we can do. He wouldn't believe us if we said anything bad about Kit because he doesn't want to believe us. You would not have believed me if I had said anything bad about Miranda, would you?" Raistlin asked with a tinge of bitterness.

"No, I guess not." Caramon sighed massively. He still maintained his heart was broken, although he was now involved with three girls, at last count. "Isn't there anything we can do about Kit?"

"We watch her, my brother. We watch her very carefully."

8

SUMMER DAYS DRIFTED BY IN A HAZE OF SMOKE FROM COOKING FIRES, dust kicked up by travelers along the Solace road, and the morning mists that wound like wraiths among the boles of the vallenwood trees.

Flint kept to his bed, a surprisingly docile patient, though he grumbled enough for thirty dwarves, as Tasslehoff said, and complained that he was missing out on all the fun. He had, in fact, a very easy life of it. The kender waited on him hand and foot. Caramon and Sturm took turns visiting him every afternoon after their sword practice to demonstrate their newfound skills. Raistlin came by daily to rub oil of wintergreen into the dwarf's tight muscles, and even Kit dropped by occasionally to entertain Flint with accounts of fighting goblins and ogres.

Flint was so comfortable that Tanis was beginning to worry that the dwarf was enjoying his leisure too much. The pain in his back and leg had nearly subsided, but it was beginning to look as if Flint might never walk again.

Tanis called his friends together, hatched a plot to cause the dwarf to leave his bed, "without the use of gnome powder," as the half-elf put it.

"I hear there's a new metalsmith moving to Solace," Tasslehoff Burrfoot announced one morning as he fluffed up the dwarf's pillows.

"What's that?" Flint looked startled.

"A new metalsmith," the kender repeated. "Well, it's only to be expected. Word has gone out that you've retired."

"I have not!" Flint said indignantly. "I'm only taking a bit of a rest. For my health."

"I hear it's a dwarf. From Thorbardin."

Leaving this poisoned shaft inside the wound, guaranteed to rankle,

Tasslehoff left on his daily tour of Solace to see who was new in town and, more important, what interesting objects might find their way into his pouches.

Sturm was next to arrive, with a pot of hot soup sent by his mother. In regard to the dwarf's anxious questions, Sturm replied that he had "heard something about a new metalsmith coming to town" but added that he rarely paid attention to gossip and couldn't provide any more details.

Raistlin was a good deal more forthcoming, providing a great many details about the Thorbardin metalsmith, down to his clan and the length and color of his beard, also adding that the main reason the Thorbardin dwarf had chosen Solace as a place to locate his business was that "he'd heard they'd had no good metalwork done here in a long, long while."

By the time Tanis arrived late that afternoon, he was pleased but not terribly surprised to find Flint in his workshop, firing up the forge that been cold all summer long. The dwarf still walked with a limp (when he remembered) and still complained of pain in his back (particularly when he had to go rescue Tasslehoff from any number of minor disasters). But he never took to his bed again.

As for the Thorbardin metalsmith, he found that the air of Solace didn't agree with him. At least that's what Tanis said.

The summer had been a long one and a prosperous one for the people of Solace. Large numbers of travelers, the most travelers anyone could remember, passed through the town. The roads were relatively safe. There were thieves and footpads, certainly, but that was a fact of life on the road and not considered to be more than a nuisance. War was the great disrupter of travel, and no wars were being fought anywhere on Ansalon at this time, nor were any expected. Ansalon had been at peace for three hundred years, and everyone in Solace assumed complacently that the peace would last for another three hundred.

Almost everyone, that is. Raistlin believed differently, and it was for this reason that he had decided to concentrate his area of study in the realm of magic on war wizardry. It was not a decision based on a young boy's idealized picture of battle as something glorious and exciting. Raistlin had never played the games of war, as had the other children. He was not enamored of a martial life, nor was he at all excited at the thought of entering into battle. His was a calculated decision, made after long deliberation, and it had to do with one object: money.

The overheard conversation of Kitiara and the stranger had a great deal to do with Raistlin's planning. He could repeat the conversation verbatim, and he went over the words in his mind almost nightly.

Up north—Sanction, presumably—a great lord with vast sums of money was interested in gaining information about Qualinesti. He was also interested in recruiting skilled warriors; he had loyal and intelligent agents working for him. A gully dwarf child could have taken this evidence and worked it to its logical conclusion.

Someday, somewhere, sometime soon, someone was going to need to put together an army to defend against this lord, and they would need to put it together fast. This unknown someone would pay highly for soldiers and even more highly for mages skilled in the art of combining sword and sorcery.

Raistlin assumed, and rightly so, that dealing death would pay him far better than mixing herbs to heal sick babies.

Having made this decision, he pondered on the best way to act upon it. He needed to acquire magical spells that were combative in nature, that much was certain. He would also need spells to defend himself, else his first fight would be his last. But what would he be defending against? What did a commander expect of a warrior mage? What would be his place in the ranks? What attack spells would be required? Raistlin knew little about soldiering, and he realized then that he needed to know more if he was going to make an effective war wizard.

The one person who might know the answers to these questions was the one person he dared not ask: Kitiara. He did not want to put ideas into her head. Asking Tanis Half-Elven was the same these days as asking his sister, for Tanis would surely discuss anything Raistlin said with Kit. Neither Sturm nor Flint would be of any help; knights and dwarves distrusted magic intensely and would never rely on a mage in a battle situation. Tasslehoff wasn't even a consideration. Anyone who asks a question of a kender deserves the answer.

Raistlin had secretly searched Master Theobald's library and found nothing useful.

"This age on Krynn will be called the Age of Peace," Master Theobald was wont to predict. "We are a changed people. War is an institution of unenlightened generations past. Nations have learned how to peacefully coexist. Humans, elves, and dwarves have learned to work together."

By pointedly ignoring each other, Raistlin thought. That is not coexistence. It is blindness.

When he looked into the future, he saw it ablaze with flame, awash in blood. He could see the coming wars so clearly, in fact, that he sometimes wondered if he hadn't inherited some of his mother's talent as a seer.

Convinced that his scheme was the right one, the one that would win him fame and fortune, Raistlin required only knowledge to put it into action. Such knowledge could come from only one source: books. Books his master did not have. How to acquire them?

The Tower of High Sorcery at Wayreth had the most extensive library of magic anywhere on Krynn. But as a novice mage, an initiate, not even yet an apprentice, Raistlin would not be permitted inside the Tower. His first entry into that fabled and dread edifice would be if and when he was invited to take the Test. The Tower of Wayreth was out of the question.

There were other sources for books of magic and books on magic: mageware shops.

Mageware shops were not numerous in this day and age, but they did exist. There was a mageware shop in Haven; Raistlin had heard Master Theobald speak of it. He knew the location, having made surreptitious inquiries.

One night, shortly after Flint's marvelous recovery, Raistlin knelt down beside a small wooden chest he kept in his room. The chest was guarded by a simple locking cantrip, one of the first magicks every mage learns, a spell that is absolutely essential in a world populated by kender.

Removing the cantrip with a single spoken command, a command that could be personalized to suit each wizard who utilized it, Raistlin opened the lid to the chest and took out of it a small leather purse. He counted the coins—completely unnecessary. He knew to the halfpence how much he had acquired. He deemed he had enough.

The next morning he broached the subject with his brother.

"Tell Farmer Sedge that you must take some time off, Caramon. We are traveling to Haven."

Caramon's eyelids opened so wide it seemed probable he might never be able to close them. He stared at his twin in wordless astonishment. The distance from Solace to Master Theobald's former school, about five miles, had been the farthest Caramon had ever traveled from his home in his life. The distance to the Lordcity of Haven was perhaps some ninety miles and seemed liked the end of the known world to Caramon.

"Flint is journeying to the Harvest Home Festival in Haven next week. I heard him tell Tanis so last night. Tanis and Kit will undoubtedly travel along. I propose that we go with them."

"You bet we will!" cried Caramon. In his joy, he performed an impromptu dance upon the door stoop, causing the entire house to shake on its tree-limb foundations.

"Calm down, Caramon," Raistlin ordered irritably. "You'll crash through the floorboards again, and we can't spare the money for repairs."

"Sorry, Raist." Caramon quieted his elation, especially as he had a sobering thought. "Speaking of money, do we have enough? Going to Haven will cost plenty. Tanis will offer to pay for it, but we shouldn't let him."

"We have enough if we are frugal. I will handle that detail. You need not worry about it."

"I'll ask Sturm if he wants to go," Caramon said, his happiness returning. He rubbed his hands together. "It will be a real adventure!"

"I trust not," Raistlin said caustically. "It is a three-day journey by wagon on well-traveled roads. I see no adventuring involved."

Which only proved that he had not inherited his mother's gift of foresight after all.

9

THE JOURNEY BEGAN AS UNEVENTFULLY AS ANYONE COULD HAVE WISHED, with the possible exception of two young and aspiring warriors eager to display their newfound skills. The weather was clear and cool, the sunshine warmed them pleasantly in the afternoons. Recent rains kept the dust down. The road to Haven was filled with travelers, for Harvest Home was the city's largest festival.

Tanis drove the wagon, which was filled to capacity with the dwarf's wares. Flint hoped to make money enough at the festival to help offset the amount he had lost over the summer. Raistlin rode up front with Tanis, to keep the half-elf company. Kitiara sometimes rode, sometimes walked. She was far too restless to ever do anyone thing for long. Flint had a place in the back of the wagon, where he was comfortably ensconced among the rattling pots and pans, keeping a close eye upon his more valued wares: silver bracers and bracelets, necklaces set with precious stones. Sturm and Caramon walked alongside, ready for trouble.

The two young men peopled the road with bands of robbers, legions of hobgoblins (despite Tanis's amused assurances that a goblin had not been seen in Solace since the time of the Cataclysm), and hordes of ravening beasts from wolves to basilisks.

Their hopes for combat (nothing serious, a minor altercation would do) were aided and abetted by Tasslehoff, who took great delight in relating every tale he'd ever heard and quite a few he made up on the spot. Tales about unwary travelers having their hearts ripped out and eaten by ogres, travelers who were dragged off by bears, travelers who were changed into undead by wraiths.

The result was that Sturm kept his hand on the hilt of his sword, coldly scrutinizing every person he met with such intensity that most of them figured Sturm himself for a thief and hurried to get out of his way. Caramon wore a perpetual scowl on his usually cheerful face, thinking that this made him look mean, though in reality, as Raistlin said, it only made him look bilious.

By the end of the first day, Sturm's hand was cramped from gripping his sword hilt, and Caramon had developed a splitting headache from keeping his jaw thrust forward at an unnatural angle. Kitiara's ribs ached from suppressed laughter, for Tanis would not allow her to openly ridicule the young men.

"They have to learn," he said. It was shortly after lunch, and Kit was riding on the wagon's seat between Tanis and Raistlin. "It doesn't hurt them to develop habits of watchfulness and caution on the road, even if they are overdoing it a bit. I remember when I was young. I was the exact opposite. I set off from Qualinesti without a care in the world or a brain in my head. I took everyone I met for a friend. It was a wonder I didn't end up in a ditch with my silly skull bashed in."

"When you were young," Kit scoffed. She squeezed his hand. "You talk like an old man. You are still young, my friend."

"In elven terms, perhaps," Tanis said. "Not in human. Don't you ever think about that, Kit?"

"Think about what?" she asked carelessly. In truth, she was not really paying attention. Having recently purchased a knife from Flint, a fine steel blade, she was engrossed in wrapping the handle with braided strips of leather.

Tanis persisted. "About the fact that I have lived well over a hundred of your human years. And that I will live hundreds more."

"Bah!" Kit bent over her work, her fingers quick at their task but not particularly efficient. The braided leather provided a better grip, but it wouldn't be much to look at. Kit didn't care how it looked. Finishing her task, she tucked the knife into the top of her boot. "You're only part elf."

"But I have an expanded life span compared to—"

"Hey, Caramon!" Kit yelled in mock alarm. "I think I saw something move over in that bush! Look at that great idiot. If anything did jump out at him, he'd pee in his pants. . . . What were you saying?"

"Nothing," Tanis said, smiling at her. "It wasn't important."

Shrugging, Kit jumped off the wagon to go tease Sturm by hinting that she was certain they were being followed by goblins.

Raistlin glanced at Tanis. The half-elf's smooth, unlined face—a face that would not be lined or wrinkled with age for perhaps another hundred years—was shadowed with unhappiness. He would be still a young man when Kitiara was an old, old woman. He would watch her age and die, while he remained relatively untouched by time.

The bards sang songs of the tragic love of elf for human. What would it be like? Raistlin pondered. To watch beauty and youth wither in those you love. To see them in their old age, in their dotage, while you are still young and vibrant. And yet, Raistlin considered, if the half-elf should fall in love with an elven woman, he would suffer a like fate, except that in this case he would be the one to age.

Raistlin regarded Tanis with new understanding and some compassion. He is doomed, the young mage reflected. He was doomed from birth. In neither world can he ever be truly happy. Talk of the gods playing a cruel joke on someone!

This brought to mind the three ancient gods of magic. Raistlin felt a twinge of conscience. He had not fulfilled his promise to them. If he truly believed in them, as he had professed to them so long ago, why was he constantly questioning and doubting his belief? He was reminded of the three gods yet again when, late in the day, the companions came upon a group of priests walking down the road.

The priests—twenty of them, men and women-walked down the center of the road in two files. They walked slowly, their expressions as solemn as if they were accompanying a body to the burial ground. They looked neither to the right nor the left, but kept their faces forward, their eyes lowered.

The slow-moving column traveling down the middle of the road had the effect—intentional or not—of seriously impeding the flow of traffic.

A great many people were on the Haven road this day. Flint was just one of several merchants traveling in that direction, transporting their stock in horse-driven carts or pushcarts or lugging bundles on their backs and heads. The wagons could not pass the priests, slowed to a funereal pace. Those traveling by foot were luckier, or so it seemed at first. They would start to circle around the double lines of the priests, walk about halfway, then suddenly stop in the road, fearful of moving, or fall hastily back.

Those on horseback who attempted to ride around the group failed when their animals shied nervously, dancing sideways into the brush, or balked completely, refusing to even come near the priests.

"What is it? What's going on?" Flint grumbled, waking from a refreshing nap in the warm autumn sun. He stood up inside the wagon, clumped his way forward. "What's the delay? At this rate, we'll arrive in Haven in time to do the May dance."

"Those priests up ahead," said Tanis. "They won't move off the road and no one can get around them."

"Maybe they don't know we're back here," Flint suggested. "Someone should tell them."

The driver of the lead wagon was attempting to do just that. He was shouting—politely shouting—for the priests to move to the side of the roadway. The priests paid no attention. They might have been deaf, everyone of them. They continued walking down the center.

"This is ridiculous!" said Kit. "I'll go talk to them."

She strode forward, her cape whipping around her, her sword rattling. Tasslehoff dashed after her.

"No, Tas, Kit! Wait—Blast!" Tanis swore softly.

Tossing the reins to the startled Raistlin, the half-elf hastily climbed out of the wagon and hurried after the two. Raistlin grappled uncertainly with the reins; he'd never driven a wagon before in his life. Fortunately Caramon jumped up on the wagon. He brought the cart to a halt, watching.

Few creatures on Krynn can move as fast as an excited kender. By the time Tanis caught up with Kitiara, Tasslehoff was far ahead of them both. Tanis shouted for Tas to stop, but few creatures on Krynn are as deaf as an excited kender. Before Tanis could reach him, Tas was alongside one of the priests, a bald man, the tallest in line, who was bringing up the rear of the file on the right-hand side.

Tas reached out his hand in order to introduce himself, and then the kender performed an extremely remarkable feat, jumping two feet in the air straight up and three feet back simultaneously, to land in a confusion of bags and pouches in the middle of a hedgerow.

Tanis and Kit reached the kender as he was extricating himself and his pouches from the clinging branches of the hedge.

"He has a snake, Tanis!" Tasslehoff cried, brushing leaves and twigs from his best orange-and-green plaid trousers. "Each one of the priests is carrying a snake wrapped around his arm!"

"Snakes?" Kit wrinkled her nose, gazed after the priests in disgust. "What are they doing with snakes?"

"It was very exciting," Tas reported. "I went up to the first priest, and I was going to introduce myself, which is only polite, you know, except that he wouldn't look at me or talk to me. I reached out my hand to pluck at his sleeve, figuring he hadn't seen me, and the snake reared up its head and hissed at me," Tasslehoff said, thrilled almost past the ability to speak. Almost.

"I was just about to ask him if I could pet it—snakes have such wonderful dry skin—when it darted out its head at me, and that's when I jumped backward. I was bitten by a snake once when I was a little kender, and while being snake-bit is certainly an interesting experience, it's not one that should be repeated too often. As you say, Tanis, it's not conducive to one's health. Especially because I think this snake was of the poisonous sort. It had a hood over its head and a forked tongue and little beady eyes. Could one of you help me get this pouch loose? It's stuck on that branch."

Tanis untangled the straps of the pouch. By this time, Flint and Raistlin and Sturm had joined them, leaving a disgruntled Caramon to guard the wagon.

"From your description, the snake would appear to be a viper," Raistlin observed. "But I've never heard of vipers being found anywhere outside the Plains of Dust."

"If so, the viper must have had its fangs drawn," said Sturm. "I cannot imagine any sane person would walk along the road carrying a poisonous snake!"

"Then you have very limited imagination, brother," said a peddler, coming up level with them. "Though I'm not saying you're right when it comes to sanity. Their god takes the form of a viper. The snake is their symbol and a test of their faith. Their god gives them power over the viper so that it won't harm them."

"In other words, they're snake charmers," said Raistlin, his lip curling.

"Don't let them hear you call them that, brother," the peddler advised, casting the line of priests an uneasy sidelong glance. He kept his voice low. "They don't tolerate any disrespect. They don't tolerate much of anything, if it comes to that. This could be a real poor Harvest Home if they have their way."

"Why? What have they done?" Kit asked, grinning. "Shut down the alehouses?"

"What was that you said?" Flint could only hear part of the conversation, which was being carried on above his head. He crowded close to hear better. "What did she say? Shut down the alehouses?"

"No, nothing like that, though the priests don't touch the stuff themselves," the peddler returned. "They know they'd never get away with anything so drastic. But they might as well. I'm sorry to see them here. I'll be surprised now if anyone even shows up at the fair. They'll all be going to temple to see the 'miracles.' I've a mind to turn around and go back home."

"What is the name of their god?" Raistlin asked.

"Belzor, or some such thing. Well, good day to all of you, if that's possible anymore." The peddler trudged gloomily off, heading back down the road the way he'd come.

"Hey! What's going on?" Caramon bellowed from the wagon.

"Belzor," Raistlin repeated grimly.

"That was the name of that god the widow woman talked about, wasn't it?" Flint said, tugging at his beard.

"The Widow Judith. Yes, Belzor was the god. She was from Haven as well. I had forgotten that." Raistlin was thoughtful. He would not have imagined he could have ever forgotten the Widow Judith, but other events in his life had crowded her out. Now the memory returned, returned in force. "I wonder if we will find her here."

"We won't," said Tanis firmly, "because we're not going anywhere near those priests. We're going to the fair, concentrate on the business at hand. I don't want any trouble." Reaching out his hand, he caught hold of the kender's shirt collar.

"Oh, please, Tanis! I just want to go have another look at the snakes."

"Caramon!" Tanis shouted, hanging onto the wriggling kender with difficulty. "Drive the wagon off the road. We're stopping for the night."

Flint seemed inclined to argue, but when Tanis spoke in that tone, even Kitiara held her tongue. She shook her head, but she said nothing aloud.

Coming level with Raistlin, Kit said offhandedly, "Judith. Was that the woman who was responsible for our mother's death?"

"Our mother?" Raistlin repeated, regarding Kit in astonishment. When Kitiara mentioned Rosamun at all, which was seldom, she was referred to as "your" mother—spoken to the twins in a scathing tone. This was the first time Raistlin had ever heard Kit acknowledge a relationship.

"Yes, Judith is the woman," he said when he had recovered from his shock sufficiently to reply.

Kit nodded. With a glance at Tanis, she leaned near to Raistlin to whisper, "If you know how to hold your tongue, we might have some fun on this trip after all, little brother."

Sturm and Caramon insisted on setting a watch on their camp that night, though Kit asked, laughing, "Where do you think we are? Sanction?"

They built a fire, spread their blanket rolls near it. Other fires flared not far away. More than one traveler had decided to let Belzor's priests get a long head start.

Flint was in charge of cooking and prepared his famous traveler's stew, a dwarven recipe made from dried venison and berries, simmered in ale. Raistlin added some herbs he had found along the road, herbs which the dwarf regarded with suspicion but was eventually persuaded to add. He would not admit that they added to the flavor; dwarven recipes needed no alteration. But he consumed four helpings, just to make certain.

They kept the fire burning to ward off the night's chill. Seated around it, they passed the ale jug and told stories until the fire burned low.

Flint took a last swallow, called it a night. He planned to sleep in the wagon, to guard his wares from thieves. Kit and Tanis moved off into the shadows, where they could be heard laughing softly and whispering together. Caramon and Sturm argued over who should keep watch first and tossed a coin. Caramon won. Raistlin wrapped himself in his blanket, prepared to spend his first night outdoors, lying on the ground beneath the stars.

Sleeping on the ground was every bit as uncomfortable as he'd imagined it would be.

Silhouetted against the dying embers of the fire, Caramon whistled softly to himself, whittling a stick as he kept watch. Raistlin's last glimpse, before he drifted off into an uneasy slumber, was of Caramon's large body blotting out the starlight.

10

THE KENDER KEPT AN EAGER LOOKOUT THE NEXT DAY FOR THE PRIESTS of Belzor, but they must have walked all night—either that or they turned off the road—because the companions did not run into them that day or the next.

The peddler may have held a pessimistic view as to the probable success of the Harvest Home Fair, but this was not the view of the general populace of Abanasinia. The road became more and more crowded, providing enough interesting subjects that Tasslehoff soon forgot all about the snakes, much to Tanis's relief.

Wealthy merchants, whose servants had been sent ahead with their wares, traveled along the road in ornate litters, borne on the shoulders of stout bearers. A noble family passed, accompanied by their retainers, the lord riding at the head on a large war-horse, the wife and daughter and the daughter's duenna following on smaller ponies. The horses were decorated in bright colored trappings, while that of the daughter was adorned with small silver bells on the bridle and silk ribbons braided into the mane.

The daughter was a lovely girl of about sixteen, who charitably bestowed a smile on Caramon and Sturm as she might have bestowed coins upon the poor. Sturm doffed his hat and made a courtly bow. Caramon winked at her and ran after the horse, hoping to speak to her. The noble lord frowned. The retainers closed ranks around the family. The duenna clucked in disapproval and, plucking a scarf over the young girl's head, admonished her in loud tones not to take notice of the riffraff one saw along the road.

Her harsh words wounded Sturm. "You behaved boorishly," he said to Caramon. "You have made us look ridiculous."

Caramon thought the episode was funny, however, and for the next mile he minced along the side of the wagon on his tiptoes, his handkerchief covering his face, feigning to be disgusted by them all and shouting "riffraff" in falsetto tones.

The trip continued uneventfully until midafternoon.

Springing up from his place in the back of the wagon, Flint shouted, "Look out!" and pummeled Tanis on the shoulder by way of emphasizing the danger. "Drive faster! Hurry! They're coming closer!"

Expecting to see no less than an army of minotaurs in hot pursuit, Tanis looked behind him in alarm. "Too late!" Flint groaned, as the wagon was immediately surrounded by a party of about fifteen laughing kender.

Fortunately for the dwarf, the kender were far more interested in Tasslehoff than they were in the dwarf's wares. Always delighted to meet more of his kind, Tas jumped off the wagon into a thicket of small, outstretched arms.

There is a proscribed ritual involved in the meeting of kender who are strangers to one another. This ritual takes place whether the meeting is between two kender or twenty.

First come handshaking all around and formal introductions by name. Since it is considered extremely rude for one kender to forget or mistake the name of another, the introductions take some time.

"How do you do? My name is Tasslehoff Burrfoot."

"Clayfoot?"

"No, Burrfoot. Burr—as in the little sharp pointy things that stick to your clothes."

"Ah, Burrfoot! Nice to meet you. I am Eider Thistledown."

"Eiderdown?"

"Thistledown. Eider comes first. And this is Hefty Warblethroat. "

"Glad to meet you, Tuftedhair Hotfoot."

"Tasslehoff Burrfoot," corrected Tasslehoff. "It is an honor to meet you, Flabby Cutthroat." And so on down the line.

Once all kender have been properly introduced and everyone knows the name of everyone else, they then move into the second phase of the ritual, which is determining if they are related. It is a known fact among kender that every kender born can trace his or her ancestry back to, around, up, or over the famous Uncle Trapspringer. Kinships are therefore easily established.

"Uncle Trapspringer was my mother's aunt's third cousin on her father's side by marriage," said Eider Thistledown.

"Isn't that amazing!" cried Tasslehoff. "Uncle Trapspringer was my father's uncle's wife's second cousin once removed."

"Brother!" cried Eider, spreading his arms.

"Brother!" Tasslehoff rushed into them.

This also continued down the line of kender, ending with the determination that Tasslehoff was closely related to every single one of the fifteen, none of whom he had ever seen before in his life.

After this came the third phase. Tasslehoff inquired politely if any of his fellows had come across any interesting or unusual objects on his or her journeys. The other kender just as politely insisted that Tasslehoff should be the one to show off his acquisitions, with the result that all the kender plunked themselves down in the middle of the road. Emptying their pouches, they began to rummage through each other's belongings while traffic backed up behind them.

"Drive on, Tanis!" Flint urged in a hoarse whisper. "Faster! Faster! Maybe we'll lose him."

Well knowing that Tas could be involved with this entertaining project for a day at least, Tanis did as the dwarf recommended, though not with any hope of losing the kender no matter how fast they traveled.

That night as they were making camp Tasslehoff turned up, tired and hungry, not even wearing the same clothes anymore, but completely happy.

"Did you miss me, Flint?" he asked, plopping down beside the dwarf.

Ignoring Flint's resounding "No!" Tas proceeded to show the companions his newfound treasures. "Look, Flint. I have a whole lot of new maps. Truly fine maps. I've never seen maps nearly as good as these. My cousin says they came all the way from Istar, which isn't there anymore. It was smashed flat in the Cataclysm. These maps have little mountains drawn on them and little roads, and here's a tiny little lake. And they have the names all written in. I've never heard of any of these places, and I don't know where they are, but if I ever want to go there, I've got this map to show me what's there when I get there."

"If you don't know where something is, what good is the map, you doorknob?" Flint demanded.

Tas thought this over, then pointed out the flaw in the dwarf's logic. "Well, I can't get there without it, now, can I?"

"But you just said you didn't know where it was, so that means you can't get there with it!" Flint fumed.

"Ah, but if I ever do get there, I'll know where I am!" Tasslehoff stated triumphantly, at which point Tanis changed the subject before the dwarf, now extremely red in the face, burst some important blood vessel.

The next day, around midday, they arrived at the gates of the Lordcity of Haven.

The residents of Haven were the ones who termed Haven, grandiosely, a Lordcity. In their minds, Haven rivaled the fabled northern metropolis of Palanthas. None of the inhabitants of Haven had ever traveled to Palanthas, which might account for this misnomer. Haven was, in reality, nothing grander than a large farming community located on extremely fertile land, whose rich soil was nourished on a semiyearly basis by the flooding of the White-rage river.

In these days of relative peace among the diverse races inhabiting Abanasinia, Haven's crops helped feed both the dwarves of Thorbardin and the humans of Pax Tharkas. The elves of Qualinesti did not relish human-grown food, but they had discovered that the vineyards on the sunny slopes of the Kharolis Mountains produced grapes of remarkable sweetness. These grapes were imported to Qualinesti to make wine that was famous throughout Ansalon. Haven hemp was much prized by the Plainspeople, who twisted it into strong, sturdy rope. Haven wood was used by the inhabitants of Solace to build their houses and businesses.

The Harvest Home Festival was therefore not only a celebration of another excellent year in the fields, but it was also a celebration of Haven itself, a tribute to its agrarian prosperity.

A wooden stockade surrounded the city, intended to keep out marauding bands of wolves more than armies. Haven had never been attacked and had no expectations of being attacked. This was the Age of Peace, after all. The gates of the wooden stockade were closed only at night, stood wide open during the day. Those manning the gates acted more as greeters than guards, exchanging friendly salutations with visitors they knew from years past and giving a hearty welcome to newcomers.

Flint and Tanis were well known and well liked. The sergeant-at-arms walked over to personally shake hands with the dwarf and the half-elf and to stare admiringly at Kitiara. The sergeant said they had missed Flint's customary visit, asked where they had been all summer. He listened with deep commiseration to Flint's tale of woe and assured the dwarf that his usual booth on the fairgrounds was waiting for him.

Tasslehoff was well known, too, apparently. The sergeant frowned at seeing the kender and suggested that Tas go lock himself up in jail right now, thereby saving everyone considerable time and trouble.

Tas said that he viewed it as extremely kind of the sergeant to make such a thoughtful offer, but the kender was forced to refuse it.

"Flint depends on me, you know," Tas said, fortunately out of the dwarf's hearing.

The sergeant welcomed the other young men, and when he heard it was their first visit to Haven, he said that he hoped they would not spend all their time working but would have a chance to see some of the sights. He shook hands once more with Flint, advised Tanis in an undertone that he was responsible for the kender, bowed to Kitiara, and then walked on to greet the next wagonload rolling through the wooden gates.

Once inside the stockade, they were accosted by a young man wearing sky-blue robes, who motioned their wagon to stop.

"What's this?" asked Tanis.

"One of those Belzor priests," Flint said, glowering.

"Does he have a snake? I want to see it!" Tasslehoff was prepared to jump off the wagon.

"Not now, Tas," Tanis said in a tone that Tas had, on occasion, actually obeyed. Just to make certain, Caramon caught the kender by the back of his green-and-purple striped vest and held on tightly.

"What can we do for you, sir?" Tanis called out over the hubbub of rolling carts, neighing horses, and jostling crowds.

"I would speak to the young man in the white robes," the priest answered, directing his attention to Raistlin. "Are you a wielder of magic, brother?"

"A novice mage, sir," Raistlin said humbly. "I have yet to take my Test."

The priest walked to the side of the wagon near where Raistlin sat, gazed up at him earnestly, intently.

"You are very young, brother. Are you aware of the evil in which you dabble—probably all unknowingly, I am sure?"

"Evil?" Raistlin leaned over the side of the wagon. "No, sir. I have no intention of doing evil. What do you mean?"

The priest clasped his hand over Raistlin's. "Come hear us outside the Temple of Belzor, brother. All will be explained. Once you understand that you are worshiping false gods, you will renounce them and their evil arts. You will strip off those foul robes and walk once more in the sunlight. Will you come, brother?"

"Gladly!" Raistlin cried. "What you say terrifies me, sir."

"Huh? But, Raist—" Caramon started to protest.

"Hush, you big ninny!" Kitiara dug her nails into Caramon's arm.

The priest gave Raistlin instructions on how to find the temple, which, he said, was the largest building in Haven, located at the very center of the city.

"Tell me, sir," Raistlin said after noting down the directions, "is there a person connected with the temple whose name is Judith?"

"Why, yes, brother! She is our most holy priestess. It is she who imparts to us the will of Belzor. Do you know her?"

"Only by reputation," said Raistlin respectfully.

"It is sad that you are a professed user of magic, brother. Otherwise I could invite you inside the temple to witness the ceremony of the Miracle. Priestess Judith will be summoning Belzor to appear among us this very night. And she will be speaking to the Blessed of Belzor who have already passed over."

"I would like to see this," said Raistlin.

"Alas, brother. Mages are not permitted to witness the Miracle. Forgive me for saying this, brother, but Belzor finds your evil ways offensive."

"I'm not a mage," said Kit, with a charming smile for the young priest. "Could I come to the temple?"

"Certainly! All the rest of you are welcome. You will see wonderful miracles performed, miracles that will astound you, erase your doubts, and make you believe in Belzor with all your heart and soul."

"Thanks," said Kit. "I'll be there."

The priest solemnly pronounced the blessing of Belzor on them all, then took his leave, moving off to question the occupants of another arriving wagon.

Flint snorted in disdain, dusted the blessing off his clothes. "I don't need the good opinion of any god who thinks well of snakes. And you, lad. I admit that I don't much take to magic—no true dwarf does—but it seems to me that you're a damn sight better off being a wizard than a follower of Belzor."

"I agree with you, Flint," Raistlin said gravely. This was not the time to remind the dwarf of his many harangues against magic in all its shapes and forms. "But it will not hurt me to talk to this priest and find out what this worship of Belzor entails. Perhaps Belzor is one of the true gods for which we have all been searching. I would like very much to see these miracles of which they speak"

"Yes, I'm interested in this Belzor myself," said Kitiara. "I think I'll go to the temple tonight. You could come, too, little brother. All you'd have to do is change clothes and likely they'd never recognize you."

"You're not going to make me go with you, are you?" Caramon asked uneasily. "No disrespect to Belzor, but I've heard the taverns of Haven are real lively, particularly during fair time, and—"

"No, my brother," Raistlin said curtly. "You do not need to come."

"None of the rest of you need to come," Kit said. "Raist and I are the spiritual members of this family."

"Well, I think you're the crazy members of the family," Caramon stated.

"Our first night in Haven, and you want to go visit a temple. And what was this business about some priestess named Judith?" He stopped, blinked. "Judith," he repeated, frowning. "Oh." He looked hard at his brother and at Kit. "I'm going."

"I'm going, too!" said Tas. "Maybe I'll get to see those snakes again, not to mention talking to those who have already passed over. What does that mean? What did they pass over? The roof?"

"I believe he means that they talk to the dead," Raistlin explained.

Tas's eyes widened. "I've never talked to dead people before. Do you suppose they'll let me speak to Uncle Trapspringer? Not that we're all that sure he's really dead, mind you. His funeral was sort of confused. The body was there one minute and gone the next. Uncle Trapspringer tended to be a bit absentminded when he got old, and some said maybe he just forgot that he was dead and wandered off. Or maybe he tried being dead and didn't like it, so he came back to life. Or it could be that the undertaker misplaced him. Anyhow, this would be one way to find out the truth."

"That settles it!" Flint grunted. "I'm not going anywhere near this Temple! It's bad enough talking to a live kender, let alone a dead one."

"I will go," said Sturm. "It is my duty to go. If they are performing miracles in the name of Belzor, I should bring such news to the knighthood."

"I'll go," said Tanis, but that was understood, since Kitiara was going.

"You're all daft" was Flint's opinion as the wagon joined the rest of those headed for the fairgrounds.

"It looks like we're not going to have quite as much fun as we thought," Kit observed to Raistlin in an undertone, with a glance in Tanis's direction.

Raistlin paid small attention to her, however. He was keeping a watch for the Herbalists Street, where, according to Master Theobald, the mageware shop was located.

11

THE STREETS OF HAVEN WERE NOT NAMED AT THIS TIME, ALTHOUGH THIS was one of the civic improvements currently under consideration, particularly after some adventurer had mentioned that the Palanthians not only named their streets but also erected signposts with the names written on them for the benefit of the confused traveler. Travelers to Haven were rarely confused; if you were tall enough, you could see from one end of the village to the other. However, the High Sheriff of Haven thought signposts an excellent idea and resolved to institute them.

Many of the roads in Haven already had names, logical names that had to do with the nature of the goods sold along that road, as in Market Street, Mill Street, Blade Street. Other names had to do with the nature of the road itself, such as Crooked Street or Three Forks, while still others were named after the families who lived on them. Herbalists Street was easy to find, more with the nose than the eyes.

Scents of rosemary, lavender, sage, and cinnamon drifted on the air, making a pleasant contrast to the strong smell of horse dung in the street. The merchant's stalls and shops of Herbalists Street were marked by bunches of dried plants hanging upside down in the sunshine. Baskets of seeds and dried leaves were arranged artfully along the roadside to tempt passersby into making purchases.

Raistlin asked Tanis to halt the wagon. "There are herbs here that I do not grow, some of which I am not familiar with. I would like to replenish my own supplies, as well as discuss their uses."

Tanis told Raistlin how to find Flint's place on the fairgrounds and bade him have fun. Raistlin jumped down from the wagon. Caramon followed, as a matter of course. Tasslehoff was in an agony of indecision, trying to decide whether to go with Raistlin or stay with Flint. Flint and the fairgrounds won out, mainly because, having peered up this street, the kender could see nothing except plants, and while plants were interesting, they just didn't compare to the wonders he knew awaited him at the fairgrounds.

Raistlin would have never permitted the kender to accompany him, but Tas's decision spared him an argument. He was not certain what to do with Caramon, however. Raistlin had planned to visit the mageware shop alone and in secret. He had told no one that he intended to go to the shop. He had told no one what he hoped to purchase. His instinct was to keep his secret, order his brother to go with Flint.

Raistlin rarely discussed his arcane art with his brother, never with his friends. He had not, since the days of his youth—days that he looked back upon and blushed over in shame—flaunted or openly displayed his magical skills.

He was well aware that his magic made some people nervous and uneasy. As well it should. Magic gave him a power over people, a power in which he reveled. He was wise enough to realize, however, that such power would be diminished if he used it repeatedly. Even magic becomes ordinary if used every day.

Raistlin's views toward people had changed over the years. Once he had sought to be loved and admired, much as his brother was loved and admired. Now, as Raistlin had come to understand himself, he faced the fact that he would never win the type of regard given his twin. In the house of Caramon's soul, the door stood always wide open, the window shutters were flung wide, the sun shone daily. anyone was welcome. There was not much furniture in Caramon's house. Visitors could see into every corner.

The house of Raistlin's soul was far different. The door was kept barred, opened only a crack to visitors, and then only a very few were permitted to cross the threshold. Once there, they were not allowed to come much farther. His windows were shut and shuttered. Here and there a candle gleamed, a warm spot in the darkness. His house was filled with furniture and objects strange and wonderful, but it was not messy or cluttered. He could instantly lay his hand on whatever was needed. Visitors could not find his corners, much less pry into them. Small wonder they never liked to stay long, were reluctant to return.

"Where are we going?" Caramon asked.

It was on the tip of Raistlin's tongue to order his brother back into the wagon. He rethought the matter, however. Without responding, he set off at a rapid walk down the street, leaving Caramon to stand flat-footed in the middle of the road.

"It is only common sense that he accompanies me," Raistlin said to himself. "I am a stranger in a strange town. I have no protection that I am willing to use, except under the most dire circumstances. I require Caramon's aid now as I will require it in the future. If I do become a war mage, as I intend, I will need to learn to fight at his side. I might as well get used to having him around."

The latter was said with something of a sigh, especially when Caramon came clomping up alongside, raising a great cloud of dust and demanding to know again where they were going, what they were looking for, and hinting that they could stop in a tavern along the way.

Raistlin halted. He turned to face his brother with a suddenness that caused Caramon to stumble backward in order not to step on his twin.

"Listen to me, Caramon. Listen to what I have to say and do not forget it." Raistlin's tone was hard, stern, and he had the satisfaction of seeing it hit Caramon like a slap in the face. "I am going to a certain place to meet a certain person and acquire certain merchandise. I am permitting you to accompany me because we are young and will consequently be taken for easy marks. But know this, my brother. What I do and what I say and what I buy are private, secret, known only to myself and to you. You will mention nothing of this to Tanis or Flint or Kitiara or Sturm or anyone else. You will say nothing of where we've been, who I've seen, what I've said or done. You must promise me this, Caramon."

"But they'll want to know. They'll ask questions. What do I say?" Caramon was clearly unhappy. "I don't like keeping secrets, Raist."

"Then you do not belong with me. Go back!" Raistlin said coldly and waved his hand. "Go back to your friends. I have no need of you."

"Yes, you do, Raist," Caramon said. "You know you do."

Raistlin paused. His steady gaze caught his brother's and held it. This was the decisive moment, the moment on which their future depended.

"Then you must make a choice, my brother. You must either pledge yourself to me or return to your friends." Raistlin held up his hand, halting his brother's quick answer. "Think about it, Caramon. If you remain with me, you must trust me completely, obey me implicitly, ask no questions, keep my secrets far better than you keep your own. Well, which will it be?"

Caramon didn't hesitate. "I'm with you, Raist," he said simply. "You're my twin brother. We belong together. It was meant to be this way."

"Perhaps," Raistlin said with a bitter smile. If that were true, he wondered very much who meant it and why. He'd like to have a talk with them someday.

"Come along then, my brother. Follow me."

☯

According to Master Theobald, the mageware shop was located at the very end of Herbalists Street, on the left-hand side as you faced the north. Standing at some distance from the rest of the shops and dwellings, it was tucked back by itself amid a grove of oak trees.

Theobald had described it. "The shop is located on the lower floor of the house, living quarters above. It is difficult to see from the road. Oak trees surround it, as does a large walled-in garden. You will see the sign outside, however—a wooden board painted with an eye in colors of red, black, and white.

"I've never had any business there myself. I acquire everything I need from the Tower at Wayreth, you know," Master Theobald had added, with a sniff. "However, I'm sure Lemuel has some small items that mages of low rank might find valuable."

If Raistlin had learned nothing else from Theobald, he had learned to hold his tongue. He swallowed the caustic retort he would have once made, thanked the master politely, and was rewarded with the following bit of information, which might prove of inestimable value.

"I've heard that Lemuel has an interest in weeds the same as you," Theobald said. "You two should get along well."

Consequently Raistlin had brought with him a couple of rare species of plants he'd discovered, dug up, and carried home, and now had seedlings to share. He hoped in this way to curry Lemuel's favor, and if the books Raistlin wanted proved beyond his means, perhaps he might persuade their owner to lower the price.

The twins walked the length of Herbalists Street; Caramon taking his new duties and responsibilities with such extreme seriousness that he nearly tripped on his brother's heels in order to guard him, glared balefully at anyone who glanced twice at them, and rattled his sword constantly.

Raistlin sighed to himself over this, but he knew there was nothing he could do. Remonstrating with his brother, urging Caramon to relax and not be so conspicuous, would probably only confuse him. Eventually Caramon would fit comfortably into his role as bodyguard, but it would take time. Raistlin would just have to be patient.

Fortunately there were not that many people on the street to see them, since most of the herbalists were in the process of setting up stalls on the fairgrounds. On reaching the end of the street, they found it abandoned, no people in sight. Raistlin located the mageware shop easily enough. It was the only building on the left side of the road. Oak trees hid it from view, and there was the garden with its high stone wall. The sign of a mageware shop, the sign of the eye, was missing, however. The door was shut up tight, the windows were closed. The house might have been abandoned, but on peering over the wall, Raistlin saw that the garden was well tended.

"Are you sure this is the place?" Caramon asked.

"Yes, my brother. Perhaps the sign blew down in a storm."

"If you say so," Caramon muttered. He had his hand on the hilt of his sword. "Let me go to the door, then."

"Absolutely not!" Raistlin said, alarmed. "The sight of you, scowling and waving that sword around, would scare any wizard witless. He might turn you into a frog or something worse. Wait here in the road until I call for you. Don't worry. There's nothing wrong," Raistlin said with more assurance than he truly felt.

Caramon started to argue. Recalling his pledge, he kept silent. The threat about the frog might also have had something to do with his quick compliance.

"Sure, Raist. But you be careful. I don't trust these magic-users."

Raistlin walked to the door. His body tingled with both anticipation and dread, excitement at the idea of obtaining what he needed, dread to think that he might have come all this way only to find the mage gone. Raistlin was in such a state of nervous excitement by the time he reached the door that at first his strength failed him; he could not lift his trembling hand to knock, and when he did, his knock was so faint that he was forced to repeat it.

No one answered the door. No face came to peer curiously out the window.

Raistlin very nearly gave way to despair. His hopes and dreams of future success had been built around this one shop; he had never imagined that it might be closed. He had looked forward to gaining the books he needed for so long, he had come so far and he was so close, that he did not think he could bear the disappointment. He knocked again, this time much louder, and he raised his voice.

"Master Lemuel? Are you home, sir? I have come from Master Theobald of Solace. I am his pupil, and—"

A small window inside the door slid open. An eye in the window peered out at Raistlin, an eye filled with fear.

"I don't care whose pupil you are!" came a thin voice through the small opening. "What do you think you're doing, shouting that you're a mage at the top of your lungs? Go away!"

The window slid shut.

Raistlin knocked again, more peremptorily, said loudly, "He recommended your shop. I have come to purchase—"

The little window slid open. The eye appeared. "Shop's closed."

The window slid shut.

Raistlin brought in his reserves for the attack. "I have an unusual variety of plant with me. I thought that perhaps you might not be familiar with it. Black bryony—"

The window slid open. The eye was more interested. "Black bryony, you say? You have some?"

"Yes, sir." Raistlin reached into his pouch and carefully drew out a tiny bundle of leaves, stems, and fruits with the roots attached. "Perhaps you'd be interested . . ."

The window slid shut again, but this time Raistlin heard a bolt being thrown. The door opened.

The man inside the door was clad in faded red robes, covered with dirt at the knees where he was accustomed to kneeling in his garden. He must have been standing on tiptoe to put his eye to the small window in the door, because he was almost as short as a dwarf, compact and round, with a face that must once have been as ruddy and cheerful as the summer sun. Now he was like a sun that is eclipsed. His eyes were puckered with worry and his brow creased. He peered nervously out into the street, and at the sight of Caramon, his eyes widened in fear and he very nearly shut the door again.

Raistlin had his foot in it, however, and was quick to seize the handle with his hand. "May I present my brother, sir? Caramon, come here!"

Caramon obligingly came over, ducking his head and grinning self-consciously.

"Are you sure he's who he says he is?" the mage asked, regarding Caramon with intense suspicion.

"Yes, I'm certain he's my brother," Raistlin replied, wondering uneasily if he was having to deal with a lunatic. "If you look at us closely, you will note the resemblance. We are twins."

Caramon helpfully tried to make himself look as much like his brother as possible. Raistlin attempted to match Caramon's open, honest smile. Lemuel studied them for several long moments, during which Raistlin thought he would fly apart from the tension of this strange interview.

"I guess so." The mage didn't sound very convinced. "Did anyone follow you?"

"No, sir," said Raistlin. "Who would there be to follow us? Most people are at the fairgrounds."

"They're everywhere, you know," observed Lemuel gloomily. "Still, I suppose you're right." He looked long and hard down the street. "Would your brother mind very much going to check to make certain no one is hiding in the shadow of that building over there?"

Caramon looked considerably astonished but, at an impatient nod from his twin, did as he was told. He walked back down the street to a tumbledown shack, searched not only the shadow but took a look inside the building itself. He stepped back out into the street, lifting his hands and shrugging to indicate that he saw nothing.

"There, you see, sir," Raistlin said, motioning his brother back. "We are alone. The black bryony is very fine. I have used it successfully to heal scars and close wounds."

Raistlin held the plant in his palm.

Lemuel regarded it with interest. "Yes, I've read about it. I've never seen any. Where did you find it?"

"If I could come inside, sir . . ."

Lemuel eyed Raistlin narrowly, gazed at the plant longingly, made up his mind. "Very well. But I suggest that you post your brother outside to keep watch. You can't be too careful."

"Certainly," said Raistlin, weak with relief.

The mage pulled Raistlin inside, slammed shut the door so rapidly that he shut it on the hem of Raistlin's white robes and was forced to open the door again to remove the cloth.

His twin gone, Caramon roamed about for a few moments, scratching his head and trying to figure out what to do. Eventually he found a seat on a crumbling stone wall and sat down to watch, wondering what it was he was supposed to watch for and what he was supposed to do if he saw it.

The interior of the mage's shop was dark. The shutters over the windows blocked out all the daylight. Lemuel lit two candles, one for himself and one for Raistlin. By the candle's light, he saw in dismay that everything was in disorder, with half-filled crates and barrels standing about. The shelves were bare, most of the merchandise had been packed away.

"A light spell would be less costly and more efficient than candles, I know," Lemuel confessed. "But their tormenting has me so upset that I haven't been able to practice my magic in a month. Not that I was all that good at it to begin with, mind you." He sighed deeply.

"Excuse me, sir," said Raistlin, "but who has been tormenting you?"

"Belzor," said the mage in a low tone, glancing about the darkened room as though he thought the god might jump out at him from the cupboard.

" Ah," said Raistlin.

"You know of Belzor, do you, young man?"

"I met one of his priests when I first came to town. He warned me that magic was evil and urged me to come to his temple."

"Don't do it!" Lemuel cried, shuddering. "Don't go anywhere near the place. You know about the snakes?"

"I saw that they carried vipers," Raistlin said. "The fangs are pulled, I suppose."

"Not so!" Lemuel shivered. "Those snakes are deadly poison. The priests trap them in the Plains of Dust. It is considered a test of faith to be able to hold the snakes without being bitten."

"What happens to those lacking in faith?"

"What do you suppose happens? They are punished. A friend told me. He was present during one of their meetings. I tried to go to one myself, but they refused to let me inside. They said I would pollute the sanctity of their temple. I was glad I didn't. That very day one of the snakes bit a young woman. She was dead within seconds."

"What did the priests do?" Raistlin asked, shocked.

"Nothing. The High Priestess said it was Belzor's will." Lemuel shook so that his candle flame wavered. "Now you know why I asked your brother to stand guard. I live in mortal fear of waking up one morning to find one of those vipers in my bed. But I won't live in fear long. They win. I'm giving up. As you see"—he waved his hand at the crates—"I'm moving out."

He held the candle near. "Might I take a closer look at that black bryony?"

Raistlin handed over the small parcel. "What have they done to you?" He had to ask the question several times and give Lemuel a gentle nudge before he could wrest the mage's attention away from examining the plant.

"The High Priestess herself came to me. She told me to close my shop or face the wrath of Belzor. At first I refused, but then they grew nasty. The priests would stand outside the shop. When anyone came, they'd shout out that I was a tool of evil.

"Me?" Lemuel sighed. "A tool of evil? Can you imagine? But the priests frightened people and they quit coming. And then one night I found a snakeskin hanging from the door. That was when I closed the shop and decided to move."

"Excuse me if I seem disrespectful, sir, but if you fear them, why did you try to go to their temple?"

"I thought it might placate them. I thought perhaps I could pretend to go along with them, just to keep them from hounding me. It didn't work." Lemuel shook his head sadly. "Moving wouldn't be so bad. The mageware shop itself never made a lot of money. It's my herbs and my plants that I'll miss. I'm trying to dig them up hoping to transplant them, but I'm afraid I'll lose most of them."

"The shop wasn't successful?" Raistlin asked, glancing around wistfully at the bare shelves.

"It might have been if I'd lived in a city like Palanthas. But here in Haven?" Lemuel shrugged. "Most of what I sold came from my father's collection. He was a remarkable wizard. An archmagus. He wanted me to follow in his footsteps, but his shoes were much too big. I couldn't hope to fill them. Just wasn't cut out for it. I wanted to be a farmer. I have a wonderful way with plants. Father wouldn't hear of it, however. He insisted that I study magic. I wasn't very good at it, but he kept hoping I'd improve with age.

"But then, when I was finally old enough to take the Test, the conclave wouldn't let me. Par-Salian told my father it would be tantamount to murder. Father was extremely disappointed. He left home that very day, some twenty years ago, and I haven't heard from him since."

Raistlin was barely listening. He was forced to admit that his trip had been in vain.

"I'm sorry," he said, but that was more for himself than the mage.

"Don't be," Lemuel said cheerfully. "I was relieved to see Father go, to tell you the truth. The day he left I plowed up the yard and put in my garden. Speaking of which, we should get this plant into water immediately."

Lemuel bustled off into the kitchen, which was located behind the shop in the back of the house. Here the shutters were open, letting in the sunlight. Lemuel blew out his candle.

"What type of wizard was your father?" Raistlin asked, blowing out his candle in turn.

"A war wizard," Lemuel replied, lovingly tending the black bryony. "This is really quite nice. You say you grew it? What sort of fertilizer do you use?"

Raistlin answered. He looked out the window onto Lemuel's garden, which, despite the fact that it was half dug up, was truly magnificent. At any other time, he would have been interested in Lemuel's herbs, but all he saw now was a blur of green.

A war wizard . . .

An idea was forming in Raistlin's mind. He was forced to discuss herbs for a few moments, but soon led the conversation back to the archmagus.

"He was considered one of the best," Lemuel said. He was obviously quite proud of his father, held no bitterness or grudges against the man. He brightened when he spoke of him. "The Silvanesti elves once invited him to come help them fight the minotaurs. The Silvanesti are very snooty. They almost never have anything to do with humans. My father said it was an honor. He was immensely pleased."

"Did your father take his spellbooks with him when he left?" Raistlin asked hesitantly, not daring to hope.

"He took some, I'm sure. The very powerful ones, no doubt. But he didn't bother with the rest. My guess is that he moved to the Tower of Wayreth, and in that case, you know, he wouldn't really need any of his elementary spellbooks. What type of soil would you recommend?"

"A bit on the sandy side. Do you still have them? The books, I mean. I would be interested in seeing them."

"Blessed Gilean, yes, they're still here. I have no idea how many there are or if they are of any importance. A lot of the mages I deal with . . . or rather used to deal with"—Lemuel sighed again—"aren't interested in war magic.

"Elves come here often, mostly from Qualinesti these days. Sometimes they have need of what they term 'human magic,' or sometimes they come for my herbs. You wouldn't think that, would you, young man? Elves being so good with plants themselves. But they tell me that I have several species that they have not been able to grow. One young man used to say that I must have elf blood in me somewhere. He's a mage, too. Perhaps you know him. Gilthanas is his name."

"No, sir, I'm sorry," Raistlin said.

"I suppose you wouldn't. And, of course, I don't have any elf blood at all. My mother was born and raised here in Haven, a farmer's daughter. She had the misfortune to be extremely beautiful, and that's how she attracted my father. Otherwise I would have been the son of some honest farmer, I'm sure. She wasn't very happy with my father. She said she lived in fear that he'd burn the house down. You say you use black bryony to close wounds? What part? The juice of the berry? Or do you grind the leaves?"

"About those books . . ." Raistlin hinted, when he had finally satisfied Lemuel as to the care, feeding, and uses of the black bryony.

"Oh, yes. In the library. Up the stairs and down the hall, second door on your left. I'll just go pot this. Make yourself at home. Do you suppose your brother would like something to eat while he keeps watch?"

Raistlin hastened up the stairs, pretending not to hear Lemuel call after him, wanting to know if the black bryony would prefer to be in direct sunlight or partial shade. He went straight to the library, drawn to it by the whispered song of magic, a teasing, tantalizing melody. The door was shut, but not locked. The hinges creaked as Raistlin opened it.

The room smelled of mold and mildew; it had obviously not been aired out in years. Dried mouse dung crunched under Raistlin's boot, dark shapes flitted into corners at his entrance. He wondered what mice found in this room to eat and hoped fervently that it wasn't the pages of the spellbooks.

The library was small, contained a desk, bookshelves, and scroll racks. The scroll racks were empty, to Raistlin's disappointment, but not his surprise. Magical spells inscribed on scrolls could be read aloud by those with the knowledge of the language of magic. They did not require nearly so much energy or the level of skill needed to produce a spell "by hand," as the saying went. Even a novice such as Raistlin could use a magical scroll written by an archmagus, provided the novice knew how to pronounce the words correctly.

Thus scrolls were quite valuable and charily guarded. They could be sold to other magi, if the owner did not have a use for them. The archmagus would have taken his scrolls with him.

But he had left behind many of his books.

Scattered and upended, some of the spellbooks lay on the floor, as if they had been considered, then discarded. Raistlin could see gaps on the shelves where the archmagus had presumably removed some valuable volume, leaving the unwanted to lie moldering on the shelf.

These remaining books, their white bindings now turned a dirty and dismal gray, their pages yellowed, had been considered valueless by their original owner. But in Raistlin's eyes, the books glittered with a radiance brighter than that of a dragon's hoard. His excitement overwhelmed him. His heart beat so rapidly that he became light-headed, faint.

The sudden weakness frightened him. Sitting down on a rickety chair, he drew in several deep breaths. The cure almost proved his undoing. The air was dusty. He choked and coughed, and it was some time before he could catch his breath.

A book lay on the floor almost at his feet. Raistlin picked it up, opened it.

The archmagus's handwriting was compact, with sharp, jutting angles. The distinctive leftward slant of the letters indicated to Raistlin that the man was a loner, preferred his own company to that of others. Raistlin was somewhat disappointed to find that this volume wasn't a spellbook at all. It was written in Common, with a smattering of what Raistlin thought might be the mercenary tongue, a cant used by professional soldiers. He read the first page and his disappointment faded.

The book gave detailed instructions on how to cast magical spells on ordinary weapons, such as swords and battle-axes. Raistlin marked the book as one of immense value—to him, at least. He set the book to one side and took up another. This was a spellbook, probably of very elementary spells, for it had no magical locks or prohibitions placed upon it. Raistlin could puzzle out a few of the words, but most were foreign to him. The book served to remind him of how much more he had yet to learn.

He regarded the book in bitterness and frustration. It had been cast aside by the great archmagus, the spells it contained beneath his notice. Yet Raistlin could not even decipher them!

"You are being foolish," Raistlin reprimanded himself. "When this archmagus was my age, he didn't know nearly as much as I do. Someday I will read this book. Someday I will cast it aside."

He laid the book down on top of the first and proceeded with his investigations.

Raistlin became so absorbed that he completely lost track of time. He was aware that twilight was coming on only when he found that he was having to hold the books to his nose to be able to read them. He was about to set off in search of candles when Lemuel tapped at the door.

"What do you want?" Raistlin demanded irritably.

"Excuse me for disturbing you," Lemuel said meekly, poking his head inside. "But your brother says that it will be dark soon and that you should be going."

Raistlin remembered where he was, remembered that he was a guest in this man's house. He jumped to his feet in shame and confusion. One of the precious volumes slid from his lap and tumbled to the floor.

"Sir, please forgive my rudeness! I was so interested, this is so fascinating, I forgot that I was not in my own home—"

"That's quite all right!" Lemuel interrupted, smiling pleasantly. "Think nothing of it. You sounded just like my father. Took me back in time. I was a boy again for a moment. Did you find anything of use?"

Raistlin gestured at the three large stacks of books near the chair.

"All these. Did you know that there is an account of the minotaur battle for Silvanesti in here? And this is a description of how to use battle spells effectively, without endangering your own troops. These three are books of spells. I have yet to look through the others. I would offer to buy them, but I know I do not have the means." He gazed sadly at the pile, wondering despairingly how he would ever manage to save up enough money.

"Oh, take them," Lemuel said, waving his hand casually around the room.

"What? Really, sir? Are you serious?" Raistlin caught hold of the back of the chair to steady himself. "No, sir," he said recovering. "That would be too much. I could never repay you."

"Pooh! If you don't take them, I'll have to move them, and I'm running out of crates." Lemuel spoke very glibly about leaving his home, but even as he tried to make this small joke, he was gazing sadly around him. "They'll only go into an attic, to be eaten by mice. I would much rather they were put to good use. And I think it would please my father. You are the son he wanted."

Tears stung Raistlin's eyes. His fatigue from the three days of travel, which included not only time on the road but also time spent climbing the mountains of hope and plummeting into the valleys of disappointment, had left him weak. Lemuel's kindness and generosity disarmed Raistlin completely. He had no words to thank the man and could only stand in humble, joyous silence, blinking back the tears that burned his eyelids and closed his throat.

"Raist?" Caramon's anxious voice came floating up the staircase. "It's getting dark and I'm starved. Are you all right?"

"You'll need a wagon to cart these home in," observed Lemuel.

"I have . . . my friend . . . wagon . . . at the fair . . ." Raistlin didn't seem to be able to manage a coherent sentence.

"Excellent. When the fair is ended, drive over here. I'll have these books all packed for you and ready to go."

Raistlin drew out his purse, pressed it into Lemuel's hand. "Please, take this. It isn't much, it doesn't nearly begin to cover what I owe, but I would like you to have it."

"Would you?" Lemuel smiled. "Very well, then. Although it's not necessary, mind you. Still, I recall my father saying once that magical objects should be purchased, never given as gifts. The exchange of money breaks whatever hold the previous owner may have had on them, frees them up for the next user."

"And if by chance you should ever come to Solace," Raistlin said, casting one more lingering look into the library as Lemuel shut the door, "I will give you slips and cuttings of every plant I have in my garden."

"If they are all as excellent as the black bryony," said Lemuel earnestly, "then that is more than payment enough."

12

Night had fallen by the time the brothers reached the fairgrounds, which were located about a mile outside the town's stockade. They had no difficulty finding their way. Campfires as numerous as fireflies marked the campsites of the vendors, their light warm and inviting. The fair itself was filled with people, though none of the stalls were open and would not be until the next day. Vendors continued to arrive, their wagons rolling down the rutted road. They called out greetings to friends and exchanged pleasant banter with rivals as they unloaded their wares.

Many of the buildings on the site were permanent. They had been built by those vendors who attended the fair frequently, were boarded up during the rest of the year. Flint's was one of these—a small stall with a sheltering roof. Hinged doors swung wide to permit customers a good view of the merchandise, displayed to best advantage on tables and shelves. A small room in back provided sleeping quarters.

Flint had an ideal location, about halfway into the fairgrounds, near the brightly colored tent of an elven flute maker. Flint complained a lot about the constant flute music that resonated from the tent, but Tanis pointed out that it drew customers their direction, so the dwarf kept his grumbling to himself. Whenever Tanis caught Flint tapping his toe to the music, the dwarf would maintain that his foot had gone to sleep and he was only attempting to revive it.

There were some forty or fifty vendors at the fair, plus various venues for entertainment: beer tents and food vendors, dancing bears, games of chance designed to part the gullible from their steel, rope walkers, jugglers, and minstrels.

Inside the grounds, those merchants who had already arrived had unpacked and set up their merchandise, ready for tomorrow's busy day. Taking their leisure, they rested near their fires, eating and drinking, or ventured around the grounds to see who was here and who wasn't, exchanging gossip and wineskins.

Tanis had provided the twins with directions to Flint's booth; a few additional questions asked of fellow vendors led the two straight to the location. Here they found Kitiara pacing back and forth in front of the stall, which was closed up for the night, its doors bolted and padlocked.

"Where have you been?" Kitiara demanded irritably, her hands on her hips. "I've been waiting here for hours! You're still planning to go to the temple, right? What have you been up to?"

"We were—" Caramon began.

Raistlin poked his brother in the small of the back.

"Uh . . . just looking around town," Caramon concluded with a guilty blush that must have betrayed his lie if Kit hadn't been too preoccupied to notice.

"We didn't realize how late it was," Raistlin added, which was true enough.

"Well, you're here now, and that's what matters," Kit said. "There's a change of clothing for you, little brother, inside that tent. Hurry up."

Raistlin found a shirt and a pair of leather breeches belonging to Tanis. Both were far too big for the slender young man, but they would do in an emergency. He secured the breeches around his waist with the rope belt from his robe or they would have been down around his knees. Tying back his long hair and tucking it up beneath a slouch hat belonging to Flint, Raistlin emerged from the tent to chortles of raucous laughter from Caramon and Kitiara.

The breeches chafed Raistlin's legs, after the freedom of the comfortable robes; the shirt's sleeves kept falling down his thin arms, and the hat slid over his eyes. All in all, Raistlin was pleased with his disguise. He doubted if even the Widow Judith would recognize him.

"Come along, then," said Kit impatiently, starting off toward town. "We're going to be late as it is."

"But I haven't eaten yet!" Caramon protested.

"There's no time. You better get used to missing a few meals, young man, if you're going to be a soldier. Do you think armies lay down their arms to pick up frying pans?"

Caramon looked horrified. He had known that soldiering was dangerous, the life of a mercenary a rough one, but it had not occurred to him that he might not be fed. The career he had been looking forward to ever since he was six suddenly lost a good deal of its luster. He stopped at a water well, drank two gourdfuls, hoping to quiet the rumblings of his stomach.

"Don't blame me," he said in an undertone to his twin, "if these growls scare the snakes."

"Where are Tanis and Flint and the others?" Raistlin asked his sister as they retraced their steps back into Haven.

"Flint's gone to the Daft Gnome, his favorite alehouse. Sturm went on ahead to the temple, not knowing if you two were going to honor us with your presence or not. The kender vanished—good riddance, I say." Kit never made any pretense of the fact that she considered Tasslehoff a nuisance. "Thanks to the kender, I managed to get rid of Tanis. I didn't think we wanted him along."

Caramon shot an unhappy glance at his brother, who frowned and shook his head, but Caramon was upset and doggedly ignored his twin's subtle warning.

"What do you mean, you got rid of Tanis? How?"

Kit shrugged. "I told him that a messenger had come by with word that Tasslehoff had been thrown into prison. Tanis promised the town guard that he'd be responsible for the kender, so there wasn't much he could do but go see to the matter."

"There's the temple—where that bright light is shining." Raistlin pointed, hoping his brother would take the hint and drop the subject. "I suggest we turn down this road." He indicated the Hostlers Street.

Caramon persisted. "Is Tas in prison?"

"If he's not now, he soon will be," Kit answered with a grin and wink. "I didn't tell much of a lie."

"I thought you liked Tanis," Caramon said in a low voice.

"Oh, grow up, Caramon!" Kit returned, exasperated. "Of course I like Tanis. I like him better than any other man I've ever known. Just because I like a man doesn't mean I want him hanging around every minute of every hour of every day! And you have to admit that Tanis is a bit of a spoilsport. There was this time I captured a goblin alive. I wanted to have some fun, but Tanis said—"

"I believe that this is the temple," Raistlin stated.

The temple of Belzor was a large and imposing structure, built of granite wrested from the nearby Kharolis Mountains and dragged into Haven on ox-drawn skids. The building had been erected hastily and possessed neither grace nor beauty. It was square in shape, short, and squat, topped with a crude dome. The temple had no windows. Carvings—not very good carvings—of hooded vipers adorned the granite walls. The building had been designed to be functional, to house the various priests and priestesses who labored in Belzor's name, and to hold ceremonies honoring their god.

About twenty priests formed a double line outside the temple, funneling the faithful and the curious into the open door. The priests held blazing torches in their hands and were friendly and smiling, inviting all to come inside to witness the miracle of Belzor. Six huge wrought-iron braziers, their iron legs made in the image of twisted snakes, had been placed on either side of the doorway. The braziers were filled with coal that, by the smell, had been sprinkled with incense. Flames leapt high, sending sparks flying into the night sky, filling the air with smoke laced with a cloying scent.

Kit wrinkled her nose. Caramon coughed; the smoke seemed to seize him by the throat. Raistlin sniffed, choked. "Cover your nose and mouth! Quickly!" he warned his brother and sister. "Don't breathe the smoke!"

Kit clapped her gloved hand over her nose. Raistlin covered his face with his shirt sleeve. Caramon fumbled for a handkerchief, only to find it missing. (It would be discovered the next day, inside Tasslehoff's pocket, where the kender had put it for safekeeping.)

"Hold your breath!" Raistlin insisted, his voice muffled by his sleeve.

Caramon tried, but just as he was entering the temple, shuffling along with a crowd of people going the same way, an acolyte used a gigantic feather fan to waft the smoke directly into Caramon's face. He blinked, gasped, and sucked in a huge breath.

"Get that thing away from us!" And when the acolyte didn't move fast enough to please her, Kit gave the youth a shove, nearly knocking the youngster down.

Kit caught hold of Caramon, who had veered drunkenly off to the right. Dragging him along, she swiftly mingled with the crowd entering the temple. Raistlin slid through the press of bodies, keeping close to his brother and sister.

They entered a wide corridor, which opened into a large arena located directly beneath the dome. Granite benches formed a circle around a recessed center stage. Priests guided the people to their seats, urging them to move to the center in order to accommodate the crowd.

"There's Sturm!" said Kit.

Ignoring a priest's instructions, she barged down several stairs to reach the front of the arena.

Caramon stumbled after her. "I feel awful strange," he said to his twin. He put his hand to his head. "The room's going round and round."

"I told you not to breathe in the smoke," Raistlin muttered, and did what he could to guide his brother's fumbling steps.

"What was that stuff?" Kit asked over her shoulder.

"They are burning poppy seeds. The smoke brings about a feeling of pleasant euphoria. I find it interesting to note that Belzor apparently likes his worshipers in a state of befuddlement."

"Yes, isn't it," Kit agreed. "What about Caramon? Will he be all right?"

Caramon wore a foolish grin on his face. He was humming a little song to himself.

"The effects will wear off in time," said Raistlin. "But don't count on him for any action for a good hour or so. Sit down, my brother. This is neither the time nor the place for dancing."

"What's been going on in here?" Kit asked Sturm, who had saved front row seats, right next to the arena.

"Nothing of interest," he said.

There was no need to lower their voices, the noise in the chamber was deafening. Affected by the smoke, people were giddy, laughing and calling out to friends as the priests directed them to their seats.

"I arrived early. What's the matter with everyone?" Sturm gazed about in disapproval. "This looks more like an alehouse than a temple!" He cast Caramon a reproving glance.

"I'm not drunk!" Caramon insisted indignantly and slid off the bench onto the floor. Rubbing his buttocks, he stood up, giggling.

"Those braziers burning outside. They're giving off some sort of poisoned smoke," Kit explained. "You didn't get a whiff of it, did you?"

Sturm shook his head. "No, they were just preparing the fires when I entered. Where is Tanis? I thought he was coming."

"The kender got himself arrested," Kit replied with an easy shrug. "Tanis had to go rescue him from jail."

Sturm looked grave. Although he was fond of Tasslehoff, the kender's "borrowing" distressed him. Sturm was always lecturing Tas on the evils of theft, citing passages from a Solamnic code of law known as the Measure. Tas would listen with wide-eyed seriousness. The kender would agree that stealing was a terrible sin, adding that he couldn't imagine what sort of wicked person would walk off with another person's most prized possessions. At this point, Sturm would discover he was missing his dagger or his money belt or the bread and cheese he was intending to eat for lunch. The missing objects would be found on the person of the kender, who had taken advantage of the lecture to appropriate them.

In vain, Tanis advised Sturm that he was wasting his time. Kender were kender and had been that way since the time of the Graygem, and there was no changing them. The aspiring knight felt it his duty to try to change at least one of them. So far he wasn't having much luck.

"Perhaps Tanis will come later," Sturm said. "I will save him a seat."

Kit caught Raistlin's eye, smiled her crooked smile.

Once they were settled, with the drugged Caramon seated between Kit and himself, where his twin could keep a firm hand on him, Raistlin was free to inspect his surroundings. The inside of the arena was very dimly lit by four braziers which stood on the floor of the arena itself. Raistlin sniffed carefully, trying to detect the odor that had first warned him of the presence of an opiate. He smelled nothing unusual. Apparently the priests wanted their audience relaxed, not comatose.

The brazier's light illuminated a large statue of a hooded snake, which loomed at the far end of the arena. The statue was crudely carved and, in direct light, would have looked grotesque, even humorous. Seen by the flickering firelight, the statue was rather imposing, particularly the eyes, which were made of mirrors and reflected the light of the fires. The gleaming eyes gave the giant viper a very lifelike and frightening aspect. Several children in the audience were whimpering, and more than one woman screamed on first sighting it.

A rope stretched around the arena prohibited entry. Priests stood guard at various points, preventing the crowd from venturing inside. The only other object in the center of the arena was a high-backed wooden chair.

"That's some big snake, huh?" said Caramon in loud tones, staring glassy-eyed at the statue.

"Hush, my brother!" Raistlin pinched the flesh of his twin's arm.

"Shut up!" Kit muttered from the other side, digging her elbow into Caramon's ribs.

Caramon subsided, mumbling to himself, and that was all they heard out of him until his head lolled forward onto his broad chest and he began to snore. Kit propped him against the granite riser of the seat behind them and turned her attention to the arena.

The outer doors slammed shut with a resounding boom, startling the members of the audience. The priests called for silence. With much shuffling, coughing, and whispering, the crowd settled down to await the promised miracles.

Two flute players entered the arena and began to play a dolorous tune. Doors on either side of the statue opened, and a procession of priests and priestess clad in sky-blue robes entered. Each carried a viper coiled in a basket. Raistlin examined the priestess closely, searching for the Widow Judith.

He was disappointed not to find her. The flute music grew livelier. The vipers lifted their heads, swaying back and forth with the motion of their handlers. Raistlin had read an account in one of Master Theobald's books on snake charming, a practice developed among the elves, who killed no living thing if they could help it but used the charming to rid their gardens of deadly serpents.

According to the book, the charm was not magical in nature. Snakes could be put into trances by means of music, a fact Raistlin had found difficult to credit. Now, watching the vipers and their reactions to the changes in the flute music, he began to think there might be something to it.

The audience was impressed. People gasped in awe and thrilled horror. Women gathered their skirts around their ankles and pulled children onto their laps. Men muttered and grasped their knives. The priests were unconcerned, serene. When their dance in honor of the statue concluded, they set the baskets containing the snakes on the floor of the arena. The vipers remained inside the baskets, their heads moving back and forth in a sleepy rhythm. Those people seated in the front rows watched the snakes warily.

The priests and priestesses formed a semicircle around the statue and began to chant. The chanting was led by a middle-aged man with long, gray-streaked black hair. His robes were a darker color than the robes of the other priests, were made of a finer cloth. He wore a gold chain around his neck, a chain from which hung the image of a viper. Word whispered around the room that this was the High Priest of Belzor.

His expression was genial, serene, though Raistlin noted that the man's eyes were much like the eyes of the statue; they reflected the light, gave none of their own. He recited the chants in a somnambular monotone that was punctuated with an occasional shout at odd moments, shouts perhaps intended to jolt into wakefulness members of the audience who had dozed off.

The chanting droned on and on. From mildly annoying, it soon became quite irritating, rasping on the nerves.

"This is intolerable," Sturm muttered.

Raistlin agreed. Between the echoing noise, the smoke of the fires burning in the braziers, and the stench of several hundred people crowded into a single windowless room, he was finding it increasingly difficult to breathe. His head ached, his throat burned. He didn't know how much longer he could stand this and hoped it would end soon. He feared he might fall ill and have to leave, and he had yet to find Judith. He had yet to witness these purported miracles.

The chanting ceased abruptly. An audible sigh whispered among the audience, whether of reverence or relief, Raistlin couldn't tell. A hidden door located inside the statue opened up, and a woman entered the arena.

Raistlin leaned forward, regarded her intently. There was no mistaking her, though it had been many years since he had last seen her. He had to make absolutely certain. Grabbing hold of Caramon's arm, Raistlin shook his twin into wakefulness.

"Huh?" Caramon gazed around dazedly. His eyes focused, he sat upright. His gaze was fixed on the priestess who had just entered, and Raistlin could tell from the sudden rigidity of his brother's body that Caramon had also recognized her.

"The Widow Judith!" Caramon said hoarsely.

"Is it?" Kit asked. "I only saw her once. Are you sure?"

"I'm not likely to ever forget her," Caramon said grimly.

"I recognize her as well," Sturm stated. "That is the woman we knew as the Widow Judith."

Kit smiled, pleased. Crossing her arms over her chest, she settled back comfortably, her bent leg propped over one knee, and stared at the priestess to the exclusion of anyone else in the temple.

Raistlin also watched Judith attentively. though the sight of her brought back intensely painful memories. He waited to see her perform a miracle.

The High Priestess was clad in sky-blue robes similar to those the others wore, with two exceptions: Hers were trimmed in golden thread, and whereas the sleeves on the robes of the others fit tightly over their arms, her sleeves were voluminous. When she spread her arms wide, the sleeves made a rippling motion, providing her with an eerie, not-of-this-world aspect. This was further enhanced by her extremely pale complexion, a pallor that Raistlin suspected was probably enhanced by the skillful use of chalk. She had darkened her eyelids with kohl, rubbed coral powder on her lips to make them stand out in the flickering light.

Her hair was drawn back from her head, pulled back so tightly that it stretched the skin over her cheekbones, erasing many of her wrinkles, making her look younger. She was an impressive sight, one that the audience, in their opiated state, appreciated to the fullest. Murmurs of admiration and awe swept through the arena.

Judith raised her hands for silence. The audience obeyed. All was hushed, no one coughed, no baby whimpered.

"Those supplicants who have been deemed acceptable may now come forward to speak to those who have passed beyond," the High Priest called out. He had an oddly high-pitched voice for a man his size.

Eight people, who had been herded into a sort of pen on one side of the arena, now shuffled down the stairs in single file, guided by the priests. The supplicants were not permitted to step onto the floor of the arena itself, but were kept back by ropes.

Six were middle-aged women, dressed in black mourning clothes. They looked pleased and self-important as they entered behind the priests. The seventh was a young woman not much older than Raistlin, who looked pale and worn and sometimes put her hand to her eyes. She was also wearing mourning clothes, her grief was obviously fresh. The eighth was a stolid farmer in his forties. He stood rock still, stared straight ahead, his face carefully arranged so as to betray no emotion. He was not dressed in mourning and looked extremely out of place.

"Step forward and make your requests. What is it you would ask Belzor?" the High Priest called out.

The first woman was escorted to the fore by a priest. Standing in front of the High Priestess, she made her request.

She wanted to speak to her deceased husband, Arginon. "I want to make sure he's fine and wearing his flannel weskit to keep off the chill," she said. "This being what kilt him."

High Priestess Judith listened, and when the woman finished, the High Priestess made a gracious bow. "Belzor will consider your request," she said.

The next woman came forward with much the same desire, to speak to a dead husband, as did the four who came after.

The High Priestess was gracious to each, promising that Belzor was listening.

Then the priests led forward the young woman. She pressed her hands together, gazed earnestly at the High Priestess.

"My little girl died of . . . of the fever. She was only five. And she was so afraid of the dark! I want to make sure . . . it's not dark . . . where she is. . . ." The bereaved mother broke down and sobbed.

"Poor girl," said Caramon softly.

Raistlin said nothing. He had seen Judith frown slightly, her lips compress in a tight, forbidding smile that he remembered very well.

The High Priestess promised, in a tone somewhat colder than that she had used with the others, that Belzor would look into the matter. The young woman was helped back to her place in line, and the priests led forth the farmer.

He appeared nervous but determined. Clasping his hands, he cleared his throat. In a loud and booming voice, speaking very rapidly, without a pause for breath or punctuation, he stated, "My father died six months ago we know he had money when he died 'cause he spoke of it when the fit was on him he must have hid it but we can't none of us find it what we want to know is where the money is hid thank you."

The farmer gave a curt nod and stepped back in line, nearly trampling the priest who had come up to escort him.

The audience murmured at this; someone laughed and was immediately stifled.

"I am surprised he was permitted to come forward with such an ignoble request," Sturm said in a low voice.

"On the contrary," Raistlin whispered, "I imagine that Belzor will look upon his request with favor."

Sturm looked shocked and tugged on his long mustache. He shook his head.

"Wait and see," Raistlin advised.

The High Priestess once more raised her hands, commanding silence. The audience held its breath, an air of excited expectation electrified the crowd. Most had been in attendance many times previous. This was what they had come to see.

Judith lowered her arms with a sudden dramatic gesture, which caused the voluminous sleeves to fall and cover her hands, hiding them from sight. The High Priest began to chant, calling upon Belzor. Judith tilted her head. Her eyes closed, her lips moved in silent prayer.

The statue moved.

Raistlin's attention had been focused on Judith; he caught sight of the movement out of the corner of his eye. He shifted his gaze to the statue, at the same time drawing his brother's attention to it with a nudge.

"Huh?" Caramon gave a violent start.

The crude stone statue of the viper had come to life. It twisted and writhed, yet as Raistlin narrowed his gaze to focus on the statue, he was not convinced that the stone itself was moving.

"It's like a shadow," he said to himself. "It is as if the shadow of the snake has come to life . . . I wonder . . ."

"Do you see that?" Caramon gasped, awe-struck and breathless. "It's alive! Kit, do you see that? Sturm? The statue is alive!"

The shadowy form of the snake, its hood spread wide, slithered forward across the arena. The viper was enormous, the swaying head brushed the high domed ceiling. The viper, tongue flickering, crawled toward the High Priestess. Women cried out, children shrieked, men called hoarse warnings.

"Do not be afraid!" cried the High Priest, raising his hands, palm outward, to quiet the worshipers. "What you see is the spirit of Belzor. He will not harm the righteous. He comes to bring us word from beyond."

The snake slithered to a halt behind Judith. Its hooded head swayed benignly over her, its gleaming eyes stared out into the crowd. Raistlin glanced at the priests and priestesses in the arena. Some, especially the young, gazed up at the snake with wonder, utterly believing. The audience shared that belief, reveled in the miracle.

A subdued Kit was grudgingly impressed. Caramon was a firm believer. Only Sturm remained doubtful, it seemed. It would take more than a stone statue come to life to displace Paladine.

Judith's head lifted. She wore an expression of ecstasy, her eyes rolled back until only the whites showed, her lips parted. A sheen of sweat glistened on her forehead.

"Belzor calls forth Obadiah Miller."

The widow of the late Miller stepped nervously forward, her hands clasped. Judith shut her eyes, stood slightly swaying on her feet, in rhythm with the snake.

"You may speak to your husband," said the High Priest.

"Obadiah, are you happy?" asked the widow.

"Most happy, Lark!" Judith replied in an altered voice, deep and gravely.

"Lark!" The widow pressed her hands to her bosom. "That was his pet name for me! It is Obadiah!"

"And it would please me very much, my dear," the late Obadiah continued, "if you would give a portion of the money I left you to the Temple of Belzor."

"I will, Obadiah. I will!"

The widow would have spoken with her husband further, but the priest gently urged her to step back, permitting the next widow to take her place.

This one greeted her late husband, wanted to know if they should plant cabbages next year or turn the parcel of land on the sunny slope over to turnips. Speaking through Judith, the late husband insisted on cabbages, adding that it would please him very much if a certain portion of all their produce should be given to the Temple of Belzor.

At this, Kit sat up straight. She cast a sharp, questioning look at Raistlin.

He glanced at her sidelong, nodded his head once very slightly.

Kit lifted her brows, silently interrogating him.

Raistlin shook his head. Now was not the time.

Kit sat back, satisfied, the pleased smile again on her face.

The other widows spoke to their dead. Each time the deceased husband came forth, he managed to say something that only a wife would know. The husbands all concluded by requesting money for Belzor, which the widows promised, wiping away happy tears, to grant.

Judith asked that the farmer searching for his lost heritage come forward.

After a brief exchange between father and son concerning the ravages of the potato grub, an exchange which Belzor—speaking through Judith—appeared to find somewhat tedious, Judith brought the subject back to the hidden wealth.

"I have told Belzor where to find the money," said Judith, speaking for the late farmer. "I will not reveal this aloud, lest some dishonest person take advantage of the knowledge while you are away from home. Return tomorrow with an offering for the temple and the information will be imparted to you."

The farmer ducked his head several times, as grateful as if Belzor had handed him a chest of steel coins on the spot. Then it was the turn of the bereaved young mother.

Recalling the forbidding expression on Judith's face, Raistlin tensed. He could not imagine that Belzor would extract much of an offering from this poor woman. Her clothes were worn. Her shoes were clearly castoffs from someone else, for they did not fit. A ragged shawl covered her thin shoulders. But she was clean, her hair was neatly combed. She had once been pretty and would be pretty again, when time rounded off the sharp corners of her bitter loss.

Judith's head rolled and lolled. When she spoke, it was in the high-pitched voice of a little child, a terrified child.

"Mama! Mama! Where are you? Mama! I'm afraid! Help me, Mama! Why don't you come to me?"

The young woman shuddered and reached out her hands. "Mother is here, Mia, my pet! Mother is here! Don't be frightened!"

"Mama! Mama! I can't see you! Mama, there are terrible creatures coming to get me! Spiders, Mama, and rats! Mama! Help me!"

"Oh, my baby!" The young woman gave a heartrending cry and tried to rush forward into the arena. The priest restrained her.

"Let me go to her! What is happening to her? Where is she?" the mother cried.

"Mama! Why don't you help me?"

"I will!" The mother wrung her hands, then clasped them together. "Tell me how!"

"The child's father is an elf, is he not?" Judith asked, speaking in her own voice, no longer that of a child.

"He—he is only part elven," the young woman faltered, startled and wary. "His great-grandfather was an elf. Why? What does that matter?"

"Belzor does not look with favor upon the marriage of humans with persons of lesser races. Such marriages are contrived, a plot of the elves, intended to weaken humanity so that we will eventually fall to elven domination."

The audience murmured in approval. Many nodded their heads.

"Because of her elven blood," Judith continued remorselessly, "your child is cursed, and so she must live in eternal darkness and torment!"

The wretched mother moaned and seemed near to collapsing.

"What folly is this?" Sturm demanded in a low, angry voice.

Several of his neighbors, overhearing, cast him baleful glances.

"Dangerous folly," said Raistlin and clasped his thin fingers around his friend's wrist. "Hush, Sturm! Say nothing. Now is not the time."

"You and your husband are not wanted in Haven," Judith stated. "Leave at once, lest more harm befall you."

"But where will we go? What will we do? The land is all we have, and that is not much! And my child! What will become of my poor child?"

Judith's voice softened. "Belzor takes pity on you, sister. Make a gift of your land to the temple, and Belzor might be prevailed upon to bring your child from darkness into light."

Judith's head lowered to her chest. Her arms fell limp to her sides. Her eyes closed. The shadowy form of the viper retreated until it blended in with the statue, then vanished.

Judith raised her head, looked around as if she had no idea where she was or what had happened. The High Priest took hold of her arm, supported her. She gazed out upon the audience with a beatific smile.

The High Priest stepped forward. "The audience with Belzor is concluded."

The priests and priestesses picked up the baskets containing the charmed vipers. Forming into a procession, they circled the arena three times, chanting the name of Belzor, then they left through the door in the statue. Acolytes circulated among the crowd, graciously accepting all offerings made in Belzor's name, with Belzor's blessing.

The High Priest led Judith to the door leading out of the temple. Here she greeted worshipers, who begged for her blessing. A large basket stood at the floor at Judith's feet. Blessings were granted as the steel coins clinked.

The young mother stood bereft and alone. Catching hold of one of the acolytes, she begged, "Take pity on my poor child! Her heritage is not her fault."

The acolyte coldly removed her hand from his sleeve. "You heard the will of Belzor, woman. You are fortunate our god is so merciful. What he asks is a very small price to pay to free your child from eternal torment."

The young mother covered her face with her hands.

"Where'd the snake go?" asked Caramon, weaving unsteadily on his feet.

Raistlin kept firm hold on his brother, dissuaded him from making a foray into the arena in search of the giant viper. "Kitiara, you and Sturm take Caramon back to the fairgrounds and put him to bed. I will meet you there."

"I do not want to believe in this miracle," Sturm said, gazing at the statue, "but neither can I explain it."

"I can, but I'm not going to," Raistlin said. "Not now."

"What will you do?" Kit asked, catching hold of the reeling Caramon by the shirttail.

"I'll join you later," Raistlin said and left them before Kit could insist on coming with him.

He pushed his way through the roving acolytes with their offering baskets to the arena, where the mother of the dead child stood alone. One man, passing her, gave her a shove, called out, "Elven whore." A woman came up to her to say loudly, "It is well your child died. She would have been nothing but a pointy-eared freak!" The mother shrank away from these cruel words as from a blow.

Anger burned in Raistlin, anger kindled from words shouted long ago, words the weak use against those weaker than themselves. An idea formed in hot forge-fire of his rage. It emerged from the flames as steel, heated and ready for slagging. In the space of three steps, he had forged the plan in his mind, the plan he would use to bring High Priestess Judith to ruin, discredit all the false priests of Belzor, bring about the downfall of the false god.

Drawing near the unfortunate mother, Raistlin put out a hand to detain her. His touch was gentle, he could be very gentle when he wanted, yet the woman still shivered beneath his grasp in fright. She turned fearful eyes upon him.

"Leave me alone!" she pleaded. "I beg of you. I have suffered enough."

"I am not one of your tormentors, madam," Raistlin said in the quiet, calming tones he used to soothe the sick. His hand clasped over the mother's, and he could feel her shaking. Stroking her hand reassuringly, he leaned near and whispered, "Belzor is a fraud, a sham. Your child is at peace. She sleeps soundly, as though you had rocked her to sleep yourself."

The woman's eyes filled with tears. "I did rock her. I held her, and at the end, she was at peace, as you have said. 'I feel better now, Mama,' she told me, and she closed her eyes." The woman clutched frantically at Raistlin. "I want to believe you! But how can I? What proof can you give me?"

"Come to the temple tomorrow night."

"Come back here?" The mother shook her head.

"You must," said Raistlin firmly. "I will prove to you then that what I've told you is the truth."

"I believe you," she said and gave him a wan smile. "I trust you. I will come."

Raistlin looked back into the arena, at the long line of worshipers fawning over Judith. The coins in the basket gleamed in the light of the braziers, and more money continued to flow in. Belzor had done well for himself tonight.

One of the acolytes came up, rattled the collection basket in front of Raistlin hopefully.

"I trust we will see you at tomorrow night's ceremony, brother."

"You can count on it," said Raistlin.

13

RAISTLIN RETURNED TO THE FAIRGROUNDS, MULLING OVER HIS PLAN IN his mind. The forge-fire in his soul had burned very hot but the flames died quickly when exposed to the cool night air. Plagued with self-doubt, he regretted having made his promise to the bereaved mother. If he failed, he would be laughed out of Haven.

Shame and derision were far more difficult for Raistlin to contemplate than any physical punishment. He pictured the crowd hooting with mirth, the High Priest hiding his smugly pitying smile, the High Priestess Judith regarding his downfall in triumph, and he writhed at the thought. He began to think of excuses. He would not go to the temple tomorrow. He wasn't feeling well. The young mother would be disappointed, left bitterly unhappy, but she would be no worse off than she was now.

The right and proper thing to do would be to make a report to the Conclave of Wizards. They were the people most capable of dealing with the matter. He was too young, too inexperienced. . . .

Yet, he said to himself, think of the triumph if I succeed!

Not only would he ease the suffering of the mother, but he would also distinguish himself. How fine it would be to report not only the problem to the conclave, but to add modestly that he had solved it. The great Par-Salian, who had undoubtedly never heard of Raistlin Majere before, would take notice. A thrill came over Raistlin. Perhaps he would be invited to attend a meeting of the conclave! By this act, he would prove to others and to himself that he was capable of using powerful magicks in a crisis situation. Surely they would reward him. Surely the prize was worth the risk.

"In addition, I will be fulfilling my promise to the three gods who once took an interest in me. If I cannot prove their existence to others, at least I can shatter the image of this false god who is attempting to usurp them. In that way, I will draw their favorable attention as well."

He went over his plan in his mind again, this time eagerly, excitedly, searching for flaws. The only flaw that he could see lay within himself. Was he strong enough, skilled enough, brave enough? Unfortunately none of those questions would be answered until the time came.

Would his friends back him up? Would Tanis, who was nominally their leader, permit Raistlin to even try his scheme?

"Yes, if I approach them the right way."

He found the others gathered around a campfire they had built in back of Flint's stall.

Tanis and Kit sat side by side. Evidently the half-elf had not yet discovered Kit's deception. Caramon sat on a log, his head in his hands. Flint had returned from the tavern a bit tipsy, having fallen in with some hill dwarves from the Kharolis Mountains, who, though not of his clan, had traveled near his old homeland and were happy to share gossip and ale. Tasslehoff squatted by the campfire, roasting chestnuts in a skillet.

"You're back," said Kit as Raistlin appeared. "We were getting worried. I was just about to send Tanis to find you. He's already been out rescuing the kender."

Kit winked when Tanis wasn't looking. Raistlin understood. Caramon did, too, apparently. Lifting his head, his brow puckered, he looked at his twin, sighed, and lowered his head to his hands again.

"My head aches," he mumbled.

Tanis explained that he had found Tasslehoff, along with twenty other kender, incarcerated in the Haven jail. Tanis paid the fine levied on those who "knowingly and willingly associate with kender," extricated Tas from prison, and brought him forcibly back to the fairgrounds. Tanis trusted that tomorrow the distractions of the fair would keep the kender occupied and out of the town proper.

Tasslehoff was sorry to have missed the evening's adventure, especially the giant snake and the intoxicating smoke. The Haven jail had been a disappointment.

"It was dirty, Raistlin, and it had rats! Can you believe it? Rats! For rats I missed a giant snake and intoxicating smoke. Life is so unfair!"

Tas could never stay unhappy for long, however. Upon reflecting that he couldn't possibly be two places at the same time (except Uncle Trapspringer, who had done it once), the kender cheered up. Forgetting the chestnuts (which soon burned past eating), Tas sorted through all his newfound possessions, then, worn out by the day's excitement, he fell asleep, his head pillowed on one of his own pouches.

Flint shook his head at the story of Belzor. He stroked his long beard and said it didn't surprise him in the least. He expected nothing better of humans, present company excepted.

Kit considered it a fine joke.

"You should have seen Caramon," she told them, laughing. "Staggering about like a great drunken bear."

Caramon groaned and rose unsteadily to his feet. Mumbling something about feeling sick, he staggered off in the direction of the men's privies.

Sturm frowned. He did not approve of Kit's levity on serious subjects. "I do not like these followers of Belzor, but you must admit that we did see a miracle performed in that arena. What other explanation can there be, except that Belzor is a god and his priests have miraculous powers?"

"I'll give you an explanation," Raistlin said. "Magic."

"Magic?"

Kit laughed again. Sturm was disapproving. Flint said, "I knew it," though no one could figure out how.

"Are you certain, Raistlin?" Tanis asked.

"I am," Raistlin answered. "I am familiar with the spell she cast."

Tanis appeared dubious. "Forgive me, Raistlin. I'm not casting doubt on your knowledge, but you are only a novice."

"And as such I am fit for nothing except washing out my master's chamber pot. Is that what you are saying, Tanis?"

"I didn't mean—"

Raistlin dismissed the apology with an irritated wave of his hand. "I know what you meant. And what you think of me or my abilities makes no difference to me. I have further evidence that what I say is true, but it is obvious that Tanis does not care to hear it."

"I want to hear it," said Caramon stoutly. He had returned from his short jaunt, seemed to be feeling better.

"Tell us," said Kit, her dark eyes glinting in the firelight.

"Yes, lad, let us hear your evidence," said Flint. "Mind you, I knew it was magic all along."

"Bring me a blanket, my brother," Raistlin ordered. "I will catch my death, sitting on this damp ground." When he was comfortable, seated on a blanket near the fire and sipping at a glass of mulled cider, which Kit brought him, he explained his reasoning.

"My first indication that something might be wrong was when I heard that the priests were forbidding users of magic to enter the temple. Not only that, but they are actively persecuting the one wizard who lives in Haven, a Red Robe named Lemuel. Caramon and I met him this afternoon. The priests forced him to close his mageware shop. They have frightened him into fleeing his home, the house where he was born. In addition to this, the priests have prohibited all mages from entering their temple when the 'miracle' is performed. Why? Because any magic-user, even a novice such as myself," Raistlin added in acid tones, "would recognize the spell Judith casts."

"Why did they force that friend of yours, that Lemuel, to close down his mageware shop?" Caramon asked. "How could a shop hurt them?"

"Shutting down Lemuel's mageware shop insures that the wizards who frequented that shop—wizards who might expose Judith—will no longer have a reason to come to Haven. When Lemuel leaves town, the priests will consider themselves safe."

"But then why did that priest invite you to the temple, little brother?" Kit asked.

"In order to make certain I would not be a nuisance," Raistlin replied. "Remember, he said that I would not be allowed inside to witness the 'miracle.' Undoubtedly, had I gone, they would have urged me to renounce magic and embrace Belzor."

"I'd like to embrace him," Caramon growled, flexing his big hands. "I've got the worst hangover I've ever had in my life, and I never touched a drop. Life's not fair, as the kender says."

"But those people who spoke to Belzor." Sturm was arguing in favor of the miracle. "How did the Widow Judith know all those things about them? A husband's pet name for his wife, where that farmer hid his money?"

"Remember, those people who appeared before Belzor were handpicked," Raistlin replied. "Judith probably interviewed them in advance. Through skillful questioning, she could elicit information from them, information about their husbands and family, information they don't realize they are providing. As for the farmer and the hidden money, they did not tell him publicly where to find it. When he comes to the temple, they'll tell him to search under the mattress. If that fails, they'll tell him he lacked faith in Belzor, and if he contributes more money, they'll offer him another place to search."

"There's something I don't understand," said Flint, thinking things over. "If this widow woman is a wizardess, why did she attach herself to your mother, then denounce her at your father's funeral?"

"That puzzled me, too, at first," Raistlin admitted. "But then it made sense. Judith was trying to introduce the worship of Belzor into Solace.

Her first act when she arrived in town would be to seek out any magi who might prove to be a threat. My mother, who had some reputation as a seer, was an obvious choice. All the while Judith lived in Solace, she endeavored to build up her following. She was not performing any 'miracles' then. Perhaps she had not yet mastered the technique, or perhaps she was waiting until she had a suitable location and audience. Before she could proceed, however, you and Tanis thwarted her plan. Judith realized at my father's funeral that the people of Solace were not likely to fall in with her schemes.

"As we saw tonight, Judith and the High Priest of Belzor, who is probably her partner in this scheme, feed on people's worst qualities: fear, prejudice, and greed. The residents of Solace tend to be less fearful of strangers, more accepting of others simply because the town is a crossroads."

"It is an ugly game that widow woman's playing, bilking people out of what little they have," Flint stated grimly. He looked quite fierce, his brows bristled. "Not to mention tormenting that poor lass who lost her babe."

"It is an ugly game," Raistlin concurred. "And one I believe that we can end."

"I'm in," said Kit immediately.

"Me, too," Caramon said promptly, but that was a foregone conclusion. If his twin had proposed setting off on an expedition to find the Graygem of Gargath, Caramon would have started packing.

"If these 'miracles' are in reality nothing more than the deceitful tricks of a mage, then it is my duty to expose her," Sturm said.

Raistlin smiled grimly, and bit back a sharp retort. He had need of the erstwhile knight.

"I wouldn't mind giving that widow a black eye," said Flint reflectively. "What do you say, Tanis?"

"I want to hear Raistlin's plan first," Tanis stated with his customary caution. "Attacking people's faith is dangerous, more dangerous than attacking them physically."

"Count me in," said Tasslehoff, sitting up and rubbing his eyes. "What are we doing?"

"Whatever it is, we don't need a kender," Flint said grumpily. "Go to sleep. Or, better yet, why don't you go back and tell 'em how to run their jail."

"Oh, I already did that," Tas said, sensing the excitement and waking up quickly. "They were extremely rude, even when I offered my most helpful suggestions. Can I come, too, Raistlin? Please? Where are we going?"

"No kender," said Flint emphatically.

"The kender may come," Raistlin said. "As a matter of fact, Tasslehoff is the key to my plans."

"There! You see, Flint!" Tas jumped to his feet, tapped himself proudly on the chest. "Me! I'm the key to the plan!"

"Reorx help us!" Flint groaned.

"I hope he will," Raistlin replied gravely.

14

RAISTLIN WAS UP EARLY THE NEXT DAY; HE HAD BEEN AWAKE MUCH OF the night, finally falling into an uneasy sleep in the early hours of the morning. He woke from a dream he could not recall, but which left a feeling of disquiet in his mind. He had the impression he'd been dreaming about his mother,

Flint and Tanis were up early as well, arranging and rearranging the wares to best advantage. They had placed the bracers, with their beautiful engravings of griffins, dragons, and other mythical beasts, on a front shelf. Necklaces of silver braid, fine and delicate work, were laid out on red velvet. Silver and gold lover's rings, made to resemble clinging ivy, gleamed in wooden cases.

Flint was not happy with the way the wares were displayed, however. He was certain that the morning sun would cast a shadow over the stall, and that therefore the silver must go here, not there, Tanis listened patiently, reminded Flint that they'd been through this yesterday, and due to the shadow of an overhanging oak, the sun rays would fall on the silver and set the jewels sparkling only if it remained where it was.

They were still arguing when Raistlin went to the men's privies to perform his ablutions, splashing cold water from a communal bucket over his face and body. Shivering, he dressed quickly in his white robes. Caramon remained asleep inside their tent, snoring off the effects of the opiated smoke.

The air was chill and crisp, the sun was reddening the mountain peaks, already white from a smattering of snow. No clouds marred the sky. The day would warm pleasantly; the crowds at the fair would be brisk.

Flint called out for Raistlin to come settle the argument on the placement of the jewelry. Raistlin, who cared nothing about the matter and would have just as soon seen the jewelry on the roof as anyplace else, managed to escape by pretending he hadn't heard the dwarf's bellow.

He made his way through the fairgrounds, watched the activity with interest. Shutters were coming down, handcarts were being wheeled to the proper locations. The smells of bacon and fresh bread filled the air. The grounds were quiet, compared to the noise and confusion expected later in the day. Vendors called out to wish each other luck, or gathered together to share food and stories, or bartered for each other's work.

The vendors had only been here a day, and already they had formed their own community, complete with leaders, gossip, and scandals, bound together by the feeling of camaraderie, an "us against them" mentality. "Them" meant the customers, who were spoken of in the most disparaging terms and who would later be met with gracious smiles and servile attitudes.

Raistlin viewed this little world with amused cynicism until he came to the booth of one of the bakers. A young woman was arranging fresh, hot muffins in a basket. Their spicy cinnamon smell made a pleasant accompaniment to the smell of wood smoke from the brick ovens and tempted Raistlin to walk over and ask the price. He was fumbling for his few remaining pennies, wondering if he had enough, when the young woman smiled at him and shook her head.

"Put your money away, sir. You're one of us."

The muffin warmed his hands as he walked; the taste of apples and cinnamon burst on his tongue. It was undoubtedly the best muffin he had ever eaten, and he decided that being part of the small community was very pleasant, even if it all was a bit odd.

The streets of Haven were beginning to waken. Small children came bursting out of doors, squealing with excitement that they were going to go to the fair. Their harassed mothers darted out to retrieve them and wash their grimy faces. The town guard walked about with an important air, mindful of strangers visiting Haven and determined to impress.

Raistlin kept a watch out for any of the blue-robed priests of Belzor. When he saw some in the distance, he ducked hastily into the next block to avoid them. It was unlikely that any would have recognized him as the shabbily clad peasant from the night before, but he dared not take the chance. He had considered putting on the same disguise today, but reflected that he would have to explain the reason for the disguise to Lemuel, something he did not want to do if it could be avoided. The meek little man would most certainly try to dissuade Raistlin from going through with his plan.

Raistlin did not feel equal to hearing any more arguments. He'd heard them all already from himself.

The sun's rays were melting the frost on the leaves in the street when Raistlin reached Lemuel's house. The house was quiet, and though this was not unusual for the reclusive mage, Raistlin realized uneasily that it was still very early in the morning. Lemuel might still be asleep.

Raistlin prowled about outside the house for several moments, not liking to wake the mage, but not liking the idea of leaving, of wasting all this time and energy. He walked around to the back of the house, hoping he could see inside one of the near windows. He was pleased and relieved to hear noises coming from the garden.

Finding a protruding brick in the lower portion of the garden wall, Raistlin set his foot upon it and hoisted himself up.

"Excuse me, sir. Lemuel," he called out softly, trying not to startle the nervous man.

He failed. Lemuel dropped his trowel and stared about him in consternation. "Who . . . who said that?" he demanded in a quavering voice.

"It's me, sir . . . Raistlin." He was conscious of his undignified position, clinging precariously to the wall, holding on with both hands.

After a moment's search, Lemuel saw his guest and greeted Raistlin most cordially, greetings which were cut short by Raistlin's foot slipping from the brick, causing him to disappear from the mage's sight with a startling abruptness. Lemuel opened the garden gate and invited Raistlin to enter, asking him anxiously as he did so if he'd seen any snakes near the house.

"No, sir," Raistlin answered, smiling. He had grown to like the nervous, fussy little man. Part of his motivation for proceeding with his plan—the unselfish part of his motives—was the determination that Lemuel should stay with his beloved garden. "The priests are down at the fairgrounds, finding new converts. So long as the fair runs, I do not think they will bother you, sir."

"We should be grateful for small blessings, as the gnome said when he blew off his hand when it might have been his head. Have you had breakfast? Do you mind very much if we take our food into the garden? I have a great deal of work to do there."

Raistlin indicated that he had already eaten and that he would be perfectly happy to go into the garden. He found the plots about a fourth of the way dug up, with plants arranged in neat bundles, ready for transport.

"Half of them won't survive the trip, but some of them will make it, and in a few years, I daresay I will have my old garden back again," Lemuel said, trying to be cheerful.

But his gaze roved sadly to the blackberry bushes, the cherry and apple trees, the enormous lilac bush. The trees and plants he could not take with him could never be replaced.

"Perhaps you won't have to leave, sir." Raistlin said. "I have heard rumors that some people think Belzor is a fraud and that they intend to expose him as such."

"Really?" Lemuel's face brightened, then fell again into shadow. "They won't succeed. His followers are much too powerful. Still, it is kind of you to give me hope, even if only for a moment. Now, what is it you want, young man?" Lemuel regarded Raistlin shrewdly. "Is someone ill? Do you need some of my medicines?"

"No, sir." Raistlin flushed slightly, embarrassed that he was so transparent. "I would like to look over your father's books again, if you don't mind."

"Bless you, young man, they're your books now," Lemuel said warmly, with such kindness that Raistlin determined then and there to bring down Belzor no matter what the cost and without a thought to his own ambition. He left the mage roving unhappily about his garden, trying to decide what could be safely transplanted and what should be left behind, hoping that the next owner would properly water the hydrangea.

Inside the library, Raistlin spent a moment looking fondly and proudly on the books—his books, soon to be his library—and then he set to work. He found the spell he was seeking without difficulty; the war mage had been a man of precise habits and had noted down each spell and its location in a separate volume. Upon reading a description of the spell—which the war mage had also included, apparently for his own reference—Raistlin was convinced beyond doubt that this indeed was the spell the High Priestess was casting.

He was further confirmed in his belief on noting that the spell required no components—no sand sprinkled over the eyes or bat guano rolled in the fingers. Judith had only to speak the words and make the appropriate gestures in order to work the magic. This was the reason for the voluminous sleeves.

The question now was, could he cast this same spell?

The spell was not exceptionally difficult, it did not require the skills of an archmage to cast. The spell would be easily accessible to an apprentice mage, but Raistlin was not even that. He was a novice, would not be permitted to apprentice himself until after he had taken the Test. By the laws of the conclave, he was forbidden to cast this spell until that time. The law was quite specific on that point.

The laws of the conclave were also quite specific on another point: If ever a mage met a renegade wizard, one who was operating outside the law of the conclave, it was the duty of that mage to either reason with the renegade, bring the renegade to justice before the conclave, or—in extreme cases—end the renegade's life.

Was Judith a renegade? This was a question Raistlin had spent the night pondering. It was possible she might be a black-robed wizard, using her evil magic to fraudulently obtain wealth and poison people's minds. Practitioners of evil magic, the Order of the Black Robes, worshipers of Nuitari, were an accepted part of the conclave's ranks. Though few outsiders could understand or accept what they considered a pact with the forces of darkness.

Raistlin recalled an argument he had presented to Sturm over this very point.

"We mages recognize that there must be balance in the world," Raistlin had tried to explain. "Darkness follows the day, both are necessary for our continued existence. Thus the conclave respects both the dark and the light. They ask that, in turn, all wizards respect the conclave's laws, which have been laid down over the centuries in order to protect magic and those who practice it. The loyalty of any wizard must be to the magic first, to all other causes second."

Needless to say, Sturm had not been convinced.

By Raistlin's own argument, it was possible that a black-robed wizardess could practice evil magic in disguise and still be condoned by the conclave, with one important exception: The conclave would most certainly frown upon the use of magic to promote the worship of a false god. Nuitari, god of the dark moon and darker magicks, was known to be a jealous god, one who demanded absolute loyalty from those who sought his favor. Raistlin could not imagine Nuitari taking kindly to Belzor under any circumstances.

In addition, Judith was slandering magic, threatening magic-users and endeavoring to persuade others that the use of magic was wrong. That alone would condemn her in the eyes of the conclave. She was a renegade, of that Raistlin had little doubt. He might run afoul of the conclave's laws in casting a spell before he was an accepted member of their ranks, but he had a solid defense. He was exposing a fraud, punishing a renegade, and, by so doing, restoring the repute of magic in the world.

Doubts at rest, his decision made, he started to work. He searched the library until he found a piece of lamb's skin, rolled up with others in a basket. He stretched the skin out on the desk, holding it flat beneath books placed at the corners. Unfortunately the vials containing lamb's blood, which he would need to use for ink, had all dried up. Having foreseen that this might be the case, Raistlin drew out a knife he had borrowed from his brother and laid it on the table, ready for use.

This done, he prepared to laboriously transfer the spell in the book to the lamb's skin. He would have liked to be able to cast the spell from memory, but as complex as the spell was—far more complex than any he had yet learned—he dared not trust himself. He had never yet performed magic in a crisis situation, and he had no idea how he would react to the pressure. He liked to think he would not falter, but he must not fall prey to overconfidence.

He had the time and solitude necessary to his work. He could concentrate his energy and skill into the transference of the spell to the scroll. He could study the words beforehand, make certain he knew the correct pronunciation, for he would have to speak the words—and speak them correctly—both when he copied the spell and when he cast it.

Settling down with the book, Raistlin pored over the spell. He spoke each letter aloud, then spoke each word aloud, repeating them until they sounded right in his ear, as a minstrel with perfect pitch tunes his lute. He was doing very well, and was feeling rather proud of himself, until he came to the seventh word. The seventh word in the spell was one he had never heard spoken. It might be pronounced any of several different ways, each with its own variant meaning. Which way was the right way?

He considered going to ask Lemuel about it, but that would mean having to tell Lemuel what he planned to do, and Raistlin had already ruled out that option.

"I can do this," he said to himself. "The word is made up of syllables, and all I have to do is to understand what each syllable does, then I will be able to pronounce each syllable correctly. After that, I will simply combine the syllables to form the word."

This sounded easy, but it proved far more difficult than he had imagined. As soon as he had the first syllable settled in his mind, the second appeared to contradict it. The third had nothing to do with the previous two. Several times Raistlin very nearly gave up in despair. His task seemed impossible. Sweat chilled on his body. He lowered his head to his hands.

"This is too hard. I am not ready. I must drop the whole idea, report her to the conclave, let some archmage deal with her. I will tell Kitiara and the rest that I have failed. . . ."

Raistlin sat up. He looked down at the word again. He knew what the spell was supposed to do. Surely, using logical deduction as well as studying related texts, he could determine which meanings were the ones required. He went back to work.

Two hours later, two hours spent searching through texts for every example of the use of the word or parts of the word in a magical spell that he could find, hours spent comparing those spells with each other, looking for patterns and relations, Raistlin sagged back in his chair. He was already weary, and the most difficult part—the actual copying—was before him. He felt a certain satisfaction, however. He had the spell. He knew how it was spoken, or at least he thought he did. The real test would come later.

He rested a few moments, reveling in his victory. His energy restored, he sliced open a cut about three inches long on his forearm, and, holding his arm over a dish he'd placed on the table for the purpose, he collected his own blood to use for ink. When he had enough, he pressed on the wound to stop the bleeding, wrapped his arm with a handkerchief.

He had just completed this when he heard footsteps advancing down the hall. Raistlin hurriedly drew his sleeve over his injured arm, flipped open the book to another page.

Lemuel peered in the door. "I hope I'm not disturbing you. I thought you might like some dinner. . . ." Seeing the dish of blood and the lamb's skin on the desk, the elder mage paused, looked quite startled.

"I'm copying a spell," Raistlin explained. "I hope you don't mind. It's a sleep spell. I've been having a bit of trouble with it, and I thought if I copied it, I could learn it better. And thank you for the offer, but I'm not really hungry."

Lemuel smiled, marveled. "What a very dedicated student you are. You would have never found me cooped up with my books on a sunny day during Harvest Home." He turned to leave, paused again. "Are you sure about dinner? The housekeeper has fixed rabbit stew. She's part elf, you know. Comes from Qualinesti. The stew is quite good, flavored with my own herbs—thyme, marjoram, sage . . ."

"That does sound good. Perhaps later," said Raistlin, who was not the least bit hungry but didn't want to hurt the mage's feelings.

Lemuel smiled again and hurried off, glad to return to his garden.

Raistlin went back to work. Flipping through the pages, he located the correct spell. He picked up the quill pen, made of the feather of a swan, the point tipped with silver. Such a writing instrument was rather extravagant, not necessary to the making of the scroll, but it showed that the archmage had been prosperous in his line of work. Raistlin dipped the pen's point in the blood. Whispering a silent prayer to the three gods of magic—not wanting to offend anyone of them—he put the pen to the scroll.

The elegant quill wrote most smoothly, unlike other quills that would balk or sputter, causing the ruin of more than one scroll. The first letter seemed to glide effortlessly upon the lamb's skin.

Raistlin resolved to someday own such a pen. He guessed that Lemuel would have given it freely if Raistlin had asked, but Lemuel had already given his new friend a great deal. Pride forbade asking for more.

Raistlin copied out the spell, pronouncing each word as it was written. The work was painstaking and time-consuming. Sweat formed beneath his hair, trickled down his neck and breast. He had to stop writing after each word to rub the cramp from his hand, cramps that came from clutching the pen too tightly, and to wipe the sweat from his palm. He wrote the seventh word with fear in his heart and the thought as he completed the scroll that this might have been all for naught. If he had mispronounced that word, the entire scroll and all his careful work were worthless.

Reaching the end, he hesitated a moment before adding the final period. Closing his eyes, he again asked a prayer of the three gods.

"I am doing your work. I am doing this for you. Grant me the magic!"

He looked back on his work. It was perfect. No wobble in the *os*. The curls on the *s* were graceful but not overdone. He cast an anxious glance at the seventh word. There was no help for it. He had done his best. He put the fine silver point of the quill to the lamb's wool and added the period that should start the magic.

Nothing happened. Raistlin had failed.

His eye caught a tiny flicker of light. He held his breath, wanting this as he had wanted his mother to live, willing this to happen as he had willed her to continue breathing. His mother had died. But the flicker of the first letter of the first word grew brighter.

It was not his imagination. The letter glowed, and the glow flowed to the second letter, and then to the second word, and so on. The seventh word seemed to Raistlin to absolutely blaze with triumph. The final dot sparked and then the glow died away. The letters were burned into the lamb's skin. The spell was ready for casting.

Raistlin bowed his head, whispered fervent, heartfelt thanks to the gods who had not failed him. Rising to his feet, he was overcome by dizziness, and nearly passed out. He sank back into the chair. He had no idea what time it was, was startled to see by the position of the sun that it was midafternoon. He was thirsty and hungry and had an urgent need for a chamber pot.

Rolling up the scroll, he tucked it carefully in a scroll case, tied the case securely to his belt. He pushed himself to his feet, made his way downstairs. After using the privies, he hungrily devoured two bowls of rabbit stew.

Raistlin could not recall having eaten so much in his entire life. Shoving aside his bowl, he leaned back in his chair, intending to rest for only a brief moment.

Lemuel found him sound asleep. The mage kindly covered the young man with a blanket, then left him sleeping.

15

RAISTLIN WOKE IN LATE AFTERNOON, GROGGY AND STUPID FROM A NAP he had never intended to take. He had a stiff neck, and the back of his head ached where he had leaned against the chair. A sudden fear seized him that he had slept too long and missed the "miracle" slated for tonight at the temple. A glance at a pool of sunshine, meandering lazily through a screen of window-climbing ivy, reassured him. Rubbing the back of his neck, he threw off the blanket and went in search of his host. Fortunately he knew where to find him.

Lemuel was in his garden, working diligently, although he did not appear to have made much progress in his preparations for moving.

He confessed as much to Raistlin. "I start to do one thing, and then I think of another and I drop the first and move to the second, only to recall that I simply must do a third before either of them, so I leave to attend to that, only to recall that the first had to be done in advance. . . ." He sighed. "I'm not getting along very fast."

He gazed sadly at the upheaval that surrounded him—overturned pots, mounds of dirt, holes where plants had been uprooted. The plants themselves, looking forlorn and naked, lying on the ground with their roots shivering.

"I suppose it's because I've never been anywhere else but here. And I don't want to be anywhere else. To tell you the truth, I haven't even decided yet where I'm going. Do you think I would like Solace?"

"Perhaps you won't have to move after all," Raistlin said, unable to witness Lemuel's suffering without making some attempt to alleviate it. He couldn't tell his intent, but he could hint. "Perhaps something will happen that will cause Belzor's faithful to leave you alone."

"A second Cataclysm? Fiery mountains raining down on their heads?" Lemuel smiled wanly. "That's too much to hope for, but thank you for the thought. Did you find what you were looking for?"

"My studies went well," said Raistlin gravely.

"And will you stay for supper?"

"No thank you, sir. I must return to the fairgrounds. My friends will be concerned about me. And please, sir," Raistlin said by way of farewell, "do not give up hope. I have a feeling you will be here long after Belzor has gone."

Lemuel was considerably astonished at this and would have asked more questions had not Raistlin pointed out that the tulip bulbs were in danger of being carried away by a squirrel. Lemuel dashed off to the rescue. Raistlin checked for the twentieth time to make certain the scroll case hung from his belt, took his grateful leave, and departed.

"I wonder what he's up to . . ." Lemuel mused. Having chased off the thief, he watched Raistlin walk up the road in the direction of the fairgrounds. "He wasn't copying out any sleep spell, that's for certain. I may not be much of a mage, but even I could pull off a snooze without writing it down. No, he was copying something far more advanced, well beyond his novitiate rank. And all that about something happening to the Belzorites . . ."

Lemuel chewed worriedly on a sprig of mint. "I suppose I should try to stop him. . . ." He considered this option, shook his head. "No. It would be like trying to stop a gnomish juggernaut once it's in gear and rolling downhill. He would not listen to me, and of course there's no reason why he should. What do I know? And he might have a chance of succeeding. There's a lot going on behind those fox-fire eyes of his. A lot going on."

Muttering to himself, Lemuel started to return to his digging. He stood a moment, holding the trowel and staring down at his once tranquil garden, now in a state of chaos.

"Perhaps I should just wait and see what tomorrow brings," he said to himself, and after covering the roots of the plants he had already dug up, making certain that they were warm and damp, he went inside to eat his supper.

❸

Raistlin arrived back at the fairgrounds just in time to prevent Caramon from turning out the town guard in search of him.

"I was busy." he replied testily, in response to his brother's persistent questioning. "Have you done as I ordered?"

"Kept hold of Tasslehoff?" Caramon heaved a long-suffering sigh. "Yes, between Sturm and me, we've managed, but I never want to have to go through anything like that again so long as I live. We had him occupied this morning, or at least we thought we did. Sturm said he wanted to look at Tas's maps. Tas dumped them all out, and he and Sturm spent an hour going over them. I guess I must have dozed off. Sturm got interested in looking at a map of Solamnia, and by the time I woke up and we realized what was what, the kender was gone."

Raistlin frowned.

"We went after him," Caramon said hurriedly. "And we caught up with him. Luckily he hadn't gone far—the fair is pretty interesting, you know. We found him, and after we took the monkey back to its owner, who'd been searching high and low for it . . . The monkey does tricks. You should see it, Raist. It's real cute. Anyway, the owner was hopping mad, although Tas said over and over that the monkey had accompanied him voluntarily, and the monkey did seem to like him—"

"Kindred spirits," observed Raistlin.

"—so by this time, the monkey's owner was yelling for the town guard. Tanis showed up about then, and we made off with Tas while Tanis explained it had all been a mistake and settled with the owner for a couple of steel for his trouble. Sturm decided then that a little military discipline was what was called for, so we took Tas to the parade ground and marched up and down for an hour. Tas thought that was great fun and would have kept it up, but due to the hot sun and the fact that we'd forgotten to bring any water, Sturm and I had to call it quits. We were about done in. The kender, of course, was feeling fine.

"We no more than got back to the fairgrounds when he sees some woman swallowing fire—she really did, Raist. I saw it, too. Tas runs off and we chase after him, and by the time we caught up, he'd lifted two pouches and a sugar bun and was just about to try putting hot coals into his mouth. We took the coals away and returned the pouches, but the sugar bun was gone except for some crumbs around Tas's lips. And then—"

Raistlin held up his hand. "Just answer me this: Where is Tasslehoff now?"

"Tied up," said Caramon wearily. "In the back of Flint's booth. Sturm's standing guard over him. It was the only way."

"Excellent, my brother," said Raistlin.

"Absolute hell," Caramon muttered.

Flint was doing quite well for himself at the fair. People crowded into his stall, kept the dwarf busy pulling rings from the cases and lacing on bracers. He had taken in a goodly quantity of steel, which he kept in a locked iron money box, as well as many items taken in trade. Bartering was an accepted practice at the fair, especially among the vendors. Flint had acquired a new butter churn (which he would trade to Otik for brandy), a washtub (his had sprung a leak), and a very fine tooled-leather belt. (His current belt was a tad too small. Flint claimed it had shrunk when he fell into Crystalmir Lake. Tanis said no, the belt was fine. It was the dwarf who had expanded.)

Raistlin avoided the crowd in the front of the booth, entered the back to find the kender tied securely to a chair, with Sturm seated in a chair opposite. If one were to judge by the expressions on the faces of the two, one might have guessed that Sturm was the prisoner. Tasslehoff, quite enjoying the novelty of being tied hand and foot, was passing the time by entertaining Sturm.

"—and then Uncle Trapspringer said, 'Are you sure that's your walrus?' And the barbarian said—Oh, hello, Raistlin! Look at me! I'm tied to a chair. Isn't this exciting? I'll bet Sturm would tie you up if you asked him politely. Would you, Sturm? Would you tie up Raistlin?"

"What happened to the gag?" Caramon asked.

"Tanis made me take it off. He said it was cruel. He doesn't know the meaning of the word," Sturm replied. He eyed Raistlin grimly as though he would have liked to take the kender up on his offer. "I trust this will be worth it. I doubt now that anything short of the return of the entire pantheon of gods to denounce Belzor would be sufficient to recompense us for the day we've spent."

"Something less than that, perhaps, but just as effective," Raistlin replied. "Where is Kitiara?"

"She went off to look around the fairgrounds, but she promised she'd be back in time." Caramon quirked an eyebrow. "She said the atmosphere was too cold for comfort, if you take my meaning."

Raistlin nodded in understanding. She and Tanis had quarreled last night, a quarrel that had probably been overheard by most of the vendors and perhaps half the town of Haven. Tanis had kept his voice low; no one could hear what he was saying, but Kit had no such scruples.

"What do you take me for? One of your namby-pamby little elf maids who has to be clinging to you every second? I go where I please, when I please, and with whom I please. To tell you the truth, no, I didn't want you along. You can be such an old man sometimes, always trying to spoil my fun."

The quarrel had gone on long into the night.

"Did they make up this morning?" Raistlin asked his brother, glancing at Tanis's back. The half-elf stood behind the booth, counting money, answering questions, taking measurements, and noting down special orders.

"Silver and amethyst, if you please," a noble lady was dictating. "And a pair of earrings to match."

"No, not a chance," Caramon replied. "You know Kit. She was ready to kiss and make up, but Tanis . . ."

As if aware that they were talking of him, Tanis turned from dropping another three steel into the money box.

"Are you still planning to go through with this?" he asked.

"I am," Raistlin said.

Tanis shook his head. He had gray smudges beneath his eyes and looked tired. "I don't like it."

"No one asked you to," Raistlin returned.

An uncomfortable silence fell. Caramon flushed and bit his lip, embarrassed for his brother, yet too loyal to say anything. Sturm gave Raistlin a look of haughty disapproval, reminded Raistlin silently that he was not to be disrespectful to his elders. Tas was going to tell another Uncle Trapspringer story, but he couldn't think of one that seemed to fit, and so he kept quiet, wiggled unhappily in his chair. The kender would have run cheerfully into a dragon's open mouth and never turned a hair on his topknot, but anger among his friends always made him feel very uncomfortable.

"You are right, Raistlin. No one did ask me," Tanis said. He started to turn away, to go back to the front of the booth.

"Tanis," Raistlin called out. "I'm sorry. I had no right to speak to you—my elder—in that manner, as the knight here would remind me. I can offer as my excuse only that I have an extremely difficult task ahead of me tonight. And I remind you and everyone here"—his gaze swept them all—"that if I fail, I will be the one to pay the penalty. None of the rest of you will be implicated."

"And yet I wonder if you realize the enormous risk you're running," Tanis said earnestly. "This false religion is making Judith and her followers wealthy. By exposing her, you may be putting yourself into considerable danger. I think you should reconsider. Let others deal with her."

"Aye," said Flint, coming back behind the booth to bring more money for the iron box. He had overheard the latter part of the conversation. "If you'll take my advice, laddie, which you never do, I say we keep our noses out of this. I was thinking on this last night, and after what you told me about the people tormenting that poor lass who lost her babe, it is my opinion that the humans of Haven and Belzor deserve each other."

"You can't be serious, sir!" Sturm protested, shocked. "According to the

Measure, if a person has knowledge of a law being broken and that person does nothing to halt it, then that person is as guilty as the lawbreaker. We should do everything in our power to stop this false priestess."

"We do that by reporting her to the proper authorities," Tanis argued.

"Who won't believe us," Caramon pointed out.

"I think—"

"Enough! I have made my decision!" Raistlin put an end to the arguments, which were making him doubt himself, undermining his carefully built fortifications. "I will go ahead with the plan. Those who want to help me can do so. Those who don't may go about their business."

"I will help," said Sturm.

"Me, too," Caramon replied loyally.

"And me! I'm the key!" Tas would have jumped up and down, except he found that jumping was difficult when it involved bringing along the chair to which he was tied. "Don't be mad, Tanis. It will be fun!"

"I'm not mad," Tanis said, his weary face relaxing into a smile. "I'm pleased that you young men are willing to risk danger for a cause you think is right. I trust that is why you're doing this," he said, with a pointed glance at Raistlin.

Never mind my motives, Raistlin advised the half-elf silently. You wouldn't understand them. So long as I achieve an outcome that pleases you and is beneficial to others, what do you care why I do what I do?

Annoyed, he was turning away when Kitiara strolled through the door of the stall. Elbowing aside several customers, who glared at her resentfully, she made her way behind the counter.

"I see we're all here. Ready to go feed Judith to the snakes?" she asked, grinning. "I'm among the chosen, by the way, baby brother. I've asked to speak to our dead mother, and the High Priestess has kindly granted my request."

This was not part of the plan. Raistlin had no idea what Kit was up to, but before he could question her, she draped her arm around Tanis, ran her hand caressingly over his shoulder. "Are you coming along to help us tonight, my love?"

Tanis pulled away from her touch.

"The fairgrounds don't shut down until dark," he said. "I have work to do here."

Kit drew close, nibbled at his ear. "Is Tanis still mad at Kitiara?" she asked in a playful tone.

He gently shoved Kit away. "Not here," he said, adding in a low voice, "We have a lot of things to talk over, Kit."

"Oh, for the love of—Talk! That's all you ever want to do!" Kit flared. "All last night, talk, talk, talk. So I told you a harmless little lie! It wasn't the first time, and it won't be the last. I'm sure you've lied to me plenty!"

Tanis paled. "You don't mean that," he said quietly.

"No, of course I don't. I say things I don't mean all the time. I'm a liar. Just ask anyone."

Kit strode angrily around the counter, giving Caramon a kick when he didn't move out of her way fast enough to suit her. "Are the rest of you coming?"

"Untie the kender," Raistlin ordered. "Sturm, you're in charge of Tas. And you, Tas"—he fixed the kender with a stern eye—"you must do exactly as I say. If you don't, you might be the one fed to the vipers."

"Ooh, how excit—" Tas saw by Raistlin's swiftly contracting brows that this was not the right response. The kender was suddenly extremely solemn. "I mean, yes, Raistlin. I'll do whatever you tell me to do. I won't even look at a snake unless you say to," he added with what he considered truly heroic self-sacrifice.

Raistlin suppressed a sigh. He could see great gaps opening in his plan, envision any number of things going wrong. For one, he was counting on a kender, which anyone in Krynn would tell him was sheer madness. Two, he was trusting in a would-be knight, who put honor and honesty over every other consideration, including common sense. Three, he had no idea what Kitiara was plotting on her own, and that was perhaps the most dangerous gap of all—a veritable chasm, into which they all might tumble.

"I'm ready, Raist," said Caramon stoutly. His loyalty was comforting to his brother, but then Caramon spoiled it by tugging proudly on his collar and adding, "I won't breathe the smoke. I wore this big shirt specially, so that I could pull it up over my head."

Presented with a vision of Caramon entering the temple with his shirt hiked up over his head, Raistlin shut his eyes and silently prayed to the gods—the gods of magic, and all true gods everywhere—to walk with him.

16

T HEY ARRIVED AT THE TEMPLE IN TIME TO MINGLE WITH THE THRONG surging inside. The crowd was far larger tonight, word of Judith's "miracle" having circulated among the fairgoers, and included hill dwarves, several of the barbaric, feather-decorated Plainsmen, and a number of noble families, clad in fine clothes, accompanied by their servants.

Raistlin also saw, much to his dismay, several of their neighbors from Solace. He drew his shapeless felt hat low over his face, huddled into the thick black cloak he wore over his robes. He was actually glad to see that Caramon had his shirt pulled up to his ears, making him resemble a gigantic tortoise. Raistlin hoped none of their neighbors would recognize them and make some reference to their fellow villager's magic.

Raistlin was somewhat daunted by the turnout. People from all parts of Abanasinia would be witness to his performance. It had not occurred to him until now that he would be performing before a large audience. The thought was not a comfortable one. At that moment, if someone had appeared before him and offered him a bent penny to flee, he would have grabbed the coin and run.

Pride goaded him on. After his confrontation with Tanis, his fine talk before his siblings and friends, Raistlin could not back down now. Not without forfeiting their respect and losing any hold he might once again wield over them.

Crowding close behind Caramon, Raistlin used his brother's large body as a shield as they made their way through the crowd. Sturm kept near them, shepherding Tasslehoff with one hand on the kender's shoulder and the other plucking Tas's wandering fingers out of the worshipers' pouches and bags.

"I have to go down in front with the priests. It's a great seat! Good luck," Kit called and waved her hand.

"Wait!" Raistlin struggled out from behind Caramon to try to reach his sister, but they were caught in a press of people and it was too late. Kitiara had seized hold of one of the priests and was now being led by him through the crowd.

What was she going to do?

Raistlin cursed his sister for her distrustful, secretive nature, but even as he muttered the words, he was forced to bite them off. Blood to blood, as the dwarves say. He might as well curse himself. He had said nothing of his plans to Kitiara.

"You can put your shirt down now!" he snapped at Caramon, nervousness making him irritable.

"Where do you want us?" Sturm asked.

"You and the kender go to the very back wall," Raistlin said, pointing to the upper tiers of seats in the arena. He gave them their final instructions. "Tas, when I shout 'Behold,' you start walking down the aisle. Walk slowly and keep your mind on what you're doing. Don't allow yourself to get distracted by anything, do you understand? If you obey me, you will see such wonderful magic as you've never seen in your entire life."

"I will, Raistlin," Tas promised. " 'Behold.' " He repeated the word several times, in order not to forget it. " 'Behold, behold, behold.' I saw a beholder once. Did I ever tell you—"

"No kender allowed," said a blue-robed priest, descending on them.

Unable and unwilling to lie, Sturm stood with his hand on the kender's shoulder. Raistlin's breath caught in his throat. He dared not intervene, dared not draw attention to himself. Fortunately for all of them, Tasslehoff was accustomed to being thrown out of places.

"Oh, he's just escorting me off now, sir," the kender said with a beaming smile.

"Is that true?"

Sturm, his mustaches bristling, inclined his head the merest fraction, the closest he had come in his entire life to telling a falsehood. Perhaps the Measure sanctioned lies in a good cause.

"Then I'm sorry for interfering with you, sir," said the priest in mollifying tones. "Please don't let me keep you from your task. The doors are in that direction." He waved his hand.

Sturm bowed coldly and dragged Tasslehoff away, shushing the kender's remarks with a stern "Silence!" and a shake of the small shoulder to emphasize the point.

Raistlin drew breath again.

"Where to?" Caramon asked, peering over the heads of the crowd.

"Somewhere near the front."

"Keep close behind me," Caramon advised.

Thrusting out with his elbows, he shouldered and jostled and eventually cleared a path through the throng. People scowled, but on noting his size, they kept any angry remarks they had been about to make to themselves.

The lower seats near the arena were filled. There was perhaps room for one person—and that a small person—at the end of the aisle. "Watch this," Caramon said to his brother with a wink.

Caramon plunked himself down on the empty seat, shifting and bumping his body against that of his neighbor, a wealthy woman, finely dressed, who glared at him. Coldly and pointedly, she moved away from his touch. Raistlin was wondering what this was going to accomplish, for there was still no room for him, when Caramon suddenly let out a great belch and then noisily passed gas.

People in the vicinity grimaced, regarded Caramon with disgust. The woman beside him clapped her hand over her nose and glared at Caramon, who gave a shamefaced grin.

"Beans for dinner," he said.

The woman rose to her feet. Sweeping her silk skirts, she favored him with a scathing glance and the comment, "Clod! I can't think why they permit your kind in here! I shall certainly protest!" She flounced off up the stairs, searching for one of the priests.

Caramon waved his brother to come sit down in the empty place beside him. "I had not realized you could be so subtle, my brother," Raistlin murmured as he took his seat.

"Yeah, that's me! Subtle!" Caramon chuckled.

Raistlin searched the crowd and soon located Sturm, standing in the shadow of a pillar near an aisle. Tasslehoff was not visible, Sturm had probably stashed the kender in the shadows.

Sturm had been searching for Raistlin as well. Sighting him, Sturm gave a brief nod, jerked his thumb. A small hand shot out from behind Sturm's back, waved. Kender and knight were in position.

Raistlin turned to face the arena. He had no difficulty at all finding his sister. Kitiara stood in the pen in front of the arena, alongside the others who had been invited to speak to their dead kin.

As if aware of his gaze upon her, Kit grinned her crooked grin. Raistlin realized with some bitterness that she was calm, relaxed, even having fun.

He was not.

When the last stragglers had been hurried to their seats, the doors shut. The Temple grew dark. Fire sprang up from the braziers on the arena floor. The chanting began. The priests and priestess entered, bearing the charmed vipers in the baskets. Soon Judith would make her entrance. Raistlin's moment to act was fast approaching.

He was terrified. He knew very well what ailed him, recognized the symptoms—stage fright.

Raistlin had experienced stage fright before, but only very mildly, prior to his performances at the small fairs in Solace. The fear had always vanished the moment he began his act, and he had not worried about it.

He had never before performed to an audience of this size, an audience that must be considered hostile. He had never performed for stakes this large. His fear was a hundredfold greater than anything he'd previously experienced.

His hands were chilled to the bone, the fingers so stiff he did not think he could move them enough to draw the scroll from the case. His bowels gripped, and he thought for one horrible moment that he was going to be forced to leave to go find the privies. His mouth dried up. He could not speak a word. How was he to cast the spell if he couldn't talk? His body was drenched in sweat, he shivered with chills. His stomach heaved.

His performance was going to end in ignominy and shame, with him being sick all over himself.

The High Priest began his introduction. Raistlin didn't pay heed. He sat hunched over, miserable and deathly ill.

High Priestess Judith appeared in her blue robes. She was making her welcoming speech to the audience. Raistlin couldn't hear the words for the roaring in his ears. The time was fast approaching. Caramon was looking at him expectantly. Somewhere in the darkness, Kit was watching him. Sturm was waiting for his signal, so was Tasslehoff. They were waiting for him, counting on him, depending on him. They would understand his failure. They would be kind, never reproach him. They would pity him. . . .

Judith had lowered her arms. The sleeves cascaded down around her hands. She was preparing to cast the spell.

Raistlin fumbled at the scroll case, forcing his numb fingers to unfasten the lid. He drew forth the scroll, his hand shaking so he nearly dropped it. Panicked, afraid he would lose it in the darkness and not be able to recover it, he clenched his fist over it.

Slowly, trembling, Raistlin cast off his black cloak, rose to his feet. His neighbors glared at him in irritation. Someone behind him hissed loudly for him to sit down. When he didn't, more voices were raised. The commotion caused others to look in his direction, including one of the priests in the arena.

Raistlin searched his mind frantically for his carefully worded, oft-rehearsed speech. He couldn't recall any of it. Dazed by debilitating fear, he unrolled the scroll and looked at it, hoping it might give him some clue.

The letters of the magical words glowed faintly, pleasantly, as if they had been illuminated, the brush tipped with fire. The warmth of the magic spread from the scroll through his chilled fingers and brought with it reassurance. He possessed the ability to cast the spell, the skill to wield the magic. He would work his will on these people, hold them under his sway.

The knowledge enflamed him. An updraft of power consumed his fear.

His voice, when he spoke, was unfamiliar. Generally soft-spoken, he had not expected to sound so strong. He pitched his voice to where the acoustics would best amplify his words, and the result was dramatic. He startled even himself.

"Citizens of Haven," he called, "friends and neighbors. I stand before you to warn you that you are being duped!"

Mutterings and murmurs rumbled through the crowd. Some were angry, shouted for him to stop insulting the god. Others were annoyed, worried that he was going to disrupt the promised miracle. A few clapped, urged him on. They'd come to see a show, and this guaranteed that they'd get more than their money's worth. People craned their necks to see him, many stood up in their seats.

The priests and priestesses in the arena looked uncertainly at their leader, wondering what to do. At a signal from the High Priest, they raised their voices to try to drown out Raistlin's words with their chanting. Caramon was on his feet, standing protectively beside his brother, keeping a baleful eye upon the acolytes, who had grabbed torches and were hastening down the aisle toward them.

Raistlin paid no attention to the uproar. He was watching Judith. She had ceased her spell-casting. Locating him in the crowd, she stared at him. In the semidarkness, she did not recognize him. She saw his white robes, however, and immediately recognized her own danger. She was confounded, but only for a moment. Quickly she regained her composure.

"Beware the wizard!" she cried. "Seize him and take him away. His kind are forbidden in the temple. He comes to work his evil magic among us!"

"Let us hear more about evil magic, Widow Judith," Raistlin shouted.

She knew him then. Her face suffused with the blood of her rage. Her eyes widened, the white rims visible around the dilated pupils. Her pallid lips moved without speech. She stared at him, and he was appalled at the hatred he saw in her eyes, appalled and alarmed. His conviction wavered.

She sensed him faltering, and her lips parted in a terrible smile. She did what she should have done at first. Disdainfully she turned from him, ignored him.

The acolytes clattered down the steps toward him. Fortunately some of the audience had moved into the aisle, hoping to see better, and were blocking the way. Caramon, fists clenched, was ready to hold the acolytes off, but it would be only a matter of time before he was overwhelmed by sheer numbers.

"I can prove my accusations are true!" Raistlin cried. His voice cracked. People began to boo and hiss.

Embarrassed, feeling his audience slipping away, he struggled to retain his desperate hold. "The woman who calls herself a High Priestess performs what she calls a miracle. I say it is magic, and to prove it, I will cast the very same spell. Watch as I bring you another so-called god! Behold!"

Raistlin did not need the scroll. The words of the spell were in his blood. The magic formed a pool of fire around his fast-beating heart, his blood carried the magic into every part of his body. He recited the words of magic, pronouncing each correctly and precisely. reveling in the exhilarating sensation as the magic flowed like molten steel through his fingers, his hands, his arms.

Drawing on the energies of those watching him, utilizing even the hatred and fury of his enemies to his own advantage, Raistlin cast forth the magic. The spell streamed out of him, seemed to uplift him, carry him along on radiating waves of heat and fire.

A giant appeared before the audience. A fearful giant, a giant with a topknot, wearing green plaid pants and a purple silk shirt, a giant draped with pouches, a giant trying his very best to look as if he appreciated the enormity of the situation.

"Behold!" Raistlin called again. "The Giant Kender of Balifor!"

People gasped, then someone tittered. Someone else giggled, the nervous giggle of tense situations. The giant kender began moving down the aisle, his face so solemn and serious that his nose quivered with the effort.

"Summon Belzor!" cried one wit. "Sic Belzor on the kender!"

"My money's on the kender!" cried another.

Gales of merriment rippled through the crowd, most of whom had come to see a spectacle and were feeling well rewarded. A few of the faithful cried out in anger, demanded that the wizard cease his sacrilege, but the laughter, once started, was difficult to halt.

Laughter—a weapon as deadly as any spear.

"In this corner, Belzor . . ." cried out someone.

Roars of laughter. Four acolytes had made it down the stairs, were attempting to seize hold of Raistlin. Caramon pushed the acolytes back, knocking them aside with his bare hands.

Their neighbors, who were enjoying the show and didn't want it to end, joined in the shoving match. Some of the faithful sided with the acolytes. Three men who had come to the temple straight from the beer tent leapt eagerly into the fray, not caring whose side they took. A small riot erupted around Raistlin.

Shouts and screams and cries drew the attention of the Haven town guards who were in attendance. They had been glancing nervously at their captain, fearing that at any moment they might be ordered to arrest the giant kender. The captain himself was considerably baffled. He had sudden visions of the giant kender incarcerated in the Haven jail, with most of his torso and his topknotted head and shoulders sticking up through the hole they would have to cut in the roof.

Under these circumstances, a riot—plain and simple—was extremely welcome. Ignoring the giant kinder, the captain ordered his men to quell the riot.

The giant kender continued to march down the aisle, but few were paying attention to him anymore. By this time, most of the people in the arena were on their feet.

The prudent, seeing that the situation was quickly getting dangerously out of hand, gathered up their families and headed for the exits.

Thrill-seekers stood on their seats, trying to obtain a better view. Young men in the audience charged gleefully across the arena to take part in the fight. Several children, escaping their frantic mothers, were in hot pursuit of the giant kender.

A group of visiting dwarves were taking on all comers and swearing that this was the best religious meeting they had attended since before the time of the Cataclysm.

Raistlin stood on the marble seat, where he had taken refuge. The knowledge that he had wrought this confusion, that he had fomented this chaos, appalled him. And then, it thrilled him.

He tasted the power and its taste was sweet, sweeter to him than love, sweeter than gain. Raistlin saw for himself the fatal flaws in his fellow mortals. He saw their greed and prejudice, their gullibility, their perfidy, their baseness. He despised them for it, and he knew, in that instant, that he could make use of such flaws for his own ends, whatever those ends might be. He could use his power for good, if he chose. He could use it for ill.

He turned, in his triumph, to the High Priestess.

She was gone. Kitiara was gone, too, Raistlin realized in consternation.

He caught hold of the back of Caramon's shirt—the only part of him he could reach—and gave it a jerk. Caramon was wrestling two of the acolytes. He held one at arm's length, his hand at the throat of another. All the while he was telling them over and over that they should just settle down and leave honest people alone. The jerk on his collar half-strangled Caramon, caused him to twist his head around.

"Let them go!" Raistlin shouted. "Come with me!"

Fists flailed around them, men heaved and shoved and shouted and swore. In their attempt to restore order, the guards increased the confusion. Raistlin took a moment to search the crowd for Sturm, but couldn't find him. The giant kender had disappeared, the spell faded as the audience's readiness to believe in the illusion subsided. Tasslehoff, returned to his normal size, was buried beneath an avalanche of small boys.

The magic was gone from Raistlin as well, leaving him drained, as if he had cut open an artery, spilled his life's blood. Every movement took an effort, every word spoken required concentrated thought. He longed desperately to curl up under a soft blanket and sleep, sleep for days. But he dared not. Yet when he took a step, he swayed and nearly fell.

Caramon took firm hold of his brother's arm. "Raist, you look terrible! What's the matter? Are you sick? Here, I'll carry you."

"You will not! Shut up and listen to me!" Raistlin had neither the time nor the energy to waste on Caramon's nonsense. He started to thrust aside Caramon's supportive arm, then realized that he might well collapse without it. "Help me walk, then. Not that way, ninny! The door beneath the snake! We must find Judith!"

Caramon glowered. "Find that witch? What for? Good riddance. The Abyss take her!"

"You don't know what you're saying, Caramon," Raistlin gasped, foreboding sending a shudder through him. "Come with me or I will go myself."

"Sure, Raist," Caramon said, subdued, impressed by his brother's urgent tone. "Out of our way!" he cried, and punched a skinny town guardsman, who was trying ineffectually to get his hands around Caramon's thick neck.

Caramon helped Raistlin climb down from the seats, assisted him over the rope used to keep the faithful from entering the arena.

"Watch out for the vipers!" Raistlin warned, leaning on Caramon's strong arm. "The charm that held them is ended."

Caramon gave the snakes, swaying in their baskets, a wide berth. The High Priest and his followers had wisely fled the arena, leaving the vipers behind. Even as Raistlin spoke his warning, one of the snakes slid out of its basket and slithered across the floor.

People spilled into the arena, some trying to flee the melee, others seeking new opponents. A guard bumped into a brazier, spilling burning coals onto the straw which had been spread to deaden the noise. Gouts of flame shot up, wisps of smoke coiled into the air, further increasing the pandemonium as someone shouted hysterically that the building was on fire.

"This way!" Raistlin gestured toward the narrow doorway inside the stone statue of the snake.

The two entered a corridor of stone, lit by flickering torches. Several doors opened off the corridor on both sides. Raistlin looked into one of these, a large room, splendidly furnished, lit by hundreds of wax candles. In these rooms, Belzor's priests lived—lived well, by the looks of it—and worked. He had hoped to find Judith, but the room was empty, as was this part of the corridor. The followers of Belzor had deemed it wise to abandon the temple mob.

Glancing around in haste, Raistlin discovered that not all the faithful had fled. A lone figure crouched in a shadowed corner. He drew near to see it was one of the priestesses. Either she was injured or she had collapsed out of fear. Whatever the reason, the other servants of Belzar had abandoned her, left her huddled against the stone wall, weeping bitterly.

"Ask her where to find Judith!" Raistlin instructed. He deemed it wiser if he remained out of sight, hidden in the shadows behind his brother.

Caramon gently touched the priestess on the hand, to draw her attention. She started at his touch, lifted her tear-streaked face to stare at him fearfully.

"Where is the High Priestess?" Caramon asked.

"It wasn't my fault. She lied to us!" the girl said, gulping. "I believed her."

"Sure you did. Where—"

A scream, a scream of anger, rising shrilly to fear, was suddenly cut off, in a horrible gurgle. Raistlin was chilled to the bone with horror at the dreadful sound. The girl screamed herself, covered her ears with her hands.

"Where is Judith?" Caramon persisted. He had no idea what was going on, but he had his instructions. He wasn't going to let anything distract him. He shook the frightened girl.

"Her waiting room . . . is down there." The girl whimpered. She crouched on her knees. "You have to believe me! I didn't know . . ."

Caramon didn't wait to hear more. Raistlin was already moving down the corridor in the direction the girl had indicated. Caramon caught up with his twin at the end of the hall. Here the corridor branched off, ran in two different directions, forming a **Y**. The torches on the left side of the corridor, the side where Judith's room was located, had been doused. That portion of the temple was in darkness.

"We need light!" Raistlin commanded.

Caramon grabbed a torch from an iron sconce on the wall. He held it high.

Smoke from the burning straw in the arena had drifted through the doorway. The smoke slid in sinuous curls across the floor. The light shone on a single door which stood at the end of the dark corridor, gleamed off the symbol of the serpent made of gold which adorned the door.

"Did you hear that scream, Raist?" Caramon whispered uneasily, coming to a halt.

"Yes, and we weren't the only ones to hear it," Raistlin answered impatiently, casting his brother an annoyed glance. "What are you standing there for? Hurry up! People will be coming to investigate. We don't have much time."

Raistlin continued walking down the hall. After a moment's hesitation, Caramon hurried to his brother's side.

Raistlin rapped sharply on the door, only to find that it swung open at his touch.

"I don't like this, Raist," Caramon said, nervous and shaken. "Let's go."

Raistlin pushed on the door.

The room was brightly lit. Twenty or thirty thick candles stood on a ledge of stone inside the small chamber. Thick velvet curtains, hung from an interior door, closed off another room in the back, probably Judith's sleeping chamber. Wine in a pewter goblet and bread and meat, sustenance intended for the priestess's refreshment after her performance, had been placed on a small wooden table.

Judith no longer had need of food. Her performances were ended. The wizardess lay on the floor beneath the table. Blood covered the stone floor. Her throat had been slashed with such violence that the killer had almost severed the head from the neck.

At the horrible sight, Caramon retched, covered his eyes with his hands.

"Oh, Raist! I didn't mean it!" he mumbled, sickened. "About the Abyss! I didn't mean it!"

"Nevertheless, my brother," Raistlin said, regarding the corpse with terrible calm, "we may safely assume that the Abyss is where the Widow Judith is now residing. Come, we should leave immediately. No one must find us here."

As he started to turn away, he caught a flash out of the corner of his eye—torchlight glinting off metal. Looking closely, he saw a knife lying on the floor near the body. Raistlin knew that knife, he'd seen it before. He hesitated a split second, then, bending down, he snatched up the knife, slipped it into the sleeve of his robe.

"Quickly, my brother! Someone's coming!"

Outside, booted feet clattered; the girl was shrilly guiding the town guard to the High Priestess's chambers. Raistlin reached the door just as the captain of the guard entered, accompanied by several of his men. They stopped short at the sight of the body, alarmed and amazed. One guard turned away to be quietly sick in a corner.

The captain was an old soldier who'd seen death in many hideous aspects and was not unduly shocked by this one. He stared first at Judith, whom he had come to question about bilking money out of the good citizens of Haven, then he turned a stern gaze to the two young men. He recognized them both immediately as the two who had precipitated the evening's disastrous events.

Caramon, nearly as pale as the blood-drained corpse, said brokenly, "I—I didn't mean it."

Raistlin kept quiet, thinking quickly. The situation was desperate, circumstances were against them.

"What's this?" The captain pointed to a smear of blood on Raistlin's white robes.

"I have some small reputation as a healer. I bent down to examine her." Raistlin started to add, "to see if there were any signs of life." Glancing at the body, he realized how ludicrous that statement would sound. He clamped his mouth shut.

He was acutely aware of the knife clutched tightly in his hand. The blood on the hilt was sticky, was gumming his fingers. He was repulsed, would have given anything to have been able to wash it off.

Taking that knife had been an act of unbelievable stupidity. Raistlin cursed himself for his folly, couldn't imagine what had prompted him to do something so ill-judged. Some vague and instinctive desire to protect her, he supposed. She would have never done as much for him.

"The weapon's not here," said the captain after another glance at Raistlin's bloodstained robes and a cursory look around the room. "Search them both."

One of the guardsman seized hold of Raistlin, grabbed him roughly, pinned his arms. Another guard rolled up Raistlin's long sleeves, revealing the bloody knife, held fast in his blood-covered hand.

The captain smiled, grimly triumphant.

"First a giant kender, and now murder," he said. "You've had a busy night, young man."

17

THE HAVEN JAIL WAS NOT A PARTICULARLY NICE JAIL, AS TASSLEHOFF had complained. Located near the sheriff's house, the jail had once been a horse barn. It was drafty and cold, the dirt floors were strewn with refuse. The place stank of both horse and human piss and dung, mingled with vomit from those who had indulged too freely in dwarf spirits at the fair.

Raistlin didn't notice the smell, at least not after the first few seconds. He was too tired to notice. They could have hanged him—hanging being the penalty for murder in Haven—and he would not have protested. He sank down on a filthy straw mattress and fell into a sleep so deep that he didn't feel the rats skitter over his legs.

His dreamless, untroubled sleep provided much conversation among the jail's two guards. One held that such sleep was indicative of a mind innocent of murder, for all knew that a guilty conscience could never slumber peacefully. The other guard, older, scoffed at this notion. It proved the young man to be a hardened criminal, since he could sleep that soundly with the blood of his victim still on his hands.

Raistlin did not hear their arguments, nor did he hear the noisy voices of his fellow prisoners, mostly kender. The kender were filled with excitement, for this had been an eventful day, complete with a riot, a conflagration, a murder, and, most wonderfully, one of their own transformed into a giant. Not even Uncle Trapspringer had been known to accomplish such a magnificent feat. The giant kender was to become a celebrated figure in kender song and story ever after that, often seen striding across the oceans and hopping from mountaintop to mountaintop. If there was ever a night when the silver and red moons didn't rise, it was widely known that the giant kender had "borrowed" them.

Eager to discuss this momentous occasion, the kender were constantly in and out of each other's cells, picking the locks almost before the cell doors were shut. As soon as the guards had one kender locked up, two more were out roaming around.

"He's shivering," observed the young guard, glancing into Raistlin's cell during one of the few lulls given them by the kender, a lull that was quite ominous, if only they'd thought about it. "Should I get him a blanket?"

"Naw," said the jailkeep with a leer. "He'll be warm enough. Too warm, if you take my meaning. They say it's hotter'n the smithy's forge in the Abyss."

"I guess there'll be a trial first, before they hang him," said the young guard, who was new to the area.

"The sheriff will hold one, for form's sake." The jailer shrugged. "Myself, I don't see the need. He was caught with the knife in his hand standing over the body." He dredged up a filthy blanket. "Here, you can cover him up if you want. 'Twould be a shame if he caught cold and died before the hanging. Hand over the keys."

"I don't have the keys. I thought you had the keys." As it turned out, the kender had the keys. They poured out of their cells and were soon having a picnic in the middle of the jail.

Intent on endeavoring to persuade the kender to return their keys, the jailer and the lone guard were too distracted to notice the flare of torchlight approaching the prison, nor could they hear over the shouts of the kender, the shouts of the approaching mob.

Raistlin, exhausted from the spellcasting and the sheriff's questioning, had fallen into a comatose-like sleep and heard nothing.

☻

Caramon did not see the torchlight either. He was far from the jail, running as fast as he possibly could for the fairgrounds.

Caramon had narrowly escaped being made a prisoner himself. When questioned by Haven's sheriff, Caramon steadfastly denied all knowledge of the crime, denied it in the name of himself and his brother. Raistlin had wearily repeated his own story. He had knelt beside the body to examine the victim. He had no idea why he had picked up the knife or why he had tried to hide it. He had been in a state of shock, did not know what he was doing. He added, emphatically, that Caramon was not involved.

Fortunately a witness, the young priestess, came forward to claim that she had been speaking to Caramon in the hallway when they heard Judith scream. Caramon swore that his twin had been with him at the time, but the girl said she had seen only one of them.

Due to this alibi, the sheriff reluctantly released Caramon. He gave his brother one loving, anxious, worried look—a look that Raistlin ignored—and then hurried off to the fairgrounds.

On his way, Caramon mulled things over in his mind. People accused him of being dull-witted, slow. He was not dull-witted, but he was slow, though not in the popular use of the term, meaning stupid. He was a thinker, a slow and deliberate thinker, one who considered every aspect of a problem before finally arriving at the solution. The fact that he invariably arrived at the right solution often went unnoticed by most people.

Caramon had several miles to consider this terrible predicament. The sheriff had been quite candid. There would be a trial as a matter of form, though its outcome was a foregone conclusion. Raistlin would be found guilty of murder, he would pay for his crime by hanging. The hanging would likely take place that very day, as soon as they could assemble the gallows.

By the time he reached the fairgrounds, Caramon had come to a decision. He knew what he had to do.

The fairgrounds were quiet. Here and there a light shone from behind the shutters of a booth, although it was well into the morning hours. Some craftsmen were still hard at work replenishing their stock for tomorrow's opening. Tomorrow would be the last day of the fair, the last day to entice customers, the last day to urge the buyer to part with his steel.

Word of the excitement in Haven had either not yet reached the fairgrounds, or, if it had, the participants had listened to it as a good story, little thinking it would have any effect on them. They would feel differently in the morning. If there was a murder trial and a hanging tomorrow, attendance at the fair would fall to almost nothing, sales would be down.

Caramon found Flint's stall by tracing the lumpy outlines of the various buildings, silhouetted against the lambent light of stars and the red moon, which was full and exceedingly bright. Caramon took this as a good omen. Though Raistlin wore white robes, he had once remarked that he favored Lunitari.

Caramon looked for Sturm, but he was nowhere to be found, nor was Tasslehoff around. Caramon went to Tanis's tent, hesitated at the tent flap.

Desperate, Caramon had no compunction about interrupting any sort of pleasurable activity that might be taking place inside. Listening, he could hear nothing. He lifted the flap, peeked in. Tanis was alone, asleep, though not peacefully. He murmured something in an unknown language, probably elven, tossed restlessly. Evidently the quarrel remained unresolved. Caramon lowered the flap, backed away.

Entering the tent he shared with his twin, Caramon was not surprised to find Kitiara inside, rolled up in a blanket. By her even breathing, she was sleeping soundly and contentedly. Red moonlight flowed in after Caramon, as though Lunitari herself was intent on being present at this interview. Anger and awe vied for the uppermost position in Caramon's soul.

Squatting down, he touched Kit's shoulder. He had to shake her several times to rouse her, and by this and the poor job of acting she did on rolling over and feigning not to immediately recognize him, he concluded that she had been shamming, playing possum. Kit was not one to let anyone sneak up on her, as Caramon himself knew from past painful experience.

"Who is that? Caramon?" Kit affected a yawn, ran her hand through her tousled hair. "What do you want? What time is it?"

"They've arrested Raistlin," Caramon said.

"Yes, well, I'm not surprised. We'll pay his fine and get him out of jail in the morning." Kit drew the blanket over her shoulders, turned away.

"They've arrested him for murder." Caramon spoke to his sister's back. "For the murder of the Widow Judith. We found her dead in her chambers. Her throat had been cut. There was a knife beside the body. Raistlin and I both recognized that knife. We'd seen it before—on your knife belt."

He fell silent, waiting.

Kitiara held still a moment, then, throwing off the blanket, she sat up. She was dressed in her hose and long-sleeved shirt. She had removed her leather vest, but she was wearing her boots.

She was nonchalant, easy, even slightly amused. "So why did they arrest Raistlin?"

"They found him holding the knife."

Kit grimaced. "That was stupid. Baby brother usually doesn't make stupid mistakes like that. As for recognizing the knife"—she shrugged—"there are a lot of knives in this world."

"Not many with Flint's mark, or the way you wrap the hilt with braided leather. It was your knife, Kit. Both Raistlin and I know it."

"You do, do you?" Kit quirked an eyebrow. "Did Raistlin say anything?"

"No, of course not. He wouldn't." Caramon was grim. "Not until I talked to you about it. But he's going to."

"They won't believe him."

"Then you're going to say something. You killed her, didn't you, Kit?"

Kitiara shrugged again, made no reply. The red moonlight, reflected in her dark eyes, never wavered.

Caramon stood up. "I'm going to tell them, Kit. I'm going to tell them the truth." He bent down, started to duck out the tent.

Kit twisted to her feet, seized hold of his sleeve. "Caramon, wait! There's something you have to consider. Something you haven't thought about." She tugged him back inside the tent, closed the flap, shutting out the moonlight.

"Well"—Caramon regarded her coldly—"what's that?"

Kit drew closer to Caramon. "Did you know Raistlin could do magic like that?"

"Like what?" Caramon was puzzled.

"Cast a spell like the one he cast tonight. It was a powerful spell, Caramon. I know. I've been around magic-users some, and I've seen . . . Well, never mind what I've seen, but trust me on this. What Raistlin did he shouldn't have been able to do. Not as young as he is."

"He's good at magic," Caramon said, still not comprehending what this was all about. He might have added, in the same tone, that Raistlin was good at gardening or at cooking fried eggs, for that was how Caramon viewed it.

Kit made an impatient gesture. "Are you part gully dwarf to be so thickheaded? Can't you understand?" She lowered her voice to a hissing whisper. "Listen to me, Caramon. You say Raistlin is good at magic. I say he's too good at magic. I hadn't realized it until tonight. I thought he was just playing at being a wizard. How could I know he was this powerful? I didn't expect—"

"What are you saying, Kit?" Caramon demanded, starting to lose patience.

"Let them have him, Caramon," Kitiara said, soft, quiet. "Let them hang him! Raistlin is dangerous. He's like one of those vipers. As long as he's charmed, he'll be nice. But if you cross him . . . Don't go back to the prison, Caramon. Just go to bed. In the morning, if anyone asks you about the knife, say it was his. That's all you have to do, Caramon. And everything will be over with quickly."

Caramon was struck dumb, her words hitting him like a blow that left him too dazed to think what to say.

Kit couldn't read the blank expression on his face in the darkness. Judging him by her own standards, she guessed that he was tempted.

"Then it's you and me, Caramon," she continued. "I've had an offer of a job up north. The pay is good, and it will keep getting better. It's mercenary work. What we always talked about doing, you and I. I'll put in a good word for you. The lord will take you on. He's looking for trained soldiers. You'll be free of Solace, free of entanglements"—she cast a narrow-eyed glance in the direction of Tanis's tent, then looked back to her half-brother—"free to do what you want. What do you say? Are you with me?"

"You want me . . . to let Raistlin . . . die?" Caramon asked hoarsely, the last word nearly choking him.

"Just let whatever's going to happen, happen," Kit said soothingly, spreading her hands. "It will be for the best."

"You can't mean that!" He stared, incredulous. "You're not serious."

"Don't be an idiot, Caramon!" Kit said sternly. "Raistlin's using you! He always has, he always will! He doesn't care a Flotsam penny for you. He'll use you to get what he wants, then when he's finished with you, he'll throw you away as if you were a bit of rag he'd use to wipe his ass. He'll make your life hell, Caramon! Hell! Let them hang him! It won't be your fault."

Caramon backed away from her, nearly taking down the tent post. "How can you . . . No, I won't do it!" He began fumbling with the tent flap, trying desperately to get out.

Kit lunged at him, dug her nails into his flesh. Her face loomed close to his, so close that he could feel her breath hot on his cheek. "I would have expected such an answer from Sturm or Tanis. But not you! You're not a sap, Caramon. Think about what I've said!"

Caramon shook his head violently. He felt nauseous, the same way he'd felt when he'd first seen the murdered corpse. He was still trying to get out of the tent, but he was so flustered and upset that he couldn't find his way.

Kit regarded him in silence, her hands on her hips. Then she gave a exasperated sigh.

"Quit it!" she ordered irritably. "Stop thrashing about! You're going to knock the tent over. Just calm down, will you? I didn't mean it. It was all a joke. I wouldn't let Raistlin hang."

"That's your idea of a joke?" Caramon wiped the chill sweat from his brow. "I'm not laughing. Are you going to tell them the truth?"

"What the hell good will that do?" Kit demanded, adding with a flash of anger, "You want to see me hang instead? Is that it?"

Caramon was silent, miserable.

"I didn't kill her," Kit said coldly.

"Your knife—"

"Someone stole it in the confusion in the temple. Took it from my belt. I would have told you if you had asked me, instead of accusing me like that. That's the truth. That's what happened, but do you think anyone will believe me?"

No, Caramon was quite certain no one would believe her.

"Come along," Kit ordered. "We'll wake Tanis. He'll know what to do."

She laced on her leather vest. Her sword lay on the floor, next to where she'd been sleeping. Grabbing hold of it, she buckled the belt around her waist.

"Not a word about my little joke to the half-elf," she said to Caramon, lightly stroking his arm. "He wouldn't understand."

Caramon nodded his head, unable to speak. He wouldn't tell anyone, ever. It was too shameful, too horrible. Perhaps it had been a joke—gallows humor. But Caramon didn't think so. He could still hear her words, the vehemence with which they were spoken. He could still see the eerie light in her eyes. He drew away from her. Her touch made his flesh crawl.

Kit patted him on the arm, as if he were a good child who had eaten all his porridge. Shoving past him, she strode out the tent, yelling Tanis's name as she walked.

Caramon was heading for the booth to wake up Flint when he heard a loud voice shouting, echoing through the fairgrounds.

"There's going to a wizard-burning! Come and see! They're going to burn the wizard!"

18

RAISTLIN STARTED TO WAKEFULNESS, A SENSE OF DANGER BURSTING LIKE lightning on his sleep, jolting him out of terrifying dreams. Instinctively he kept still, shivering beneath a thin blanket, until his mind was awake and active and he had located the source of the danger.

He smelled the smoke of burning torches, heard the voices outside the prison, and lay immobilized, listening fearfully.

"And I tell you men," the guard was saying, "the wizard's trial'll be held tomorrow. Today, that is. You'll have your say then before the High Sheriff."

"The High Sheriff has no jurisdiction in this case!" a deep voice responded. "The wizard murdered my wife, our priestess! He will burn this night, as all witches must burn for their heinous crimes! Stand aside, jailer. There's only two of you and more than thirty of us. We don't want innocent people to get hurt."

In the adjacent cells, the kender were chattering with excitement, shoving benches over to the windows in order to see and lamenting the fact that they were locked up in prison and would miss the wizard's roasting. At this, someone suggested they once again pick the lock. Unfortunately, following the theft of their keys, the guards had added a chain and padlock to the kenders' cell door, which considerably raised the level of difficulty. Nothing daunted, the kender set to work.

"Rankin! Go fetch the captain," the jailkeep ordered. There came the sound of a scuffle outside, shouts, cursings, and a cry of pain.

"Here are the keys," said the same deep voice. "Two of you, enter the jail and bring him out."

"What about the captain of the guard and the sheriff?" a voice asked. "Won't they try to interfere?"

"Some of our brethren have already dealt with them. They will not trouble us this night. Go fetch the wizard."

Raistlin jumped to his feet, trying desperately to quell his panic and think what to do. His few magic spells came to mind, but the jailer had taken away the pouches containing his spell components. Between his extreme weariness and his fright, he doubted if he had strength or wit enough to cast them anyway.

And what good would they do me? he reflected bitterly. I could not send thirty people to sleep. I might be able to cast a spell that would hold the cell door shut, but as weak as I am, I could not maintain it for long. I have no other weapons. I am helpless! Completely at their mercy!

The priests in their sky-blue robes appeared, holding their torches high, searching one cell after another. Raistlin fought the wild, panicked urge to hide in a shadowy corner. He pictured them finding him, dragging him out ignominiously. He forced himself to wait in stoic calm for them to reach him. Dignity and pride were all he had left. He would maintain them to the end.

He thought fleetingly, hopefully, of Caramon, but then dismissed the hope as being unrealistic. The fairgrounds were far from the prison. Caramon had no way of knowing what was going on. He would not return until morning, and by then it would be too late.

One of the priests stood in front of Raistlin's cell.

"Here he is! In here!"

Raistlin clasped his hands together tightly to keep from revealing how he trembled. He faced them defiantly, his face a cold, proud mask to conceal his fear.

The priests had keys to the cell; the jailer had not put up much of a fight. Ignoring the pleadings and wailings of the kender, who were having a difficult time removing the padlock, the priests opened Raistlin's cell. They seized hold of him, bound his hands with a length of rope.

"You'll not work any more of your foul magic on us," said one.

"It's not my magic you fear," Raistlin told them, speaking proudly, pleased that his voice did not crack. "It is my words. That is why you want to kill me before I can stand trial. You know that if I have a chance to speak, I will denounce you for the thieves and charlatans that you are."

One of the priests struck Raistlin across the face. The blow rocked him backward, knocked loose a tooth and split open his lip. He tasted blood. The cell and the priests wavered in his sight.

"Don't knock him unconscious!" scolded the other priest. "We want him wide awake to feel the flames licking him!"

They took hold of Raistlin by the arms, hustled him out of the cell, moving so rapidly that they nearly swept him off his feet. He stumbled after them, forced to almost run to keep from falling. Whenever he slowed, they jerked him forward, gripping his arms painfully.

The jailkeep stood huddled by the door, head down and eyes lowered. The young guard, who had apparently made some attempt to defend the prisoner, lay unconscious on the ground, blood forming a pool beneath his head.

The priests gave a cheer when Raistlin was brought forth. The cheer ceased immediately, at a sharp command from the High Priest. Quietly, with deadly intent, they surrounded Raistlin, looked to their leader for orders.

"We will take him back to the temple and execute him there. His death will serve as an example to others who may have it in mind to cross us.

"After the wizard's dead, we will claim that none of us saw the giant kender. We will send out our claque to make the same pronouncements. Soon those who did see it will begin to doubt their senses. We will maintain that the wizard, frightened of the power of Belzor, started a riot in order that he might slip away unnoticed and murder our priestess."

"Will that work?" asked someone dubiously. "People saw what they saw."

"They'll soon change their minds. Seeing the charred body of the wizard in front of the temple will help them reach the right decision. Those who don't will face the same fate."

"What about the wizard's friends? The dwarf and the half-elf and the rest of them?"

"Judith knew them, told me all about them. We have nothing to fear. The sister's a whore. The dwarf's a drunken sot who cares only for his ale mug. The half-elf's a mongrel, a sniveling coward like all elves. They won't cause any trouble. They'll be only too happy to slink out of town. Start chanting, someone," the High Priest snapped. "It will look better if we do this in the name of Belzor."

Raistlin managed a bleak smile, though it reopened the wound on his split lip. At the thought of his friends, his despair lessened and he grew hopeful. The priests didn't want him dead nearly as much as they needed the drama of his death, needed it to instill the fear of Belzor in the minds of the populace. This delay could work to his advantage. The noise and the light and the uproar in the town must be noticed, even as far away as the fairgrounds.

Taking up the chant, shouting praise to Belzor, the priests dragged Raistlin through the streets of Haven. The sound of loud chanting and the light of flaring torches brought people from their beds to the windows. Seeing the spectacle, they hastily donned their clothes, hurried out to watch. The ne'er-do-wells in the taverns left their drinking to see what all the commotion was about. They were quick to join the mob, and fell in behind the priests. Drunken shouts now punctuated the priests' chanting.

The pain of his swelling jaw made Raistlin's head ache unbearably. The ropes cut into his flesh, the priests pinched his arms. He struggled to remain on his feet, lest he fall and be trampled. It was all so unreal, he felt no fear.

Fear would come later. For now, he was in a nightmare existence, a dreamworld from which there would be no awakening.

The torchlight blinded him. He could see nothing but an occasional face—mouth leering, eyes gleefully staring—illuminated in the light, vanishing swiftly in the darkness, only to be replaced by another. He caught a glimpse of the young woman who had lost the child, saw her face, grieved, pitying, afraid. She reached out her hand to him as if she would have helped, but the priests shoved her brutally back.

The Temple of Belzor loomed in the distance. The stone structure had not been damaged in the fire, apparently, only portions of the interior. A crowd had gathered on the broad expanse of grass in front of the temple to watch a man in blue robes drive a large wooden pole into the ground. Other priests tossed faggots of wood around the stake.

Many of Haven's citizens were assisting the priests to build the pyre. Some of the very same citizens, who had only hours before jeered the priests, laughed at him and mocked him. Raistlin was not surprised. Here again was evidence of the ugliness of mankind. Let them be subjugated, robbed, and hoodwinked by Belzor. He and his followers deserved each other.

The priests and the mob hauled Raistlin down the street leading to the temple. They were very close to the stake now, and where was Caramon? Where were Kit and Tanis? Suppose the priests had managed to intercept them, waylay them? Suppose they were battling for their lives inside the fairgrounds, with no way to reach him? Suppose—chilling thought—they had seen that rescue was hopeless, had given up?

The mob picked up the chant, shouting, "Belzor! Belzor!" in an insane litany. Raistlin's hopes died, his fear sprang horribly to life. Then a voice rang out over the wild chanting and the shrieks and laughter.

"Halt! What is the meaning of this?"

Raistlin lifted his head.

Sturm Brightblade stood in the center of the street, blocking the priests' way, standing between the stake and its victim. Illuminated by the light of many torches, Sturm was an impressive sight. He stood tall and unafraid, his long mustaches bristling. His stern face was older than its years. He held naked steel in his hand; torchlight flared along the blade as if the metal had caught fire. He was proud and fierce, calm and dignified, a fixed point in the center of swirling turmoil.

The crowd hushed, from awe and respect. The priests in the vanguard halted, daunted by this young man who was not a knight but who was made knightly by his demeanor, his stance, and his courage. Sturm seemed an apparition, sprung from the legendary time of Huma. Uncertain and uneasy, the priests in front looked to the High Priest in the back for orders.

"You fools!" the High Priest shouted at them in fury. "He's one man and alone! Knock him aside and keep going!"

A rock sailed out from the midst of the watching mob, struck Sturm in the forehead. He clapped his hand over the wound, staggered where he stood. Yet he did not leave his place in the road, nor did he drop his sword. Blood poured from his face, obliterating his vision in one eye. Lifting his sword, he advanced grimly on the priests.

The mob had tasted blood, they were eager for more, so long as it wasn't their own. Several ruffians ran from the crowd, jumped on Sturm from behind. Yelling and cursing, kicking and pummeling, the men bore him to the ground.

The priests hustled their captive to the stake. Raistlin cast a glance at his friend. Sturm lay groaning in the road, blood covered his torn clothing. And then the mob surged around Raistlin and he could see his friend no more.

He had quite given up hope. Caramon and the others were not coming. The knowledge came to Raistlin that he was going to die, die most horribly and painfully.

The wooden post thrust up from the center of the pile of wood, dry wood that snapped underfoot. The jutting branches caught on Raistlin's robes, tearing the cloth as the priests shoved him near the stake. Roughly they turned him around, so that he faced the crowd, which was all gleaming eyes and gaping, hungry mouths. The dry wood was being doused with liquid—dwarf spirits, by the smell of it. This was not the priests' doing, but some of the more drunken revelers.

The priests tied Raistlin's wrists together behind the stake, then they wound coils of rope around his chest and torso, binding him tightly He was held fast, and though he struggled with all his remaining strength, he could not free himself. The High Priest had been going to make a speech, but some eager drunk flung a torch on the wood before the priests had finished tying up their prisoner, nearly setting the High Priest himself on fire. He and the others were forced to jump and skip with unseemly haste away from the pyre. The liquor-soaked wood caught quickly. Tongues of flame licked the tinder, began to devour it.

Smoke stung Raistlin's eyes, filled them with tears. He closed them against the flames and the smoke and cursed his feebleness and helplessness. He braced himself to endure the agonizing torment when the flames reached his skin.

"Hullo, Raistlin!" chimed a voice directly behind him. "Isn't this exciting? I've never seen anyone burned at the stake before. 'Course, I would much rather it wasn't you—"

All the while that Tasslehoff prattled, his knife cut rapidly through the knots on the rope that bound Raistlin's wrists.

"The kender!" came hoarse, angry shouts. "Stop him!"

"Here, I thought this might help!" Tas said hurriedly.

Raistlin felt the hilt of a knife shoved into his hand.

"It's from your friend, Lemuel. He says to—"

Raistlin was never to know what Lemuel said, because at that moment an enormous bellow broke over the crowd. People screamed and shouted in alarm. Steel flared in the torchlight. Caramon loomed suddenly in front of Raistlin, who could have broken down and wept with joy at the sight of his brother's face. Oblivious to the pain, Caramon snatched up whole bundles of burning wood and flung them aside.

Tanis had placed his back to Caramon's, swung the flat of his blade, knocking away torches and clubs. Kitiara fought at her lover's side. She was not using the flat of her blade. One priest lay bleeding at her feet. Kit fought with a smile on her lips, her dark eyes bright with the fun of it all.

Flint was there, wrestling with the priests who had hold of Tasslehoff and were trying to drag him into the temple. The dwarf attacked them with such roaring ferocity that they soon let loose of the kender and fled. Sturm appeared, wielding his sword with dispatch, the blood forming a mask on his face.

Haven's citizens, though sorry to see that the wizard wasn't going to go up in flames, were diverted and entertained by the daring rescue. The fickle mob turned against the priests, cheered the heroes. The High Priest fled for the safety of the temple. His cohorts—those who remained standing, at least—followed in haste. The mob hurled rocks and made plans to storm the temple.

Relief and the realization that he was safe, that he was not going to die in the fire, flooded through Raistlin in a tidal surge that left him faint and dazed. He sagged against his bonds.

Caramon snatched the ropes from around Raistlin's body and caught hold of his fainting brother. Lifting Raistlin in his arms, Caramon carried him away from the stake and laid him on the ground.

People crowded around, eager to help save the young man whom they had been just as eager to see burn to death only moments earlier.

"Clear off, you buggers!" Flint roared, waving his arms and glowering. "Give him air."

Someone handed the dwarf a bottle of fine brandy "to give to the brave young man."

"Thankee," Flint said and took a long pull to fortify himself, then handed over the bottle.

Caramon touched the brandy to Raistlin's lips. The sting of the liquor on his cut lip and the fiery liquid biting into his throat brought him to consciousness. He gagged, choked, and thrust the brandy bottle away.

"I have narrowly escaped being burned to death, Caramon! Would you now poison me?" Raistlin coughed and wretched.

He struggled to his feet, ignoring Caramon's protestations that he should rest. The mob had surrounded the temple, shouting that the priests of Belzor should all be burned.

"Was the young man hurt?" came a worried voice. "I have an ointment for burns."

"It's all right, Caramon," Raistlin said, halting his brother, who was attempting to shoo away the curious. "This is a friend of mine."

Lemuel gazed at Raistlin anxiously. "Did they hurt you?"

"No, sir. I have taken no hurt, thank you. I am only a little dazed by it all."

"This ointment"—Lemuel held up a small jar. "I made it myself. It comes from the aloe—"

"Thank you," said Raistlin, accepting the jar. "I don't need it, but I believe that my brother could use it."

He cast a glance at Caramon's hands, which were burned and blistered. Caramon flushed and grinned self-consciously, thrust his hands behind his back.

"Thank you for the knife," Raistlin added, offering to return it. "Fortunately I had no need to use it."

"Keep it! It's the least I can do. Thanks to you, young man, I won't have to leave my home."

"But you have given me your books," Raistlin argued, holding out the knife.

Lemuel waved the knife away. "It belonged to my father. He would have wanted a magus like you to have it. It certainly does me no good, although

I did find it useful to aerate the soil around my gardenias. There's a quaint sort of leather thong that goes with it. He used to wear the knife concealed on his arm. A wizard's last defense, he called it."

The knife was a very fine one, made of sharp steel. By the slight tingle he experienced holding it, Raistlin guessed that it had been imbued with magic. He thrust the knife into his belt and shook hands most warmly with Lemuel.

"We'll be stopping by later for those books," Raistlin said.

"I should be very pleased if you and your friends would take tea with me," Lemuel replied, with a polite bow.

After more bows and further introductions and promises to drop by on their way out of town, Lemuel departed, eager to put his uprooted plants back in the ground.

This left the companions alone. The citizens who had surrounded the temple were dispersing. Rumor had it that the priests of Belzor had escaped by way of certain underground passages and were fleeing for their lives into the mountains. There was talk of forming a hunting party to go after them. It was now almost dawn. The morning was raw and chill. The drunks were dull-headed and sleepy. Men recalled that they had to work in the fields, women suddenly remembered their children left home alone. The citizens of Haven straggled off, left the priests to the goblins and ogres in the mountains.

The companions turned their steps back to the fairgrounds. The fair lasted for one more day, but Flint had already announced his intention of leaving.

"I'll not spend one minute longer than need be in this foul city. The people here are daft. Just plain daft. First snakes, then hangings, now burnings. Daft," he muttered into his beard. "Just plain daft."

"You'll miss a day's sales," Tanis observed.

"I don't want their money," the dwarf said flatly. "Likely it's cursed. I'm seriously considering giving away what I've already taken."

He didn't, of course. The strongbox containing the money would be the first object the dwarf packed, stowing it securely and secretly underneath the wagon's seat.

"I want to thank you all," Raistlin said as they walked along the empty streets. "And I want to apologize for putting you at risk. You were right, Tanis. I underestimated these people. I didn't realize how truly dangerous they were. I will know better next time."

"Let's hope there isn't a next time," Tanis said, smiling.

"And I want to thank you, Kitiara," Raistlin said.

"For what?" Kit smiled her crooked smile. "For rescuing you?"

"Yes," said Raistlin dryly. "For rescuing me."

"Anytime!" Kit said, laughing and slapping him on the shoulder. "Anytime."

Caramon looked upset at this, and solemn. He turned his head away.

Battle suited Kitiara. Her cheeks were flushed, her eyes glittered, her lips were red, as if she had drunk the blood she spilled. Kit, still laughing, took hold of Tanis's arm, hugged him close. "You are a very fine swordsman, my friend. You could earn a good living with that blade of yours. I'm surprised you haven't considered something in the mercenary line."

"I earn a good living now. A safe living," he added, but he was smiling at her, pleased by her admiration.

"Bah!" Kit said scornfully. "Safety's for fat old men! We fight well together, side by side. I've been thinking . . ."

She drew Tanis away, lowered her voice. Apparently the quarrel between the two was forgotten.

"Aren't you going to thank me, too, Raistlin?" Tasslehoff cried, dancing around Raistlin. "Look at this." The kender sadly twitched his topknot over his shoulder. The smell of burnt hair was very strong. "I got a bit singed, but the fight was worth it, even if I didn't get to see you being burned at the stake. I'm pretty disappointed about that, but I know you couldn't help it." Tas gave Raistlin an conciliatory hug.

"Yes, Tas, I do thank you," Raistlin said and removed his new knife from the kender's hand. "And I want to thank you, Sturm. What you did was extremely brave. Foolhardy, but brave."

"They had no right to try to execute you without first giving you a fair trial. They were wrong, and it was my duty to stop them. However . . ."

Sturm came to a halt in the road. Standing stiffly, his hand pressed against his injured ribs, he faced Raistlin. "I have given the matter serious thought as we've been walking, and I must insist that you turn yourself over to the High Sheriff of Haven."

"Why should I? I've done nothing wrong."

"For the murder of the priestess," Sturm said, frowning, thinking Raistlin was being flippant.

"He didn't kill the Widow Judith, Sturm," Caramon said quietly, calmly. "She was dead when we entered that room."

Troubled, Sturm looked from one twin to the other. "I have never known you to lie, Caramon. But I think you might if your brother's life depended on it."

"I might," Caramon agreed, "but I'm not lying now. I swear to you on the grave of my father that Raistlin is innocent of this murder."

Sturm gazed long at Caramon, then nodded once, convinced. They resumed walking.

"Do you know who did kill her?" Sturm asked.

The brothers exchanged glances.

"No," Caramon said and stared down at his boots, kicking up dust in the road.

❂

It was daylight by the time they reached the fairgrounds. The vendors were opening their stalls, preparing for the morning's business. They received Raistlin as a hero, lauded his exploits, applauded as the companions walked to Flint's shop. But no one spoke to them directly.

Flint did not open his stall. Leaving the shutters closed, he began to move his wares to the wagon. When several of the other vendors, overcome by curiosity, did finally drop by to hear the tale, they were gruffly repulsed by the dwarf and went away, offended.

There was one more visitor, one more scare. The High Sheriff himself appeared, looking for Raistlin. Kit drew her sword, told her brother to make himself scarce, and it seemed as if there was going to be yet another fight. Raistlin told her to put away her weapon.

"I'm innocent," he said, with a significant look for his sister.

"You were nearly a crispy innocent," Kit returned angrily, sheathing her sword with an impatient thrust. "Go on, then. And don't expect me to save you this time."

But the sheriff had come to apologize. He did so, grudgingly and awkwardly. The young priestess had come forth to admit that she had seen Raistlin in company with his twin at the time the murder was committed. She had not told the truth before, she said, because she hated the wizard for what he had done to instigate Belzor's downfall. She was horrified by the High Priest's actions, wanted nothing more to do with any of them.

"What will happen to her?" Caramon asked worriedly.

"Nothing." The sheriff shrugged. "The young ones were like the rest of us—fooled completely by the murdered woman and her husband. They'll get over it. We all will, I suppose."

He fell silent, squinted into the sun that was just topping the trees, then said, not looking at them, "We don't take kindly to mages in Haven. Lemuel, now—he's different. He's harmless. We don't mind him. But we don't need any more."

"He should have thanked you," Caramon said, puzzled and hurt.

"For what?" Raistlin asked with a bitter smile. "Destroying his career? If the sheriff didn't know that Judith and the rest of Belzor's followers were frauds, then he's one of the biggest fools in Abanasinia. If he did know, then he was undoubtedly being paid well to leave them alone. Either way, he's finished. You had better let me put some ointment on those burns, my brother. You are obviously in pain."

Once he had treated Caramon, cleaning the burns and covering them with the healing salve, Raistlin left the others to finish the packing, went to lie down in the wagon. He was completely and utterly exhausted, so tired he was almost sick. He was just about to climb inside when a stranger clad in brown robes approached him.

Raistlin turned his back on him, hoping the man would take the hint and leave. The man had the look of a cleric, and Raistlin had seen clerics enough to last him a lifetime.

"I want just a moment, young man," the stranger said, plucking at Raistlin's sleeve. "I know you have had a trying day. I want to thank you for bringing down the false god Belzor. My followers and I are eternally in your debt."

Raistlin grunted, pulled his arm away, and climbed into the wagon. The man hung on to the wagon's sides, peered over them.

"I am Hederick, the High Theocrat," he announced with a self-important air. "I represent a new religious order. We hope to gain a foothold here in Haven now that the rogues of Belzor have been driven away. We are known as the Seekers, for we seek the true gods."

"Then I hope very much that you find them, sir," Raistlin said.

"We are certain of it!" The man had missed the sarcasm. "Perhaps you'd be interested—"

Raistlin wasn't. The tents and bedrolls had been stacked in one corner of the wagon. Unfolding a blanket, he spread it out over the pile of tenting, lay down.

The cleric hung about, yammering about his god. Raistlin covered his head with the hood of his robe and, eventually, the cleric departed. Raistlin thought no more of him, soon forgot the man entirely.

Lying in the wagon, Raistlin tried to sleep. Every time he closed his eyes, he saw the flames, felt the heat, smelled the smoke, and he was wide awake, awake and shivering.

He recalled with terrifying clarity his feeling of helplessness. Resting his hand on the hilt of his new knife, he wrapped his fingers around the weapon, felt the blade, cold, sharp, reassuring. From now on, he would never be without it. His last measure of defense, even if it meant his life was his to take and not his enemy's.

His thoughts went from this knife to the other knife, the bloody knife he'd found lying beside the murdered woman. The knife he had recognized as belonging to Kitiara.

Raistlin sighed deeply, and at last he was able to close his eyes, relax into slumber.

Rosamun's children had taken their revenge.

BOOK 5

The aspiring magus, Raistlin Majere, is hereby summoned to the Tower of High Sorcery at Wayreth to appear before the Conclave of Wizards on the seventh day of the seventh month at the seventh minute of the seventh hour. At this time, in this place, you will be tested by your superiors for inclusion into the ranks of those gifted by the three gods, Solinari, Lunitari, Nuitari.

—The Conclave of Wizards

RAISTLIN
CHRONICLES

1

THAT WINTER WAS ONE OF THE MILDEST SOLACE HAD KNOWN, WITH RAIN and fog in place of snow and frost. The residents packed away their Yule decorations for another year, took down the pine boughs and the mistletoe, and congratulated themselves on having escaped the inconveniences of a hard winter. People were already talking of an early spring when a terrifying and most unwelcome visitor came to Solace. The visitor was Plague, and accompanying him was his ghastly mate, Death.

No one was certain who invited this dread guest. The number of travelers had increased during the mild winter, anyone of them might have been a carrier. Blame was also ascribed to the standing bogs around Crystalmir Lake, bogs that had not frozen as they should have during the winter. The symptoms were the same in all cases, beginning with a high fever and extreme lethargy, followed by headache, vomiting, and diarrhea. The disease ran its course in a week or two; the strong and healthy survived it. The very young, the very old, or those in weak health did not.

In the days before the Cataclysm, clerics had called upon the goddess Mishakal for aid. She had granted them healing powers, and the plague had been virtually unknown. Mishakal had left Krynn with the rest of the gods. Those who practiced the healing arts in these days had to rely on their own skill and knowledge. They could not cure the disease, but they could treat the symptoms, try to prevent the patient from becoming so weak that he or she developed pneumonia, which led inevitably to death.

Weird Meggin worked tirelessly among the sick, administering her willow bark to break the fever, dosing the victims with a bitter concoction the consistency of paste, which seemed to help those who could be persuaded to choke it down.

Many of Solace's residents derided the old crone, terming her "cracked" or a witch. These very same people were among the first to ask for her the moment they felt the fever grip them. She never failed them. She would come at any time, day or night, and though her manner was a little strange—she talked constantly to herself and insisted on the unusual practice of washing her hands continually and forced others in the sickroom to do so as well—she was always welcome.

Raistlin began by accompanying Weird Meggin on her rounds. He assisted her in sponging the feverish bodies, helped persuade sick children to swallow the bad-tasting medicine. He learned how to ease the pain of the dying. But as the plague spread and more and more of Solace's citizens were caught in its lethal grip, Raistlin was forced by sheer necessity to tend patients on his own.

Caramon was among the first to catch the disease, a shock to the big man, who had never been sick in his life. He was terrified, certain he was going to die, and nearly wrecked the bedroom in his delirium, fighting snakes carrying torches, who were trying to set him on fire.

His strong body threw off the contagion, however, and since he had already survived the disease, he was able to assist his brother in caring for others. Caramon worried constantly that Raistlin would catch the plague. Frail as he was, he would not survive it. Raistlin was deaf to his brother's pleas to remain safely at home. Raistlin had discovered to his surprise that he gained a deep and abiding satisfaction in helping those stricken with the illness.

He did not work among the sick out of compassion. In general, he cared nothing for his neighbors, considered them dull and boorish. He did not treat the sick for monetary gain; he would go to the poor as readily as the rich. He found that what he truly enjoyed was power—power he wielded over the living, who had come to regard the young mage with hope bordering on reverence. Power he was sometimes able to wield over his greatest, most dread foe, Death.

He did not catch the plague, and he wondered why. Weird Meggin said it was because he made certain to wash his hands after tending to the sick. Raistlin smiled derisively, but he was too fond of the crazy old woman to contradict her.

At length, Plague slowly opened his clenched skeletal fingers, released Solace from his deadly grip. Solace's residents, acting under Weird Meggin's instructions, burned the clothes and bedding of those who had been ill. The snow came at last, and when it did, it fell on many new graves in Solace's burial ground.

Among the dead was Anna Brightblade.

It is written in the Measure that the duty of the lady wife of a knight is to feed the poor and tend to the sick of the manor. Though she was far from the land where the Measure was written and obeyed, Lady Brightblade was faithful to the law. She went to the aid of her sick neighbors, caught the disease herself. Even when she felt its first effects, she continued to nurse until she collapsed.

Sturm carried his mother home and ran to fetch Raistlin, who treated the woman as best he could, all to no avail.

"I'm dying, aren't I, young man?" Anna Brightblade asked Raistlin one night. "Tell me the truth. I am the wife of a noble knight. I can bear it."

"Yes," said Raistlin, who could hear the popping and crackling sounds of fluid gathering in the woman's lungs. "Yes, you are dying."

"How long?" she asked calmly.

"Not long now."

Sturm knelt at his mother's bedside. He gave a sob and lowered his head to the blanket. Anna reached out her hand, a hand wasted from the fever, and stroked her son's long hair.

"Leave us," she said to Raistlin with her customary imperiousness. Then, looking up at him, she smiled wanly, her stern expression softened. "Thank you for all you have done. I may have misjudged you, young man. I give you my blessing."

"Thank you, Lady Brightblade," Raistlin said. "I honor your courage, madam. May Paladine receive you." She looked at him darkly, frowned, thinking he blasphemed, and turned her face from him.

In the morning, as Caramon fixed his twin a bowl of hot gruel to sustain him through the rigors of the day, there came a knock on the door. Caramon opened it to admit Sturm. The young man was haggard and deathly pale, his eyes red and swollen. He was composed, however, had control of himself.

Caramon ushered his friend inside. Sturm sank into a chair, his legs collapsing beneath him. He had slept little since the first day of his mother's illness.

"Is Lady Brightblade . . ." Caramon began, but couldn't finish.

Sturm nodded his head.

Caramon wiped his eyes. "I'm sorry, Sturm. She was a great lady."

"Yes," said Sturm in a husky voice. He slumped in the chair. A tremor of a dry sob shuddered through his body.

"How long has it been since you ate anything?" Raistlin demanded.

Sturm sighed, waved an uncaring hand.

"Caramon, bring another bowl," Raistlin ordered. "Eat, Sir Knight, or you will shortly follow your mother to the grave."

Sturm's dark eyes flashed in anger at Raistlin's flippant tone. He started to refuse the food, but when he saw that Caramon had picked up the spoon, was intending to feed him like a baby, Sturm muttered that perhaps he could manage a mouthful. He ate the entire bowl, drank a glass of wine, and the color returned to his wan cheeks.

Raistlin shoved aside his own bowl only half eaten. This was customary with him, however; Caramon knew better than to protest.

"My mother and I talked near the end," Sturm said in a low voice. "She spoke of Solamnia and my father. She told me that she had long ago ceased believing he was alive. She had kept up the pretense only for my sake."

He lowered his head, pressed his lips tightly together, but shed no tears. After a moment, his composure regained, he looked at Raistlin, who was gathering his medicines, preparing to set out.

"Something strange happened at . . . the end. I thought I would tell you, to see if you had ever heard the like. Perhaps it is nothing but a manifestation of the disease."

Raistlin looked up with interest. He was making notes on the illness, recording symptoms and treatments in a small book for future reference.

"My mother had fallen into a deep sleep, from which it seemed that nothing could rouse her."

"The sleep of death," Raistlin said. "I have seen it often with this illness. Sometimes it can last for several days, but whenever it comes, the patient never wakes."

"Well, my mother did wake," Sturm said abruptly.

"Indeed? Tell me precisely what occurred."

"She opened her eyes and looked, not at me, but beyond me, to the door to her room. 'I know you, sir, do I not?' she said hesitantly, adding querulously, 'Where have you been all this time? We've been expecting you for ages.' Then she said, 'Make haste, Son, bring the old gentleman a chair.'

"I looked around, but there was no one there. 'Ah,' my mother said, 'you cannot stay? I must come with you? But that will mean leaving my boy all alone.' She seemed to listen, then she smiled. 'True, he is a boy no longer. You will watch over him when I am gone?' And then she smiled, as if reassured, and drew her last breath.

"And this is the strangest part. I had just risen to go to her when I thought I saw, standing beside her, the figure of an old man. He was a disreputable old man, wearing gray robes with a shabby sort of pointed hat." Sturm frowned. "He had the look of a magic-user. Well? What do you think?"

"I think that you had gone a long time without food or sleep," Raistlin replied.

"Perhaps," Sturm said, still frowning, puzzled. "But the vision seemed very real. Who could the old man have been? And why was my mother pleased to see him? She had no use for magic-users."

Raistlin headed for the door. He had been more than patient with the bereaved Sturm and he was tired of being insulted. Caramon cast him an apprehensive glance, fearing that his brother might lash out, make some sarcastic comment, but his twin departed without saying another word.

Sturm left soon after, to arrange for his mother's burial. Caramon heaved a doleful sigh and sat down to finish off the remainder of his brother's uneaten breakfast.

2

SPRING PERFORMED ITS USUAL MIRACLE. Green leaves sprouted on the vallenwoods, wildflowers bloomed in the graveyard; the small vallenwoods planted on the graves grew at the rapid pace customary to the tree, bringing solace to the grief-stricken. The spirits of those who had died flourished, were renewed in the living tree.

This spring brought another disease into Solace—a disease known to be carried by kender, a disease that is often contagious, especially among the young, who had just come to realize that life was short and very sweet and should be experienced to the fullest. The disease is called wanderlust.

Sturm was the first to catch it, although his other friends had exhibited the same symptoms. His case had been coming on ever since the death of his mother. Bereft and alone, his thoughts and dreams looked northward, to his homeland.

"I cannot give up the hope that my father still lives," he confessed to Caramon one morning. It was now his custom to join the twins for breakfast. Eating alone, in his own empty house, was too much to bear. "Though I admit that my mother's argument has some merit. If my father is alive, why did he never once try to contact us?"

"There could be lots of reasons," said Caramon stoutly. "Maybe he's being held prisoner in a dungeon by a mad wizard. Oh, sorry, Raist. I didn't mean that the way it sounded."

Raistlin snorted. He was occupied in feeding his rabbits, paying scant attention to the conversation.

"Whatever the case," Sturm said, "I intend to find out the truth. When the roads are open, within the month, I plan to travel north to Solamnia."

"No! Name of the Abyss," exclaimed Caramon, startled.

Raistlin, too, was amazed. He turned from his work, cabbage leaves in his hand, to see if the young man was serious.

Sturm nodded his head. "I have wanted to make such a journey for the past three years, but I was loath to leave my mother for an extended period of time. Now there is nothing to hold me. I go, and I go with her blessing. If, in fact, my father is dead, then I have my inheritance to claim. If he lives—"

Sturm shook his head, unable to complete the expression of the dream, too wonderful to possibly come true.

"Are you going alone?" Caramon asked, awed.

Sturm smiled, a rare thing for the usually solemn and serious young man. "I had hoped that you would come with me, Caramon. I would ask you, too, Raistlin," he added more stiffly, "but the journey will be long and difficult, and I fear it might tax your health. And I know that you would not want to be so far from your studies."

Ever since their return from Haven, Raistlin had spent every moment he could spare studying the tomes of the war magus. He had added several new spells to his spellbook.

"On the contrary, I am feeling unusually strong this spring," Raistlin remarked. "I would be able to take my books with me. I thank you for the offer, Sturm, and I will consider it, as will my brother."

"I'm going," Caramon said. "So long as Raist comes, too. And as he says, he has been really strong. He hasn't been sick hardly at all."

"I am glad to hear it," Sturm said, though without much enthusiasm. He knew very well that the twins would not be separated, although he had hoped against all reason to be able to persuade Caramon to leave Raistlin behind. "I remind you, Raistlin, that magic-users are not venerated in my country. Although, of course, you would be accorded the hospitality due any guest."

Raistlin bowed. "For which I am deeply grateful. I will be a most accommodating guest, I assure you, Sturm. I will not set the bed linens on fire, nor will I poison the well. In fact, you might find certain of my skills useful on the road."

"He's a really good cook," stated Caramon.

Sturm rose to his feet. "Very well. I will make the arrangements. My mother left me some money, although not much. Not enough for horses, I fear. We will have to travel on foot."

The moment the door closed behind Sturm, Caramon began capering around the small house, upsetting the furniture and wreaking havoc in his delight. He even had the temerity to give his brother a hug.

"Have you gone mad?" Raistlin demanded. "There! Look what you've done. That was our only cream pitcher. No, don't try to help! You've caused enough damage. Why don't you go polish your sword or sharpen it or whatever you do to it?"

"I will! A great idea!" Caramon rushed off to his bedroom, only to run back a moment later. "I don't have a whetstone."

"Go borrow one from Flint. Or better still, take your sword to Flint's and work on it there," Raistlin said, mopping up spilled cream. "Anything to get you out from underfoot."

"I wonder if Flint would like to come along. And Kit and Tanis and Tasslehoff! I'll go see."

His brother gone and the house quiet, Raistlin picked up the pieces of the broken pitcher and threw them away. He was as excited over the prospect of a journey to new and distant lands as his brother, though he had more sense than to smash the crockery over it. He was considering which of his herbs to pack, which he might find along the roadside, when there came a knock at the door.

Thinking it might be Sturm, Raistlin called out, "Caramon has gone to Flint's."

The knock was repeated, this time with the sharp rapping of an impatient visitor.

Raistlin opened the door, regarded his guest in amazement and surprise and not a little concern.

"Master Theobald!"

The mage stood upon the boardwalk outside the house. He wore a cloak over his white robes and carried a stout staff, indications that he had been traveling.

"May I come in?" Theobald asked gruffly.

"Certainly. Of course. Forgive me, Master." Raistlin stood aside, ushered his guest across the threshold. "I was not expecting you."

That was quite true. In all the years that Raistlin had attended the master's school, Theobald had never once paid a visit to Raistlin's home, nor evinced the slightest inclination to do so.

Bemused and somewhat apprehensive—his exploits in Haven had been widely reported throughout Solace—Raistlin invited his master to be seated in the only good chair in the house, the chair that happened to be his mother's rocking chair. Theobald declined all offers of food and wine.

"I do not have time to linger. I have been gone for a week, and I have not yet been home. I came here immediately. I have just returned from the Tower at Wayreth, from a meeting of the conclave."

Raistlin's uneasiness increased. "Isn't a meeting of the conclave at this early time of year somewhat unusual, Master? I thought they were always held in the summer."

"It is indeed unusual. We wizards had matters of great import to discuss. I was specially sent for," Theobald added, stroking his beard.

Raistlin made suitable comments, all the while wishing impatiently and with increasing nervousness that the provoking old fart would come to the point.

"Your doings in Haven were among the topics of discussion, Majere," Theobald said, glowering at Raistlin, brows bristling. "You broke many rules, not the least of which was casting a spell far above your capability."

Raistlin would have pointed out that the spell was obviously not above his capability to cast, since he had cast it, but he knew that this would be lost on Theobald.

"I did what I thought was right under the circumstances, Master," Raistlin said, as meekly and contritely as he could.

"Rubbish!" Theobald snorted. "You know what was right under the circumstances. You should have reported the wizardess to us as a renegade. We would have dealt with the matter in time."

"In time, Master," Raistlin emphasized. "Meanwhile, innocent people were being bilked out of what little they had, others were being driven from their homes. The charlatan priestess and her followers were causing irreparable harm. I sought to end it."

"You ended it, all right," Theobald said with dark implications.

"I was exonerated from her murder, Master," Raistlin returned, his tone sharp. "I have a writ from the High Sheriff of Haven himself proclaiming my innocence."

"So who did kill her?" Theobald asked.

"I have no idea, Master," Raistlin replied.

"Hunh," Theobald grunted. "Well, you handled the matter badly, but, still, you handled it. Damn near got yourself killed in the process, I understand. As I said, the conclave discussed the matter."

Raistlin kept silent, waited to hear his punishment. He had already determined that if they forbade him to practice magic, he would defy them, become a renegade himself.

Theobald withdrew a scroll case. He opened the lid, taking an unconscionable length of time about it, fussing and fumbling clumsily until Raistlin was tempted to leap across the room and wrest the case from the man's hand. Finally the lid came off. Theobald removed a scroll, handed it across to Raistlin.

"Here, pupil. You might as well see this for yourself."

Now that the scroll was in his hands, Raistlin wondered if he had the courage to read it. He hesitated a moment to insure that his hands did not tremble and betray him, then, with outward nonchalance masking inward apprehension, he unrolled the scroll.

He tried to read it, but his nervousness impaired his eye sight. The words would not come into focus. When they did, he did not comprehend them.

Then he could not believe them.

Amazed and aghast, he stared at his master. "This . . . this can't be right. I am too young."

"That is what I said," Theobald stated in nasty tones. "But I was overruled."

Raistlin read the words again, words that, though they were not in the least magical, began to glow with the radiance of a thousand suns.

> The aspiring magus, Raistlin Majere, is hereby summoned to the Tower of High Sorcery at Wayreth to appear before the Conclave of Wizards on the seventh day of the seventh month at the seventh minute of the seventh hour. At this time, in this place, you will be tested by your superiors for inclusion into the ranks of those gifted by the three gods, Solinari, Lunitari, Nuitari.
>
> To be invited to take the Test is a great honor, an honor accorded to few, and should be taken seriously. You may impart knowledge of this honor to members of your immediate family, but to no others. Failure to accede to this injunction could mean the forfeiture of the right to take the Test.
>
> You will bring with you your spell book and spell components. You will wear robes representing the alliance of your sponsor. The color of the robes you will wear, if and when you are apprenticed—i.e., your allegiance to one of the three gods—will be determined during the Test. You will carry no weapons, nor any magical artifacts. Magical artifacts will be provided during the Test itself in order to judge your skill in the handling of said artifacts.
>
> In the unfortunate event of your demise during the Test, all personal effects will be returned to your family.
>
> You may be provided with an escort to the Tower, but your escort should be aware that he or she will not be permitted to enter the Guardian Forest. Any attempt by the escort to force entry will result in most grievous harm to the escort. We will not be held responsible.

That last sentence had been written, then crossed out, as if the writer had experienced second thoughts. An addendum had been inserted.

> *An exception to this rule is made in regard to Caramon Majere, twin brother to the aforementioned contestant. Caramon Majere is expressly desired to attend his brother's testing. He will be admitted into the Guardian Forest. His safety will be guaranteed, at least during the time he is inside the forest.*

Raistlin lowered the scroll, let it roll back upon itself. His hands lacked the strength to hold it up, keep it open. To be invited to take the Test so young, to be even considered capable of taking the Test at his novitiate stage, was an honor of incredible magnitude. He was overcome with joy, joy and pride.

Of course, there was that cautionary phrase, *In the event of your demise.* Later, in the small hours of the night, when he would lie awake, unable to sleep for his excitement, that sentence would rise up before him, a skeletal hand reaching out to grasp him, drag him down. But now, filled with confidence in himself, proud of his achievements and the fact that these achievements had evidently impressed the members of the conclave, Raistlin had no fear, no qualms.

"I thank you, Master," he began when he could control his voice sufficiently to speak.

"Don't thank me," Theobald said, standing. "It is likely that I am sending you to your doom. I won't have your death on my conscience. I told Par-Salian as much. I go on record as being opposed to this folly."

Raistlin accompanied his guest to the door. "I am sorry you have so little faith in me, Master."

Theobald made an impatient gesture with his hand. "Come to me if you have any questions on your spellbook."

"I will do so, Master," said Raistlin, privately resolving that he would see Theobald in the Abyss first. "Thank you."

After the master had gone and Raistlin had shut the door behind him, it was now Raistlin's turn to caper about the house. Transported with happiness, he lifted the skirts of his robes and performed several of the round-dance steps Caramon had struggled for years to teach him.

Entering at that moment, Caramon stared openmouthed at his brother. His astonishment increased tenfold when Raistlin ran over to his twin, flung his arms around him, embraced him, then burst into tears.

"What's wrong?"

Caramon misread his brother's emotions, his heart almost stopped in terror. He dropped his sword, which fell to the floor with a resounding clang, to clutch at his twin. "Raistlin! What's wrong? What's the matter? Who died?"

"Nothing is the matter, my brother!" Raistlin cried, laughing and drying his tears. "Nothing in the world is the matter! For once, everything is right."

He waved the scroll, which he still held in his hand, pranced about the small room until he collapsed, out of breath but still laughing, in his mother's rocking chair.

"Shut the door, my brother. And come sit beside me. We have a great deal to discuss."

3

Swearing Caramon to secrecy regarding the Test proved a difficult task. In his exuberance, Raistlin showed Caramon the precious document summoning them both to the Tower at Wayreth. Caramon came across the unfortunate line *in the event of your demise* and was extremely upset. So upset that, at first, he vowed Raistlin should not go, that he would have Tanis and Sturm and Flint and Otik and half the population of Solace sit on Raistlin before he should take a Test where the penalty for failure was death.

Raistlin was at first touched by Caramon's very genuine concern. Exhibiting unusual patience, Raistlin tried to explain to his twin the reasoning behind such drastic measures.

"My dear brother, as you yourself have seen, magic wielded by the wrong hands can be extremely dangerous. The conclave wants only those among their ranks who have proven that they are disciplined, skillful, and—most important—dedicated body and soul to the art. Thus those who merely dabble in magic, who practice it for their own amusement, do not want to take the Test, because they are not prepared to risk their lives for the magic."

"It is murder," Caramon said in a low voice. "Murder, plain and simple."

"No, no, my brother." Raistlin was soothing. Thinking of Lemuel, Raistlin smiled as he added, "Those deemed not suitable for taking the Test are prohibited from doing so by the conclave. They permit only those magi who have an excellent chance of passing to take the Test. And, my dear brother, very, very few fail. The risk is extremely minor and, for me, no risk at all. You know how hard I have worked and studied. I can't possibly fail!"

"Is that true?" Caramon lifted his pale, haggard face, regarded his twin with a searching, unblinking gaze.

"I swear it." Raistlin sat back in the rocker, smiled again. He couldn't keep from smiling.

"Then why do they want me to come with you?" Caramon asked suspiciously.

Raistlin was forced to pause before answering. Truth to tell, he didn't know why Caramon should be invited to come along. The more Raistlin thought about it, the more he resented the fact. Certainly it was logical for his brother to escort him as far as the forest, but why should he come farther? It was extremely unusual for the conclave to permit entry to their Tower to any person outside their ranks.

"I'm not sure," Raistlin admitted at last. "Probably it has something to do with the fact that we are twins. There is nothing sinister about it, Caramon, if that's what you are thinking. You will merely accompany me to the Tower and wait until I have finished the Test. Then we will return home together."

Envisioning that triumphant journey back to Solace, Raistlin's spirits, which had been shadowed a moment before, were elevated to the heavens and sparkled bright as the stars.

Caramon was dolefully shaking his head. "I don't like it. I think you should discuss it with Tanis."

"I tell you again, I am not permitted to discuss it with anyone, Caramon!" Raistlin said angrily, losing patience at last. "Can't you get that through your gully-dwarf skull?"

Caramon looked unhappy and uneasy, but still defiant.

Raistlin left the rocking chair. Hands clenched to fists, he stood over his brother, stared down at him, spoke to him with passionate intensity.

"I am commanded to keep this secret, and I will do so. And so will you, my brother. You will not mention this to Tanis. You will not mention this to Kitiara. You will not mention this to Sturm or anyone else. Do you understand me, Caramon? No one must know!"

Raistlin paused, drew a breath, then said quietly, so that there could be no doubt of his sincerity, "If you do—if you ruin this chance for me—then I have no brother."

Caramon went white to the lips. "Raist, I—"

"I will disown you," Raistlin pressed on, knowing that the iron must strike to the heart. "I will leave this house, and I will never come back. Your name will never be spoken in my presence. If I see you coming down the road, I will turn and walk the opposite direction."

Caramon was hurt, deeply hurt. His big frame shuddered, as if the point Raistlin had driven home was in truth steel.

"I guess . . . it means a lot . . . to you," Caramon said brokenly, lowering his head, staring at his clasped hands.

Raistlin was softened by his brother's anguish. But Caramon had to be made to understand. Kneeling beside his twin, Raistlin stroked his brother's curly hair.

"Of course this means a lot to me, Caramon. It means everything! I have worked and studied almost my entire life for this chance. What would you have me do—cast it aside because it is dangerous? Life is dangerous, Caramon. Just stepping out that door is dangerous! You cannot hide from danger. Death floats on the air, creeps through the window, comes with the handshake of a stranger. If we stop living because we fear death, then we have already died.

"You want to be a warrior, Caramon. You practice with a real sword. Isn't that dangerous? How many times have you and Sturm very nearly sliced off each other's ears? Sturm has told us of the young knights who die in the tourneys held to test their knighthood. Yet if you had the chance to fight in one of those, wouldn't you take it?"

Caramon nodded. A tear fell on the clasped hands.

"What I do is the same thing," Raistlin said gently. "The blade must be forged in the fire. Are you with me, my brother?" He pressed his hand over Caramon's. "You know that I would stand at your side, should you ever fight to prove your mettle."

Caramon lifted his head. In his eyes, there was new respect and admiration. "Yes, Raist. I'll stand with you. I understand, now that you've explained it. I won't say a word to anyone. I promise."

"Good." Raistlin sighed. The elation had drained away. The battle with his brother had sapped his energy, leaving him weak and exhausted. He wanted to lie down, to be quiet and alone in the comforting darkness.

"What do I tell the others?" Caramon asked.

"Whatever you choose," Raistlin returned, heading for his room. "I don't care, so long as you make no mention of the truth."

"Raist . . ." Caramon paused, then asked, "You wouldn't do what you said, would you? Disown me? Claim that you never had a brother?"

"Oh, don't be such an idiot, Caramon," Raistlin said and went to his bed.

4

CARAMON INFORMED STURM THE NEXT DAY THAT NEITHER HE NOR HIS brother could accompany him to Solamnia. Sturm tried arguing and persuading, but Caramon remained adamant, though he could give no clear reason for his change of heart. Sturm marked Caramon as being worried and preoccupied about something. Assuming that Raistlin had decided not to go and had forbidden his brother to go without him, Sturm—though offended and hurt—said no more about the matter.

"If you want a traveling companion, Brightblade, I'll go with you myself," Kitiara offered. "I know the fastest and best routes north. Plus, from what I've heard, there's dark doings happening up that way. We shouldn't either of us travel alone, and since we're heading the same direction, it makes sense that we travel together."

The three were in the Inn of the Last Home, drinking a glass of ale. Having stopped by her brother's home, Kit had recognized immediately that the twins were up to something and was angry when they maintained that nothing unusual was going on. Well aware that she would never be able to pry the secret from Raistlin, she hoped to be able to tease the truth out of the more pliable Caramon.

"You and Tanis would be most welcome, Kitiara," Sturm said, recovering from his initial astonishment at her offer. "I did not ask you at first because I knew Tanis planned to accompany Flint on his summer journeys, but—"

"Tanis won't be going with me," Kit said tonelessly, flatly. She drained her tankard of ale and loudly called out for Otik to bring her another.

Sturm looked over at Caramon, wondering what was going on. Tanis and Kitiara had been together all winter, closer and more affectionate than ever.

Caramon shook his head to indicate that he had no idea.

Sturm was troubled. "I'm not certain—"

"Fine. It's settled. I'm coming," Kit said, refusing to listen to any arguments. "Now, Caramon, tell me why you and that wizard brother of yours won't come with us. Four traveling the road is much safer. Besides, there's some people up north I want you to meet."

"Like I told Sturm, I can't go," Caramon said.

His usually cheerful face was shadowed, grave. He hadn't drunk even a sip of his ale, which had by now gone flat. Shoving it aside, he stood up, flung a coin on the table, and left.

He didn't feel comfortable around Kitiara anymore. He was glad she was leaving, relieved that Tanis wasn't going with her. He had often felt that he should tell Tanis the truth about that night. Tell Tanis that Kit had been the one to murder Judith. Tell Tanis that she had urged Caramon to let Raistlin take the blame, to let Raistlin die.

She had claimed that she was joking. Still . . .

Caramon gave a relieved sigh. She would leave, and if they were lucky, she would not return. Caramon was worried about Sturm, who would be traveling in Kit's company, but on reflection, Caramon decided that the young knight, bolstered by his reliance on the Oath and the Measure, could look after himself. Besides, as Kit said, traveling alone was dangerous.

Caramon's main concern was for Tanis, who would be terribly hurt by Kit's decision to leave. Caramon figured—logically—that Kitiara, the restless firebrand, was the one who had ended the relationship.

It was Raistlin who discovered the truth.

Although he had several months to wait before he and Caramon would undertake their journey to the Tower, Raistlin began immediately to make preparations. One of these involved the retooling of the leather thong that held the knife on Raistlin's wrist, concealed beneath his robes. A flick of that wrist was supposed to cause the knife to drop down, unseen, into the mage's hand.

At least that was how the thong was designed to work. Raistlin's wrist was far thinner than the wrist of the war mage who had originally worn it, however. When Raistlin tried wearing the contraption, the thong itself dropped into his hand. The knife fell to the floor. He took it to Flint, hoping the dwarf could fix it.

Flint, looking the thong over, was impressed with the workmanship, thought it might be dwarven. According to Lemuel, the Qualinesti elves had made the knife and the thong as a gift to their friend, the war mage. Raistlin made no mention of this, however. He agreed with the dwarf that the thong was undoubtedly constructed by some great dwarven leather-worker. Flint offered to adjust the size if Raistlin would leave the thong with him for a week or two.

Raistlin had his hand on the doorknocker, was about to knock, when he heard faint voices inside. The voices belonged to Tanis and Flint. Raistlin could distinguish only a few words, but one was "Kitiara."

Certain that any conversation about his sister would cease if he were introduced into it, Raistlin carefully and quietly lowered his hand from the knocker. He looked to see if anyone was in sight. Finding that he was alone, Raistlin slipped around the side of the house to Flint's workshop. The dwarf had opened the window to let in the soft spring breeze. Hidden from view by a fall of purple clematis, which grew up the side of the workshop, Raistlin stood to one side of the window.

Any qualms he might have had about eavesdropping on his friends were easily settled. He had often wondered how much Tanis knew about Kit's activities: midnight meetings with strangers, the murder of the priestess . . . Was Kit fleeing danger? Had Tanis threatened to denounce her? And where did that leave Raistlin if this were the case? Quite understandably, he had small faith in his sister's loyalty.

"We've been arguing for days," Tanis was saying. "She wants me to come north with her."

The conversation was interrupted by a moment's furious hammering. When that was finished, the talk resumed.

"She claims to have friends who will pay large sums to those skilled with bow and blade."

"Even half-elves?" Flint grunted.

"I pointed that out, but she says—rightly so—that I could hide my heritage if I wanted. I could grow a beard, wear my hair long to cover my ears."

"A fine sight you'd look with a beard!"

Flint plied the hammer again.

"Well? Are you going?" he asked when the hammering had stopped.

"No, I'm not," Tanis said, speaking reluctantly, loath to share his feelings even with his longtime friend. "I need time away from her. Time to think things through. I can't think when I'm around Kitiara. The truth is, Flint, I'm falling in love with her."

Raistlin snorted, almost laughed. He swallowed his mirth, fearing to give himself away. He would have expected something inane like this from Caramon, but not the half-elf, who had certainly lived long enough to know better.

Tanis spoke more rapidly, relieved to be able to talk about it. "The one time I ever even hinted at marriage, Kit laughed me to scorn. She scolded me about it for days after. Why did I want to ruin all our fun? We shared a bed, what more could I want? But I'm not happy just sharing my bed with her, Flint. I want to share my life with her, my dreams and hopes and plans. I want to settle down. She doesn't. She feels trapped, caged. She's restless and bored. We quarrel continually, over stupid things. If we stayed together, she would come to resent me, perhaps even hate me, and I couldn't bear that. I will miss her terribly, but it's better this way."

"Bah! Give her a year or two with those friends of hers up north and she'll be back. Maybe then she'll be receptive to your proposal, lad."

"She may come back." Tanis was silent a moment, then he added, "But I won't be here."

"Where are you going, then?"

"Home," Tanis replied quietly. "I haven't been home in a long time. I know this means I won't be with you on the first part of your travels, but we could meet in Qualinesti."

"We could, but . . . well . . . The truth of it is, I won't be going that way, Tanis," Flint said, clearing his throat. He sounded embarrassed. "I've been meaning to talk this over with you, but I never seemed to find the right time. I guess this is as good as any.

"That fair at Haven soured me, lad. I saw the ugly faces beneath the masks humans wear, and it left a bad taste in my mouth. Talking to those hill dwarves made me start thinking of my own home. I can never go back to my clan. You know the reason for that, but I've a mind to visit some of the other clans in the vicinity. It will be a comfort to me, being with my own kind. I've been thinking about what that young scamp Raistlin says about the gods. I'd like to find out if Reorx is around somewhere, maybe trapped inside Thorbardin."

"Searching for some sign of the true gods . . . It's an interesting idea," Tanis said. He added with a sigh, "Who knows? In looking for them, I might find myself along the way."

The pain and sadness in the half-elf's voice made Raistlin ashamed of having listened in on this private conversation. He was leaving his post, heading for the front door, prepared to announce himself by conventional means, when he heard the dwarf say dourly,

"Which of us has to take the kender?"

5

IT WAS THE LAST DAY OF THE MONTH OF SPRING BLOSSOM TIME. The roads were open. Travelers were abroad, once more filling the Inn of the Last Home to capacity. They ate Otik's potatoes, praised his ale, and told stories of gathering trouble in the world, stories of armies of hobgoblins on the march, of ogres moving down from their hidden holdings in the mountains, hints of creatures more fearsome than these.

Sturm and Kit were planning to leave the first of Summer Home. Tanis was leaving that day, too, explaining somewhat lamely that he wanted to be in Qualinesti in time for some sort of elven celebration involving the sun. Truth was, he knew very well that he could not go back to his empty house, the house that would always echo with her laughter. Flint was to accompany his friend part of the way, and so he, too, was setting off the next day.

It was known now among the companions that Raistlin and Caramon were making a journey themselves—a fact discovered by Kit, who was consumed with curiosity regarding Caramon's unusual circumspectness and who consequently bullied and teased him until he let fall that much.

Fearful that Kitiara would break his twin's resolve in the end, force him to reveal his secret, Raistlin hinted that they were going to seek out their father's relations, who had presumably come from Pax Tharkas. If their friends had looked at a map, they would have noted that Pax Tharkas was located in exactly the opposite direction from the Wayreth Forest.

No one did look at a map, because the only maps available were in the possession of Tasslehoff Burrfoot, who was not present. One of the reasons the companions had come together this last night, other than to bid each other farewell and safe roads, was to determine what to do about the kender.

Sturm began by stating in no uncertain terms that kender were not welcome in Solamnia. He added that any knight seen traveling in the company of a kender would be ruined, his reputation damned and blasted forever.

Kit said shortly that her friends in the north had no use for kender whatsoever, and she made it clear that if Tasslehoff valued his skin, he'd find some other route to travel. She fixed her gaze pointedly and haughtily upon Tanis. Relations between the two were strained. Kit had thought for certain that Tanis would beg her to stay, either that or travel with him. He had done neither, and she was angry.

"I cannot take Tas into Qualinesti," Tanis said, avoiding her gaze. "The elves would never permit it."

"Don't look at me!" Flint stated, alarmed to see them do just that. "If any of my clansmen were to so much as set eyes upon me in company with a kender, they'd lock me up for a crazy Theiwar, and I would be hard pressed to say they were wrong. Tasslehoff should go with Raistlin and Caramon to Pax Tharkas."

"No," said Raistlin with a finality in his tone that boded no argument. "Absolutely not."

"What do we do with him, then?" Tanis asked in perplexity.

"Bind him and gag him and stash him in the bottom of a well," Flint advised. "Then we sneak off in the middle of the night, and he might—I repeat, he might—not find us."

"Who are you stashing at the bottom of a well?" came a cheerful voice. Tasslehoff, having sighted his friends through the open window, decided to save himself the wearisome walk around to the front door. Hoisting himself up onto the window ledge, he climbed inside.

"Mind my ale mug! You nearly kicked it over! Get off the table, you doorknob!" Flint caught his ale mug, held it close to his chest. "If you must know, it's you we're talking of stashing in the well."

"Are you? How wonderful!" Tas said, his face lighting up. "I've never been at the bottom of a well before. Ah, but I just remembered. I can't."

Reaching out, Tas kindly patted Flint's hand. "I appreciate the thought. I truly do, and I'd almost stay behind to do it, but you see, I'm not going to be here."

"Where are you going?" Tanis asked the question with trepidation.

"Before I start, I want to say something. I know you've been arguing over who takes me along, haven't you?" Tas looked sternly around at the group.

Tanis was embarrassed. He had not meant to hurt the kender's feelings. "You can come with us, Tas," he began, only to be interrupted by a horrified "He cannot!" from Flint.

Tas raised his small hand for silence. "You see, if I go with one of you, then that will make the others feel bad, and I wouldn't like that to happen. And so I've decided to go off on my own. No! Don't try to make me change my mind. I'm going back to Kendermore, and, no offense"—Tas looked quite severe—"but the rest of you just wouldn't fit in there."

"You mean the kender wouldn't allow us to enter their land?" Caramon asked, insulted.

"No, I mean you wouldn't fit in. Especially you, Caramon. You'd take the roof off my house the moment you stood up. Not to mention squashing all my furniture. Now, I could make an exception for Flint. . . .".

"No you couldn't!" said the dwarf hurriedly.

Tasslehoff went on to describe the wonders of Kendermore, painting such an interesting picture of that carefree shire, where the concepts of private property and personal possessions are completely unknown, that every person at the table firmly resolved never to go anywhere near it.

The issue of the kender settled, there was nothing left but to say good-bye.

The companions sat for a long time at their table. The setting sun gleamed a fiery ball in the red portion of the stained-glass windows, shone orange in the yellow, and a strange sort of green in the blue. The sun seemed to linger as long as the companions, spreading its golden light throughout the sky, before slipping down past the horizon, leaving a warm afterglow behind.

Otik brought candles and lamps to drive away the shadows, along with an excellent supper of his famous spiced potatoes, lamb stew, trout from Crystalmir Lake, bread, and goat's cheese. The food was excellent; even Raistlin ate more than his usual two or three nibbling bites, actually devouring an entire trout. When every speck was eaten—nothing ever went to waste, with Caramon there to finish off the leftovers—Tanis called Otik over to settle the bill.

"The meal is on the house, my friends—my very dear friends," Otik said. He wished them all a safe journey and shook hands with everyone of them, including Tasslehoff.

Tanis invited Otik to share a glass, which he did. Flint invited him to share another, and another after that. Otik shared so many glasses that eventually, when his services were required in the kitchen, young Tika had to help him stagger off.

Other Solace residents stopped by the inn, came to their table to say good-bye and offer their good wishes. Many were Flint's customers, sorry to hear of his leaving, for he had sold out all his stock and let it be known that he expected to be gone as long as a year. Many more came to say farewell to Raistlin, much to the secret astonishment of the rest of the company, who had no idea that the caustic, sharp-tongued, and secretive young man had so many friends.

These were not friends, however. They were his patients, come to express their gratitude for his care. Among these was Miranda. No longer the town beauty, she was wan and pale in her black mourning clothes. Her baby had been among the first to perish with the plague. She gave Raistlin a sweet kiss on his cheek and thanked him, in a choked voice, for being so gentle with her dying child. Her young husband also offered his thanks, then led away his grieving wife.

Raistlin watched her depart, thankful in his heart that he had been warned away from following down that pretty, rose-strewn path. He was uncommonly nice to his brother that night, much to the astonishment of Caramon, who couldn't imagine what he had done to earn Raistlin's gratitude.

Strangers at the inn noticed the odd assortment of friends, mainly due to the fact that either Tanis or Flint dropped by to return valuables that had been appropriated by the kender. The strangers shook their heads and raised their eyebrows.

"It takes all kinds to make this world," they said, and by the disparaging tones in which they spoke, it was obvious that they didn't believe the old homily in the slightest. In their view, it took their kind and no other.

The night deepened. Darkness gathered around the inn. The shadows crept into the inn itself, for the other customers were gone to their beds, taking their lamps or candles with them to light their way. A pleasantly soused Otik had long ago rolled into his bed, leaving the cleaning up to be done by Tika, the cook, and the barmaids.

They scrubbed the tabletops and swept the floor; the clatter of crockery could be heard coming from the kitchen. Still the companions sat at their table, loath to part, for each felt, in his or her own heart, that this parting would be a long one.

At length, Raistlin, who had been nodding where he sat for some time, said quietly, "It is time for us to go, my brother. I need my rest. I have much studying to do tomorrow."

Caramon made some unintelligible response. He had drunk more than his share of ale. His nose was red, and he was at that stage of drunkenness in which some men fight and others blubber. Caramon was blubbering.

"I, too, must take my leave," said Sturm. "We need to make an early start, put several miles behind us before the heat of the day sets in."

"I wish you would change your mind and come with us," Kitiara said softly, her eyes on Tanis.

Kit had been the loudest, brashest, liveliest person in the group, except when her gaze would fall on Tanis, and then her crooked smile would slip a little. Moments later, her smile would harden, and her laughter would blare out harshly, the noisiest person at the table. But as the jollity waned and the inn grew quieter, the shadows deepened around them, Kit's laughter died away, her stories began but never came to a close. She drew nearer and nearer to Tanis, and now she clasped his hand tightly beneath the table.

"Please, Tanis," she said. "Come north. You will find glory in battle, wealth, and power. I swear it!"

Tanis hesitated. Her dark eyes were warm and soft. Her smile trembled with the intensity of her passion. He had never seen her look more lovely. He was finding it more and more difficult to give her up.

"Yes, Tanis, come with us," Sturm urged warmly. "I cannot promise you wealth or power, but glory must surely be ours."

Tanis opened his mouth. It seemed he would say "yes." Everyone expected him to say "yes," including himself. When the "no" came out, he looked as startled as anyone at the table.

As Raistlin would say later to Caramon, on their way home that night, "The human side of Tanis would have gone with her. It was the elven side of him that held him back."

"Who wants you along anyway?" Kit flared, angry, her pride hurt. She had not anticipated failure. She slid away from him, stood up. "Traveling with you would be like traveling with my own grandfather. Sturm and I will have lots more fun without you."

Sturm appeared somewhat alarmed at this statement. The pilgrimage to his homeland was a sacred journey. He wasn't going north to "have fun." Frowning, he smoothed his mustaches and repeated that they needed to make an early start.

An uncomfortable silence fell. No one wanted to be the first to leave, especially now, when it seemed likely that their parting would end on a discordant note. Even Tasslehoff was affected. The kender sat quiet and subdued, so unhappy that he actually returned Sturm's money pouch. Tas returned the pouch to Caramon, but the thought was there.

"I have an idea," said Tanis at last. "Let us plan to meet again in the autumn, on the first night of Harvest Home."

"I might be back, I might not," said Kit, shrugging with a careless air. "Don't count on me."

"I trust I will not be back," Sturm said emphatically, and his friends knew what he meant. A return to Solace in the autumn would mean his quest to find his father and his heritage had failed.

"Then we will meet every year after, on the first night of Harvest Home in the fall, those of us who are here," Tanis suggested. "And let us take a vow that five years from now we will return here to the inn, no matter where we are or what we are doing."

"Those of us who are still alive," Raistlin said.

He had intended his words as a joke, but Caramon sat up straight, the shock of his brother's words penetrating his alcohol-induced befuddlement. He cast his twin a frightened glance, a glance that Raistlin deflected with narrowed eyes.

"It was only a small attempt at humor, my brother."

"Still, you shouldn't say things like that, Raist," Caramon entreated. "It's bad luck."

"Drink your ale and keep silent," Raistlin returned irritably.

Sturm's stern expression had eased. "That is a good idea. Five years. I pledge myself to return in five years."

"I'll be back, Tanis!" Tas said, hopping about in excitement. "I'll be here in five years."

"You'll likely be in some jail in five years," Flint muttered.

"Well, if I am, you'll bail me out, won't you, Flint?" The dwarf swore it would be a cold day in the Abyss before he bailed the kender out of jail one more time.

"Are there cold days in the Abyss?" Tasslehoff wondered. "Are there any sort of days at all in the Abyss, or is it mostly dark and spooky like a giant hole in the ground, or is it filled with blazing fire? Don't you think the Abyss would be a great place to visit, Raistlin? I'd really like to go there someday. I'll bet not even Uncle Trapspringer has—"

Tanis called for silence, just in time to prevent Flint from upending his ale mug over the kender's head. Tanis placed his hand, palm down, in the center of the table.

"I vow on the love and friendship I feel for all of you"—his gaze touched each of his friends, gathered them together— "that I will return to the Inn of the Last Home on the first night of Harvest Home five years hence."

"I will be back in five years," said Kit, resting her hand over Tanis's. Her expression had softened. Her grip on him tightened. "If not sooner. Much sooner."

"I vow on my honor as the knight I hope to become that I will return in five years," Sturm Brightblade said solemnly. He placed his hand over Tanis's and Kit's.

"I'll be here," said Caramon. His large hand engulfed the other hands of his friends.

"And I," said Raistlin. He touched the back of his brother's hand with his fingertips.

"Don't forget me! I'll be here!" Tasslehoff crawled on top of the table to add his small hand to the pile.

"Well, Flint?" Tanis said, smiling at his old friend.

"Confound it, I may have more important things to do than come back to this place just to see your pasty faces," Flint grumbled.

He took hold of the hands of all his friends in his own gnarled and work-hardened hands. "Reorx walk with you until we meet again!" he said, then turned his head, stared very hard out the window at nothing.

The inn's door had long ago been locked for the night. A yawning barmaid was on hand to let them out. Raistlin said his good-byes quickly. He was eager to go home to his rest, and he waited impatiently at the door for his brother. Caramon embraced Sturm, the two longtime friends holding each other close. They parted in silence, both unable to speak. Caramon shook hands with Tanis, and he would have hugged Flint, but the dwarf, scandalized, told him to get along home." Tasslehoff flung his arms as far as they would go around Caramon, who playfully tweaked the kender's topknot in return.

Kitiara stepped forward to embrace her brother, but Caramon seemed not to see her. Raistlin was now tapping his foot in irritation. Caramon hurried off, brushing past Kit without a word. She stared after him, then grinned, shrugged. Sturm's good-byes were brief and formal, accompanied by low and respectful bows for Tanis and Flint. Kit arranged a meeting place and then Sturm left.

"I think I'll stay a little longer," said Tas. He was just about to upend his pouches to look over his day's "findings" when there came a heavy knock on the door.

"Oh, hullo, Sheriff," Tas called cheerfully. "Looking for someone?"

Tasslehoff departed in the company of the sheriff. The kender's last words were for someone to remember to get him out of jail in the morning.

Kit stood in the doorway, waiting for Tanis.

"Flint, you coming?" Tanis asked.

The barmaid had taken the candles away. Flint sat in the darkness. He made no response.

"The girl's wanting to close up," Tanis urged.

Still no response.

"I'll take care of him, sir," the barmaid said softly.

Tanis nodded. Joining Kit, he put his arm around her, drew her close. The two walked side by side into the night.

The dwarf sat there, by himself, until dawn.

BOOK 6

The blade must pass through the fire, else it will break.

—Par-Salian

1

I T WAS THE SIXTH DAY OF THE SEVENTH MONTH. Antimodes stood in the window of his room in the Tower of Wayreth gazing out into the night. His room was one of many rooms in the tower open to mages arriving to study, to confer, or—as was Antimodes—to participate in giving the Test, which would be held on the morrow.

The tower's accommodations were of various sizes and designs, from small cell-like rooms for the apprentice mages to larger and more lavish rooms reserved for the archmagi. The room in which Antimodes was comfortably ensconced was his customary room, his favorite. Since the archmage was fond of travel, known to drop by at unexpected times, Par-Salian saw to it that the room was always kept ready for his friend's arrival.

Located near the top part of the tower, the suite consisted of a bedroom and a parlor, with a small balcony that sometimes overlooked the Forest of Wayreth and sometimes did not, depending on where the magical forest happened to be at the moment.

If the forest was not there, Antimodes would often conjure up a view himself. Vast fields of yellow wheat, or perhaps crashing surf, depending on what he felt in the mood for that day. The forest was not there this night, but since it was dark and Antimodes was tired from his day's travel, he did not bother with landscaping. He had been standing on the balcony, cooling himself in the evening breeze. Leaving the shutters open to keep the air circulating—it was unusually hot that night—he returned to a small desk, continued his frowning perusal of a scroll, a perusal which already had been interrupted by dinner.

A knock on the door again interrupted him.

"Enter," he called in an irritated tone.

The door opened silently. Par-Salian thrust his head inside.

"Am I disturbing you? I can come back. . . ."

"No, no. My dear friend." Antimodes rose hastily to his feet to greet his visitor. "Come in, come in. I am very glad to see you. I was hoping we might have a chance to talk before tomorrow. I would have gone to you, but I feared to disturb you at your work. I know how busy you are just prior to a testing."

"Yes, and this Test will prove more difficult than most. You are studying a new spell?" Par-Salian glanced at the scroll on the desk, which was partially unrolled.

"It is one I bought," said Antimodes with a grimace. "And as it turns out, I believe I was swindled. It is not what the man promised me."

"My dear Antimodes, didn't you read it first?" Par-Salian asked, shocked.

"I only glanced over it quickly. The fault is mine, a fact which merely increases my annoyance."

"I don't suppose you could return it."

"Afraid not. One of those deals in an inn. I should know better, of course, but I have been searching for this spell for a long time, and she was so very kind, not to mention pretty, and assured me that this would do precisely what I wanted." He shrugged. "Ah, well. Live and learn. Please, sit down. Will you have some wine?"

"Thank you." Par-Salian tasted the pale yellow liquid, rolled it on his tongue. "Conjured or purchased?"

"Purchased," Antimodes said. "Conjured lacks body, to my mind. Only the Silvanesti elves know how to do it right, and it's becoming harder and harder to acquire good Silvanesti wine these days."

"Too true," Par-Salian agreed. "King Lorac used to bring me several bottles whenever he visited, but it has been many years since he has been to see us."

"He's sulking," Antimodes observed. "He thought he should have been elected head of the conclave."

"I don't think that is it. Yes, he did feel he deserved the position, but he readily admitted that he was extremely busy with his duties as ruler of the Silvanesti. If anything, I think he wanted to be granted the honor so that he could have politely turned it down."

Par-Salian frowned thoughtfully. "Do you know, my friend, I have the strangest feeling that Lorac is hiding something from us. He doesn't come to see me anymore because he fears discovery."

"What do you think it is? Some powerful artifact? Is there one missing?"

"Not to my knowledge. I could be wrong. I hope I am."

"Lorac was always one to act on his own, the conclave be damned," Antimodes observed.

"Still, he abided by our rules as much as any elf ever abides by rules not of his own making." Par-Salian finished his wine, permitted himself another glass.

Antimodes was silent and thoughtful, then he said abruptly, "The gods grant Lorac good of it, then. He'll need it, I fear. Whatever it is. You received my last report?"

"I did." Par-Salian sighed. "I want to know this: Are you absolutely certain of your facts?"

"Certain? No, of course not! I will never be certain until I see with my own eyes!" Antimodes waved his hand. "It is rumor, hearsay, nothing more. Yet . . ." He paused, then said softly, "Yet I believe it."

"Dragons! Dragons returning to Krynn. Takhisis's dragons, no less! I hope, my friend," Par-Salian said earnestly, "I hope and pray that you are wrong."

"Still, it fits in with what facts we do know. Did you approach our black-robed brethren about this as I advised?"

"I discussed the matter with Ladonna," Par-Salian said. "Not mentioning where or how I had heard anything. She was evasive."

"Isn't she always?" Antimodes said dryly.

"Yes, but there are ways to read her if you know her," Par-Salian said.

Antimodes nodded. He was an old friend, a trusted friend. There was no need between them to mention that Par-Salian knew Ladonna better than most.

"She has been in fine spirits for the last year," Par-Salian continued. "Happy. Elated. She has also been extremely busy with something, for she has visited the tower only twice, and that to go through our collection of scrolls."

"I do have verification for my other news," Antimodes said. "As I had heard, a wealthy lord in the north is recruiting soldiers, and he is not being very particular about the type of soldiers he recruits. Ogres, hobgoblins, goblins. Even humans willing to trade their souls for loot. A friend of mine attended one of his rallies. Vast armies are being raised, armies of darkness. I even have a name for this lord—Ariakas. Do you know him?"

"I seem to remember something of him—a minor magus, if I'm not mistaken. Far more interested in gaining what he wanted quickly and brutally by the sword than by the more subtle and elegant means of sorcery."

"That sounds like the man." Antimodes sighed, shook his head morosely. "The sun is setting. Night is coming, my friend, and we cannot stop it."

"Yet we may be able to keep a few lights burning in the darkness," Par-Salian said quietly.

"Not without help!" Antimodes clenched his fist. "If only the gods would give us a sign!"

"I'd say Takhisis has already done just that," Par-Salian said wryly.

"The gods of good, I mean. Will they let her walk over them?" Antimodes demanded, impatient and exasperated. "When will Paladine and Mishakal finally make known their presence in the world?"

"Perhaps they are waiting for a sign from us," Par-Salian observed mildly.

"A sign of what?"

"Of faith. That we trust in them and believe in them, even though we do not understand their plan."

Antimodes regarded his friend narrowly. Then, leaning back in his chair, continuing to keep his gaze on Par-Salian, Antimodes scratched his raspy jaw. Par-Salian bore up under the intense scrutiny. He smiled to let his friend know that his thinking was traveling along the right road.

"So that is what this is all about," Antimodes said after a moment.

Par-Salian inclined his head.

"I wondered. He is so very young. Skilled, admittedly, but very young. And inexperienced."

"He will gain in experience," Par-Salian said. "We have some time before us, do we not?"

Antimodes considered the matter. "These ogres and goblins and humans must be trained, molded into a fighting force, which may prove extremely difficult. As it stands now, they would just as soon kill each other as the enemy. Ariakas has a monumental job on his hands. If rumor is true and the dragons have returned, they must also be controlled in some manner, although it will take those of strong will and courage to accomplish that! So, yes, in answer to your question, I say that we have time. Some time, but not much. The young man will never wear the white robes. You know that, don't you?"

"I know that," Par-Salian replied calmly. "I've been listening to Theobald rant and rave about Raistlin Majere for years, practically ever since he started school as a child. I know his faults: He is secretive and conniving, arrogant, ambitious, and hungry."

"He is also creative, intelligent, and courageous," Antimodes added. He was proud of his ward. "Witness his deft handling of that renegade witch, Judith. He cast a spell far above his level of ability, a spell he should not have even been able to read, let alone command. And he cast it by himself, without help."

"Which only goes to prove that he will bend rules, even break them if it suits his purpose," Par-Salian said. "No, no. Don't feel the need to defend him further. I am aware of his merits as I am aware of his weaknesses. That is why I invited him to take the Test, rather than bring him up before the Conclave on charges, as I should do by rights, I suppose. Do you think he murdered her?"

"I do not." Antimodes was firm. "If for no other reason than cutting someone's throat is not Raistlin's style. Far too messy. He is a skilled herbalist. If he had wanted her dead, he would have slipped a little nightshade into her tarbean tea."

"You believe him capable of murder, then?" Par-Salian asked, frowning.

"Who among us is not, given the right set of circumstances? There is a rival tailor in my town, an odious man who cheats his customers and spreads vicious lies about his competitors, including my brother. I myself have been tempted more than once to send Bigby's Crushing Hand knocking on his door." Antimodes looked quite fierce when he said this.

Par-Salian hid a smile in another glass of wine.

"You yourself used to say that those who walk the paths of night had better know how to see in the dark," Antimodes continued. "You don't want him bumbling about blindly, I suppose."

"That was part of my reasoning. The Test will teach him a few things about himself. Things he might not like to know, but which are necessary to his understanding of himself and the power he wields."

"The Test is a humbling experience," Antimodes said with something between a sigh and shudder.

Their faces lengthened, they cast surreptitious glances at each other to see if their thoughts were once more traveling in similar directions. It seemed that the thoughts were concurrent, as evidenced by the fact that they had no need to name the personage about whom they now spoke.

"He will undoubtedly be there," said Antimodes in a low voice. He glanced around guardedly, as if he feared they might be overheard in the chamber, a chamber that stood alone in the topmost part of the tower, a chamber to which no one but the two of them had access.

"Yes, I fear so," said Par-Salian, looking grave. "He will take particular interest in this young man."

"We should finish him, once and for all."

"We've tried," Par-Salian said. "And you know the results as well as I do. We cannot touch him on his plane of existence. Not only that, but I suspect that Nuitari guards him."

"He should. He never had a more loyal servant. Talk of murders!" Leaning forward, Antimodes spoke in a conspiratorial undertone. "We could limit the young man's access to him."

"And what of freedom of will? That has always been the hallmark of our orders. A freedom many have sacrificed their lives to protect! Do we throw the right to choose our own destinies to the Abyss?"

Antimodes was chastened. "Forgive me, friend. I spoke in haste. I am fond of the young man, though. Fond and proud of him. He has done me great credit. I would hate to see harm befall him."

"Indeed he has done you credit. And he will continue to do so, I hope. His own choices will lead him on the path he is to walk, as our choices led us. I trust they may be wise ones."

"The Test will be hard on him. He is a frail youth."

"The blade must pass through the fire, else it will break."

"And if he dies? What of your plans then?"

"Then I will look for someone else. Ladonna spoke to me of a promising young elf magus. His name is Dalamar. . . ."

Their conversation turned to other matters, to Ladonna's pupil, dire events in the world, and eventually to the area that interested them most—magic.

Above the Tower, silver Solinari and red Lunitari shone brightly. Nuitari was there as well, a dark hole in the constellations. The three moons were full this night, as was necessary for the Test.

In the lands beyond the tower, far, far away from the room where the two archmagi sipped their elven wine and spoke of the fate of the world, the young mages who were traveling to the Tower to take the Test slept restlessly, if they slept at all. In the morning, the Forest of Wayreth would find them, lead them to their fate.

Tomorrow some might sleep, never to wake again.

2

THE TWINS' JOURNEY TO THE TOWER TOOK THEM OVER A MONTH.
They had expected it would take longer, for they had thought they
would be traveling on foot. Shortly after their friends had left Solace,
a messenger arrived to say that two horses had been delivered to the
public stables in the name of Majere. The horses were gifts from Raistlin's
sponsor, Antimodes.

The young men traveled southwest through Haven. Raistlin stopped
to pay his respects to Lemuel, who reported that the temple of Belzor had
been razed, its stone blocks used to build homes for the poor. This had
been accomplished under the auspices of a new and apparently harmless
religious order known as the Seekers. Lemuel had reopened his mageware
shop. He showed Raistlin the black bryony, which was flourishing. He
asked where they were bound. Raistlin replied that they were traveling
for fun, taking a roundabout route to Pax Tharkas.

Lemuel looked very grave at this, wished them luck and a safe road many
times, and sighed deeply when they left.

The two continued their journey, riding south along the western slopes
of the Kharolis Mountains, skirting the borders of Qualinesti.

Although they kept close watch, they saw no elves. Yet the two were always
aware of the elves watching them. Caramon suggested visiting Tanis, seeing
the elven kingdom. Raistlin reminded him that their journey was secret, they
were supposed to be in Pax Tharkas. Besides, he doubted if they would be
able to convince the elves to admit them. The Qualinesti took more kindly
to humans than did their cousins, the Silvanesti, but with evil rumors flying
on dark wings from the north, the Qualinesti were wary of strangers.

On the last morning of their journey along the border, the two woke to find an elven arrow embedded at the foot of each of their bedrolls. The Qualinesti's message was clear: We have allowed you to pass, but don't come back.

The brothers breathed a little easier once they were out of elven lands, but they could not relax their vigilance, for now began their search for the wayward Forest of Wayreth. The lands in this part of Abanasinia were wild and desolate. Once the two were set upon by thieves, another time a band of goblins passed by so near that the twins could have reached out and smacked one on its scaly hide.

The bandits had thought to jump defenseless young travelers. Caramon's sword and Raistlin's fiery spells soon apprised them of their mistake. The bandits left one of their number dead on the road, the rest dashed off to bind their wounds. The goblins proved too numerous to fight, however. The brothers took refuge in a cave until the troop had marched past, heading northward at a rapid pace.

The twins spent four days searching for the forest. Caramon, frustrated and nervous, said more than once that they ought to turn back. He consulted three maps—one given him by Tasslehoff, one provided by an innkeeper in Haven, and another taken from the body of the thief. Not one of the maps showed the forest in the same location.

Raistlin soothed his brother's concerns with as much calm as he could muster, though he himself was starting to worry. Tomorrow was the seventh day, and they had seen no sign of the forest.

That night they spread their bedrolls in a clearing of scraggly pines. They awakened to find themselves lying beneath the huge, spreading bows of enormous oak trees.

Caramon almost fled then and there. The oak trees were not ordinary oak trees. He saw eyes in the knotholes, he heard spoken words in the rustling of the leaves. He heard words in the songs of the birds as well. Though he couldn't understand them clearly, the birds seemed to him to be warning him to leave.

The twins gathered their belongings, mounted their horses. The oak trees stood shoulder to shoulder, stalwart guards blocking their path. Raistlin regarded the trees in silence a moment, summoning his courage. He urged his horse forward. The oaks parted, forming a clear path that led straight to the tower.

Caramon tried to ride after his brother. The trees glared at him with hatred, the leaves rustled in anger. His courage failed him. Fear took hold of him, wrung him, left him weak and helpless, powerless to move.

"Raist!" he cried hoarsely.

Raistlin turned. Seeing his brother's predicament, he rode back. He reached out, took hold of his brother's hand.

"Do not be afraid, Caramon. I am with you."

The two entered the forest together.

❂

On the seventh day of the seventh month, seven magi were ushered into a large courtyard at the base of the Tower of High Sorcery.

Four men and three women: Four were human, two elven, and one appeared to be half-human, half-dwarf, a rather unusual combination for a magic-user. The youngest by almost five years was Raistlin Majere, the only one to arrive with an escort. The others glanced askance at the young mage, observed his delicate features, his pallor, and the excessive thinness that made him appear younger than he was.

They wondered why he was here, and why he was permitted to have a family member with him. The elves were open in their disdain. The half-dwarf suspected the young man of having sneaked in uninvited, though he could not say how.

The garden courtyard in the Tower of High Sorcery was an eerie place, crisscrossed with corridors of magic. Magi passed through here regularly, traveling the magic pathways on errands to the tower or on business of their own. Those standing in the garden could not see the travelers on their hidden pathways, but it seemed to them that they could feel the breath of their passing.

The older, more experienced magi who frequented the tower grew accustomed to the sudden shifting eddies of magic that swirled about the courtyard. This being the first occasion any of the novices had visited the tower, they found the voices that spoke from nothingness, the sudden whiffs of air down the back of the neck, the half-seen flash of a hand or foot, most disturbing.

The initiates and the single lone warrior stood in the courtyard, waiting for what they hoped would be the beginning of their lives as one of this elite group of wizards. The initiates tried not to think about the fact that this might be the last day of their lives.

Caramon jumped, with a clatter of sword and leather armor, and whipped around to stare fearfully behind him.

"Hold still! You are making a fool of yourself, Caramon," Raistlin admonished as they stood waiting in the courtyard.

"I felt a hand touch my back," Caramon said, pale and sweating.

"Very probably," Raistlin murmured, unperturbed. "Pay it no mind."

"I don't like this place, Raist!" Caramon's voice sounded unnaturally loud in the whispering stillness. "Let's go back home. You're a good enough mage without having to put up with this!"

His words carried quite clearly. The other initiates turned to stare. The upper lip of one of the elves curled in a sneer.

Raistlin felt the hot blood flood his face. "Hush, Caramon!" he rebuked, his voice quivering with anger. "You are shaming us both!"

Caramon shut his mouth, bit his lip.

Raistlin deliberately turned his back on his twin. He could not fathom why the conclave had insisted on Caramon's being a part of his brother's testing.

"Unless they plan on aggravating me to death," Raistlin muttered to himself.

He tried to ignore Caramon's presence, concentrating on banishing his own nervous fears. There was no reason he should be afraid. He had studied his spellbook, he knew it inside out, could have recited his spells backward while standing on his head, if that was what the judges might require. He had proven that he could work his magic under pressure. He would not fall apart, nor would his spell fall apart, in tense situations.

He need not be concerned about his abilities to perform magic during the Test. Nor was he particularly worried about the intangible portions of the Test, the part wherein the mage learns more about himself. Introspective from birth, Raistlin was confident that he knew all there was to know about his own inner workings.

For him, the Test would be a mere formality.

Raistlin relaxed, discovered that he was actually looking forward to the Test. His worries eased, he spent the time waiting for the judges to arrive in studying the fabled Tower of Wayreth.

"I will see it often in the future," he said to himself and envisioned traveling the unseen pathways, tending herbs in the garden, studying in the great library.

The tower at Wayreth was in actuality two towers, constructed of polished black obsidian. The main towers were surrounded by a wall in the shape of an equilateral triangle, with three smaller towers located at each of the angles. The wall surrounded the garden, where grew many varieties of herbs used not only for spell components, but also for healing and cooking.

The tops of the walls had no battlements, for the tower was protected by strong magicks. The forest would not permit the entry of anyone unless he had been invited by the conclave. If an enemy did, by some mischance, manage to stumble into the forest, the magical creatures roaming within would deal with the foe.

There was need for such precautions. Long ago there had been five Towers of High Sorcery, centers for magic on Ansalon. During the rise of Istar, the Kingpriest, who secretly feared magic and the power of wizards, outlawed magic. He caused mobs to rise against the wizards, hoping to eradicate them.

The wizards might have fought back, and some advocated the use of force, but the conclave deemed such drastic action unwise. Defending themselves would result in tragic loss of life on both sides. The Kingpriest and his followers wanted bloody conflict. Then they could point an accusing finger at the wizards and say, "We were right! They are a menace and should be destroyed!"

The conclave made a bargain with the Kingpriest. The wizards would abandon their towers, retreat to a single tower located in Wayreth. Here they would continue to study unmolested. The Kingpriest, though disappointed that the wizards chose not to fight, agreed. He had already taken control of the Tower of High Sorcery at Istar, and now he looked forward to gaining the exquisitely lovely tower in Palanthas. He planned to make it a temple to his greatness.

As he entered the tower to claim it, a black-robed wizard, purportedly insane, leapt from one of the tower's upper windows. The wizard impaled himself upon the sharp barbs of the iron fence below. With his dying breath, he cast a curse upon the tower, saying that none should inhabit it except the Master of Past and Present.

Who was this mysterious master? No one could say. Certainly it was not the Kingpriest. As he watched, horrified, the tower altered in appearance, becoming so hideous in aspect that those looking at it were constrained to cover their eyes. Even then, those who saw it were forever haunted by the dreadful sight.

The Kingpriest sent for powerful clerics to try to lift the curse. Surrounded by the Shoikan Grove, a forest of fear, the tower was guarded by the dark god Nuitari, who paid no attention to prayers uttered to any god except himself. The clerics of Paladine came, but they ran whimpering from the site. The clerics of Mishakal tried to enter. They barely escaped with their lives.

When the gods cast down the fiery mountain on Ansalon, the Cataclysm sent Istar to the bottom of the Blood Sea. Quakes broke the continent of Ansalon, ripping it apart, forming new seas, creating new mountain ranges. The city of Palanthas shook on its foundations, houses and buildings toppled. Yet not a leaf in the Shoikan Grove so much as shivered.

Dark, silent, empty, the tower waited for its master, whoever that maybe.

Raistlin pondered the history of the towers. In his mind, he was already walking the halls of the Tower of Wayreth, an accepted and revered wizard, when an unseen bell chimed seven times.

The seven initiates, who had been walking in the garden, visiting with each other, or standing apart, reciting their spells to themselves, came to a halt. All talking ceased.

Some faces paled in fear, others flushed in excitement. The elves, priding themselves on showing no emotion before humans, appeared nonchalant, bored.

"What's that?" Caramon asked, hoarse with nervousness.

"It is time, my brother," Raistlin said.

"Raist, please . . ." Caramon began.

Seeing the expression on his brother's face—the narrowed eyes, the frowning brows, the hard, firm set of the lips—Caramon swallowed his final plea.

A disembodied hand appeared, floating above the roses in the center of the garden.

"Oh, shit!" Caramon breathed. His hand closed convulsively over the hilt of his sword, but he did not need his brother's warning glance to understand that he should not draw any weapon on these grounds. He doubted if he could have found the strength to do so.

The hand beckoned. The initiates drew their hoods over their heads, placed their hands in the sleeves of their robes, and silently walked in the direction the hand indicated, heading for a small tower located between the two larger towers.

Raistlin and his brother, who had been the last to arrive, brought up the rear of the line.

The hand pointed at the door in the foremost tower, a door whose knocker was the head of a dragon. No one was required to knock to gain entry. The door opened silently as they approached.

One by one, each of the initiates filed inside. Leaving the sunlit garden, they entered a darkness so thick that all were temporarily blinded. Those in front halted, uncertain where to go, afraid to go anywhere that they could not see. Those coming behind them bunched up inside the doorway. Caramon, entering last, blundered into all of them.

"Sorry. Excuse me. I didn't see—"

"Silence."

The darkness spoke. The initiates obeyed. Caramon was silent, too, or tried to be. His leather creaked, his sword rattled, his boots clattered. His stentorian breathing echoed throughout the chamber.

"Turn to your left and walk toward the light," ordered the voice that was as disembodied as the hand.

The initiates did as commanded. A light appeared, and they moved toward it with quiet, shuffling steps, Caramon tromping along loudly behind.

A small corridor of stone, lit by torches whose pale fire burned steadily, gave no warmth and made no smoke, opened into a vast hall.

"The Hall of Mages," Raistlin whispered, digging his nails into the flesh of his arms, using the pain to contain his excitement.

The others shared his awe, his elation. The elves dropped their stoic masks. Their eyes shone, their lips parted in wonder. Each one of the initiates had dreamed of this moment, dreamed of standing in the Hall of Mages, a place forbidden, a place most people on Krynn would never see.

"No matter what happens, this is worth it," Raistlin said silently.

Only Caramon remained unaffected, except by fear. He hung his head, refused to look to left or right, as if hoping that if he did not look, it would all go away.

The chamber walls were obsidian, shaped smooth by magic. The ceiling was lost in shadow. No pillars supported it.

Light shone, white light that illuminated twenty-one stone chairs, arranged in a semicircle. Seven of the chairs bore black cushions, seven of them red cushions, and seven white cushions. Here was the meeting place of the Conclave of Wizards. A single chair stood in the center of the semicircle. This chair was slightly larger than the rest. Here sat the head of the conclave. The cushion on the chair was white.

At first glance, the chairs were empty.

At second glance, they were not. Wizards occupied them, men and women of different races, wearing the different colors suitable to their orders.

Caramon gasped and lurched unsteadily on his feet. Raistlin's hand closed viciously over his twin's arm, probably hurting his brother as much as it supported him.

Caramon was having a very bad time of it. He had never taken either magic or his brother's gift for magic seriously. To him, magic was coins dribbling from the nose, bunnies popping up unexpectedly, giant kender. Even that spell had impressed Caramon only moderately. When it came down to it, the kender had not really turned into a giant at all. It was only illusion, trickery. Trickery and magic had been all muddled up in Caramon's mind.

This was not trickery. What he witnessed was a raw display of power, intended to impress and intimidate. Caramon continued to fear for his brother. If he could have, he would have snatched Raistlin from that place and fled. But somewhere in the depths of Caramon's mind, he was finally beginning to understand the high stakes for which his brother gambled, stakes high enough that it might be worth betting his life.

The wizard in the center chair rose to his feet.

"That is Par-Salian, head of the conclave," Raistlin whispered to his brother, hoping to save Caramon from yet another gaffe. "Be polite!"

The initiates bowed respectfully, Caramon along with the rest.

"Greetings," said Par-Salian in a kind and welcoming tone.

The great archmage was in his early sixties at the time, though his long white hair, wispy white beard, and his stooped shoulders made him look older. He had never been robust, had always preferred study to action. He worked constantly to develop new spells, refine and enhance old ones. He was eager for magical artifacts as a child is eager for sugarplums. His apprentices spent much of their time traveling the continent in search of artifacts and scrolls or in tracking down rumors of such.

Par-Salian was also a keen observer and participant in the politics of Ansalon, unlike many wizards who held themselves above the trivial, everyday dealings of an ignorant populace. The head of the conclave had contacts in every single government of any importance on Ansalon. Antimodes was not Par-Salian's only source of information. He kept most of his knowledge secret and to himself, unless it benefited his plans to do otherwise.

Though few knew the full extent of his influence in Ansalon, an aura of wisdom and power surrounded Par-Salian with an almost visible halo of white light, shining so brightly that the two Silvanesti elves, who held most humans in the same regard as other races held kender, bowed low to him and then bowed again.

"Greetings, initiates," Par-Salian repeated, "and guest."

His gaze went to Caramon, seemed to strike right to the big man's heart and set him trembling.

"You have each come at the appointed time by invitation to undergo tests of your skills and your talent, your creativity, your thought processes, and, most importantly, the testing of yourself. What are your limits? How far can you push beyond those limits? What are your flaws? How might those flaws impede your abilities? Uncomfortable questions, but questions we each must answer, for only when we know ourselves—faults and strengths alike—will we have access to the full potential that is within us."

The initiates stood silent and circumspect, nervous and awed and anxious to begin.

Par-Salian smiled. "Don't worry. I know how eager you are, and therefore I will not indulge in long speeches. Again I want to bid you welcome and to extend my blessing. I ask that Solinari be with you this day."

He lifted his hands. The initiates bowed their heads. Par-Salian resumed his seat.

The head of the Order of Red Robes stood up, moved briskly on to the business at hand.

"When your name is called, step forward and accompany one of the judges, who will take you to the area where the testing will begin. I am certain you are all familiar with the criteria of the testing, but the conclave requires me to read it to you now, so that none can later claim he or she entered into this unknowingly. I remind you that these are guidelines only. Each Test is specially designed for the individual initiate and may include all or only a part of what the guidelines call for.

" 'There shall be at least three tests of the initiate's knowledge of magic and its use. The Test shall require the casting of all of the spells known to the initiate, at least three tests that cannot be solved by magic alone, and at least one combat against an opponent who is higher in rank than the initiate.' Do you have any questions?"

Not one of the initiates did; the questions were locked in each person's heart. Caramon had a great many questions, but he was too awed to be able to ask them.

"Then," said the Red Robe, "I ask that Lunitari walk with you."

He sat back down.

The head of the Order of Black Robes rose to her feet. "I ask that Nuitari walk with you." Unfurling a scroll, she began to read off names.

As each name was called, the initiate stepped forward, to be met by one of the members of the conclave. The initiate was led in silence and with the utmost solemnity into the shadows of the hall, then vanished.

One by one, each of the initiates departed until only one, Raistlin Majere, remained.

Raistlin stood stoically, with outward calm, as the numbers of his fellows dwindled around him. But his hands, inside his sleeves where they could not be seen, clenched to fists. The irrational fear came to him that perhaps there had been some mistake, that he was not supposed to be here. Perhaps they had changed their minds and would send him off. Or perhaps his loutish brother had done something to offend them, and Raistlin would be dismissed in shame and ignominy.

The Black Robe finished reading the names, shut the scroll with a snap, and still Raistlin stood in the Hall of Mages, except that now he stood alone. He maintained his rigid pose, waited to hear his fate.

Par-Salian rose to his feet, came forward to meet the young man. "Raistlin Majere, we have left you to the last because of the unusual circumstances. You have brought an escort."

"I was requested to do so, Great One," Raistlin said, the words coming in a whisper from his dry mouth. Clearing his throat, he said, more forcefully, "This is my twin brother, Caramon."

"Welcome, Caramon Majere," said Par-Salian. His blue eyes, in their maze of wrinkles, peered deep into Caramon's soul.

Caramon mumbled something that no one heard and subsided into unhappy silence.

"I wanted to explain to you why we requested the presence of your brother," Par-Salian continued, shifting his astute gaze back to Raistlin. "We want to assure you that you are not unique, nor have we singled you out. We do this in the case of all twins who come to the testing. We have discovered that twins have an extremely close bond, closer than most siblings, almost as if the two were in reality one being split in twain. Of course, in most cases, both twins take up the study of magic, both having a talent for it. You are unusual in this respect, Raistlin, in that you alone show a talent for the art. Have you ever had any interest in magic, Caramon?"

Called upon to speak, to answer such a startling question, one that he had in truth never even considered, Caramon opened his mouth, but it was Raistlin who answered.

"No, he has not."

Par-Salian looked at the two of them. "I see. Very well. Thank you for coming, Caramon. And now, Raistlin Majere, will you be so good as to accompany Justarius? He will take you the area where the Test begins."

Raistlin's relief was so great that he was momentarily faint and dizzy, obliged to close his eyes until he regained his balance. He paid scant attention to the Red Robe who stepped forward, aware only that it was an older man who walked with a pronounced limp.

Raistlin bowed to Par-Salian. Spellbook in hand, he turned to accompany the Red Robe.

Caramon took a step to follow his twin.

Par-Salian was quick to intervene. "I am sorry, Caramon, but you cannot accompany your brother."

"But you told me to come," Caramon protested, fear giving him the voice he had lacked.

"Yes, and it will be our pleasure to entertain you during your brother's absence," Par-Salian said, and though his tone was pleasant, there was no arguing with his words.

"Good . . . good luck, Raist," Caramon called out awkwardly.

Raistlin, embarrassed, ignored his brother, pretended he had not heard him. Justarius led the way into the shadows of the hall.

Raistlin was gone, walking where his brother could not follow.

"I have a question!" Caramon cried. "Is it true that sometimes the initiates die—"

He was talking to a door. He was inside a room, a very comfortable room that might have been lifted from one of the finest inns in Ansalon. A fire burned on the hearth. A table, loaded with food, all of Caramon's favorite dishes, and a most excellent ale.

Caramon paid no attention to the food. Angry at what he considered high-handed treatment, he tried to open the door.

The handle came off in his hands.

Now extremely fearful for his brother, suspecting some sort of sinister intent on Raistlin's life, Caramon was determined to rescue his twirl. He hurled himself at the door. It shook beneath his weight but did not budge. He beat at the door with his fists, shouting for someone to come and release him.

"Caramon Majere."

The voice came from behind him.

Startled and alarmed, Caramon turned around so fast that he tripped over his own feet. Stumbling, he clutched at the table and stared. Par-Salian stood in the center of the room. He smiled reassuringly at Caramon.

"Forgive my dramatic arrival, but the door is wizard-locked, and it's such a bother removing the spell and then putting it on again. Is the room comfortable? Is there anything we might bring you?"

"Damn the room!" Caramon thundered. "They told me he might die."

"That is true, but he is aware of the risks."

"I want to be with him," said Caramon. "I'm his twin. I have that right."

"You are with him," said Par-Salian softly. "He takes you everywhere."

Caramon didn't understand. He wasn't with Raistlin, they were trying to trick him, that's all. He brushed the meaningless words aside.

"Let me go to him." He glowered and clenched his fists. "Either you let me go or I'll tear down this Tower stone by stone."

Par-Salian stroked his beard to hide his smile. "I'll make a bargain with you, Caramon. You permit our tower to remain standing, unharmed, and I'll permit you to watch your brother as he takes his Test. You will not be allowed to help or assist him in any way, but perhaps watching him may alleviate your fears."

Caramon thought it over. "Yeah. All right," he said. Once he knew where Raistlin was, Caramon figured he could go to him if he needed help.

"I'm ready. Take me to him. Oh, and thanks, but I'm not thirsty now."

Par-Salian was pouring water from a pitcher into a bowl.

"Sit down, Caramon," he said.

"We're going to go find Raist—"

"Sit down, Caramon," Par-Salian repeated. "You want to see your twin? Look into the bowl."

"But it's only water. . . ."

Par-Salian passed his hand over the water in the bowl, spoke a single magic word, scattered a few crumbled leaves of plants into the water.

Sitting down, planning to first humor the old man and then grab him by his scrawny throat, Caramon looked into the water.

3

RAISTLIN TRUDGED DOWN A LONELY, LITTLE-TRAVELED ROAD ON THE outskirts of Haven. Night was falling, a stiffening breeze swayed the treetops, sent autumn leaves flying. There was a smell of lightning in the humid air. He had been traveling all day on foot, he was tired and hungry, and now a storm was approaching. All thought of spending the night sleeping on the ground vanished from his mind.

A tinker he had met earlier had told him, in response to a question, that there was an inn up ahead, an inn with the droll name of the Inn Between. The tinker added the warning that the inn had an evil reputation, was known to be frequented by the wrong sort of crowd. Raistlin didn't care what sort of crowd drank there, so long as the inn had a bed beneath a roof and they let him sleep in it. He had little fear of thieves. It must be obvious from his shabby robes that he carried nothing of value. The very sight of those robes—the robes of a magic-user—would make the ordinary footpad think twice before accosting him.

The Inn Between, so called because it was located equidistant between Haven and Qualinesti, did not look propitious. The paint on its hanging sign was faded past recognition—no great loss to the art community. The owner, having expended his wit on the name, had not been able think of any way to illustrate it beyond a huge red **X** in the middle of a squiggle that might have been a road.

The building itself had a sullen and defiant air, as if it were tired of being teased about its clever name and would, in a fit of ill temper, tumble down upon the head of the next person who mentioned it. The shutters were half closed, giving its windows a suspicious squint. Its eaves sagged like frowning brows.

The door opened with such reluctance that Raistlin, on the first try, thought the inn might have closed down. He could hear voices and laughter inside, smell the scent of food. A second, more forceful push, caused the door to relinquish. It opened grudgingly, with a screech of rusted hinges, slammed shut quickly behind him, as much as to say, "Don't blame me. I did my best to warn you."

The laughter stopped at Raistlin's entrance. The inn's guests turned their heads to look at him, consider him, prepare to take whatever action they deemed appropriate. The bright light of a roaring fire partially dazzled him. He could see nothing for a moment until his eyes adjusted, and therefore he had no idea whether any of the guests had taken an unusual interest in him. By the time he could see, they had all gone back to doing whatever it was they were doing.

Most of them, that is. One group, consisting of three cloaked and hooded figures, seated on the far side of the room, paid him considerable attention. When they resumed their conversation, they put their heads together, talking excitedly, occasionally lifting their heads to cast glittering-eyed glances in his direction.

Raistlin found an empty booth near the fire, sat down thankfully to rest and warm himself. A glance at the plates of his fellow guests showed that the food was plain fare. It didn't look particularly tasty, but didn't appear likely to poison him either. Stew being the only dish offered, he ordered that, along with a glass of wine.

He ate a few bites of unnameable meat, then pushed the bits of potato and coagulated gravy around with his spoon. The wine was surprisingly good, with a taste of clover. He relished it and was regretting that his meager purse could not afford him a second glass when a cool pitcher appeared at his elbow.

Raistlin lifted his head.

One of the cloaked men who had been so interested in Raistlin stood at his table.

"Greetings, stranger," the man said, speaking Common with a slight accent, an accent that reminded Raistlin of Tanis.

Raistlin was not surprised to see an elf, though he was extremely surprised to hear the elf add, "My friends and I noticed how much you enjoyed the wine. It comes from Qualinesti, as do we. My friends and I would like to share this pitcher of our fine wine with you, sir."

No respectable elf would be found drinking in a human-owned tavern. No respectable elf would initiate a conversation with a human. No respectable elf would buy a human a pitcher of wine. This gave Raistlin a pretty good idea of the status of his new acquaintances.

They must be dark elves—those who have been "cast from the light" or exiled from the elven homelands, the worst possible fate that can befall an elf.

"What you drink and with whom you drink is your prerogative, sir," Raistlin said warily.

"It's not prerogative," the elf returned. "It's wine."

He smiled, thinking himself clever. "And it's yours, if you want it. Do you mind if I sit down?"

"Forgive me for seeming rude, sir. I am not in the mood for company."

"Thank you. I accept the invitation." The elf slid into the seat opposite.

Raistlin rose to his feet. This had gone far enough. "I bid you good evening, sir. I am in need of rest. If you will excuse me . . ."

"You're a magic-user, aren't you?" the elf asked. He had not removed the hood that covered his head, but his eyes were visible. Almond-shaped, they gleamed hard and clear, as if the liquid orbs had frozen.

Raistlin saw no need to answer such an impertinent and perhaps dangerous question. He turned away, intending to bargain with the innkeeper for a patch of floor near the fire in the common room.

"Pity," said the elf. "It would be your good fortune if you were—a magic-user, I mean. My friends and I"—he nodded his head in the direction of his two hooded companions—"have in mind a little job where a wizard might come in handy."

Raistlin said nothing. He did not leave the table, however, but remained standing, regarded the elf with more interest.

"There's money to be had," the elf said, smiling.

Raistlin shrugged.

The elf was puzzled at his reaction. "Odd. I thought humans were always interested in money. It seems I was wrong. What might tempt you? Ah, I know. Magic! Of course. Artifacts, enchanted rings. Spellbooks."

The elf rose gracefully to his feet. "Come meet my brethren. Hear what we've got in mind. Then if you happen to run across a mage"—the elf winked—"you could let him know he could make his fortune by joining up with us."

"Bring the wine," Raistlin said. Walking through the inn, he joined the other two elves at their table.

The elf, smiling, picked up the pitcher and brought it along.

Raistlin knew something about the Qualinesti from Tanis, probably knew more than most humans, for he had questioned the half-elf extensively on elven ways and practices. The three were tall and slender, as are all elves, and though most elves look alike to humans, Raistlin thought he detected a certain resemblance between them. All three had green eyes and peculiarly jutting, pointed chins. They were young, probably around two hundred. They wore short swords beneath their cloaks—he could hear the metal strike the chairs occasionally—and probably carried knives. He could hear the creak of leather armor.

He wondered what crime they had committed that was vile enough to be sent into exile, a punishment worse than death to elves. He had the feeling he was about to find out.

The elf who had spoken to Raistlin was the spokesman for the group. The other two rarely opened their mouths. Perhaps they didn't speak Common. Many elves did not, scorned to learn a human language.

"I am Liam." The elf made introductions. "This is Micah and Renet. And your name would be? . . ."

"Of little interest to you, sir," Raistlin replied.

"Oh, but I assure you, it is, sir," Liam returned. "I like to know the name of any man with whom I'm drinking."

"Majere," Raistlin said.

"Majere?" Liam frowned. "One of the ancient gods was called by that name, I believe."

"And so am I." Raistlin sipped at his wine. "Though I do not claim godhood. Please explain the nature of this job, sir. I don't find the company of dark elves so appealing that I want to prolong this interview."

An angry glint came into the eye of one of the other elves, the one called Renet. His fist clenched, he started to stand. Liam snapped words in elven, shoved his friend back down in his seat. Raistlin's question was answered, however. At least one of the other elves understood Common.

Raistlin himself spoke a smattering of Qualinesti, having learned the language from Tanis. He did not let on that he understood what was being said, however, thinking he might pick up useful information if the elves imagined they could speak freely among themselves in their own tongue.

"This is no time to be thin-skinned, Cousin. We need this human," Liam said in elven.

Shifting to Common, he added, "You must forgive my cousin, sir. He's a bit hot-tempered. I think you might be a little friendlier toward us, Majere. We're doing you a big favor."

"If you are looking for friends, I suggest you talk to the barmaid," Raistlin said. "She looks as if she could accommodate you. If you want to hire a mage, then you should explain the job."

"You are a mage, then," Liam asked with a sly grin.

Raistlin nodded.

Liam eyed him. "You look very young."

Raistlin was growing irritated. "You are the one who approached me, sir. You knew what I looked like when you invited me to join you." He started to rise. "It seems I have wasted my time."

"All right! All right! I don't suppose it matters how young you are, so long as you can do the work." Liam leaned forward, lowered his voice. "Here is the proposal. There's a mage living in Haven who owns a mageware shop. He's human, like yourself. His name is Lemuel. You know him?"

Raistlin did in fact know Lemuel, having had dealings with him in the past. He considered Lemuel a friend, hoped to find out what these unsavory elves wanted, with a view toward warning him.

Raistlin shrugged. "Whom I know is my own affair and none of yours."

Micah, jerking a thumb at Raistlin, muttered in elven, "I don't much like this mage of yours, Cousin."

"Nobody's asking you to like him," Liam returned in elven, scowling. "Drink your wine and keep your mouth shut. I do the talking."

Raistlin watched blandly, with the vacant expression of one who has no idea what is being said.

Liam shifted back to Common. "Now then, our plan is this: We enter the mage's house in the night, steal the valuables from his shop, turn them into good, hard steel. That's where you come in. You'll know what's worth the taking and what isn't, plus you'll know where to sell the goods and get us a fair price. You will receive your share, of course."

Raistlin was scornful. "As it happens, sir, I have frequented the shop of this Lemuel, and I can tell you right now that you are wasting your time. He has nothing of value. His entire collection is worth twenty steel at most, hardly fit payment for your trouble."

Raistlin assumed that this would end the conversation, that he had discouraged the thieves from pursuing their nefarious scheme. At all events, he would warn Lemuel to take suitable precautions.

"If you gentlemen will excuse me . . ."

Liam reached out, grabbed hold of Raistlin's wrist. Feeling the mage stiffen, Liam let go, though his strong, thin-fingered hand hovered near. He exchanged glances with his cousins, as if asking their agreement to proceed. Reluctantly both nodded.

"You are right about the shop, sir," Liam admitted. "But perhaps you are not familiar with what the mage has hidden in his cellar below the kitchen."

As far as Raistlin knew, Lemuel had nothing hidden in the cellar. "What does he have hidden?"

"Spellbooks," Liam answered.

"Lemuel once had a few spellbooks in his possession, but I know for a fact that he sold them."

"Not all of them!" Liam sunk his voice to beneath a whisper. "He has more. Many more. Ancient spellbooks from back before the Cataclysm! Spellbooks that many thought were lost to this world! That is the true prize!"

Lemuel had never mentioned such books to Raistlin. He had, in fact, pretended that Raistlin had acquired all the books in the older mage's possession. Raistlin felt betrayed.

"How do you know this?" he asked sharply.

Liam smiled unpleasantly. "You are not the only one with secrets, sir."

"Then, once more, I bid you good night."

"Oh, for the love of the Queen, tell him!" said one of the cousins in Qualinesti. "We are wasting time! Dracart wants those spellbooks delivered within the fortnight!"

"Dracart forbade us—"

"Tell him part of the truth, then,"

Liam turned back to Raistlin. "Micah visited the shop on the pretext of buying herbs. If you know this Lemuel, you know that he is stupid and naive, even by human standards. He left Micah alone in the shop while he went to his garden. Micah made a wax impression of the key to the front door."

"How do you know of the existence of the spellbooks?" Raistlin persisted.

"I tell you again, that must be our secret," Liam said, a hard and dangerous edge to his voice.

Guessing that this Dracart, whoever he was, had knowledge of the books, Raistlin tried another question, asking as innocently as he could, "And what do you intend to do with these spellbooks?"

"Sell them, of course. What possible use could they be to us?" Liam smiled. His cousins smiled. The elf's tone was persuasive, he did not blink an almond eye.

Raistlin considered. He was angered that Lemuel had lied about the existence of such valuable spellbooks. But he wanted no harm to come to the mage, for all that.

"I will not be party to murder," Raistlin said.

"Nor will we!" Liam stated emphatically. "This Lemuel has many friends in the elven lands, guest friends who would feel obligated to avenge his death. The mage is not at home. He has left to visit these friends of his in

Qualinost. The house is empty. An hour's work and we will be rich men! As for you, you can either take your share in magic artifacts or we will pay you in hard steel."

Raistlin wasn't thinking of money. He wasn't thinking of the fact that the elves were lying to him, that they were undoubtedly intending to use him and then find a way to conveniently get rid of him. He was thinking of spellbooks—ancient spellbooks, perhaps spellbooks that had been stolen from the besieged Tower of High Sorcery in Daltigoth, or rescued from the drowned Tower of Istar. What wealth of magic lay within their covers? And why was Lemuel keeping them secret, hidden away?

Raistlin had the answer immediately. These must be books of black magic. That was the only logical explanation. Lemuel's father had been a war wizard of the White Robes. He could not destroy the books. By strictest law, no member of one order could willfully destroy any magical artifact or spellbook belonging to another. Magical knowledge, no matter from whence it came, who produced it, or whom it might benefit, was precious and deserved protection. But he might have been tempted to conceal those spellbooks he considered evil. By hiding such books away. he could both preserve them and keep them from falling into the hands of his enemies.

It is my duty to look into this matter, Raistlin convinced himself. Besides, if I do not go with these elves, they will only find someone else, someone who might harm the books.

Thus Raistlin rationalized, but in his heart was the undeniable longing to see these books, to hold them and feel their power. Perhaps unlock their secrets . . .

"When do you propose to do this?" Raistlin asked.

"Lemuel left town two days ago. We are pressed for time. Tonight? Are you with us?"

Raistlin nodded. "I am with you."

4

THE RED AND SILVER MOONS SHONE BRIGHTLY; THE ORBS WERE CLOSE this night, as if the two gods were leaning their heads together, to whisper and laugh over the follies they viewed from high above. The silver and red light shone down on the thieves. Raistlin cast two shadows as he walked along the road. The shadows stretched before him. One shadow, tinged with silver, went to his right; the other, haloed by red, to his left. He could have almost imagined diverging paths, except that, in essence, both shadows were black.

They took a roundabout way to Lemuel's house to avoid passing through town. Raistlin did not recognize the route. They were coming from a different angle, and he was startled—startled and ill at ease—to suddenly see the mage's house loom in front of him before he was expecting it. The house was the same as Raistlin remembered, held the same appearance of being abandoned that it had worn the first time he had visited Lemuel. No lights shone in the windows, nor was there a single sound of anything living within. Lemuel had been at home then. What if he were at home now?

These dark elves would have no compunction about killing him.

Micah produced the skeleton key he had made, fitted it into the lock. The other two elves kept watch. Their cloaks were cast aside, providing easy access to their weapons. They were well equipped with daggers and knives, the weapons of thieves, weapons of assassins.

Raistlin felt a deep loathing for these dark elves, a loathing that extended to himself, for he was standing in the moonlight in the dead of night alongside them, preparing to enter a man's house without his knowledge or his permission.

I should turn right now and walk away, he thought to himself.

The door opened soundlessly. Beyond, it was dark and still. Raistlin hesitated only a moment, then he slipped inside.

He could have rationalized the situation. He had come too far to back out, the dark elves would never let him escape alive. He might have continued to pretend that he was doing this for Lemuel's own good to relieve him of books which must be a burden on the mage's soul.

Now that he was here, now that he was committed, Raistlin scorned to do either. He already loathed himself for the crime that he was about to commit, he didn't intend to add to that loathing by lying about his motives. He hadn't come here out of fear or constraint, he wasn't here in the name of loyalty and friendship.

He was here for the magic.

Raistlin stood in the darkness in the mageware shop with the elves, his heart beating fast with excitement and anticipation.

"The human cannot see in the dark," Liam said in Qualinesti. "We don't want him falling over something and breaking his neck."

"At least not until we are finished with him," Micah said, with a trilling, musical laugh that accorded oddly with his dire words.

"Strike a light."

One of the elves produced quickmatch, put the match to a candle standing on the counter. The elves politely handed the candle to Raistlin, who just as politely took it.

"This way." Micah led them from the shop.

Raistlin could have supplied himself with light, magical light, but he did not mention this to the elves. He chose to save his energy. He was going to need it before this night was out.

The four left the shop, entered the kitchen, which Raistlin remembered from his first visit. They continued through the pantry, entered a door, and passed into a small storage room containing a veritable thicket of mops and brooms. Working swiftly and silently, the elves cleared these to one side.

"I see no spellbooks," Raistlin remarked.

"Of course you don't," Liam grunted, barely biting off the appellation "fool." "I told you. They are hidden in the cellar. The trapdoor is beneath that table."

The table in question was a butcher's block, used to cut meat. Made of oak, it was stained with the blood of countless animals. Raistlin was amused to see that the sight and smell disgusted the dark elves, who were prepared to murder humans without compunction, but who looked queasy over the idea of steaks and lamb chops. Holding their breaths against what must have been to them a malodorous stench, Micah and Renet hauled the table to one side. Both hastily wiped their hands on a towel when they had finished.

"We will put back all as we have found it when we leave," Liam said. "This Lemuel is such a stupid, unobservant little man. He will likely go for years without noticing that the books have been discovered and removed."

Raistlin admitted the truth of this statement. Lemuel cared for nothing except his garden, took little interest in magic unless it pertained to his herbs. He had probably never even looked at these books, was merely obeying his father's injunction to keep them hidden.

When Raistlin took the books to the tower at Wayreth—which he fully intended to do, confessing his own sins at the time—the conclave could inform Lemuel that the books had been removed. As for what the conclave might do to Raistlin, he considered it likely that they would reprimand him for thievery, but probably nothing more severe. The conclave would not take kindly to the fact that these valuable spellbooks had been concealed all these years. Of the two crimes, they would consider concealment the greater.

Raistlin hoped their sanctions would fall on the father, if he still lived, not on the son.

Micah tugged at the handle of the trapdoor. It did not budge, and at first the elves thought it might be locked, either with bolts or magic. The elves checked for bolts, Raistlin cast a minor spell which would ascertain the presence of magic. No bolts were visible, neither was there a wizard-lock. The trapdoor was stuck tight, the wood having swelled with the damp. The elves wrenched and tugged and eventually the door popped open.

Cold air, cold and dank as the breath of a tomb, flowed up out of the darkness below. The air had a foul smell that caused the elves to wrinkle their noses and back off. Raistlin covered his mouth with the sleeve of his robe.

Micah and Renet cast furtive glances at Liam, fearful he was going to order them to walk down into that chancy darkness. Liam himself looked uneasy.

"What is that stench?" he wondered aloud. "It's like something died down there. Surely books on magic, even human books on magic, could not smell that bad."

"I am not afraid of a bad smell," Raistlin said scornfully. "I will go down to see what is amiss."

Micah was not happy at this; he took offense at Raistlin's suggestion of cowardice, though not offense enough to enter the cellar. The elves discussed the matter in their own language. Raistlin listened, diverted by their arrogance. They did not even consider the possibility that a human might be able to understand their language.

Renet concluded that Raistlin should go down alone. It was possible the spellbooks might have a guardian. Raistlin was a human and therefore expendable. Micah argued that since Raistlin was a mage, he might grab several of the spellbooks and abscond with them, traveling the corridors of magic, where the elves could not follow.

Liam had a solution to that problem. Giving gracious permission for Raistlin to enter the cellar first, the elf posted himself at the top of the stairs, armed with a bow and a nocked arrow.

"What is this?" Raistlin demanded, feigning ignorance.

"In order to protect you," Liam replied smoothly. "I am an excellent shot. And although I do not speak the language of magic, I understand a little of it. I would be able to tell, for example, if someone in that cellar were to try casting a spell that would make him disappear. I doubt if he would have time to complete the spell before my arrow struck him through the heart. But do not hesitate to call out if you find yourself in danger."

"I feel safe in your hands," Raistlin said, bowing to hide his sardonic smile.

Lifting the skirts of his robes—gray-colored robes, now that he looked at them—holding the candle high, he cautiously descended the steps that led into the darkness.

The staircase was a long one, longer than Raistlin had anticipated, leading deep under the ground. The stairs were carved of stone, a stone wall extended along on the right side, the stairs were open on his left. He shifted the candle as he walked, sending its pale light into as many portions of the cellar as it would reach, trying to catch a glimpse of something—anything. He could make out nothing. He continued his descent.

At last his foot touched dirt floor. He looked back up the stairs to see the elves small and diminished, a far distance away, almost as if they stood upon another plane of existence. He could hear their voices faintly; they were perturbed that he had passed beyond their sight. They decided that they would go down to find him.

Flashing the candle about, Raistlin tried to see as much as he could before the elves arrived. The candle's feeble light did not extend far. Expecting to hear the elves' soft footfalls, Raistlin was startled to hear a deep booming sound instead. A blast of air extinguished his candle, leaving him trapped in a darkness so deep and impenetrable that it might have been the darkness of Chaos, out of which the world was formed.

"Liam! Micah!" Raistlin called, and was alarmed when the names echoed back to him.

Nothing more than echoes. The elves did not answer.

Trying his best to hear over the rush of blood to his head, Raistlin distinguished faint sounds, as of someone pounding on a door. He gathered by this and the fact that the elves hadn't responded to his call that the trapdoor had inexplicably slammed shut, leaving him on one side and the elves on the other.

Raistlin's first panicked impulse was to use his magic for light. He stopped himself before casting the spell. He would not act on impulse. He would think the situation through calmly, as calmly as possible. He decided that it was best to remain in the darkness. Light would reveal to him whatever was down here. But light would also reveal him to whatever was down here.

Standing in the dark, he pondered the situation. The first notion that came to him was that the elves had lured him down here to leave him to his death. He abandoned this quickly. The elves had no reason to kill him. They had every reason to want to get into the cellar. They hadn't lied about the spellbooks, that much he had ascertained from their private conversations. The continued pounding on the trapdoor reassured him. The elves wanted to open that door as much as he wanted it open.

This decided, he took the precaution of moving, as quietly as he could, to put the stone wall at his back. His sight gone, he relied on his other senses, and almost immediately, now that he was calmer, he could hear breathing. Someone else's breathing. He was not alone down here.

It was not the breathing of a fearsome guardian, not the deep, harsh snufflings of an ogre, not the husky, whistling breaths of a hobgoblin. This breathing was thin and raspy, with a slight rattle. Raistlin had heard breathing like this before-in the rooms of the sick, the elderly.

Although somewhat reassuring, the sound shattered his calculations as to what he might find down in the cellar. The first wild thought was that he was about to meet the owner of the books, Lemuel's father. Perhaps the old gentleman had chosen to retire to the cellar, to spend his life with his precious books. Either that or Lemuel had locked his father in the cellar, a feat which, considering the father was a respected archmagus, was highly unlikely.

Raistlin stood in the dark, his fear diminishing by the moment as nothing untoward happened to him, his curiosity increasing. The breathing continued, uneven, fractured, with a gasp now and again. Raistlin could hear no other sounds in the cellar, no jingle of chain mail, creak of leather, rattle of sword. Above, the elves were hard at work. By the sounds of it, they were attacking the trapdoor with an ax.

And then a voice spoke, very near him. "You're a sly one, aren't you?" A pause, then, "Clever, too, and bold. It is not every man who dares stand alone in the darkness. Come! Let's have a look at you."

A candle flared, revealing a plain wooden table, small and round. Two chairs stood opposite each other, the table in between. One of the chairs was occupied. An old man sat in the chair. One glance assured Raistlin that this old man was not Lemuel's father, the war magus who fought at the side of elves.

The old man wore black robes, against which his white hair and beard shone with an eerie aura. His face arrested attention; like a landscape, its crevices and seams gave clues to his past. Fine lines spreading from the nose to the brow might have represented wisdom in another. On him, the lines ran deep with cunning. Lines of intelligence around the hawk-black eyes tightened into cynical amusement. Contempt for his fellow beings cracked the thin lips. Ambition was in his outthrust jaw. His hooded eyes were cold and calculating and bright.

Raistlin did not stir. The old man's face was a desert of desolation, harsh and deadly and cruel. Raistlin's fear smote him full force. Far better that he should fight an ogre or hobgoblin. The words to the simple defensive spell that had been on Raistlin's lips slipped away in a sigh. He imagined himself casting it, could almost hear the old man's mocking, derisive laughter. Those old hands, large-knuckled, large-boned, and grasping, were empty now, but those hands had once wielded enormous power.

The old man understood Raistlin's thoughts as if he'd spoken them aloud. The eyes gazed in Raistlin's direction, though he stood shrouded in the darkness.

"Come, Sly One. You who have swallowed my bait. Come and sit and talk with an old man."

Still Raistlin did not move. The words about bait had shaken him.

"You really might as well come sit down." The old man smiled, a smile that twisted the lines in his face, sharpening mockery into cruelty. "You're not going anywhere until I say you may go." Lifting a knotted finger, he pointed it straight at Raistlin's heart. "You came to me. Remember that."

Raistlin considered his options: He could either remain standing in the darkness, which was obviously not offering him much protection, since the old man seemed to see him clearly. He could make a desperate attempt to escape back up the steps, which would probably be futile and make him look foolish, or he could grasp his courage and assert what dignity remained, confront the old man, and find out what he meant by his strange references to bait.

Raistlin walked forward. Emerging out of the darkness into the candle's yellow light, he took a seat opposite the old man. The old man studied Raistlin in the light, did not appear particularly pleased with what he saw.

"You're a weakling! A sniveling weakling! I've more strength in my body than I see in yours, and my body is nothing but ashes and dust! What good will you do me? This is just my luck! Expecting an eagle, I am given a sparrow hawk. Still"—the old man's mutterings were only barely audible—"there is hunger in those eyes. If the body is frail, perhaps that is because it feeds the mind. The mind itself is desperate for nourishment, that much I can tell. Perhaps I judged hastily. We will see. What is your name?"

Raistlin had been clever and glib with the dark elves. In the company of this daunting old man, the young one answered meekly, "I am Raistlin Majere, Archmagus."

"Archmagus . . ." The old man lingered over the word, tasting it in his mouth. "I was once, you know. The greatest of them all. Even now they fear me. But they don't fear me enough. How old are you?"

"I have just turned twenty-one."

"Young, young to take the Test. I am surprised at Par-Salian. The man is desperate, that much is apparent. And how do you think you've done thus far, Raistlin Majere?" The old man's eyes crinkled, his smile was the ugliest thing Raistlin had ever seen.

"I'm sorry, sir, I don't know what you're talking about. What do you mean, how have I done? Done—"

Raistlin caught his breath. He had the sensation of rousing from a dream, one of those dreams that are more real than waking reality. Except that he had not dreamed this.

He was taking the Test. This was the Test. The elves, the inn, the events, the situations were all contrived. He stared at the candle flame and thought back frantically, wondering, as the old man had asked, how he had done.

The old man laughed, a chuckle that was like water gurgling beneath the ice. "I never tire of that reaction! It happens every time. One of the few pleasures I have left. Yes, you are taking the Test, young magus. You are right in the middle of it. And, no, I am not part of it. Or rather I am, but not an officially sanctioned part."

"You mentioned bait. 'I came to you,' that was what you said." Raistlin kept fast hold of his courage, clenching his hands so that no shiver or tremor should betray his fear.

The old man nodded. "By your own choices and decisions, yes, you came to me."

"I don't understand," Raistlin said.

The old man helpfully explained. "Some mages would have heeded the tinker's warning, never entered such a disreputable inn. Others, if they had entered, would have refused to have anything to do with dark elves. You went to the inn. You spoke to the elves. You fell in with their dishonest scheme quite readily." The old man again raised the knotted finger. "Even though you considered the man you were about to rob a friend."

"What you say is true." Raistlin saw no point in denying it. Nor was he particularly ashamed of his actions. In his mind, any mage, with the possible exception of the most bleached White Robe, would have done the same. "I wanted to save the spellbooks. I would have returned them to the conclave."

He was silent a moment, then said, "There are no spellbooks, are there?"

"No," replied the old man, "there is only me."

"And who are you?" Raistlin asked.

"My name is not important. Not yet."

"Well, then, what do you want of me?"

The old man made a deprecating gesture with the gnarled and knotted hand. "A little favor, nothing more."

Now it was Raistlin who smiled, and his smile was bitter. "Excuse me, sir, but you must be aware that since I am taking the Test, I am of very low ranking. You appear to be—or have been—a wizard of immense skill and power. I have nothing that you could possibly want."

"Ah, but you do!" The old man's eyes gleamed with a hungry, devouring light, a flame that made the candle's flame dim and feeble by contrast. "You live!"

"For the time being," Raistlin said dryly. "Perhaps not much longer. The dark elves will not believe me when I tell them there are no ancient spellbooks down here. They will think that I have magically spirited them away for my own use." He glanced around. "I don't suppose there is any way to escape from this cellar."

"There is a way—my way," said the old man. "My way is the only way. You are quite right, the dark elves will kill you. They're not thieves as they pretend, you know. They are high-ranking wizards. Their magic is exceptionally powerful."

Raistlin should have recognized that at once.

"Not giving up, are you?" the old man asked with a sneer.

"I am not." Raistlin lifted his head, gazed steadily at the old man. "I was thinking."

"Think away, young magus. You're going to have to think hard to overcome three-to-one odds. Make that twelve-to-one, since each dark elf is four times as powerful as yourself."

"This is the Test," Raistlin said. "It is all illusion. Admittedly some magi die taking the Test, but that is through their own failure or inadvertence. I have done nothing wrong. Why should the conclave kill me?"

"You have talked to me," the old man said softly. "They are aware of that, and that may well prove your downfall."

"Who are you, then," Raistlin asked impatiently, "that they fear you so?"

"My name is Fistandantilus. Perhaps you've heard of me."

"Yes," said Raistlin.

Long ago, in the turbulent and desperate years following the Cataclysm, an army of hill dwarves and humans laid siege to Thorbardin, the great underground city of the mountain dwarves. Leading this army, instrumental in its formation, intending to use the army to achieve his own driving ambition, was a wizard of the Black Robes, a wizard of immense power, a renegade wizard openly defying the conclave. His name was Fistandantilus.

He built a magical fortress known as Zhaman and from there launched his attack against the dwarven stronghold.

Fistandantilus fought the dwarves with his magic, his armies fought with ax and sword. Many thousands died on the plains or in the mountain passes, but the wizard's army faltered. And the dwarves of Thorbardin claimed victory.

According to the minstrels, Fistandantilus plotted one last spell, a spell of catastrophic power that would split the mountain, lay Thorbardin open to conquest. Unfortunately the spell was too powerful. Fistandantilus could not control it. The spell shattered the fortress of Zhaman. It collapsed in upon itself and was now known as Skullcap. Thousands of his own army died in the blast, including the wizard who had cast it.

That is what the minstrels sang, and that is what most people believed. Raistlin had always imagined there was more to the story than that. Fistandantilus had gained his power over hundreds of years. He was not elven, but human. He had, so it was rumored, found a way to cheat death. He extended his life by murdering his young apprentices, drawing out their life-force by means of a magical bloodstone. He had not been able to survive the shattering effects of his own magic, however. At least, that's what the world supposed. Evidently Fistandantilus had once again cheated death. Yet he would not do so for long.

"Fistandantilus—the greatest of all magi," Raistlin said. "The most powerful wizard who has ever lived."

"I am," said Fistandantilus.

"And you are dying," Raistlin observed.

The old man did not like this. His brows contracted, the lines of his face drew together in a dagger point of anger, his outrage bubbled beneath the surface. But every breath was a struggle. He was expending an enormous amount of magical energy merely to hold this form together. The fury ceased to boil, a pot under which the fire was put out.

"You speak the truth. I am dying," he muttered, frustrated, impotent. "I am nearly finished. They tell you that my goal was to take over Thorbardin." He smiled disdainfully. "What rot! I played for far greater stakes than the acquisition of some stinking, filthy dwarven hole in the ground. My plan was to enter the Abyss. To overthrow the Dark Queen, remove Takhisis from her throne. I sought godhood!"

Raistlin was awed listening to this, awed and amazed. Awed, amazed, and sympathetic.

"Beneath Skullcap is . . . or shall we say was, for it is gone now"— Fistandantilus paused, looked extremely cunning—"a means of entering the Abyss, that cruel netherworld. Takhisis was aware of me. She feared me and plotted my downfall. True, my body died in the blast, but I had already planned my soul's retreat on another plane of existence. Takhisis could not slay me, for she could not reach me, but she never ceases to try. I am under constant assault and have been for centuries. I have little energy left. The life-force I carried with me is almost gone."

"And so you contrive to enter the Test and lure young mages like me into your web," said Raistlin. "I would guess that I am not the first. What has happened to those who came before me?"

Fistandantilus shrugged. "They died. I told you. They spoke to me. The conclave fears that I will enter into the body of a young mage, take him over and so return to the world to complete what I began. They cannot allow that, and so each time they see to it that the threat is eliminated."

Raistlin gazed steadily at the old man, the dying old man. "I don't believe you. The mages died, but it was not the conclave who killed them. It was you. That is how you've managed to live for so long-if you call it living."

"Call it what you will, it is preferable to the great nothingness I see reaching out for me," Fistandantilus said with a hideous grin. "The same nothingness that is reaching out for you, young mage."

"I have little choice, it seems," Raistlin replied bitterly. "Either I die at the hands of three wizards or I am to be sucked dry by a lich."

"It was your decision to come down here," Fistandantilus replied.

Raistlin lowered his gaze, refused to allow the old man's probing hawk eyes to gain admittance to his soul. He stared at the wooden table and was reminded of the table in his master's laboratory, the table on which the child Raistlin had written, so triumphantly, I, Magus. He considered the odds he faced, thought about the dark elves, wondered at their magic, wondered if what the old man had said about them was true or if it was all lies, lies intended to trap him. He wondered about his own ability to survive, wondered if the conclave would kill him simply because he had spoken to Fistandantilus.

Raistlin lifted his gaze, met the hawk eyes. "I accept your offer."

Fistandantilus's thin lips parted in a smile that was like the grin of a skull. "I thought you might. Show me your spellbook."

5

RAISTLIN STOOD AT THE BOTTOM OF THE CELLAR STAIRS, WAITING FOR the old man to release the trapdoor from the enchantment that held it shut. He wondered that he felt no fear, only the razor-edged pain of anticipation.

The elves had halted their assault on the cellar doors; they had figured out that magic held them. He allowed himself the hope that perhaps they had gone. The next moment he laughed at himself for his foolishness. This was his Test. He would be required to prove his ability to use magic in battle.

Now! came a voice in Raistlin's head.

Fistandantilus had disappeared. The physical form the old man had taken had been illusory, conjured up for Raistlin's benefit. Now that the form was no longer required, the old man had abandoned it.

The cellar doors swung violently open, falling with a resounding boom on the stone-flagoned floor.

Raistlin trusted that the elves would be caught off guard by the sudden opening of the door. He planned to use these few moments of confusion to launch his own attack.

To his dismay, he discovered that the dark elves had been prepared for just such an occurrence. They were waiting for him.

An elven voice spoke the language of magic. Light blazed, a globe of fire illuminated Liam's face. The instant the door flew open, the flaming ball, trailing sparks like the blazing tail of a comet, hurtled through the air.

Raistlin was not prepared for this attack; he had not imagined the dark elves would react so quickly. There was no escape. The flaming ball would fill the room with fiery death. Instinctively he flung his left arm up to protect his face, knowing all the while there could be no protection.

The fireball burst on him, over him, around him. It burst harmlessly, its effects dissipated, showering him with sparks and globs of flame that struck his hands and his astonished face and then vanished in a sizzle, as if they were falling into standing water.

"Your spell! Quickly!" came the command.

Raistlin had already recovered from his startlement and his fear; the spell came immediately to his lips. His hand performed the motions, tracing the symbol of a sun in the air. Sparks from the fireball still glimmered on the cellar floor at his feet. He noticed, as he moved his hand, that his skin had a golden cast to it, but he did not let himself do more than remark upon this as a curiosity. He dared not lose his concentration.

Symbol drawn, he spoke the words of magic. The symbol flashed brightly in the air; he had spoken the words correctly, accurately. From the fingers of his outstretched right hand streaked five small flaming projectiles, a puny response to the deadly weapons of the powerful archmages.

Raistlin was not surprised to hear the dark elves laughing at him. He might as well have been tossing gnome crackers at them.

He waited, holding his breath, praying that the old man kept his promise, praying to the gods of magic to see to it that the old man kept his promise. Raistlin had the satisfaction, the deep abiding satisfaction, of hearing elven laughter sucked away by indrawn breaths of astonishment and alarm.

The five streaks of flame were now ten, now twenty. No longer smidgens of flame, they were crackling, sparkling white-hot stars, stars shooting up the stairs, shooting with unerring accuracy for Raistlin's three foes.

Now it was the dark elves who had no escape, no defensive spells powerful enough to protect them. The deadly stars struck with a concussive force that knocked Raistlin off his feet, and he was standing some distance from the center of the blast. He felt the heat of the flames all the way down the cellar steps. He smelled burning flesh. There were no screams. There had not been time for screams.

Raistlin picked himself up. He wiped dirt from his hands, noting once more the peculiar golden color of his skin. The realization came to him that this golden patina had protected him from the fireball. It was like a knight's armor, only much more effective than armor; a plate and chain-mail clad knight would have fried to death if that fiery ball had struck him, whereas Raistlin had suffered no ill effects.

"And if that is true," he said to himself, "if this is armor or a shield of some magical type, then it could aid me considerably in the future."

The storage room was ablaze. Raistlin waited until the worst of the flames had died down, taking his time, recovering his strength, bringing his next spell to mind. Holding the sleeve of his robe over his nose against the stench of charred elf, Raistlin mounted the stairs, prepared to face his next foe.

Two bodies lay at the top of the cellar stairs, black lumps burned beyond recognition. A third body was not visible, perhaps it had been vaporized. Of course, this is all illusion, Raistlin reminded himself. Perhaps the conclave had simply miscounted.

Emerging from the cellar, he gathered up the skirt of his robes, stepped over the body of one of the elves. He cast a swift glance around the storage room. The table was a pile of ash, the mops and brooms were wisps of smoke. The image of Fistandantilus hovered amidst the ruins. His illusory form was thin and translucent, almost indistinguishable from the smoke. A good stiff puff of breath could blow him away.

Raistlin smiled.

The old man stretched out his arm. It was cloaked in black. The hand was shriveled, wasted, the fingers little more than bare bones.

"I will take my payment now," said Fistandantilus.

His hand reached for Raistlin's heart.

Raistlin took a step backward. He raised his own hand protectively, palm out. "I thank you for your assistance, Archmagus, but I rescind my part of the bargain."

"What did you say?"

The words, sibilant, lethal, coiled around inside Raistlin's brain like a viper in a basket. The viper's head lifted; eyes, cruel, malignant, merciless, stared at him.

Raistlin's resolve shook, his heart quailed. The old man's rage crackled around him with flames more fierce than those of the fireball.

I killed the elves, Raistlin reminded himself, seizing hold of his fast-fleeing courage. The spell belonged to Fistandantilus, but the magic, the power behind the spell, was my own. He is weak, drained; he is not a threat.

"Our bargain is rescinded," Raistlin repeated. "Return to the plane from which you've come and there wait for your next victim."

"You break your promise!" Fistandantilus snarled. "What honor is this?"

"Am I a Solamnic knight, to concern myself with honor?" Raistlin asked, adding, "If it comes to that, what honor is there in luring flies to your web, where you entangle and devour them? If I am not mistaken, your own spell protects me from any magic you may try to cast. This time the fly escapes you."

Raistlin bowed to the shadowy image of the old man. Deliberately he turned his back, began to walk toward the door. If he could make it to the door, escape this charnel room, this room of death, he would be safe. The way was not far, and though part of him kept expecting to feel the touch of that dread hand, his confidence grew with each step he took nearer the exit.

He reached the doorway. When the old man's voice spoke, it seemed to come from a great distance away. Raistlin could barely hear it.

"You are strong and you are clever. You are protected by armor of your own making, not mine. Yet your Test is not concluded. More struggles await you. If your armor is made of steel, true and fine, then you will survive. If your armor is made of dross, it will crack at the first blow, and when that happens, I will slip inside and take what is mine."

A voice could not harm him. Raistlin paid no heed to it. He continued walking, reached the door, and the voice drifted away like the smoke in the air.

6

RAISTLIN WALKED THROUGH THE DOORWAY OF LEMUEL'S STORAGE ROOM and stepped into a dark corridor made of stone. At first he was startled, taken aback. He should have been standing inside Lemuel's kitchen. Then he recalled Lemuel's house had never truly existed except in his mind and the minds of those who had conjured it.

Light gleamed on the wall near him. A sconce in the shape of a silver hand held a globe of white light, akin to the light of Solinari. Next to that, a hand made of brass held a globe of red light, and beside that hand, a hand of carven ebony held nothing—in Raistlin's eyes, at least. Those mages dedicated to Nuitari would see their way clearly.

Raistlin deduced from these lights that he was back in the Tower of Wayreth, walking one of the many corridors of that magical building. Fistandantilus had lied. Raistlin's Test was over. He had only to find his way back to the Hall of Mages, there to receive congratulations.

A breath of air touched the back of his neck. Raistlin started to turn. Burning pain and the nerve-jarring sensation of metal scraping against bone, his own bone, caused his body to jerk with agony.

"This is for Micah and Renet!" hissed Liam's vicious voice.

Liam's arm, thin, strong, tried to encircle Raistlin's neck. A blade flashed.

The elf had intended his first blow to be his last. He had tried to sever Raistlin's spinal cord. That breath of air on his neck had been enough to alert Raistlin. When he turned, the blade missed its mark, slid along his ribs. Liam was going to make another try, this time going for the throat.

Raistlin's panic-stripped mind could not come up with the words of a spell. He had no weapon other than his magic. He was reduced to fighting like an animal, with tooth and claw. His fear was his most powerful tool, if he did not let it debilitate him. He remembered vaguely watching Sturm and his brother in hand-to-hand combat.

Clasping his hands together, Raistlin drove his right elbow with all the force his adrenaline-pumping body could manage into Liam's midriff.

The dark elf grunted and fell back. But he was not injured, just short of breath. He leapt back to the fight, his knife slashing.

Frantic and terrified, Raistlin grabbed hold of his attacker's knife hand. The two grappled, Liam trying to stab Raistlin, Raistlin struggling to wrench the knife from the dark elf's grip.

They lurched about the narrow corridor. Raistlin's strength was ebbing fast. He could not hope to keep up this deadly contest for long. Staking his hopes on one desperate move, Raistlin concentrated his remaining energy, smashed the elf's hand-the hand holding the knife—against the stone.

Bones cracked, the elf gasped in pain, but he clung tenaciously to his weapon.

Panic seized hold. Again and again Raistlin struck Liam's hand against the hard stone. The knife's handle was slippery with blood. Liam could not hold on to it. The knife slipped from his grip and fell to the floor.

Liam made a lunge to try to recover his weapon. He lost it in the shadows, apparently, for he was down on all fours, frantically searching the floor.

Raistlin saw the knife. The blade burned with red fire in Lunitari's bright light. The elf saw it at the same time, made a lunge for it. Snatching the knife from beneath the elf's grasping fingers, Raistlin drove the blade into Liam's stomach.

The dark elf screamed, doubled over.

Raistlin yanked the blade free. Liam tumbled to his knees, his hand pressed over his stomach. Blood poured from his mouth. He pitched forward, dead, at Raistlin's feet.

Gasping, each breath causing him wrenching agony, Raistlin started to turn, to flee. He could not make his legs work properly and collapsed to the stone floor. A burning sensation spread from the knife wound throughout his nerve endings. He was nauseated, sick.

Liam would have his revenge after all, Raistlin realized in bitter despair. The dark elf's knife blade had been tipped with poison.

The lights of Solinari and Lunitari wavered in his sight, blurred together, and then darkness overtook him.

Raistlin woke to find himself lying in the same corridor. Liam's body was still there, beside him, the elf's dead hand touching him. The body was still warm. Raistlin had not been unconscious long.

He dragged himself away from the dead body of the dark elf. Wounded and weak, he crawled into a shadowy corridor and slumped against a wall. Pain coiled around his bowels. Clutching his stomach, he retched and heaved. When the vomiting subsided, he lay back on the stone floor and waited to die.

"Why are you doing this to me?" he demanded through a haze of sickness.

He knew the answer. Because he had dared to bargain with a wizard so powerful that he had once thought of overthrowing Takhisis, a wizard so powerful that the conclave feared his power even after he was dead.

If your armor is made of dross, it will crack at the first blow, and when that happens, I will slip inside and take what is mine.

Raistlin almost laughed. "What little life I have left, you are welcome to, archmagus!"

He lay on the floor, his cheek pressed against the stone. Did he want to survive? The Test had taken a terrible toll, one from which he might never recover. His health had always been precarious. If he survived, his body would be like a shattered crystal, held together by the force of his own will. How would he live? Who would take care of him?

Caramon. Caramon would care for his weak twin.

Raistlin stared into Lunitari's red, flickering light. He couldn't imagine such a life, a life of dependency on his brother. Death was preferable.

A figure materialized out of the shadowy darkness of the corridor, a figure illuminated by Solinari's white light.

"This is it," Raistlin said to himself. "This is my final test. The one I won't survive."

He felt almost grateful to the wizards for ending his suffering. He lay helpless, watching the dark shadow as it drew closer and closer. It came to stand next to him. He could sense its living presence, hear its breathing. It bent over him. Involuntarily, he closed his eyes.

"Raist?"

Gentle fingers touched his feverish flesh.

"Raist!" The voice sobbed. "What have they done to you?"

"Caramon," Raistlin spoke, but he couldn't hear his own words. His throat was raw from the smoke, the retching.

"I'm taking you out of here," his brother said.

Strong arms slipped under Raistlin's body. He smelled Caramon's familiar smell of sweat and leather, heard the familiar sound of creaking armor, his broadsword clanking against the stone.

"No!" Raistlin tried to free himself. He pushed against his brother's massive chest with his frail, fragile hand. "Leave me, Caramon! My Test is not finished! Leave me!" His voice was an intelligible croak. He gagged, coughed.

Caramon lifted his brother, cradled him in his arms. "Nothing is worth this, Raist. Rest easy."

They walked beneath the silver hand, holding the white light. Raistlin saw tears, wet and glistening, on his brother's cheeks. He made one last attempt.

"They won't permit me to leave, Caramon!" He fought for breath enough to speak. "They'll try to stop us. You're only putting yourself in danger."

"Let them come," Caramon said grimly. He walked with firm, unhurried steps down the corridor.

Raistlin sank back, helpless, his head resting on Caramon's shoulder. For an instant, he allowed himself to feel comforted by his brother's strength. The next moment he cursed his weakness, cursed his twin.

"You fool!" Raistlin said silently, lacking the strength to speak the words aloud. "You great, stubborn fool! Now we'll both die. And, of course, you will die protecting me. Even in death, I will be indebted to you. . . ."

"Ah!"

Raistlin heard and felt the sharp intake of breath into his brother's body. Caramon's pace slowed. Raistlin raised his head.

At the end of the corridor floated the disembodied head of an old man. Raistlin heard whispered words.

If your armor is made of dross . . .

"Mmmmm . . ." Caramon rumbled deeply in his chest—his battle cry.

"My magic can destroy it!" Raistlin protested as Caramon laid his brother gently on the stone floor. That was a lie. Raistlin did not have energy enough to pull a rabbit from a hat. But he'd be damned if Caramon was going to fight his battles, especially against the old man. Raistlin had made the bargain, he had been the one to benefit, he must pay.

"Get out of my way, Caramon!"

Caramon did not respond. He walked toward Fistandantilus, blocked Raistlin's view.

Raistlin put his hands to the wall. Propping his body against the stone, he pushed himself to a standing position. He was about to expend his strength in one last shout, hoping to warn off his brother. Raistlin's shout was never uttered. His warning died in a rattle of disbelief.

Caramon had dropped his weapons. Now, in place of his sword, he held a rod of amber. In the other hand, his shield hand, he clasped a bit of fur.

He rubbed the two together, spoke the magic. Lightning streaked from the amber, sizzled down the corridor, struck the head of Fistandantilus.

The head laughed and hurtled straight at Caramon. He did not blench, but kept his hands raised. He spoke the magic again. Another bolt flashed.

The old man's head exploded in blue fire. A thin cry of thwarted anger screamed from some far distant plane, but it died away to nothing.

The corridor was empty.

"Now we'll get out of here," Caramon said with satisfaction. He tucked the rod and the fur into a pouch he wore at his belt. "The door is just ahead."

"How—how did you do that?" Raistlin gasped, sagging against the wall.

Caramon stopped, alarmed by his brother's wild, frenzied stare.

"Do what, Raist?"

"The magic!" Raistlin cried in fury. "The magic!"

"Oh, that." Caramon shrugged, gave a shy, deprecating smile. "I've always been able to." He grew solemn, stern. "Most of the time I don't need the magic, what with my sword and all, but you're hurt really bad, and I didn't want to take the time fighting that lich. Don't worry about it, Raist. Magic can still be your little specialty. Like I said, most of the time I don't need it."

"This is not possible," Raistlin said to himself, struggling to think clearly. "Caramon could not have acquired in moments what it took me years of study to attain. This doesn't make sense! Something's not right. . . . Think, damn it! Think!"

It wasn't the physical pain that clouded his mind. It was the old inner pain clawing at him, tearing at him with poisoned talons. Caramon, strong and cheerful, good and kind, open and honest. Caramon, everyone's friend.

Not like Raistlin—the runt, the Sly One.

"All I ever had was my magic," Raistlin said, speaking clearly, thinking clearly for the first time in his life. "And now you have that, too."

Using the wall for support, Raistlin raised both his hands, put his thumbs together. He began speaking the words, the words that would summon the magic.

"Raist!" Caramon started to back away. "Raist, what are you doing? C'mon! You need me! I'll take care of you—just like always. Raist! I'm your brother!"

"I have no brother!"

Beneath the layer of cold, hard rock, jealousy bubbled and seethed. Tremors split the rock. Jealousy, red and molten, coursed through Raistlin's body and flamed out of his hands. The fire flared, billowed, and engulfed Caramon.

Caramon screamed, tried to beat out the flames, but there was no escaping the magic. His body withered, dwindled in the fire, became the body of a wizened old man. An old man wearing black robes, whose hair and beard were trailing wisps of fire.

Fistandantilus, his hand outstretched, walked toward Raistlin.

"If your armor is dross," said the old man softly. "I will find the crack."

Raistlin could not move, could not defend himself. The magic had sapped the last of his strength.

Fistandantilus stood before Raistlin. The old man's black robes were tattered shreds of night, his flesh was rotting and decayed, the bones were visible through the skin. His nails were long and pointed, as long as those of a corpse, his eyes gleamed with the radiant heat that had been in Raistlin's soul, the warmth that had brought the dead to life. A bloodstone hung from a pendant around the fleshless neck.

The old man's hand touched Raistlin's breast, caressed his flesh, teasing and tormenting. Fistandantilus plunged his hand into Raistlin's chest and seized hold of his heart.

The dying soldier clasps his hands around the haft of the spear that has torn through his body. Raistlin seized hold of the old man's wrist, clamped his fingers around it in a grip that death would not have relaxed.

Caught, trapped, Fistandantilus fought to break Raistlin's grip, but he could not free himself and retain his hold on the young man's heart.

The white light of Solinari, the red light of Lunitari, and the black, empty light of Nuitari—light that Raistlin could now see—merged in his fainting vision, stared down at him, an unwinking eye.

"You may take my life," Raistlin said, keeping fast hold of the old man's wrist, as Fistandantilus kept hold of young man's heart. "But you will serve me in return."

The eye winked, and blinked out.

7

H E KILLED HIS OWN BROTHER?" ANTIMODES REPEATED THE INFORMATION Par-Salian had just given him, repeated it in disbelief.

Antimodes had not been involved in Raistlin's Test. Neither teacher nor mentor of an initiate is allowed to participate. Antimodes had handled the testing of several of the other young magi. Most had gone quite well, all had passed, though none had been as dramatic as Raistlin's. Antimodes had been sorry he missed it. He had been until he heard this. Now he was shocked and deeply disturbed.

"And the young man was given the Red Robes? My friend, are you in your right mind? I cannot conceive of an act more evil!"

"He killed an illusion of his brother," Par-Salian emphasized. "You have siblings of your own, I believe?" he asked, with a meaningful smile.

"I know what you're saying, and, yes, there have been times I would have been glad to see my brother engulfed in flames, but the thought is a long way from the deed. Did Raistlin know it was an illusion?"

"When I asked him that question," Par-Salian replied, "he looked straight at me and said in a tone that I shall never forget, 'Does it matter?' "

"Poor young man," Antimodes said, sighing. "Poor young men, I should say, since the other twin was a witness to his own fratricide. Was that truly necessary?"

"I deemed it so. Odd as it may seem, though he is the stronger of the two physically, Caramon is far more dependent on his brother than Raistlin is on him. By this demonstration, I had hoped to sever that unhealthy connection, to convince Caramon that he needs to build a life of his own. But I fear that my plan did not succeed. Caramon has fully exonerated his brother.

Raistlin was ill, not in his right mind, not to be held responsible for his own actions. And now, to complicate matters, Raistlin is more dependent upon his brother than ever."

"How is the young man's health?"

"Not good. He will live, but only because his spirit is strong, stronger than his body."

"So there was a meeting between Raistlin and Fistandantilus. And Raistlin agreed to the bargain. He has given his life's energy to feed that foul lich!"

"There was a meeting and a bargain," Par-Salian reiterated cautiously. "But I believe that this time Fistandantilus may have got more than he bargained for."

"Raistlin remembers nothing?"

"Nothing whatsoever. Fistandantilus has seen to that. I do not believe that he wants the young man to remember. Raistlin may have agreed to the bargain, but he did not die, as did the others. Something kept him alive and defiant. If Raistlin ever does remember, I think it is Fistandantilus who might be in considerable danger."

"What does the young man believe happened to him?"

"The Test itself shattered his health, left him with a weakness in his heart and lungs that will plague him the remainder of his life. He attributes that to the battle with the dark elf. I did not disabuse him of the notion. Were I to tell him the truth, he would not believe me."

"Do you suppose he will ever come to know the truth?"

"Only if and when he comes to know the truth about himself," Par-Salian answered. "He has to confront and admit the darkness within. I have given him the eyes to see with, if he will: the hourglass eyes of the sorceress Raelana. Thus he will view time's passing in all he looks upon. Youth withers before those eyes, beauty fades, mountains crumble to dust."

"And what do you hope to accomplish by this torture?" Antimodes demanded angrily. He truly thought the head of the conclave had gone too far.

"To pierce his arrogance. To teach him patience. And as I said, to give him the ability to see inside himself, should he turn his gaze inward. There will be little joy in his life," Par-Salian admitted, adding, "but then I foresee little joy for anyone in Ansalon. I did compensate for what you deem my cruelty, however."

"I never said—"

"You didn't need to, my friend. I know how you feel. I have given Raistlin the Staff of Magius, one of our most powerful artifacts. Though it will be a long time before he knows its true power."

Antimodes was bitter, refusing to be mollified. "And now you have your sword."

"The metal withstood the fire," Par-Salian replied gravely, "and came out tempered and true, with a fine cutting edge. Now the young man must practice, he must hone the skills he will need in the future and learn new ones."

"None of the conclave will apprentice him, not if they think he is somehow tied to Fistandantilus. Not even the Black Robes. They would not trust him. How, then, will he learn?"

"I believe he will find a master. A lady has taken an interest in him, a very great interest."

"Not Ladonna?" Antimodes frowned.

"No, no. Another lady, far greater and more powerful." Par-Salian cast a glance out the window, where the red moon shone with a ruby's glittering brilliance.

"Ah, indeed?" Antimodes said, impressed. "Well, if that's the case, I suppose I need not worry about him. Still, he's very young and very frail, and we don't have much time."

"As you said, it will be some years before the Dark Queen can muster her forces, before she is prepared to launch her attack."

"Yet already the clouds of war gather," Antimodes remarked ominously. "We stand alone in the last rays of the setting sun. And I ask again, where are the true gods now that we need them?"

"Where they have always been," Par-Salian replied complacently.

8

RAISTLIN SAT IN A CHAIR BEFORE A DESK IN THE TOWER OF HIGH SORCERY. He had been a resident of the tower for several days, Par-Salian having given the young man permission to remain in the tower for as long as he deemed necessary to recover from the effects of the Test.

Not that Raistlin would ever truly recover. He had never before been physically strong or healthy, but in comparison to what he was today, he looked back upon his former self with envy. He spent a moment recalling the days of his youth, realized regretfully that he had never fully appreciated them, never fully appreciated his energy and vigor. But would he go back? Would he trade his shattered body for a whole one?

Raistlin's hand touched the wood of the Staff of Magius, which stood at his side, was never far from his side. The wood was smooth and warm, the enchantment within the staff tingled through his fingers, an exhilarating sensation. He had only the vaguest idea what magic the staff could perform. It was requisite that any mage coming into possession of a magical artifact search out such power himself. But he was aware of the staff's immense magical power, and he reveled in it.

Not much information on the staff existed in the tower; many of the old manuscripts concerning Magius, which had been kept in the Tower of Palanthas, had been lost when the magi evacuated to the tower at Wayreth. The staff itself had been retained, as being of far more value, though it had—according to Par-Salian—remained unused all these centuries.

The time had not been right for the staff's return to the world, Par-Salian had said evasively in answer to Raistlin's question. Until now the staff had not been needed. Raistlin wondered what made the time right now, right for a staff that had purportedly been used to help fight dragons. He was not likely to find out. Par-Salian kept his own counsel. He would tell Raistlin nothing about the staff, beyond where to find the books that might provide him with knowledge.

One of those books was before him now, a smallish quarto written by some scribe attached to Huma's retinue. The book was more frustrating than helpful. Raistlin learned a great deal about manning battlements and posting guards, information that would be useful to a war mage, but very little about the staff. What he had learned had been inadvertent. The scribe, writing an account of Magius, described the mage leaping from the topmost tower of the besieged castle to land unharmed among us, much to our great astonishment and wonder. He claimed to have used the magic of his staff. . . .

Raistlin wrote in his own small volume: *It appears that the staff has the ability to allow its owner to float through the air as lightly as a feather. Is this spell inherent in the staff? Must magical words be recited in order to activate this spell? Is there a limit to its usage? Will the spell work for anyone other than the magus who is in possession of the staff?*

All these were questions that must be answered, and that was just for one of the staff's enchantments. Raistlin guessed there must be many more bound within the wood. In one sense, it was frustrating not to know. He would have liked to have had them delineated. Yet if the nature of the staff's powers had been presented to him, he still would have pursued his studies. The old manuscripts might be lying. They might be deliberately withholding information. He trusted no one but himself.

His studies might take him years, but . . .

A spasm of coughing interrupted his work. The cough was painful, debilitating, frightening. His windpipe closed, he could not breathe, and when the paroxysms were very bad, he had the terrible feeling that he would never be able to breathe again, that he would suffocate and die.

This was one of the bad ones. He fought, struggled to breathe. He grew faint and dizzy from lack of air, and when at last he was able to draw a breath with a certain amount of ease, he was so exhausted from the effort that he was forced to rest his head on his arms on the table. He lay there, almost sobbing. His injured ribs hurt him cruelly, his diaphragm burned from coughing.

A gentle hand touched his shoulder.

"Raist? Are . . . are you all right?"

Raistlin sat upright, thrust aside his brother's hand.

"What a stupid question! Even for you. Of course I am not all right, Caramon!" Raistlin dabbed at his lips with a handkerchief, drew it back stained with blood. He swiftly concealed the handkerchief in a secret pocket of his new red robes.

"Is there anything I can do to help?" Caramon asked, patiently ignoring his brother's ill humor.

"You can leave me alone and quit interrupting my work!" Raistlin returned. "Are you packed? We leave within the hour, you know."

"If you're sure you're well enough . . ." Caramon began. Catching his brother's irritated and baleful gaze, he bit his tongue. "I'll . . . go pack," he said, though he was already packed and had been for the past three hours.

Caramon started to leave, tiptoeing out of the room. He fondly imagined that he was being extremely quiet. In reality, with his rattling, jingling, clanking, and creaking, he made more noise than a legion of mountain dwarves on parade.

Reaching into the pocket, Raistlin drew forth the handkerchief, wet with his own blood. He gazed at it for a dark, brooding moment.

"Caramon," he called.

"Yes, Raist?" Caramon turned around, pathetically anxious. "Is there something I can do for you?"

They would have many years together, years of working together, living together, eating together, fighting together. Caramon had seen his twin kill him. Raistlin had seen himself kill.

Hammer blows. One after the other.

Raistlin sighed deeply. "Yes, my brother. There is something you can do for me. Par-Salian gave me a recipe for a tisane that he believes will help ease my cough. You will find the recipe and the ingredients in my pouch, there on the chair. If you could mix it for me . . ."

"I will, Raist!" Caramon said excitedly. He couldn't have looked more pleased if his twin had bestowed a wealth of jewels and steel coins upon him. "I haven't noticed a teakettle, but I'm sure there must be one around here somewhere. . . . Oh, here it is. I guess I didn't see it before. You keep working. I'll just measure out these leaves . . . . Whew! This smells awful! Are you sure? . . . Never mind," Caramon amended hurriedly. "I'll make the tea. Maybe it'll taste better than it smells."

He put on the kettle, then bent over the teapot, mixing and measuring the leaves with as much care as a gnome would take on a Life Quest.

Raistlin returned to his reading.

Magius struck the ogre on the head with his staff I charged in to save him, for ogre's are notoriously thick-skulled, and I could not see that the wizard's walking staff would inflict much damage. To my surprise, however, the ogre keeled over dead, as if it had been struck by a thunderbolt.

Raistlin carefully noted the occurrence, writing: *The staff apparently increases the force of a blow.*

"Raist," said Caramon, turning from watching for the teapot to boil, "I just want you to know. About what happened . . . I understand . . ."

Raistlin lifted his head, paused in his writing. He did not look at his brother, but gazed out the window. The Forest of Wayreth surrounded the tower. He looked out upon withering leaves, leafless branches, rotted and decayed stumps.

"You are never to mention that incident to me or to anyone else, my brother, so long as you live. Do you understand?"

"Sure, Raist," Caramon said softly, "I understand." He turned back to his task. "Your tea's almost ready."

Raistlin closed the book he had been reading. His eyes burned from the strain of trying to decipher the scribe's old-fashioned handwriting, he was weary from the effort involved in translating the mixture of archaic Common and the military slang spoken among soldiers and mercenaries.

Flexing his hand, which ached from gripping the pen, Raistlin slid the volume about Magius into his belt for perusal during their long journey north. They were not returning to Solace. Antimodes had given the twins the name of a nobleman who was hiring warriors and who would, Antimodes said, be glad to hire a war mage as well. Antimodes was heading in that direction. He would be glad to have the young men ride with him.

Raistlin had readily agreed. He planned to learn all he could from the archmagus before they parted. He had hoped that Antimodes would apprentice him, and had even been bold enough to make the request. Antimodes had refused, however. He never took apprentices, or so he said. He lacked the patience. He added that there was little opportunity in the way of apprenticeships open these days. Raistlin would be far better studying on his own.

This was a prevarication (one could not say that a White Robe lied). The other mages who had taken the Tests had all been apprenticed. Raistlin wondered why he was the exception. He decided, after considerable thought, that it must have something to do with Caramon.

His brother was rattling the teapot, making a most ungodly racket, slopping boiling water all over the floor and spilling the herbs.

Would I go back to the days of my youth?

Then my body had seemed frail, but it was strong in comparison to this fragile assembly of bones and flesh that I now inhabit, held together only by my will. Would I go back?

Then I looked on beauty and I saw beauty. Now I look on beauty and

I see it drowned, bloated, and disfigured, carried downstream by the river of time. Would I go back?

Then we were twins. Together in the womb, together after birth, still together but now separate. The silken cords of brotherhood, cut, dangle between us, never to be restrung. Would I go back?

Closing the volume of his precious notations, Raistlin picked up a pen and wrote on the cover:

I, Magus.

And, with a swift, firm stroke, he underlined it.

CODA

ONE EVENING, WHILE I WAS ABSORBED IN MY USUAL TASK OF CHRONICLING the history of the world, Bertram, my loyal but occasionally inept assistant, crept into my study and begged leave to interrupt my work.

"Whatever is the matter, Bertram?" I demanded, for the man was as pale as if he'd encountered a gnome bringing an incendiary device into the Great Library.

"This, Master!" he said, his voice quavering. He held in his trembling hands a small scroll of parchment, tied with a black ribbon and sealed with black ink. Stamped upon the ink was the imprint of an eye.

"Where did this come from?" I demanded, though I knew immediately who must have sent it.

"That's just it, Master, " Bertram said, holding the scroll balanced on the tips of his fingers. "I don't know! One minute it wasn't there. And the next minute it was."

Knowing I would get nothing more intelligent from Bertram than this, I told him to place the scroll on the desk and to leave. I would peruse it at my leisure. He was clearly reluctant to leave the missive, thinking no doubt that it would burst into flame or some other such nonsense. He did as I requested, however, and left with many a backward glance. Even then, he waited, hovering outside my door with—as I learned later—a bucket of water nearby, intending, no doubt, to fling it on me at the first puff of smoke.

Breaking the seal and untying the ribbon, I found this letter, of which I have included a portion.

> *To Astinus,*
>
> *It may be that I am about to undertake a daring enterprise.[2] It is highly probable that I will not return from this undertaking (should I decide to undertake it) or if I do, it will be an altered state. If it should occur that I meet my demise upon this quest, then I give you leave to publish the true account of my early life, including that which has always been kept most secret, my Test in the Tower of High Sorcery. I do this in response to the many wild tales and untruths being circulated regarding me and my family. I grant you permission on the condition that Caramon also agrees with my decision . . . .*

I did not forget about Raistlin's charge to me, as some have implied. Neither Caramon nor I deemed the time right for publication of his book. Now that his nephew Palin has grown to manhood and has taken his own Test in the Tower, Caramon has given his permission for the book to be published.

This is the true account of Raistlin's early life. Astute readers will note discrepancies between this account and others which have come before. I trust those readers will take into consideration the fact that the name of Raistlin Majere had become legend over the years. A great deal that has been written, told, and sung about the great mage is either false or a distortion of the truth.

I am guilty of some of this myself, for I deliberately misled people in regard to certain aspects of Raistlin's life. The Test in the Tower of High Sorcery—the Test that proved to have such a devastating and fateful influence on him—is one of the most important. Other accounts exist of his Test, but this is the first time the true account has been written.

The Conclave of Wizards has long decreed that the nature of the Test be kept secret. Following Raistlin's "death," certain wild and destructive rumors began to circulate regarding him. Caramon asked for permission from Par-Salian to lay these rumors to rest. Since the rumors appeared likely to damage the reputations of all magic-users on Krynn, the Conclave granted permission for the story to be told, but only if certain of the facts were altered.

Thus Caramon caused to be written an abbreviated story of Raistlin's Test, which came to be known as the *Test of the Twins*. In essence, the story is true, though you will see that the actual events are a great deal different form those earlier portrayed.

2 The enterprise to which he refers is his attempt to enter the Abyss and overthrow Takhisis. Those interested may find this tale in the Great library, in the books marked "Dragonlance Legends."

I finish with the conclusion of Raistlin's letter.

*. . . I break the silence now because I want the facts known. If I am
to be judged by those who come after me, let me be judged for the truth.
I dedicate this book to the one who gave me life.*

Raistlin Majere

BROTHERS
IN ARMS

RAISTLIN
CHRONICLES

MARGARET WEIS
& DON PERRIN

"*Warp*: The threads which are extended lengthwise in the loom, usually twisted harder than the weft, or woof, with which these threads are crossed to form the web or piece.

"*Weft*: The threads that cross from side to side of a web, at right angles to the warp threads, with which they are interlaced."

—*Oxford English Dictionary* (Second Edition)

BOOK 1

"I don't care about your name, Red. I don't want to know your name. If you survive your first three or so battles, then maybe I'll learn your name. Not before. I used to learn the names, but it was a goddamned waste of time. Soon as I'd get to know a puke, he'd up and die on me. These days I don't bother."

—Horkin, Master-at-Wizardry

1

Mists shrouded the Tower of High Sorcery at Wayreth, and a light rain fell. The rain shimmered on the mullioned windows. Drops welled up on the thick stone ledges of the windows, overflowed to trickle down the black obsidian walls of the Tower, where the raindrops collected in puddles in the courtyard. In that courtyard stood a donkey and two horses loaded with blanket rolls and saddlebags, ready for travel.

The donkey's head was lowered, her back sagged, her ears drooped. She was a spoiled donkey, fond of dry oats, a snug stable, a sunlit road, and a slow and easy pace. Jenny knew of no reason why her master should travel on such a wet day and had stubbornly resisted all attempts to drag her from her stall. The burly human who had attempted to do so was now nursing a bruised thigh.

The donkey would still be in her warm stall, but she had fallen victim to a ruse, a foul trick played on her by the big human. The fragrant smell of carrot, the lush scent of apple—these had been her temptation and her downfall. Now she stood in the rain, feeling much put upon and determined to make the big human suffer, make them all suffer.

The head of the Conclave, the master of the Tower of Wayreth, Par-Salian, gazed down upon the donkey from the window of his chambers in the North Tower. He saw the donkey's ears twitch, and he winced involuntarily as her left hind hoof lashed out at Caramon Majere, who was endeavoring to secure a pack onto the donkey's saddle. Caramon had fallen victim to the donkey once this day and he was on the lookout. He, too, had seen the telltale ear twitch, understood its portent, and managed to dodge the kick. He stroked the donkey's neck and produced another apple, but the donkey lowered her head. By the look of her, Par-Salian thought—he knew something about donkeys, though few would have believed it—the ornery beast was contemplating rolling on the ground.

Blissfully unaware that all his careful packing was on the verge of being dislodged and squashed flat, not to mention soaked in a puddle, Caramon began loading the two horses. Unlike the donkey, the horses were glad to be away from the confinement and boredom of the stalls, were looking forward to a brisk canter and the chance to stretch their muscles, see new sights. The horses frisked and stamped and danced playfully on the flagstone, blowing and snuffling at the rain, and looking eagerly out the gates at the road beyond.

Par-Salian, too, looked at the road beyond. He could see where it led, could see the road far more clearly than others at that time on Krynn. He saw the trials and travails, he saw the danger. He saw hope, too, though its light was dim and wavering as the magical light cast by a crystal atop a young mage's staff. Par-Salian had purchased this hope, but at a terrible cost, and, at the moment, hope's light did little more than reveal to him more dangers. He must have faith, however. Faith in the gods, faith in himself, faith in the one he had chosen as his battle sword.

His "battle sword" stood in the courtyard, miserable in the rain, coughing fitfully, shivering and chilled as he watched his brother—limping slightly from his bruised thigh—ready the horses for their journey. A warrior such as the brother would have rejected such a sword outright, for it was, to all appearances, weak and brittle, liable to break at the first pass.

Par-Salian knew more about this sword than did the sword itself, perhaps. He knew that the iron will of the young mage's soul, having been tempered with blood, heated by fire, shaped by fate's hammer, and cooled with his own tears, was now finest steel, strong and sharp. Par-Salian had created a fine-honed weapon, but like all weapons, it had a double edge. It could be used to defend the weak and the innocent, or to attack them. He did not know yet which way the sword would cut. He doubted if the sword knew.

The young mage, wearing his new red robes—plain homespun robes without adornment, for he had no money to purchase better—stood huddled beneath a rose tree blooming in the courtyard, finding what shelter he could from the rain. The thin shoulders of the young man shook occasionally, he coughed into a handkerchief. At every cough, his brother, hale and robust, would pause in his work to glance back at his frail twin anxiously. Par-Salian could see the young man stiffen with irritation, could see his lips move and almost hear his curt admonition for his brother to get on with his task and leave him be.

Another person bustled out into the courtyard, just in time to prevent the donkey from spilling her load. A neat and dapper man of middle years, wearing gray robes—he would not spoil his white robes with the stains of travel—and a hooded cloak, Antimodes was a welcome sight. His cheerful air seemed to dispel the gloom of the day as he chided the donkey, all the while fondling her ears, and instructed the robust twin on some point of packing, to judge by the hand-waving and gesticulating. Par-Salian could not hear their conversation, but he smiled at the sight. Antimodes was old friend, mentor, and sponsor to the young mage.

Antimodes lifted his head and gazed at the North Tower, looking up at Par-Salian looking down. Though Antimodes could not see the Head of the Order from where he stood in the courtyard, he knew perfectly well that Par-Salian was there and that he was watching. Antimodes frowned and glowered, making certain that Par-Salian was aware of his ire and disapproval. The rain and the mist were Par-Salian's doing, of course. The Head of the Conclave controlled the weather around the Tower of High Sorcery. He could have sent his guests off in sunshine and springtime had he chosen to do so.

In truth, Antimodes was not that upset about the weather. It was merely an excuse. The real reason for Antimodes's ire was his disapproval of the way Par-Salian had handled the young mage's Test in the Tower of High Sorcery. Antimodes's disapproval was so strong that it had cast a cloud over the two men's long friendship.

The rain was Par-Salian's way of saying, "I understand your concern, my friend, but we cannot live all our days in sunshine. The rose tree needs the rain to survive, as well as the sun. And this gloom, this dreary darkness is nothing, my friend, nothing compared to what is yet to come!"

Antimodes shook his head, as if he had heard Par-Salian's thoughts, and turned grumpily away. A practical and pragmatic man, he didn't appreciate the symbolism, and he resented being forced to start out on his journey wet to the bone.

The young mage had been watching Antimodes closely. When Antimodes turned away and went back to placating his irate donkey, Raistlin Majere turned his own gaze to the North Tower, to the very window where stood Par-Salian. The archmage felt the gaze of those eyes—golden eyes, whose pupils were the shape of hourglasses—touch him, prick his flesh as though the tip of the sword's blade had sliced across his skin. The golden eyes, with their accursed vision, gave no hint of the thoughts behind them.

Raistlin did not understand fully what had happened to him. Par-Salian dreaded the day when Raistlin would come to understand. But that had been part of the price.

Was the young mage bitter, resentful? Par-Salian wondered. His body had been shattered, his health ruined. From now on, he would be sickly, easily fatigued, in pain, reliant on his stronger brother. Resentment would be natural, understandable. Or was Raistlin accepting? Did he believe that the fine steel of his blade had been worth the price? Probably not. He did not yet know his own strength. He would have time to learn, the gods willing. He was about to receive his first lesson.

All the archmages in the Conclave had either participated in Raistlin's Test or they had heard about what had occurred during the Test from their colleagues.[1] None of them would accept him as an apprentice.

"His soul is not his own," said Ladonna of the Black Robes, "and who knows when the buyer will come to claim his property."

The young mage needed instruction, needed training not only in magic, but in life. Par-Salian had done some discreet investigation and found a teacher whom he hoped would provide a suitable course of study. A rather unlikely instructor, but one in whom Par-Salian had a lot of faith, though this instructor would have been astounded to hear so.

Acting under Par-Salian's instructions, Antimodes inquired if the young mage and his brother would be interested in traveling east during the spring-time, to train as mercenaries with the army of the renowned Baron Ivor of Langtree. Such training would be ideally suited to the young mage and his warrior brother, who needed to earn their bread and butter, all the while honing their martial skills.

Skills they would need later, unless Par-Salian was very much mistaken.

There was no need for hurry. The time of the year was early fall, the season when warriors begin to think of putting away their weapons, start searching for a comfortable place to spend the cold winter days by the fire, telling tales of their own valor. Summer was the season of war, spring the season of preparing for war. The young man would have all winter to heal. Or rather, he would have time to adapt to his handicap, for he would never heal.

Such legitimate work would prevent Raistlin from exhibiting his talents in the local fairs in exchange for money, something he'd done in the past, much to the shock of the Conclave. It was all very well for illusionists or unskilled practitioners of the art to make spectacles of themselves before the public, but not for those who had been accepted into the Conclave.

---

1 The story of Raistlin's Test in the Tower of High Sorcery is related in *The Soulforge,* TSR publisher, 1998.

Par-Salian had yet another motive for sending Raistlin to the baron, a motive the young man would never—if he was lucky—come to know. Antimodes had his suspicions. His old friend Par-Salian never did anything just for the doing of it, all his means were aimed at a specific end. Antimodes had endeavored to find out, for he was man who loved secrets as a miser loves his coins, liked to count them over in the night, fondle them and gloat over them. But Par-Salian was closemouthed, would not fall victim to even the most cunningly laid snare.

The small group was at last ready to set out. Antimodes climbed upon his donkey. Raistlin mounted his horse with assistance from his brother, assistance that he accepted churlishly and with an ill grace, by the looks of it. Caramon, with exemplary patience, made certain his brother was settled and comfortable, and then he swung himself easily into the saddle of his own large-boned steed.

Antimodes took the lead. The three headed toward the gate. Caramon rode with his head down against the slashing rain. Antimodes left with a backward glare for the North Tower window, a glare expressive of his extreme discomfort and irritation. Raistlin halted his horse at the last moment, turned in the saddle to gaze at the Tower of High Sorcery. Par-Salian could guess what was going through the young man's mind. Much the same had gone through his mind, when he had been young.

How my life has changed in only a few short days! I entered this place strong and confident. I leave it weak and shattered, my vision cursed, my body frail. Yet, I leave this place triumphant. I leave with the magic. To gain that, I would have traded away my very soul. . . .

"Yes," Par-Salian said quietly, watching until the three had ridden into the magical Forest of Wayreth and there vanished from his mortal sight. His mind's eye kept them in view much longer. "Yes, you would have. You did. But you don't know that yet."

The rain fell harder. Antimodes would be cursing his friend heartily now. Par-Salian smiled. They would have sunshine when they left the forest. The sun's heat would bake them dry, they would not have to ride long in wet clothes. Antimodes was a wealthy man, fond of his comforts. He would see to it that they slept in a bed in a reputable inn. He would pay for it, too, if he could find a way to do so that would not offend the twins, who had only a few meager coins in their purses, but whose pride could have filled the royal coffers of Palanthas.

Par-Salian turned from the window. He had too much to do to stand there, staring out into a curtain of rain. He cast a wizard-lock spell upon the door, a strong spell that would keep out even the most powerful mages, mages such as Ladonna of the Black Robes. Admittedly, Ladonna had not visited the Tower in a long, long time, but she took great delight in arriving unexpectedly and at the most inopportune moments. It would never do for her to find him involved in these particular studies. Nor could he allow any of the other mages who lived in or frequented the Tower to find out what he was doing.

The time was not right to disclose what little he knew. He did not yet know enough. He had to learn more, to discover if what he had begun to suspect was true. He had to learn more, to ascertain if the information he had gleaned from his spies was accurate.

Certain that no one short of Solinari, God of White Magic, could break the spell cast upon the door, Par-Salian seated himself at his desk. On the desk—which was of dwarf-make, a present from one of the thanes of Thorbardin in return for services rendered—lay a book.

The book was old, very old. Old and forgotten. Par-Salian had found the book only by references made to it in other texts, else he himself would not have known of its existence. At that, he'd been forced to search for it for a great many hours, search through the library of the Tower of High Sorcery, a library of reference books and spellbooks and magical scrolls, a library so vast that it had never been catalogued. Nor would it ever be catalogued, except in Par-Salian's mind, for there were dangerous texts there, texts whose existence must be carefully guarded, texts known only to the Heads of the Three Orders, certain texts known only to the Master of the Tower himself. There were also texts of whose existence even he was not aware, as proven by the book in front of him, a book he had finally discovered in a corner of a storage room packed either mistakenly or by design in a box labeled "Child's Play."

Judging from the other artifacts to be found in the box, the box itself had come from the Tower of High Sorcery in Palanthas and dated back to the time of Huma. The box had undoubtedly been among those hastily packed when the mages had swallowed their pride and abandoned their Tower, rather than declare all-out war upon the people of Ansalon. The box marked "Child's Play" had been shoved into a corner and then forgotten in the chaos following the Cataclysm.

Par-Salian brushed his hand gently over the leather cover of the old book, the only book to be found in the box. He brushed away the dust and mouse-droppings and cobwebs that had partially obliterated the book's embossed title, a title whose letters he felt as bumps beneath his fingertips. A title that raised bumps on his flesh.

2

THE TREES OF WAYRETH FOREST, WAYWARD AND MAGICAL GUARDIAN OF the Tower of High Sorcery, lined up like soldiers on parade duty, stood tall and silent and stern beneath the lowering clouds.

"Guards of honor," said Raistlin.

"For a funeral," muttered Caramon.

He did not like the forest, which was no natural forest but a wandering and unexpected forest, a forest that was nowhere in sight of a morning and all around you in the evening. A dangerous forest to those who entered it unawares. He was thankful when they finally left the forest, or perhaps it was the forest who finally left them.

Whichever way it was, the trees took the clouds with them. Caramon removed his hat and lifted his face to the sun, basking in the warmth and the radiance.

"I feel like I haven't seen the sun in months," he said in a low voice with a baleful, backward glance at the Wayreth Forest, now a formidable wall of wet, black-boled trees, shrouded in gray mist. "It's good to be away from that place. I never want to go back, not as long as I live."

"There's absolutely no reason you should, Caramon," Raistlin said. "Believe me, you will not be invited back. Nor," he added an undertone, "will I."

"That's good, then," Caramon said stoutly. "I don't know why you'd want to go back. Not after"—he glanced at his brother, saw his grim expression, the eyes glinting, and faltered—"not after . . . well . . . what they did to you."

Caramon's courage, which had been squashed flat in the Tower of High

Sorcery, was reviving wonderfully in the warm sunshine, out from under the shadows of the watching, distrustful trees.

"It's not right what those mages did to you, Raist! I can say it now that we're away from that horrible place. Now that I'm sure no one's going to turn me into a beetle or an ant or something just for speaking my mind.

"I mean no offense, sir," Caramon added, shifting his attention to their traveling companion, the white-robed archmagus, Antimodes. "I appreciate all you've done for my brother in the past, sir, but I think you might have tried to stop your fiends from torturing him. There was no need for that. Raistlin could have died. He very nearly did die. And you didn't do a thing. Not a damn thing!"

"Enough, Caramon!" Raistlin admonished, shocked.

He glanced anxiously at Antimodes, who, fortunately, did not appear to have taken offense at Caramon's blunt statement. It almost appeared as if the archmagus agreed with what had been said. Still, Caramon was behaving like a buffoon, as usual.

"You forget yourself, my brother!" Raistlin stated angrily. "Apologize—"

Raistlin's throat constricted, he could not breathe. He let fall the reins to grip the pommel of the saddle, so weak and dizzy he feared he might fall from the horse. Leaning over the pommel, he tried desperately to clear his throat. His lungs burned, just as they had during the time years back when he'd been so sick, the time he'd collapsed in his mother's grave. He coughed and coughed but could not catch his breath. Blue flame flickered before his eyes.

This is the end! he thought in terror. I cannot survive this one!

The spasm eased suddenly and Raistlin drew in a shuddering breath, another, and another. His vision cleared. The burning pain subsided. He was able to sit upright. Fumbling for a handkerchief, he spit out the phlegm and the blood, used the handkerchief to wipe his lips. His hand closed over the handkerchief quickly, stuffed it back into the silken cord belt he wore around his waist, tucked the stained cloth in the folds of his red robes so that Caramon did not see it.

Caramon was off his horse, standing at Raistlin's side, regarding him with anxiety, arms outstretched, ready to catch him should he fall. Raistlin was angry at Caramon, but more angry at himself, angry at the momentary twinge of self-pity that wanted to sob out, "Why *did* they do this to me? Why?"

He gave his brother a scathing look. "I am quite capable of sitting a horse without assistance, my brother," he said caustically. "Make your apologies to the archmagus and then let us proceed. And put your hat back on! The sun will fry what few brains you have left."

"No need for you to apologize, Caramon," Antimodes said mildly, though his gaze, when it fell upon Raistlin, was grave. "You spoke your heart. No harm in that. Your care and concern for your brother are perfectly natural. Laudable, in fact."

And that is intended as a rebuke to me, Raistlin said to himself. You *know*, don't you, Master Antimodes? Did they let you watch? Did you watch me kill my twin? Or what turned out to be the illusion of my twin. Not that it matters. The knowledge that I have it within me to commit such a heinous act is the same as the deed. I horrify you, don't I? You don't treat me as you used to. I'm no longer the prize discovery, the young and gifted pupil you were so proud to exhibit. You admire me—grudgingly. You pity me. But you don't like me.

He said none of this aloud. Caramon remounted his horse in silence, and in silence the three rode off slowly. They had not traveled ten miles when Raistlin, weaker than he'd anticipated, stated that he could go no farther. The gods alone knew how he had pushed himself this far, for he was so weak that he was forced to allow Caramon to help ease him from the saddle, half-carry him inside.

Antimodes fussed over Raistlin, ordering the best room in the inn— though Caramon said many times over that the common room would do for them both—and recommending the broth of a boiled chicken to settle the stomach.

Caramon sat by Raistlin's bed, gazing at him helplessly, until Raistlin, annoyed beyond endurance, ordered his brother to go about his business and leave him to rest.

But he could not rest. He was not sleepy, his mind was active, if his body was not. He thought of Caramon—downstairs flirting with the barmaids and drinking too much ale. Antimodes would be down there, too, eavesdropping on conversations, picking up information. The fact that the white-robed wizard was one of Par-Salian's spies was an open secret among the denizens of the Tower, a secret not hard to deduce. A powerful archmagus, who could whisk himself from place to place with a few words of magic, did not travel the dusty roads of Ansalon on the back of a donkey unless he had good reason to want to dawdle in inns and gossip with the innkeepers, all the while keeping an eye on who came in and who went out.

Raistlin left his bed to sit at a small table next to a window, a window looking out onto a wheat field, bright gold against the green of the trees beneath a sun-filled blue sky. In his eyes—the cursed hourglass eyes of enchantment, first inflicted in ancient days as a lesson on the arrogant and dangerous renegade sorceress Relanna—Raistlin saw the wheat turning brown with the coming of autumn, drying up, its stalks stiff and brittle, to break beneath the snow. He saw the leaves on the trees wither and die, drift down to lie in the dust until they were blown away on cold winter winds.

He shifted his gaze from the dismal view. He would spend this precious time, this time alone, on study. He opened and laid out on the table the small quarto that contained information about the precious Staff of Magius, the magical artifact given to him by Par-Salian as . . . what? Compensation?

Raistlin knew better than that. Taking the Test had been his choice. He had known going into the Test that it would change him. All candidates are given that warning. Raistlin had been going to remind Caramon of this fact before the coughing fit seized him and wrung him like a dog wrings a knotted dishtowel. Mages had died during the Test before this, and the only compensation their families received was the mage's clothes sent home in a neat bundle with a letter of condolence from the Head of the Conclave. Raistlin was one of the fortunate ones. He had survived with his life, if not his health. He had survived with his sanity, although he sometimes feared his hold on that was tenuous.

He reached out to touch the staff, which was never far from his grasp. During their days in the Tower, Caramon had rigged a means of carrying the staff on horseback, lashing the staff on the back of the saddle, always near to Raistlin's hand. The smooth wood tingled with the lightning feel of magic beneath his fingers, acted as a tonic, easing his pain—pain of body, pain of mind, pain of soul.

He meant to read the book, but he found himself distracted, pondering this strange weakness with which he was afflicted. He had never been strong, not like his hale and robust twin. Fate had played him a cruel joke, had given his twin health and good looks and a guileless, winning nature; had given Raistlin a weak body, nondescript looks, native cunning, a quick mind, and a nature incapable of trust. But in compensation, Fate—or the gods—had given him the magic. The tingle of the feel of the magical staff seeped into his blood, warming it pleasantly, and he did not envy Caramon his ale or his barmaids.

But this weakness, this burning of fever in his body, this constant cough, this inability to draw a breath, as if his lungs were filled with dust, the blood on the handkerchief. The weakness would not kill him, at least so Par-Salian had assured him. Not that Raistlin believed everything Par-Salian told him— white-robed mages did not lie, but they did not necessarily tell you the truth either. Par-Salian had been extremely vague when it came to explaining to Raistlin just exactly what was wrong with him, what it was that had happened to him during the Test to have left him in such a weak and pitiful condition.

Raistlin remembered the Test clearly, most of it, at least. The magical Tests were designed to teach the mage something about himself, also to determine the color of the robes he wore, to which of the gods of the magic he pledged his allegiance. Raistlin had gone into the Test wearing white robes to honor his sponsor, Antimodes. Raistlin had come out wearing red, the robes of neutrality, honoring the goddess Lunitari. Raistlin did not walk the paths of light, nor did he walk the shadowed paths of darkness. He walked his own path, in his own way, of his own choosing.

Raistlin remembered fighting with a dark elf. He remembered—a terrible memory—the elf stabbing him with a poisoned dagger. Raistlin remembered pain, remembered his strength ebbing. He remembered dying, remembered being glad to die. And then Caramon had come to rescue him. Caramon had saved his twin with the use of his twin's one gift—the magic. It was then, in a jealous rage, that Raistlin had killed his brother. Except that it had only been an illusion of his brother.

And Caramon had seen his brother slay him.

Par-Salian had permitted Caramon to watch this part of the Test, the last part. Caramon now knew the darkness that twisted and writhed in his twin's soul. Caramon should, by rights, hate his twin for what he'd done to him. Raistlin wished Caramon would hate him. His brother's hatred would be so much easier to bear than his pity.

But Caramon did not hate Raistlin. Caramon "understood," or so he said.

"I wish I did," Raistlin said bitterly.

He remembered the Test, but not all of it. A part was missing. When he looked back on the Test in his mind, it was like looking at a painting that someone has deliberately marred. He saw people, but the faces were blotted out, smeared over with black ink. And ever since the Test, he had the oddest feeling; the feeling that someone was following him. He could almost feel a hand about to touch his shoulder, the whiff of a cold breath on the back of his neck. Raistlin had the impression that if he could just turn around quickly enough, he'd catch a glimpse of whatever it was that lurked behind him. He'd caught himself more than once whipping his head around, staring over his shoulder. But there was never anyone there. Only Caramon, with his sad and anxious eyes.

Raistlin sighed and banished the questions, which wearied him for no good reason, for they led him nowhere. He set himself to read the book, which had been written by a scribe attached to Huma's army, and which occasionally mentioned Magius and his wondrous staff. Magius—one of the greatest wizards ever to have lived, a friend to the legendary Knight Huma—Magius had assisted Huma in his battle against the Queen of Darkness and her evil dragons.

Magius had placed many enchantments on the staff, but he had left no record of them, a common practice among magi, particularly if the artifact was exceptionally powerful and they feared it might fall into the wrong hands. Generally the master passed the artifact and the knowledge of its power on to a trusted apprentice, who would hand it on in turn. But Magius had died before he could hand over the staff. Whoever used the staff now would have to puzzle out its abilities for himself.

After only a few days' study, Raistlin had already learned from his reading that the staff gave the possessor the ability to float in the air as lightly as thistledown and that, if used as a club, its magic would increase the force of a blow, so that even someone as weak as Raistlin could deal considerable harm to an enemy. These were useful functions, but Raistlin was quite certain the staff was far more powerful. The reading was slow going, for the language was a mixture of Solamnic, which he had learned from his friend Sturm Brightblade, and Common and a slang used by soldiers and mercenaries. It would often take Raistlin an hour to figure out the meaning of a single page. He read again a passage, which he was certain was important, but one that he had yet to understand the meaning of.

We knew the black dragon was nearby, for we could hear the hissing of solid rock dissolving in the deadly acid of the foul wrym's spittle. We could hear the creak of its wings and its claws scrape against the castle walls as it climbed over them in search of us. But we could see nothing, for the dragon had cast upon us some sort of evil magic, which quenched the sunshine and made all dark as the wrym's own heart. The dragon's plan was to come upon us in this darkness and slay us before we could battle it.

Huma called for torchlight, but no flame could we kindle in the thick air, which had been poisoned by the fumes from the dragon's deadly breath. We feared that all was lost and that we would die in this unholy darkness. But then Magius came forward, bearing light! I know not how he accomplished it, but the crystal of the staff he bore drove away the darkness and let us see the terrible monster. We had a target for our arrows and, by Huma's command, we launched our attack. . . .

Several pages detailed the killing of the dragon, which Raistlin skipped over impatiently as information he would probably never need to know. No dragon had been seen on Krynn since Huma's time, and there were those who were now saying that even then they were only creatures of myth. That

Huma had made it all up in order to glorify himself, that he'd been nothing but a showman, a self-aggrandizing liar.

I asked a friend how Magius had caused his staff to shine with such a blessed light. The friend, who had been standing near the wizard at the time, said that Magius spoke but a single word of command. I asked what the word was, for I thought it might be of use to the rest of us. He maintained that the word was "shark," which is a type of monstrous fish that lives in the sea and bites men in twain, or so I have heard sailors tell. I do not think he is right, for I tried the word myself, secretly, one night when Magius had left his staff propped up in a corner, and I could not make the crystal light. I can only suppose that the word is a foreign one, perhaps elvish in nature, for Magius is known to have dealings with their kind.

Shark! Raistlin sniffed. Elvish! What a fool. The word was obviously spoken in the language of magic. Raistlin had spent a frustrating hour in the Tower trying every phrase that he could think of in the arcane tongue, every word that bore even a remote resemblance to "shark." He had about as much luck causing the crystal atop the staff to light as had that long-dead and unknown soldier.

A burst of laughter came from downstairs. Raistlin could distinguish Caramon's booming guffaw among the shriller voices of the women. At least his brother was pleasantly occupied and not likely to barge in and disturb him.

Raistlin turned to look at the staff. "*Elem shardish*," he said, which meant, "By my command," a standard phrase used to activate the magic in many an artifact.

But not this one. The crystal, held fast in a golden replica of a dragon's claw, remained dark.

Frowning, Raistlin looked down at the next phrase he'd noted on his list. *Sharcum pas edistus*, another common magical command, which meant roughly "Do as I say." The command did not work either. The crystal gleamed, but only with a beam of reflected sunlight. He continued on through the list, which included *omus sharpuk derli*, for "I will it to be so," to *shirkit muan*, which meant "Obey me."

Raistlin lost patience. "*Uh, Lunitari's idish, shirak, damen du!*"

The crystal atop the staff burst into brilliant, radiant light.

Raistlin stared, astonished, and tried to recall what he'd said, the exact words. His hand trembling, his gaze divided between the wondrous, magical light and his work, he wrote down the phrase, *Uh, Lunitari's idish, shirak, damen du!* and its translation, *Oh, for god's sake, light, damn you!*

And there was the answer.

Raistlin felt his skin burn in embarrassment and was extremely thankful he had not mentioned his puzzlement to anyone, especially Antimodes, as he'd considered doing.

"*I* am the fool," he said to himself. "Making something simple into something difficult. 'Shark.' '*Shirak*.' 'Light.' That is the command. And to douse the light. '*Dulak*.' 'Dark.'"

The magical light in the crystal blinked out.

Triumphant, Raistlin unpacked his writing equipment, a small quill made of a trimmed goose feather and a sealed bottle of ink. He was entering his discovery in his own small journal when his throat seemed to thicken and swell, shutting off the windpipe. He dropped the quill, causing an inkblot upon the journal, and coughed and choked and struggled for breath. When the spasm passed, he was exhausted. He lacked the strength to lift the feather quill. Barely able to creep back to his bed, he lay down thankfully, resentfully, to wait for the dizziness, the weakness to pass.

Downstairs, another roar of laughter. Caramon was in rare form, apparently. Out in the hallway, Raistlin heard two pairs of footfalls and Antimodes's voice. "I have a map in my room, friend. If you could just be so good as to show me the location of that goblin army. Here is some steel for your trouble. . . ."

Raistlin lay in his bed and struggled to breathe while life went on around him. The sun moved across the sky, the shadows of the window frame slid across the ceiling. Raistlin watched them and wished for a cup of the tea he drank that would ease his pain and wondered fretfully that Caramon did not come to check up on him, to see if there was anything he needed.

But when Caramon did come, late in the afternoon, doing his best to creep into the room without making any noise, he knocked over a pack and woke Raistlin from the first peaceful sleep he'd had in days, for which mistake Caramon received a bitter tongue-lashing and was ordered out of the room.

Ten miles in a single day. Hundreds of miles to go to reach their destination.

The journey was going to be a long one.

3

RAISTLIN FELT BETTER, STRONGER THE NEXT FEW DAYS. He was able to travel more hours during the day. They reached the outskirts of Qualinesti in good time. Although Antimodes assured them that there was no hurry, that the baron would not muster his army until springtime, the twins hoped to reach the baron's headquarters, a fortress built on an inlet of New Sea, far to the east of Solace, before winter set in. They hoped to be able to at least have their names entered upon the rolls, to perhaps find a way to earn some money in the baron's service, for the twins were now desperately short of coins. Their plans were thrown awry, however. A river crossing proved disastrous.

They were fording the Elfstream when Raistlin's horse slipped on a rock and went down, throwing his rider into the water. Fortunately, the river was slow and sluggish in mid-autumn, after the rushing of the snowmelt in the spring. The water broke his fall, and Raistlin received no greater injury than loss of dignity and a dunking. But a soaking rainstorm that night prevented him from drying off. A chill set in and struck through to the bone.

The next day, he rode shivering beneath a hot sun and by nightfall had fallen into feverish delirium. Antimodes, who had rarely been sick in his life, knew nothing about treating illness. Had Raistlin been conscious, he could have helped himself, for he was a skilled herbalist, but he wandered in dark dreams, horrifying dreams, to judge by his cries and his moans. Desperate with worry for his twin, Caramon risked entering the woods of the Qualinesti elves, hoping to be able to find some among them who would come to his brother's aid.

Arrows fell thick as wheat stalks at his feet, but that did not deter him. He shouted to the unseen archers, "Let me talk to Tanis Half-Elven! I am a friend of Tanis's! He will vouch for us! My brother is dying! I need your aid!"

Unfortunately, the mention of Tanis's name seemed to make matters worse, not better, for the next arrow pierced Caramon's hat, and another grazed his arm, drawing blood. Admitting defeat, he cursed all elves heartily (though under his breath) and retreated from the woods.

The next morning, Raistlin's fever had abated somewhat, enough to permit him to speak rationally. Clutching Caramon's arm, Raistlin whispered, "Haven! Take me to Haven! Our friend, Lemuel, will know what to do for me!"

They traveled to Haven with speed, Caramon holding his ill brother in his arm, propped up in front of him on his saddle, Antimodes galloping behind, leading Raistlin's horse by the reins.

Lemuel was a mage. He was an inept mage, a reluctant mage, but he was a mage, and he and Raistlin had developed an odd sort of friendship on an earlier, ill-fated trip to Haven. Lemuel still held a fondness for Raistlin and readily welcomed him and his brother and the archmagus to his house. Giving Raistlin the very best bedroom, Lemuel saw to it that Antimodes and Caramon were comfortable in other rooms of the large house, then set about doing what he could to help the gravely ill young man.

"He is very sick, there's no doubt about that," Lemuel told the distraught Caramon, "but I don't believe there is cause for alarm. A cold that flew to his chest. Here is a list of some herbs I need. You know where to find the herbalist shop? Excellent. Run along. And don't forget the ipecac."

Caramon left, almost staggering with fatigue but unable to sleep or rest until he was assured his twin was being treated.

Lemuel made certain that Raistlin was resting as comfortably as possible, then went to the kitchen to fetch some cool water, to lave the young man's skillet-hot body, make some attempt to reduce the fever. He encountered Antimodes, enjoying a cup of tea.

Antimodes was a middle-aged human, dapper in his dress, wearing fine, expensive robes. He was a powerful mage, though economic with his power. He didn't like to soil his clothes, as the saying went. By contrast, Lemuel was short, tubby, of a cheerful disposition. He liked nothing better than to work in his garden. As for magic, he had barely enough to boil water.

"Excellent brew this," said the archmagus, who had, in fact, boiled the water himself. "What is it?"

"Chamomile with a touch of mint," said Lemuel. "I picked the mint this morning."

"How is the young man?" Antimodes asked.

"Not good," said Lemuel, sighing. "I didn't like to say anything with his brother around, but he has pneumonia. Both lungs are filled with fluid."

"Can you help him?"

"I will do what I can for him. But he is very ill. I am afraid . . ." Lemuel's voice trailed off. He shook his head again.

Antimodes was silent a moment, sipping at his tea and frowning at the teapot. "Well, perhaps it is better this way," he said at last.

"My dear sir!" Lemuel exclaimed, shocked. "You can't mean that! He's so young!"

"You see how he has changed. You know that he took the Test."

"Yes, Archmagus. His brother told me. The change is . . . quite . . . remarkable." Lemuel shivered. He cast the archmagus a sidelong glance. "Still, I suppose the Order knows what it is doing."

He cocked an ear down the hallway, listening for his patient, whom he had left in a fitful, troubled sleep.

"You'd like to think so, wouldn't you," Antimodes muttered gloomily.

Lemuel was uncomfortable at this, not certain how to reply. Filling his basin with water, he started to leave.

"You knew Raistlin before, I believe," Antimodes stated abruptly.

"Yes, Archmagus," Lemuel said, turning back to his guest. "He has visited me several times."

"What do you think of him?"

"He performed a very great service for me, sir," Lemuel replied, flushing. "I am in his debt. Perhaps you have not heard that story? I was being driven out of my home by a cult of fanatics who worshiped a snake god. Belzor, I think his name was, or some such thing. Raistlin was able to prove that the magic the cultists claimed came from the gods was actually ordinary, run-of-the-mill magic. He very nearly died—"

Antimodes used the sugar spoon to wave away death and gratitude. "I know. I heard. Aside from that, what do you think of him?"

"I like him," said Lemuel. "Oh, he has his faults. I admit that. But then, which of us does not? He is ambitious. I was ambitious once myself at that age. He is completely and wholly dedicated to the art—"

"Some might say obsessed," Antimodes observed darkly.

"But then so was my father. I believe you knew him, sir?"

Antimodes bowed. "I had the honor. A fine man and an excellent wizard."

"Thank you. I myself was a sad disappointment to my father, as you can imagine," Lemuel said, with a self-deprecating smile. "When I first met

Raistlin, I said to myself, 'This is the son my father wanted.' I felt a kind of brotherly feeling toward him."

"Brother! Be thankful you are *not* his brother!" Antimodes said sternly.

The archmagus frowned so darkly, spoke in such a solemn tone that Lemuel, who could make nothing of this strange statement, excused himself by saying that he had to go check on his patient and left the kitchen with haste.

Antimodes remained at the table, so absorbed in his thoughts that he forgot the tea in the cup. "Near to death, is he? I'll wager he doesn't die. You" —he glowered at the thin air, as if it held a disembodied spirit—"you won't let him die, will you? Not without exerting every effort to save him. For if he dies, you die. And who am I to judge him, after all? Who has foreseen the role he is destined to play in the terrible times that are fast approaching? Not I, that is for certain. And not Par-Salian, either, though he would like very much for us to think so!"

Antimodes looked gloomily into the teacup, as if he could read the future in the leaves.

"Well, well, young Raistlin," he said after a moment, "I am sorry for you, that much I can say. Sorry for you and sorry for your brother. The gods—if there be gods—help you both. Here's to your health."

Antimodes raised the teacup to his lips and took a sip. Finding the tea cold, he immediately spit it back out.

☻

Raistlin did not die. Whether it was Lemuel's herbs, Caramon's patient nursing, Antimodes's prayer, or the watchful care of one on another plane of existence, one whose life-force was inextricably bound up with the life of the young mage, or whether it was none of these and Raistlin's will alone that saved him, no one could say. One night, after a week during which he hovered in a no-man's-land between life and death, life won the battle. The fever broke, he breathed easier, and sank into a restful sleep.

He was weak—incredibly weak, so weak that he could not lift his head from the pillow without his brother's strong arm to support him. Antimodes postponed his own journey, lingered in Haven long enough to see that the young man had pulled through. Certain that Raistlin would live, the archmagus left for his own home, hoping to reach Balifor before winter storms made the roads impassable. He gave Caramon a letter of introduction to be given to Baron Ivor in Antimodes's absence.

"Don't kill yourselves getting there," said Antimodes on the day of his departure. "As I tried telling you before, the baron will not be happy to see you now anyway. He and his soldiers will sit idle all winter, and you two would be just two more mouths to feed. In the spring, he will begin receiving offers for his army's services. Never fear that you will lack work! The Baron of Langtree and his mercenaries are well known and well respected throughout this part of Ansalon. He and his soldiers are in high demand."

"Thank you very much, sir," said Caramon gratefully. He helped Antimodes mount the recalcitrant Jenny, who had taken quite a liking to Lemuel's sweet apples and was in no hurry to resume her journey. "Thank you for this and for everything that you have done for us." Caramon flushed. "About what I said back there, when we were riding out of the forest. I'm sorry. I didn't mean it. If it hadn't been for you, sir, Raist never would have fulfilled his dream."

"Ah, dear me, my young friend," Antimodes said with a sigh, resting his hand on Caramon's shoulder. "Don't lay that burden on me, as well."

He gave Jenny a flick of the riding crop on her broad rump, which did nothing to improve her temper, and the donkey trotted off, leaving Caramon standing in the middle of the road, scratching his head.

Raistlin's health mended slowly. Caramon worried that they were a burden to Lemuel and hinted more than once that he thought his brother could make the trip back to their home in Solace. But Raistlin had no desire to return to their home, not yet. Not while he was still weak, his appearance so terribly altered.

He could not bear the thought of any of their friends seeing him like this. He envisioned Tanis's concern, Flint's shock, Tasslehoff's prying questions, Sturm's disdain. He writhed at the thought and vowed by the gods of magic, by all three gods of magic, that he would never return to Solace until he could do so with pride in himself and with power in his hand.

In answer to Caramon's concerns, Lemuel invited the two young men to stay as long as they needed, to stay all winter if they wanted. The shy and diffident mage enjoyed the company of the two young men. He and Raistlin shared an interest in herbs and herb lore and, when Raistlin was stronger, the two of them spent the days quite pleasantly pounding up leaves with a mortar and pestle, experimenting with various ointments and salves, or exchanging notes on such topics as how best to rid roses of aphids and chrysanthemums of spider mites.

Raistlin was generally in a better humor when he was in Lemuel's company. He curbed his sarcastic tongue in Lemuel's presence, was much kinder and more patient with Lemuel than he was with his own brother.

Prone to self-analysis, Raistlin wondered why this should be so. One obvious reason was that he genuinely liked the cheerful and unassuming mage. Unfortunately, he also found that part of his kindness stemmed from a vague sense of guilt in regard to Lemuel. Raistlin couldn't define his guilt or understand the reason for it. So far as he could remember, he had never done or said anything to Lemuel for which he need apologize. He had committed no ungenerous act. But he felt as if he had, and the feeling bothered him. Oddly enough, Raistlin discovered that he could not walk into Lemuel's kitchen without experiencing an overwhelming sense of dread, which always brought the image of a dark elf to mind. Raistlin could only assume that Lemuel had somehow been involved in his Test, but how or why he had no idea, and, search his mind as he might, he could not dredge up the memory.

Once assured that Raistlin was out of danger and that Lemuel really wanted them to stay, that he wasn't just being polite, Caramon settled down to enjoy the winter in Haven. He earned a few coins by doing odd jobs for people—chopping wood, repairing roofs damaged in the fall rains, helping bring in the harvest, for he and Raistlin insisted on helping with Lemuel's household expenses. Thus Caramon came to know a great many of the town's citizens, and it was not long before the big man was as popular and well liked in Haven as he had been in Solace.

Caramon had girl friends by the score. He fell in love several times a week and was always on the verge of marrying someone, but never did. The girls always ended up marrying someone else, someone richer, someone who did not have a wizard for a brother. Caramon's heart was never truly broken, although he swore it was often enough and would spend the afternoon telling Lemuel in dolorous tones that he was finished with women for good, only to be entwined in a pair of soft, warm arms that very night.

Caramon discovered a tavern, the Haven Arms, and made that his second home. The ale was almost as good as Otik's, and the scrapple, made with scraps of pork, stewed with meal and pressed into cakes, was much better than Otik's, although Caramon would have allowed himself to be stewed with meal before he admitted it. Caramon never went to the tavern, he never went out to work, never left the house before making certain that there was nothing he could do for his brother.

Relations between the two—strained almost to the breaking point after the terrible incident in the Tower—eased over the winter. Raistlin had forbidden Caramon ever to mention the occurrence, and the two never discussed it.

Gradually, after thinking it over, Caramon came to believe that his apparent murder at the hands of his twin was his fault, a belief that Raistlin did not dispute.

I deserved death at my brother's hands, was the thought lurking somewhere in the back of Caramon's mind. He did not blame his brother in the least. If somewhere deep inside him, some part of Caramon was grieved and unhappy, he took care to trample on that part until he had stomped it into the soil of his soul, covered it with guilt, and watered it generously with dwarf spirits. He was the strong twin, after all. His brother was frail and needed protection.

Deep inside himself, Raistlin felt shame for his jealous rage. He was appalled to learn that he had the capability within him to kill his brother. He, too, trampled on his emotions, smoothed out the soil, so that no one—least of all himself—would ever find out anything had been buried there. Raistlin comforted himself with the idea that he'd known all along the image of Caramon wasn't real, that he'd murdered nothing but an illusion.

By Yule time, the relationship between the twins was almost back to what it had once been before the infamous Test. Raistlin did not like the cold and snow. He never ventured out of Lemuel's comfortable house, and he enjoyed listening to Caramon's gossip. Raistlin enjoyed proving to his own satisfaction that his fellow mortals were fools and idiots, while Caramon took immense pleasure in bringing a smile—albeit it a sardonic smile—to his twin's lips, lips that were too often stained with blood.

Raistlin spent his winter months in study. He knew now at least some of the magic contained within the staff of Magius, and though he found it frustrating to know that there were more spells that he did not know, perhaps would never know, he reveled in the knowledge that he possessed the staff and others did not. He worked on his war wizard spells, as well, in preparation for the day soon coming when he and Caramon would join up with the mercenary army, there to make their fortunes—of that both young men were firmly convinced.

Raistlin read numerous texts on the subject—many of them left behind by Lemuel's father—and he practiced combining his magic with Caramon's swordsmanship. The two killed a great many imaginary foes and a tree or two (several of Raistlin's early fire-based spells having gone awry), and were soon confident that they were already as good as professionals. Congratulating themselves on their skill, they agreed between them that they could take on an army of hobgoblins all by themselves. They half hoped that such an army might attack Haven during the winter and when no hobgoblins ventured near, the twins expressed resentment against the entire race of hobgoblins, a soft race, who would apparently rather skulk about in warm caves than go to battle.

☻

Spring came to Haven, returning with the robins, the kender, and other wayfarers, bringing proof that the roads were open and the traveling season had begun. It was time for the twins to head east, to find a ship to take them to Langtree Manor, located in the town of Langtree on the Green, the largest city in the barony of Langtree.

Caramon packed clothes and food for the trip. Raistlin packed his spell components, and the two made ready to leave. Lemuel was genuinely sorry to see them go and would have made Raistlin a present of every plant in the garden had Raistlin permitted it. The tavern Caramon frequented nearly shut down from sorrow, and the road out of Haven was literally paved with weeping women, or so it seemed to Raistlin.

His health had improved over the winter, either that or he was learning to cope. He sat his horse with confidence and with ease, enjoying the soft spring air, which seemed better for his lungs to breathe than the sharp, cold air of winter. The knowledge that Caramon was keeping a watchful eye on his twin caused Raistlin to make light of any weakness he felt. He felt so well that they were soon able to ride almost ten leagues in a day.

Much to Caramon's dismay, they skirted Solace, taking a little-known animal trail discovered when they were children.

"I can smell Otik's potatoes," said Caramon wistfully, sitting up in the saddle, sniffing. "We could stop at the Inn for dinner."

Raistlin could also smell the potatoes—or at least he imagined he could—and he was suddenly overwhelmed with homesickness. How easy it would be to return! How easy to relapse once more into that comfortable existence, to make his living tending colicky babies and treating old men's rheumatism. How easy to sink into that cozy, warm feather bed of a life. He hesitated. His horse, sensing its rider's indecision, slowed its pace. Caramon looked at his twin hopefully.

"We could spend the night at the Inn," he urged.

The Inn of the Last Home. Where Raistlin had first met Antimodes. Where he had first heard the mage tell him of the forging of a soul. The Inn of the Last Home. Where people would stare at him, would whisper about him . . .

Raistlin drove the heels of his boots hard into his horse's flanks, causing the animal—unaccustomed to such treatment—to break into a trot.

"Raist? The potatoes?" Caramon cried, his horse galloping to catch up.

"We don't have the money," Raistlin returned shortly, coldly. "Fish in Crystalmir Lake are free to eat. The woods charge nothing for us to sleep in them."

Caramon knew very well that Otik would not ask them to pay, and he sighed deeply. He brought his horse to a halt, turned to look back longingly at Solace. He couldn't see the town, which was hidden in the trees, except in his mind. The mental image was all the more vivid.

Raistlin checked his horse. "Caramon, if we went back to Solace now, we would never leave. You know that, as well as I."

Caramon didn't respond. His horse shuffled nervously.

"Is that the life you want?" Raistlin demanded, his voice rising. "Do you want to work for farmers all your life? With hay in your hair and your hands steeped in cow dung? Or do you want to come back to Solace with your pockets filled with steel, with tales of your prowess on your lips, displaying scars of your battles to adoring barmaids?"

"You're right, Raist," Caramon said, turning his horse's head. "That's what I want, of course. I felt a sort of tugging feeling, that's all. Like I was being pulled back. But that's silly. There's no one left in Solace anymore. None of our old friends, I mean. Sturm's gone north. Tanis is with the elves, Flint with the dwarves. And who knows where Tasslehoff is?"

"Or cares," Raistlin added caustically.

"One person might be there, though," Caramon said. He glanced sidelong at his twin. Raistlin understood the unspoken thought.

"No," said Raistlin. "Kitiara is not in Solace."

"How do you know?" Caramon asked, astonished. His brother had spoken with unshaken conviction. "You're not . . . not having visions, are you? Like . . . well . . . like our mother."

"I am not suffering from second sight, my brother. Nor am I given to portents and premonitions. I base my statement on what I know of our sister. She will never come back to Solace," Raistlin said firmly. "She has more important friends now. More important concerns."

The trail between the trees narrowed, forcing the two to ride single file. Caramon took front, Raistlin fell in behind. The two rode in silence. Sunlight filtered through the tree limbs, casting barred shadows across Caramon's wide back, shadows that slid over him as he rode in and out of the sunshine. The scent of pine was sharp and crisp. The way was slow, the path overgrown.

"Maybe it's wrong to think this, Raist," Caramon said after a very long silence. "I mean, Kit's our sister and all. But . . . I don't much care if I ever see her again."

"I doubt we ever will, Caramon," Raistlin replied. "There is no reason why our paths should cross."

"Yeah, I guess you're right. Still, I get a funny feeling about her sometimes."

"A 'tugging' feeling?" Raistlin asked.

"No, more of a jabbing feeling." Caramon shivered. "Like she was poking at me with a knife."

Raistlin snorted. "You are probably just hungry."

"Of course I am." Caramon was complacent. "It's nearly dinnertime. But that's not the kind of feeling I mean. A hungry feeling is an empty feeling in the bottom of your stomach. It sort of gnaws at you. This other kind of feeling is like when all the hair on your arms stands up—"

"I was being sarcastic!" Raistlin snapped, glaring out from beneath the rim of his red hood, which he wore pulled up over his head in case they happened across someone they knew.

"Oh," Caramon returned meekly. He was quiet a moment, fearing to further irritate his brother. The thought of food was too much. "Say, how are you going to cook the fish tonight, Raist? My favorite way is when you put onions and butter on it and wrap it in lettuce leaves and put it on a really hot rock. . . ."

Raistlin let his twin ramble on about the various methods of cooking fish. He was quiet, thoughtful, and Caramon did not intrude on his thoughts. The two camped on the banks of Crystalmir Lake. Caramon caught the fish, fourteen or so small lake perch. Raistlin cooked the perch—not with lettuce leaves, the lettuce being mostly underground at this time of year. They shook out their bedrolls. Caramon, his stomach full, soon fell asleep, his face bathed in the warm, laughing light of the red moon, Lunitari.

Raistlin lay awake, watching the red light of the moon play upon the water, dancing on the wavelets, teasing him to come join in their revels. He smiled to see them but kept to the comfort of his blanket.

He truly believed what he had told Caramon. He would never see Kitiara again. The threads of their lives had once been a whole cloth, but the fabric of their youth had frayed, unraveled. Now he pictured the thread of his own life unwinding before him, running straight and true toward his goals.

Little did he think that at this moment the weft of his sister's life, advancing at right angles to his own, would cross the warp of his life and his brother's to form a web, strange and deadly.

4

It was springtime in Sanction. Or rather, it was springtime in the rest of Ansalon, almost a year to the date from the time the companions had come together in the Inn of the Last Home to say their good-byes and to pledge to meet again five years in the fall. Spring did not come to Sanction. Spring brought no budding trees, no daffodils yellow against the melting snow, no sweet breezes, no cheery birdsong.

The trees had been cut down to feed Sanction's forge-fires, the daffodils had died in the poisonous fumes of the belching mountains known as the Lords of Doom. And if there had ever been birds, they had long since been wrung, plucked, and eaten.

Spring in Sanction was Campaign Season, celebrated for the fact that the roads were now open and ready for marching. The troops under the command of General Ariakas had spent the winter in Sanction huddled in their tents, half-frozen, fighting each other for scraps of food tossed to them by their commanders, who wanted a lean and hungry army. To the soldiers, spring meant the chance to raid and loot and kill, steal food enough to fill their shriveled bellies, and capture slaves enough to do the menial work and warm their beds.

Warriors made up the bulk of the population of Sanction, and they were in good spirits, roaming the town, bullying the inhabitants, who got their revenge by charging exorbitant prices for their wares, while the abused innkeepers served up rotgut wine, watered-down ale, and dwarf spirits made of toadstools.

"What a god-awful place," said Kitiara to her companion, as the two walked the crowded, filthy streets. "But it does sort of grow on you."

"Like scum on a pond," said Balif with a laugh.

Kitiara grinned. She had certainly been in prettier places, but what she'd said was true—she found herself liking Sanction. Rough, coarse, and crude, the city was also exciting, interesting, entertaining. Excitement appealed to Kitiara, who had been laid up for the past few months, forced to lie abed and do nothing except hear rumors of great events taking shape, and fret and fume and curse her ill luck that she could not be part of them. She had since rid herself of the minor inconvenience that had momentarily incapacitated her. Free of entanglements, she was free to pursue her ambitions.

Before Kit was even out of the birthing bed, she had sent a message to a disreputable inn known as The Trough in Solace. The message was to a man named Balif, who passed through town every so often and who had been waiting months for a message from Kit.

Her missive was short: *How do I meet this general of yours?*

His reply was equally terse and to the point. *Come to Sanction.*

When she was able to travel, Kitiara had done just that.

"What is that foul smell?" she asked, wrinkling her nose. "Like rotten eggs!"

"The sulfur pits. You get used to it," Balif answered, shrugging. "After a day or two, you won't notice it. The best part of Sanction is that no one comes here who doesn't belong here. Or, if they do, they don't stay long. Sanction's safe, and it's secret. That's why the general chose it."

"The city is aptly named, though. Sanction—it's a punishment to live here!"

Kit was pleased with her own little joke. Balif laughed dutifully, glanced at her admiringly as she strode along the narrow streets at his side. She was thinner than she had been when he'd last seen her over a year ago, but her dark eyes were still as bright, her lips still as full, her body lithe and graceful. She wore her traveling clothes, for she'd only just arrived in Sanction—fine leather armor over a brown tunic, which came to mid-thigh, revealing shapely legs in green stockings, leather boots that came to her knees.

Kitiara saw Balif look, understood the proposition, and—shaking her short, dark curls—she returned a veiled promise with her eyes. She was looking for diversion, amusement, and Balif was handsome in a cold, sharp-edged sort of way. What was equally important, he was a high-ranking officer in General Ariakas's new-formed army, a most trusted spy and assassin. Balif had the general's ear and access to his presence, an honor that Kit could not hope to achieve on her own, not without wasting valuable time, requiring resources she did not possess. Kitiara was flat broke.

She'd been forced to pawn her sword to provide money enough to travel to Sanction, and most of that money had gone to pay her passage on the ship across New Sea. She had no money at all now and had been wondering where she would spend the night. That problem was now solved. Her smile, the crooked smile that she could make so charming, widened.

Balif had his answer. He licked his lips and moved a step closer, put his hand on her arm to steer her around a drunken goblin, stumbling down the street.

"I'll take you to the inn where I'm staying," Balif said, his grip on her tightening, his breath coming faster. "It's the best in Sanction, though I admit that's not saying a lot. Still, we can be alo—"

"Hey, Balif." A man wearing black leather armor halted in front of them, blocking their path along the cracked and broken street. Eyeing Kitiara, the man leered. "What have we here? A fine-looking wench. I trust you'll share with your friends?" He reached out to grab hold of Kitiara. "Come here, sweetheart. Give us a kiss. Balif won't mind. He and I have slept three to a bed before—ugh!"

The man doubled over, groaning and clutching his crotch, his ardor deflated by the toe of Kitiara's boot. A swift chop to the back of his neck drove him to the broken stones of the street, where he lay unmoving. Kit nursed a cut hand—the bastard had been wearing a spiked leather collar around his neck—and snatched her knife from her boot.

"Come on," she said to the man's two friends, who had been about to back him up, but who were now reconsidering their options. "Come on. Who else wants to sleep three to a bed with me?"

Balif, who had seen Kit's work before, knew better than to interfere. He leaned against a crumbling wall, his arms folded, watching with amusement.

Kitiara balanced lightly on the balls of her feet. She held the knife with easy, practiced skill. The two men facing her liked women who shrank from them in fear and terror. There was no fear in the dark eyes that watched their every move. Those eyes gleamed with keen anticipation of the fight. Kit darted forward, lashing out with the knife, moving so fast that the blade was a flashing blur in the few rays of weak sunlight that managed to struggle through the smoke-laden air. One of the men stared stupidly at a bloody slash across his upper arm.

"I'd sooner bed a scorpion," he snarled, and putting his hand over the cut to try to stanch the flow of blood, he gave Kit a vicious look and slouched away, accompanied by his friend. They left their third companion in the street, where the unconscious man was immediately set upon by goblins, who stripped him of every valuable he owned.

Kit sheathed her knife in her boot and turned to Balif, regarded him with approval. "Thanks for not 'helping.'"

He applauded. "You're a joy to watch, Kit. I wouldn't have missed that for a bag of steel."

Kit put her wounded hand to her mouth.

"Where's this inn of yours?" she asked, slowly licking the blood from the cut, her eyes on Balif.

"Near here," he answered, his voice husky.

"Good. You're going to buy me dinner." Kit slid her hand through his arm, pressed close to him. "And then you're going to tell me all about General Ariakas."

☻

"So where have you been all this time?" Balif asked. His pleasure sated, he lay next to her, tracing over the battle scars on her bare breast with his hand. "I expected to hear from you last summer or at least by fall. Nothing. Not a word."

"I had things to do," said Kit lazily. "Important things."

"They said you went north to Solamnia, in company with a boy knight. Brightsword, or some such name."

"Brightblade. Yes." Kitiara shrugged. "We traveled on the same errand, but we soon parted company. I could no longer stomach his prayers and vigils and sanctimonious prattling."

"He may have started on that trip a boy, but I'll wager he was a man by the time you were finished with him," Balif said with a salacious wink. "So where did you go after that?"

"I wandered around Solamnia for a while, looking for my father's family. They were landed noblemen, or so he always said. I figured they'd be glad to see their long-lost granddaughter. So glad they'd part with a few of the family jewels and a chest of steel. But I couldn't find them."

"You don't need some moldy old blue blood's money, Kit. You'll earn your own fortune. You've got brains and you've got talent. General Ariakas is looking for both. Who knows, someday you might rule Ansalon." He fondled the scars on her right breast. "So you finally left that half-elf lover you were so taken with."

"Yes, I left him," Kitiara said quietly. Drawing the sheet up around her, she rolled to the other side of the bed. "I'm sleepy," she said, her voice cold. "Blow out the candle."

Balif shrugged and did what he was told. He had her body, he didn't care what she did with her heart. He was soon fast asleep. Kitiara lay with her back to him, staring into the darkness. She hated Balif at that moment, hated him for reminding her of Tanis. She had worked hard to put the half-elf out her mind, and she had very nearly done so. She did not ache for his touch at night anymore. The touch of other men eased her longing, though she still saw his face whenever any other man loved her.

Her seduction of the boy Brightblade had been out of frustration and anger with Tanis for leaving her; she meant to punish him by taking his friend for her lover. And when she'd laughed at the boy, ridiculed him, tormented him, she was, in her mind, tormenting Tanis. But in the end, she had been the one punished.

Her tryst with Brightblade had left her with child, and too sick and weak to rid herself of the unwanted pregnancy. The labor was hard, she had very nearly died. In her pain, in her delirium, she had dreamed only of Tanis, dreamed of crawling to him, begging his forgiveness, dreamed of agreeing to be his wife, of finding peace and contentment in his arms. If only he had come to her then! How many times she had almost sent him a message!

Almost. And then she would remind herself that he had rebuffed her, he had turned down her proposal to head north to join up with "certain people who knew what they wanted from life and weren't afraid to take it." He had, in essence, sent her packing. She would never forgive him.

Love for Tanis was strong when she was weak and in low spirits. Anger returned with her strength. Anger and resolve. She'd be damned if she'd go crawling back to him. Let him stay with his pointed-eared kin. Let them snub him and make a mockery of him and sneer at him behind his back. Let him make love to some little elven bitch. He had mentioned a girl in Qualinesti. Kit could not recall her name, but the she-elf was welcome to him.

Kitiara lay in the darkness, her back to Balif, as far from him as she could get without falling out of bed, and cursed Tanis Half-Elven bitterly and with vehemence until she fell asleep. But in the morning, when she was only half-awake, drowsy with sleep, it was Tanis's shoulder that she caressed.

5

Y OU WERE GOING TO TELL ME ABOUT GENERAL ARIAKAS," KIT REMINDED
Balif.

The two had lingered in bed until the morning. Now they walked through
the streets of Sanction, heading for the armed camp north of town where
the general had established his headquarters.

"I meant to fill you in last night," Balif said. "You gave me other things
to think about."

General Ariakas had never been far from Kit's mind, but she mixed
business with pleasure only when absolutely necessary. Last night had been
pleasure. Today was business. Balif was an agreeable companion, a skilled
lover, and thankfully, he didn't make a nuisance of himself by wanting to
walk with his arm around her or holding hands with her, claiming her as
his own personal possession.

But Kitiara was far too hungry to be satisfied with the small fish she had
lured to her net. When the time was right, she would toss him back and wait
for a bigger catch. She was not worried about hurting Balif's feelings. For
one, he had no feelings to hurt. For another, he was under no illusions. He
knew where he stood with her. She had rewarded him for his efforts, and
she guessed he would use her to gain a more valuable reward from General
Ariakas. Kit knew Balif too well to believe that he had kept track of her out
of the goodness of his heart.

"Shall I tell you what I know of Ariakas or what is rumored?" Balif asked,
speaking to her but not looking at her. His watchful and distrustful gaze
focused on each passing person as he came toward him, glanced at each as

he passed behind him. You watched your front and your back in Sanction."

"Both," Kit replied, doing the same.

The soldiers she encountered regarded her with respect, stepping aside to allow her room to pass and regarding her with admiration.

"Looks like you're the talk of the town," Balif observed.

Kitiara was feeling especially good this morning, and she gave her admirers her crooked smile and a toss of her curls in reply.

"'If truth is the meat, rumor is the sauce,'" she said, quoting the old saying. "How old a man is Ariakas?"

"Oh, as to that, who knows?" Balif shrugged. "He's not young, that's for certain, but he's no grandfather, either. Somewhere in the middle. He's a brute of a man. A minotaur once accused General Ariakas of cheating at cards. Ariakas strangled the minotaur with his bare hands."

Kitiara arched her dark eyebrow skeptically. In this instance, rumor was a bit hard to swallow.

"The truth! I swear it by Her Dark Majesty!" Balif averred, raising his hand to the oath. "A friend of mine was there and saw the fight. Speaking of Her Majesty, our Queen is said to favor him." He lowered his voice. "Some say that he was her lover."

"And how did he manage that?" Kit asked mockingly. "Did he travel to the Abyss for this rendezvous? Which of her five heads did he kiss?"

"Hush!" Balif was scandalized, reproving. "Don't say such things, Kit. Not even in jest. Her Dark Majesty is everywhere. And if she is not, her priests are," he added, with a baleful glance at a black-robed figure, skulking among the crowd. "Our Queen has many forms. She came to him in his sleep."

Kit had heard other terms for encounters of this sort, but she refrained from mentioning them. She had little use for other women in general, and that included a so-called Queen of Darkness. Kitiara had been raised in a world where the gods did not exist, a world where a man was on his own, to make of himself what he would. She had first heard rumors about this newly arrived Queen of Darkness years ago, on her various travels throughout Ansalon. She had discounted such rumors, figuring this Dark Queen to be another creation of some charlatan priest, out to swindle the gullible. Just like that foul priestess of the phony snake god Belzor, a priestess who had died by Kit's hand, with Kit's knife at her throat. To Kitiara's surprise, the worship of the Queen of Darkness had not petered out. Her cult had grown in numbers and in power, and now there was talk of this Takhisis trying to break free from the Abyss, where she had long been imprisoned, returning to conquer the world.

Kit was quite willing to conquer the world, but she intended to do it in her own name.

"Is this Ariakas a good-looking man?" she asked.

"What did you say?" Balif returned.

They were passing the slave market, and both of them put their hands over their noses to avoid the stench. They waited to resume their conversation until they were well away from the area.

"Phew!" said Kit. "And I thought the rotten-egg smell was bad. I asked if Ariakas was a good-looking man."

Balif appeared disgusted. "Only a woman would ask such a question. How the devil should I know? He's not my type, for certain. He's a magic-user," he added, as if one went along with the other.

Kit frowned. Her people were from Solamnia, her father had been a Knight of Solamnia before his misdeeds caused him to be cast out. Kitiara had inherited her family's distrust and dislike of wizards.

"That's no recommendation," she said shortly.

"What's the matter with him being a wizard?" Balif demanded. "Your own baby brother dabbled in the art. You were the one who got him started, as I recall."

"Raistlin was too weak to do anything else," Kit returned. "He had to have some way to survive in this world. I knew it wouldn't be by the sword. From what you've told me, this General Ariakas has no such excuse."

"He doesn't practice his magic that much," Balif said defensively. "He's a warrior through and through. But it never hurts to have another weapon at hand. Like you keeping a knife in your boot."

"I suppose," Kitiara said grudgingly. So far, she was not much impressed by what she'd heard of this General Ariakas.

Balif saw this, understood, and was just about to launch into another tale of his admired general, a tale he was sure Kit would appreciate—how Ariakas had risen to power by the murder of his own father. But he had lost Kit's attention. She had come to a halt outside a smithy, was gazing with rapt attention at a shining sword displayed on a wooden rack outside the shop.

"Look at that!" she said, reaching out her hand.

The sword was a bastard sword, also known as a hand and a half sword, for its blade was longer and narrower than that of a traditional bastard sword—a factor Kit appreciated, since male opponents tended to have longer arms. Such a sword would compensate for her shorter reach.

Kitiara had never seen such a marvelous sword, one that appeared to have been made for her and her alone. She removed it carefully from its stand, almost afraid of testing it, fearful of finding some imperfection. She tried her hand around the leather-wrapped grip. Most grips on bastard swords were made for a man's hand, were too thick for hers. Her fingers wrapped lovingly around this grip, it fit her perfectly.

She checked the balance, making certain that the blade was not too heavy, which would lead to an aching elbow, or too light, tested to see that the pommel balanced the weight of the blade. The balance was ideal; the sword seemed an extension of herself.

She was falling in love with this blade, but she had to be careful, cool, not rush into this blindly. She held the sword to the light, examined all the parts—tugging on them, shaking them—to make certain that nothing rattled or wobbled. This test passed, she checked to see how the swept hilt fit her hand. Kit checked the clearance between guard and hand, making small testing movements with her wrist. The guard bars were ornately carved and lovely to look at, but appearance counts for nothing if the bars dig into your hand or forearm.

She stepped into the street, took up her fighting stance. She held the blade out in front of her, taking note of the length and the feel of the sword when extended. She tried a couple of test swings, halting them abruptly in mid-swing to determine the momentum and to see whether a movement, once begun, could easily be changed.

Finally, she placed the sword tip against the ground. Holding the sword in both hands by the guard, she applied pressure until the blade curved in a shallow arc. You don't want a blade so brittle it will break or one that will bend and stay bent. The blade was supple as a lover's caress.

The smith was banging away at his work inside the shop. His assistant, who had been keeping an eye out for potential customers and to shoo away kender, hurried to the door.

"We have much finer blades inside the shop, sir," he said, bowing officiously and gesturing inside to the hot and smoky interior. "If you'd care to step inside, sir—I beg your pardon, madam—I can show you the master's work."

"Is this some of your master's work?" Kit asked, keeping a fast grip on the sword.

"No, no, madam," the assistant said, looking scornful. "Note these other blades. These are the master's work. Now, if you'll only step inside . . ." He tried again to lure her into the shop, where he would have her at his mercy.

"Who made this sword?" Kitiara asked, having duly noted the other blades, noted the poor quality of the steel and the shoddy workmanship.

"What was his name?" The assistant frowned, trying to recall such an unimportant detail. "Ironfeld, I believe. Theros Ironfeld."

"Where is *his* shop?" Kitiara asked.

"Burned down," the assistant said, rolling his eyes. "Not an accident, if you take my meaning. He was too high and mighty for the likes of some in Sanction. Thought too well of himself. He had to be taught a lesson. We would not normally carry such inferior work, but the poor fellow who sold it to us was down on his luck, and the master is a most generous man. You appear to be a woman of discriminating taste. We can do much better for you. Now, if you'll just step inside the shop . . ."

"I want this sword," Kit said. "How much?"

The assistant pursed his lips in disapproval, spent several more moments trying to dissuade her, then named a price.

Kit lifted her eyebrows. "That's a lot for a sword of such poor quality," she said.

"It's been taking up shelf space," the assistant said sullenly. "We paid too much for it, but the poor fellow was—"

"Down on his luck. Yes, you mentioned that." Kitiara haggled with the man. Eventually she agreed to pay the price he asked, if he threw in a leather sheath and belt for free.

"Pay him," she told Balif. "I'll pay you back when I have the money."

Balif brought forth his purse and counted out the coins, all of them steel and all marked with the likeness of General Ariakas.

"What a bargain!" Kit said, buckling the belt around her waist, adjusting the fit to where it was comfortable and the sword was in easy reach on her hip. Had she been an inch shorter, the long blade would have dragged the ground. "This sword is worth ten times the amount that fool wanted for it! I *will* pay you back," she added.

"No need," said Balif. "I'm doing well for myself these days."

"I won't be in debt to any man," Kitiara said with a flash of her dark eyes. "I pay my own way. Either you agree or you take back the sword." She put her hand to the buckle, as if she would strip it off then and there.

"All right!" Balif shrugged. "Have it your way. Here, we go this direction, across the lava flow. The general's headquarters is inside a great temple built to honor the Dark Queen. The Temple of Luerkhisis. Very impressive."

A long, wide natural bridge made of granite spanned the Lava River, as it was known by the few natives left in Sanction after the arrival of the Dark Queen's forces. The river flowed down from the Doom range of the Khalkist Mountains that surrounded Sanction on three sides to pour, hissing, into the New Sea. The city was isolated, well protected, for only two passes led through the mountains, and these were heavily guarded. Anyone caught walking those paths was captured and taken into Sanction, to a second temple built to honor the Dark Queen and her evil cohorts, the Temple of Huerzyd.

Here all those entering Sanction were questioned, and those who gave the right answers were free to go. For those who did not have the right answers, there were the prison cells, with the torture chamber located conveniently nearby, "just a hop, skip, and a jump" (a kender's last words) from the morgue.

Those leaving Sanction by more pleasant and less permanent means needed a pass signed by General Ariakas himself. All others were detained and either forced to remain in Sanction or were escorted to the dread Temple of Huerzyd.

Balif had provided Kitiara with a letter of safe passage and a password, so she had been permitted to enter Sanction without making any side trips. She had arrived by ship, the only other way in and out of Sanction.

Sanction's harbor was blockaded by ships of Ariakas's army, which watched the surface, and by fearsome sea monsters, which guarded the deep. All pleasure craft and small fishing vessels belonging to Sanction's inhabitants had been seized and burned so that people could not use them to sneak past the blockade. Thus General Ariakas kept his troop buildup secret from the rest of Ansalon, who probably would not have believed it anyway.

At this time, almost four years prior to the start of what would become known as the War of the Lance, General Ariakas was just starting to gather his forces. Agents such as Balif, wholly loyal and completely dedicated, traveled in secret throughout Ansalon, making contact with all those inclined to walk the paths of darkness, appealing to their greed, their hatreds, promising them loot, plunder, and the destruction of their enemies if they would sign their lives over to Ariakas and their souls to Queen Takhisis.

Bands of goblins and hobgoblins, harried for years by the Solamnic Knights, came to Sanction, vowing revenge. Ogres were lured out of the mountain strongholds by promises of slaughter. Minotaurs came to earn honor and glory in battle. Humans arrived, hoping for a share of the wealth to be won when the elves were driven from their ancient homelands and the rest of Ansalon ground beneath the heel of General Ariakas. Dark clerics reveled in their newfound clerical power—a power given to no one else on Ansalon, for Queen Takhisis had kept her return to the world a secret from the other gods, with the exception of one, her son, Nuitari, god of dark magic. In his name, black-robed wizards worked their arcane arts in secret and prepared for the glorious return of their Queen to the world.

Nuitari had two cousins, Solinari, the son of the god Paladine and goddess

Mishakal, and Lunitari, the daughter of the god Gilean. Solinari was god of white magic, Lunitari daughter of red or neutral magic. The three gods of magic were close, bound by their love of magic. Their three moons—the white, the red, and the black—orbited Krynn, so it was difficult for one to keep something hidden from the others, even one as cold and dark and secret as Nuitari.

And so there were those on Ansalon who saw the shadows cast by dark wings and who had begun to make their own preparations. When the Dark Queen finally struck, four years hence, the forces of good would not be taken completely by surprise.

That day was not here yet, only foreseen.

The stone bridge spanned the Lava River, opened onto the grounds of the Temple of Luerkhisis. The bridge was guarded by Ariakas's own personal troops—at the time, the only well-trained force in Sanction. Kitiara and Balif waited in line behind a wretched merchant who was insisting that he had to talk with General Ariakas.

"His men wrecked my establishment!" he said, wringing his hands. "They smashed my furniture and drank my best wine. They insulted my wife, and when I ordered them to leave they threatened to burn down my inn! They told me General Ariakas would pay for the damage. I am here to see him."

At this, the guards laughed loudly. "Sure, General Ariakas will pay," said one. Removing a coin from his purse, he tossed it on the ground. "There's your payment. Pick it up."

The merchant hesitated. "That's not nearly enough. I want to see General Ariakas."

The guard frowned, said harshly, "Pick it up!"

The merchant gulped, then bent to pick up the steel coin. The guard kicked the man in the rear end, sent him sprawling in the dirt.

"Take your payment and be gone with you. General Ariakas has better things to do than listen to you snivel about a few pieces of broken furniture."

"Any more complaints from you," said the other guard, getting in a kick for himself, "and we'll find some other place to do our drinking."

The merchant struggled to his feet, clutching the coin, and limped off toward the town.

"A very good day to you, Lieutenant Lugash," said Balif, approaching the guard post. "It's good to see you again."

"Captain Balif." The lieutenant saluted, stared hard at Kitiara.

"My friend and I have an audience this afternoon with General Ariakas, Lieutenant."

"What's your friend's name?" asked Lugash.

"Kitiara uth Matar," Kit answered. "And if you have a question, ask me. I can speak for myself."

Lugash grunted, regarded her appraisingly. "Uth Matar. Sounds Solamnic."

"My father was a Knight of Solamnia," Kitiara said, lifting her chin, "but he wasn't a fool, if that's what you're implying."

"Thrown out of the knighthood," Balif said in an undertone. "Gambling, working for the wrong people."

"So she told you, sir." Lugash sneered. "The daughter of a Solamnic. She could be a spy."

Balif stepped between the lieutenant and Kitiara, who had drawn her new sword halfway from its sheath.

"Simmer down, Kit," Balif advised, laying a restraining hand on her arm. "These are Ariakas's own personal troops. They're not like that piss-pants who tried to manhandle you yesterday. They're veterans who've proven themselves in battle, earned his respect. You'll have to do that, too, Kit." Balif glanced sidelong at her. "It won't be easy."

He turned back to the lieutenant. "You know about the information I gave the general on Qualinesti. You were there when I related it to him."

"Yes, sir," said Lugash, his hand on his own sword, his gaze dark on Kit. "What of it?"

"She's the one who came by it," Balif said, nodding his head in Kit's direction. "The general was very impressed. He asked to meet her. As I said, Lieutenant, we have an audience with him. Let us cross—both of us—or I will report you to your superior."

The lieutenant was not to be bullied. "I have my orders, Captain. My orders state that no one is to be allowed across the river today unless they're part of the army. You can go across, sir, but I'm going to have to detain your friend."

"Damn your eyes!" Balif cursed, frustrated.

The lieutenant was implacable, unmoving.

Balif turned to Kit. "You wait here. I'll go find the general."

"I'm beginning to think it's not worth it," Kitiara said, glowering at the soldiers.

"It's worth it, Kit," Balif said quietly. "Be patient. There's just been some sort of mix-up. I won't be gone long."

He hastened across the bridge. The guards returned to their posts, both of them keeping their eyes on Kitiara. Taking care to appear uncaring, she sauntered over to the edge of the bridge, stared across the Lava River to the great Temple of Luerkhisis.

Balif had termed the temple impressive. Kitiara was forced to agree with him. The side of the mountain had been carved into the likeness of the head of an enormous dragon. The dragon's nostrils formed the entrance to the temple. Two huge incisors were observation towers, or so Balif had told her. The great audience hall was inside the dragon's mouth. Formerly the Queen's dark clerics had resided there, but they had been displaced by the arrival of the army. General Ariakas had taken over quarters for himself in the temple and established a barracks for his own personal bodyguard. The dark clerics remained, but they had had to make do with less sumptuous quarters.

What must it be like to hold *that* much power? Kitiara wondered. Leaning on the parapet of the stone bridge, she stared over the turgid red river of lava at the temple, feeling the heat radiate from the river, a heat the dark clerics did their best to disperse, but which could not be cooled entirely. Nor did Ariakas want it cooled. The heat would enter the blood of his soldiers, send them pouring into Ansalon, a red river of death.

Kitiara's hands clenched tightly in longing. Someday, I'll know the answer, she vowed silently to herself. Someday such power will be mine.

Realizing she was gaping at the temple like a country-born yokel, Kitiara began to amuse herself by tossing stones down into the lava flow. Though the river was far below the bridge, she was soon bathed in sweat. Balif was right, though. One did get used to the smell.

Balif returned, bringing with him one of Ariakas's aides.

"The general says that Uth Matar is to be allowed to pass," said the aide. "And the general wants to know why he is being bothered by this."

Lieutenant Lugash paled, but he answered stoutly, "I thought—"

"That was your first mistake," said the captain dryly. "Uth Matar, I greet you in the name of General Ariakas. The general is not holding audience in the temple this day. He is engaged in training this afternoon. He asked that I escort you to his command tent."

"Thank you, Captain," said Kitiara, with a charming smile. Accompanying the aide and Balif across the bridge, Kitiara glanced at the lieutenant, memorized every feature on his ugly face.

Someday he'd pay for that sneer.

6

THOUSAND MEN WERE ASSEMBLED ON THE PRACTICE FIELD IN FRONT of the Temple of Luerkhisis in ranks four deep and two hundred and fifty long. They stood at the guard position—left foot forward, right foot back, shield up and sword at the ready. The sun blazed down on the troops from a clear blue sky. The heat from the Lava River roiled over them. Sweat collected under their heavy steel helmets, dripped down their faces. Their bodies, encased in padding and practice armor, were soaked.

In front of the line stood a single officer, wearing ornate bronze armor, a polished bronze helm, and a blue cloak, attached by large golden hasps at the shoulders. The cloak was thrown back, leaving his muscular arms bare. He was a large man, large-boned, muscular. Black hair, wet with sweat, flowed from beneath his helmet. He wore a sword at his side but did not draw it.

"Prepare to thrust," he ordered. "Thrust!"

Every soldier took a pace forward and lunged with his sword, then froze in that position. A thousand voices shouted out the short attack yell. An uneasy silence fell. The officer was frowning, his brows lowering beneath his bronze helm. The men glanced sidelong at each other and panted in the glaring sun.

General Ariakas had noticed several men in the front rank who, either from nervousness or eagerness to please, jumped before he gave the order, thrust their swords out too far. They had been off by only a few seconds, but it showed a lack of discipline.

Ariakas pointed at one of the offending soldiers.

"Company Master Kholos, take that man in the front rank and have him flogged. Never anticipate the word of command until it is given."

A human with the sallow skin and slavering jaws that bespoke some sort of goblin ancestry—one of four officers who stood behind the regiment—escorted the offending soldier to the side of the practice field. At his gesture, two sergeants, armed with whips, took their places.

"Remove your armor," the company master ordered.

The soldier did so, stripping off his practice armor and the heavy padding beneath it.

"Stand at attention."

The soldier, his face set rigid, stood stiff and straight. The company master nodded. The sergeants raised their whips and, one after the other, each struck the man's bare back three lashes. The soldier tried to stifle his cries, but at the sixth, with the blood trickling down his back, he gave a strangled yell.

The sergeants, their duty done, coiled their whips and stepped back along the sidelines. The soldier gritted his teeth against the pain as the salt sweat ran into his fresh wounds. Moving as rapidly as he could under the baleful eye of Ariakas, the soldier replaced his padding, which was quickly soaked in blood, and put the armor back on over it.

The company master nodded again, and the soldier hastened to take up his position in the ranks, assuming the same stance as the other soldiers around him, who were still holding the thrust-forward stance. Arms and legs quivered with the strain.

"Prepare to recover," Ariakas commanded. "Recover!"

Each man pulled back on his sword, as if recovering it from the belly of some phantom enemy, returning to the guard position. Resting, they waited tensely for the next order.

"Better," Ariakas stated flatly. "Prepare to thrust. Thrust! Prepare to recover. Recover!"

The drill went on for nearly an hour. Twice more Ariakas paused to have men flogged. This time, he chose men in the rear ranks—a sign that he was watching more than just the front rank. At the end of an hour, he was almost satisfied. The soldiers were moving as a single unit, every man's foot placed correctly, every shield held in the proper position, every sword exactly where it should be.

"Prepare to thrust—" Ariakas began, then stopped. The words hung in the hot air.

One soldier had not obeyed. Stepping forward, moving out of the front rank of the formation, the soldier tossed his sword into the dirt. He yanked off his helmet, threw it into the ground in front of him.

"I didn't sign up for this shit," he said, loud enough for everyone to hear. "I quit!"

None of the other soldiers said a word. After one swift glance, they looked away, fearing that they might be taken for accomplices. Their faces stony, they kept their eyes forward.

Ariakas nodded once, coolly.

"Front rank, fourth company," he said, addressing the rebellious soldier's comrades. "Kill that man."

The doomed man turned to his friends, raised his hands.

"Boys, it's me! C'mon!"

They stared at him, through him.

The man turned to flee, but he stumbled over his own armor, fell to the ground. Sixty-one men moved at once. Three of them, the three nearest the doomed man, performed just as they had practiced.

Prepare to thrust. Thrust.

The man screamed as three swords pierced his body.

Prepare to recover. Recover.

The soldiers jerked their weapons from the bloody corpse, fell back into position. The man's screams ended abruptly.

"Very good," said Lord Ariakas. "That's the first time I've seen any sign of disciplined behavior in the lot of you. Company Masters, have your companies break for twenty minutes, and make sure that the men are given water."

General Ariakas was conscious that he now had an audience—a young woman stood on the edge of the parade field, watching. Her hands were on her hips, her head tilted slightly to one side, a crooked smile on her lips. Removing his helmet, wiping the sweat from his face, Ariakas strode from the field to his command tent, a large tent over which flew his flag bearing a black eagle with outstretched wings. Company masters hurried onto the grounds, ordering the men to break out of formation. The thirsty men surged for the horse troughs that stood at the side of the parade ground. Dipping their hands into the tepid, sulfurous-tasting water, the men gulped it down and then splashed it over their bodies. Then they sank to the ground, exhausted, to watch the sergeants drag the dead body off to another area of the camp. The camp dogs would eat well this night.

Inside his command tent, Ariakas took off the cloak, tossed it into a corner. An aide assisted him to remove the heavy bronze breastplate.

"Damn, that was hot work!" Ariakas groaned and massaged his tight back muscles.

A slave brought in a large gourd filled with water. Ariakas drank it, sent the slave back for another, drank part of that, and dumped the remainder over his head. He lay down on his bunk, ordered the slave to remove his boots.

The four company masters came to the tent, knocked on the center pole.

"Enter." Ariakas remained lying at ease on the bunk.

The company officers removed their helmets, saluted, and stood at attention, waiting. They were tense, wary.

Kholos, Fourth Company Master, spoke first. "Lord Ariakas, I apologize for the insubordination—"

Ariakus waved his hand. "No, don't worry about it. We're trying to beat buffoons and ruffians into some semblance of a decent fighting force. We've got to expect some setbacks. In fact, I commend you, Company Master. Your men behaved very well. All the men are shaping up better than I had hoped. They're not to know that, though. The men should think I am disgusted with them. In fifteen minutes, go back out and commence company drill. The same thing—thrust and recover. Once they have that perfected, they can learn anything."

"Sir," said the Second Company Master. "Should we order the sergeants to flog the men if necessary?"

Ariakas shook his head. "No, Beren, flogging is my tool. I want them to fear me. With fear comes respect." He grinned. "Content yourselves with being hated, gentlemen. Make do with stern looks and a few choice words. If any of the men disobey, send them to me, and I will deal with them."

"Yes, sir. Any other orders, sir?"

"Yes. Drill for at least another hour and a half, then break for evening meal, let the men retire for the night. When it's good and dark and the men are sound asleep, rouse them out of bed and have them shift their tents from the north to the south side of the camp. They must learn to wake quickly when the alarm sounds, learn to work in the dark and to keep organized so that they can break camp any time in any weather."

The four officers turned to leave.

"One more thing," Ariakas called after them. "Kholos, you will be taking command of this regiment in two weeks' time. I will be forming a new regiment with all new recruits then. Beren, you will stay with me as my senior company master, and you other two will go with Kholos. I'll promote new officers to fill the rest of the positions. Clear?"

All four saluted and returned to their companies. Kholos looked particularly pleased. It was a good promotion and, after the unfortunate incident, showed that Ariakas still had confidence in him.

Ariakas shifted his position on the bunk, groaned again as he willed the muscles in his back to relax. He recalled the days of his youth, when he had marched ten miles wearing thirty pounds of chain mail and a heavy steel breastplate over that and still had energy enough to enjoy the clash of battle—to revel in the exhilarating love of life that comes only when you may be about to lose your life, to hear again the thunderous crash when the front ranks come together, to recall the fierce struggle to determine who would live and who would die. . . .

"Sir. Are you awake, sir?" His aide hovered at the tent pole.

"Am I some old man, to indulge in an afternoon nap?" Ariakas sat bolt upright, glared at the aide. "Well, what is it?"

"Captain Balif here, sir. As requested. And he has brought a visitor."

"Ah, yes." Ariakas recalled the comely young woman standing on the edge of the parade ground. By the gods, he *was* getting old to have forgotten about her! He was clad only in his boots and the short skirt made of strips of leather, which he wore beneath his chain mail, but if the stories he had heard about this woman were true, she would not be disturbed by the sight of a half-naked man. "Send them in."

The woman entered the tent first, followed by Balif, who saluted and stood at attention. The woman took in her surroundings at a glance, then her gaze fixed on Ariakas. Here was no shy maiden, with modest downcast lashes. Here was no brazen whore, either, whose fluttering lashes concealed the hard glint of greed. This woman's gaze was bold, unabashed, penetrating, and fearless. Ariakas, who had expected—naturally enough—to be the one doing the judging, found that he himself was being judged. She was sizing him up, appraising him, and if she didn't like what she saw, she'd leave.

At any other time, Ariakas might have been offended, even insulted, but he was pleased with the way the troops had performed today, and this woman with her curly hair, her well-formed figure, and her dark eyes intrigued him mightily.

"Sir," said Balif, "I present Kitiara uth Matar."

Solamnic. So that's where she came by that proud, defiant air, as if daring the world to do its damnedest. Someone had taught her to wear a sword, to wear it with ease, as if it were just one more part of her body, and such a fine body at that. Yet there was something fey about this Kitiara. That crooked smile was not born of a self-righteous Knight.

"Kitiara uth Matar," said Ariakas, clasping his hands over the girdle of his leather skirt, "welcome to Sanction." His gaze narrowed. "I have met you before, I believe."

"I cannot claim the honor, sir," said Kitiara. The crooked smile widened slightly. In the dark, smoky eyes was a flicker of fire. "I am certain I would have remembered."

"You have seen her, sir," interjected Balif, whose presence Ariakas had nearly forgotten. "You two did not meet. It was in Neraka. Last year, when you were there overseeing the construction of the great temple."

"Yes! I recall now. You'd been scouting out Qualinesti, as I recall. Commander Kholos was quite pleased with your report. You will be glad to know that we intend to put the information you gave us to good use against the heathen elves."

The crooked smile stiffened a moment, then hardened. The fire in the dark eyes flared, then was quickly quenched. Ariakas wondered what rock he'd struck his flint against, to cause such a spark.

"I am glad to have been of service to you, sir," was all she said, however, and her tone was cool, respectful.

"Please, be seated. Andros!" Clapping his hands, Ariakas summoned one of the slaves, a boy of about sixteen, captured during a raid on some unfortunate town, who bore the marks of his hard life and ill usage on his bruised face. "Bring in wine and meat for our guests. You will share my supper, will you not?"

"With pleasure, sir," said Kitiara.

Another slave was dispatched to find more folding camp chairs. Ariakas shoved a map of Abanasinia off a table onto the ground and the three took their seats.

"Forgive the crudeness of the repast." Ariakas spoke to both his guests, though his eyes were fixed on only one. "When you come to visit me in my headquarters, I will serve you one of the finest meals in all of Ansalon. One of my slaves is a most excellent cook. Her cooking saved her life, and so she puts her heart into it."

"I look forward to that, sir," said Kitiara.

"Eat! Eat!" Ariakas said, waving to the haunch of freshly roasted venison, which slaves brought in on a sizzling platter and placed on the table. Drawing his knife from his belt, he cut off a hunk of meat. "Do not stand on ceremony. By Her Dark Majesty, I am hungry! We had hot work out there today."

He glanced at the woman, to see what she would say.

Kitiara, her own knife in her hand, cut off meat for herself.

"You are a strict disciplinarian, sir," she observed, eating the greasy meat with the relish of a longtime campaigner who is never certain when or where she will find her next meal. "And you have troops to spare, it would appear. Either that or you plan to raise another army of the dead."

"Those who join my army are well paid," Ariakas replied. "And I pay on time. Unlike some commanders, I don't lose half my troops in the spring so that they can go home to put in their crops. My soldiers are not required to live off the towns they capture and loot—that's a bonus. Regular pay gives a man pride; it's a reward for a job well done. But even then"—he shrugged his massive shoulders—"I still have malcontents, like any commander. Best to get rid of them right away. If I start to coddle them, cater to them, the rest will slack off. They'll lose respect for me and my officers and next they'll lose respect for themselves. And when an army loses respect for itself, it's finished."

Kitiara had stopped eating to listen to him, was giving him the compliment of her full attention. When he was finished, she paid him a further compliment by considering his words, then she nodded once, abruptly, in agreement.

"Tell me about yourself, Kitiara uth Matar," Ariakas said, gesturing to the slave to refill their wine cups. He noted that Kitiara drank hers neat and that she enjoyed it, but she could put the cup aside. Unlike Balif, who had drained his first and gulped his second and was now starting on a third.

"Not much to tell, sir," she said. "I was born and raised in Solace in Abanasinia. My father was Gregor uth Matar, a Solamnic of noble birth, a Knight. He was one of their best warriors," she added, a statement of fact, not bragging. "But he couldn't stomach their petty little rules, the way they try to run a man's life. He sold his sword and his talents where he chose to sell it. He took me to see my first battle when I was five and taught me to use a sword, taught me how to fight. He left home when I was young. I haven't seen him since."

"And you?" Ariakas asked.

Kitiara lifted her chin. "I'm my father's daughter, sir."

"Meaning you don't like rules?" He frowned. "You don't like to obey orders?"

She paused, thinking out her words carefully, shrewd enough to know her future depended on them, but with strength and pride and confidence enough to tell the truth.

"If I found a commander I admired, a commander in whom I could place my trust and my respect, a commander who had both common sense and intelligence, I would obey the orders given by such a commander. And . . ." She hesitated.

"And?" Ariakas repeated, urging her on with a smile.

She lowered her dark lashes, her eyes glimmered beneath them. "And, of course, such a commander must make it worth my while."

Ariakas leaned back from the table and laughed. He laughed long and loud, banging his cup on the table, laughed until one of his aides—defying all convention—peered inside the tent to see what had so captured his lordship's fancy. Ariakas was not generally celebrated for his good humor.

"I think I can promise you a commander who can satisfy all your requirements, Kitiara uth Matar. I have need of several more officers. I think you will fill the bill. You must prove yourself, of course. Prove your courage, your skill, your resourcefulness."

"I am ready, sir," Kitiara said coolly. "Name your task."

"Captain Balif, you have done well," said Lord Ariakas. "I will see to it that you are rewarded." Writing on a small scrap of paper, Ariakas yelled for his aide, who entered with alacrity. "Take Captain Balif to the counting room. Give the pursers this." He handed over the chit. "Come back to see me tomorrow, Captain. I have another assignment for you."

Balif rose somewhat unsteadily to his feet. He accepted his dismissal with good humor, having caught sight of the amount written down on the chit. He knew well enough that he'd lost Kitiara, that she'd moved to a higher level, a level where he could not follow. He also knew her well enough to guess that she was not likely to exert herself in the future on his behalf. He'd had his reward. He rested his hand on her shoulder as he passed. She shrugged off his touch, and so they parted.

Having rid himself of his aide and Captain Balif, Ariakas pulled shut the tent flaps. He came up behind Kitiara, grabbed hold of a handful of dark, crisp curls, pulled her head back, and kissed her on the lips, kissed her hard, roughly.

His passion was returned, returned with a force that startled him. She kissed him fiercely, her nails digging into the bare flesh of his arms. And then, when he would have taken more, she broke free of him.

"Is this how I am to prove myself, sir?" she asked. "In your bed?"

"No, damn it! Of course not," he said harshly. Grabbing hold of her around her waist, he pulled her body close to his. "But we might as well enjoy ourselves!"

She leaned away from him, arching her back, her hands on his chest. She was not being coy, she wasn't fighting him. Indeed, to judge by her glistening eyes and quickened breathing, she was fighting her own desires.

"Think, sir! You say you want to make me an officer?"

"I do. I will!"

"Then if you take me to your bed now, it will be whispered among the soldiers that you have made an officer of your toy, a plaything. You said yourself that the men should have respect for their officers. Will they have respect for me?"

Ariakas regarded her in silence. He had never before met a woman like this, a woman who could meet him—and best him—on his own ground. Still, he did not release her. He had never before met a woman who so tantalized him.

"Let me prove myself to you, sir," Kitiara continued, not drawing away from him, but nestling close, close enough that he could feel her warmth, the quivering tension in her body. "Let me make a name for myself in your army. Let your soldiers speak of my courage in battle. Then they will say that Lord Ariakas takes a warrior to his bed, not a whore."

Ariakas ran his hand through her curly hair, entangling his fingers. His hand clenched in her curls, pulling her hair painfully. He saw the involuntary tears start to her eyes. "Never before has any woman said 'no' to me and lived to tell of it," he said.

He gazed at her long, waiting to see a flicker of fear in those dark eyes. If he had seen it, he would have snapped her neck.

She regarded him calmly, steadfastly, with a hint of the crooked smile on her lips.

Ariakas laughed, somewhat ruefully, and released her. "Very well, Kitiara uth Matar. What you say makes sense. I will give you a chance to prove yourself. I have need of a messenger."

"I suppose you have plenty of message boys," Kitiara said, looking displeased. "I seek glory in battle."

"Let us say that I *had* plenty of message boys," Ariakas said with an unpleasant smile. He poured two cups of wine, to blunt the edge of their unfulfilled desire. "Their numbers are dwindling. I have sent four prior to this and not a single one has returned."

Kitiara's good humor returned. "This sounds more promising, sir. What is the message and to whom is it to be delivered?"

Ariakas's heavy black brows drew together, his expression stern and grim. His hand clenched over the wooden wine cup. "This is the message. You will say that I, Ariakas, general of the armies of Her Dark Majesty, command him, in the name of Her Dark Majesty, to report to me here in Sanction. You will tell him that I have need of him, that Her Dark Majesty has need of him. You will tell him that he defies me—and his Queen—at his peril."

"I will carry your message, sir," said Kitiara. She arched an eyebrow. "But the man may need persuading. Do I have your permission to do what I need to do in order to force his compliance?"

Ariakas smiled slyly. "You have my permission to *try* to force him to obey me, Kitiara uth Matar. Though you may not find that an easy task."

Kitiara tossed her head. "I have never met the man who said 'no' to me, sir, and lived to tell of it. What is his name? And where do I find him?"

"He lives in a cave in the mountains near Neraka. His name is Immolatus."

Kitiara frowned. "Immolatus. An odd name for a man."

"For a man, yes," said Ariakas, pouring out another cup of wine. He had the feeling she was going to need it. "But not for a dragon."

7

KITIARA LAY BENEATH HER BLANKETS, HER ARMS BENEATH HER HEAD, glowering up at the red moon, the laughing red moon. Kit knew very well why the moon laughed.

"Snipe hunt," Kitiara fumed aloud, with a vicious snap of her teeth over the words. "It's a goddam snipe hunt!"

Tossing off the blankets, for she could not sleep, she stomped around the small fire, drank some water, then, bored and frustrated, she sat back down, to poke at the red-glowing charred logs with a stick. Sending a shower of sparks into the night sky, she accidentally doused what remained of the small blaze. Kitiara was remembering a snipe hunt, remembered the prank, which had been played on the gullible Caramon.

All the companions were in on the prank, with the exception of Sturm Brightblade, who, if he had been told about it, would have lectured them interminably and ended by spoiling their fun. He would have let the snipe out of the bag, so to speak.

Whenever the friends came together, Kitiara, Tanis, Raistlin, Tasslehoff, and Flint spoke of the glories of the snipe hunt, of the excitement of the chase, the ferocity of the snipe when cornered, the tenderness of snipe meat, which was said to rival chicken in flavor. Caramon listened with round eyes, open mouth, and growling stomach.

"The snipe can only be caught by the light of Solinari," Tanis said.

"You must wait in the woods, quiet as a sleepwalking elf, with a bag in your hand," Flint counseled. "And you must call, 'Come to the bag for a treat, snipe! Come to the bag for a treat!' "

"For you see, Caramon," Kitiara told her brother, "snipes are so gullible that when they hear these words, they will hurry straight to you and run right into the bag."

"At that point, you must tie the ends of the sack together swiftly," Raistlin instructed, "and hold the bag fast, for once the snipe realizes he has been tricked, he will try to free himself and, if he does, he will tear apart his captor."

"How big are they?" Caramon asked, looking a little daunted.

"Oh, no larger than a squirrel," Tasslehoff assured him. "But they have teeth sharp as a wolf and claws sharp as a zombie's and a great spiked tail like a scorpion."

"Be sure to take a good strong sack, lad," Flint advised, and was then forced to muzzle the kender, who was suddenly overcome with a severe attack of the giggles.

"But aren't the rest of you coming?" Caramon asked, surprised.

"The snipe is sacred to elves," Tanis said solemnly. "I am forbidden to kill one."

"I'm too old," Flint said with a sigh. "My snipe hunting days are over. It is for you to uphold the honor of Solace."

"*I* killed *my* snipe when I was twelve," Kitiara said proudly.

"Gee!" Caramon was impressed, also downcast. He was already eighteen and had never heard of a snipe before now. He held up his head. "I won't let you down!"

"We know you won't, my brother," Raistlin said, laying his hand on his twin's broad shoulder. "We are all very proud of you."

How they laughed that night, all of them together in Flint's house, picturing Caramon standing out there all night, pale and quivering in the darkness, calling out, "Come to my bag for a treat, snipe!" And they laughed still more in the morning, when Caramon appeared, breathless with excitement, holding up a bag containing the elusive snipe, which was wriggling a great deal.

"Why's it giggling?" Caramon asked, peering at the sack.

"That's a sound made by all captured snipe," Raistlin said, barely able to speak for his suppressed laughter. "Tell us of your hunt, my brother."

Caramon told them how he had called and how the snipe had come rushing out of the darkness and jumped into his sack, how he—Caramon—had bravely pulled together the end of the sack and, after a struggle, subdued the vicious snipe.

"Should we hit it over the head before we let it out?" Caramon asked, brandishing a stick.

"No!" the snipe squeaked.

"Yes!" Flint roared, making an unsuccessful attempt to snatch the stick from Caramon.

At this, Tanis, feeling the prank had gone far enough, freed the snipe, who looked very much like Tasslehoff Burrfoot.

No one laughed louder than Caramon, once the joke was explained to him, all of them assuring him that they had fallen for it. All except Kit, who said that she, for one, had never been such a booby as to go on a snipe hunt.

At least not until now.

"I might as well be standing in these blasted mountains with a sack in my hand calling 'Here, dragon, here! I have a treat for you!'" She swore in disgust, kicked irritably at the charred remains of the log and wondered again as she had wondered for the past seven days—ever since she had left Sanction—why General Ariakas had sent her on this ridiculous mission. Kitiara believed in dragons about as much as she believed in snipes.

Dragons! She snorted in disgust. The people of Sanction talked of nothing else but dragons. People claimed to worship dragons, the Temple of the Dark Queen was formed in the image of a dragon, Balif had once asked Kit if she would be afraid to meet a dragon. Yet, to Kitiara's knowledge, none of these people had ever set eyes upon a dragon. A real fire-breathing, brimstone-eating dragon. The only dragon they knew was a dragon carved from the cold stone of a mountain.

When Ariakas had first told her she was meeting a dragon, Kit had laughed.

"It is no joke, uth Matar," General Ariakas had told her, but she had seen his dark eyes glint.

Then, still thinking it was a joke and he was making sport of her, she had been angry. The glint had disappeared from the general's dark eyes, cold and cruel and empty.

"I have given you a mission, uth Matar," General Ariakas had told her, his voice as cold and empty as his eyes. "Take it or leave it."

She had taken it—what choice did she have? She had requested an escort of soldiers. General Ariakas had refused brusquely. He could not, he said, afford to lose any more men on this mission. Did uth Matar feel incapable of handling this assignment on her own? Perhaps he would find someone else. Someone more interested in gaining his favor.

Kitiara had accepted General Ariakas's challenge to go into the Khalkist mountains, where this alleged dragon named Immolatus lived. The dragon had lived here for centuries, or so Ariakas told her, prior to being awakened by the Queen of Darkness. Kitiara had no choice but to accept.

Her first three days out of Sanction, Kitiara had been on her guard, watching for the ambush she was certain was coming, the ambush ordered by Ariakas, the ambush meant to test her fighting skills. She vowed that she would not be the one left holding the bag, or, if she was, that there would be heads inside.

But three days passed quietly. No one sprang at her out of the darkness, no one jumped her from behind a bush except an irate chipmunk, disturbed in his springtime foraging.

Ariakas had provided her with a map showing her destination, a map he said came from the priests of the Temple of Luerkhisis, a map revealing the location of the cavern of the supposed dragon. The nearer she drew to her destination, the more desolate became the countryside. Kitiara began to be uneasy. Certainly if she had chosen a location where one might find a dragon, this would be it. On the fourth day, even the few hopeful vultures that had been keeping a hungry eye on her since Sanction disappeared with ominous-sounding croaks as she climbed farther up the side of the mountain.

Not a bird, not an animal, not a bug did Kit see on her fifth day. No flies buzzed around her meal of dried trail beef. No ants came to drag off the crumbs of waybread. She had traveled far and fast. Sanction was out of sight behind the peaks of the second mountain, its peak hidden by the perpetual cloud of steam that hung over the Lords of Doom. Sometimes she could feel the ground tremble beneath her feet. She had put this down to the rumblings of the unquiet mountains, but now she wondered. Perhaps it was the rumbling of a great wyrm, turning and twisting in his dreams of treasure, dreams of death.

On the sixth day, Kitiara began to feel truly alarmed. The ground on which she walked was empty of life, barren. Admittedly she was up past the tree line and had left spring's warmth far below. But she should have found a few scraggly bushes clinging precariously to the rocks in the sunshine, patches of snow in the shadows. No snow remained, and she wondered what had caused it to melt. The one bush she did find on the trail was blackened, the rocks scorched, as if a forest fire had swept the side of the mountain. But there could not be a forest fire in an area where there were no trees.

She was puzzling over this phenomenon, had just about decided it must have been a lightning strike, when she rounded a gigantic granite boulder and stumbled upon the corpse.

Kit started and fell back a pace. She had seen plenty of dead men before, but none quite like this. The body had been consumed in fire, a blaze so hot that it had left behind only the larger bones of the body, such as the skull and the ribs, the spine and the legs. Smaller bones, those of the toes and fingers, were burned away.

The corpse lay facedown. He had been fleeing his enemy when the fire blasted him, searing the flesh from his body. Kitiara recognized the emblem on the blackened helm that still covered the head. The same emblem was on his sword, which lay several paces behind him. She guessed that if she turned over the corpse to look at the breastplate in which lay his bones, like a rib roast on a metal platter, she would see the same emblem yet again—the black-feathered eagle with outstretched wings, the emblem of General Ariakas.

Kitiara began to believe.

"You might have the last laugh after all, Caramon," she said ruefully, squinting in the sunlight to scan the top of the mountain.

She saw nothing except blue sky, but feeling exposed and vulnerable on the side of the steep mountain, she crouched behind the granite boulder, noted as she did so that where the boulder itself had been touched by the flames, the rock had started to melt.

"Damn it all to the Abyss and back," Kit said to herself, as she sat down on the ground in the boulder's shadow, with the charred corpse keeping her gloomy company. "A dragon. I'll be damned. A real, live dragon.

"Oh, stop it, Kit," she scolded herself. "It's impossible. You'll be believing in ghouls next. The poor bastard was hit by lightning."

But she was lying to herself. She could see the man clearly, fleeing from pursuit, flinging down his sword in his panicked flight, its blade of good solid steel, useless against such a terrible enemy.

Kitiara reached her hand into a leather pouch marked with the emblem of the black eagle and pulled out a small scroll—vellum rolled tight and thrust through a ring. She regarded the scroll with frowning thoughtfulness, chewing her nether lip. General Ariakas had given her the scroll, telling her that she was to deliver it to Immolatus.

Furious at the deceit being played upon her, Kit had taken the scroll without looking at it, thrust it angrily into her pouch. She had listened with barely concealed scorn to Ariakas telling her what he knew of dragons, just as she herself had told Caramon all she knew of snipes.

Kitiara examined the ring carefully. It was a signet ring. A signet in the shape of a five-headed dragon.

"Whew, boy," said Kitiara. She wiped the sweat from her brow. The five-headed dragon, ancient symbol for Queen Takhisis. Kit hesitated a moment, then slid the scroll from out the ring. Carefully, gingerly, she unrolled it, took a quick look at what it said.

Immolatus, I command you to obey the summons I send to you by this messenger. Four times before you have spurned my command. There will not be a fifth. I am losing patience. Take upon yourself human form and return to Sanction with the bearer of this, my ring, there to receive your orders from General Ariakas, soon to be general of my dragonarmies.

This order scribed by Wyrllish, High Cleric of the Black Robes, in the name of Takhisis, Queen of Darkness, Queen of the Five Dragons, Queen of the Abyss, and soon to be Queen of Krynn.

"Oh, damn!" said Kitiara. "Oh, damn it all."

Propping her elbows on her bent knees, she bowed her head in her hands. "I'm a dolt! An idiot! But who would have guessed? What have I done? How did I get myself into this?

"So much," she added, lifting her head to look at the corpse, her crooked smile straight and hard and bitter, "for all my hopes, all my ambitions. This is where it will end. On the side of a mountain, my bones fused to the rock. But who would have guessed Ariakas was telling the truth? A dragon. And I'm to be its goddam messenger!"

She sat for a long time on the summit of the desolate mountainside, gazing out into the empty blue sky that seemed so near, watched the sun slide from the sky, looking as if it were setting beneath her, so far was she above the horizon. The air was starting to cool off rapidly. She shivered, the gooseflesh raised on her arms beneath the finespun wool tunic she wore underneath her chain-mail corselet. She had brought with her a woolen cloak, lined with shaggy wool, but she did not unpack it.

"The air is liable to warm up soon," she said to herself, and a hint of the crooked smile returned. "Too soon and too warm for comfort."

Shaking off her lethargy, she pulled the cloak from her bag and, wrapping the sheepskin around her shoulders, she settled down to study—with more attention—the map given her by General Ariakas. She located all the landmarks: the mountain peak, which was split in twain, as if by some giant axe blade; a jutting crag, thrusting out of the side of the mountain, looking like a hooked nose.

Now that she knew where to look, she located the cave without too much difficulty. The opening to the dragon's lair was hidden beneath the overhang, not far from where she sat. A short walk over some rough terrain, but not difficult to reach. Solinari was waning this night, but would shed light enough for her to find her way among the rocks. Kit rose to her feet, looked down the side of the mountain. It had been in her mind to take the easy way out, to simply step off the edge and into the void below. The easy way out . . . the coward's way out.

"Lie, cheat, steal—the world winks at such faults," her father had once told her. "But the world despises a coward."

This might be her last battle, but she was determined it would be a glorious one. She turned her back on the sun and looked ahead, into the gathering darkness.

She had no plan of attack; she couldn't see that a plan would be of any great use. Nothing to do except barge in the front door. Placing her hand on the hilt of her sword, she set her jaw, gritted her teeth, and took a determined step forward.

An immense beast appeared at the edge of the lip beneath the overhang. Spreading its wings—massive wings, wings that dwarfed the eagle—the beast took flight, soaring into the air. Red scales caught the last of the afterglow, glinting and gleaming and sparking like cinders flying up from the blazing log or a gentlewoman's rubies, cast into the sunlight, or drops of blood. A snout; a tail, long and sinuous; a body so ponderous and heavy that it seemed impossible the wings could lift it; a spiked mane, black against the garish, dying light; enormous, powerful legs and feet with long, sharp claws; a seeking eye of flame.

For the first time in her twenty-eight years of life, Kit tasted fear. Her stomach clenched, sending hot bile surging into her dry mouth. Her leg muscles spasmed; she nearly collapsed. Her hand on her sword hilt went wet and nerveless. The only thought her brain could think was "run, hide, flee!" If there had been a hole nearby, she would have crawled into it. At that moment, even the leap into the void off the side of the mountain appeared to her to be a wise and prudent thing to do.

Kitiara crouched down in the shadow of the boulder and huddled there, shivering, the cold sweat beading on her forehead. Her chest was tight, her heart raced, she found it difficult to breathe. She could not take her eyes from the dragon, a sight that was awful, beautiful, appalling. He was forty feet long, at least. Stretched out end to end, he would have covered the parade ground and still lapped over into the temple.

She feared the dragon had seen her.

Immolatus had no idea she was there. She might have been a gnat plastered against the rock for all he knew or cared. He was flying out into the night to hunt. Several days had passed since his last meal, a meal that had, by great good fortune, come to him. After dining on the messenger, Immolatus had been too lazy to seek more food until hunger woke him from his pleasant dreams, dreams of plunder and fire and death. Feeling his shriveled stomach flapping against his ribs, he waited hopefully to see if another toothsome morsel might enter his cave.

None did. Immolatus fretted a bit, deeply regretted having indulged in sport with one of the soldiers, chasing the terror-stricken man down the cliff face, watching him burn like a living torch. If the dragon had been thinking ahead, he would have kept his captive alive until he was ready to dine again.

Ah, well, the dragon mused grumpily. No use crying over spilt blood. He took to the air, circled once around his peak to make certain all was well.

Kitiara held perfectly still, frozen like a rabbit when it sees the dogs. She ceased to breathe, willed her heart not to beat so loudly, for it seemed to echo around her like thunder. Kit willed the dragon to fly away, fly far away. It seemed he would do so, for he wheeled as if to catch the warm air currents rising up the mountainside. Kit was close to sobbing with relief, when suddenly her throat constricted.

The dragon shifted his flight. He sniffed the air, his huge head with its red eyes turning this way and that, looking for the scent that made his mouth water.

Sheep! This blasted sheepskin cloak! Kitiara knew as well as if she had been sitting between the dragon's shoulder blades that the beast smelled sheep, that he had an appetite for sheep for dinner, but would not be too disappointed to discover his mistake—a human in sheep's clothing.

The huge snout turned in her direction, and Kitiara could see the sharp fangs as the mouth opened in anticipation.

"Queen of Darkness," Kit prayed, asking for help for the first time in her life, "I am here by your command. I am your servant. If you want this mission to succeed, then you sure as hell better do something!"

The dragon drew nearer, darker than night, blotting out the first pale stars with its enormous wings. The deeper the darkness, the redder its baleful eyes. Helpless, unable to move, unable even to draw her sword, Kitiara watched death fly closer.

There came a frantic bleating, hooves beat against rock. The dragon dove. The wind of its passing flattened Kit against the boulder. The wings gave a single flap, a death cry echoed among the rocks. The dragon's tail twitched back and forth in violent pleasure. The dragon wheeled in the sky, flew back over her. Warm blood dripped onto Kitiara's upturned face. A freshly killed mountain goat dangled from the dragon's claws.

Immolatus was pleased with his catch and his luck—he had never before known a mountain goat to venture this near his cave. He hauled the bleeding carcass back into his cavern where he could dine at his leisure. He wondered a little about the strong scent of sheep he had detected on the mountainside, an odd scent, mingled with human, but he much preferred goat meat to mutton any day. Or human, for that matter. There was generally little meat on human bones and he had to work hard for what was there, ripping away the armor to get at it, armor that always left the taste of metal in his mouth. Back in his lair, he settled his large body onto the rocks, which should have been treasure—or so he always thought resentfully—and tore into the goat.

For the moment Kitiara was safe. Weak with relief, she huddled on the ground beneath the boulder, unable to move. Her muscles, tight with adrenaline, remained clenched. She could not loosen her hand from the hilt of her sword. By sheer effort of will, she forced herself to relax, calmed her racing heartbeat, caught her gasping breath.

First, she had a debt to pay. "Queen Takhisis," Kitiara said humbly, looking up into the night sky sacred to the goddess, "thank you! Stay with me, and I will not fail you!"

Her score settled, Kitiara pulled the sheepskin more closely around her and, lying in the starlit darkness, thought back on her talk with General Ariakas, a talk to which she had paid scant attention. She forced herself to try to remember what he had told her about dragons.

8

THE GOAT HAD BEEN A NICE, PLUMP ONE. Pleased with his meal and the fact that he hadn't had to work overly hard to catch it, Immolatus settled down upon his rocky bed. Imagining his rocks were piles of treasure, he went back to sleep, sought refuge once more in his dreams.

Most of the other dragons dedicated to the service of the Queen of Darkness had been pleased when Takhisis woke them from their long, enforced sleep. Not so Immolatus.

His dreams of the past century had been dreams of fire, of driving hapless humans and elves, dwarves and kender before him, of blasting their miserable dwellings to kindling, of scooping up their children in his great maw and crunching down on their tender flesh, of toppling castles and impaling screaming Knights upon his sharp claws, claws that could tear through the strongest armor. Dreams of sifting through the rubble, after it had cooled, picking up the sparkling jewels and silver chalices, magical swords and golden bracers, piling them onto the few wagons he had taken care not to set ablaze and then carrying the wagons in his claws back to his lair.

His cave had once been stuffed with treasure, so stuffed that he could hardly squeeze his own body inside. Huma—that wicked devil-Knight Huma and his accursed wizard Magius—had put an end to Immolatus's fun. They had nearly put an end to Immolatus.

The Dark Queen, curse her black heart, had called on Immolatus to join her in what was supposed to have been the war to end all wars. A war wherein the irritating scourge of Solamnic Knights would be obliterated, their foul kind wiped from the face of the long-suffering world. The Dark

Queen had assured her dragons that they could not lose, that they were invincible. Immolatus had thought this sounded like fun—he was a young dragon then. He had left his treasure trove and gone to join his brethren: blue dragons, red and green, the white dragons of the snow-capped south, black dragons of the shadows.

The war had not gone as planned. The cunning humans had invented a weapon, a lance whose bright and magical silver metal was as painful to the dragon's eyes as its sharp tip was deadly to the dragon's heart. The horrid Knights carried this terrible weapon into battle. Immolatus and his kind fought valiantly, but, in the end, Huma and his dragonlance forced Queen Takhisis to retreat from this plane of existence, forced her to make a desperate pact. Her dragons would not be put to death but would sleep the centuries away and, so as not to upset the balance of the world, the good dragons, those of silver and of gold, would also sleep.

Immolatus's right wing had been torn by the cruel lance, his left hind leg ripped by the horrible lance, his stomach slashed by the infamous lance. The dragon limped back to his cave, his blood falling like rain on the ground, and there he found that, in his absence, thieves had stolen away his treasure!

His bellows of outrage split the mountain peak. He vowed, before he went to sleep, that he would never again have anything to do with humans, unless it was to rip off their heads and munch on their bones. He would have nothing more to do with the Queen of Darkness, either. The Queen who had betrayed her servants.

His wounds healed during his centuries-long sleep. His body regained its strength. He did not forget his vow. Seven years ago, the spirit of Queen Takhisis, now trapped in the Abyss, had come to her dragons, had called upon Immolatus to waken from his long sleep and join her once again in yet another war to end all wars.

The spirit of Queen Takhisis stood in his cave, his pitifully empty cave, and made her demands.

Immolatus tried to bite her. Unable to do so (it is difficult to sink one's teeth into a spirit), the dragon rolled over and went back to sleep, back to his lovely dreams of mangled humans and a cave filled with gold and pearls and sapphires.

But sleep wouldn't come or, if it did, he wasn't allowed to enjoy it. Takhisis was always about, annoying him, sending messengers with orders and dispatches. Why couldn't the woman just leave him alone? Hadn't he sacrificed enough for her cause? How many of her messengers did he have to torch to make his point?

He was recalling fondly the last human he had watched go up in smoke, was smiling over the memory of the scent of roasting human flesh, when Immolatus's pleasant dream shifted. He began to dream of fleas.

Dragons are not bothered by fleas. Lesser animals are bothered by fleas, animals not blessed with scales, animals with skin and fur. Yet Immolatus dreamed of fleas, dreamed of a flea biting him. The bite was not painful, but it was annoying, stinging. The dragon dreamed of the flea, dreamed of scratching the flea, and drowsily lifted a hind leg for the purpose. The flea ceased biting, and the dragon settled down, once more at peace, when that damnable stinging began again, this time in a different spot. The flea had jumped from one place to another.

Now seriously annoyed, Immolatus roused suddenly and angrily from his sleep. Early morning sunlight brightened his cavern, filtering through an air shaft that opened into the side of the mountain. Immolatus twisted his huge head, eyes glaring around to discover the pest, which was somewhere on his left shoulder, his jaws snapping to make short work of it. Immolatus was astounded to see, not a flea on his shoulder, but a human.

"Eh?" he roared, taken completely by surprise.

The human was clad in armor and a sheepskin cloak and sat perched upon Immolatus's great shoulder, sat there as coolly as one of those god-cursed Knights astride a war-horse. Immolatus glared, shocked beyond measure at such audacity, and the human jabbed the point of a sword painfully into the dragon's flesh.

"You have a loose scale here, my lord dragon," said the human, lifting the scale, which was the size of a large piece of flagstone and about as heavy. "Did you know that?"

His mind fuddled with his dream and the soporiferous effects of goat meat, Immolatus sucked in a deep breath, prepared to blast this irritating creature into the next plane of nonexistence. The brimstone breath caught in his throat, however, as his mind woke up a bit more and informed him that he would not only fry the unwelcome intruder but his left shoulder as well.

Immolatus gargled a bit, swallowed the flame that had been bubbling in his stomach. He had other weapons, a goodly number of magical spells, although these required effort to use on the dragon's part, and he was too lazy to bring to mind the complicated words required for their casting. His best and most effective weapon was fear. His enormous red eyes—their pupils were larger than the human's head—stared into the dark eyes of the human, and he brought into that small mind images of her own death. Death by fire, death by tooth and claw, death by rolling over on her and squashing her into a bloody pulp.

The human wavered beneath this assault, she shivered and grew pale, but, at the same time, the sword blade bit deeper.

"I don't suppose, my lord," said the human, with a slight quaver in her voice, a quaver she controlled and suppressed, "that you've ever cut up a chicken for a stewpot. Am I right? I thought so. A pity. Because if you had cut up a chicken, my lord, you would know that this tendon, which runs right along here"—jab, jab, poke, poke with the sword blade—"controls your wing. If I were to cut this tendon"—the blade dug in a little deeper—"you could not fly."

Immolatus had never cut up a chicken—he generally ate them whole, several dozen at a time—but he was well acquainted with the construction of his own body. He was also well acquainted with injuries to his wings, injuries that left him a prisoner in his cave, unable to fly and to hunt, suffering the pangs of hunger and of thirst.

"You are powerful, my lord," said the human. "You are skilled in magic. You could kill me with a snap of your jaws. But not before I have inflicted a considerable amount of damage on you."

By now, Immolatus had lost his irritation. He had overcome his rage. He wasn't hungry, the goat had seen to that. The dragon was beginning to be fascinated.

The human was respectful, deferring to him as "my lord." Most appropriate and suitable. The human had been afraid, but she had conquered her fear. Immolatus applauded such courage. He was impressed with her intelligence, her ingenuity. He wanted to continue their conversation, which he found intriguing. He could always kill her later.

"Climb down off my shoulder," he said. "I'm getting a crick in my neck trying to see you."

"I am sorry for that, my lord," said the human. "But you must see that moving would put me at a considerable disadvantage. I will deliver my message from here."

"I won't harm you. For the time being, at least."

"And why would you spare me, my lord?"

"Let us say that I am curious. I want to know why in the name of our fickle Queen you are here! What do you want of me? What is so important that you risk death to speak to me?"

"I can tell you all that from where I sit, my lord," said the human.

"Confound it!" the dragon roared. "Come down at eye level! If I do decide to slay you, I will give you fair warning first. I will allow you to put up your pitiable defense, if for nothing else than for my own amusement. Agreed?"

The human considered the proposal, decided to accept it. She jumped lightly from the dragon's shoulder to land on the stone floor of his cave—the oh, so empty stone floor of his cave.

Immolatus regarded the emptiness with gloomy melancholy. "It cannot be the lure of my treasure that brought you. Not unless you have a burning desire to collect rocks." Sighing deeply, he rested his gigantic head upon a stone pillow, which placed the human level with his eyes. "That is better. More comfortable. Now, who are you and why have you come?"

"My name is Kitiara uth Matar—" she began.

Immolatus rumbled. "Uth Matar. It sounds Solamnic." He glowered, having second thoughts about slaying her later rather than sooner. "I have little love for Solamnics."

"Yet you respect us," said Kitiara proudly. "As we respect you, my lord." She bowed. "Not like the rest of the foolish world, who laugh when dragons are mentioned and claim that they are no more than kender tales."

"Kender tales!" Immolatus reared his head. "Is that what they say of us?"

"Indeed, my lord."

"No songs of conflagration, of holocaust? No tales of burning cities and scorched bodies, no stories of murdered babies and stolen treasure? We are . . . " Immolatus could barely speak for his indignation. "We are *kender* tales!"

"That is what you have become, my lord. Sadly," Kitiara added.

Immolatus knew that he and his brothers and sisters and cousins had been asleep for many decades—centuries, even—but he had thought that the awe in which dragons were held, the stories of their magnificent deeds, the fear and loathing they engendered would have been passed down through the ages.

"Think back to the old days," Kitiara continued. "Think back to the days of your youth. How many times did parties of Knights seek you out to slay you?"

"A great many," Immolatus said. "Ten or twenty at a time, arriving at least twice a year."

"And how many times did thieves enter your lair, bent on securing your treasure, my lord?"

"Monthly," said the dragon, his tail twitching at the memories. "More often than that if there happened to be a goodly number of dwarves in the area. Pesky creatures, dwarves."

"And how often, in this day and age, have thieves tried to sneak in and steal your treasure?"

"I have no treasure to steal!" Immolatus shouted in pain.

"But the thieves don't know that," Kitiara argued. "How many times have you been attacked in your cave? I would venture to guess the answer is none, my lord. And why is that? It is because no one believes in you anymore. No one knows of your existence. You are nothing but a myth, a legend, a story to be laughed at over a mug of cold ale."

Immolatus roared, a bellow that shook the walls and sent rivulets of rock dust cascading down from the cavern's ceiling, a bellow that caused the ground to quake and forced the human to cling to a handy stalactite for support.

"It is true!" The dragon gnashed his teeth savagely. "What you say is true! I never thought of it that way before. I sometimes wondered, but I had always supposed it was fear that kept them away. Not . . . not . . . obliviousness!"

"Queen Takhisis intends to see to it that they remember, my lord," Kitiara said coolly.

"Does she?" Immolatus muttered and shifted his great bulk. He scraped his claws across the stone floor, leaving gouge marks in the rock. "Perhaps I misjudged her. I thought . . . well, never mind. It is not important. And so she has sent you with a message for me?"

Kitiara bowed. "I am sent by General Ariakas, head of the Army of Queen Takhisis, with a message to Immolatus, greatest and most powerful of Her Majesty's dragons." Kitiara proffered the scroll. "Will it please your lordship to read it?"

Immolatus waved a claw. "You read it to me. I have difficulty deciphering the chicken scratches of humans."

Kitiara bowed again, unrolled the scroll, and read the words. When she came to, "*Four times before you have spurned my command. There will not be a fifth. I am losing patience,*" Immolatus cringed a bit, in spite of himself. He could hear quite distinctly his Queen's furious voice behind those words.

"But how was I supposed to know that the world had come to such a pass?" Immolatus muttered to himself. "Dragons forgotten! Or worse— laughed at, despised!"

"*Take upon yourself human form and return to Sanction with the bearer of this, my ring, there to receive your orders from Ariakas, soon to be general of my dragonarmies.*"

"Human form!" Immolatus snorted a gout of flame from his nostrils. "I won't," he said grimly. "The world has forgotten dragons, has it? Then they will soon come to recognize their error. They will see me in my glory. I will fall upon them like a thunderbolt! They will come to know dragons then, by our Dark Queen! They will think that she has snatched the fiery sun from the heavens and hurled it into their midst!"

Kitiara pursed her lips.

Immolatus glared at her. "Well, what is it? If you think I am worried about disobeying the orders of Takhisis, I'm not," he said petulantly. "Who is she to name herself Queen over us? The world was given to *us* to do with as we liked. And then she came among us, making promises, a different promise with each of her five mouths. And where did those promises lead us? To the sharp end of some Knight's lance! Or worse—torn to pieces by some god-cursed gold dragon!"

"And that is precisely what will happen if you proceed with your plan, my lord," said Kitiara.

Immolatus growled and the mountain creaked. Smoke curled from between his fangs, his lips pulled back. "You are beginning to bore me, human. Take care. I find that I am starting to hunger."

"Go out there into the world and what will you do?" Kitiara asked, gesturing toward the exit hole of the dragon's cavern. "Destroy a few houses, burn some barns. You may even wreck a castle or two. A few hundred people die." She shrugged. "And what happens? You cannot kill everyone. The survivors band together. They come looking for you and they find you—alone, without support, abandoned by your brethren, forgotten by your Queen. The gold dragons come, too. And the silver. For there is nothing to stop them. You are mighty, Lord Immolatus, but you are one and they are many. You will fall."

Immolatus's tail lashed, and the mountain shuddered. The human was not daunted. She took a step forward, daring to come nearer the huge teeth that could have bitten her in twain with a single snap of the dragon's jaws. Though his anger burned like brimstone in his gut, Immolatus could not help but be impressed with the human's courage.

"Great lord, listen to me. Her Majesty has a plan." Kitiara explained, "She has wakened her dragons—*all* her dragons. When the time is right, she will call all her dragons to war. Nothing on Krynn will be able to withstand her fury. Krynn will fall to her might. You and your kind will rule the world in the Queen's name."

"And when will that glorious time come?" Immolatus demanded.

"I do not know, my lord," said Kitiara humbly. "I am only a messenger and therefore not privy to my commander's secrets. But if you come back with me to the camp of General Ariakas in human form, as Her Majesty recommends—for it is requisite that we keep all knowledge of your return secret—you will undoubtedly learn all there is to know."

"Look at me!" Immolatus snarled. "Look at my magnificence! And you have the audacity to ask me to diminish and demean myself by squeezing into a weak, soft, flabby, puny, squishy body such as the one you inhabit?"

"*I* do not ask such a sacrifice of you, my lord," said Kitiara, bowing.

"Your Queen asks of you. I can tell you this, my lord Immolatus—you are Her Majesty's chosen. You alone have been asked to come forth into the world at this time to accept this difficult challenge. None of the others have been so honored. Her Majesty required the best, and she came to you."

"*None* of the others?" Immolatus asked, surprised.

"None, my lord. You are the only one of her dragons to be entrusted with this important task."

Immolatus heaved a deep sigh, a sigh that stirred up centuries of rock dust, enveloping the human in a cloud and setting her coughing and choking. Just another example of the pitiful nature of the form he was being asked to assume.

"Very well," said Immolatus. "I will take on human form. I will accompany you to the camp of this commander of yours. I will listen to what he has to say. Then I will decide whether or not to proceed."

The human attempted to make some response, but she was having difficulty catching her breath.

"Leave me," said the dragon. "Wait for me outside. Altering form is demeaning enough without having you standing there gawking at me."

The human bowed again. "Yes, my lord."

She laid her hand upon the end of a rope dangling down from the air shaft—a rope the dragon had not noticed until now. Grasping hold, she climbed it nimbly to the top of the cavern and crawled out the air shaft, hauling the rope up after her.

Immolatus watched this proceeding grimly. After the human had disappeared, he grasped a boulder in his red claw and jammed the boulder into the air shaft, wedging it in the hole tightly so that no other intruder could again sneak inside.

The cavern was now darker than he liked it and less airy; the sulfurous fumes of his own breath were starting to make the place stink. He'd have to open another air shaft, at considerable cost and trouble to himself. Humans! Blast them! Nuisances. They deserved to be burned. All of them.

He'd see to that later. In the meantime, it was only right and natural that Queen Takhisis should turn to him for aid. Though he considered her selfish and scheming, arrogant and demanding, Immolatus could not fault Her Majesty's intelligence.

☙

Kitiara waited on the mountainside for the dragon to join her. The experience had been a grueling one; she freely admitted that she never wanted to undertake another like it so long as she lived. She was exhausted; the strain of controlling her fear, of trying to outwit the quick-thinking creature, had drained her almost past her endurance. She felt as weak as if she had marched twelve leagues in full plate armor and fought a prolonged battle in the process. Slumping down among the rocks, she gulped water from her flask, then rinsed her mouth, trying to rid herself of the taste of fire.

Tired though she was, she was pleased with herself, pleased with the success of her plan. Pleased, but not surprised. Kitiara had yet to meet the male of any species, dragon or otherwise, who was immune to flattery. And she would have to keep piling it on thick during the journey back to Sanction in order to keep her arrogant and potentially lethal companion tractable.

Kitiara slumped down on a boulder, rested her head in her arms. A man in armor came running toward her. His mouth open, screaming, his face contorted with fear and pain, but she knew him.

"Father!" Kitiara sprang to her feet.

He rushed straight for her. He was on fire, his clothes burning, his hair burning. He was being burned alive. His flesh sizzling and bubbling. . . .

"Father!" Kitiara screamed.

The touch of a hand woke her.

"Come along, worm," said a grating voice.

Kitiara rubbed the sleep from her eyes, wished she could rub its grit from her brain. She looked closely at the corpse, as she passed it. She was relieved to see that the man had been a foot shorter than Gregor uth Matar. Still, Kit could not repress a shudder. The dream had been very real.

The dragon poked her in the back with a long, sharp nail. "Keep moving, slug! I want to be done with this onerous task."

Kitiara wearily increased her pace. The next five days were going to be long. Very long indeed.

9

IVOR OF LANGTREE WAS KNOWN THROUGHOUT THE SURROUNDING countryside as the Mad Baron. His neighbors and tenants did truly think he was crazy. They loved him, they nearly worshiped him, but as they watched him ride his galloping steed through their villages, jumping hay carts and scattering chickens, waving his plumed hat as he dashed past, they would shake their heads when he was gone, clean up the debris, and say to themselves, "Aye, he's daft, is that one."

Ivor Langtree was in his late thirties, scion of a Solamnic Knight, Sir John of Langtree, who'd had the good sense to pack up his household and quietly leave Solamnia during the turmoil following the Cataclysm, traveling south with his family to an inlet on the New Sea. Finding a secluded valley, he'd built a wooden stockade and established his home. He worked the land, while his lady wife took in, fed, and clothed the poor exiles driven from their homelands when the fiery mountain fell upon Krynn. A great many of the exiles chose to live near the stockade and helped defend it against marauding goblins and savage ogres.

The years passed. The eldest Langtree son succeeded his father; the younger sons went off to war, fighting for causes that were just and honorable. If these causes happened to pay well, the sons brought their fortune home to the family coffers. If not, the sons had the satisfaction of knowing that they had acted nobly, and when they returned home, the family coffers supported them. The daughters worked among the people, easing poverty and helping the sick, until they married and went forth to spread the good work their lady mother had begun.

The land prospered. The fortress became a castle, surrounded by a small city, the city of Langtree. Several small towns and villages sprang up in the wide valley, more were established in a neighboring valley, all of their people swearing allegiance to the Langtree family. So prosperous did the Langtrees become that John III decided to call himself baron and deem his land holdings a barony. The villagers and city dwellers were proud to consider that they belonged to a barony and were more than willing to make their lord happy by so doing.

After the first baron of Langtree, sons came and sons went—mostly went, for the Langtrees loved nothing more than a thumping good battle and were always being carried back to the castle by their grieving comrades, half or wholly dead. The current baron was a second son. He had not expected to become baron, but had ascended to that title on the untimely death of his older brother, who had fallen while defending one of the outlying holdings against a tribe of hobgoblins.

As a younger son, Ivor had been expected to earn his living with his sword. This he had done, though not quite according to time-honored fashion. Having taken stock of his abilities and natural gifts, Ivor had come to the conclusion that he would do better hiring other men to fight with him than he would by hiring himself out to other men.

Ivor was an excellent leader, a good strategist, brave but not foolhardy and a firm believer in the Knight's Oath, "My honor is my life," if not the grinding and binding rules of the Measure. A small man—some mistook him for a kender, a mistake they did not make more than once—Ivor was slender and dark, with a swarthy complexion, long black hair, and large brown eyes. Men were wont to say of Ivor that though he was only five foot two, his courage stood six foot four.

Ivor was wiry and tough, clever in battle and deceptively strong. His plate armor and chain mail weighed more than some full-grown men. He rode one of the largest horses in the barony or out of it and rode it well. He loved to fight and he loved to gamble, he loved ale and he loved women, mostly in that order, which was the way he'd come by his nickname, the Mad Baron.

Having been most reluctantly made a baron by the death of his brother, Ivor had interviewed the stewards and the secretaries who undertook the daily running of the barony and, finding they were sound in their jobs and trustworthy, he placed them in charge and continued to do what he liked to do best—train men for battle and then find battles for them to fight.

Thus the barony thrived, and so did Ivor, whose exploits were the stuff of legend and whose mercenaries were much in demand. He had no need of money, he was offered more jobs than he could possibly accept and chose only those that suited him. The promise of steel had no power to sway him. He would turn his back on a sum large enough to build another castle if he deemed the cause unjust. He would spend money like water and his own blood in the same manner to fight for those who could pay only with their grateful blessings. Another reason he was called mad.

There was a third reason, too. Ivor, Baron of Langtree, worshiped an ancient god, a god known to have left Krynn long ago. This god was Kiri-Jolith, formerly a god of the Solamnic Knights. Sir John of Langtree had never lost faith in Kiri-Jolith. The Knight had carried his faith from Solamnia with him, and he and his family had kept that faith alive, a sacred fire in their hearts, a fire that was never permitted to die.

Ivor made no secret of his faith, though he was often ridiculed for it. He would laugh good-naturedly, and—just as good-naturedly—give the jokester a buffet on the head. Ivor would then pick up his detractor, brush him off, and, when the jokester's ears had ceased ringing, advise him to have respect for another's beliefs, if he could not respect those beliefs himself.

His men might not believe in Kiri-Jolith, but they believed in Ivor. They knew he was lucky, for they had seen him escape death in battle by a whisker more times than they could count. They watched their Mad Baron pray openly to Kiri-Jolith before he rode into battle, though never a sign or a word did he have that the god answered those prayers.

"It is not a general's business to take time to explain to every blasted foot soldier his plans for the battle," the Mad Baron used to say with a laugh. "So I don't suppose that it is the Immortal General's business to explain his plans to me, ha, ha, ha!"

Soldiers are a superstitious lot—anyone gambling on a daily basis with death tends to put his trust in luck-bringing objects, in rabbits' feet and charmed medallions and locks of ladies' hair. More than one, therefore, whispered a little prayer to Kiri-Jolith before the charge, more than one carried a bit of bison fur into the fray—the bison being an animal sacred to Kiri-Jolith. While it might not help, it could not hurt.

The Mad Baron was the nobleman to whom Caramon and Raistlin were going to present themselves. Caramon carried in a small leather pouch that he wore next to his skin the precious letter of introduction and recom-mendation written by Antimodes, addressed to Baron Ivor of Langtree. More valuable than steel to the brothers, the letter represented the hopes and plans of both the twins. This letter was their future.

Antimodes had not told them much about Ivor of Langtree (he had not told them his nickname, thinking that they might find this disquieting). The twins were considerably disconcerted, therefore, when they disembarked from their ship and asked for the way to the barony of Ivor of Langtree. They were met with wide grins and shaking heads and knowing looks and the pronouncements, "Ah, here's another couple of loonies come to join the Mad Baron."

"I do not like this, Caramon," said Raistlin one night, about two days' journey from the baron's castle where, according to one peasant, the Mad Baron was "making a mustard."

"I don't think the fellow meant 'mustard,' Raist," said Caramon. "I think he meant 'muster.' It's what you do when you recruit men for—"

"I know what the fool meant!" Raistlin interrupted impatiently. He paused a moment to give his complete attention to the rabbit simmering in the stewpot. "And that's not what I was talking about. What I don't like is the way we are met with winks and gibes whenever we mention Ivor of Langtree. What did you hear about him in town?"

Raistlin disliked entering towns, where he was certain to draw stares and gapes and gasps, to become the object of pointing fingers, hooting children, and barking dogs. The twins had taken to making their nightly camp off the road outside of villages, where Raistlin would either rest from the day's travels or, if he felt well enough, would roam the fields and the woods, searching for herbs that he used for spell components, healing, and cooking. Caramon walked into town for news, supplies, and to check to make certain they were traveling in the right direction.

At first, Caramon was reluctant to leave his twin alone, but Raistlin assured him that he was in very little danger, and this was true. More than one potential footpad, seeing the sun glisten on Raistlin's golden skin and glitter in the crystal ball atop the obviously magical staff, had skulked off to try his luck elsewhere. Indeed, the twins were rather disappointed that they had not had a chance to try their newfound martial talents on anyone during the long journey.

Caramon sniffed hungrily at the rabbit. The twins, short on money, were reduced to eating one meal a day and that was one they had to catch themselves. "Isn't it done, yet? I'm starving. It looks done to me."

"A hare sunning itself on a rock would look done to you," Raistlin returned. "The potatoes and onions are nowhere near cooked enough, and the meat must stew another half hour, at least."

Caramon sighed and tried to forget the rumblings in his stomach by answering his brother's earlier question.

"It is kind of odd," he admitted. "Whenever I ask about Ivor of Langtree, everyone laughs and makes cracks about the Mad Baron, but they don't seem to talk about him in a bad way, if you know what I mean."

"No, I do not," Raistlin said, glowering. He had a low opinion of his brother's powers of observation.

"The men smile, and the woman sigh and say he's a lovely gentlemen. And if he's mad, then some other parts of Ansalon we've been through could use his kind of madness. The roads here are maintained, the people are well fed, their houses are well built and kept in repair. No beggars in the streets. No bandits on the highways. Crops in the fields. Here's what I've been thinking—"

"You! Thinking!" Raistlin snorted.

Caramon didn't hear. He was concentrating on the pot, trying to hurry the rabbit.

"*What* were you thinking?" Raistlin asked at last.

"Huh? I dunno. Let me see . . . Yeah, I remember. I was thinking that maybe they called this Ivor the Mad Baron the same way we used to call Weird Meggin, Weird Meggin. I mean, *I* always thought the woman was cracked, but you said she wasn't and that she was malingered."

"Maligned," Raistlin corrected, casting a severe eye on his brother.

"That's it!" Caramon returned, nodding sagely. "That's what I meant to say. They mean the same thing, don't they?"

Raistlin gazed out to the road, where a steady stream of men, young and old, walked or rode, all headed for Langtree Castle, where the baron had his training grounds. Many of the men were obviously veterans, such as the two Raistlin was watching now. Both wore chain-mail corselets over leather tunics, lined with strips of leather at the bottom, which formed a short skirt. Swords rattled at their hips, their arms and faces and legs—bare beneath the tunic—were seamed with great ugly weals. The two veterans had come across a friend, apparently, for the three men flung their arms around each other, slapped each other on the back.

Caramon let out a wistful sigh. "Would you look at those battle scars! Someday—"

"Hush!" Raistlin ordered peremptorily. "I want to listen to what they're saying." He drew back his hood in order to hear better.

"So, it looks like you did well for yourself over the winter," said one of the men, eyeing his friend's broad stomach.

"Too well!" said the other, groaning. He wiped sweat from his forehead, though the sun was setting and the night air was cool. "Between Marria's cooking and the tavern's ale"—he shook his head gloomily—"and the fact that my chain mail shrank—"

"Shrank!" His friends hooted in derision.

"So it did," said the other, aggrieved. "You remember that time at the Munston siege when I had to stand guard duty in the pouring rain? The damn chain mail's pinched me ever since. My brother-in-law's a black-smith, and he said he'd seen many a mail shirt shrink in the wet. Why do you think the smith dunks his swords in water when he's forging them, answer me that?" He glared at his comrades. "To make the metal tighten up, that's why."

"I see," said one of the men, winking at the other. "And I'll bet he also told you to throw out that old chain mail and order a whole new set."

"Well, sure," said the rotund soldier. "I couldn't be joining up with the Mad Baron wearing shrunken chain mail now, could I?"

"No, no!" said his friends, rolling their eyes and grinning out of the corners of their mouths.

"Besides," said the other, "there were the moth holes."

"Moth holes!" one said, about to burst from suppressed laughter. "Moth holes in your armor?"

"Iron moths," said the soldier with dignity. "When I found holes in my mail, I thought they were caused by defective links, but my brother-in-law said that no, the links were fine. It's just that there are these moths that eat iron. . . ."

This proved too much. One of the men collapsed in the road, wiping his streaming eyes. The other leaned weakly against a tree.

"Iron moths," said Caramon, deeply impressed. He glanced worriedly at his own brand-new, shiny chain-mail corselet, which he had purchased prior to leaving Haven and of which he was enormously proud. "Raist, take a look, will you? Are there any—"

"Hush!" Raistlin shot his brother a furious glance, and Caramon meekly subsided.

"Well, don't worry," said one of the men, slapping his chubby friend on the back. "Master Quesnelle will march that lard off you soon enough."

"Don't I know it!" The man sighed deeply. "What's in store for us this summer? Any jobs in the offing? Have either of you heard?"

"Naw." One of the men shrugged. "Who cares? The Mad Baron picks his fights well. So long as the pay's good."

"Which it will be," said another. "Five steel a week, per man."

Caramon and Raistlin exchanged glances.

"Five steel!" said Caramon, awed. "That's more in a week than I earned in months working on the farm."

"I am beginning to think you are right, my brother," said Raistlin quietly. "If this baron is mad, there should be more lunatics like him."

Raistlin continued to watch the veterans. All this time, they had been standing in the road, laughing and exchanging the latest gossip. Eventually they fell into step—by force of habit—and marched down the road. No sleeping out-of-doors for these men, Raistlin reflected. No dining on scrawny rabbit and seed potatoes, which the twins had purchased with the last of their money from a farmer's wife. These men had steel in their purses, they would spend the night in a comfortable inn.

"Raist . . . can we eat yet?" Caramon asked.

"If you do not mind undercooked rabbit, I suppose we can. Watch out! Use the—"

"Ouch!" Caramon snatched back burned fingers, stuck them in his mouth. "Hot," he mumbled, sucking on them.

"It's one of the characteristics of boiling water," Raistlin observed caustically. "Here! Use the ladle! No, I don't want any meat. Just some of the broth and potatoes. And when you are finished, fix my tea for me."

"Sure, Raist," said Caramon between mouthfuls. "But you should eat some meat. Keep up your strength. You'll need it when it comes to fighting."

"I will not be involved in any actual physical fighting, Caramon." Raistlin smiled disdainfully at his brother's ignorance. "From what I have read, the war wizard stands off to the sidelines, a good distance from the battle, surrounded by soldiers to protect him. This enables him to cast spells in relative safety. Since spellcasting requires such intense concentration, the wizard cannot risk being distracted."

"I'll be there to watch out for you, Raist," Caramon said, when he could speak, having rendered himself momentarily speechless by shoving a whole potato in his mouth.

Raistlin sighed and thought back to the time when he had been so sick with pneumonia. He remembered his twin tiptoeing into the room in the night, drawing the blankets up around Raistlin's shoulders. There had been times when Raistlin was shivering with chills, when this attention had been most welcome. But there had been other times, when the fever burned hot, that Raistlin thought the blankets were meant to suffocate him.

In memory of his illness, he began to cough, coughed until his ribs ached and tears stood in his eyes. Caramon was all concern, watched him anxiously.

Raistlin cast aside the bowl containing his uneaten broth and wrapped himself, shivering, in his cloak. "My tea!" he croaked.

Caramon jumped to his feet, spilling the wooden dish with the remainder of his dinner onto the ground and hastened to fix the strange, ill-tasting and ill-smelling tisane, which eased his twin's cough, soothed his throat, and dulled the unceasing pain.

Huddled in his blanket, Raistlin cupped his hands over the wooden mug that held his tea, sipped it slowly.

"Is there anything else I can get for you, Raist?" Caramon inquired, regarding his brother in concern.

"Make yourself useful," Raistlin ordered peevishly. "You irritate me to death! Leave me in peace, and let me get some rest!"

"Sure, Raist," said Caramon softly. "I'll . . . I'll just clean up the dishes. . . ."

"Fine!" Raistlin said without a voice. He closed his eyes.

Caramon's footsteps thudded all around him. The stewpot clanged, the wooden bowls rattled. Wet wood, tossed on the fire, hissed and spat. Raistlin lay down, pulled his blanket up over his head. Caramon was actively working at being quiet.

Caramon is like this tea, Raistlin thought to himself as he drifted off to sleep. My feelings for him are mixed with guilt, tainted with jealousy. The flavor is bitter, it is hard to swallow. But once taken, a pleasant warmth pervades my system, my pain eases, and I can sleep, secure in the knowledge that he is there beside me in the night, watching over me.

10

THE CITY OF LANGTREE HAD SPROUTED UP AROUND THE BARON'S CASTLE, which afforded protection for the city's inhabitants and also, in the early days, a market for goods and services. The city was now prosperous with a small but burgeoning population that produced goods and services for itself as well as the castle and its inhabitants. Excitement and bustle were in the air, for it was spring muster and the city's population was swelling with the return of the veterans and the arrival of new volunteers.

Langtree was a peaceful place during the winter, when the chill winds blew down from the distant mountains, bringing sleet and snow. A peaceful city, but not a sleepy one. The blacksmith and his assistants spent the winter days working hard at the forge, making the swords and daggers, chain mail and plate armor, spurs and wagon wheels and horseshoes, which would be in high demand when the soldiers came back in the spring.

Farmers who could not see their fields for the snow covering them turned to a second craft. The winter was the time for fine leatherwork, and the hands that wielded the hoe in the summer now sewed belts, gloves, and tunics, fashioned sheaths for sword and knife. Most were plain and serviceable, but some were made with intricate, hand-tooled designs, which would command high prices. The farmers' wives pickled eggs and pigs' feet and laid up jams and jellies and jars of honeycomb to sell at the open-air markets. Millers ground flour and corn to make bread. Weavers worked at their looms, making cloth for blankets, cloaks, and shirts, all embroidered with the baron's crest—the bison.

Tavern owners and innkeepers spent the dull winter months cleaning and refurbishing and laying up quantities of ale and wine and mead, brewed cordials, and caught up on their sleep, which was always in short supply when the troops came to town. Jewelers and gold- and silversmiths fashioned objects of beauty to tempt the soldiers to spend their steel. Everyone in town looked forward to spring muster and summer campaign season. During this frantic, exciting time, they would make money enough to live on the remainder of the year.

Caramon and Raistlin had been to the Harvest Home Fair held at Haven every year—a gathering of people they both considered impressive. But they were not prepared for anything like spring muster in Langtree. The population of the town swelled fourfold. Soldiers filled the town— good-naturedly jostling each other in the streets, raising the roofs off the taverns with their laughter and their singing, thronging to the Street of Swords, haranguing the blacksmiths, teasing the barmaids, bargaining with the vendors, or cursing the kender, who were everywhere they didn't belong.

The baron's guards patrolled the streets, keeping a watchful eye on the soldiers, ready to intervene if there was trouble. Trouble was rare. The baron always had more volunteers than he needed. Anyone who made a misstep was out of his favor for good. The soldiers took care of each other, hustling drunken comrades out the back door, breaking up fights before they spilled out onto the street, and making certain that the tavern owners were well paid for any damages.

Reunions among friends happened on every street corner, with much laughter and reminiscing and the occasional sorrowful shake of the head remembering one who "ate his pay," which the twins discovered did not mean that he had gulped down steel coins for breakfast, but had taken a steel blade in the gut.

The language the mercenaries spoke was a jumble of Common, their own jargon, some Solamnic (spoken with a terrible accent that would have made it unrecognizable to a true resident of Solamnia), some dwarven—mainly to do with weapons—and even a bit of elven when it came to archery. The twins understood one word out of about five, and those words made little sense.

The twins had hoped to be able to slip into the city unnoticed, avoid attention. This proved difficult. Caramon stood head and shoulders above most of Langtree's population, while Raistlin's red robes, though stained with travel, caused him to stand out like a cardinal among sparrows in the more somberly dressed crowd.

Caramon was very proud of his shining new chain mail, his new sword, and its new sheath. He wore them ostentatiously and never failed to display them to what he assumed were admiring beholders. Now, he realized, to his deep chagrin, the very newness of which he'd been so proud marked him a raw recruit. He gazed with envy on the battered chain mail worn with such ease by the veterans and would have sold his new sword seven times over for one with a notched blade indicative of many hard-fought battles.

Though he could not understand the gist of most of the comments aimed his direction—many of which had to do with "pukes," which he couldn't fathom at all, even the occasionally obtuse Caramon could tell the remarks were not complimentary. He wouldn't have minded much on his own account—Caramon was used to being kidded and took teasing good-naturedly—but he was starting to grow angry over what they were saying about his twin.

Raistlin was accustomed to people regarding him with suspicion and dislike—people still distrusted wizards, in this day and age—but at least in the past they had viewed him with respect.

Not in Langtree. The soldiers appeared to dislike his calling as much as anyone and didn't have a particle of respect for him either. They certainly did not fear him, to judge by the gibes thrown his direction.

"Hey, witch boy, what you got under those fancy red robes?" called out one grizzled soldier.

"Not much, by the look of him!"

"The witch boy stole his mama's clothes. Maybe she'd pay to get them back!"

"The clothes, maybe. Not him!"

"Ooh, look out, Shorty. You're gonna make the witch boy mad. He's gonna turn you into a frog!"

"No, a lunkhead. That's what happened to the big guy with him." The soldiers laughed and hooted.

Caramon glanced at his brother uneasily. Raistlin's face was set and grim, the golden skin burnished with a sheen of red as the blood mounted to his cheeks.

"You want me to pound 'em, Raist?" Caramon asked in a low voice, glowering at their detractors.

"Keep walking, Caramon," Raistlin admonished. "Keep walking and pay them no mind."

"But, Raist, they said—"

"I know what they said!" Raistlin snapped. "They're trying to provoke us into starting a fight. Then *we'll* be the ones who get into trouble with the baron's guards."

"Yeah, I guess you're right," said Caramon unhappily. They were out of range of the teasing now, the soldiers having found something else to amuse them. But more soldiers filled the streets, and being in high spirits, they were looking for fun, and the young men were easy targets. They were forced to endure insults and derogatory remarks at every street corner.

"Maybe we should leave this place, Raist," Caramon said. He had entered the city proudly, filled with excitement. Now, completely crushed, he hung his head, hunched his shoulders, and tried to make himself as small as possible. "No one wants us here."

"We have not come this far to give up before we start," Raistlin returned with more confidence than he felt. "Look, my brother," he added quietly. "We're not alone."

A young man of indeterminate age, somewhere between fifteen and twenty, walked on the opposite of the street. Carrot-red hair, ragged and lanky, fell past his shoulders. His clothes were patched and too small for him; he had outgrown them but probably could not afford to purchase new. As he came near the twins, his attention fixed on Raistlin. The youngster stared at the mage with frank and open curiosity.

A soldier emerged from a tavern, his face flushed with drink. The long carrot-red hair proved too great a temptation. The soldier reached out, grabbed hold of a hank of hair and twisted, jerking the young man backward.

The youngster yelped and grabbed hold of his head. He must have felt as if his hair was being yanked out at the roots.

"What have we here?" the soldier demanded, chortling.

Wildcat was the answer.

Moving with marvelous agility, the youngster twisted in the man's grasp and lashed out at his molester, spitting and clawing and kicking. The attack was so savage and sudden, so completely unexpected, that the youngster landed four punches on the soldier's face and two kicks—one to the shin and one to the knee—before the man knew what had hit him.

"Look at that!" His drunken cohorts roared. "Rogar's been whipped by a baby!"

Furious, blood dribbling from a broken nose, the soldier landed a punch on the jaw that sent the youngster tumbling head over heels into the gutter.

Straddling his victim, the enraged soldier grabbed hold of the boy's shirt—tearing it—and yanked him, groggy and dazed and bleeding, out of the gutter. The soldier raised a meaty fist—his next blow might well kill the young man.

"I don't like this, Raist," said Caramon sternly. "I think we should do something."

"This time I agree with you, my brother." Raistlin was already opening one of the many small pouches that hung from his belt, pouches that held his spell components. "You take care of the bully. I will deal with his friends."

Rogar was intent on his prey, his friends were intent upon their wit. Rogar never saw Caramon, who loomed up from behind him, his large shadow falling over the man like a thundercloud passing before the sun, his fist landing on him like a bolt from the heavens. The soldier fell facefirst into the gutter. He would later waken with a ringing in his ears, swearing he'd been struck by lightning.

Rogar's two friends had their mouths open, laughing. Raistlin tossed a handful of sand into their faces, recited the words to a spell. The soldiers slumped to the street and lay there, snoring loudly.

"Fight!" screamed a barmaid, coming to the door with a tray of mugs, which she promptly dropped with a crash.

Soldiers clambered to their feet, jostling with each other to be first out the door, eager to join the fray. From down the street came whistles and shouts, and someone yelled that the guards were coming.

"Let's go!" Raistlin cried to his brother.

"Aw, c'mon, Raist! We can handle these bastards!" Caramon's face was flushed with pleasure. His fists clenched, he was ready to take on all comers.

"I said, we are going, Caramon!"

When Raistlin spoke in that tone, sharp and cold as a chunk of ice, Caramon knew better than to disobey. Reaching out, he caught hold of the youngster, who was swaying on his feet, and hauled him off as easily as if the young man had been a sack of potatoes.

Raistlin dashed off down the street, his red robes flapping around his ankles, clutching the Staff of Magius in his hand. He could hear Caramon thudding behind him and a parcel of drunken soldiers haring along after them.

"This way!" he yelled and, veering suddenly, made a sharp right turn and darted into a shadowy alley.

Caramon followed. The alley opened into another bustling street, but Raistlin halted about halfway down, in front of a wall made of wooden planks. The smell of horse and hay was strong. Raistlin tossed the Staff of Magius over the wall. Caramon heaved the young man, arms and legs flying, over afterward.

"Give me a boost!" Raistlin ordered, reaching up his hands to catch hold of the top of the wall.

Caramon grabbed hold of his twin around his waist and boosted him with such energy that Raistlin missed his grasp and shot over the wall to land headfirst in a bale of straw. Caramon lifted himself by his hands, peered over the wall.

"You all right, Raist?"

"Yes! Yes! Hurry up before they see you!"

Caramon heaved himself up and over, tumbled into the straw.

"They went down the alley!" yelled a voice.

The clamor came their direction. The brothers crouched deeper into the straw. Raistlin put his finger to his lips, counseling silence. The young man Caramon had rescued lay in the straw beside them, gasping quietly for breath and watching them both with bright, dark eyes.

Booted feet stomped past the stable. Their pursuers ran by, burst into the street at the end of the alley, where someone shouted that the three had been seen heading toward the city gate.

Raistlin relaxed. By the time the soldiers realized they had lost their prey, they would have found another tavern. As for the guards, all they cared about was restoring order, not making arrests. They would not waste their time tracking down the participants in a bar fight.

"We are safe now," Raistlin was about to say, when dust from the dry straw flew into his mouth and set him coughing.

The spasm was a bad one, doubling him over in pain. He was thankful the attack had not struck him as he was fleeing, wondered vaguely that he had been able to run with such ease, run without even thinking about his infirmity.

Both Caramon and the young man they had rescued watched Raistlin anxiously.

"I am all right!" Raistlin gasped, striking away his brother's solicitous hand. "It's this blasted straw! Where's my staff?" he demanded suddenly, looking for it and not finding it. A pang of unreasoning terror constricted his heart.

"Here it is," said the young man, squirming and fishing for something beneath him. "I think I'm sitting on it."

"Don't touch it!" Raistlin demanded in a half-choked voice, lunging forward and thrusting out his hand.

Startled, recoiling from the mage as if he'd been a striking snake, the young man—wide-eyed—moved his hand away from the staff.

Raistlin clutched at it, and only when he had the staff safely in hand did he relax.

"I am sorry if I startled you," Raistlin said gruffly, clearing his throat. "The staff is quite valuable. We should leave here before someone comes. Are you all right?" he asked the young man curtly.

The young man glanced over his legs and arms, wiggled his fingers and his bare toes. "Nothing broken. Just a split lip. And I've had worse than this from Pa," he added cheerfully, wiping away blood.

Caramon peered out the front of the horse stall. A long line of stalls stretched off in both directions, another row stood across from them. About half the stalls were filled. Horses snorted and snuffled and shuffled their feet, munched hay. In the stall across from theirs, a big bay companionably rubbed heads with a chestnut. Sparrows flew in and out of the eaves, darting into the stalls to snitch a bit of straw for nest repair.

"No one around," Caramon reported.

"Excellent. Caramon, pick the hay out of your hair."

Raistlin brushed off his robes, the young man assisting him helpfully. After a brief inspection, Raistlin pronounced them in suitable condition to leave. Caramon took one more look, then the three emerged from the stall and walked along the row of horses.

"I really miss Nightsky," said Caramon, heaving a sigh. The sight and smell of horses brought back his loss. "He was a great horse."

"How did he die?" asked the young man in sympathetic tones.

"He didn't," Raistlin said. "We sold our horses to have money to buy our passage across New Sea. Ah," he added loudly, "thank you for allowing us to look around, sir!"

A stable hand clad in leather breeches and homespun shirt was leading two horses, saddled and bridled, out of their stalls. Two men, well dressed, waited in the stable yard. The stable hand came to a dead stop on seeing the odd-looking trio.

"Hey, what the—"

"We saw nothing we liked," Raistlin said, waving his hand. "I thank you all the same. Caramon, give the man something for his trouble."

With a courteous nod, Raistlin passed by the stable hand, who stared at them open-mouthed.

"Here you are, my good man," said Caramon, handing over one of their precious coins with as much nonchalance as if he scattered gold through the streets on a daily basis.

The three sauntered out of the stables. The stable hand glanced at his coin suspiciously and, finding it good, thrust it into a pocket with a grin.

"Come again!" he called out loudly. "Anytime!"

"There goes a night's lodging," Caramon said gloomily.

"Worth the price, my brother," Raistlin returned. "Otherwise we might have lodged in the baron's dungeons." He cast a sidelong glance from out his hood at the young man who walked alongside them.

In Raistlin's cursed vision, the young man seemed to wither and age and die as Raistlin watched. But as the flesh melted from the bones and the skin stretched taut, Raistlin detected some interesting features in the young man's face. A thin face, far too thin and older than the boy's years, which Raistlin guessed at about fifteen. He had a thin body, an oddly constructed body. The young man was short, he came to about Raistlin's shoulder. Fine-boned hands hung from large wristbones, his bare feet were small for his height. His clothes were worn and ill assorted, but they were clean—at least they had been before he'd landed in a gutter and hidden in a stable. Now that he came to think of it, Raistlin noticed that all of them bore a distinct odor of manure and horse piss.

"Caramon," Raistlin announced, pausing at the door to a likely-looking tavern, "the unaccustomed exercise has made me hungry. I propose that we stop for supper."

Caramon stared, gaping, at his brother. Never in their twenty-one years together had he ever heard his twin—who didn't eat enough to keep a good-sized cricket alive—say that he was hungry. Admittedly, it had been a long time since Caramon had seen his twin run like that; in fact, he couldn't recall ever having seen Raistlin run anywhere. Caramon was about to say something expressive of his astonishment when he saw Raistlin's eyes narrow, a frown line crease his brow.

Caramon knew immediately that something was going on, something beyond his comprehension and that he was not to do or say anything that might imperil the situation.

"Uh, sure, Raist," Caramon said, gulping, adding weakly, "This seems like a decent enough place."

"I guess this is good-bye, then. Thanks for the help," said the young man, holding out his thin hand to each of them. He cast a wistful glance at the tavern. The smell of fresh-baked bread and smoked meats filled the air. "I'm here to join the army. Perhaps we'll see each other again." Shoving his hands in his pockets, his empty pockets, he stared down at his feet. "Well, good-bye. Thanks again."

"We are here to join the baron's army, as well," Raistlin said. "Since we are all strangers in town, we could dine together."

"No, thanks, I couldn't," said the young man. He stood straight, his head tossed back. Pride flushed his thin cheeks.

"You would be doing my brother and me a great favor," Raistlin said. "We have traveled a long distance, and we grow weary of each other's company."

"That's true enough!" said Caramon enthusiastically. A little too enthusiastically. "Raist and I, we sure do get tired of talking to each other. Why, only the other day—"

"That will do, Brother," Raistlin said coldly.

"C'mon," said Caramon, putting his arm around the young man's shoulders, the big man's arm practically swallowing him up. "Don't worry about money. You'll be our guest."

"No, please, really—" The young man stubbornly stood his ground. "I don't want charity. . . ."

"It's not charity!" Caramon said, looking shocked at the mere suggestion. "We're brothers-in-arms now. Men who've spilt blood together share everything. Didn't you know that? It's an old Solamnic tradition. Who knows? Maybe next time Raist and I won't have any money, and then it'll be your turn to take care of us."

The young man's face flushed again, this time with shy pleasure. "Do you mean that? Are we really brothers?"

"Sure we are. We'll take the oath. What's your name?"

"Scrounger," said the young man.

"That's an odd sort of name," Caramon said.

"It's my name, nonetheless," the young man returned cheerfully.

"Oh, well. Each to his own." Caramon drew his sword, lifted it solemnly, the hilt in the air. His voice was deep and reverent. "We have spilt blood together. By Solamnic tradition, we are bound closer than brothers. What you have is mine. What I have is yours."

"That may be truer than you know, Brother," Raistlin said wryly, plucking at Caramon's sleeve as the three entered the tavern with Scrounger in the lead. "In case you hadn't noticed, our new young friend is part kender."

11

THE TAVERN, LOCATED ON A SIDE STREET, WAS KNOWN AS THE SWELLING Ham and featured a pink and apoplectic-looking pig on its hinged sign. To judge by the smell, the Swelling Ham had only one thing to recommend it and that was the cheap prices, which were posted on a board in the window.

The Swelling Ham attracted a poorer crowd than the more prosperous taverns along the main street. There were few veterans, only those who had squandered their earnings, but many hungry hopefuls. Caramon looked over the crowd carefully before entering, saw no one who looked familiar, and pronounced it safe to enter.

The three found seats at a dirty table. Caramon was forced to appropriate a chair, first removing a slumbering drunk from it and depositing him on the floor. The barmaids, busy and distracted, let the drunk lie, stepping either on him or over him. One of the barmaids hurled three bowls of ham and beans in their direction and left to draw two ales for Caramon and Scrounger and a glass of wine for Raistlin.

"My mother was a kender," said Scrounger readily, talking between mouthfuls of white beans and ham and corn bread. "Or at least mostly kender. I think there was human blood in her somewhere, for she was like me, she looked more human than she did kender. If there was human blood in her, she didn't let it hinder her. She was kender through and through. Like everything else in her life, she had no idea how she came by me. That tasted really good." He shoved aside his empty bowl regretfully.

Raistlin passed his bowl, still full, to the young man.

"No, thank you." Scrounger shook his head.

"Take it. I am finished," Raistlin said. He had eaten only three mouthfuls. "It would go to waste otherwise."

"Well, if you're sure you don't want any more . . ." Scrounger seized the bowl, scooped up a large spoonful of beans, and chewed on it with a deep sigh of satisfaction. "I can't tell you when I've eaten anything that tastes this good!"

The beans were underdone, the ham rancid, the bread moldy. Raistlin cast an expressive glance at his brother, who was devouring his food with as much gusto as Scrounger. Caramon paused with the spoon to his mouth. Raistlin jerked his head at the young man.

Caramon looked stricken. "Ah, but, Raist . . ."

Raistlin's eyes narrowed.

Caramon sighed. "Here you go," he said, shoving his half-full bowl over to the young man. "I ate a big lunch."

"Are you sure?"

Caramon eyed the bowl sadly. "Yes, I'm sure."

"Gee, thanks!" Scrounger started in on his third bowl. "What were we talking about?"

"Your mother," Raistlin prompted, sipping at his wine.

"Oh, yeah. Mother had sort of a vague memory of a human having been kind to her once, but she couldn't remember where or when or even his name. She didn't know I was coming until one day I just popped out. She was never so surprised in her life. But she thought it was great fun, having a baby, and she took me with her, only sometimes she'd forget about me and leave me behind. But people would always find me and run after her to return me. She was glad to have me back, though I think that sometimes she didn't exactly remember who I was. When I got older, I used to return myself, which worked out fine.

"Then one day, when I was eight, I guess, she left me outside an herb shop to wait for her while she went in to try to sell the herbalist some mushrooms we'd found. We'd walked a long way that day. It was warm and sunny outside the shop, and I fell asleep. The next thing I knew, Mother was running out of the shop, with the shopkeeper yelling that they weren't mushrooms, they were toadstools and that she was going to poison him.

"I tried to keep up with her, but mother had a good head start, and I lost sight of her. The shopkeeper quit the chase and came back, cursing, for it seems that Mother had made off with a jar of cinnamon sticks in the bargain. I was going to follow her, but when the shopkeeper saw me, he was so mad that he knocked me down. I hit my head on a door stoop, and when I woke up it was night and Mother was long gone. I looked for her all along the road, but I never did find her."

"That's too bad," said Caramon sympathetically. "We lost our mother, too."

"Did you?" Scrounger was interested. "Did she leave you behind?"

"So to speak," said Raistlin with an angry glance for his twin. "You mentioned your 'pa,'" he added, changing the subject before Caramon could say any more. "Did you then find your father?"

"Oh, no." Scrounger shoved away the third empty bowl. Sitting back in the booth, he gave a contented belch. "That's just what he made us call him. He was a miller who took in stray kids to work in his shop. He said it was cheaper to feed us than it was to pay hired help. I was tired of roaming around, and he gave me a good meal at least once a day, so I stayed with him."

"Was he mean to you?" Caramon asked, frowning at this.

Scrounger thought this over. "No, not really. He'd hit me sometimes, but I guess I deserved it. And he saw to it that I could read and write Common, because he said stupid children made him look bad in front of the customers. I stayed with him until I was about nineteen. I thought I might be there forever. He was going to make me shop foreman.

"But then one day a really strange feeling came over me. My feet got real itchy, and I couldn't sit still, and I began to see the road in my dreams." Scrounger smiled, stared past them, out the window. "That road. Out there. I saw it stretch before me, and at the end I saw high mountains with snow on their peaks and green valleys covered with wildflowers and dark, spooky forests, cities with high walls and castles shining in the sun, vast seas with foam-flecked waves. The dreams were wonderful, and when I woke up and found myself surrounded by four walls, I was so sad I'd almost burst out crying.

"Then one day a new customer came into the shop. He was a very wealthy man who'd bought up several of the local farms and he wanted to sell us his grain. I started to talk to him and found out he'd been a soldier, a mercenary. That was how he'd earned his money. He told me exciting stories, all about his adventures, and that was when I made up my mind. I said that if he ever heard about anyone wanting to hire on soldiers, to let me know. He promised he would, and he was the one who told me about the Mad Baron. The baron was an excellent commander, so he told me, and a good soldier, and I could do worse than learn from him. So I left the mill and started out. That was last fall. I've been on the road about six months."

"Six months! Where do you come from then?" Caramon asked, amazed.

"Southern Ergoth," said Scrounger complacently. "The trip was fun, most of the time. I worked my way on board a ship across the New Sea, landed near Pax Tharkas, and walked the rest of the way from there."

"You said you are nineteen?" Raistlin found this hard to believe. "That would make you close to our age." He nodded at his twin.

"Give or take a year," said Scrounger. "Mother had no idea of the date when I was born. One day I asked her how old I was. Mother asked me how old I wanted to be. I thought it over and said it seemed to me that six sounded like a pretty good age, and she said six was fine with her, and so I was six. I began counting from there."

"And how did you come by your name?" Raistlin asked. "I have to assume that Scrounger is not your given name."

"It might be, for all I know," Scrounger replied with shrug. "Mother always called me whatever took her fancy at the time. The miller mostly called me 'kid' until I began to show a talent for acquiring things that he needed."

"Stealing?" said Caramon, looking severe.

"Not 'stealing,' " said Scrounger, shaking his head. "No, and not 'borrowing' either. It's like this. Everyone has something someone else wants. Everyone has something he doesn't need anymore. What I do is find out what those somethings are, and I make sure that everyone ends up with something he wants in exchange for something he doesn't."

Caramon scratched his head. "I dunno. It doesn't sound legal to me."

"It is. I'll show you."

"That'll be sixpence for the beans," said the barmaid, dragging her straggling hair out of her face in order to read the marks she'd chalked on their table. "Sixpence for the ale, and fourpence for the wine."

Caramon reached for the money purse. Scrounger's thin fingers closed over his arm, halting him.

"We don't have the money," said Scrounger brightly.

The barmaid glowered. "Ragis!" she called out ominously.

A big man standing behind the bar filling ale mugs looked her direction.

"But," Scrounger added hurriedly, "I see your fire is almost out." He gestured toward the large fireplace in which a charred log feebly sputtered.

"So? No one's got time to chop firewood, have they?" The barmaid returned defiantly. "And where do you come off complaining, scum? Ragis'll use you for firewood unless you hand over what you owe!"

Scrounger smiled at her. Even with his split lip, he had a most charming and disarming smile. "We'll pay with something worth more than money."

"There's nothin' worth more than money," said the barmaid sulkily, but she was intrigued.

"Yes, there is. Time and muscles and brains. Now, my friend

here"—Scrounger rested his hand on Caramon's bulging arm—"is the fastest and best woodchopper in all of Ansalon. I am an expert at waiting tables. If you'll give us a bed for the night, my other friend—a wizard of great renown—has a magical spice that will make your beans a culinary masterpiece. Everyone will come to your tavern just to eat them."

"Our beans ain't culinary!" the barmaid said indignantly. "They ain't never made anyone sick!"

"No, no. I mean that this spice will make them taste as good as the beans eaten by the Lord of the City of Palanthas. Even better. When His Grace comes to hear of them—and I'll be sure to tell him—he'll journey all this way just to try them."

The barmaid smiled grudgingly. "Well, the customers *have* been complaining some. Not our fault, mind you. The cook got into the sherry, fell down the cellar stairs, and broke her ankle, which means Mabs and I've had to do the cooking *and* the cleaning *and* the table waiting. We're run off our feet, and Ragis can't leave the bar, not with this thirsty crowd."

She eyed Caramon, her gaze softening. "You *are* a strong one, ain't you? What's sixpence if we can't keep the fire going or bring up a new cask of ale from the cellar? All right. You chop the wood, and you, wizard"—she cast Raistlin a disparaging glance—"what have you got?"

Raistlin removed one of his pouches, reached in his hand, and brought out a bulbous white object with a strong and heady smell. "This is the magic ingredient," he said. "Peel it and chop it fine and put it into the beans. I guarantee you will bring customers in off the street."

"We're not suffering from lack of customers. But I grant you it'd be nice to serve a meal they don't throw back in my face." She sniffed at the white bulb. "That does smell good. You guarantee it won't poison no one?"

"My brother here will volunteer to eat the first bowlful," said Raistlin, and Caramon cast him a grateful glance.

"Well . . ."

"The Lord of Palanthas," Scrounger remarked dreamily. He took her red, work-worn hand and kissed it. "Vowing yours are the best beans he ever ate in his life."

The barmaid giggled and gave Scrounger's red hair a teasing yank. "Lord of Palanthas, my ass! You, wizard, go into the kitchen and add your magic spice."

She leaned over the table, showing a fine expanse of bosom framed by a dirty, frilly blouse, and erased the marks scrawled on the wood with her forearm.

"And there'll be a little something extra in this for you, my dear," said

Caramon, resting his hand amorously over the barmaid's.

"Get along with you!" she cried, snatching back her hand, all the while bending over to whisper, "We close at midnight." With an arch look and a shake of her bedraggled hair, she flounced off in answer to a chorus of yells for more ale. "Yeah, yeah, I'm comin'! Keep your pants on!"

"For the time being," Caramon said beneath his breath, grinning. He went off, whistling, to the back lot to chop wood.

"Well done, Scrounger," said Raistlin, rising to his feet, preparatory to taking his "magic spice," otherwise known as garlic, to the kitchen. "You have saved us the price of a meal and a night's lodging. One question—how did you know what I had in my pouches?"

Scrounger's thin cheeks flushed, his eyes sparkled impishly. "I didn't forget everything my mother taught me," he said, slipping off to wait tables.

❂

The next morning, the twins and Scrounger joined a long line of men forming a double column in the courtyard outside the baron's castle. A large plank of wood set on two trestles made a table. A piece of parchment had been nailed to the table, to keep the parchment from blowing away in the strong, offshore breeze. When the officers arrived, they would take the men's names, then send them off to the training camp.

Here the men would be fed and sheltered for a week at the baron's expense, undergoing rigorous training that was a test of their strength, their agility, and their ability to obey orders. Those who did not make the grade were weeded out during this week and sent packing with a small sum to thank them for their trouble. Those who survived the first week were given a week's pay. Those who survived after a month were accepted into the army. Of one hundred men who marked down their names on the list, eighty would be around after the first week. Fifty would be left by the time the army was ready to march.

The recruits had begun lining up at dawn. The day was going to be a hot one for spring. In the distance, clouds gathered on the horizon. There would be rain by afternoon. The hopefuls standing in line began to sweat before the morning was half over.

The twins arrived early. Caramon was so eager that he would have left before dawn, had not Raistlin, who foresaw a long day ahead of them, persuaded him to at least wait until the sun was up. Caramon had not spent the night with the barmaid after all—much to her disappointment. He had spent the night polishing his equipment, and by morning, clad in his new armor, he outshone the sun. He was too excited to eat more than one breakfast, sat fidgeting at the table, rattling his sword and asking every five minutes if they weren't going to be late. Finally Raistlin said that they could go, only because, as he said, Caramon was annoying him to the point of madness.

Scrounger was nearly as excited as Caramon. Raistlin doubted the baron would accept the thin and childlike youngster into the army, feared that Scrounger might be in for a severe disappointment. Such was the young man's ebullient nature that Raistlin guessed Scrounger would not be downcast for long.

The tavern owner was sorry to see them leave, particularly Raistlin. The garlic in the beans had proven quite magical, the smell luring customers in off the street. The owner had tried to prevail upon Raistlin to remain behind in the capacity of cook. Raistlin, though flattered, politely refused. The barmaid kissed Caramon. Scrounger kissed the barmaid, and they set off to the mustering grounds.

They took their places in line, waiting in the bright sunshine. About twenty-five men were already there ahead of them. They waited about an hour, during which some of those in line began to chat with their neighbors. Caramon and Scrounger were talking with the man behind them.

The man standing in front of Raistlin glanced at him, as if wanting to start a conversation. Raistlin pretended not to notice. He could already feel the dust from the road start to tickle his throat; he feared that he would suffer one of his coughing spasms, could imagine being cast out of the line in ignominy. He avoided the man's friendly gaze by studying the baron's fortifications with as much interest as if he intended to besiege them.

A sergeant, a cocky bantam of a man, bowlegged and missing one eye, arrived, escorted by five veteran soldiers. The sergeant cast a glance over the hundred or so now in line. By the squint in his eye and the sardonic shake of his head, he wasn't impressed. He said something to his comrades, who laughed boisterously. Those in line fell suddenly and uncomfortably silent. The first man in line paled and shrank to almost nothing.

The sergeant took his place behind the table. The soldiers stood behind him, their arms crossed over their chests, wide grins on their faces. The sergeant's single eye was like a gimlet, boring through the first man in line to get a look at the second and so on until it seemed he was able to see through each recruit to the very last one. Pointing a grimy finger at the paper, he said to the first man in line, "Write yer name. If you can't write, mark your **X**. Take your place over there to my left."

The man, dressed in a farmer's smock and clutching a shapeless felt hat in his hand, shuffled forward. He humbly marked down his X and walked meekly over to stand where indicated. One of the veterans began to call out, "Here piggie, piggie, piggie." The others laughed appreciative. The farmer cringed and ducked his head, undoubtedly wishing the Abyss would open up and swallow him.

The next man in line hesitated before approaching. He seemed to be of two minds, one of which was telling him to run for his life. He took courage, however, and stepped forward.

"Write yer name," said the sergeant, already sounding bored. "If you can't write, mark your **X**. Take your place in line."

The litany continued. The sergeant said the same thing in the same tone to every man. The sergeant's comrades made comments about each recruit. The men took their places in line with their ears and cheeks burning. Most took it meekly enough, but the young man ahead of Raistlin grew angry. Flinging down the quill pen, he glowered at the veterans, fists clenched, and took a threatening step forward.

"Steady, son," said the sergeant coolly. "It's death to strike a superior officer. Take your place in line."

The young man, who was better dressed than most and who was one of the few to write his name, glared at the veterans, who grinned back at him. Lifting his head proudly, he stalked over and took his place in line.

"Fighting spirit," Raistlin heard one of them say, as he approached. "He'll be a good soldier."

"Can't control his temper," said another. "He'll be gone in a week."

"Bet?"

"Bet." The two clasped hands.

Raistlin's turn. He could see plainly enough that the object of this exercise was not only to enroll new recruits but to humiliate them, intimidate them. Having read up on training methods, he was aware that commanders used such means to tear a man apart, reduce him to nothing so that the officers could build him back up again into a good soldier, one who would obey orders without thinking, one who had confidence in himself and in his comrades.

"All very well for the common foot soldier," Raistlin thought disdainfully. "But it will be different with me."

As it happened, the sergeant had lowered his head to search for the name of the angry young recruit, thinking of taking a part of the bet. He was staring at the paper with his one good eye, trying to read the name upside down, when the name and the paper were obscured by a loose-flowing red sleeve and a hand and arm that gleamed with a golden sheen.

The men behind the sergeant give a low murmur, nudged each other with their elbows. The sergeant snapped his head up. The single eye focused on Raistlin, who said politely, "Where do *I* sign, sir? I am here to enroll as war wizard."

"Well, well," said the sergeant, squinting in the sun, "this is a new one. We ain't had one of your kind for quite a spell." He laughed and leered. "Spell. That's a joke."

"Where do I sign, sir?" Raistlin asked. The dust and heat were stifling. He could feel his throat starting to close, dreaded having a coughing fit now, before these grinning veterans. He pulled his hood low, keeping his face and eyes hidden. He did not want to give these men any more fodder for their jokes than was necessary. As it was, they already found him humorous enough.

"Where'd you get that gold skin, boy?" asked one of the veterans. "Maybe your mama was a snake, huh?"

"A lizard, most likely," said another, and they laughed. "Lizard-boy. That's his name, Sarge. Write that down for him."

"He'll be a cheap recruit," said the first. "All he eats is flies!"

"Bet he's got a long red tongue to catch 'em. Stick out your tongue for us, Lizard-boy."

Raistlin felt the cough seizing him. "Where do I sign?" he demanded, half-choked.

The sergeant, peering up, caught a sudden glimpse of the strange, hourglass eyes. "Go tell Horkin," he said over his shoulder to one of the men behind him.

"Where is he?"

"The usual."

The soldier nodded and left on his assignment.

Raistlin couldn't help himself. He began to cough. Fortunately, the spasm wasn't a bad one and passed quickly. But it was enough to set the sergeant frowning.

"What's the matter with you, boy? You sick? It ain't catchin,' is it?"

"My infirmity is not contagious," Raistlin said through gritted teeth. "Where do I sign?"

The man indicated the paper. "With all the rest," he said, his lip curling. He obviously didn't think much of this new recruit. "Go stand with the others."

"But I am here——"

"I know why you're here." The sergeant dismissed him from sight and mind. "Do as you're told."

His cheeks burning, Raistlin walked over to take his ignominious place with the other recruits, who were now all staring at him, as were most of those still waiting in line. Stoically, Raistlin ignored them all. His hope now was that Caramon wouldn't do or say anything to draw attention to himself. Knowing Caramon, that was a forlorn hope at best.

"Write yer name," said the sergeant, yawning. "If you can't write, mark your **X**. Take your place over there to my left."

"Sure thing, Sergeant," said Caramon cheerfully. He wrote his name with a flourish on the parchment.

"Big as an ox," said one of the veterans. "Probably about as bright, too."

"I like 'em big," said his comrade. "They stop more arrows that way. We'll put him in the front ranks."

"Thank you kindly, sir," said Caramon, pleased. "Oh, by the way," he added modestly, "I don't really need any training. I can just skip all that part."

"Oh, you can, can you?" said the sergeant.

Raistlin groaned. Shut up, Caramon! his twin said mentally. Shut up and walk away!

Caramon was charmed by the attention, however. "Yes, I know everything there is to know about fighting. Tanis taught me."

"Tanis taught you, did he?" said the sergeant, leaning forward. His friends covered their mouths with their hands, rocked back on their heels, enjoying the sport. "And who would this Tanis be?"

"Tanis Half-Elven," said Caramon.

"An elf. An elf taught you to fight."

"Well, really, it was mostly his friend, Flint. He's a dwarf."

"I see." The sergeant stroked his grizzled chin. "An elf *and* a dwarf taught you to fight."

"Me and my friend Sturm. He's a Solamnic Knight," Caramon added proudly.

Shut up, Caramon! Raistlin urged silently, desperately.

"And then there was Tasslehoff Burrfoot," Caramon went on, not heeding his twin's mental command. "He's a kender."

"A kender." The sergeant was awed. "An elf, a dwarf, *and* a kender taught you to fight." He turned to his fellows, who were red-faced with suppressed laughter. "Boys," he said solemnly, "tell the general to resign. We have his replacement."

At this, one of the men groaned and stomped his foot, trying desperately to contain his mirth. The other lost his composure and had to turn his back. His shoulders shook, he wiped away the tears streaming down his cheeks.

"Oh, that won't be necessary, sir," Caramon hastened to assure them. "I'm not that good yet."

"Oh, so the general can stay?" the sergeant asked. One corner of his mouth twitched.

"He can stay," said Caramon magnanimously.

Raistlin closed his eyes, unable to watch anymore.

"Thank you. We appreciate it," said the sergeant with deep gratitude. "And now"—the sergeant looked at the list—"Caramon Majere—" He paused. "Or would that be *Sir* Caramon Majere?"

"No, I'm not the Knight," said Caramon, anxious that there should be no misunderstanding. "That was Sturm."

"I see. Well, take your place in line with the others, Majere," said the sergeant.

"But, I told you, you really don't need to waste time training me," Caramon said.

The sergeant stood up, leaned forward and said softly, "I don't want to make the others feel bad. They might get discouraged and quit. So just play along, will you, Sir Caramon?"

"Sure. I can do that." Caramon was accommodating.

"Oh, and by the way, Majere," said the sergeant, as Caramon was walking over to join his chagrined twin, "if the drillmaster—that would be Master Quesnelle—makes any mistakes, you be sure and tell him. He'll appreciate the help."

"Yes, sir. I'll do that," said Caramon. Smiling, he joined Raistlin. "Gee, that sergeant's a nice guy."

"You are the world's biggest idiot," Raistlin said softly, furiously.

"Huh? Me? What'd I do?" Caramon demanded, amazed.

Raistlin refused to discuss it, however. He turned his back on his twin to watch as Scrounger approached the table.

The sergeant eyed him. "Look, kid, why don't you run along home. Come back in ten years when you've grown up."

"I'm grown up enough," Scrounger said confidently. "Besides, Sergeant, you need me."

The sergeant rubbed his forehead. "Oh, yeah. Give me one good reason."

"I'll give you several. I'm a scrounger and a good one. Whatever you need, I can get it. What's more, I can climb any wall standing. I can fit into tunnels mice would refuse to enter. I'm quick and I'm fast and I'm good with a knife in the dark. I can walk through the woods so quiet that compared to me caterpillars make the ground shake. I can slip into a three-story window and take the golden locket from around milady's throat and kiss her into the bargain, and she'll never hear me or see me. That's what I can do for you, Sergeant," said Scrounger. "And more."

The veterans had quit laughing. They were regarding Scrounger with interest. So was the sergeant.

"And you can talk the wings off a fly." The sergeant gazed at the young man intently. "All right. Put your name down. If you live through training, you might be of some use to the baron after all."

Feeling a touch on his shoulder, Raistlin turned.

"You the mage?" asked the soldier unnecessarily, since Raistlin was the only man in the compound wearing wizard's robes. "Come with me."

Raistlin nodded and stepped out of line. Caramon stepped out after him.

"You a mage, too?" the soldier asked, coming to a halt.

"No, I'm a soldier. I'm his brother. Where he goes, I go."

"Not now, Caramon!" Raistlin said in a low voice.

The soldier shook his head. "I have orders to bring the mage. Take your place back in line, Puke."

Caramon frowned. "We're never separated."

"Caramon!" Raistlin turned to his twin. "You have shamed me enough this day. Do as you are told. Get back in line!"

Caramon's face went red, then white. "Sure, Raist," he mumbled. "Sure. If that's what you want. . . ."

"That is what I want."

Caramon, hurt, returned to line, took his place beside Scrounger.

Raistlin accompanied the soldier through the gate and into the baron's castle.

12

THE SOLDIER LED RAISTLIN INTO THE COURTYARD, WHICH WAS BUSTLING with activity. Soldiers stood about in groups laughing and talking, or squatted on the ground, playing at knucklebones, a game involving tossing the foot bones of a sheep up in the air and catching them in a prescribed fashion, or pitching coins against the side of a wall.

Grooms led horses into or out of stalls, dogs were everywhere underfoot. A servant had hold of a yelping kender by the ear and was dragging him out of the main entryway. Some of the soldiers cast curious glances at Raistlin as he passed, others rudely stared. Coarse comments accompanied him through the castle gate and into the courtyard.

"Where are we going, sir?" Raistlin asked.

"The barracks," said his guide, indicating a row of low stone buildings lined with windows.

The soldier entered the main door to the barracks, led Raistlin down a cool, dark hallway off which were the rooms where the soldiers billeted. Raistlin was impressed with the neatness and cleanliness of the building. The stone floor was still wet from its morning scrub-down, fresh straw had been spread on the floors of the sleeping rooms, bedrolls were tightly wrapped and stowed in an orderly manner. Each man's personal possessions were wrapped in his bedroll.

At the end of the hall they came to a set of stone stairs spiraling downward. The soldier descended the stairs. Raistlin followed along behind. At the end of the stairs stood a wooden door. Halting, the soldier gave a thunderous knock. There came a crash from inside, as of glass breaking.

"You whore's son!" yelled an irritated voice. "You've made me drop my potion! What in the Abyss do you want?"

The soldier grinned, winked at Raistlin. "I have the new mage, sir. You said I was to bring him here."

"Well, who the devil thought you'd be so blasted quick about it!" the voice grumbled.

"I can take him away, sir," said the soldier, speaking in respectful tones.

"Yes, do that. No, don't. He can clean up this mess, since he was the cause of it."

There came the sound of footsteps, a door bolt lifting with a clank. The door swung open.

"Meet Master Horkin," said the soldier.

Expecting a war wizard, Raistlin expected height, power, intelligence. He expected to be awe-inspired, or at least inspired. Lemuel's father had been a war wizard. Lemuel had often described his father, and Raistlin had discovered a portrait of him hanging in the Tower of High Sorcery—a tall man, with black hair streaked with white, a hawk nose and hawk eyes, and the long-fingered, slender-boned hands of the artist. That was his dream of what a war wizard would look like.

At the sight of the mage standing in the doorway, glaring at him, Raistlin's dream cracked down the center, spilling its contents in a flood of disappointment.

The mage was short, he came to about Raistlin's shoulder, but what he lacked in height he made up for in girth. He was relatively young, in his late forties, but there was not a hair on his head, not a hair anywhere, not an eyebrow or an eyelash. He was thick-necked, thick-shouldered, with ham-fisted hands—small wonder he had dropped the delicate potion bottle. He was red-faced, choleric, with fierce blue eyes whose blueness was emphasized by the redness of his face.

But it was not his odd looks that caused Raistlin to stiffen, caused his lip to curl. The mage—and to term him so was to pay him a compliment he likely did not deserve—wore brown robes. Brown robes—the mark of those who had never taken the Test in the Tower of High Sorcery, the mark of a mage who did not possess skill enough to pass or lacked the ambition to try to pass or was, perhaps, afraid. Whatever the reason, this mage had not committed himself to magic, had not given himself to it. Raistlin could have no respect for a man such as this.

He was consequently startled and piqued to see his own disdain reflected right back at him. The brown-robed mage was regarding Raistlin with no very amiable air.

"Oh, for Luni's sake, they've sent me a blasted Tower mage," Horkin growled.

To his deep chagrin, Raistlin was seized with a coughing fit. Fortunately it was short-lived, but it did nothing to impress Horkin.

"And a sickly one at that," he said in disgust. "What the hell are you good for, Red?"

Raistlin opened his mouth, proud to name his accomplishments.

"I'll bet you can cast a sleep spell," Horkin said, answering his own question. "A fine lot of good that'll do us. Give the enemy a nice little nap on the battlefield. They wake up refreshed and ready to slit our guts open. What the devil are you gawking at?" This to the soldier. "I assume you have work to do."

"Yes, sir, Master Horkin." The soldier saluted, turned, and departed.

Horkin grabbed hold of Raistlin's arm, yanked him inside the laboratory with a jerk that nearly took him off his feet, and slammed the door shut behind him. Raistlin looked around disparagingly, his worst fears realized. The so-called laboratory was a dark and shadowy subterranean room made of stone. A few battered spellbooks stood forlornly on a shelf. Various weapons hung on the wall—bludgeons, maces, a battered-looking sword, and some other wicked-looking implements Raistlin did not recognize. A beat-up, stained cabinet contained bottles filled with spices and herbs.

Horkin let go of the young mage, gazed at him speculatively, eyeing Raistlin as he might have eyed a carcass in the butcher's stall. He obviously did not think much of what he saw.

Raistlin stiffened beneath the insulting inspection.

Horkin put his meaty hands on his hips or at least in that general vicinity. He was built like a wedge, his shoulders and chest the most massive part.

"I am Horkin, *Master* Horkin to you, Red."

"My name is—" Raistlin began stiffly.

Horkin held up a warning hand. "I don't care about your name, Red. I don't want to know your name. If you survive your first three or so battles, then maybe I'll learn your name. Not before. I used to learn the names, but it was a goddamned waste of time. Soon as I'd get to know a puke, he'd up and die on me. These days I don't bother. Clutters up my mind with useless information."

His blue eyes shifted away from Raistlin.

"Now that is a damn fine staff," Horkin said, regarding the staff with far more interest and respect than he had regarded the young mage. Horkin reached out a thick-fingered hand.

Raistlin smiled to himself. The Staff of Magius knew its true and rightful owner, would not permit another to touch it. More than once, Raistlin had heard the crackle of the staff's magic, heard subsequent yelps and shrieks (mostly from kender) and seen the malefactor who had attempted to either touch the staff or make off with it wring a burned hand. Raistlin made no move to stop Horkin from seizing the staff, did not warn him.

Horkin took hold of the Staff of Magius, ran his hand up and down the wood, nodded approvingly at the feel. He held the crystal to his eye, examined it with one eye shut, peered through it. Holding the staff in two hands, he made a few passes with it, lunging out in a motion that stopped just short of cracking the amazed Raistlin in the ribs.

Horkin handed the staff back. "Well balanced. A fine weapon."

"This is the Staff of Magius," Raistlin said indignantly, holding the staff protectively.

"Oh, the Staff of *Magius*, is it?" Horkin grinned. He had a leering grin, thrusting out his lower jaw, with the result that his lower canines jutted up over his top lip. He moved closer to Raistlin to whisper. "I'll tell you what, Red. You can buy a dozen of those staves for two steel in any mageware shop in Palanthas."

Horkin shrugged. "Still, there is a mite of magic packed in that thing. I can feel it twizzle my hand. I don't suppose you have any idea of what the staff can do, do you, Red?"

Raistlin was too appalled to speak. Two steel in Palanthas! The magic—the powerful magic, the compensation given to Raistlin for his shattered body—dismissed as a "mite" that "twizzled"! True, Raistlin didn't yet know all the magic of which the staff was capable, but still—

"Thought not," said Horkin.

He turned his back, walked over to a stone table, and lowered his massive body onto a stool, which appeared incapable of supporting his weight. He placed a pudgy finger on the page of a leather-bound book that lay open on a stone table.

"I suppose there's no help for it. I'll have to start over again." Horkin motioned to a broken beaker that had spilled its contents over the stone floor. "Clean up the mess, Red. There's a mop and a bucket in the corner."

Anger seethed in Raistlin, bubbled over. "I will *not!*" he cried, thumping the toe of the staff into the stone floor to emphasize his ire. "I will *not* clean up your mess. I will not subordinate myself to a man who is beneath me. *I* took the Test in the Tower of High Sorcery! *I* risked my life for the magic! I was not afraid—"

"Afraid?" Horkin interrupted the torrent. He looked up from his perusal of the tome, grimly amused. "We'll see who's afraid, by Luni."

"When you are in my presence," said Raistlin coldly, nothing daunted, "you will refer to the goddess Lunitari with the respect she is due—"

Horkin could move rapidly for such a big man. One moment he was seated on the stool, the next he seemed to materialize right in front of Raistlin like some imp bursting up out of the Abyss.

"Listen to me, Red," Horkin said, jabbing his finger in Raistlin's thin chest. "First, you do not give me orders. I give you orders, and I expect you to obey those orders. Second, you will refer to me as Master Horkin or sir or master or master sir. Third, I can refer to the goddess any damn way I feel like. If I call her Luni it's because I have the right to call her Luni. Many's the night we've sat drinking together beneath the stars, passing the bottle, she and I. I wear her symbol over my heart."

He moved the finger from Raistlin's chest to his own, pointing at a badge with the symbol of Lunitari embroidered upon it, which he wore on his left breast, a badge Raistlin had not noticed. "And I wear her emblem around my neck."

Horkin drew forth a silver pendant from beneath his robes, held it up for Raistlin to see, shoving it in his face so that Raistln was forced to draw back to avoid having it jammed up his nose.

"Luni, the darling, gave me this with her own fair hands. I have seen her, I have talked to her." Horkins moved an impossible step closer, until he was practically standing on Raistlin's toes. The elder mage glared up at Raistlin, into him, through him.

"I may not wear her symbol," said Raistlin, standing his ground, refusing to fall back farther, "but I wear her color, which, as you have so astutely noted, is red. And she has spoken to me, as well."

Silence as charged as a thunderbolt crackled between them. Raistlin looked closely at the symbol of Lunitari. Made of solid silver, the symbol of the goddess was old, very old, and finely crafted, glimmered with latent power. He could almost believe that it had come from Lunitari.

Horkin looked closely at Raistlin, and perhaps the elder mage was thinking almost the very same thoughts as the younger.

"Lunitari herself has spoken to you?" Horkin asked, lifting the finger he'd been using to jab Raistlin, holding it in the air, pointing to the heavens. "This you swear?"

"Yes," said Raistlin calmly. "By the red moon, I swear."

Horkin grunted. He thrust his face another impossible inch nearer Raistlin. "Yes, *what*, soldier?"

Raistlin hesitated. He did not like this man, who was crude and uneducated, who probably did not possess a tenth of the magical power

Raistlin possessed, and who would, nonetheless, force Raistlin to treat him as his superior. This man had belittled Raistlin, had insulted him. For a kender copper, Raistlin would have turned and stalked out of the laboratory. But in that last question, Raistlin detected a change of tone, a subtle note—not a tone of respect but of acceptance. Acceptance into a brotherhood, a hard brotherhood, a deadly brotherhood. A brotherhood that, if it accepted him in turn, would embrace him and hold to him with fierce, undying loyalty. The brotherhood of Magius and Huma.

"Yes . . . Master Horkin," Raistlin said. "Sir."

"Good." Horkin grunted again. "I might make something of you, after all. None of the others have ever even known who I was talking about when I mentioned Luni, dear Luni."

He raised what would have been his eyebrows, if he'd had any eyebrows to raise. "Now, Red" —Horkin pointed at the broken beaker— "clean up the mess."

13

WAITING IN LINE WITH THE OTHER NEW RECRUITS IN THE HOT SUNSHINE, Caramon watched his brother depart with considerable anxiety. In situations like this—new and unfamiliar—Caramon felt oppressed and uneasy when separated from his twin. Caramon had become accustomed to looking to his brother for guidance, was uncertain and unsure when Raistlin was not with him. Caramon was also concerned about his weaker twin's health and even ventured to ask one of the officers if he might go see if his brother was all right.

"Since all we're doing is standing in line," Caramon added, "I thought I could go see if Raistlin—"

"You want your mommy, too?" asked the soldier.

"No, sir," Caramon replied, flushing. "It's just that Raist's not very strong—"

"Not very strong!" the officer repeated, amazed. "What did he think he was joining? The Fine Ladies of Palanthas Embroidery and Hot Muffin Society?"

"I don't mean he's not strong," Caramon said, attempting to correct his mistake, hoping fervently his twin never came to hear what he'd said. "He's very strong in magic. . . ."

The officer's expression darkened.

"I think you should be quiet now," Scrounger whispered at Caramon's elbow.

Caramon considered this excellent advice. He fell silent, and the officer, shaking his head and muttering, walked off.

When the new recruits had all made their mark or signed the roll sheet, the sergeant ordered Caramon and the other recruits to march into the courtyard of the castle. Shuffling their feet and tripping over one another, they entered the courtyard and lined up in wavering, uneven rows. An officer brought them to what passed for attention, subjected them to a long list of rules and regulations, the infraction of any of which would bring about all sorts of dire occurrences.

"They say the gods dropped a fiery mountain on top of Krynn," said the officer, summing up. "Well, that ain't nothin' compared to what you'll get from me if you screw up. And now Baron Langtree would like to say a few words. Three cheers for the baron!"

The recruits shouted lustily. The Mad Baron took his place before them. He was jaunty, cocky, his tall leather boots, which came up over his thighs, would have swallowed him, but for his large plumed hat. Despite the heat, he wore a thick, padded doublet. His black beard and mustache emphasized his wide grin, his long black hair curled on his shoulders. He bore an immense sword, which seemed always on the verge of tripping him or becoming entangled in his legs, but, miraculously, it never did. Putting his hand on the sword's massive hilt, the Mad Baron made his customary welcoming speech, which had the advantage of being short and to the point.

"You're here to join an elite force of fighting men and women. The best in Krynn. You look like a pretty scabby group to me, but Master Quesnelle here will do his best to try to turn you into soldiers. Do your duty, obey orders, fight bravely. Good luck to you all, and let me know where to send your pay in the event that you don't survive to collect it! Ha, ha, ha!" The Mad Baron laughed uproariously and, still laughing, walked back to the castle.

After that, the new recruits were each handed a small loaf of bread, which, though heavy and hard to chew, was surprisingly good, and a hunk of cheese. Devouring his food, Caramon considered it a good beginning and wondered when the rest of the meal was going to be served. He and his stomach were doomed to disappointment. The men were permitted to drink their fill of water, then the sergeant marched the recruits off to the barracks—low buildings made of stone with large rooms, the same buildings through which Raistlin had passed. The recruits were given sleeping rolls and other equipment, including boots. All that they received was marked down against their names, the money for their equipment would be docked from their pay.

"This is your new home," the sergeant announced. "It will be your home for the next month. You will keep it clean and tidy at all times." The sergeant cast a disparaging glance at the well-swept floor and the new straw that covered it.

"Right now," he announced, "it's worse than a pigsty. You will spend the rest of the afternoon cleaning up."

"Excuse me, sir," said Caramon, raising his hand in the air. He honestly thought the sergeant had made a mistake. Perhaps the man was nearsighted. "But the room is already clean, sir."

"You think that floor's clean, Majere?" the sergeant asked with deceptive solemnity.

"Yes, sir," said Caramon.

The sergeant reached out, grabbed a slop bucket from a corner, and dumped its foul contents onto the stone floor, soaking the straw that covered the floor.

"Now do you think the floor's clean, Majere?" the sergeant asked.

"No, but you—"

"No, what, Majere?" the sergeant roared.

"No, sir," said Caramon.

"Clean it up, Majere."

"Yes, sir," said Caramon, subdued. The other recruits were now mopping and scrubbing most industriously. "If I could have a mop, sir—"

"Mop?" The sergeant shook his head. "I wouldn't soil a good mop with this filth. A good mop's hard to come by. But you're different, Majere. You're expendable. Here's a rag. Get down on your hands and knees."

"But, sir—" Caramon grimaced. The smell was nauseating.

"Do it, Majere!" the sergeant shouted.

Trying to hold his breath to avoid the stench, Caramon took the rag and got down on his hands and his knees. He continued to hold his breath until he saw stars, then gulped in the quickest breath he could manage. The next moment he was reaching for the slop bucket, to deposit the contents of his stomach.

The floor was suddenly deluged with a flood of water, which effectively diluted the horrible smell, washed away much of the filth, and sloshed over the sergeant's boots.

"Sorry, sir," said Scrounger, looking apologetic.

"Let me wipe those off for you, sir," said Caramon, solicitously daubing at the toes of the wet boots with his rag.

The sergeant glared at the two of them, but there was a glint of laugher in his eyes and a hint of approval. Turning, he yelled at the other recruits, who were standing around, staring. "What the hell are you looking at? Get busy, the sorry lot of you! I want to be able to eat my dinner off this floor, and I want it clean before sundown!"

The recruits jumped to work. The sergeant strode out of the barracks, his face twitching in the grin he had worked hard to suppress. Discipline must be maintained.

The recruits removed the fresh straw, swept the floor with brooms made of rushes, poured water on the floor, mopped it until the stone was so clean that, as Caramon announced proudly on the sergeant's return, "You can see your face in it, sir!"

The sergeant grudgingly pronounced the work satisfactory. "At least until you're taught to do better," he added.

Caramon waited for the sergeant to announce that it was time to eat, either on the floor or off it, Caramon didn't care which, so long as he was given food and lots of it. The sergeant glanced at the setting sun, then glanced back thoughtfully at the men.

"Well, now, you're done early, so I'm going to give you a little reward."

Caramon smiled happily, anticipating extra rations.

"Pick up your bedrolls. Strap them to your back. Pick up your swords and your shields, put on your breastplates and your helmets, and"—he pointed to a hill in the distance—"run to the top."

"Why, sir?" Scrounger asked, interested. "What's up there?"

"Myself, with a whip," said the sergeant. Rounding on his heel, he caught hold of Scrounger's shirt and gave him a shake. "Listen to me, Puke. And this goes for all the rest of you." He glowered around at them, no hint of laughter in his eyes. "This is the first thing you will learn, and you will learn it now. When I give an order, you obey that order. You don't question it. We don't discuss it. We don't take a vote on it. You do it. Why? I'll tell you why. And this is the only time I will ever tell you why you are doing something.

"Because there will come a time when you're in battle, and the arrows are whistling around your ears, and the enemy is rushing down on you yelling and screaming like demons freed from the Abyss. The trumpets are shrieking, and hot, bloody metal slashes the air, and I'm going to give you an order. And if you take even one second to think about that order or to question that order or decide whether or not you're going to obey that order, you'll be dead. And not only will you be dead, but your buddies'll be dead. And not only will they be dead, but the battle will be lost.

"Now . . ." The sergeant let loose of Scrounger, dumped him on the stone floor. "Now, we'll start over again. Pick up your bedrolls. Strap them to your back. Pick up your swords and your shields, put on your breastplates and your helmets, and run to the top of that hill. You will notice," he added with a grin, "that I'm wearing my helm and my plate and carrying my sword and shield. Now, get those sorry asses moving!"

The order was obeyed, though with considerable confusion. None of the recruits had any idea how to fasten their bedrolls around their bodies. They fumbled at knots and, in several instances, watched in dismay as their bedrolls uncoiled out behind them. The sergeant went from man to man, bullying and shouting, but all the time instructing. Eventually, they were all more or less ready, with their helmets perched at odd angles on their heads, their swords clanking against their legs—occasionally tripping those unaccustomed to wearing a weapon—sweating under the heavy breastplates. Scrounger could not see from beneath his helmet, which was too large and fell down over his eyes, and he rattled around in the breastplate like a stick in an empty ale mug. The shield he carried dragged the ground.

Clad in his armor, his sword at this side, Caramon cast a longing, regretful glance in the direction of the eating hall, where he could hear the clatter of plates and smell the delicious odor of roast pig.

With a yell, the sergeant started his recruits on their way.

Night had fallen by the time they returned—at a run—from the hill. Six recruits had decided on the way that a military career was not for them, no matter how much it paid. They handed in their equipment—what they hadn't dropped on the trail—and limped, exhausted and footsore, back into town. The rest of the recruits staggered into the courtyard, where several collapsed and where several more learned why new recruits were termed "pukes."

The sergeant took a head count, discovered that two were missing. He shook his head and started out to see if he could find the bodies.

✲

"What's this?" The Mad Baron paused on his way from touring the camp to look at an unusual sight.

Flaring torches and a huge bonfire lit the compound. Into the light came a very large and muscular young man with curly brownish-red hair and a handsome, open face. This young man carried, slung over his shoulder, a very thin and scrawny young man, who still clung gamely to a sword he had clutched in one hand and a shield, which he held in the other and which knocked the big man in the back of the legs whenever he took a step. The two were the last to make it down the hill.

Upon reaching the other recruits, who stood at sagging attention, the big man deposited the smaller man gently on the ground. The smaller man staggered, almost fell, but—digging the end of the shield into the ground—he used his shield to prop himself up and managed a triumphant, if exhausted, smile. The big man, who had carried his own shield and sword as well as his comrade, took his place in line. He did not look particularly worn out or winded. He just looked hungry.

"Who are those two?" the baron asked the sergeant.

"Two of the new recruits, sir," said sergeant. "Just back from a run up old Heave-Your-Guts. I saw the whole thing. The boy there collapsed about halfway up the hill. He wouldn't quit, though. Got to his feet and tried again. Made it a few steps and down he went. Damned if he didn't stand up and make another go at it. It was then that the big guy grabbed hold of him, slung him over his shoulder, and hauled him up the hill. Hauled him back down, too."

The baron peered closely at the pair. "There's something odd about that boy. Does he look like a kender to you?"

"The good Kiri-Jolith protect us! I hope not, sir!" the sergeant said fervently.

"No, he looks more human," said the baron on reflection. "He'll never make a soldier. He's too little."

"Yes, sir. Shall I muster him out, sir?"

"I suppose you better. Still," the baron added, "I like his pluck. And that big man. I like his loyalty. Let the skinny fellow stay. We'll see how he does in training. He may surprise us all."

"He may, at that, sir," said the sergeant, but he did not look convinced. The baron's comment about kender had shaken the officer badly. He made a mental note to count the metal plates and the wooden spoons, and if there was one missing, by the gods, the skinny fellow was gone, pluck or no pluck.

The recruits were sent to their dinners. They staggered into the mess hall, where several fell asleep over the meal, too tired to eat. Not liking to see food go to waste, Caramon took it upon himself to eat their dinners for them. But even Caramon had to admit that the stone floor felt as good to him as the softest feather bed when he was finally permitted to lie down to sleep.

He had closed his eyes for only a moment, or so it seemed, when he woke to a trumpet blast that brought him sitting bolt upright on the straw-covered floor, his heart thudding. His fuddled brain had no idea where he was or what was happening or why it should be happening to him at this ungodly hour. The barracks was pitch dark. Outside the windows—slits cut into the stone walls—he could still see the stars, though there might have been the faintest hint of dawn in the paling night sky.

"Huh? What? What?" Caramon mumbled and lay back down.

Flaring torches lit the barracks room. The torches glowed ruddily on the faces of those carrying them, faces that were grinning and jovial.

"Reveille! Up and at 'em, you lazy rotters!"

"No! It's still night!" Caramon groaned and piled straw over his head.

A booted toe slammed into Caramon's midriff. He woke wide awake this time, woke with a grunt and whoof.

"On your feet, you sons of gully dwarves!" the sergeant roared in his ear. "You're going to start earning that five steel!"

Caramon sighed deeply. He no longer considered the amount he was being paid generous.

The stars had disappeared by the time the recruits had dressed themselves in worn blue-and-gray tabards, gulped a hasty and highly inadequate breakfast, and marched to the training grounds—a large field located about a mile from the castle. Seemingly as sleepy as the men, the sun peeped above the horizon for a few moments, then, as if tired out by the effort, crawled under a blanket of heavy gray clouds and went back to sleep. A soft, soaking spring rain pattered down on the metal helmets of the sixty men, who had been bullied and cajoled into forming three ranks of twenty men each.

The sergeant and his staff handed out equipment—a practice shield and wooden sword.

"What's this, sir?" Caramon asked, eyeing the wooden sword with disdain. Lowering his voice, he said in confidential tones, so that the other recruits wouldn't feel bad, "I know how to use a real sword, sir."

"You do, do you?" the soldier said, grinning. "We'll see."

"No talking in the ranks!" snapped out the sergeant.

Caramon sighed. Hefting the wooden sword, he was astonished to find that it weighed twice as much as a good steel blade. The shield, also weighted, was extremely heavy. Scrounger could barely lift the shield off the ground. A second soldier passed among the ranks, handing out battered arm bracers. Caramon's arm bracer would not fit over his large forearm. Scrounger's slid off and fell into the mud.

Once every man was more or less accoutered, the sergeant saluted an older man who was standing on the sidelines.

"They're all yours, Master Quesnelle, sir," said the sergeant in the same dour and hopeless tones he might have used to announce that plague rats had sneaked into the castle.

Master Quesnelle grunted. Walking slowly and deliberately through the rain, the master-at-arms took his place in front of the troops.

He was sixty years old. His beard and hair, flowing beneath his helm, were iron-gray. His face was scarred from sword and knife wounds, deeply tanned from years of campaigning. He, too, was missing an eye—a patch covered the empty socket. The other eye was deep-set and glittered beneath the shadow of his helm. The eye seemed to shine more brightly than a normal eye, as if it sparked for two. The master held in his hand the same wooden sword and the same practice shield as the men. He had a voice that could carry over the din of battle, could probably be heard over a kender reunion at a midsummer's fair.

Master Quesnelle studied the recruits, and his face grew grim.

"I'm told that some of you think you know how to use a sword." His single eye roved among them, and those it touched found it convenient to stare at their boots. Master Quesnelle sneered. "Yeah. You're all real tough bastards—every one of you. You remember one thing, and one thing only. You know *nothing!* You know *nothing,* and you know *nothing* until I tell you that you know something."

No one moved, no one spoke. The ranks, which had started relatively straight, now straggled all over the field. The men stood glumly, the heavy wooden swords in their sword hands, shields in the other, the rain dripping off the nose guards of their helms.

"I was introduced as Master Quesnelle. I am Master Quesnelle only to my friends and my comrades. You slugs will call me by my first name, which is Sir! Got that?"

Half the men in line, feeling the stinging eye upon them, said "Yes, sir" in despondent tones. The rest, not knowing that they were meant to answer, hastily threw in "Yes, sir" at the last moment, while one unfortunate made the mistake of saying, "Yes, Master Quesnelle."

Master Quesnelle was on him like a cat on a stinkbug. "You! What did you say?"

The poor fellow realized his error. "Yes, s-s-sir," he stammered.

Master Quesnelle nodded. "That's better. Just to impress that on your feeble mind, I want you to run around this field ten times, repeating to yourself, 'Sir, sir, sir.' Move!"

The recruit stared, his mouth opened. The sergeant loomed up in front of him, glaring. The recruit dropped his sword and shield to the ground and prepared to run.

The sergeant halted him, handed him his heavy sword and his very heavy shield. The recruit staggered off, began running around the perimeter of the training ground, yelling, "Sir, sir, sir" at intervals.

The master lowered his sword, the wooden blade dug into the ground.

"Did I make a mistake?" he asked, and he sounded almost plaintive. "I was under the impression you men were here because you wanted to be soldiers. Was I wrong?"

Master Quesnelle's eye ranged over the recruits, who shrank down behind their shields or tried to hide behind the men standing in front of them. The master frowned.

"When I ask a question, I want a battle roar back from you. Is that understood?"

Half the men caught on, responded with a growl. "Yes, sir."

"Is that understood?" the master bellowed.

This time the response was loud, unified, and direct. A great shout burst from the group. "Yes, sir!"

Master Quesnelle nodded briefly. "Well, it looks like we have some spirit here after all." He raised his wooden sword. "Do you know what to do with this?" he asked.

Several looked blank. A few, Caramon among them, remembered the drill and shouted back, "Yes, sir!"

Master Quesnelle appeared exasperated. "Do you know what to do with this?" he yelled, shaking his sword in the air.

The roar was near-deafening.

"No, you don't," he said calmly. "But you will by the time we're finished. Before you learn to use the weapon, you need to learn to use your body. Take your sword in your right hand. Place your right foot behind your left foot and put your weight on it. Bring your shield up like this." He lifted his shield in a defensive posture, held it to protect the vulnerable side of his body. "When I yell 'thrust,' you give me that roar, and you step forward and give the enemy in front of you a good running-through. You freeze in that position. When I yell 'recover,' you return to the ranks. Thrust!"

The master threw in the command on the heels of the word before it, tripping up all but the most attentive. Half the ranks thrust, and the others wavered, uncertain what to do. Scrounger was quick off the mark, and so was Caramon, whose blood was stirring and who was starting to enjoy himself. He stood in the second row on the end. His tabard hung on him like a dirty dishcloth, soaked through and chafing his arms. He gleefully thrust and yelled, and, after a moment, the rest of the ranks joined in.

"Freeze!" Master Quesnelle yelled. "Nobody move."

The recruits were poised at an awkward angle, holding their swords horizontal to the ground as if they had just made an attack. The master waited, looking them over complacently. Soon arm muscles began to burn, then to quiver trying to hold the weight of the heavy sword. Still no one moved. Caramon was starting to feel a bit of discomfort. He glanced at Scrounger, saw his friend's arm shaking, the sword wobbling. Sweat mingled with the rain. Scrounger clamped his teeth over his lower lip with the effort to hold the sword, whose tip was weaving and bobbing. Slowly the blade started to drop toward the ground. Scrounger watched in agony, helpless, his strength gone.

"Recover!" Master Quesnelle yelled.

Every man shouted in relief, the best battle yell any of them had made thus far.

"Thrust!"

Mercifully, the wait time before the recover was less.

"Recover!"

"Thrust!"

"Recover!"

Scrounger was gasping, but he held on to the sword grimly. Caramon was beginning to feel a bit worn. The man who had been running around yelling "sir" took his place back in line and began the exercise. After an hour, Quesnelle permitted the men to stand at the recover for a few moments, giving them time to catch their breath and ease their aching muscles.

"Now, do any of you slugs know why we fight in ranks?" the master asked.

Feeling that here was his chance to offer needed assistance to the master-at-arms, Caramon was the first to raise his sword in the air.

"So that the enemy can't break through and attack us from the side and rear, sir," Caramon replied, proud of his knowledge.

Master Quesnelle nodded, looked surprised. "Very good. Majere, isn't it?"

Caramon's chest swelled. "Yes, sir!"

Quesnelle extended his shield arm to one side, the arm holding his sword to the other. Keeping both arms fully extended—shield in one hand, sword in the other—he charged toward the front rank, who eyed him with trepidation, not knowing what to do, expecting him to halt when he reached them.

The master continued charging straight into the men. His shield flattened one recruit, who had not moved out of the way fast enough, the master's sword struck another full in the face. The master broke through the first rank and bore down on the second, who began ducking and dodging and trying to avoid being hit.

Master Quesnelle battered his way straight toward Caramon.

"You're in for it now," cried Scrounger, dropping down behind the huge shield.

"What'd I do?" Caramon demanded in dismay.

The master stood in front of Caramon, nose-to-nose, or rather, nose-to-breastbone. The master lowered his arms and glared up at Caramon, who had never been so frightened by anything in his life, not even a disembodied hand he had encountered at the Tower of High Sorcery at Wayreth.

"Tell me, Majere," the master shouted, "if these men are standing in ranks, how in the name of Kiri-Jolith did I just charge through them to get to you?"

"You're very good, sir?" was Caramon's weak reply.

Master Quesnelle held out his arms and turned. His shield whacked Caramon hard in the chest, knocked him backward. Quesnelle snorted and charged to the front, bashing and battering and scattering recruits as he went.

He turned to face the now disorganized company.

"I have just shown you why professional soldiers keep very tight ranks. *Tighten ranks! Move! Move! Move!*"

The men shuffled closer together until they stood shoulder to shoulder, the distance between shields only six inches at the maximum.

Master Quesnelle looked them over, grunted in satisfaction. "Thrust!" he shouted, and the exercise began again. "Recover! Thrust! Recover!"

The recruits kept this up for a good half-hour, then the master called a halt. The men stood at recover, bodies rigid. The rain had ceased, but there was no sign of the sun, which was apparently in no mood to rise any time soon.

Quesnelle extended his arms, sword and shield again, and hurled himself on the front rank. This time, the recruits were ready for him. The master's chest hit the center man's shield. He tried to go through, but the center man, exerting all his force, held the master-at-arms at a standstill. Quesnelle backed up a pace and tried to dodge between shields, but the men locked their shields in place.

The master retreated. Seemingly satisfied, he tossed his sword and shield onto the ground. The recruits relaxed, thinking the practice was at an end. Suddenly, without warning, the master turned on his heel, lurched forward and launched himself bodily straight into the front rank.

The front rank was startled but knew what to do. They brought their shields up to meet the master. He hit the front and fell back to stand before them. Quesnelle's single eye glinted.

"I think we may have some soldiers here after all."

Picking up his weapons, he took his place at the head of the company.

"Thrust!"

The men lunged forward in unison.

"Recover!"

The men fell back. Though tired, they were pleased with themselves, proud of the master's praise. It occurred to Caramon at that moment—and not before—to wonder what had become of his twin.

14

FOR A BENT PENNY, RAISTLIN WOULD HAVE WALKED AWAY, LEFT THIS army, left this town. He had spent his first night staring into the bleak darkness, toying with the temptation. The situation was intolerable. He had come here hoping to learn battle magic, and what did he find? A crude and bullying man who knew less about magic than Raistlin did, yet who was not the least impressed by Raistlin's credentials.

Raistlin had cleaned up the broken beaker and its sticky contents, which had a strong smell of maple syrup and which Raistlin more than half suspected of being intended for Horkin's supper. After that, Horkin took him to view their quarters.

Raistlin was more fortunate than his twin, in that he and Horkin spent the night in the castle, not in the barracks. Admittedly, they were quartered in a small dungeonlike room below ground level, but they were given cots, were not forced to sleep on the stone floor. The cot was not in the least comfortable, but Raistlin came to appreciate it as he heard the rats skittering and screeching in the night.

"The Mad Baron likes mages," Horkin had told his new subordinate. "We get better food than the soldiers, we're treated better, too. 'Course, we deserve it. Our work's harder and more dangerous. I'm the only mage left in the baron's company. He started out with six of us. Some of them real corkers, too. Tower mages, like yourself, Red. Ironic, ain't it? Old Horkin, the stupidest of them all, the only one to survive."

Though exhausted, Raistlin could not sleep. Horkin snored so loudly that Raistlin half-expected the castle's other inhabitants to come running to see if a quake were shaking the castle walls.

By midnight, he had resolved to leave the next day. He would find Caramon and together they would depart, head back . . . where? Back to Solace? No, out of the question. To go back to Solace would be to go back in defeat. But there were other towns, other castles, other armies. His sister had spoken often of a great army forming in the north. Raistlin played with that idea for a while, eventually abandoned it. To go north was to run into Kitiara, and he had no desire to see her. They might try Solamnia. The Knights were reportedly looking for warriors and would probably be glad to take Caramon. But the Solamnics did not take kindly to magi of any sort.

Raistlin tossed and turned on his cot, which was barely wide enough to accommodate his slender frame. Horkin overlapped his cot by about six inches all around. Lying there, listening to what sounded like rats chewing on the cot legs, Raistlin realized suddenly that he'd suffered only one severe coughing spasm all day. Generally, he could count on having five or more.

He pondered this. "Can this hard life actually be beneficial to me?" he wondered. "The damp, the cold, the foul water, the putrid swill they term food . . . I should be half-dead by now. Yet, I have rarely felt more alive. My breath comes easier, the pain in my lungs is diminished. I have not drunk my tea all day."

He reached down to touch the Staff of Magius, which he kept lying beside the bed, always close to hand. He felt the slight tingle in the wood, the warmth of the magic spread through his body. "Perhaps it is because for the first time in many months, I am not dwelling on myself," he admitted. "I have other things to think about than if I am going to be able to draw the next breath."

By the advent of dawn, Raistlin had decided to stay. At the very least, he might be able to learn some new spells from the little-used spellbooks he had seen standing on the shelves. He fell asleep to the sound of Horkin's rumbling snore.

That morning, Raistlin was ordered to perform yet more menial tasks—sweeping the laboratory, washing empty beakers in a tub of soapy water, carefully wiping the dust from the books on the shelves. He enjoyed the dusting, mainly because he had a chance to study the spellbooks, and he was impressed by some of what he found. His hopes had been revived. If Horkin was able to utilize these books, he might not be the amateur he appeared.

Raistlin's hopes were dashed almost the next moment, when Horkin appeared at his elbow.

"Quite a few spellbooks here," Horkin said carelessly. "I've read only one, couldn't make much sense of it."

"Why do you keep them, then, sir?" Raistlin asked in frozen tones.

Horkin shrugged and winked. "They'll make good weapons if we're ever besieged." Lifting one of the larger, thicker books, he thumped it disrespectfully. "Put one of these tomes in a catapult and launch it, and it'll do some damage, by Luni."

Raistlin stared, appalled.

Horkin chuckled, gave Raistlin a painful nudge in the ribs with an elbow. "I'm joking, Red! I'd never do anything like that. These books are too valuable. I could probably get—oh, six or seven steel for the lot. They're not mine, you know. Most were captured during the Alubrey expedition six years ago.

"Now, you take this fancy black one." Horkin removed a book from the shelf, stood looking at it fondly. "I took it from a Black Robe last campaign season. He was running fast—to the rear, mind you—but I guess he thought he needed to run a bit faster, 'cause he flung aside the book, which must have been weighing him down. I picked it up and brought it back."

"What spells does it contain?" Raistlin asked, his hands itching to snatch the book from his master's hands.

"Beats the heck out of me," Horkin said cheerfully. "I can't even read the runes on the cover. I never looked inside. Why waste my time with a bunch of gobbledygook? Must have some choice spells though. Maybe someday you can take a look at it."

Raistlin would have given up half the years of his life to be able to read that book. He could not make out the runes either, but with study he was certain he could come to understand them. Just as, with study, he could come to understand the spells inside the book, a book Horkin could never read. A book that was nothing more to him than the price of a mug of ale.

"Perhaps if you let me take it back to my quarters—" Raistlin began.

"Not now, Red." Horkin tossed the book carelessly back on the shelf. "No time to waste puzzling out Black Robe spells that you, being a Red Robe, probably couldn't use anyway. We're running low on bat guano. Scout around the castle walls and pick up all you can find."

Raistlin had seen the bats leaving the castle's towers last evening in pursuit of insects. He left in pursuit of the bats' droppings, the runes on the spellbook burning in his mind.

"You can never have too much bat guano," Horkin remarked on his way out with a wink.

Raistlin spent two hours picking up the poisonous bat guano and putting it into a bag. He was careful to wash his hands well, then reported back to the laboratory, where he found Horkin eating supper.

"You're just in time, Red," Horkin mumbled, crumbs from the maize bread dribbling from the corners of his mouth. He mourned the loss of the syrup he usually poured over the hard, dry, yellow mass. "Eat up." He gestured to a second plate. "You're going to need your strength."

"I am not hungry, sir," Raistlin said diffidently.

Horkin did not stop chewing. "That's an order, Red. I can't have you passing out in the middle of a battle 'cause your belly's empty."

Raistlin pecked at the maize bread, was surprised to find that it actually tasted good to him. He must be hungrier than he imagined. He ate two large hunks and ended by conceding that maple syrup poured over the bread would have made a treat. Their meal finished, he cleaned up the dishes, while Horkin puttered around in a corner of the laboratory.

"Well," Horkin said, when Raistlin had completed his task, "are you ready to begin your training?"

Raistlin smiled scornfully. He could not imagine that Horkin had anything to teach him. Raistlin guessed that the session would probably end with Horkin begging Raistlin to teach him. As to Horkin's story of the six deceased Tower mages who had gone before him, Raistlin didn't believe a word of it. It was simply not possible that an unschooled, itinerant magic-user could have survived where skilled, trained magi could not.

"Let me get my equipment," said Horkin.

Raistlin expected the magic-user to bring along spell components, perhaps a scroll or two. Instead, Horkin picked up two wooden dowels, two inches in diameter and three feet long. Grabbing a bundle of rags from the table, he stuffed the rags in a pocket of his brown robes.

"Follow me." He led Raistlin out into the rain, which had started again, after a brief letup. "Oh, and leave your staff here. You won't be needing it today. Don't worry," he added, seeing Raistlin hesitate. "It'll be safe enough."

Raistlin had not let the staff out of sight—and barely out of touch—since the day he'd received it from Par-Salian's hand. He started to protest, but then he thought how silly he would look, fussing over the staff like a mother afraid of leaving her newborn babe in the care of others. Raistlin leaned the staff against a wall on which hung some of the weapons, with the rather absurd notion (he blushed to think of it) that Magius's staff would feel at home in such martial company.

Pulling his cowl over his head, Raistlin slogged through the mud. A mile's walk brought them to the training grounds, where a company of soldiers were practicing at the far end of the field. The soldiers all wore the same blue-and-gray tabard, but Raistlin recognized Caramon, who stood head and shoulders above the rest. The soldiers didn't appear to be doing anything useful that Raistlin could see. Just yelling and jabbing with their swords and yelling some more.

The rain soaked through his robes. Soon he was shivering with the cold and was beginning to regret his decision to stay.

Horkin shook off the water like a dog. "All right, Red, let's see what they taught you in the mighty Tower of Wayreth."

He slashed the air with the two dowel rods, holding one in each hand, whipping them through the rain. Raistlin could not imagine what Horkin intended to do with the rods, which were not part of any spell that Raistlin could bring to mind. He was beginning to think that Horkin was slightly mad.

The war-mage turned and pointed to the opposite end of the field, a part far away from where the soldiers were lunging and yelling.

"Now, Red, what's one of your best spells, aside from sleep?" Horkin rolled his eyes.

Raistlin ignored the comment. "I am proficient in the launching of incendiary projectiles, sir."

"Incendi-whats?" Horkin looked bemused. He patted Raistlin on the shoulder. "You can speak Common, Red. We're all friends here."

Raistlin gave a deep sigh. "Magical bolts, sir."

"Ah, good." Horkin nodded. "Launch one of your bolts at the fence post on the far end of the field there. Do you see it?"

Raistlin put his left hand into the pouch he wore on the side of his belt, brought forth the small patch of fur—the spell component he would need to cast the spell. Locating the distant fence post, he withdrew into himself, seeking the words that would form the incantation necessary to produce a fiery bolt made of magic.

The next moment, he was on the ground, doubled over on his hands and knees, gasping for breath. Horkin stood over him with a dowel, which had just whacked Raistlin in the stomach.

Shocked by the painful and unexpected blow, Raistlin stared in blank astonishment, gasping for air and trying to calm his pounding heart.

Horkin stood over him, waiting, not offering to help. Eventually, Raistlin regained his feet.

"Why did you do that?" he demanded, shaking with anger. "Why did you strike me?"

"Why did you strike me, *sir?*" Horkin said sternly.

Raistlin, too furious to repeat the words, glared grimly at Horkin.

The war-mage lifted the dowel rod, used it this time as a pointer.

"Now you see the danger, Red. Do you think the enemy's going to stand there and wait while you go into a trance and sing 'la-de-da' and wiggle your fingers in the air and rub some fur on your cheek? Hell, no! You planned on casting the most powerful, the most perfect magical bolt that ever was, didn't you? You were gonna split that post in half, weren't you, Red? In reality, you cast nothing. In reality, you would have been dead, 'cause the enemy wouldn't be using a dowel rod. He'd be yanking his sword out of your scrawny belly.

"Lesson Number Two, Red—don't take too long to cast a spell. Speed is the name of the game. Oh, and Lesson Number Three—don't try to cast a complicated spell when there's an adversary breathing down your neck."

"I did not know you were an adversary, sir," Raistlin said coldly.

"Lesson Number Four, Red," Horkin said with a gape-toothed grin. "Get to know your comrades well before you trust your life to them."

Raistlin's stomach was sore, breathing was painful. He wondered if Horkin had cracked a rib, considered it likely.

"Try for the post again, Red," Horkin ordered. "Or if you can't manage to hit the post, somewhere in the general vicinity will be fine. Don't take all day."

Grimly, Raistlin clutched the bit of fur and tried to gather the words hastily in his mind.

Horkin lifted the other dowel rod, jabbed at Raistlin. The latter continued with his spell-casting, but then he saw, to his astonishment, a flicker of flame burst out of the base of the rod. The flame sizzled along the rod toward Raistlin, who tried desperately to ignore it. The flame neared the end of the rod.

His spell was almost complete. He was about to cast it when bright, blinding light flared. A loud bang nearly deafened him.

He flung up his arm to shield his face from the blast, only to see, out of the corner of his eye, Horkin swinging the other dowel rod. He struck Raistlin on the back, sent him sprawling facefirst into the mud.

Slowly, painfully, Raistlin picked himself up. His knees were scraped and bruised, his hands scratched. He wiped mud from his face and looked at Horkin, who was rocking back on his heels, mightily pleased with himself.

"Lesson Five, Red," said Horkin. "Never turn your back on an enemy."

Raistlin wiped mud and blood from his hands. He inspected the scratches, removed a small sharp pebble that had lodged beneath the skin.

"I believed that you skipped Lesson One, sir," Raistlin said, barely keeping his anger in check.

"Did I? Perhaps I did. Think about it," said Horkin.

Raistlin didn't want to think about it. He wanted to escape this crazed fool. There was no doubt in Raistlin's mind that Horkin was mentally deranged. Raistlin wanted to go back to a warm fire and dry clothes. He was certain he would catch his death out here in the wet. He would go find Caramon. Find Caramon and tell Caramon what this fiend had done to him. He had never seen Horkin cast the spell that blinded him.

Raistlin forgot his pain, forgot his discomfort. The spell! What was that spell? Raistlin didn't recognize it. He had no idea how it was cast. He had not seen Horkin reach for any spell components. He had not heard Horkin utter a word, recite any incantations.

"How did you do that spell, sir?" Raistlin asked.

Horkin's grin widened. "Well, now, so maybe there is a bit of magic you can learn from the sorry old mage who never took his Test. Stick with me this campaign season, Red, and I'll teach you all sorts of tricks. I'm not the last surviving mage in this gods-forsaken regiment because I was the best." He winked. "Just the smartest."

Raistlin had taken enough abuse. He started to turn away, when he felt Horkin's heavy hand upon his shoulder. Raistlin whipped around, anger cracking.

"By the gods, if you hit me again—"

"Simmer down, Red. I want you to look at something."

Horkin pointed to the training field. The recruits had been given leave to take a break, the men gathering around a water barrel. How they could possibly want more water was beyond Raistlin. The rain was falling harder. His robes were so wet that water ran in a steady trickle down his bare back. The recruits seemed to be in excellent humor, however, laughing and talking despite the rain.

Caramon demonstrated his sword technique, lunging out and falling back with such energy that he very nearly skewered Scrounger, who held his shield over his head, using it as a canopy to protect him from the rain. Horkin's expression altered, his bantering tone changed.

"We're an infantry regiment, Red. We fight. We die. Someday those men over there are going to be depending on you in battle. If you fail, you not only fail yourself, you fail your comrades. And if you fail them, they'll die. I'm here to teach you how to fight. If you're not here to learn how to fight, then just what the hell are you here for?"

Raistlin stood in silence, the rain thudding onto his wet robes, drumming on his head. Water dripped from his hair, hair that was prematurely white, a result of the terrors of the Test he'd undergone. Water ran down his hands, slender hands with long, nimble fingers, hands that shone with the sheen of gold, another mark of the Test. Yes, he had passed, but just barely. Though he could not remember all that had happened, he knew in his heart that he had come close to failing. He looked through the rain's gray curtain at Caramon, at Scrounger and the others whose names he did not know yet. His comrades.

Raistlin felt humbled. He regarded Horkin with new respect, realizing he had learned more from this man—this uneducated, low-level magic-user, whose kind is generally seen at fairs, pulling coins from their noses—than he had learned in all his years of schooling.

"I offer my apologies, sir," Raistlin said quietly. He lifted his head, blinked the rainwater from his eyes. "I believe that you have a great deal to teach me."

Horkin smiled, a warm smile. His hand exerted friendly pressure on Raistlin's shoulder, and Raistlin did not flinch away from the touch.

"We might make a soldier of you yet, Red. That was Lesson Number One. You ready to continue?"

Raistlin's gaze shifted to the dowel rods. He straightened his thin shoulders. "Yes, sir."

Horkin saw the look. Laughing, he tossed the dowel rods to the ground. "I don't think we'll be needing these anymore." He regarded Raistlin thoughtfully, then suddenly reached out and plucked the bit of fur, which Raistlin was still holding, from his hand.

"Now cast the spell."

"But I can't, sir," Raistlin protested. "I don't have another piece of fur, and that is the prescribed spell component."

Horkin shook his head. "Tsk, tsk. You're standing in the middle of a battle, being pushed and shoved from all directions, arrows whizzing over your head, men yelling and screaming. Someone jostles you, and down goes that bit of fur into the muck and blood, trampled beneath stomping feet. And you can't cast the spell without it." He shook his head again, sighed. "I guess you're dead."

Raistlin pondered. "I could try to find another bit of fur. Some soldier's fur cloak, perhaps."

Horkin pursed his lips. "The time is midsummer, you fight beneath the blazing sun. It's hot enough to roast a kender with your shield as a skillet. I don't think many soldiers are going to be wearing their fur cloaks into battle, Red."

"Then what do I do, sir?" Raistlin demanded, exasperated.

"You cast the spell without the fur," said Horkin.

"But it can't be done. . . ."

"It can, Red. I know because I've done it myself. I've always speculated," Horkin continued, musing, "that the old magi put that requirement in there as a bit of a wheeze. Or perhaps to give the fur trade in Palanthas a boost."

Raistlin was skeptical. "I've never seen the spell done without the component, sir."

"Well, now," said Horkin, "you're about to."

He lifted his right hand, muttered several words of magic, all the while twitching the fingers of his left hand in a complex pattern. Within seconds, a bolt of magic flame crackled from his fingers, flared across the field, and struck the fence post, setting it ablaze.

Raistlin gasped, amazed. "I did not think it possible! How did you manage to cast it without the fur?"

"I play a little trick on myself. That scene I described to you really happened to me once. An enemy arrow took the fur from my hand just as I was about to cast my spell." Horkin held out his hand, exhibited a long, jagged white scar, which ran across his palm. "I was scared and I was desperate and I was mad. 'It's just a stupid piece of fur,' I said to myself. 'I don't need it. By the gods, I can cast this spell without it!' " He shrugged. "And I did. Nothing has ever smelled quite so fine to me as burnt hobgoblin did that day. Now, you try it."

Raistlin peered across the field, and tried to mentally trick himself into believing that the fur was in his hand. He spoke the words, made the symbol.

Nothing happened.

"I don't know how you do it, sir," said Raistlin, chagrined, "but the rules of magic state—"

"Rules!" Horkin snorted. "Does the magic control you, Red? Or do you control the magic?"

Raistlin blinked, startled.

"Maybe I've misjudged you, Red," Horkin continued, a shrewd glint in his eyes, "but it's my guess that you've broken one or two rules before in your life." He tapped Raistlin's hand, tapped the golden skin that covered it. "If you never break rules, you're never punished. And it looks to me as if you've taken some punishment in your life."

Horkin nodded to himself, said softly, "Try it."

I control the magic, said Raistlin inwardly. *I* control the magic.

He raised his hand. Magic flared from his fingers, shot across the field. A second fence post burst into flame.

"That was fast!" Raistlin said, exhilarated.

Horkin nodded approvingly. "I've never seen it faster."

The recruits ended their practice for the day. They quick-marched down the road, chanting a cadence to keep in step.

"They're headed back for dinner," said Horkin. "We better go, too, otherwise there won't be any food left. You hungry, Red?"

To his vast astonishment, Raistlin—customarily a picky eater—was so hungry that even the thought of the tasteless stew served up by the camp cook was tantalizing. The two walked back across the muddy field, heading for the barracks.

"Begging your pardon, sir, but you didn't tell me the spell you used to distract me."

"You're right, Red," Horkin agreed. "I didn't."

Raistlin waited, but the mage just grinned to himself and said nothing.

"It must be a very complex spell," Raistlin observed. "The flame crawled along the wood rod, exploded when it reached the end. I've never heard of a spell like it. Is it one of your own magicks, sir?"

"You could say that, Red," said Horkin solemnly. He glanced sidelong at Raistlin. "I'm not sure you're ready for it."

Laughter, joyous laughter—laughter at himself of all things!—bubbled in Raistlin's throat. He forced himself to swallow the laugh, not wanting to disturb the mood, not just yet. He couldn't believe it, couldn't understand it. He had been beaten, mauled, mistreated, duped. He was covered with mud, soaked to the skin, and he'd never felt so good in his life.

"I believe that I am ready, sir," he said respectfully, and he meant it.

"Flash powder." Horkin cracked the two dowel rods together liked drumsticks, keeping his own cadence. "It wasn't a spell at all. You didn't know that, though, did you, Red? Fooled you completely, didn't I?"

"Yes, sir, you did," said Raistlin.

15

THE RAIN FELL IN SANCTION, FELL ON THE HOT LAVA FLOWING SLUGGISHLY and incessantly from the Lords of Doom, splashed with a hissing sound on the molten rock, and turned to steam. The steam coiled into the air, roiled around the ground; a thick fog hid the bridge guards from each other's sight, though they stood no more than ten paces from one another.

No training exercises this day. The men could not have seen their commanders, could not have seen each other. Ariakas had put them to work filling in the old latrines, digging new ones—a task where the less seen the better. The men would grumble, but it was a soldier's lot in life to grumble.

Ariakas sat in his command tent, writing out dispatches by the light burning from a wick set in a dish of tallow. Water leaked through the tent roof, dripped monotonously into an upended helm he'd placed under the drip to keep it from spreading over the tent floor. He wondered why he bothered. Due to the fog, his tent was almost as wet inside as out. The fog crept inside, licked its gray tongue over his armor, over the tent posts, over his chair and the table, left them glistening in the lamplight.

Everything was wet, damp, and gray. He could not tell what time of day it was, time had been swallowed up by the fog. Outside, he could hear the crunch of booted feet passing, men coming and going, cursing the rain and the fog and each other.

Ariakas paid them no attention, continued to work. He could have left this dripping tent, returned to the warmth of his office in the Temple of Luerkhisis. He might now be seated at his desk with a cup of hot mulled wine. He put the thought from his mind. Rarely did soldiers fight battles in warm, cozy rooms. They fought in the rain and the mud and the fog. Ariakas was training himself as much as his men, toughening himself to endure the rigors of campaign life.

"My lord." One of his aides knocked on the tent post.

"Yes, what is it?" Ariakas did not look up from his writing.

"That woman is back, my lord."

"What woman?" Ariakas was irritated at the interruption. These orders had to be clear and precise and detailed. He could not afford any mistakes. Not on this mission.

"The warrior woman, my lord," said his aide. "She asks to see you."

"Kitiara!" Ariakas looked up, laid down his pen. His work was not forgotten, but it could wait.

Kitiara. She had been on his mind ever since she'd left on her journey well over a month ago. He was pleased she had returned alive, though not particularly surprised, despite the fact that four others he'd sent to accomplish the same mission had either died or deserted. Kitiara was different, out of the ordinary. There was a sense of destiny about her, or so it seemed to him. He was gratified to find that he had been right.

Of course, she'd failed in her mission. That was only to be expected. The task on which he'd sent her had been impossible to achieve. He'd agreed to it merely to humor his Dark Queen. Perhaps now Takhisis would listen to him. Ariakas looked forward to hearing Kit's excuses. He considered it impressive that she'd had the courage to come back.

"Send her in at once," said Ariakas.

"Yes, my lord. She has a red-robed human magic-user with her, my lord," the aide added.

"She has *what?*" Ariakas was baffled. What would Kitiara be doing in the company of a red-robed wizard? And how dare she bring one into his camp? Who could it be? That half-brother of hers? After their first meeting, Ariakas had questioned Balif about Kitiara. The general knew that she had twin half-brothers, one of whom was a dolt and the other a young wizard, a Red Robe at that.

"He's a strange-looking cove, that one, my lord," said the aide, lowering his voice. "Red from head to toe. And something dangerous about him. The guards would have never permitted him to enter camp—in fact they wanted to slay him on the spot—but the woman protected him, insisted that she was acting on your orders."

Red . . . from head to toe . . .

"By our Queen!" Ariakas exclaimed, rising to his feet as the truth hit him a stunning blow. "Send them both to me at once!"

"*Both* of them, my lord."

"Both! Immediately!"

The aide departed.

Some time passed—the guards must have been holding the two down by the bridge. Then Kitiara entered the tent, ducking beneath the dripping flap. She smiled to see him, a smile that was wider on one side of her mouth than the other, a smile that showed a flash of white teeth on only one side. A crooked smile, as he had noticed the first time he'd seen her. A mocking smile, as if she were laughing at fate, daring it to do its damnedest. Her dark eyes met his. She informed him of her triumph in that one single glance.

"General Ariakas." She saluted him. "I have brought Lord Immolatus, as ordered."

"Well done, uth Matar," said Ariakas. "Or should I say, Regimental Commander uth Matar."

Kitiara grinned. "Thank you, sir."

"Where is he?"

"Outside, sir. He waits to be properly introduced."

She rolled her eyes, quirked an eyebrow. Ariakas took the hint.

Kit turned toward the entrance to the tent and bowed low. "General Ariakas, I have the honor to present His Eminence, Immolatus."

Ariakas gazed with some impatience at the tent flap. "His Eminence!" Ariakas snorted. "What's he waiting for?"

"Sir!" Kit whispered urgently, "I respectfully suggest that you should bow when he enters. He expects nothing less."

Ariakas frowned, crossed his arms across his massive chest. "I bow to no one except my Queen."

"Sir," Kit returned in a harsh whisper, "how badly do you want the services of this dragon?"

Ariakas didn't want the dragon's services at all. Personally he could have done quite well without them. Queen Takhisis had decided that Ariakas wanted the dragon. Ariakas, rumbling a growl, bent his body a fraction of a degree.

A human male dressed in long robes the color of flame entered the tent. Everything about him was red. His hair was fiery red, his skin had an orangish tint to it, his eyes were red as sparking cinders. His features were elongated, sharp, pointed—pointed chin, pointed nose. His teeth were also sharp and pointed and rather more prominent than was quite comfortable to look upon. He walked with slow and stately step. His red-eyed gaze, noting everything, was bored by everything he noted.

He gave Ariakas a disdainful glance. "Be seated," said Immolatus.

Ariakas was not normally accustomed to receiving orders in his own command tent and he very nearly choked on the rage that surged up from his belly. Kitiara's hand, cool and strong, closed over his wrist, exerted gentle pressure. Even in this critical moment, her touch aroused him. Water droplets glittered in her dark hair, her wet shirt clung tantalizingly to her skin, her leather armor glistened.

Later, Ariakas thought, and reminded by Kitiara's touch of the other woman in his life—Her Dark Majesty—he sat down in his chair. He eased himself slowly into the seat, however, slowly and deliberately, clearly implying that he sat down of his own volition, not because he was obeying Immolatus.

"Will you be seated, my lord?" Ariakas asked.

The dragon remained standing, which allowed him to look down his extraordinarily long nose at the mortals beneath him. "You humans have so many lords, so many dukes and barons, princes and kings. What are you, with your short and dreary lives, compared to me? Nothing. Less than nothing. Worm. Spelt with an 'o.' I am eminently superior. You will therefore refer to me as Eminence."

Ariakas's fingers curled in on themselves. He was fondly imagining those same strong fingers curling around His Eminence's neck. "My Queen, give me patience," he muttered and managed a dark-visaged smile. "Certainly, Your Eminence." He was wondering how he would explain the dragon's presence to his men. Rumor's black wings were probably already flapping around the campfires.

"And now," said Immolatus, folding his hands, "you will tell me this plan of yours."

Kitiara rose to her feet. "I am certain that you will excuse me, my lord—"

Ariakas caught hold of her forearm. "No, Commander uth Matar. You will remain."

Kitiara smiled on him, the crooked smile that was like fire in his blood, a fire that burned painfully in his groin.

"I am sending you on this mission, as well, uth Matar," Ariakas continued, relinquishing her reluctantly. "Close the tent flap. Tell the guards to form a perimeter around this tent, let no one pass." He cast a stern glance at both Kit and the dragon. "What I say in this tent goes no farther, on peril of your lives."

Immolatus was amused. "My life? Forfeit for a human secret? I should like to see you try!"

"The secret is not mine," said Ariakas. "The secret is Her Majesty's. Queen Takhisis. It is to Her Majesty you will be forced to answer if you permit the secret to escape."

Immolatus did not find this quite so amusing. His lip curled in a sneer, but he said nothing more, and he actually deigned to take a seat in a folding camp chair. The dragon leaned his elbow on General Ariakas's table, knocking the neat pile of dispatches onto the floor, and drummed his long, pointed fingers on the table, expressive of his extreme boredom.

Kitiara carried out her orders. He could hear her dismissing the guards, ordering them to form a perimeter around the tent some thirty paces away.

"Check to make certain there is no one outside," Ariakas commanded on her return.

Kitiara exited the tent again, made a complete circuit—he could hear her booted footfalls. She returned, shaking the water from her hair. "No one, my lord. You may proceed. I will keep watch."

"You can hear me from the tent flap, uth Matar?" Ariakas asked. "I do not want to raise my voice."

"My hearing is excellent, my lord," Kit replied.

"Very well." Ariakas was silent a moment. He frowned down at his disordered dispatches, sorting his thoughts.

Immolatus, his curiosity piqued by these precautions—as Ariakas had intended—was looking slightly less bored.

"Well, get on with it," the dragon growled. "The sooner I am able to abandon this weak and puny form I am forced to inhabit, the better."

"There is a city located in the very southernmost part of the Khalkist Mountains. The city is called by the somewhat prophetic name of Hope's End. It is inhabited by humans, and—"

"You want me to destroy it," said Immolatus with a flash of his sharp teeth.

"No, Your Eminence," said Ariakas. "Her Majesty's orders are quite specific. Only a few people, a very few, have been granted the knowledge that dragons have returned to Krynn. The day will come when Her Dark Majesty will permit you to unleash your fury upon the world, but that day is distant. Our armies are not yet trained, not yet prepared. The mission on which you are being sent is far more important than the mere destruction of a city. Your mission has to do"—Ariakas lowered his voice—"with the eggs of the dragons of Paladine."

The sound of that cursed name, the name of the god who reigned in heaven in opposition to Queen Takhisis, the name of the god of those who had done Immolatus so much damage, caused the dragon's flesh to twitch. He hissed in anger. "I do not permit that name to spoken in my presence, human! Speak it again and I will see to it that your tongue rots in your head!"

"Forgive me, Your Eminence," said Ariakas, undaunted. "I had need to speak it once, so that you could understand the gravity of the mission. I have no need to speak it again. According to reports from Her Majesty's clerics, the eggs of these dragons, which I shall henceforth refer to as 'metallic,' lie beneath the city of Hope's End."

Immolatus's red eyes narrowed. "What is this trickery, human? I have reason to know you are lying. Don't ask me to tell you how I know!" He raised a long-fingered hand. "Such knowledge is not for worms."

Ariakas was forced to exert all his self-control to keep from throttling his guest. "Your Eminence refers, no doubt, to the raid conducted by your kind upon the Isle of the Dragons in the year 287. A raid that did procure many eggs of the metallics. Many, but not all. It seems the metallics are not the fools we thought. They actually hid away some of the rarer, more precious eggs—those of gold and silver dragons."

"I am to destroy these eggs, then," said Immolatus. "It will be a pleasure."

"A pleasure deferred, I am sorry to say, Your Eminence," said Ariakas coolly. "Her Majesty has need of the eggs whole and intact."

"Why? For what purpose?" Immolatus demanded.

Ariakas smiled. "I suggest that you ask Her Majesty. If her *wyrms* require such information, I presume she will tell them."

Immolatus rose in anger, seeming to fill the tent with his swelling fury. Heat radiated from his body, warming the tent to such an extent that the water droplets on Kit's armor sizzled. Kitiara did not hesitate. Drawing her sword, she stepped between Ariakas and the dragon. Confident, self-possessed, she stood ready to defend her commander with her blade and with her body.

"His lordship meant no insult, Great Immolatus," said Kitiara, though it was quite plain that his lordship had.

"Indeed, I did not, Your Eminence," said Ariakas, taking his cue from Kit. Even in human form, the dragon could cast any number of potent magical spells. Spells that could set ablaze Ariakas, reduce his camp and the city of Sanction itself to smoldering ashes.

He could never win a war against this powerful, arrogant monster, but Ariakas was pleased with his small victory. It put him in a conciliatory mood. He could afford to humble himself. "I am soldier, not a diplomat, Your Eminence. I am accustomed to speaking bluntly. If I have offended, I did not intend it. You have my apology."

Somewhat appeased, Immolatus resumed his seat. The heat in the tent returned to a more comfortable level. Ariakas wiped the sweat from his face. Kitiara sheathed her sword and resumed her place at the tent flap as though she had done nothing remarkable or out of the ordinary.

Ariakas followed her movements, as graceful as those of a stalking cat.

Never had he known a woman like her! The lamplight glittered on her armor, cast dark shadows behind her, shadows that seemed to embrace her as he longed to embrace her. He ached to seize her, crush her to him, free himself of this pleasurable pain.

"Shall we get back to business?" Immolatus said. He was well aware of Ariakas's desire, scornful of the weakness of human flesh. "What does Her Dark Majesty require me to do with these eggs?"

Ariakas tamped down his lust. Anticipation would make the culmination that much more exciting.

"Her Majesty requests that you travel to Hope's End in company of one of my officers." Ariakas glanced at Kitiara, whose eyes flashed with pride and pleasure. "I am thinking of sending uth Matar, if you have no objections, Eminence."

"She is tolerable, for a human," said the dragon with a curl of his lip.

"Good. Once there, it will be your task to ascertain if the reports of the dragon eggs are true. It seems that though the clerics have strong evidence of the eggs' existence, the clerics cannot find them. The god whose name I may not pronounce has kept the knowledge of the whereabouts of these eggs concealed even from Her Majesty. Her Majesty believes that only another dragon can discover their whereabouts."

"And so she needs me to come in and do that which she cannot do herself," said Immolatus. A coil of smoke curled from one nostril, hung motionless in the thick and fetid air. "And what do I do once the eggs have been located?"

"You will return, inform me of the location and of the numbers and types of eggs you have found."

"And so I am to be Her Majesty's egg peddler!" Immolatus returned angrily. "A task any farm wench could perform!" He grumbled a bit, then added in growl, "I suppose there will be some fun. For, of course, you will want me to destroy the city and its inhabitants."

"Not exactly," said Ariakas. "True, no one must know about our search. No one must know the real reason you are in the city of Hope's End. But no one must know that dragons have returned to Krynn. The city will be destroyed, but it will be destroyed by other means, means less likely to draw attention to ourselves and to you, Eminence. We are therefore creating a diversion.

"Hope's End is just one city in the kingdom of Blödehelm. The king of Blödehelm, King Wilhelm, is now under the control of dark clerics. Acting on their 'advice,' he has imposed a tax upon the city of Hope's End, a completely unfair and ruinous tax, a tax that has the population rising up in revolt against him. King Wilhelm has requested that my armies aid him in quelling the revolt. We will be providing troops as requested. I will be sending in two of my newly formed regiments along with a mercenary force that King Wilhelm has hired—"

"Outsiders," said the dragon. "*Not* under your control."

"I am aware of that, Your Eminence," Ariakus returned testily, "but I do not yet have troops enough to obtain the objective. This is a training mission, as it is. I need the men blooded, and this war provides the perfect opportunity."

"And what is the objective? If we are not to destroy the city and butcher its inhabitants—"

"Ask yourself, Eminence. What purpose does a dead human serve? Nothing. He rots away, making a great stink and spreading contagion. Live humans, on the other hand, are extremely useful. The men work in the iron mines. The older children work in the fields. The young women provide my troops amusement. The very young and the very old obligingly die off, so one doesn't have to worry about them. Our objective, therefore, will be to capture the city and enslave its citizens. Once Hope's End is empty, Her Majesty may do what she will with the dragon eggs."

"And what of the mercenaries? Will they enslave or be enslaved? I should think they would be valuable to you, if you are, as *you* say, short on manpower."

The dragon was goading him, hoping to force him to lose his temper. Ariakas replied with deliberate calm, "The leader of these mercenaries is a Solamnic by ancestry. He knows King Wilhelm to be a man of honor and has been convinced that the cause for which he and his men fight is a good one. If this mercenary leader were to learn the truth, that he has been duped, he would be a threat to us. Yet, I need him. He is one of the best. He hires only the best soldiers—so my reports indicate. You see my predicament, Your Eminence."

"I do." Immolatus smiled, showing a vast number of sharp teeth, rather more teeth than was normal for a human.

"Once the city falls, these mercenaries are expendable." Ariakas waved a gracious hand. "I give them to you, Your Eminence. You may do with them what you wish . . . provided"—the hand became a warding hand—"that you do not reveal your true nature, your true form."

"You have taken most of the fun out of it," Immolatus complained petulantly. "Still, there is the challenge, the creative genius—"

"Precisely, Your Eminence."

"Very well." The dragon leaned back in his chair, crossed one leg over the other. "Now we can discuss my payment. I gather that this mission is of considerable importance. It must be worth a great deal to Her Majesty."

"You will be well rewarded for your time and trouble, Your Eminence," said Ariakas.

"How well?" Immolatus's eyes narrowed.

Ariakas paused, uncertain.

"If I may, my lord?" Kitiara intervened, her voice dark and sweet as chocolate.

"Yes, uth Matar?"

"His Eminence suffered a terrible loss during the last war. He was robbed of his treasure, while he was away fighting for Her Majesty's cause against the Solamnic Knights."

"The Solamnic Knights?" Ariakas frowned. He could not recall a war with the Solamnic Knights, who had fallen in disfavor and disrepute at the time of the Cataclysm and who had never really recovered their former glory. "What Solamnic Knights?"

"Huma, my lord," Kitiara said with a straight face.

"Ah!" Ariakas forced his mind to think more nearly along the lines of the long-lived dragon. Huma was a recent foe to Immolatus. "*That* Solamnic Knight."

"Perhaps Her Majesty might see fit to compensate His Eminence for at least some his loss—"

"*All* of his loss," Immolatus corrected. "I know the amount, down to the last silver chalice." Reaching into the sleeve of his robes, he withdrew a scroll, tossed it on the desk. "I have here an accounting. I want payment in kind, none of your steel coins. Filthy things, steel coins. Impossible to form into a really comfortable bed. And I don't trust steel to hold its value. Nothing is more reliable than gold. Nothing quite so suited to peaceful sleep as gold. Silver and precious gems are, of course, acceptable. Sign here." He indicated a line at the bottom of the document.

Ariakas frowned down at it.

"The city of Hope's End will undoubtedly have a considerable amount of treasure in its vaults, my lord," Kitiara hinted. "As well as what you will take from the merchants and the inhabitants."

"True," said Ariakas.

He had counted on that money for his treasury. Raising an army—an army capable of conquering all of Ansalon—was an expensive proposition. The wealth that would be handed over to this fool of an arrogant, greedy dragon would have forged a lot of swords, fed a lot of soldiers.

Provided he had a lot of soldiers to feed, which at the moment, he did not.

His Queen had promised him that more troops were coming. Ariakas was one of only a handful of people who knew of the secret experiments going on in the bowels of the mountains known as the Lords of Doom. He knew what the black-robed archmagus Drakart, the dark cleric Wyrllish, and the ancient red dragon Harkiel the Bender were attempting to create, perverting the eggs of the good dragons into creatures that would one day live to slay their unwitting parents.

Ariakas—a sometime magic-user himself—had his doubts as to the practicality of such an ambitious experiment. But if new troops, new and powerful and invincible troops, were to come from these dragon eggs, they would be worth the price of handing over a city's treasure.

Ariakas scrawled his name on the line. Rolling up the scroll, he handed it back to Immolatus. "My army is on the march. You and uth Matar will leave in the morning."

"I am prepared to depart immediately, sir," said Kitiara.

Ariakas frowned. "I said you would leave *in the morning*." He placed strong emphasis upon the words.

Kitiara was respectful but firm. "His Eminence and I should travel under the cover of darkness, sir. The fewer who see us the better. His Eminence attracts a considerable amount of attention."

"I can imagine," Ariakas muttered. He eyed Kitiara. He wanted her so badly, the pain was unendurable. "Your Eminence, would you be so kind as to wait a moment outside. I want a word in private with uth Matar."

"My time is valuable," said the dragon. "I agree with the female. We should set out immediately."

He rose majestically to his feet. Gathering his robes in one hand, he swept out of the tent, paused at the entrance to glance behind. He raised the scroll, pointed it at Ariakas. "Do not test my patience, worm." He departed, leaving behind a faint smell of sulfur.

Ariakas seized Kitiara around the waist, pressed her body against his, nuzzled her neck.

"Immolatus is waiting, sir," said Kitiara, allowing herself to be kissed but again not yielding.

"Let him wait!" Ariakas breathed, his passion overtaking him.

"You will not like me like this, sir," Kit said softly, seductively, even as she fended off her seducer. "I will bring you victories. I will bring you power. No one and nothing will be able to withstand us. I will be the thunder to your lightning, the smoke to your devouring fire. Together, side by side, we will rule the world."

She put her hand over his questing lips. "I will serve you as my general. I will honor you as my leader. I will lay down my life for you, if you require it. But I am master of my love. No man takes by force what I do not choose to give. But know this, my lord. When I surrender to you at last, our pleasure on that night will be well worth the wait."

Ariakas kept firm and painful hold on her for another instant. Slowly he released her. He found pleasure in bed, but he found far more pleasure in battle. He enjoyed all aspects of war: the strategy, the tactics, the buildup, the clash of arms, the exhilaration of overcoming a foe, the final triumph. But the sweet feeling of victory came only when he fought a foe as skilled as himself, defeated an opponent worthy of his steel. He took no real pleasure in butchering unarmed civilians. Likewise, he found no real pleasure in making love to slaves, women who yielded to him out of terror, who lay shivering in his arms, limp and lifeless as corpses. In love as in war, he wanted—he needed—an equal.

"Go!" he said to Kitiara gruffly, turning aside, turning his back on her. "Go now! Leave while I am still master of myself!"

She did not leave immediately, did not flaunt her victory. She lingered. Her hand caressed his arm. Her touch sent fire through his veins.

"The night I return in victory, my lord, I am yours." She kissed his bare shoulder, then left him, opening the tent flap and slipping out into the rain to join the dragon.

That night, to the astonishment of his servants, Lord Ariakas took no woman to his bed. Nor did he, for many nights to come.

16

THE TWINS' TRAINING CONTINUED WITHOUT LETUP, WEEK AFTER WEEK. The food was monotonous, the training monotonous, the same practice day after day, until Caramon could have performed the maneuvers while sleepwalking with a bag over his head.

He knew this because they were up so early every morning, he felt as if he were sleepwalking, and one day Master Quesnelle ordered bags to be put over their heads and told them to go through the same drill—thrust, recover, thrust, recover. Except by this time, they'd added pivot left, pivot right, lockstep, sidestep, retreat in formation, lock shields, and a whole host of other commands.

Not only did they drill every day, they cleaned their barracks every day, hauling off the straw from the day before, mopping the stone floor, shaking out their blankets, and replacing the straw. They bathed every day in a cold, rushing stream—a novelty to some of the men, who took baths once a year on Yule whether they needed it or not. One symptom of the Mad Baron's madness was that he insisted that cleanliness of the body and the living environs reduced the possibility of disease and the spread of fleas and lice—the soldier's customary companions.

The men marched up and down Heave Gut hill every day, carrying their heavy packs and weapons. Every man could make it now without difficulty, with the exception of Scrounger. His body was too light, and though he did as Caramon advised and ate twice as much of the tasteless, monotonous food as any other man in the ranks, Scrounger did not gain in either height or bulk. He refused to admit defeat. Every day he collapsed in a gasping heap on the trail, half-buried beneath his shield, but Scrounger was always proud to point out that he'd gone "quite a bit farther today than yesterday, Master Quesnelle, sir."

The master-at-arms was impressed with Scrounger's spirit. Quesnelle confided to the Mad Baron in the weekly commanders' and officers' meeting that he wished to the gods the lad's body was as big as his heart.

"The men like him, and they cover for him, especially the big guy, Majere. He carries Scrounger's pack when he thinks I'm not looking. He holds back when they fight one on one or pretends that the little fellow's struck a blow that would have served an ogre proud. I've turned a blind eye to it so far. But there's no way he will make a foot soldier, my lord," said the master, shaking his head. "His friends are doing him no favors. He'll end up getting himself and the rest of us killed."

The other officers agreed, nodding their heads. The weekly meetings were held in the baron's castle, in an upper-level room that provided a fine view of the parade ground below, where the troops could be seen working on their equipment, oiling the leather straps to keep them supple, making certain that the sharp eyes of the sergeants could not detect a speck of rust on sword or knife.

"Don't muster him out yet," said the baron. "We'll find something for him to do. We just have to figure out what it is. Speaking of weaklings, how is our new mage shaping up, Master Horkin?"

"Better than expected for a Tower mage, Baron," Horkin replied, comfortably settling his bulk in his chair. "He seems a sickly chap. I passed through the mess hall the other night and heard him coughing until I thought he would hack up a lung. When I spoke to him about his illness, suggested that he was too weak to be part of my army, he gave me a look that shriveled me to ashes and swept me into the dustbin."

"The other men don't like him, my lord, and that's a fact," said Master Quesnelle, his expression dark. "I don't much blame them. Those eyes of his give me the creeps. He has a way of looking at you as if he sees you lying dead at his feet and he's about to throw dirt into the grave. The men say"—the master lowered his voice—"that he's bartered his soul in the marketplace of the Abyss."

Horkin laughed. Folding his hands calmly over his rotund belly, he shook his head.

"You may laugh, Horkin," said the master-at-arms dourly, "but I'm warning you that I think it likely one day we'll find your young mage lying dead in the forest with his head on backward."

"Well, what do you say, Horkin?" The baron turned to the

master-at-wizardry. "I admit that I agree with Quesnelle. I do not much like this mage of yours."

Horkin sat up straight. His keen blue eyes boldly confronted each of the officers, not sparing the baron.

"What do I say, sir?" Horkin repeated. "I say that I never knew the army was a midsummer's picnic, my lord."

The baron was perplexed. "Explain yourself, Horkin."

Horkin coolly obliged. "If you're holding a contest to name the Queen of the May, my lord, then I admit that my young mage will not be a candidate. But I don't think you want the Queen of the May joining us in battle, do you, my lord?"

"That's all very well, Master Horkin, but his sickness—"

"Is not of the body, my lord. It is not catching," said Master Horkin, "nor is it curable. No, not even if the clerics of old were to return and place their healing hands upon him and call on the power of the gods could they restore Raistlin Majere to health."

"Is the sickness magical in nature?" The baron frowned. He would have been more comfortable with an ordinary, run-of-the-mill plague.

"It is my belief, my lord, that the young man's sickness *is* the magic!" Horkin nodded sagely.

The commanders and officers were dubious, they shook their heads and grumbled. Horkin's forehead furrowed in thought, furrowed so deeply that it seemed to draw his whole scalp into the process. He looked to the master-at-arms.

"Quesnelle, you wanted to be a soldier all your life?"

"Yes," said the master, wondering what this had to do with anything. "I guess you could say I've *been* a soldier all my life. My mother was a camp follower, my cradle was my father's shield."

"Just so." Horkin nodded again. "You wanted to be a soldier from childhood up. You, like our lord here, are a Solamnic by birth. Did you never think of becoming a Knight?"

"Naw!" Quesnelle appeared disgusted.

"Why not, if I may ask?" Horkin asked mildly.

Quesnelle considered. "Truth to tell, such a thing never crossed my mind. For one, I was not of noble birth—"

Horkin waved that aside. "There have been Knights in the past who were not of noble birth, who rose through the ranks. Legend says that the great Huma himself was one of these."

"What has this to do with the mage?" Quesnelle demanded irritably.

"You will see," said Horkin.

Quesnelle looked at the baron, who quirked a black eyebrow, as much as to say, "Humor him."

"Well"—Quesnelle's brow furrowed—"well, I guess that the main reason would be that when you're a Knight you have two commanders. One's a flesh-and-blood commander, and the other commander is a god. And you have to answer to both of them. If you're lucky, they both agree. If you're not . . ." Quesnelle shrugged. "Which do you obey? The torment of that question can rip a man's heart in two."

"True," murmured the baron, almost to himself. "Very true. I had never thought it about like that before."

"Me, I like my orders coming from only one place," said Quesnelle.

"I feel the same," said Horkin, "and that is why I am, in the ranks of magic, a humble infantryman. But our young mage, he's a Knight."

The baron's black eyebrows shot up into his thick curling black hair.

"Oh, I don't mean literally, my lord." Horkin chuckled. "No, no. The Solamnics would curl up and die first. I mean that he is a knight of magic. He hears two voices calling to him—the voice of man and the voice of the god. Which of them, in the end, will he choose to follow? I don't know. If, indeed, he chooses either of them," Horkin added, scratching his hairless chin. "I wouldn't be surprised to learn that he ends up turning his back on both, walking his own road."

"Yet, you've tipped a bottle with the goddess yourself from time to time, I believe," said the baron, with a smile.

"I am an acquaintance, my lord," Horkin replied gravely. "Raistlin Majere is her champion."

The baron was silent a moment, digesting this. "Let us return to our original discussion. Do you think it advisable for me to keep Raistlin Majere in my employ? Will he be of benefit to this company?"

"Yes and yes, my lord," said Horkin stoutly.

"Master-at-arms?" The baron looked to Quesnelle. "What do you say?"

"If Horkin vouches for the mage and will keep an eye on him, then I have no objection to his remaining," said Quesnelle. "I'm just as glad of it, in fact, for if the one twin left, we should lose the other. And Caramon Majere is shaping into a fine soldier. Far better than he gives himself credit for. I was thinking of transferring him to Flank Company."

He cast a glance at Master Senej, the commander of Flank Company, who nodded, interested.

"So be it," said the baron. He reached for the pitcher of cold ale that always ended the officers' meeting. "By the way, gentleman, we have our marching orders for our first battle."

"Where is that, my lord?" both officers asked eagerly. "And when?"

"We leave in two weeks' time." The baron poured the ale. "We are marching at the request of King Wilhelm of Blödehelm, a fine king, a good king. A city under his rule has been taken over by hotheaded rebels, demanding that they be permitted to break away from Blödehelm and become an independent city-state. The rebels have, unfortunately, convinced most of the citizens to join them in their cause. King Wilhelm is gathering his own forces, he will be sending in two regiments to deal with the rebels. We will be there to assist. His hope is that once they see the force of our might arrayed against them, the rebels will realize that they cannot win and give up."

"A damn siege," said Quesnelle grumpily. "Nothing I hate worse than a boring old siege."

"There may be hot work for us yet, Master," said the Mad Baron soothingly. "According to my sources, the rebels are the type who would rather die fighting than be hung for traitors."

"Come now," said Quesnelle, brightening. "That's more like it! What do we know about these other two regiments?"

"Nothing." The baron shrugged. "Nothing at all. I guess we'll find out when we get there." He winked. "If they're not any good, we'll show them how to fight." He raised his ale mug. "Here's to Hope's End."

"What?" The commanders stared, dismayed.

"That's the name of the city, gentlemen," said the baron with a grin. "Hope's End for our enemies!"

The commanders drank the toast—and many more after that—with relish.

17

GOOD NEWS, RED," SAID HORKIN, ENTERING THE LABORATORY, MORE OR less steady on his feet. He smelled very strongly of ale. "We have our marching orders. Two weeks we leave." He heaved a beery sigh. "That doesn't give us much time. Lots of work to do between now and then."

"Two weeks!" Raistlin repeated, feeling a little flutter in his stomach. He told himself the flutter was excitement and it was—partly. He looked up from the mortar and pestle he was wielding. His assigned duty this day was to grind up spices, which were to be used by the cook for their meals. Raistlin wondered why he bothered. Thus far the most exciting thing he'd found in his rabbit stew—which appeared to be cook's only known recipe—had been a cockroach. And it was dead. Probably of food poisoning.

"What is our objective, sir?" he asked, proudly using the military term he'd learned from the Magius book.

"Objective?" Horkin wiped the back of his hand across his mouth, mopping up the froth that still lingered on his lips. "Only one of us needs to know the objective, Red. And that's me. All you need to know is to go where you're told, do what you're told, when you're told to do it. Got that?"

"Yes, sir," Raistlin replied, swallowing his ire.

Horkin was perhaps hoping to set the young mage off so that he would have a chance to slap him down again. The knowledge helped Raistlin exert unusual self-control. He went back to pounding his spices, putting such effort into it that the cinnamon sticks smashed into bits, filling the air with their pungent scent.

"Pretending that's me in there, eh, Red?" Horkin asked, chuckling. "Want to see old Horkin smashed into a pulp, do you? Well, well. Put away the spices for today, Blasted cook! I don't know what he does with them anyway. Probably sells them. I know darn good and well he doesn't cook with them!"

Muttering, he waddled over to the shelf where the spellbooks stood, newly dusted, and reached up an unsteady hand to grasp the "fancy black one" as he termed it. "Speaking of selling things, I'm headed into town to the mageware shop to sell these books. Now that I have a Tower mage to read that black book for me, I want you to examine it and tell me how much you figure I should ask for it."

Raistlin clamped his teeth over his lips to keep his frustration from bursting out. The book was far more valuable for its spells than the piddling amount Horkin was likely to receive for it at the Langtree mageware shop. Shopkeepers generally paid little for spellbooks belonging to the followers of Nuitari, god of the Dark Moon, mainly because they were difficult to resell. Few black-robed wizards had the temerity to walk boldly into a shop and browse through the spellbooks belonging to their kind, spellbooks dealing with necromancy, curses, tortures, and other evils.

Like other wizards, Black Robes were well aware that truly powerful spellbooks were not likely to be found in mageware shops. Oh, you would hear tell now and then of a wizard who happened across a wondrous spell-book of old, lost to the ages, lying forgotten under a layer of dust on the shelf of some backwater shop in Flotsam. But such occurrences were rare. A wizard who wanted a powerful spellbook did not waste his time going from shop to shop, but traveled to the Tower of High Sorcery at Wayreth, where the selection was excellent and no questions were asked.

Horkin tossed the spellbook down upon the laboratory table and spent a moment admiring it—the spoils of battle—his bald head cocked to one side. Raistlin gazed at the book as well, but with a critical eye and a ravening curiosity to see what wonders it might contain. The thought occurred to him that perhaps he could buy it from Horkin himself, save up his pay until he was able to afford it.

There was small chance he would be able to read any of the spells yet, spells that were undoubtedly far too advanced for him. And most of the spells, especially the spells of evil, were spells he had no intention of casting. But he could always learn from the book. All spells—good, bad, and indifferent—were constructed using the same letters of the magical alphabet, which went together to form the same words. It was the way those words were spoken and arranged that affected the spellcasting.

He had another reason for wanting to study this spellbook. The book had been in possession of a Black Robe war wizard. Raistlin might have to someday defend against these very spells. Knowing how a spell was constructed was essential to knowing how to deconstruct it or how to protect oneself from its effects. All sound reasons. But, as Raistlin was forced to admit to himself, the true reason he was interested in this book was his passion for knowledge of his art. Any source—even an evil source—that would provide such knowledge was precious in his sight.

The book was quite new. The black leather of its binding was still shiny and showed few signs of wear. And the book's binding was fancy. Horkin's word was an apt description. The binding of most spellbooks was plain and unostentatious. Those who made them did not intend that they should attract the eye and hand of every curious kender. Far from it. Spellbooks were quiet, unassuming, glad to fade into the shadows, hoping to remain hidden, overlooked.

This book was different, The words, "Book of Arcane Lore and Power" were stamped in garish silver on the front in the Common language for anyone to read. The symbol of the Eye—a symbol sacred to magic-users— was embossed in each of the four corners, embellished with gold leaf. It was surrounded by the runes Raistlin had noted earlier, runes of magic. A red ribbon marker flowed from the closed tome like a rivulet of blood.

"If the inside's as pretty as the outside," said Horkin, reaching out his hand to open it, "perhaps I'll keep it just for the pictures."

"Wait, sir! What are you doing?" Raistlin demanded, putting out his own hand to stop Horkin's.

"I'm going to open the book, Red," said Horkin, impatiently shoving Raistlin's hand away.

"Sir," said Raistlin, speaking hurriedly and with the utmost respect, but also the utmost urgency, "I beg you to proceed cautiously. We are taught in the Tower," he added, in apologetic tones, "to test the magical emanations of any spellbook before attempting to open it."

Horkin snorted and shook his head, muttering beneath his breath about "highfalutin foolery," but seeing that Raistlin was adamant, the elder mage waved his approval. "Test away, Red. Mind you, just so you know, I picked the book up from the battlefield and carried it around for weeks, and it did no harm to me. No fiery jolts or anything like that."

"Yes, sir," said Raistlin. He smiled slyly. "Lesson Number Seven. It never hurts to err on the side of caution."

He stretched out his hand, held his hand over the book, about a finger's breadth from the surface, careful not to touch the binding. He held his hand there for a count of five indrawn and exhaled breaths, opening his mind, alert for the smallest sensation of magic. He had seen the magi in the Tower of High Sorcery at Wayreth practice this skill, but he had never had a chance to try it himself. Not only was he eager to see if this procedure worked, but there was something about this book he found disconcerting.

"How very odd," Raistlin murmured.

"What?" Horkin asked eagerly. "What? Do you feel anything?"

"No, sir," said Raistlin, frowning with puzzlement, "I don't. And that's what I find odd."

"You mean there's no magic at all in there?" Horkin scoffed. "That doesn't make any sense! Why would a Black Robe carry around a spellbook that had no spells in it!"

"Exactly, sir," Raistlin insisted. "That's why it's odd."

"C'mon, Red!" Horkin said, elbowing Raistlin out of the way. "Forget that Tower malarkey. The best way to find out what's inside the damn thing is to open it—"

"Sir, please!" Raistlin went so far as to close his gold-skinned, slender hand over Horkin's browned and pudgy wrist. Raistlin eyed the book warily, with increasing suspicion. "There is a great deal that I find disturbing about this book, Master Horkin."

"Such as?" Horkin was clearly dubious.

"Think about it, sir. Have you ever before known a war wizard to cast down his spellbook? His *spellbook*, sir—his only weapon! To let it fall into the hands of his enemy! Is that likely, sir? Would you do that yourself? It would be tantamount to . . . to a soldier throwing down his sword, leaving himself defenseless!"

Horkin appeared to consider this argument. He glanced askance at the book.

"And there is this, sir," Raistlin continued. "Have you ever seen a spellbook that so blatantly announces it is a spellbook! Have you ever seen a spellbook that advertises its mysteries to all and sundry."

Raistlin waited tensely. Horkin was staring at the book, intently now, scowling, his mind not so befuddled with ale that he could not follow his apprentice's reasoning. He removed his hand from book's binding.

"You're right about one thing, Red," said Horkin. "This blasted book *is* decked out fancier than a Palanthas whore."

"And for perhaps the same reason, sir," said Raistlin, trying hard to keep the proper note of humility in his tone. "Seduction. May I suggest that we practice a little experiment on the volume?"

Horkin was clearly disapproving. "More Tower magic?"

"No, sir," said Raistlin. "No magic at all. I will need a skein of silken thread, sir, if you have some handy."

Horkin shook his head. He seemed on the verge of opening the book just to prove that he was not going to be counseled by some upstart young pup. But, as he had told Raistlin, he had not survived in this outfit by being stupid. He was willing to concede that Raistlin had advanced some cogent arguments.

"Confound it!" Horkin grumbled. "Now you've got me curious. Carry on with your 'experiment,' Red. Though where you'll find silk thread around an army barracks is past my understanding!"

Raistlin already knew where to look for silk thread, however. Where there were embroidered insignia, there had to be silk embroidery thread.

He went to the castle, begged a skein from one of the housemaids, who gave it to him readily, asking him, with a simper and a giggle, if the rumors were true, was he really twin to the handsome young soldier she'd seen on parade and, if he was, would he would please tell his brother that she had a night off every second week.

"Got your thread? Now what?" Horkin asked on Raistlin's return. The elder mage was clearly beginning to enjoy himself—perhaps with the thought of the young mage's eventual discomfiture. "Maybe you're thinking of taking the book into a field and flying it, like one of those kender kites."

"No, sir," Raistlin said. "I am not going to 'fly' it. However, the suggestion of a field is an excellent idea. We should conduct this experiment in a secluded place. The training ground where we practice our magic would be ideal."

Horkin heaved an exaggerated sigh and shook his head. He started to reach for the book, halted. "I guess it'll be safe enough to carry it? Or should I fetch the fire tongs?"

"The fire tongs will not be necessary, sir," said Raistlin, ignoring the sarcasm. "You have carried the book before now without harm. However, I would suggest that you put the book into a conveyance of some sort. Perhaps this basket? Just to prevent its being opened accidentally."

Chuckling, Horkin lifted the book—handling it gingerly, Raistlin noted—and placed it gently into a straw basket. But Raistlin heard the elder mage mutter as they were leaving, "I hope no one sees us! Proper fools we must look, walking about with a book in a basket."

Due to the officers' meeting, the troops were not practicing this day. They had spent the morning cleaning their equipment. Now they were scrubbing down and whitewashing the outside walls of the barracks. Raistlin saw Caramon, but he pretended not to see Caramon's waving hand or hear his cheerful yell, "Hey, there, Raist! Where you going? On a picnic?"

"That your brother?" Horkin asked.

"Yes, sir," Raistlin answered, staring straight ahead.

Horkin swiveled his thick neck to take another glance. "Someone told me you two were twins."

"Yes, sir," Raistlin said evenly.

"Well, well," said Horkin, glancing at the young mage. "Well, well," he said again.

Arriving at the training ground, the mages discovered to their disappointment that the field was not deserted as they had anticipated. The Mad Baron was in the field practicing.

Mounted on his horse, a lance in his hand, the baron had leveled his lance and was riding straight at an odd-looking contraption consisting of a wooden crosspiece mounted on a base in such a way that it would swivel when hit. A battered shield had been nailed to one of the arms of the crosspiece. A large sandbag swung from the opposite end.

"What is this, sir?" Raistlin asked.

"The quintain," said Horkin, watching with pleasure. "The lance must strike the shield just so or— Ah, there, Red. That's what happens."

The baron missed his aim, struck the shield a glancing blow, and was now picking himself up off the ground.

"You see, Red, if you miss hitting the shield squarely, the off-center blow causes the sandbag to whip around and hit you squarely between the shoulder blades," said Horkin, when he could speak for laughter.

The baron uttered some of the most colorful and original expletives Raistlin had ever been favored to hear and stood rubbing his rump. His horse gave a low whinny that sounded very much like a snicker.

The baron fished a sodden pulpy mass from his pocket, a mass that had once been an apple, but which his fall had squashed flat. "You will suffer as I do, my friend," he said to the horse. "This would have been yours had we hit the mark."

The horse eyed the mashed fruit with distaste, but was not too proud to accept it.

"That machine will be the death of you, yet, my lord!" Horkin called out.

The Mad Baron turned, not at all disconcerted to find that he had an audience. He left his horse to munch on the maltreated apple and limped over to converse.

"By the gods, I smell like a cider press!" Baron Ivor looked back at the quintain, shook his head ruefully. "My father could hit dead center every time. Instead, it hits me dead center every time!" He laughed heartily at himself and his failure. "All that talk about knights put me in mind of him. I thought I would come out and set up the old machine, give it a tilt."

Raistlin would have died of shame had he been caught in such an undignified position by underlings. He was beginning to understand how the Mad Baron came by his appellation.

"But what are you up to, Horkin? What's in the basket? Something good, I hope! A little wine, maybe, some bread and cheese! Good!" The Baron rubbed his hands. "I'm starving." He peered into the basket, raised an eyebrow. "Doesn't look very appetizing, Horkin. Cook's given you worse than usual."

"Don't touch it, sir," Horkin was quick to warn. At the baron's querying glance, the warmage's face flushed. "Red here thinks that maybe there's more to this Black Robe's spellbook than meets the eye. He's"—Horkin jerked a thumb at Raistlin—"going to conduct a little experiment on it."

"Are you?" The baron was intrigued. "Mind if I watch? It's not any sort of wizardly secret stuff, is it?"

"No, sir," said Raistlin.

He had been plagued by self-doubt ever since they left the castle grounds, had been on the verge of admitting that he'd been mistaken. The book looked so very innocent riding along in the basket. He had no reason to suspect it was anything other than what it purported to be. Horkin had lugged it around and nothing untoward had happened to him. Raistlin was going to look a fool, not only in front of his commander—who already had very little use for him—but now in front of the baron, who might be mad but whose respect Raistlin was suddenly fiercely desirous of earning. He was about to humbly admit he'd been mistaken and to retreat with what dignity he had remaining, when his gaze fell once again on the book.

The spellbook with its gaudy cover and gilt-leaf edges and blood red ribbon . . . a Palanthas whore . . .

Raistlin seized hold of the basket. "Sir," he said to Horkin, "what I am about to do might be dangerous. I respectfully suggest that you and His Lordship remove yourselves to that stand of trees. . . ."

"An excellent idea, my lord," said Horkin, planting his feet firmly and crossing his arms over his chest. "I'll join you there myself in a moment."

The baron's black eyes sparked, his grin widened, his teeth gleamed stark white against his black beard. "Let me move my horse," he said and dashed away, stiffness and soreness forgotten in the prospect of action.

He led the horse at a running trot to the grove of trees, tied the animal to a branch and ran back, his face aglow with excitement. "Now what, Majere?"

Raistlin looked up, surprised and gratified that the baron had actually remembered his name. He hoped fervently that the baron would remember that name after all this was over, remember with something other than laughter.

Seeing that neither Horkin nor the baron was going to take his advice and retreat to a place of safety, Raistlin reached with extreme care into the basket, lifted the spellbook. For just an instant, he felt a tingle in the nerve endings of his fingers. The tingle dissipated rapidly, leaving him to doubt that he had felt it at all. He paused a moment, concentrating, but the tingle did not return, and he was forced to conclude, with an inward sigh, that he had felt it only because he wanted so desperately to feel it.

He laid the book down on the ground. Removing the skein of silk thread from a pocket, Raistlin formed a loop in the end of the thread. Moving with extreme caution, trying to refrain from lifting the book's cover, he prepared to pass the loop around the upper right-hand corner of the binding. The work was delicate. If what he suspected was right, the least false move might be his last.

He was alarmed to notice his fingers trembling, and he forced himself to calm down, to clear his mind of fear, to concentrate on the task at hand. Holding the loop of thread around his thumb and the first and second finger of his right hand, Raistlin slowly, slowly, slowly slipped the thread between the cover and the first page. He held his breath.

A rivulet of sweat trickled down the back of his neck. To his horror, he felt his chest close, felt a hacking cough rise up, ready to seize him by the throat. He choked it back, half-strangling, and, exerting all the control he possessed, held the thread steady. He slid the thread over the corner, secured it, and quickly drew back his hand.

The tightness eased, the need to cough passed. Looking up, he saw Horkin and the baron watching in tense anticipation.

"Now what, Majere?" the baron asked, his voice hushed.

Raistlin drew in a shaky breath, tried to speak, but found his voice was gone. He cleared his throat, rose trembling to his feet.

"We must go back to the trees," Raistlin said. Reaching down, he very gently lifted the skein of thread, began to carefully unroll it. "Once we have reached safety, I will open the book."

"Here, let me unroll the thread, Majere," the baron offered. "You look about done in. Don't worry, I'll be careful. By Kiri-Jolith," he said, backing up, allowing the thread to slide through his fingers, "I didn't know you wizards led such exciting lives. I thought it was all bat shit and rose petals."

The three reached the stand of trees, where the horse stood grazing and rolling its eyes as if it thought every one of them deserved to bear the baron's moniker. "We should be safe enough. What do you think might happen, Horkin?" The baron put his hand to his sword hilt. "Shall we be fighting a flock of demons from the Abyss?"

"I have no idea, my lord," Horkin replied, reaching into his pouch for a spell component. "This is Red's show."

Raistlin had no breath left to comment. Kneeling down, so that he was level with the book, he slowly and carefully tugged on the thread until it was taut in his hand. Raistlin looked around, motioned with his hand for the officers to crouch down. They did so, their mouths agape with wonder and excitement and expectation, their weapons ready in their hands.

Holding his breath, Raistlin said to himself, "Now or never" and pulled on the silk thread. The loop tightened around the corner of the book, held it fast. Working carefully, so as not to dislodge the thread, Raistlin tugged on the silk. The book's cover began to rise.

Nothing happened.

Raistlin continued to pull on the thread. The cover opened. He held the cover upright. The cover remained in that position, wavering a moment, and then fell. The silk thread slipped off the corner. The spellbook was open, its flyleaf, with large letters done in gold and red and blue inks, as gaudy as the front cover, winked derisively in the slanting sunlight.

Raistlin lowered his head so that the two men could not see his shame-filled face. He looked back at the book—sitting there so calmly, so benignly—with hatred. Behind him, he heard Horkin give an embarrassed cough. The baron, heaving a sigh, started to stand up.

A slight breeze ruffled the pages of the book . . .

The force of the blast knocked Raistlin backward into Horkin and flattened the baron against a tree. The horse neighed in terror, jerked loose his tether, and galloped off for the safety of his stall. He was a battle-trained horse, but he was used to screams and shouts and blood and clashing swords. He could not be expected to put up with exploding books. Or if he was, he deserved something a damn sight better than mashed apple.

"Lunitari take me," said Horkin in awe. "Are you hurt, Red?"

"No, sir," said Raistlin, his head ringing from the blast. He picked himself up. "Just a little shaken."

Horkin staggered to his feet. His normally ruddy face was gray and moist as clay on the potter's wheel, his eyes wide and staring. "To think I carried that . . . that thing around with me . . . for days!"

He looked at the gigantic hole blown in the ground and sat down again quite suddenly.

Raistlin went to assist the baron, who was trying to extricate himself from the smashed branches of the young tree he had taken down in his fall.

"Are you all right, my lord?" Raistlin asked.

"Yes, yes, I'm fine. Damn!" The baron drew in a breath, heaved it out in a gusty sigh. He stared out across the field. Wisps of smoke from the blackened grass drifted past on the breeze. "What in the name of all that is holy and all that is not holy was that?"

"As I suspected, my lord, the book was trapped," Raistlin said, trying, but not succeeding, in keeping the triumphant tone out of his voice. "The Black Robe placed the deadly spell inside the book, then surrounded the lethal spell with another spell that effectively shielded the first. That's why neither Master Horkin nor myself"—Raistlin felt he could be generous in victory—"could sense the magic emanating from it. I guessed that it must take the opening of the book to activate the spell.

"What I didn't realize," he admitted, his pride deflating a bit, "was that lifting the cover itself would not activate the spell. Pages had to be turned as well, probably a certain number of pages. Of course, now that I think about it, that would be only logical."

Raistlin gazed out at the blackened grass, at the bits of ash, all that was left of the book, floating in the air. "A very elegant weapon," he said. "Simple, subtle. Ingenious."

"Humpf!" Horkin growled. Recovering from his shock, he walked out with the baron and Raistlin to inspect the damage. "What's so blamed ingenious about it?"

"The very fact that you carried the book away, sir. The Black Robe could have arranged for the spell to go off the moment you picked it up, but he didn't. He wanted you to take the book back to camp, take it among your own troops. Then, when you opened it . . ."

"By Luni, Red! If what you say is true"—Horkin passed a trembling hand over a brow now daubed in cold sweat—"we've all had a narrow escape!"

"It would have killed a lot of men," the baron agreed, peering into the deep hole. He clapped his arm affectionately around Horkin. "Not to mention my best mage."

"One of your best mages, my lord," said Horkin, giving Raistlin a nod and an expansive grin. "One of them."

"True," said the baron, and he reached out to shake Raistlin by the hand. "You've more than earned a place among us, Majere. Or perhaps"—he looked at Horkin and winked—"I should say 'Sir Majere.'"

The baron straightened, turned to see his horse disappearing down the road. "Poor old Jet. Books exploding under his nose. He'll be halfway to Sancrist by now. I best go see if I can find him and calm him down. A pleasant evening to you, gentleman."

"And to you, my lord," said Horkin and Raistlin, both bowing.

"Red, I've got to hand it to you," said Horkin, draping his arm companionably around Raistlin's shoulders. "You saved old Horkin's bacon. I'm grateful. I want you to know that."

"Thank you, sir," said Raistlin, adding modestly, "I have a name, you know, sir."

"Sure you do, Red," said Horkin, giving him a slap on the shoulder that nearly bowled him over. "Sure you do."

Whistling a merry tune, Horkin lumbered off after the baron.

18

"WAKE UP, LITTLE BOYS!" CAME A LILTING, MOCKING FALSETTO VOICE. "Up, little boys, and greet the new day!" The voice altered to a gravelly shout, "I'm your mamma now, lads, and mamma says it's time to wake up!"

Well aware that a swift kick to his behind was the sergeant's gentle means of prodding his recruits to action, Caramon rolled out of his bedding, scattering straw left and right, and jumped to a standing position. Around him, men scrambled to obey. The barracks was still dark, but birds were up already—the fools—which meant that dawn was not far off.

Caramon was used to waking early. Many and many were the days of his youth when he'd rolled out of bed before even the birds were awake to trudge to the farm fields, timing his arrival just as dawn was breaking in order to lose none of the precious daylight. But Caramon never left his bedroll, never left his mound of straw, without deep regret.

Caramon loved sleep. He savored it. He craved it. Caramon had come to the conclusion long ago that a person spent more time sleeping than doing anything else in this life and therefore, Caramon decided, he should be good at it. He practiced at it all he could.

Not so his twin. Raistlin actually seemed to resent sleep. Sleep was some wicked thief, sneaking up on him before he was ready, stealing the hours of his life from him. Raistlin was always up early in the morning, even on holidays, a phenomenon Caramon couldn't understand. And many were the nights Caramon had found his twin slumped over his books, too tired to remain awake, yet refusing to deliver up his precious time to the stealthy robber, forcing sleep to wrestle him into submission.

Rubbing his eyes, trying to goad his mind, still relishing a pleasant dream, into wakefulness, Caramon thought sadly that for a man who enjoyed sleeping, he'd picked the wrong career. When he was a general himself someday, he'd sleep until noon, and anyone who would dare wake him would get a poke in the ribs . . . a poke in the ribs . . .

"Caramon!" Scrounger was poking him in the ribs.

"Huh?" Caramon blinked.

"You were sleeping standing up," Scrounger said, regarding his friend with admiration. "Like a horse. Sleeping standing up!"

"Was I?" Caramon asked with pride. "I didn't know a person could do that. I'll have to tell Raist."

"Helmets, shields, and weapons!" the sergeant bawled. "Outside in ten minutes."

Scrounger yawned a huge yawn.

It didn't seem possible a fellow that skinny could open his mouth that wide. "You're going to split your head in half if you do that too much," Caramon said worriedly.

"Majere," said the sergeant in a nasty tone, "are you going to favor us with your presence today? Or do you plan to spend the day filling in the latrines!"

Caramon dressed quickly, then donned his helmet, strapped on his sword belt, and hefted his shield.

The recruits dashed outside just as the first rays of light straggled past some low-lying clouds on the horizon. They lined up on the road in front of the barracks, forming three ranks. They'd done the same every morning since they had arrived, and by now they were good at it.

Master Quesnelle strode out to take his place in front of the assembled soldiers. Caramon waited expectantly for the order to march. The order did not come.

"Today, men, we are dividing you into companies," the master-at-arms announced. "Most of you will remain with me, but some of you have been chosen to join Company C, the skirmishers, under the leadership of Master Senej. When I call out your name, take two steps forward. Ander Cobbler. Rav Hammersmith. Darley Wildwood." The list continued. Caramon stood in semiwakefulness, letting the sun warm muscles stiff from sleeping on the stone floor. He wasn't expecting to be called. Company C was where they sent the very best men. Caramon started to drift off.

"Caramon Majere."

Caramon woke with a start. His feet took two practiced and precise steps forward, acting in advance of his sleep-fuddled brain. He glanced sidelong at Scrounger, smiled, and waited for them to call his friend's name.

Master Quesnelle rolled up the list with a snap. "Those men whose names I have just called, fall out and report to Sergeant Nemiss over there." The master pointed to a lone soldier standing in the middle of the road.

The other recruits wheeled expertly and marched off. Caramon remained where he was. He looked unhappily back at Scrounger, whose name had not been called.

"Go on!" Scrounger urged him, not daring to speak aloud but mouthing the words. "What are you doing, you big idiot? Go!"

"Majere!" Master Quesnelle's voice grated. "Have you gone deaf? I gave you an order! Move that big ass of yours, Majere!"

"Yes, sir!" Caramon shouted. He wheeled, stepped out, and with his left hand grabbed hold of Scrounger by the collar of his shirt. Lifting the young man off his feet, Caramon brought Scrounger along with him.

"Caramon, what— Caramon, stop it! Caramon, lemme go!" Scrounger twisted and pulled, trying desperately to break Caramon's hold, but he could not free himself of the big man's firm grasp.

Master Quesnelle was just about to come down on Caramon with the cold force and fury of an avalanche, when he caught sight of the Mad Baron, standing in the background, watching with interest. The Mad Baron made a small sign with his hand. Master Quesnelle, turning red in the face, snapped his mouth shut.

Caramon marched double-quick time. "You forgot to call his name out, sir," he said in meek, apologetic tones as he hastened past the irate master-at-arms.

"Yes, I guess I did," Quesnelle said, grumbling.

The rest of the company carried on with the normal routine: morning run, breakfast, basic maneuver practice. The twelve recruits whose names had been called stood rigidly at attention in front of their new officer.

Sergeant Nemiss was a medium-sized woman with the dusky black complexion of those who came from Northern Ergoth. She had luminous brown eyes and a sweet, pretty face, which, as the new recruits were about to discover, had nothing whatsoever to do with her true personality. Sergeant Nemiss was, in fact, a mean drunk with a fiery temper, continually getting into brawls—one reason she was a sergeant and would remain a sergeant for the rest of her days.

Sergeant Nemiss stood and stared at the twelve—thirteen, counting Scrounger—for a good long time. Her gaze fixed on poor Scrounger, who withered beneath it. The sergeant's expression didn't alter, except perhaps to grow rather sorrowful. "You," she said, pointing, "stand over there."

Scrounger gave Caramon a look and a smile, which said, "Well, we tried."

He marched out to stand by himself at the side of the road.

Sergeant Nemiss shook her head and turned back to face the rest.

"You men have been chosen to join my company. Master Senej commands the company. I am his second-in-command. It is my job to train any new recruits in Master Senej's company. Do I make myself clear?"

The twelve yelled out, "Yes, sir!" in unison. Scrounger started to say, "Yes, sir," from force of habit but dried up when the sergeant glared at him.

"Good. You men have been chosen not because you're better than the rest but because you're not as bad as the rest." Sergeant Nemiss scowled. "Don't get it into your fat heads that this means you're good. You're not good until I tell you you're good, and just standing here looking at you reprobates, I can tell right away that you're not even good enough to lick the boots of good soldiers."

The recruits stood sweating in the sun, not saying a word.

"Majere, fall out. The rest of you, go back to the barracks, gather up your things, and meet me here in five minutes. You're all moving to Master Senej's company barracks. Questions? Good, now move! Move! Move! Majere, over here."

The sergeant motioned Caramon to come stand beside Scrounger, who smiled hesitantly, ingratiatingly, and hopefully at the officer.

Sergeant Nemiss was not impressed. She eyed them both, particularly Scrounger, taking in his slender build, his quick, long-fingered hands, his unfortunately slightly pointed ears. Sergeant Nemiss's frown deepened.

"Just what the hell am I supposed to do with you—what's your name?"

"Scrounger, sir," said Scrounger in respectful tones.

"Scrounger? That's not a name!" The sergeant glowered.

"It's my name, sir," said Scrounger cheerfully.

"And that's what you can do with him, sir," said Caramon. "Scrounger here's an expert at scrounging."

"Stealing, you mean," said the sergeant. "I'll have no thieves in my outfit."

"No, sir," said Scrounger, shaking his head emphatically, keeping his eyes straight ahead as he'd been taught. "I don't steal."

The sergeant stared meaningfully at Scrounger's ears. Scrounger shifted his glance sideways, focused on the sergeant for an instant. "I don't 'borrow' things, either, sir."

"He's a scrounger, sir," said Caramon helpfully.

"You'll forgive me, Majere," said the sergeant, looking exasperated, "if I don't understand just what that term means or how the devil it's going to be of any use to me!"

"It's really pretty simple, sir," said Scrounger. "I find things for people that they want and they're willing to trade other things in return. It's a gift, sir," he added modestly.

"Is it?" The sergeant's lip curled. She paused, considering. "All right. I'll give you one chance. You bring me something I can use for the outfit—something of value, mind you—by this time tomorrow morning and I'll let you remain with this company. If you fail, you're out of here. Fair enough?"

"Yes, sir," said Scrounger, his face flushed with pleasure.

"Since this was your idea, Majere, you're detailed to go with him." The sergeant held up a warning finger. "No thievery involved. If I found out you've stolen anything, soldier, I'll string you up to that apple tree you see standing over there. We don't tolerate thieves in this army. The baron's worked hard to develop good relations with the townsfolk, and we intend to keep it that way. Majere, I'm holding you responsible. That means that if he steals, the same thing happens to you that will happen to him. If he so much as heists a peanut, you'll both swing for it."

"Yes, sir. I understand, sir," said Caramon, though he gulped a little when the sergeant wasn't looking.

"May we leave now on our assignment, sir?" asked Scrounger eagerly.

"Hell, no, you may not leave!" the sergeant snapped. "I have only two weeks to whip you clods into shape, and I'm going to need every second. The new recruits are going to be given leave tonight to go into town—"

"We are, sir?" Caramon interrupted, overjoyed.

"All but you two," said the sergeant coolly. "You two can carry out your assignment tonight."

"Yes, sir." Caramon sighed deeply. He'd been looking forward to going back to the Swelling Ham.

"Now go get your things, and report back here on the double!"

"I'm sorry you have to miss leave time, Caramon," said Scrounger, shaking straw out of his blanket.

"Bah! That's all right." Caramon shrugged off the thought of cold ale and warm, accommodating women. "Do you think you can pull this off?" he asked anxiously.

"It'll be tough," Scrounger admitted. "Usually when I do a trade, I know what I'm trading for." He gave the matter thoughtful, serious consideration. "But, yes, I think I can do it."

"I hope so," Caramon said to himself. He gave the apple tree a nervous glance.

Sergeant Nemiss led the men to a building located on the far side of the compound, halted them in front of the barracks.

An officer mounted on a coal-black stallion came from around the corner of the barracks. He was a tall man with dark hair and a jaw that looked as if it had been sawed off square, planed, and sanded.

He reined in his steed, looked over the men lined up in front of him. "My name is Master Senej. Sergeant Nemiss tells me you're not as bad as all the other recruits. What I want to know is this—are you good enough to join Company C?"

He roared out the name of the company, was answered by a deep-throated savage yell that came from inside the barracks. Soldiers dashed out, each man wearing a breastplate, helmet, tabard, carrying shield and sword. Caramon braced himself, thinking that the soldiers were about to attack. Instead, acting without any orders that Caramon had heard, the men of Company C came to a halt, forming into perfectly straight and orderly ranks. Their polished metal armor shone in the sunlight.

In less than one minute, the entire company of ninety men was in battle formation. All stood at the ready, shields up.

Senej turned back to the thirteen recruits. "As I said, I want to know if you're good enough to join my company. My company is the best company in the regiment, and I intend to keep it that way. If you're no good, you're going back to the training company. If you're good, you've got a home for as long as you live."

Caramon thought that he had never wanted anything so much in his life as to join this force of proud, confident soldiers. His chest swelled with pride to think he had been chosen to try for it, but his pride got lodged in his throat as he considered that he might not be good enough to make the cut.

"Fall out, men. Sergeant Nemiss will show you where you bunk."

The recruits had been assigned to wooden cots with at least twice the distance between sleeping areas as in their old quarters. Each man had a barracks box at the foot of his bunk in which to store personal items. Caramon thought he'd never seen such luxury.

After breakfast, Sergeant Nemiss ordered the thirteen new recruits off to the side.

"Now, you're doing well so far. A word of advice. Don't get friendly with the other lads just yet. They don't like new boys until you've proven yourselves. Don't take it personal. Once you've been through a campaign season with them, you'll be getting invitations to weddings for the rest of your life."

One of the men raised his hand.

"Yes, Manto, what is it?" the sergeant asked.

"I was wondering, sir, what does Master Senej's company do that makes it so special?"

"Oddly enough," said the sergeant, "that question isn't as stupid as it sounds. Our company is special because we're given all the special duties. We're the flank company. When the baron asks for skirmishers to advance out in front of the line, we're the ones. When there's an enemy to find, and he's playing slippery with us, we're the soldiers who go and find him. We fight in the line when we're ordered, but we do all the other dirty jobs that come up, too.

"Today, you're going to be issued a new weapon to go along with your sword. Now don't get all excited. It's just a spear. Nothing glamorous." The sergeant reached out, hefted a spear that had been leaning against a wall, and held it out in front of her. "Where you go the spear goes until your training's done."

Caramon held up his hand. "Uh, Sergeant. When's our training done?"

"You're done when I say you're done, Majere," said the sergeant. "You'll be done or washed out before we begin to march, and that's only a couple of weeks away. You've got lots to do and lots to learn in the meantime. Stick close to me and do as I tell you, and you'll come through just fine."

Nemiss took the thirteen out to the practice field, all carrying their new spears, all of the spears double-weight, just like their other practice equipment. Caramon hefted the spear with ease, but Scrounger could barely lift his. The butt end of Scrounger's spear dragged the ground, forming a long furrow behind him all the way to the training ground. Sergeant Nemiss just looked at him and rolled her eyes.

The rest of that day, they practiced with shield and spear. In the afternoon, they practiced throwing the spears. By day's end, Caramon's arm was so weak and trembly from the unaccustomed exertion that he doubted if he'd be able to lift a spoon to eat his dinner.

Scrounger had gamely tried to throw the spear, but after hurling himself right along with it a couple of times—landing flat on his face the first time and nearly spearing Caramon the second—he'd been excused from duty. Sergeant Nemiss employed him in fetching and carrying buckets of water for the men. It was plain to see that she didn't expect to have to deal with the young man in the future.

The thought of leave, of being able to spend a few hours in town, cheered the recruits considerably. Of their own accord, they ran back to the barracks, carrying their spears with them, singing a lively, bawdy marching song Sergeant Nemiss taught them.

The men gulped down their dinner and then left to scrub themselves raw, comb their hair, trim their beards, and put on their best clothes. Caramon started to follow their example—he was hoping to snatch a quick pint of ale before starting his scrounging—but he noted that Scrounger was lying down on his bunk, his hands beneath his head.

"Aren't we going into town with the rest of them?" Caramon asked.

"Nope." Scrounger shook his head.

"But . . . how are you going to scrounge for anything?"

"You'll see," Scrounger promised.

Caramon heaved a sigh that came from his toes. He put down the comb he'd been dragging painfully through his curly hair and, sitting disconsolately on his bunk, watched the rest of the men set off joyfully for town. Nearly all the soldiers who were off duty had been given leave this night. Only those standing guard or who had other assignments stayed behind. Caramon saw his brother leave in the company of Master Horkin. He overheard the two of them talking about visiting a mageware shop, then Horkin telling Raistlin that he knew of a tavern that served the finest ale in all of Ansalon.

Caramon had never felt so low-spirited in his life.

"We can at least get a couple of hours sleep," said Scrounger, once the barracks was silent. So very silent.

Which only goes to prove, Caramon thought, closing his eyes and snuggling into the straw mattress on the bunk, that things were never as bad as they seemed.

19

"CARAMON!"

Someone, it seemed, was always waking him.

"Huh?"

"It's time!"

Caramon sat up. Forgetting he was now sleeping on a bunk and not a bed of straw, he rolled over as usual. The next thing he knew, he was lying on the floor with no very clear notion of how he'd arrived there. Scrounger bent over him anxiously, shining a dark lantern full into his eyes.

"Are you hurt, Caramon?"

"Naw! And shut the cover on that damn thing!" Caramon growled, half-blinded.

"Sorry." Scrounger slid shut the cover, and the light vanished.

Caramon rubbed his bruised hip, his heart pounded. "'S all right," he mumbled incomprehensibly. "What time's it?"

"Close to midnight. Hurry up! No, no armor. It makes too much noise. Besides, it's intimidating. Here, I'll shine the light."

Caramon dressed rapidly, eyeing his friend all the while.

"You've been somewhere. Where've you been?" Caramon asked.

"To town," said Scrounger. He was in high spirits. His eyes sparkled, and he was grinning from pointed ear to pointed ear. His glee had the unfortunate tendency to emphasize his kender heritage. Caramon, looking at his friend, thought of the apple tree, and quaked.

"We're in luck tonight, Caramon. Absolute, positive luck," Scrounger said. "But then, I've always been lucky. Kender generally are. Have you ever noticed that? Mother used to say it was because once upon a time the kender were the favorites of some old god named Whizbang or something like that. Of course, he's not around anymore. According to her, this god got mad at some uppity priest and threw a rock at his head and had to leave town in a hurry before the guards came after him. But the luck he gave the kender rubbed off, and so they still have it."

"Really?" Caramon was owl-eyed. "Is that so? I'll have to tell that to Raist. He collects stories about the old gods. I don't think he ever heard of one called Whizbang. He'll likely be interested."

"Here, let me help you with that boot. What was I saying? Oh, yes. Luck. There are two trading caravans in town! Think of that! One dwarven and one human. They're here to sell supplies to the baron. I've just been to pay a visit to each of them."

"So you have a plan?" Caramon felt relief wash over him.

"No, not exactly." Scrounger hedged. "Trading is like bread dough. You have to give the yeast a chance to work."

"What does that mean?" Caramon asked, suspicious.

"I know how to start it out, but the trade has to grow all on its own. C'mon."

"Where to?"

"Hush, not so loud! Our first stop's the stables."

So they were going to ride into town. Caramon thought that a good idea. His arm was stiff and sore from spear chucking, and now his rump hurt from the tumble he'd taken. The less exercise he had this night the better.

The two crept out of the barracks. Solinari and Lunitari were both out, one full and one waning. Thin, high clouds draped across the moons like silken scarves, so that neither gave much light, smudging the stars.

Guards walked the walls of the baron's castle, stopping now and then to grouse good-naturedly about missing the fun in town. Their watch was outside the castle courtyard, not inside, and so they didn't notice the two figures slipping from shadow to shadow, heading for the stables. Caramon wondered how Scrounger had managed to convince someone to give them horses, but every time he started to ask, Scrounger shushed him.

"Wait here! Keep a lookout," Scrounger ordered and, leaving Caramon at the stable door, the half-kender slipped inside.

Caramon waited nervously. He could hear sounds from inside the stable, but he couldn't place them. One of them was a loud thud, accompanied by the jingling of metal. Then the sound of something heavy scraping across a floor. Finally Scrounger emerged, panting but triumphant, hauling a leather saddle with him.

Caramon eyed the saddle, conscious that something was missing. "Where's the horse?"

"Just take this, will you?" Scrounger said, dumping the heavy object at Caramon's feet. "Whew! I didn't think it would be that heavy. The saddle was up on a post. I had to haul it off, and it was a struggle. You can carry that, though, can't you?"

"Well, sure, I can," said Caramon. He looked at it more intently. "You know, this looks like the saddle Master Senej uses on his horse."

"It is," said Scrounger.

Caramon grunted, pleased that he'd recognized it. He lifted the saddle without a great deal of effort. A thought occurred to him. "Carry it where?" he asked.

"Into town. This way." Scrounger started off.

"No, sir!" Caramon flung the saddle down on the ground. "No, sir. Sergeant Nemiss said no stealing, and she said I was responsible, and while I really don't think that the apple tree would bear my weight if they were to hang me from it, there's probably an oak around that would."

"It's not stealing, Caramon," Scrounger argued. "It's not borrowing either. It's *trading*."

Caramon remained skeptical. He shook his head. "No, sir."

"Look, Caramon, I guarantee that the company commander will sit on his horse on a saddle tomorrow, just like he sat on his horse on a saddle today. I guarantee it. You have my word. I don't like the looks of that apple tree any more than you do."

"Well . . ." Caramon hesitated.

"Caramon, I have to make this trade," said Scrounger. "If I don't, they'll throw me out of the army. The only reason I've lasted this long is because the baron thinks I'm a novelty. But that won't last once we go campaigning. Then I'll have to earn my keep. I have to prove to them that I can be a valuable member of the company, Caramon. I have to!"

The glee had gone from Scrounger's face. He was serious, in desperate earnest.

"It's against my better judgment"—Caramon heaved a sigh and picked up the saddle, grunting at the strain on his sore arm—"but all right. How do we get out of here?"

"The front gate," said Scrounger unconcernedly.

"But the guards—"

"Let me do the talking."

Caramon groaned but said nothing. Hoisting the saddle onto his head, he accompanied Scrounger to the gate.

"Where do you two think you're going?" asked the gate guard, looking considerably amazed at what appeared to be a giant sprouting a saddle for a head.

"Master Senej sent us, sir," said Scrounger, saluting. "This stirrup's loose. He told us to take it into town first thing in the morning."

"But it's night," the guard protested.

"*After* midnight, sir," said Scrounger. "Morning now. We're only obeying orders, sir." He lowered his voice. "You know what a stickler Master Senej can be."

"Yes, and I know he thinks the world of that saddle," said the guard. "Go along then."

"Yes, sir. Thank you, sir."

Scrounger marched out the gate. Caramon plodded dolefully after him. The guard's last statement—about the master thinking the world of this saddle—had caused his heart to get tangled up with his socks.

"Scrounger," he began.

"Yeast, Caramon," said Scrounger, shining the lantern on the road. "Just think of yeast."

Caramon tried to think of yeast, he truly did. But that only reminded him that he was hungry.

❽

"There are the caravans," said Scrounger, sliding the cover over the dark lantern.

Bonfires blazed in both camps. Tall humans passed back and forth in front of one fire; short, stout dwarves walked past the other.

Caramon dropped the saddle, glad for a chance to rest. One camp was made up of a circle of large covered wagons with horses tethered off to one side. The other camp was a circle of smaller wagons, none of them covered, all with ponies standing beside them, tethered to their respective wagons.

As the two watched, a tall man left the first camp and crossed over to the second.

"Reynard!" he shouted, speaking Common. "I need to talk to you!"

A dwarf stood up from the fire and clumped out to meet the human.

"Are you ready to meet my price?"

"Look, Reynard, you know I don't have that much steel on me."

"So what's the baron paying you in—wood?"

"I have to buy supplies," the man whined. "It's a long way back to Southlund."

"And it'll be longer riding bareback. Take my offer or leave it!" the dwarf said crossly. He started to walk off.

"Are you sure we can't come to some other arrangement?" the man asked, halting him. "You can make it for me! I don't mind waiting."

"I do," the dwarf returned. "I can't spare ten days lollygagging around here losing money just to make you a saddle, and you not wanting to meet my price for the one I do have. No. Come back when you have something to offer." The dwarf returned to his fire and his ale and his companions.

Caramon looked down at the saddle. "You're not thinking—"

"It's fermenting, my friend," Scrounger whispered. "It's fermenting. Let's go."

Caramon hefted the saddle, followed Scrounger to the human camp.

"Who goes there?" A man peered at them from one of the wagons.

"A friend," Scrounger called out.

"It's a big guy and a little guy," the lookout reported. "And the big guy's got a saddle. The boss might be interested."

"A saddle!" A middle-aged man with grizzled hair and beard jumped to his feet, eyed them warily. "Seems a funny time of night for saddles to come walking into camp. What do you two want?"

"We heard from some friends of ours that you were looking for a good saddle, sir," said Scrounger politely. "We also heard that you were a little short of steel at the moment. We have a saddle—a fine one, as you can see. Caramon, put the saddle there in the firelight where these gentlemen can get a close look at it. Now, we're willing to barter. What have you got to trade me for this fine saddle?"

"Sorry," the man said. "The boss is the one who needs the saddle, and he's in his wagon. Come back tomorrow."

Scrounger shook his head sadly. "We would like to, sir, we really would. But we go on long-range patrol tomorrow. We're with the baron's army, you see. Caramon, pick up the saddle. I guess our friends were mistaken. Good evening to you, gentlemen."

Caramon reached down, picked up the saddle, and heaved it back up on his head again.

"Wait a moment!" A tall man—the same one they'd seen talking to the dwarf—jumped down out of one of the wagons. "I overheard what you said to Smitfee here. Let me have a look at that saddle."

"Caramon," said Scrounger, "put down the saddle."

Caramon sighed. He had no idea that trading was this strenuous. It was far less trouble to work for a living. He plunked down the saddle in the dirt.

The human examined it, ran his hand over the leather, peered closely at the stitching.

"Looks a little worn," he said disparagingly. "What do you want for it?"

The man's tone was cold and offhanded, but Caramon had seen the way the man's hand lingered on the fine leather, and he was certain that the sharp-eyed Scrounger had seen it, too. The master's saddle was a good one, the second finest in the company, next to the baron's own.

"Well, now," Scrounger said, scratching his head. "What are you hauling?"

The man looked surprised. "Beef."

"Do you have a lot?"

"Barrels of it."

Scrounger thought this over. "All right, I'll take my payment in beef. The saddle in exchange."

The man was wary. This seemed too easy. "How much do you want?"

"All of it," said Scrounger.

The man laughed. "I've got sixteen hundred pounds of aging prime-grade beef! I only sold the baron a couple of barrels. No saddle in Krynn is worth that."

"You drive a hard bargain, sir." Scrounger appeared disconsolate. "Very well, my friend and I will take one hundred pounds of beef, but they have to be the choicest cuts. I'll show you what we want."

The man thought it over, then nodded and thrust out his hand. "You have a deal! Smitfee, get the two their beef."

"But, Scrounger," Caramon said worriedly in a loud whisper, "The master's saddle! He's going to be—"

"Hush!" Scrounger elbowed his friend. "I know what I'm doing."

Caramon shook his head. He had just watched his friend trade away the master's saddle, the master's highly prized saddle, for a barrel of beef. His arm and his rump were sore, and he was convinced that most of the hair on top of his head had been rubbed off by the saddle. To make matters worse, between the talk of bread and beef, his stomach was sounding hollow as a drum. He had the feeling he should call a halt to this dealing right now, grab the saddle, and march back to camp. He didn't do it for two reasons: one, to do so would be to show disloyalty to his friend and two, if he never picked up that blasted saddle again, it would be too soon.

The middle-aged hand led them to one of the far wagons. Hoisting out a barrel, he manhandled it to the ground.

"Here you go, gentlemen," he said. "One hundred pounds of high-grade beef. You won't find anything better between here and the Khalkists."

Scrounger inspected the barrel closely, leaning down to peer through the slats. He stood up, put his hands on his hips, pursed his lips and looked over all the other barrels on the wagon.

"No, this won't do." He pointed. "I want the barrel there, the one near the front. The one with the white mark on the side."

Smitfee looked over toward the caravan leader, who was standing protectively, legs straddled, over the saddle, just in case the two dealers had some idea of trying a doublecross. The caravan leader nodded.

Smitfee eased down the second barrel to the ground.

"All yours, lad." Smitfee grinned and walked off.

Caramon had the terrible feeling he knew what was coming, but he made a hopeful try. "I guess we'll just leave this for the baron's men to collect tomorrow with the wagon."

Scrounger gave him an ingratiating smile, shook his head. "No, we have to take this to the dwarven camp."

"What do the dwarves want with a hundred pounds of beef?" Caramon demanded.

"Nothing, right now," Scrounger said. "I think you could roll the barrel," he added. "You don't have to carry it."

Caramon walked up to the barrel, flipped it over on its side, and began to roll it over the bumpy and uneven ground. The task wasn't as easy as one might think. The barrel wobbled and jounced, veering off in odd directions when least expected. Scrounger ran alongside, guiding as best he could. They nearly lost it once. Rolling down a slight hill, the barrel got going too fast. Caramon's heart leaped into his throat when Scrounger hurled himself bodily at the barrel in order to stop it. By the time they reached the dwarven camp, both were hot and sweating and exhausted.

They rolled the barrel into the dwarven camp, startling one of the ponies, who let out a shrill whinny. Dwarves appeared from everywhere at once. One, Caramon could have sworn, popped up from right beneath his nose, alarming him almost as much as he'd alarmed the pony.

"Good evening, good sirs," said Scrounger brightly, bowing to the dwarves. He laid his hand on the barrel, which Caramon was holding steady with his foot.

"What's in the barrel?" asked one of the dwarves, viewing it with suspicion.

"Exactly what you're looking for, sir!" Scrounger said, slapping his hand down on top of it.

"And what would that be now?" the dwarf asked. Judging by the length of his whiskers, he was the leader of the caravan. "Ale, maybe?" His eyes brightened.

"No, sir," said Scrounger disparagingly. "Griffon's meat."

"Griffon's meat!" The dwarf was clearly taken aback.

So was Caramon. He opened his mouth, shut it when Scrounger trod hard on his foot.

"One hundred pounds of the finest griffon's meat a person could ever hope to see roasting nice and juicy over a fire. Have you ever tasted griffon's meat before, sir? Some say it tastes like chicken, but they're wrong. Mouthwatering. That's the only way to describe it."

"I'll take ten pounds." The dwarf reached for his purse. "What do I owe you?"

"Sorry, sir, but I can't split up the lot." Scrounger was apologetic.

The dwarf snorted. "And what am I going to do with one hundred pounds of any kind of meat, griffon or no? The boys and I eat plain on the road. I don't have room in the wagons to waste hauling around fancy wittles."

"Not even to celebrate the Feast of the Life Tree," said Scrounger, looking shocked. "The most holy of the dwarven holidays! A day devoted to the honoring of Reorx."

"What? Eh?" The dwarf's shaggy eyebrows rose. "What feast is this?"

"Why, it's the biggest festival of the year in Thorbardin. Ah." Scrounger appeared embarrassed. "But I guess that you—being *hill* dwarves—wouldn't know anything about that."

"Who says we wouldn't?" the dwarf demanded indignantly. "I . . . I was a bit confused as to the dates, you know. All this traveling. A dwarf gets mixed up. So next week is the Festival of the . . . uh . . ."

"Life Tree," said Scrounger helpfully.

"Of course, it is," said the dwarf, glowering. He took on a cunning look. "Mind you, I know how we hill dwarves celebrate this great feast, but I don't know how they do it in Thorbardin. Not that I care particularly," he added offhandedly, "what those snooty louts do in Thorbardin. It's just that I'm curious."

"Well," said Scrounger slowly, "there's drinking and dancing."

The dwarves all nodded. That was standard.

"And they break open a fresh cask of dwarf spirits—"

The dwarves were starting to look bored.

"But the most important part of the entire feast is the Eating of the Griffon. It's well known that Reorx himself was a great lover of griffon."

"Well known," the dwarves agreed solemnly, though they shot sidelong glances at one another.

"He was said once to have downed an entire standing rib roast in one sitting, complete with potatoes and gravy, and was heard to ask for dessert," Scrounger continued.

The dwarves whipped off their hats, held them over their chests, and bowed their heads in respect.

"So, in honor of Reorx, every dwarf must eat as much griffon meat as he can possibly consume. The rest," Scrounger added piously, "he gives to the poor in Reorx's name."

One of the dwarves mopped his eyes with the tip of his beard.

"Well, now, lad," said the leader in husky tones, "since you've called our attention to the date, we will be wanting this barrel of griffon's meat after all. I'm a bit short on steel just now. What will you take in exchange?"

Scrounger thought for a moment. "What do you have that is unique? That you have only one of?"

The dwarf was caught off-guard. "Well," he began, "we have—"

"Nope." Scrounger said flatly. "Couldn't possibly."

"How about—"

Scrounger shook his head. "Won't do, I'm afraid."

"You're a hard bargainer, sir," the dwarf said, frowning. "Very well. You've driven me against the wall. I have"—he looked around, careful to see that they weren't overheard—"a suit of plate that was made in Pax Tharkas by the best dwarven metalsmiths for the renowned Sir Jeffrey of Palanthas."

The dwarf laced his hands over his belly, gazed at the two, expecting them to be impressed.

Scrounger lifted his eyebrows. "Don't you think that Sir Jeffrey might *need* his armor?"

"Not where he's going, I'm afraid." The dwarf pointed to the heavens. "Tragic accident. Slipped in the latrine."

Scrounger considered. "I assume the armor comes with the shield and saddle?"

Caramon held his breath.

"Shield yes, saddle no."

Caramon sighed deeply.

"The saddle is promised already," the dwarf added.

Scrounger mulled over the matter a good long minute before answering. "Very well, we'll take the armor and shield."

He thrust out his hand. The dwarf did the same, and they shook on the deal over the upturned barrel of sacred griffon.

The lead dwarf tromped to another wagon, returned dragging a wooden crate behind him. On top of the crate was a shield with the embossed emblem of a kingfisher on the front. Puffing, he dropped the crate at Scrounger's feet. "There you are, lad. Much obliged. That'll make room for the meat."

Scrounger thanked the dwarves and looked at Caramon, who reached down and, with much groaning, lifted the crate onto his shoulder.

"Why did you tell them it was griffon meat?" Caramon demanded.

"Because they wouldn't have been interested in plain old beef," Scrounger replied.

"Won't they know that they've been tricked when they open it?"

"If they do, they'll never admit it to themselves," Scrounger said. "They'll swear that it's the best griffon's meat they've ever eaten."

Caramon digested this for a moment, as they headed back down the road in the direction of the baron's castle.

"Do you think this armor will make up to the master for the loss of his saddle?" Caramon asked doubtfully.

"No, I shouldn't think so," Scrounger said. "That's why we're taking it back to the human camp."

"But the human's camp is back that way!" Caramon pointed out.

"Yes, but I want to get a look at the armor first."

"We can look at it here."

"No, we can't. Is that crate awfully heavy?"

"Yes," Caramon growled.

"Must be good solid armor then," Scrounger concluded.

"Lucky that you knew all about that feast in Thorbardin," Caramon said, bending double under the weight of the crate.

"What feast?" Scrounger asked. His mind had been on something else.

Caramon stared at him. "You mean—"

"Oh, that?" Scrounger grinned and winked. "We may have just started an entirely new dwarven tradition." He looked back to see how far they'd come. When the fires from the camps were only small orange dots in the darkness, he called a halt. "Come here, behind these rocks," he said, beckoning mysteriously. "Put the crate down. Can you open it?"

Caramon pried open the crate lid with his hunting knife. Scrounger shone the light from the dark lantern on the armor.

"That's the most beautiful thing I ever saw!" Caramon said, awed. "I wish Sturm could see this. Look at the kingfisher etched on the breastplate. And the roses on the beaver. And the fine leatherwork. It's perfect! Just perfect!"

"Too damn perfect," said Scrounger, chewing his lip. He glanced around, picked up a large rock, and handed the rock to Caramon. "Here, bash it a few times."

"What?" Caramon's jaw dropped. "Are you crazy? That will dent it!"

"Yes, yes!" Scrounger said impatiently. "Hurry up, now!"

Caramon bashed the armor with the rock, though he winced at every dent he put into the beautiful breastplate, feeling each almost as much if he'd been on the receiving end. "There," he said at last, breathing hard. "That should—" He stopped, stared at Scrounger, who had taken Caramon's knife and was now proceeding to make a cut on his forearm. "What the—"

"It was a desperate fight," murmured Scrounger, holding his arm over the armor, watching the blood drip onto it. "But it's comforting to know that poor Sir Jeffrey died a hero."

❂

Smitfee stopped the two at the edge of the wagons. "What now?" he demanded.

"I have a trade to propose, sir," Scrounger said politely.

Smitfee looked at Scrounger closely. "I wondered where I'd seen ears like that before. Now I remember. You're part kender, aren't you, boy? We don't take kindly to kender, diluted or no. The boss is asleep. So go away—"

The boss walked around the side of the wagon.

"I saw Barsteel Firebrand hauling that barrel of beef into his wagon. He wouldn't buy so much as a rump roast off me. How did you do it?"

"Sorry, sir," said Scrounger, cheeks flushed. "Professional secrets. But he gave me something in return. Something I think you might find interesting."

"Yeah. What's that?" The men looked at the crate curiously.

"Open it up, Caramon."

"Old beaten-up armor," said Smitfee.

Scrounger's voice took on a funereal tone. "Not just any armor, gentleman. It is the magical armor of the valiant Solamnic Knight, Sir Jeffrey of Palanthas, along with his shield. The *last* armor of the gallant Sir Jeffrey," he said with sad emphasis. "Describe the battle, Caramon."

"Oh, uh, sure," said Caramon, startled at his new role of storyteller. "Well, there were . . . uh . . . six goblins . . ."

"Twenty-six," Scrounger cut in. "And don't you mean hobgoblins?"

"Yeah, that's it. Twenty-six hobgoblins. They had him surrounded."

"There was a little golden-haired child involved, I believe," Scrounger prompted. "A princess's child. And her pet griffon cub."

"That's right. The goblins were trying to carry off the princess's child—"

"And the griffon cub—"

"And the cub. Sir Jeffrey snatched the golden-haired griffon—"

"And the child—"

"And the child from the hobgoblins and handed the child back to his mother the princess and told her to run for it. He put his back against a tree and he drew his sword"—Caramon drew his sword, to illustrate the story better—"and he slashed to the left, and he slashed to the right, and hobgoblins fell at every blow. But at last they were too much for him. It was a cursed goblin mace hit him here"—Caramon pointed—"disrupted the magic, stove in his armor, and gave him his death blow. They found him the next day with twenty-five dead hobgoblins lying all about him. And he managed to wound the last one with his dying stroke."

Caramon sheathed his sword, looking noble.

"And the golden-haired child was safe?" asked Smitfee. "And the griffon cub?"

"The princess named the cub 'Jeffrey,' " said Scrounger in tremulous tones.

There was a moment of respectful silence.

Smitfee knelt down, gingerly touched the armor. "Name of the Abyss!" he said, astonished. "The blood's still fresh!"

"We said it was magic," Caramon replied.

"This famous battle relic's wasted on the dwarves," said Scrounger. "But it occurred to me that a caravan that happened to be traveling north to Palanthas might take this armor and the tale that goes with it to the High Clerist's Tower—"

"Our route does happen to lie north," said the leader. "I'll give you another hundred pounds of beef for the armor."

"No, sir. I can't use any more of your beef, I'm afraid." Scrounger said. "What else do you have?"

"Pig's feet pickled in brine. A couple of large cheeses. Fifty pounds of hops—"

"Hops!" said Scrounger. "What kind of hops?"

"Ergothian Prost hops. Magically enhanced by the Kagonesti elves to make the best beer ever."

" 'Scuse me. Conference." He motioned Caramon off to one side.

"Dwarves don't travel much to Ergoth these days, do they?" Scrounger whispered.

Caramon shook his head. "Not if they have to go by boat. My friend Flint couldn't abide boats. Why once—"

Scrounger walked off, leaving Caramon in midstory. Scrounger thrust out his hand. "Very good, sir. I believe we have a deal."

Smitfee hauled away the armor, treating it with great respect, and returned some time later with a large crate over his shoulder. He tossed the crate on the ground in front of him and bade them both good night.

Caramon looked down at the crate, then he looked up at Scrounger.

"That was a wonderful story, Caramon," Scrounger said. "I very nearly wept."

Caramon leaned down, picked up the crate, and heaved it onto his back.

❸

"So, what have you brought me this time?" asked the dwarf.

"Hops. Fifty pounds of hops," said Scrounger triumphantly.

The dwarf appeared disgusted. "You evidently haven't met dwarves before, have you, lad? It's well known that we make the best beer in all of Krynn! We raise our own hops—"

"Not like these," said Scrounger. "Not *Ergothian* hops!"

The dwarf sucked in a deep breath. "Ergothian! Are you sure?"

"Take a whiff for yourself," said Scrounger.

The dwarf sniffed the air. He exchanged glances with his compatriots. "Ten steel coins for that crate!"

"Sorry," said Scrounger. "C'mon, Caramon. There's a tavern in town that will give us—"

"Wait!" the dwarf yelled. "What about two sets of Hylar chinaware with matching goblets. I'll throw in gold utensils!"

"I'm a military man," said Scrounger over his shoulder. "What do I need with china plates and gold spoons?"

"Military. Very well. What about eight enchanted elven longbows, handcrafted by the Qualinesti rangers themselves? An arrow fired from one of these bows will never miss its mark."

Scrounger stopped walking. Caramon lowered the crate to the ground.

"The enchanted longbows *and* Sir Jeffrey's saddle," he countered.

The dwarf shook his head. "I can't do it. I promised the saddle to another customer."

"Caramon, pick up the crate."

Scrounger resumed walking. The dwarf sniffed the air again.

"Wait! All right!" the dwarf burst out. "The saddle, too!"

Scrounger let out his breath. "Very well, sir. We have a deal."

❸

Caramon was deep in a dream, battling twenty-six golden-haired children who had been tormenting a blubbering hobgoblin. Consequently, the sound of metal clashing against metal appeared to be part of his dream, and he did not bother to wake. Not until Sergeant Nemiss held the iron pot she was banging over his head.

"Get up, you lazy bum! Flank Company's first to fight! Up I say!"

He and Scrounger had returned to camp within an hour of day's dawning. Groggy from lack of sleep, Caramon stumbled out after the others to take his place in the ranks of men lined up in front of the barracks.

The sergeant brought the company to attention and was just forming them into a marching column when the sound of galloping hooves and a voice shouting in anger brought the marching to a halt.

Master Senej reined in his excited horse, jumped from the saddle. His face was red as the morning sun, a flaming, fiery red. He glared around at the entire company, recruits and veterans. All of them shriveled away to nothing in the heat of his anger.

"Damn it! One of you bastards switched my saddle with the baron's saddle again. I'm sick and tired of this stupid prank. The baron nearly had my head on a stick the last time this happened. Now, which one of you is responsible?" Master Senej thrust his square jaw out, marched up and down the ranks, glaring each man in the face. "C'mon. 'Fess up!"

No one moved. No one spoke. If the Abyss had opened wide at his feet, Caramon would have been the first to dive in.

"No one admits it?" Master Senej snarled. "Very well. The whole company's on half rations for two days!"

The soldiers groaned, Caramon among them. This hit him where it hurt.

"Don't punish the others, sir," said a voice from the back of the orderly lines. "I did it."

"Who the hell's that?" the master demanded, peering over heads, trying to see.

Scrounger stepped out of ranks. "I'm the one responsible, sir."

"What's your name, soldier?"

"Scrounger, sir."

"This man's about to be mustered out, sir," said Sergeant Nemiss quickly. "He's leaving today, in fact."

"That doesn't excuse what he did, Sergeant. First he's going to explain to the baron—"

"Permission to speak, sir?" said Scrounger respectfully.

The master was grim. "Permission granted. What do you have to say for yourself, Puke?"

"The saddle doesn't belong to the baron, sir." Scrounger replied meekly. "If you'll check, you'll see that the baron's saddle is still in the stables. This saddle is yours, sir. Compliments of C Company."

The soldiers glanced at each other. Sergeant Nemiss snapped out a command, and they all turned eyes front again.

The master studied the new saddle closely. "By Kiri-Jolith. You're right. This *isn't* the baron's saddle. But it's in the Solamnic style—"

"The very newest style, sir," said Scrounger.

"I . . . I don't know what to say." Master Senej was touched, the red flush of anger giving way to the warm flush of pleasure. "This must have cost a small fortune. To think you men . . . went together . . ." The master could not speak for the choke in his throat.

"Three cheers for Master Senej!" shouted the sergeant, who had no idea what was going on but was more than willing to take the credit.

The soldiers responded lustily.

Mounting his horse, seating himself proudly in his new saddle, the master responded to the cheers with a flourish of his hat, then galloped up the road.

Sergeant Nemiss turned around, lightning in her eye and thunder on her face. She fixed that eye upon Scrounger, sent the bolt flashing through him.

"All right, Puke. What the devil's going on? I know darn good and well that none of us bought Master Senej a new saddle. Did *you* buy it for him, Puke?"

"No, sir," said Scrounger quietly. "I did not buy it, sir."

Sergeant Nemiss motioned. "One of you men, bring me a rope. I said what I'd do if I caught you stealing, kender. Now, march!"

Scrounger, his face set, marched over to the apple tree. Caramon stood stock still in line, controlling his face with difficulty. He only hoped that Scrounger didn't carry the joke too far.

One of the soldiers returned with a stout rope, which he handed to the sergeant. Scrounger positioned himself beneath the apple tree. The soldiers continued to stand at attention.

Swinging the rope in her hand, Sergeant Nemiss looked up into the tree, seeking a suitable branch. She stopped, stared. "What the—"

Scrounger smiled, looked down modestly at his feet.

Reaching up into the apple tree, Sergeant Nemiss grabbed hold of something, lowered it carefully. The men did not dare break formation, but all tried desperately to see what it was she held in her hands. One of the veterans forgot himself and gave a low whistle. Sergeant Nemiss was so stunned that she never noticed this breach of discipline.

In her hands, she held an elven longbow. Gazing up into the tree, she counted seven more.

Sergeant Nemiss smoothed her hand over the fine wood. "These are the best bows in all of Ansalon. They're said to be magical! The elves won't sell them to humans—at any price. Do you have any idea what these are worth?"

"Yes, sir," said Scrounger. "One hundred pounds of beef, some dented Solamnic armor, and a crate of hops."

"Huh?" Sergeant Nemiss blinked.

Caramon took a step forward. "It's true, Sergeant. Scrounger didn't steal them. There's some humans and some dwarves camped out in town who'll vouch for that. He traded for everything, fair and square."

The last was a bit of a stretch, but what the Sergeant didn't know wouldn't hurt her.

Sergeant Nemiss's face went soft, gentle, lovely. She rubbed her cheek with deep affection against the smooth, supple wood of the elven bow.

"Welcome to C Company, Scrounger," she said with tears in her eyes. "Three cheers for Scrounger!"

The men gave the cheers with a will.

"And," added Sergeant Nemiss, "three cheers for the thirteen new members of C Company."

It seemed that the cheering, once started, would never stop.

20

ARIAKAS'S TROOPS WERE ON THE MARCH. Not his own personal guard. Those men were too highly trained, too valuable to expend on this expedition. His troops had seen battle. His soldiers had captured Sanction and Neraka, plus all the surrounding lands. The men he was sending south to Blödehelm were the best of his new forces, men who had performed well during training. This was their blooding.

The mission was secret, so secret that not even the highest-ranking commanders knew the name of the objective. They received their orders for the next day's march the night before, orders delivered to them by wyverns. The troops marched at night, under the cover of darkness. They marched in silence, their boots muffled in cloth, the rings of their chain mail padded so that no one would hear the jingle. The wheels of the supply wagons were greased, the horses' harness covered with rags. Anyone unfortunate enough to stumble across the army's path was killed swiftly and without mercy. No one must be left alive to report that he had seen an army of darkness marching from the north.

Kitiara and Immolatus did not ride with the army. The two of them could travel faster than the monstrous military monster crawling across the land. Ariakas wanted them in Hope's End prior to the army's arrival, intending that they should discover the location of the eggs before the start of the battle. Their orders were to reach the city prior to the battle, enter the city in disguise, conduct their search, and leave before things got too hot.

Kitiara was glad they were on their own, away from the troops. Immolatus aroused too much curiosity, occasioned too much comment. In vain, Kit had endeavored to persuade the dragon that the garb of a red-robed wizard was not a suitable disguise for traveling in company with Her Dark Majesty's forces. Black, Kitiara hinted, was a far more attractive color.

Immolatus would not be persuaded. Red he was and red he would remain. Eventually, finding all her arguments useless, Kitiara gave up. She foresaw fights with the arrogant dragon and decided that this was a minor fray of no great consequence. She would save her strength for the battles that counted.

Kitiara wondered at the choice of the dragon—with his scathing disdain for all people regardless of race, creed, or color—for such a mission. It was not her place to question her orders, however. Particularly her last order, which had been delivered to her in secret prior to their departure from Sanction. At least she assumed the missive was an order. She supposed it could be a love letter, but Ariakas did not seem the type.

She kept that order—a hastily scrawled note from Ariakas—rolled into a small tight scroll, tucked in a pouch stowed in her saddlebag. She had not yet had a chance to read it. Immolatus demanded her constant attention. He had spent the day of their swift ride regaling her with stories of his various raids and slaughters, ransackings and lootings. When he wasn't reliving his days of glory, he was complaining bitterly about the food he was forced to eat while in his human form and how humiliating he found it to plod along on horseback when he could be soaring among the clouds.

They stopped to rest at night, and despite the fact that he was not sleeping on a bed of gold, Immolatus finally fell asleep. Fortunately, the dragon slept deeply. Much like a dog, he twitched and jerked in his dreams, snapped his teeth and ground his jaws. After watching his restless slumbers closely for long moments, Kit went so far as to shake Immolatus by the shoulder and call out his name.

He mumbled and growled but did not waken.

Satisfied that she could read her letter in private, Kitiara retrieved the scroll, read the missive by the firelight.

Commander Kitiara uth Matar

Should any circumstance arise in which it is the considered opinion of Commander uth Matar that Her Majesty's plans for the eventual conquest of Ansalon would be endangered, Commander uth Matar is hereby expressly commanded to handle the situation in any manner the commander deems suitable.

The order was signed *Ariakas, General of the Dragonarmies of Queen Takhisis.*

"Cunning bastard," Kitiara muttered with a grudging half-smile. After reading over the deliberately vague and unspecific order twice more, she shook her head, shrugged, and tucked it into her boot.

So this was the lash of the whip. She had been expecting some sort of punishment for her refusal. One did not say no to General Ariakas with impunity. But she had not expected anything so diabolically creative. Her opinion of the man rose a notch.

Ariakas had just placed responsibility for the success—or failure—of the mission on her. Should she succeed, she would be given a hero's welcome. Promotion. His lordship's favors—both in bed and out. Should she fail . . .

Ariakas was intrigued by her, fascinated by her. But he was not a man to remain intrigued or fascinated by anything long. Ruthless, power-hungry, he would sacrifice her to his ambition without a backward glance to see if her body still twitched.

Kitiara sat down near the fire, stared into the dancing flames. Slumbering near her, Immolatus snarled and snorted. The smell of sulfur was strong in the air. He must be setting fire to a city about now. She envisioned the flames devouring houses, shops. People enveloped in fire, living torches. Charred corpses, blackened ruins. The horrid smell of burning hair, seared flesh. Armies marching victorious, the ashes of the dead coating their boots.

The cleansing fire would sweep throughout Ansalon, clearing out the elven deadwood that lay rotting in the forests, burning away the tangled undergrowth of inferior races that impeded human progress, setting the spark to old-fashioned ideas such as those held by the decaying, tinder-dry knighthood. A new order would arise, phoenixlike, from the charred remains of the old.

"I will sit astride that new order," Kitiara said to the flames. "The leveling fire will burn bright in my blade. I will return to you victorious, General Ariakas.

"Or I will not return at all."

Resting her chin on her knees, Kitiara wrapped her arms around her legs and watched the flames consume the wood until all that was left were the cinders, winking at her in the darkness like the dragon's red eyes.

BOOK 2

"Nothing ever happens by chance. Everything happens for a reason. Your brain may not know the reason. Your brain may never figure it out. But your heart knows. Your heart always knows."

—Horkin, Master-at-Wizardry

RAISTLIN CHRONICLES

1

T HE CITIZENS OF HOPE'S END NEVER MEANT TO GO TO WAR. What had started as a peaceful protest over an unfair tax had escalated into full-scale rebellion, and none of the people of Hope's End quite knew how it had all gone so terribly wrong.

Rolling a pebble down a hill, they had inadvertently started a rockslide. Tossing a stick into a pond, they had created a tidal wave, a wall of water that might well drown them all. The cart of their lives, which had once been rolling so smoothly along the main road, had suddenly lost a wheel, toppled sideways, and was now careening down the cliff face.

The unfair tax was a gate tax, and it was having a ruinous effect on the businesses of Hope's End. The edict had come down from King Wilhelm (formerly known as Good King Wilhelm, now known as something not nearly as flattering). The edict required that all goods entering the city of Hope's End should be subject to a twenty-five percent tax and, in addition, all goods leaving Hope's End should be subject to the same tax. This meant that any raw materials entering the city, everything from iron ore for armor to cotton for lace petticoats, were taxed. The same armor and petticoats that left the city were also taxed.

In consequence, the price of goods from the city of Hope's End shot up higher than the latest gnome invention (a steam-powered butter churn). If the merchants did have money enough to pay for the raw materials, they had to charge so much for the finished goods that people could not afford to buy them. This meant that merchants could no longer afford to pay their workers, who no longer had money to pay for bread for their children, let alone lace petticoats.

Good King Wilhelm sent his tax collectors—hulking thuggish brutes—to see to it that the tax was levied. Those merchants who rebelled against paying the gate tax were intimidated, threatened, harassed, and sometimes physically assaulted. One enterprising entrepreneur had the idea of moving his business outside the city walls, in order to avoid the tax altogether. The thugs summarily shut down his operations, broke up his booth, set fire to his stock, and socked the enterprising citizen on the jaw.

Soon the entire economy of Hope's End was teetering on the verge of collapse.

To add insult to injury, the citizens of Hope's End discovered that their city was the only city in the realm to be so mistreated. The loathsome gate tax was levied on them alone. No other city had to pay it. The citizens sent a delegation to Good King Wilhelm requesting to know why they were being punished with this unfair tax. His Majesty refused to see the delegation, sent one of his ministers to relay his answer.

"It is the king's will."

In vain, the lord mayor sent envoys bearing letters to King Wilhelm pleading to lift the unfair tax. The envoys were turned away without ever being given audience with His Majesty. The envoys took no comfort in the rumor running through the royal city of Vantal that King Wilhelm was mad. A mad king is still king, and this one was apparently sane enough to see to it that his mad decrees were obeyed.

The situation grew steadily worse. Shops closed. The marketplace remained open, but the goods sold there were meager and few. Guild meetings—once little more than an excuse for the merchants to come together in good fellowship, share good food and drink—were now shouting matches, with each merchant demanding that something be done. Since each merchant had his own views on what that something was, each merchant was ready to heave an ale mug—now sadly filled with water—at the head of anyone who opposed him.

The Merchants Guild of Hope's End was the most powerful organization in the city. The guild held a virtual monopoly over all industry and commerce of the city. The guild supervised the smaller guilds, setting standards for crafts and seeing to it that these standards were upheld. The merchants felt, and rightly so, that shoddy workmanship reflected badly on the entire community. Any merchant caught cheating his customers was cast out of the guild and thereby lost his ability to make a living.

The Merchants Guild of Hope's End sought to improve the lot of all working men and women in the town, from seamstress and weaver to silversmith and brewer. The guild set fair wages, established the terms under which young men and women were apprenticed to trades, and arbitrated disputes between merchants. Guild members were not rabble-rousers. Their demands for better conditions for their people were not unreasonable. The guild had a cordial relationship with the lord mayor and with the high sheriff. The guild was respected throughout the city, its reputation for fairness and honesty so good that the work of craftsmen in other cities was judged by the accolade, "Good enough to be sold in Hope's End." Thus, when the edict concerning the reprehensible new tax was heralded throughout the city, the people confidently turned to the Merchants Guild to handle the situation.

In response, the guild leader, after much agonized deliberation, called a secret meeting of the guild members, a meeting held in a partially torn-down temple to a forgotten god located on the outskirts of the city.

Here, in the darkness lit by flaring torches, surrounded by his pale, determined, and resolute neighbors, associates, and friends, the guild leader made the suggestion that Hope's End secede from the realm of Blödehelm, become an independent city-state, a city-state with the ability to govern itself, pass its own laws, throw out the thugs, and end the ruinous tax.

In short—revolution.

The vote to secede had been unanimous.

The first order of business was to remove the lord mayor, replace him with a revolutionary council, which immediately elected the lord mayor as their leader. The next order of business was to drive out the thugs. Fortunately, the thugs made this simple by gathering together of an evening in their favorite tavern and drinking themselves into swinish insensibility. Most were hauled off in a drunken stupor, deposited outside the walls. Those who were sober enough to fight were subdued with ease by the city militia.

Once the thugs were gone, the gates of Hope's End were locked and barred. Messengers were sent to Good King Wilhelm informing him that the city of Hope's End had no wish to take the action it had taken but that its people had been driven to rebel. The Revolutionary Council of Hope's End offered the king one last chance to lift the heinous and unfair tax. If he did so, they would put down their arms, unlock the gates, and swear allegiance to Blödehelm and Good King Wilhelm for the rest of their days.

Figuring it would take the messenger four days of hard riding to reach the royal city of Vantal, a day to gain audience with the king, and another four days of hard riding to return, the Revolutionary Council didn't start to worry until the tenth day arrived with no sign of their messenger. Eleven days passed; worry became anxiety. On the twelfth day, anxiety flared into anger. On the thirteenth day, anger gave way to horror.

A kender arrived in the rebellious town (which only goes to show that locked and barred gates guarded by an army really *can't* keep them out!) telling the tale of a most interesting execution she'd recently witnessed in the royal city of Vantal.

"Honestly, I never saw anyone impaled in the public square before! Such a quantity of blood! I never heard such heartrending screams. I never knew a man could take so long to die. I never before saw a victim's head tossed in a cart, a cart being driven in this direction, now that I come to think of it. I never saw the sort of sign that was thrust into the victim's gaping mouth, a sign written in the victim's own blood. A sign that read . . . just give me a moment . . . I'm not all that good at reading myself, someone told me what it said . . . if only I could remember . . . oh, yes! The sign said: 'The fate of all rebels.' "

But they'd have a chance to see it for themselves, the kender added brightly. The cart was on its way to Hope's End.

Anger gave way to despair. Despair caved in to panic when scouts posted atop the city walls reported the sight of an enormous cloud of dust obscuring the northeastern horizon. Scouts, riding from Hope's End, returned with devastating news. An army, a large army, was within a day's march of their city.

The time for secrecy had passed. Ariakas's troops marched in the daylight now.

The people of Hope's End ran from house to house or stood on street corners or lined up in front of the home of the lord mayor or blocked the entrances to the Guild Hall. The people found it impossible to believe that this was happening to them and so they found it impossible to know what to do. Neighbor asked neighbor, apprentice asked master, mistress asked servant, soldier asked commander, commander asked his superiors, the lord mayor asked the guild members, who were busy asking each other: What do we do? Do we stay? Do we go? If we go, where do we go? What becomes of our homes, our jobs, our friends, our relatives?

The dust cloud grew and grew until the entire eastern sky was red at noontime, as if day were breaking with a new and bloody dawn. Some of the people decided to flee, particularly those who were new to the city, those whose roots were shallow and easily transplanted. They packed up what belongings they could carry onto carts or wrapped them in bundles and, bidding their friends farewell, trudged out the city gates and headed down the road in a direction opposite that of what everyone knew now was an approaching army. But most of the citizens of Hope's End stayed.

Like the giant oaks, their roots were sunk deep into the mountains.

Generations of them had lived and died in Hope's End. This city, whose origins dated back—or so legend had it—to the Last Dragon War, had withstood the Cataclysm.

My great-grandparents are buried here. My children were born here. I am too young to start out on my own. I am too old to start afresh somewhere else. This is the house of my youth. This is the business my grandmother started. Must I give it all up and flee? Must I kill to protect it?

A terrible choice, a bitter choice.

After the last of the refugees had fled, the gates to the city rumbled closed. Heavy wagons trundled into place behind the gates, wagons loaded with boulders and rocks to form a barricade that would halt the enemy should the gates be forced open. Every available container was filled with water to fight fires. Merchants turned soldier and spent the day at target practice. Older children were taught to retrieve spent arrows.

The citizens expected the best and prepared for the worst—at least what they considered the worst. They still had faith in their king. At best, they imagined the army marching in orderly manner down the road, setting up camp. They pictured the commander riding out politely to parley, pictured their own representatives walking out under a flag of truce to meet with the commander. He'd make threats, they would react with dignity and stand their ground. Eventually he would give some, they would give some. Finally, after maybe a day of hard and difficult negotiating, they would come to an agreement and everyone would go home to supper.

The worst, the very worst they imagined could happen, was that perhaps it would be necessary to send a few arrows over the heads of the soldiers, arrows carefully aimed, of course, so that no one was hurt. Just to show that they were serious. After that, the army commander—undoubtedly a reasonable man—would see that besieging the city was a waste of time and manpower. And after that they would negotiate.

Horns sounded the alarm throughout the city. The army of Good King Wilhelm had come into view. Everyone who could walk clambered up atop the walls.

The city of Hope's End butted up against the mountains on three sides, looked out over a fertile valley on the fourth. Small farm holdings dotted the valley. The first small seedlings of the spring planting were starting to push through the fresh-tilled ground, a silken scarf of green spread across the valley. A road cut through a mountain pass, led into the valley and from there into Hope's End. Generally, at this time of day, one might stand upon the wall and see a farmer with his oxcart driving down the road, or a party of kender, or a tinker with his wagon filled with pots and kettles or some weary traveler looking gladly at the city walls and thinking of a meal and a warm bed.

Now came pouring down the road a river of steel, whose occasional ripples and eddies, tipped by metal that flashed in the sunlight, engulfed the small farms. The steel river flowed into the valley like a fall of rushing water, booted feet shaking the ground, a cascade of drum rolls marking their advance. Soon the flicker of flames could be seen, thin wisps of smoke rising from house and barn, as the soldiers looted the granaries, butchered the animals, and either killed or enslaved the farmers and their families.

The river of steel gathered in the valley, swirled into whirlpools of activity—soldiers setting up camp, pitching tents in the fields, trampling the seedlings, chopping down trees, plundering and looting the farms. They paid scant attention to the city and the people lining its walls, people who watched with pale faces and fast-beating hearts. At length, one small knot of soldiers separated themselves from the main body and rode toward the city gates. They rode under a flag of truce, a white banner nearly hidden by the smoke of the burning fields. The soldiers halted within hailing distance of the wall. One of the soldiers, wearing heavy armor, rode forward three paces.

"City of Hope's End," shouted the commander in a deep voice. "I am Kholos, commander of the army of Blödehelm. You have two choices: surrender or die."

The citizens on the walls looked at each other in astonishment and consternation. This was certainly not what they had expected. After some jostling, the lord mayor came forward to reply.

"We . . . we want to negotiate," he cried.

"What?" the commander bawled.

"Negotiate!" the mayor yelled desperately.

"All right." Kholos sat back more comfortably on his horse. "I'll negotiate. Do you surrender?"

"No," said the lord mayor, drawing himself up with dignity. "We do not."

"Then you die." The commander shrugged. "There, we negotiated."

"What happens if we surrender?" a voice shouted from the crowd.

Kholos laughed, sneered. "I'll tell you what happens if you surrender. You make my life a whole lot easier. Here are your terms. First, all able-bodied men will put down their arms, leave the city, and form a line, so that my slave-masters may take a good look at you. Second, all young and comely women will form a line so that I may take my pick. Third, the remainder of the citizens of Hope's End will haul out their treasure and stack it up here, at my feet. Those are your terms for surrender."

"This is . . . this is unconscionable!" the lord mayor gasped. "Such terms are outrageous! We would never accept!"

Commander Kholos turned his horse's head and galloped back to his camp, his guards following him.

The people of Hope's End prepared for battle, prepared for killing, prepared to die.

They believed they defended a cause. They believed they fought against an injustice. They had no idea that the war wasn't about them, that they were nothing more than small disposable pieces in a greater cosmic game, that the dread general who had ordered this attack hadn't even known the name of the city until he looked it up on a map, that the commanders of the newly formed dragonarmies viewed this as a training exercise.

The people of Hope's End believed that at least their deaths might count for something, when in reality, the smoke rising from the ashes of the city's funeral pyres would form a single dark cloud in an otherwise lovely blue sky, a single dark cloud that would be torn to shreds in the chill wind of the waning day, vanish, and be forgotten.

2

At about the time Good King Wilhelm was disemboweling the rebellious city's ambassador, the army of the Mad Baron began its march toward that doomed metropolis. Led by the baron waving his plumed hat and laughing heartily for no good reason other than his pleasure at the prospect of action, the baron's soldiers paraded down the road amidst cheers and well-wishes from Langtree's assembled townsfolk. After the last heavily laden supply wagon had rolled out the gates, the townsfolk returned to their homes and businesses, grateful for the peace and quiet, sad for the lost revenue.

The baron gave his troops plenty of time to reach their objective. The soldiers marched no more than fifteen miles per day. He wanted his troops fresh and ready to fight, not falling over from exhaustion. Wagons carried their armor, their shields and rations, so they did not have to stop for anything along the route, except for a brief rest at midday. Anyone who dropped out of the march from exhaustion, illness, or injury was teased unmercifully but was permitted to ride in the wagons alongside the drivers.

The men were in good spirits, eager for battle and glory and the pay at the finish. They sang songs as they marched, songs led by the baron's rich baritone. They played tricks and jokes upon the new recruits. Each man knew that this battle might be his last, for every soldier knows that some-where is an arrowhead marked with his blood or a sword with his name etched on the blade. But such knowledge makes the life he is living at the moment that much sweeter.

The only person who was not enjoying the march was Raistlin. His weak body could not withstand even a moderate walking pace for very long. He grew weary and footsore after the first five miles.

"You should ride in the supply wagons, Raist," Caramon told him helpfully. "Along with the other—" He went red in the face and bit his tongue.

"Along with the rest of the weak and infirm," Raistlin finished the sentence.

"I-I didn't mean that, Raist," Caramon stammered. "You're a lot stronger now than you used to be. Not that you were weak or anything, but—"

"Just be quiet, Caramon," Raistlin said irritably. "I know perfectly well what you meant."

He limped off in high dudgeon, leaving Caramon to look after him and shake his head with a sigh.

Raistlin pictured the scornful looks of the other soldiers as they marched past him, lying recumbent on a sack of dried beans. He pictured his brother helping him out of the wagon every night, solicitous and patronizing. Raistlin resolved then and there that he would march with the rest of the army if it killed him—which it likely would. Dropping dead on the trail was preferable to being pitied.

Raistlin had lost track of Horkin during the march, supposed that the robust mage was in the front ranks, setting the pace. When the word came that Raistlin was to report to the master-at-wizardry, he was considerably astonished to find Horkin back with the supply wagons.

"I heard you were walking, Red," Horkin said.

"Like the rest of the soldiers, sir," said Raistlin, prepared to be affronted. "You needn't worry, sir. I am a little tired now, that's all. I will be better in the morning—"

"Bah! Here's your mount, Red."

Horkin indicated a donkey, tied to one of the wagons. The donkey seemed a placid sort, stood chewing hay, paying no attention to the organized confusion of making camp. "This is Lillie. She's very tractable, so long as you keep your pockets filled with apples." Horkin scratched the donkey between her ears.

"I thank you for your concern, sir," said Raistlin stiffly, "but I will continue to march on foot."

"Suit yourself, Red," said Horkin, shrugging. "But you'll have a devil of time keeping up with me that way."

He nodded toward another donkey who might have been Lillie's twin, so much did they resemble each other, even down to a black streak that ran from shoulder to rump.

"Do you ride, sir?" Raistlin asked, astonished.

Horkin was a thoroughgoing soldier, as the saying went. He had once by his own account force-marched seventy miles in one day carrying a full pack. Thirty miles per day was a stroll in the garden, according to Horkin.

"You are riding this time for my sake, aren't you, sir?" the young mage asked coldly.

Horkin placed a kindly hand on Raistlin's thin shoulder. "Red, you're my apprentice. And I'm honest when I say this. I really don't give a damn about you. I'm riding because I have a reason for riding, a reason you'll see in the morning. You could be of some assistance to me, but if you choose to march—"

"I'll ride, sir," Raistlin said, smiling.

Horkin left for the comfort of his bedroll. Raistlin remained behind, making friends with Lillie and wondering what perverse twist in his nature made him resent Caramon for caring and respect Horkin for not caring.

If Raistlin thought he was going to have an easy time of it, he learned his mistake the very next day. The two mages rode at the rear of the long column, alongside the supply wagons. Raistlin was enjoying the ride, enjoying the warm sunshine, when suddenly Horkin gave a wild shout and jerked on the reins, turned his donkey's head so violently that the animal brayed in protest. Kicking the donkey in the flanks, Horkin plunged recklessly off the trail, shouting for Raistlin to follow.

Raistlin did not have much say in the matter for Lillie did not like to be parted from her stablemate. The donkey trotted after Horkin and carried Raistlin with her. The two donkeys crashed through brush, stumbled down a steep gully, and dashed off across a meadow of clover.

"What is it, sir?" Raistlin cried.

He jounced uncomfortably on the donkey, whose gait was far different from that of a horse, his robes flapping around him, his hair streaming out behind. He was certain that Horkin was on the trail of nothing less than an army of goblins, and that his master intended on taking them on single-handed. Raistlin glanced back over his shoulder, hoping to see the rest of the army come racing along behind.

The rest of the army was, by now, out of sight.

"Sir! Where are you going?" Raistlin demanded.

He finally caught up, not through his own doing but because Lillie, apparently a most competitive animal, could not tolerate being left behind.

"Daisies!" Horkin shouted triumphantly, pointing to a field of white. He spurred his donkey on to greater efforts.

"Daisies!" Raistlin muttered, but he didn't have time for wonderment. Lillie had once again entered the race.

Horkin halted his donkey in the very midst of the field of white and yellow flowers, jumped from the saddle.

"C'mon, Red! Get off your ass!" Horkin grinned at his little joke. Grabbing an empty gunnysack from his saddle roll, he tossed it to Raistlin, took another for himself. "No time to waste. Pick the flowers and the leaves. We'll use both."

"I know that the daisy is good for easing coughs," Raistlin said, plucking flowers most industriously. "But none of the soldiers are currently suffering—"

"The daisy is what's known as a battlefield herb, Red," Horkin explained. "Grind it up, make an ointment from it, spread it on wounds, and it keeps them from putrefying."

"I didn't know this, sir," said Raistlin, gratified at learning something new.

They gathered the daisies and also some of the clover, which was good for wounds and other complaints. On the way back, Horkin again veered from the road, galloped off in search of brambles, which he said he used to cure the soldier's most common complaint—dysentery. Now Raistlin understood the need for the donkeys. By the time the two mages had completed their foraging, the army was miles ahead of them. They rode all afternoon just to catch up.

Their work did not end at night, for after a day spent in backbreaking labor harvesting the plants, Horkin ordered Raistlin to pluck the petals from the flowers or boil the leaves or pound roots into pulp. Tired as he was—and Raistlin could not remember ever feeling so exhausted—he took care each night before he slept to write down in a small book all that he had learned that day.

He had no rest on those days when their herbal work was done, for if he was not picking flowers, he was practicing his spell-casting. Prior to this time, Raistlin had always been fussily particular about his spells. He did not say the words until he was certain he could correctly pronounce each one. He did not cast the spell until he knew he could cast it perfectly. Speed was what counted now. He had to cast his spell fast, without taking time to think whether an "a" was pronounced "aaa" or "ah." He had to know the spell so well that he could recite the words rapidly, without thinking, without making a mistake. Trying to speak the words rapidly, Raistlin stammered and stuttered as badly as he had when he was eight years old. In fact, he told himself morosely, he'd said the words better at eight!

One might imagine that such practice was easy, a simple matter of repeating the words over and over as an actor memorizes his script. But an actor has the advantage of being able to rehearse his lines aloud no matter where he is, whereas the mage cannot, for fear of inadvertently casting the spell.

Raistlin was galled by the fact that Horkin—a mage of far less skill and learning—could say a spell so swiftly that Raistlin had a difficult time understanding him, cast the spell with never a miss. Raistlin persisted in his own practicing with grim determination. Whenever he had a free moment, he took himself off into the woods where he wouldn't hurt anyone if he did manage to cast an "incendiary projectile" in less than three seconds, which at this juncture did not appear likely.

His days taken up with backbreaking labor, his nights with concocting medicines and potions, writing, and studying, Raistlin was amazed that he had not collapsed from fatigue. But, in fact, he had never felt so well, so alive and interested in life. Long accustomed to holding himself up for self-evaluation, Raistlin came to the conclusion that he thrived on activity, both physical and mental; that without something to keep him occupied, his brain and body both stagnated. He coughed less frequently, though when the spasms came, they were unusually painful.

He even found Caramon less doltish than usual. Every night Raistlin joined his brother and his friend Scrounger for a supper of stewed chicken and hardtack. He actually enjoyed himself and found that he looked forward to their company.

As for Caramon, he was delighted at the change in his brother and, with his usual easygoing nature, did not spend time wondering at or questioning it. The night when Raistlin actually did manage to cast a fiery bolt, not once, but three times in rapid succession, he was so jovial during supper that Caramon secretly suspected his twin of imbibing dwarf spirits.

The march to Hope's End proceeded without incident. Company C, riding as advance scouts for the army, arrived within sight of the city on the appointed day to find the army of Good King Wilhelm camped outside the walls. The air was gray with the stench of burning, the sounds of shrieks and screams sounded eerily out of the smoke.

"Is the battle over, sir?" Caramon asked in dismay, thinking he'd missed it.

Sergeant Nemiss stood in the shadow of a large maple tree, blinking away the stinging smoke, trying to see through the pall that hung over the valley to determine what was happening. Her men gathered around her, keeping themselves concealed at the edge of the tree line.

Sergeant Nemiss shook her head. "No, we haven't missed the fight, Majere. Pah! The stuff gets in your mouth!" She swigged water from her canteen, spit on the ground.

"What's on fire, sir?" Scrounger peered into the smoke and falling ash. "What's burning?"

"They're looting the countryside," Sergeant Nemiss replied, after another drink of water. "Looting the homes and barns and setting fire to what they can't carry off. Those screams you hear—those are the women they've captured."

"Bastards!" Caramon said, his face pale. He licked dry lips, felt as though he might be sick. He had never before heard the cries of a person in torment. He gripped his sword hilt, rattled the blade in its sheath. "We'll make them pay!"

Sergeant Nemiss fixed him with an ironic eye. "Afraid not, Majere," she said dryly. "Those are our gallant allies."

❷

The baron's army established camp with disciplined efficiency, under the critical eye of the baron's second-in-command, Commander Morgon. Caramon and his company stood guard duty around the camp's perimeter. Danger would presumably come from the direction of the city, but the guards' gaze shifted constantly between the city and the camp of their allies.

"What did the baron say?" Caramon asked Scrounger, who was making the rounds of the guard posts with the waterskin.

Scrounger had yet another talent besides deal making. He was a remarkable eavesdropper, a talent that amazed everyone, since eavesdropping is perhaps the one and only fault not generally consigned to kender.

A kender overhearing a conversation feels compelled to join that conversation, deeming that he has valuable information to share on the subject under discussion, no matter how personal or private that subject may be. Whereas a good eavesdropper must be silent, circumspect. When asked how he managed to come by such skills, Scrounger said that he thought it came from deal making, wherein it is always more profitable to keep the ears open and the mouth closed.

A good eavesdropper must also be in the right place at the right time in order to see and hear to best advantage. How Scrounger managed to be in all the places he managed to be in to hear all the information he managed to hear was a marvel and a wonder to his comrades. They soon ceased to question how he came to know, however, and relied on him for information.

Scrounger reported on the conversation he'd overheard while Caramon drank the warm and brackish water thirstily. "Sergeant Nemiss told the baron that the soldiers of King Wilhelm were looting and burning the countryside. The baron said to Sergeant Nemiss, 'This is their country. Their people. They know best how to deal with the situation. The city is in rebellion. It must be taught a lesson, a hard lesson and a swift one, or the other cities in the kingdom will see that they can flout authority with imp . . . impunity. As for us, we've been hired to do a job and by the gods we're going to do it.'"

"Huh." Caramon grunted. "And what did Sergeant Nemiss say?"

"'Yes, my lord.'" Scrounger grinned.

"I mean *after* she left the baron's tent."

"You know I never use language like that," Scrounger said mockingly and, hefting the heavy waterskin, he trudged off to the next guard post.

Raistlin had no leisure to sit and ponder the odd ways of their allies. He was kept busy the moment the army arrived, assisting Horkin in setting up the war wizard's tent, which was a smaller and cruder version of Horkin's laboratory. In addition to concocting the components they used for spells, the two mages also worked with the baron's surgeon, or "leech" as he was fondly known among the troops, to provide medicines and ointments.

Currently empty, the surgeon's tent would soon be used to shelter the wounded. Raistlin had brought with him several jars of ointment, along with instructions for their use. The surgeon was busy arranging his tools, however, and curtly bade Raistlin to wait.

The tent was neat and clean and lined with cots, so that the wounded would not be forced to sleep on the ground. Raistlin examined the tools—the saw for amputating shattered limbs, the sharp knife used to cut out arrow points. He looked at the beds and suddenly he saw Caramon lying there. His brother was white-faced, beads of sweat on his forehead. They had tied his arms to the bed with leather cord and two strong men, the surgeon's assistants, were holding him down. His leg bone was shattered below the knee, broken bone protruded from the torn flesh, blood covered the bed. Caramon, breathing harshly, was begging his brother for help.

"Raist! Don't let them!" Caramon cried through teeth clenched against the pain. "Don't let them cut off my leg!"

"Hold him tight, boys," the surgeon said and lifted his saw. . . .

"You all right, Wizard? Here, you better lie down."

The surgeon's assistant hovered near him, his hand on Raistlin's arm.

Raistlin cast a glance at the cot and shuddered. "I am perfectly all right, thank you," he said.

The blood-tinged mists cleared from his eyes, the bursting stars vanished, the sick feeling passed. He pushed aside the assistant's solicitous hand and left the tent, forcing himself to walk calmly and slowly, with no unseemly show of haste. Once outside, he drew in a deep breath of smoke-tinged air and almost immediately began to cough. Still, even tainted air was preferable to the stifling atmosphere inside that tent.

"It must have been the stuffiness that overcame me," Raistlin told himself, ashamed and scornful of his weakness. "That and an overactive imagination."

He tried to banish the picture from his mind, but the image of Caramon's suffering had been extremely vivid. Since the picture would not fade, Raistlin made himself look at it long and hard. He watched in his mind's eye as the surgeon took off Caramon's leg, watched his brother linger for days in terrible agony, healing slowly. He watched his brother being carried back to the baron's castle in a wagon with other wounded. Watched his brother living the rest of his life as a cripple, his hale body wasting away beneath the pitying stares of their friends. . . .

"You would know how I feel then, my brother," Raistlin said grimly.

Realizing what he'd said and what he'd meant by saying it, he shivered.

"By the gods!" he murmured, appalled. "What am I thinking? Have I sunk so low? Am I so mean-spirited? Do I hate him that much?"

"No." Raistlin thought back to those few terrible moments in the tent. "No, I am not quite such a monster as that." His mouth twisted in a rueful smile. "I cannot imagine him in pain without feeling anguish. And yet at the same time, I cannot imagine him in pain without feeling vengeful satisfaction. What black spot on my soul—"

"Red!"

Horkin's voice boomed behind him, startling him like a sudden and unexpected drum roll. Raistlin blinked. He had been so preoccupied with his thoughts that he'd walked into the war wizard's tent without even being aware of it.

Horkin stood glaring.

"What's the matter with the ointment? Wasn't it what he wanted?" Horkin demanded. "Didn't you tell him what it was for?"

Raistlin looked down at his hands to discover he was clutching a jar of ointment with a grip Death might have envied. "I . . . That is . . . yes, he was quite pleased. He wants more, in fact," Raistlin stammered, adding, "I'll make it up myself, sir. I know how busy you are."

"Why in the name of Luni did you bring this one back?" Horkin grumbled. "Why not just leave it there for him to use until you can make up the other?"

"I'm sorry, sir," Raistlin said contritely. "I guess I didn't think of that."

Horkin eyed him. "You think too goddam much, Red. That's your trouble. You're not being paid to think. *I'm* being paid to think. You're being paid to do whatever it is I think up. Now just quit thinking and we'll get along much better."

"Yes, sir," Raistlin said with more obedience than he usually showed to his master. He found it suddenly refreshing to let go all his tormenting thoughts, watch them drift away on the air currents like so much thistledown.

"I'll bring in the rest of the supplies. You start on that ointment." Horkin paused at the tent flap, gazed loweringly at the city. "The Leech must figure it's going to be a bloody battle if he's stocking up on war-flower cream." Shaking his head, he left the tent.

Raistlin, as ordered, refused to let himself think. Reaching for the mortar and pestle, he began to crush daisies.

3

T HERE WERE MANY ALEHOUSES IN THE CITY OF HOPE'S END. The name
of this particular alehouse, an alehouse discovered by Kitiara on her
arrival to the doomed city, was the Gibbous Moon.

The tavern's signage featured a picture of a man hanging from a rope, a
picture done in lurid colors—the man's face was particularly gruesome—set
against the backdrop of a bright yellow moon. What the hanging had to do
with the alehouse's name was anybody's guess. Popular opinion held that the
owner had mixed up the word "gibbous" with the word "gibbet," but this
the owner always vehemently denied, though he could give no reason for the
noose's presence, other than that "it attracted notice."

Swinging in the breeze very like the noose it portrayed, the sign brought
many a passerby up short, caused many to stare in wide-eyed wonder, but
whether or not it induced those same passersby to taste the food or sample
the ale of a place denoted by a dangling corpse was another matter. The
tavern was not exactly overwhelmed with customers.

The owner complained that this was due to the fact that the other
tavern owners in town were "out to get him." It should be noted that this
was not necessarily true. In addition to being cursed with the stomach-
turning sign, the Gibbous Moon was situated in the oldest part of the
city, located at the very end of a crooked street lined with abandoned,
tumbledown buildings, far away from the marketplace, the merchant
streets, and Tavern Row.

The tavern was not prepossessing in appearance, being a mass of
ill-assorted wooden planks topped by a wood shingle roof and not a

single window, unless you counted the hole in the front of the alehouse where two of the planks were not on speaking terms and refused to have anything to do with one another. The building looked as if had been washed down the street in a flash flood, coming to rest smashed up against the side of the retaining wall. According to local legend, this was precisely what had occurred.

Kitiara liked the Gibbous Moon. She had searched all over the city for a place like this, something "out of the way" where a "body could find some peace and quiet," where a "person wasn't pestered to death by barmaids wanting to know if you wanted another ale."

The few customers of the Gibbous Moon did not have to put up with this inconvenience. The Gibbous Moon employed no barmaids. The tavern's owner, who was his own best customer, was generally in such a sodden stupor that the guests ended up serving themselves. One would think that this would be an open invitation to the unscrupulous to drink up their ale and leave without paying. The owner cleverly thwarted this practice by making the ale undrinkable, so that even though it might be free, it was still considered a bad bargain.

"You could not have found a more wretched pesthouse if you had searched the length and breadth of the Abyss," Immolatus complained.

He sat on the very edge of a chair, having already removed one splinter from his soft, squishy, and easily damaged human flesh. He deeply regretted the loss of his own steel-hard, shining red scales. "A demon who has spent tortured eternity roasting over hot coals would turn up his nose at the offer of a mug of that liquid, which has undoubtedly come from a horse who died of kidney disease."

"You don't have to drink it, Your Eminence," Kitiara returned testily. She was highly irritated with her companion. "Due to your 'disguise,' this is the only place in town where we can talk without having the people in the city staring at us and breathing down our necks."

She lifted the cracked mug. Ale slowly dribbled onto the floor. Kit tasted it, spit it out, and hastened the process by upending the mug. This done, she reached into her boot, removed a flask of brandy purchased from a more reputable tavern, and drank a swig. She returned the flask to her boot, not offering any to her companion, a mark of her displeasure.

"Well, Eminence," she demanded, "have you found anything? Any trace? Any hint? Any *eggs?*"

"No, I have not," Immolatus replied coolly. "I have searched every cavern I could find in these godforsaken mountains, and I can state categorically that there are no dragon eggs hidden anywhere there."

"You've searched *every* cavern?" Kitiara was skeptical.

"That I could find," Immolatus replied.

Kit was grim. "You know how important this is to Her Majesty—"

"The eggs are not hidden in any of the caverns I searched," said Immolatus.

"Her Majesty's information—" Kit began.

"Is accurate. There are eggs of the metallics hidden in the mountains. I can feel them, smell them. Gaining access to them—that's the trick. The location of the entrance to the cave is well hidden, cleverly concealed."

"Good! Now we're getting somewhere. Where is this entrance?"

"Here," said Immolatus. "In the city itself."

"Bah!" Kit snorted. "I admit that I know nothing about these so-called metallic dragons, but I can't picture them calmly laying their eggs in the middle of the town square!"

"You are right," Immolatus replied. "You know nothing about dragons. Period. May I remind you, worm, that this city is ancient, that this city was here when Huma the Accursed crawled, sluglike, upon the land. This city was here in an age and time when dragons—all dragons, chromatic and metallic—were revered, honored, feared. Perhaps I even flew over this city once in my youth," the dragon said, gazing dreamily into the distant past. "Perhaps I considered attacking it. The presence of the metallics would explain why I did not. . . ."

Kit drummed her fingers upon the table. "So what are you saying, Eminence? That gold dragons perched on the rooftops like storks? That silver dragons cackled in coops?"

Immolatus rose to his feet, fire-eyed and quivering. "You will learn to speak of even my enemies with respect—"

"Listen to me, Eminence!" Kit returned, rising to face him, her fingers curling over the hilt of her sword, "The army of Lord Ariakas has this city surrounded. Commander Kholos is preparing to attack. I'm not sure when, but it's going to be soon. I've seen what the fools in this city term their defenses. I have a pretty good idea how long this wretched place can hold out. I also know some of Commander Kholos's plans for the assault. Believe me, we don't want to be caught inside this city when that happens."

"The dragon eggs are in the mountains," said Immolatus. He grimaced, wrinkled his nose. "Somewhere. I can sense them, the way one senses a fungus beneath one's scales. It starts with an itching that you can't quite locate. Sometimes you don't feel it for days, and then one night you wake up in torment. Every time I left the city, the itch faded away. When I returned, it was strong, overpowering."

He began to absentmindedly scratch at the back of his palm. "The eggs are near here. And I will find them."

Kitiara dug her nails into her palms so that she wouldn't dig them into the dragon's throat. He'd wasted precious time on some fool kender chase! And now, when time was critical . . . Well, there was no help for it. What can't be cured must be endured, as the gnome said when he got his head stuck in his revolutionary new steam-powered grape press.

Having mastered her anger, or at least tamped it down into her belly, Kitiara muttered in no very good humor, "Well, what now, Eminence?"

They were the only customers in the alehouse. The owner had drunk himself into oblivion by suppertime and now lay sprawled upon the bar, his head on his arms. A dust-covered ray of sunshine filtered through the quarreling planks, wavered, and vanished as if appalled to find it had accidentally ventured inside.

"We have a day or two at the most remaining to us," Kitiara said. "We have to be out of here before the first assault."

Immolatus stood by the bar, frowning down at a rivulet of ale leaking from a sprung cask, forming a small pool on the hard-packed dirt floor. "Where is the old part of the city, Worm?"

Kitiara was growing extremely tired of being called that. The next time he did so, she was tempted to shove that word down his throat.

"What do you take me for, Eminence? Some ink-smeared historian from the Great Library? How should I know?"

"You've been here long enough," the dragon stated. "You might have noticed such things."

"And so should you, you arrogant—"

Kitiara washed down the next few highly descriptive adjectives with another gulp of brandy from the boot flask. This time she didn't put the flask away but left it out on the table.

Immolatus, whose hearing was excellent, smiled to himself. He grabbed hold of the lank and greasy hair of the bartender and jerked his head up off the counter.

"Slug! Wake up!" Immolatus banged the man's head several times upon the counter. "Listen to me! I have a question for you." He thumped the man's head a few more times.

The bartender winced, groaned, and opened bleary, bloodshot eyes. "Huh?"

"Where are the oldest buildings in town?"

Bang went the man's head on the counter.

"Where are they located?"

The bartender squinted, gazed up at Immolatus in drunken confusion. "Don't shout! Gods! My head hurts! The oldest buildings are on the west side. Near the old temple . . ."

"Temple!" Immolatus said. "What temple? To what god?"

"HowshouldIknow?" the man mumbled.

"A fine specimen," Immolatus said irritably and lifted the man's head again.

"What are you doing?" Kit was on her feet.

"Humanity a favor!" Immolatus stated and, with a jerk of his hand, he snapped the man's neck.

"That was brilliant," Kitiara said, exasperated. "How are we supposed to find out anything from him now?"

"I don't need him." Immolatus headed for the door.

"But what do we do with the body?" Kit asked, hesitating. "Someone might have seen us. I don't want to be arrested for murder!"

"Leave it," said the dragon. He cast a scathing look back at the dead bartender, slumped over his bar. "No one's likely to notice the change."

"Ariakas, you owe me!" Kit muttered, trailing Immolatus. "You owe me big. I expect to be made a regimental commander after this!"

4

THE STREETS GREW NARROWER AND MORE CROOKED, THE CROWDS thinned. Kitiara and the dragon had entered the old part of Hope's End. Most of the original homes and dwellings had been torn down, their stone used to make the large warehouses and granaries that replaced them. By day, tradesmen came and went. By night, vermin—both four-legged and two-legged—were the primary occupants. On rare occasions, the lord mayor, in a fit of energy and civic pride, would order the sheriff and his men to descend on the warehouse district and evict those who sought refuge there, ferreting them out of the nooks and crannies where they lay hidden.

With the coming of war, most of the two-legged vermin had abandoned ship, fleeing to safer cities. Since the warehouses held nothing in them anymore, no tradesmen walked the streets or made deals on the street corners. This part of town, the west side, was empty and deserted, or so it appeared. Still, Kit kept a watchful eye out. She couldn't imagine what Immolatus hoped to find here, unless he had some notion that the dragons had stored their eggs in a warehouse.

The day was almost finished, the sun setting in a haze of smoke from the burned fields beyond the city walls. The shadows of the mountain fell across the city, bringing early night with them. Immolatus finally called a halt, but only, it seemed to Kit, because he'd run out of street.

The dragon appeared immensely pleased with himself however. "Ah, just as I expected."

The street ran headlong into a high crumbling granite wall, or so it appeared. Catching up with the dragon, Kitiara saw that she'd been mistaken. The street actually passed through the wall, in between two tall pillars. Rusted holes in the rock indicated that iron gates might have been used to control the flow of traffic in and out of the area. Looking through the entryway, Kitiara saw a courtyard and a building.

"What is this place?" Kitiara asked, regarding the building with a disparaging frown.

"A temple. A temple to the gods. Or perhaps I should say a temple to one god." Immolatus cast the building a look of pure loathing.

"Are you sure?" Kit said, comparing it unfavorably to the grand Temple of Leurkhisis. "It's so small and . . . shabby."

"Rather like the god himself." Immolatus sneered.

The temple was small. Thirty paces would take Kit from the front to the back. In the front, three broad steps led to a narrow porch under a roof supported by six slender columns. Two windows looked out upon a courtyard paved with broken flagstones. Chickweed and some sort of choking vine were growing through the cracks. Here and there, among the weeds, a few wild rosebushes still flourished, climbing up the wall surrounding the courtyard. The roses were tiny and white and caught the last rays of the sun, the blossoms seemed to almost glow in the twilight. The roses filled the air with a sweet, spicy scent, which the dragon found offensive, for he coughed and snorted and covered his nose and mouth with his sleeve.

The temple was made of granite, and had once been covered with marble on the outside. A few slabs of marble—yellow-stained and damaged—still remained. Most of the other marble slabs had been torn off, used elsewhere. The front doors were cast in gold, they gleamed in the sunlight. A frieze, carved around the sides of the building, was almost completely obliterated, scarred with deep gouges, as if it had been attacked by picks and hammers. What images it had once portrayed had been erased.

"Eminence, how do you know what god this temple was built to honor?" Kitiara asked. "I see no writing, no symbols, nothing to indicate the name of the god."

"I know," said Immolatus, and his voice grated.

Kitiara walked past the stone pillars into the courtyard to gain a better view. The golden doors were dented and battered. She wondered that the doors were still there at all, that they hadn't been melted down for their value. Admittedly gold wasn't worth much these days, not as much as the far more practical steel. No one ever marched to war with a sword made of gold. Still, if those doors were solid gold, they would be worth something. She would remember to tell Commander Kholos, advise him to take the doors with him when he left the city.

She could see a slight crack between the two golden doors, realized that they stood partially open. Kit had the strangest idea that she was being welcomed, invited to come inside. The idea was repugnant to her. She had the strong impression that something in there wanted something from her, was out to rob her of something precious. The temple had probably become a haunt for thieves.

"What was the god called, Eminence?" Kit asked.

The dragon opened his mouth to reply, then snapped it shut. "I won't foul my mouth by pronouncing his name."

Kit smiled derisively. "One would almost think you were afraid of this god, who obviously isn't around anymore."

"Don't underestimate him," Immolatus snarled. "He's sneaky. His name is Paladine. There! I've said it and I curse it!"

A gout of flame burst from his mouth, flared briefly on the broken flagstones of the empty courtyard, burned a few weeds, then flickered out.

Kit hoped to heaven no one had seen the tantrum. Red-robed wizards, even the greatest of them, are not known to be able to spit fire.

"Well, I've never heard of him," said Kit.

"You are a worm," said Immolatus.

Kit's hand clenched over the hilt of her sword. Dragon he might be, but he was in human form, and she guessed that it would take him a moment or two to change from clothes to scales. In that moment, she could strike him dead.

"Calm down, Kit," she remonstrated with herself. "Remember all the trouble it cost you to find the beast and bring him to Ariakas. Don't let him provoke you. He wants to lash out at something, and I don't blame him. This place is unnerving."

She was starting to have an active dislike for her surroundings. There was a serenity, a peacefulness about the temple and the grounds, which she found annoying. Kitiara was not one to waste time pondering the complexities of life. Life was meant to be lived, not contemplated.

She was reminded, suddenly, of Tanis. He would have liked this place, she thought disdainfully. He would have been content here, sitting on the cracked front steps, gazing up at the sky, asking questions of the stars, foolish questions to which there could be no answer. Why was there death in the world? What happened after death? Why did people suffer? Why was there evil? Why had the gods abandoned them?

As far as Kit was concerned, the world was the way the world was. Seize your part of it, make of that part what you could, leave the rest to take care of itself. Kit had no patience with Tanis's cobweb spinning, as she termed it. His image, coming to her unbidden and unwanted, further increased her irritation.

"Well, this has been a waste of time!" she stated. "Let's leave before Kholos starts flinging molten rocks over the wall."

"No," said Immolatus, glowering at the temple and gnawing his lip. "The eggs are there. They are inside."

"You're not serious!" Kitiara stared at him incredulously. "How big are these golden dragons? Are they as big as you?"

"Perhaps," said Immolatus disdainfully. He rolled his eyes, refused to look at her, gazed off into the haze-filled sunset. "I never paid them that much attention."

"Hunh," Kit grunted. "And you expect me to believe that a creature as big or bigger than you crawled into that building"—she jabbed a finger at it—"and laid eggs inside!" Her patience snapped. "I think you're playing me for a fool. You and Lord Ariakas and Queen Takhisis! I'm finished with the lot of you."

She turned away, started back down the dead-end street.

"If the pea that you term a brain weren't rattling around inside your skull, banging off the walls, and caroming into dark corners, the truth might occur to you," said Immolatus. "The eggs were laid in the mountains and then the entrance sealed up and a watch placed on them. The temple is the guardhouse, as it were. The fools thought they would be safe here, that they would escape our knowledge. Probably intended that the priests would remain to guard them. But the priests fled before the mobs, either that or they were killed. Now no one remains to guard the eggs. No one."

The dragon's reasoning was highly logical. Turning back to face him, Kitiara surreptitiously sheathed her sword, trusting he hadn't noticed she'd drawn it.

"All right, Lord. You enter the temple, find the eggs, count them, identify them, or do whatever it is you're supposed to do with them. I will stay here and keep watch."

"On the contrary," said Immolatus, "you will enter the temple and search for the eggs. I'm certain there must be a tunnel leading to hatching chambers. Once you have found it, follow the tunnel until you discover the second entrance in the mountains. Then report back to me."

"It is not my responsibility to search for the eggs, Eminence," Kitiara returned grimly. "I don't even know what dragon eggs look like. I don't 'sense' them or smell them or whatever it is you do. This is your assignment, given to you by Queen Takhisis."

"Her Majesty could not have foreseen that the eggs would be guarded by a Temple of Paladine." Immolatus cast the temple a baleful glance. His eyes, slits of red, slid back to Kit. "I cannot go. I cannot enter."

"You won't, you mean!" Kitiara was angry.

"No, I cannot," Immolatus said. He crossed his arms over his chest, hugging his elbows. "He won't let me," he added in sulking tones, like a child banished from a game of goblin ball.

"Who won't?" Kit demanded.

"Paladine."

"Paladine! The old god?" Kit was amazed. "I thought you said he was gone."

"I thought he was. Her Majesty assured me he was." Immolatus breathed a flicker of fire. "But now I'm not so certain. It wouldn't be the first time she has lied to me." He snapped his teeth viciously. "All I know is that I cannot enter that temple. If I tried, he would kill me."

"Oh, but he'll let *me* just walk right in!"

"You are only a human. He cares nothing about you, knows nothing of you. You should have no difficulty. And if you do find trouble, I'm certain you are capable of dealing with whatever you encounter. I've seen the way you handle your sword." Immolatus grinned at her discomfiture. "And now, uth Matar, you really should be on your way. As you keep reminding me, we haven't much time. I will meet you back at Commander Kholos's camp. Remember, find the chamber where the eggs are located and the entrance in the mountains. Mark down everything in this book."

He handed her a small leather-bound volume. "And don't dawdle. This wretched city upsets my digestion."

He walked away. Kitiara permitted herself a fond image of the tip of her blade protruding from beneath the dragon's breastbone, the hilt buried in his back. She stood in the broken courtyard, enjoying the vision for long moments after the dragon had departed. Various wild thoughts entered her head. She would leave, abandon Immolatus and her mission. The hell with Ariakas, the hell with the dragonarmy. She had done well enough without them, she didn't need them, any of them.

An aching in her hand, clenched over the hilt of her sword, brought her to her senses. She had but to look out over the walls to see the myriad campfires of the army of General Ariakas, campfires whose numbers were almost as great as the stars above. And this army was but a fraction of his might. Someday he would rule all of Ansalon and she intended to rule at his side. Or perhaps in his stead. One never knew. And she would not achieve these goals, any one of them, as an itinerant sell-sword.

Which meant that, god or no god, she had to go into that blasted temple, a place that seemed so welcoming and yet at the same time filled her with a strange, cold fear, a dread foreboding.

"Bah!" said Kitiara and walked quickly across the broken courtyard.

She climbed the two stairs leading to the battered golden doors, halted at the top to have a brief argument with herself concerning this unreasoning terror, which only seemed to grow worse the closer she came to the temple.

Kitiara peered inside the opening between the doors, stared into the darkness beyond. She watched and listened. She no longer believed that thieves might be using this temple as a hideout, not unless they were thieves made of sterner stuff than herself. But Something was inside that temple and whatever the Something was, it had scared away a red dragon, one of the most powerful creatures on Krynn.

She saw nothing, but that meant nothing. The deepest night was not so dark, the Dark Queen's heart was not so dark, as this abandoned temple. Berating herself for not bringing along a torch, Kit was startled past all amazement when silver light flared suddenly, dazzling and half-blinding her.

Drawing her sword from the scabbard, she fell back on the defensive. She held her ground, she did not leave, though a panicked voice—the same voice of unreasoning fear—cried out to her to abandon the mission and run away, run far away.

Just like the dragon.

He fled. A creature far more dangerous, far more deadly, a creature far stronger than I am, Kitiara thought. Why should I go where Immolatus will not? He is not my commander. He cannot order me. So I return to General Ariakas a failure. I can lay the blame on Immolatus. Ariakas will understand. It is the dragon's fault. . . .

Kitiara stood inside the golden doors, hesitating, wavering, listening gladly to the cowardly voice inside her and hating herself for actually giving serious consideration to its suggestions. Never before had she experienced fear like this. She had never imagined that anything could frighten her so much.

If she turned and walked away, every moment from this moment until the time of her death, she would see this place whenever she closed her eyes. She would relive her fear, relive her shame, relive her cowardice. She could not live with herself. Far better to end it right now.

Sword in hand, she took a step forward into the bright, silver light.

A barrier—invisible, wispy, thin as cobweb, yet strong, as though the web had been spun from strands of steel—stretched across her chest. She pushed against it, but found her way blocked. She could not pass.

A man's voice, low and resolute, spoke from the darkness. "Enter, friend, and welcome. But first lay down your weapon. Within these walls is a sanctuary of peace."

Kitiara's breath caught in her constricting throat, her sword hand shook. The barrier kept her out, and her first thought was one of relief. Angered, she retained hold on her sword, shoved against the barrier.

"I warn you," said the man, and his voice was not threatening, but filled with compassion, "that if you enter this holy place with the purpose of doing violence, you will start down a road that will lead to your own destruction. Lay down the weapon and enter in peace and you will be welcome."

"You must take me for a fool to think I would give up my only means of defense," Kitiara called out, trying to see the person speaking, unable to make him out against the bright light.

"You have nothing to fear inside this temple except what you yourself bring into it," the voice returned.

"And what I'm bringing into it is my sword," Kitiara said.

She took a resolute step forward.

The bands pressed tight across her chest, as if they would cut into her flesh, but she did not yield. The pressure melted away with such swiftness that she was caught unsuspecting and stumbled forward into the temple, almost falling. Catlike, she regained her balance and looked swiftly about her, pivoting, holding her sword before her, prepared for an attack. She looked to the front, to either side, behind.

Nothing. No one. The silver light, which had blinded her outside the temple, was soft and diffused now that she was inside. The light illuminated all within; she could see every detail of the temple's interior in the eerie glow. Kitiara would have preferred the darkness. The light had no source that she could locate, it seemed to radiate from the walls.

The main room of the temple was rectangular in shape, devoid of decoration, and it was empty. No altar stood in front, no statue of the god, no braziers for incense, no chairs, no tables. No column cast a shadow in which an assassin could lurk. Nothing here was hidden. In the silver-white light, she could see everything.

Set in the eastern wall, the wall that butted up against the mountain, was another large door, a door made of silver. Immolatus had been right, curse him. This door must lead to the caverns within the mountain. She looked for a lock or a bolt, but saw none. The door had no handle, no means of opening. There must be a way, she had only to discover it. But she didn't want to leave an unknown enemy behind her.

"Where are you?" Kitiara demanded. The idea came to her that perhaps her enemy had absconded through the silver door. "Come out, you coward. Show yourself!"

"I stand here beside you," said the voice. "If you cannot see me, it is because you yourself are blind. Put down your sword and you will see my hand outstretched."

"Yes, with a dagger in it," Kitiara returned scornfully. "Ready to kill me once you have disarmed me."

"I repeat, friend, that whatever evil is here you have brought with you. Only the treacherous fear treachery."

Impatient at talking with empty air, Kitiara aimed at the sound of the voice, sliced her sword through what should have been the gut of her invisible enemy.

The blade met no resistance, but a paralyzing shock, as if the metal had come in contact with a lightning bolt, jolted through her sword arm. Her hand and fingers stung, a tingling sensation flashed from her palm up her arm. She gasped in pain, very nearly dropped the weapon.

"What have you done to me?" she cried angrily, clutching at the sword with both hands. "What magic do you use against me?"

"I have done nothing to you, friend. What you do, you do to yourself."

"This is some sort of spell! Coward wizard! Face me and fight!"

She whipped the blade through the air again, slashing and cutting.

The pain was like a streak of fire burning her arm. The hilt of the sword grew hot to the touch, hot as if it had come straight from the blacksmith's white-hot forge. Kitiara could not hold on to it. She flung the sword to the floor with a cry, nursed her burned hand.

"I tried to warn you, friend." The voice was sad and sorrowful. "You have taken the first steps upon the path of your own destruction. Leave now, and you may still avoid your doom."

"I am not your friend," Kitiara hissed through teeth gritted against the pain of the burn. A red and blistering welt in the shape of the sword hilt was visible on her palm. "All right, wizard. I've dropped the damn sword. Let me see you, at least!"

He stood before her. Not a wizard, as she had expected, but a Knight in silver armor, armor that was outdated and outmoded, heavy armor of a type worn about the time of the Cataclysm. The helm had no hinged visor, as did modern helms, but was made of one piece of metal and did not cover the mouth or the front of the neck.

Over his armor, the Knight wore a surcoat of white cloth on which was embroidered a kingfisher bird carrying a sword in one claw and a rose in the other. His body had a shimmering quality, was almost translucent.

For a moment Kitiara's courage failed her. Now she knew why Immolatus had not entered the temple. The temple would be guarded, he had said. What he had not said was that it would be guarded by the dead!

"I never believed in ghosts," Kit muttered to herself, "but then I never believed in dragons either. My bad luck both had to come true."

She could turn tail and run, probably should run. Unfortunately her feet were too busy shaking to do much in the way of fleeing.

"Pull yourself together, Kit!" she commanded. "It's a ghost now, but it used to be a man. And the man hasn't been born you can't handle. He was a Knight, a Solamnic. They're usually so bound up in honor that it's hard for them to take a crap. I don't suppose death would change that."

Kitiara tried to see the eyes of the spirit-knight, for an enemy's eyes will often give away his next point of attack. The Knight's eyes were not visible, however, concealed in the shadow cast by the overhanging helm. His voice sounded neither young nor old.

Forcing her stiff lips into a charming smile, Kit glanced around, located her sword lying on the floor. She could fight with her other hand, her uninjured hand, if need arose. A quick stoop, reach, grab, and she'd have her weapon again.

"A Knight!" Kitiara breathed a mock sigh of relief. She'd be damned if she was going to let this ghost know he had frightened her. "Am I glad to see you!"

She moved a step nearer the spirit, a move that she didn't want to make, but which brought her a step nearer her sword. "Listen to me, Sir Knight. Watch yourself! There is evil in this place."

"Indeed there is," said the Knight.

He did not move, but stood set and still. His fixed and unwavering attention was disconcerting.

"I guess whatever was in here has gone for the time being," Kit continued, favoring him with her crooked smile and an arch look. She was growing bolder. If the ghost meant to harm her, it would have done so before now. "You probably frightened it away. It will likely be back, however. We will fight it together, then, you and I. I will need my sword—"

"I will fight the evil with you," said the Knight. "But you do not need your sword."

"Damn it!" Kit began angrily and bit her lips to halt her hasty words.

She had to find a way to distract the spirit for only a few seconds, long enough for her to recover her sword.

"What are you doing here, Sir Knight?" Kit asked, quelling her anger, retrieving her smile. "I'm surprised that you're not out on the walls, defending your city against the invaders."

"Each of us is called upon to fight the darkness in his own way. The Temple of Paladine is my assigned post," said the Knight with solemn gravity. "The temple has been my post for two hundred years. I will not abandon it."

"Two hundred years!" Kit tried to laugh, coughed when the laugh caught in her throat. "Yeah, I guess it must seem that long, all by yourself in this godforsaken place. Or does someone share the watch with you?"

"No one shares my watch," the Knight replied. "I am alone."

"Some sort of punishment detail, I suppose," Kit said, glad to hear that the spirit had no more ghostly companions. "What's your name, Sir Knight? Perhaps I know your family. My father—" She was about to say her father had been a Solamnic Knight, then thought better of it. There was a possibility this spirit might not only know her father, but know her father's less than glorious history. "My people are from Solamnia," she amended.

"I am Nigel of Dinsmoor."

"Kitiara uth Matar." Kitiara extended her hand, shifted, twisted, dropped, made a grab for her sword.

A sword that was no longer there.

Kitiara stared at the empty place on the floor. She groped about with her hands until she realized how foolish and how frantic she must look. Slowly, she rose to her feet.

"Where is my weapon?" she demanded. "What have you done with it? I paid good steel for that sword! Give it back to me!"

"Your sword is not harmed. When you leave the temple, you will find it waiting for you."

"For any thief to steal!" Kit was fast losing her fear in her anger.

"No thief will touch it, I promise you that," said Sir Nigel. "You will also find there the knife you carried concealed in your boot."

"You are no Knight! No true Knight, at least," Kit cried, seething. "A Knight—dead or alive—would not resort to such knavery!"

"I have taken the weapons for your own good," Sir Nigel replied. "Should you try to continue to use them, far greater harm would come to you than you could do to anything else."

Baffled, thwarted, Kitiara glared in helpless frustration at this maddening ghost. She'd known few men who could stand against the fire of her displeasure, few men who could endure the scorching heat of her dark eyes. Tanis had been one of those few, and even he had come out singed on more than one occasion. Sir Nigel remained unmoved.

None of this was accomplishing the task at hand. Since anger would not work, she would try guile and charm, two weapons no one would ever take from her. She turned from the spirit, walked about the empty room, ostensibly admiring the architecture while she smoothed the bite marks from her lips, doused the fire in her eyes.

"Come, Sir Nigel," she said in wheedling tones, "we started off on the wrong foot and now we're in a hopeless tangle. I interrupted you in some pursuit of your own. You had every reason to be offended. As for my drawing a sword on you, you scared me half to death! I wasn't expecting anyone in here, you see. And there's something awful about this place," Kit added with rather more sincerity than she'd intended. She glanced about with a shudder that was not entirely faked. "It makes my flesh creep. The sooner I'm away from here the better."

She lowered her voice, moved closer to him. "I'll bet I know why you're here. Shall I make a guess? You're guarding a treasure, of course. It makes perfect sense."

"That is true," said Sir Nigel. "I am here to guard a treasure."

So that was it. Kitiara was amazed that she hadn't figured out the reason sooner. Immolatus had mentioned that the eggs would be guarded and so they were. But not by priests.

"And they've left you here all alone," said Kitiara with a sympathetic sigh. She frowned slightly. "Brave, but foolhardy, Sir Knight. I have heard tales of the commander of the enemy forces who now surround your city. Kholos is a hard man, a cruel man. Half-goblin, so they say. They also say that he can smell a steel piece at the bottom of a privy hole. He has two thousand men under his command. They will tear this temple down around your ears and there will be nothing even the dead can do to stop them."

"If these men are as cruel as you say, they will never find the treasure I guard," said Sir Nigel, and it seemed to Kit that he smiled.

"I'll bet I can find it," she said with an arch glance and a quirk of her eyebrow. "I'll bet that it's not hidden as well as you think. Let me look. If I manage to locate the treasure, you can move it to a better hiding place."

"All are free to search," said Sir Nigel. "It is not my place to stop you or anyone else from looking."

"So do you want me to look for the treasure or don't you?" Kitiara demanded impatiently, wishing for once this spirit would give her a straight answer. "And what do I do if I find it?"

"That depends entirely on you, friend," Sir Nigel replied.

He extended his arm, gestured toward the silver doors. The eerie light shone in the plate mail, glittered on his chain mail.

"I'll need a torch," she said.

"All who enter carry their own light within," Sir Nigel replied. "Unless they are truly benighted."

"You're the only one around here who's 'benighted,'" Kit said jocularly. "It's a joke. Knight. Benight—never mind."

Kit was reminded of Sturm Brightblade. This ghost was every bit as gullible and just as humorless. She couldn't believe he'd fallen for that treasure ploy. "I guess you'll be here when I get back?"

"I will be here," said the spirit.

Kitiara gave the silver doors an experimental shove, expecting resistance. To her astonishment, the doors opened easily, smoothly and silently.

Light flowed from the chamber in which she stood, washed around her and over her like in a gentle flood to illuminate a corridor before her, a corridor made of smooth white marble, which extended deeper into the mountain. She inspected the corridor closely, cocked her head for any sounds, sniffed the air. She heard nothing sinister, not even the skittering of mice. The only scent that came to her was—oddly—the scent of roses, old and faded. She saw nothing in the corridor except the white walls and the silver light. Yet fear gripped her, as she stood within the open doors, fear much like the fear she'd experienced on entering the temple, but worse, if that were possible.

She felt herself threatened, her back unprotected. She turned swiftly, hands raised to block an attack.

Sir Nigel was not there. No one was there. The temple was empty.

Kit should have felt relieved, yet still she stood trembling on the threshold, afraid to go beyond.

"Kitiara, you coward! I'm ashamed of you! Everything you want, everything you've worked for, lies before you. Succeed in this and General Ariakas will make your fortune. Fail and you will be nothing."

Kitiara walked into the darkness. The silver doors swung shut behind her, closed with a soft and whispered sigh.

5

THE REST OF THE MAD BARON'S ARMY ARRIVED OUTSIDE THE WALLS OF Hope's End the morning following Commander Kholos's arrival. Smoke was still rising from the smoldering fields, burning the eyes and stinging the nose and making breathing difficult. The officers put the men to work immediately, throwing up breastworks and digging trenches, pitching tents, unloading the supply wagons.

Commander Morgon, resplendent in his ceremonial armor, mounted his horse, which had been curried and brushed to remove the dust of the road, and left the camp, riding to the camp of their allies in order to arrange a meeting between the baron and the commander of the armies of Good King Wilhelm. The commander returned in less than an hour.

The soldiers paused in the work, hoping that the commander would let fall some word indicative of his opinion of their allies. Commander Morgon said nothing to anyone, however. Those who had served with him longest said that he looked unusually grim. He reported directly to the baron.

Scrounger lurked around the stand of maple trees located near the baron's tent, gathering wild onions and trying his hardest to hear what was being said. Commander Morgon's voice was low anyway, he had a habit of speaking into his beard. Scrounger couldn't understand a word the man said. He might have gained something from the baron's answers had they been lengthy, but the baron's replies were nothing more enlightening than "yes," "no," and "Thank you, Commander. Have the officers meet me at sundown."

At this point one of the baron's bodyguards stumbled over the half-kender, crouched in a weed patch, and shooed him away. Scrounger returned to camp empty-eared, so to speak, and smelling strongly of onion.

That evening, around sundown, everyone stopped work to watch the baron and his entourage ride toward the allied camp. Outraged, the sergeants roared into action, storming through camp to remind each soldier that he had a job to do and that job didn't include standing around gawking.

Caramon and C Company took up positions about a half-mile from the city wall, joining the line of pickets already established by their allies. This line prevented anyone inside the city from leaving and, more important, prevented anyone from outside the city from entering. Hope's End was cut off from help, should any help be in the offing.

Accompanied by three of his staff officers and a bodyguard of ten mounted men, the baron rode behind the line of pickets, using them to screen his movements from those manning the city walls.

"Never give information to your enemy for free," was one of the baron's many martial adages. "Make him pay for it."

The commander of the city forces was almost certainly watching every movement of the enemy armies. He did not need to see that the commander of the army's left flank was not part of the main body of the army, that the baron was "hired help." Such knowledge might imply a weakness in the cohesiveness of the army, a weakness the enemy might try to use to his advantage.

Leaving his own picket lines, the baron advanced into those posted by his allies. At sight of him, the first sentry came to attention, saluting with upraised fist. From here on, every fifty yards, the sentries came to attention and saluted as the baron's entourage rode past. The sentries wore full battle armor, helmet, and shield, each bearing the royal crest of Good King Wilhelm. The armor was polished and shone in the hazy twilight. Each sentry carried at his side a small hunting horn, an innovation that intrigued the baron.

"Well-disciplined troops," he said, nodding appreciatively. "Respectful. Armor so clean I could eat off that man's breastplate, eh, Morgon?" He glanced at his senior staff officer, the commander who had arranged the meeting. "And I like that idea of the sentries carrying hunting horns. If there's an alarm, the whole countryside will hear them blasting away. Much better than shouting. We'll implement that ourselves."

"Yes, my lord," Morgon replied.

"They've been busy," the baron continued, pointing to a low breastworks made of dirt that already surrounded the encampment. "Look at that."

"I see it, my lord," Morgon returned.

Everywhere they looked, men were busy. No one was idle, the

camp bustled with purposeful activity. No idlers hung about, breeding discontent. Soldiers hauled logs from the forest, timber that would be used to build siege towers and ladders. The blacksmith and his assistants were in their tent, forge fires burning brightly, hammering out dents in armor, pounding in rivets, turning out horseshoes for the cavalry. The smell of roast pig and beefsteak wafted through the camp. The baron and his men had been living on dry waybread and salt pork. The tempting odors made the mouth water.

The tents were arranged in an orderly manner, positioned so that each could catch the evening breeze. Arms were stacked neatly outside. The baron was loud in his approval.

"Look there, Morgon!" the baron said, indicating twenty soldiers wearing full battle gear lined up at attention beside a row of tents. "They have a standing ready-force like ours, except that theirs is at the full battle-ready. That's something else I think we should implement."

"Begging your lordship's pardon—that's not a standing ready-force," said Commander Morgon.

"It's not? What is it then?"

"Those men are on punishment detail, sir. They were standing there like that when I rode in this morning to arrange this meeting. There were thirty of them then. Ten must have fallen during the heat of the day."

"They just stand there?" The baron, astonished, shifted in the saddle to have a better view.

"Yes, my lord. According to the officer who escorted me, they're not allowed to eat, to rest, or drink water until their sentence time is served. That could be as long as three days. If a man collapses, he's carried off, revived and sent back out. His sentence starts over from that point."

"Good gods," the baron muttered. He continued staring until they passed out of range.

The baron and his officers halted just inside the entrance to the camp. The officers dismounted. The bodyguard remained on their horses.

"Give the men leave to stand down, Commander," the baron ordered.

"With my lord's permission, I think the men should stay mounted," Morgon returned.

"Is there something you want to tell me, Commander?" the baron demanded.

Morgon shook his head, avoided the baron's eyes. "No, sir. I just thought keeping the bodyguard ready to move out quickly would be prudent. In case Commander Kholos has urgent orders for us, my lord."

The baron stared hard at his commander but was unable to read anything from Morgon's expression except dutiful obedience. "Very well. Keep the men mounted. But see that they get some water."

An officer wearing armor covered by a tunic bearing the royal crest approached the waiting entourage and saluted. "Sir, my name is Master Vardash. I have been assigned to escort you to Commander Kholos."

The baron followed, accompanied by his officers. The entourage marched past rows of tents. Taking a right turn north of the blacksmith's works, the baron was looking over a stand of armor, approving the workmanship, when a cough from Morgon caused the baron to lift his head.

"What in the name of Kiri-Jolith is that?"

Hidden from the front of the camp by the large tent belonging to the blacksmith was a hastily constructed wooden gallows. Four bodies hung there. Three of the bodies had obviously been there since the day before—their eyes had been pecked out by carrion birds, one of whom was continuing his meal with the corpse's nose. One of the men was still alive, though he wouldn't be for long. As the baron watched, he saw the body jerk a couple of times, then quit moving.

"Deserters?" the baron asked Master Vardash.

"What, sir? Oh, that." Vardash cast the bodies an amused glance. "No, sir. Three of them thought they could get away with keeping some of the loot we took from the farmers for themselves. The fourth, there, the one who's still dancing, got caught with a young girl hidden in his tent. He said he felt sorry for her and was going to help her escape." Vardash smiled. "A likely story, wouldn't you agree, your lordship?"

His lordship had nothing to say.

"She is a pretty thing, I'll say that for him. She'll fetch a good price in San—That is"—Vardash appeared to recollect himself—"she will be handed over to the proper authorities in Vantal."

Commander Morgon cleared his throat loudly. The baron glanced at him, scratched at his beard, muttered beneath his breath, and marched on.

The command tent, marked by a large flag bearing the royal emblem of Good King Wilhelm, was flanked by a small section of six soldiers, obviously handpicked for the duty. Commander Morgon was a good six feet tall and these men towered over him. They dwarfed the short-statured baron. The guards wore armor that had obviously been specially designed, probably because no regulation armor would have fit over those hulking shoulders and bulging biceps.

These bodyguards did not wear the royal crest, the baron noted. They wore another crest, that of a coiled dragon, he thought, although he couldn't get a close look. Noting his gaze upon them, the guards very properly stiffened to attention, bringing their massive shields forward and thudding the butt end of the enormous spears they carried into the ground.

Dragons, the baron thought. A good symbol for a soldier, if rather quaint and old-fashioned.

Master Vardash announced the baron. A surly voice from within the command tent wanted to know what the devil this baron meant, interrupting him during supper. Master Vardash was apologetic, but reminded the commander that the meeting had been set for sunset. The commander gave ungracious permission for the baron to enter.

"Your sword, sir," said Master Vardash, barring the way.

"Yes, that's my sword." The baron put his hand on the hilt. "What about it?"

"I must ask you to entrust your sword to me, sir," said Vardash. "No one is allowed to enter the commander's presence carrying a weapon."

The baron was so outraged that for a minute he thought he was going to punch Master Vardash. Master Vardash apparently thought so as well, for he fell back a step, and put his hand to the hilt of his own sword.

"Our allies, my lord," said Commander Morgon softly.

The baron mastered his anger. Taking off his sword belt, he threw it in the direction of Master Vardash, who deftly caught it. "That's a valuable weapon," the baron growled. "It belonged to my father and his father before him. Take care of it."

"Thank you, sir. Your sword will be under my personal protection," the master said. "Perhaps your staff officers would be interested in seeing the rest of the camp."

"We've seen enough," said Commander Morgon dryly. "We will wait for you out here, my lord. Shout if you need us."

Grunting, the baron thrust aside the tent flap and stalked in.

He entered what he had supposed would be the usual command tent, furnished with a cot and a couple of campstools, a collapsible table covered with maps marked with the positions of the enemy. Instead, he thought for a moment he'd walked into Good King Wilhelm's front parlor. A fine rug, handwoven and embroidered, covered the ground. Elegant chairs, made of rare wood, surrounded an ornate table decorated with carved fruit and garlands. The table was loaded with food, not maps. Commander Kholos looked up from tearing apart a chicken.

"Well, you're here," Kholos said truculently by way of greeting. "Admire my furniture, do you? Perhaps you saw that manor house we burned down yesterday. If a house doesn't have walls, it doesn't need a table, does it?"

The commander chuckled and, thrusting his dirk—the handle crusted with dried blood—into half the chicken, he lifted it from his plate and popped it into his mouth, devoured it at one gulp, bones and all.

The baron mumbled an incoherent reply. He had been hungry when he'd entered, but at the sight of the commander, he lost his appetite. In some not too distant past, goblin and human had come together—one didn't want to speculate how—the result being Commander Kholos. The goblin part of his heritage was visible in his sallow, slightly green-tinged complexion, his underslung protruding lower jaw, his squinty eyes, overhung brow, and in his ruthless, brutal toughness. The human part could be seen in the cunning intelligence that burned in the squinty eyes with a pale and unnatural light, such as is given off by the decay of a loathsome swamp.

The baron could guess that the commander inspired as much fear in his own troops as he did in the enemy—perhaps more because the enemy had the good fortune of not being personally acquainted. The baron wondered why in the name of Kiri-Jolith any man would volunteer to fight under such a commander. Seeing the loot in the commander's tent and recalling Vardash's words—quickly cut off—about some captive girl "fetching a price" somewhere, the baron guessed that so long as Kholos's troops could look forward to the spoils of war, they would endure his abuse.

The baron knew King Wilhelm. He couldn't imagine what had possessed the man to hire a commander like this. Yet he'd done so, apparently, and he was king and these were their allies, damn it all to the Abyss and back. The baron sorely regretted ever putting his signature to the contract.

"How many men have you brought?" the commander demanded. "Are they any good in a fight?"

Kholos did not invite the baron to be seated, he did not offer the baron food or drink. Grabbing a mug, the commander gulped noisily, slammed it down, splashing ale over the fine table, and wiped his mouth with the back of a hairy hand. Looking at the baron, the commander belched loudly.

"Well?" he demanded.

The baron drew himself to his full height. "My soldiers are the best in Ansalon. I assume that you knew that or you wouldn't have hired us."

The commander waved a chicken leg, used it to brush aside the baron's reputation. "I didn't hire you. I never heard of you. Now I'm stuck with you. We'll see what you can do tomorrow. I need to know what sort of a fight your rabble will put up. You and your men will attack the west wall at dawn."

"Very good," the baron said stiffly. "And where will you and your men be attacking, Commander?"

"We won't," Kholos returned, grinning. He chewed and talked at the same time, dribbling bits of the chicken mixed with saliva down his chin.

"I'll be watching to see how your men perform under fire. My men have been well trained. I can't afford to have them ruined by a bunch of yelping curs who will roll over and piss themselves when the arrows start to fly."

The baron stood staring at the commander. His silence was an ominous cloud roiling black with astonishment and incredulity, lightning-charged with fury. Commander Morgon, waiting outside, would later say that he had never in his life heard anything—not even a thunderclap—louder than the baron's silence. Commander Morgon would also later report that he had his sword ready, for he assumed that the baron would kill the commander on the spot.

Kholos, seeing that the baron had nothing to say, forked another chicken.

The baron managed to throttle his desire to fork Kholos and said, speaking in a voice so unlike his own that Morgon would later swear he had no idea who was talking, "If we attack the city without support, you'll see nothing except my men dying, sir."

"Bah! The attack's just a feint. Testing the city's defenses, that's all. You can retreat if things get too hot for you." The commander took another swig of ale, belched again. "Report to me tomorrow at noon after the battle. We'll go over any improvements your men need to make then."

Kholos jerked a greasy thumb in dismissal and turned his complete attention to his meal. The meeting between allies was at an end.

The baron could not see the tent flap opening for the fiery red mist obscuring his vision. Fumbling his way out, nearly bringing down the tent in the process, he almost knocked over Vardash, who had stepped forward to assist him. The baron snatched his sword from the master, didn't take time to buckle it back on, but began walking.

"Let's get out of here," he said through gritted teeth. His officers fell into step behind, moving so rapidly that Vardash, who was supposed to escort them, had to jump to catch up.

The baron and his officers retraced their route, returned to their mounts and the bodyguard. It was now night. Despite the darkness, a company of soldiers was beginning a sword drill. Sergeants with bullwhips stood behind the ranks, waiting to correct any mistakes. The baron glanced at the punishment detail, counted eighteen men still standing. Two lay on the ground. No one paid any attention to them. One soldier, off on some errand of his own, actually stepped over the unmoving bodies. The baron quickened his pace.

The bodyguard was still mounted, ready to ride. Within minutes, the baron was out of the camp and heading back toward his own lines. He made the journey in silence, had nothing to say about the shining armor or noteworthy discipline of their gallant allies.

6

LIGHT THERE WAS ON THE OTHER SIDE OF THE SILVER DOOR, FEEBLE AND dim, but light enough for Kitiara to find her way. She advanced cautiously down the tunnel, fear walking with her. She kept expecting the spirit's bony fingers to clutch at her tunic, touch her shoulder, scrape across the back of her neck.

Kitiara was not imaginative. Even as a child, she'd laughed at stories that sent other children crying to their mamas. Assured by a playmate that monsters lived under her bed, Kitiara went after them with the fireplace poker. She was wont to say with a laugh that the only spirits she had ever encountered had been at the bottom of a wineskin. So much for that notion. The Knight wasn't the only ghost in the temple, unfortunately.

Figures in white robes walked alongside her, hastening on urgent errands or strolling slowly in meditative thought, figures that disappeared when she turned to confront them directly. Worse were the conversations, whispered echoes of long-silenced voices wisping through the corridor like smoke. At times she could almost make out distinct words, could almost catch what they were saying, but never quite. She had the impression they were talking about her, that they were saying something important. If they would only quit whispering, she could understand.

"What? What is it? What do you want?" Kitiara shouted out loud, deeply regretting the loss of her sword. "Who are you? Where are you?"

The voices whispered and murmured.

"If you've got something to say to me, come out and say it," Kitiara demanded grimly.

Apparently, the voices didn't, for they continued to whisper.

"Then shut the hell up!" Kitiara yelled and marched down the corridor.

The smooth marble floor gave way abruptly to stone. The man-made walls to the natural walls of a cavern. She walked a trail that was narrow and crooked, skirting large outcroppings of rocks that thrust up from the floor. Though rough, the path was not difficult to walk. In some places, it had been repaired or shored up to make walking easier.

She should have walked in darkness as dark as all the past ages of Krynn layered one on top of the other, for the only light to have ever penetrated this far beneath the mountain must have been the light of the sparks of Reorx's hammer. Yet down here the darkness had been banished. Light glistened on the wet stone, glinted when it touched veins of silver or of gold, illuminated columns of water-hewn rock that spiraled up to support a vast dome of sparkling crystalline formations.

The light was bright, dazzling, and try as she might, Kitiara could not locate the source. The light could not be coming from outside, for outside night had fallen.

"Stop fretting over it," Kit admonished herself. "Be grateful for the light. Otherwise it would take all night to traverse this path. There's an explanation for it. There has to be. Maybe molten lava, as in Sanction. Yes, that has to be the reason."

Never mind that this light wasn't red and garish as the flames that lit Sanction's smoke-filled skies. Never mind that this light was silver gray and cool and soft as moonlight. Never mind that there was no heat and no sign of a lava flow. Kitiara accepted her own explanation, and when that explanation became untenable—when she did not pass by any lava flows, nor did she come across any bubbling pools of magma, when the light continued to grow stronger and brighter the farther she traveled under the mountain—Kitiara ordered herself not to think about it anymore.

It seemed almost as if the white-robed figures had known she was coming and had gone out of their way to take her where she needed to go in the swiftest manner possible.

"Fools!" she said in her throat with a small, albeit nervous, chuckle and continued on.

The path wound about among the glittering stalagmites, carried her from one cavern room into another and always down, down deep into the mountain. The light never failed her, but led her on. When she was starting to feel thirsty and wished she'd thought to bring a waterskin, she came upon a clear, cold, rushing stream that looked as if it had been placed there for her convenience. But no sign of eggs, no sign of any cavern big enough to contain eggs or a dragon. The cavern ceiling was low. She could barely walk upright. A dragon could not have squeezed his little toe into this part of the cave.

She judged she had been walking about an hour and wondered how many leagues she had traveled. The path took her around a particularly large rock formation and brought her suddenly up against what appeared to be a sheer and impenetrable rock wall.

"This is more like it," Kit said, gratified and even relieved to find her way blocked. "I knew this was just too damn easy."

She searched for a way through the wall and eventually found a small archway that had been carved into the rock. A gate made of silver and gold blocked her way. In the center of the gate was wrought a rose, a sword, and a kingfisher. Looking through the gate, Kitiara saw a shadowed room, a room where the light dimmed as if in respect.

The room was a mausoleum.

A single sarcophagus stood in the center of the room. Kitiara could see the white marble of the tomb glimmer ghostly in the eerie light.

"Well, Kit, you've reached a dead end," she said, and laughed to herself at her little joke.

Not particularly wanting to disturb the rest of the dead, Kit set about looking for some other way around the wall. A half-hour's search left her hot and frustrated. It seemed impossible that there should be no more openings, no cracks through which she could squeeze. She muttered and swore and poked and kicked, now furious to find her way blocked. She would have to retrace her steps, look for some branching pathway that she must have missed.

Yet, she knew very well she had not missed anything. She had come to no crossroads. She had not once had to stop to decide which way she should take. The path led straight to this. A tomb.

She would have to examine it. If she couldn't find a way past it, she would be able to say to herself and to General Ariakas that she had done her duty. Immolatus probably wouldn't believe her, but if he doubted her word, he could jolly well come down here himself.

Kitiara entered the archway, came to stand before the gold and silver gates. No sign of a lock. The gate was fastened by a small bar, which could easily be lifted. She had only to reach out her hand.

Kitiara reached out her hand but did not touch the gate. She wanted to turn and run. Or, worse, she wanted to fall to the rock floor, curl up in a ball, and cry like a child.

"This is nonsense!" she said sternly, giving herself a mental shaking.

"What's the matter with me? Am I afraid to walk past a graveyard in the night? Open that gate this instant, Kitiara uth Matar."

Cringing, as if she expected the metal to be white hot to the touch, she lifted the latch. The gate swung aside silently on well-oiled hinges. Not giving herself time to think, Kitiara walked boldly and defiantly into the mausoleum.

Nothing happened.

And when it didn't, she grinned in relief, laughed at her fears, and took a quick investigative look around.

The mausoleum was circular, small, domed. The sarcophagus stood in the center, the only object in the room. A frieze carved around the wall portrayed scenes of battle: knights carrying lances riding on the backs of dragons fighting other knights, dragons fighting each other. Kit paid little attention to the carvings. She had no interest in the past or in tales of past glory. She had yet to win her own glory and that was all that mattered.

Her search was rewarded. Directly opposite the gate stood another wrought-iron gate, a way out. She strode past the sarcophagus, glanced at the tomb out of curiosity.

Kitiara stopped, startled.

The corpse of Sir Nigel, the ghost she had encountered in the temple, was stretched out upon the top of the tomb.

Kit had trouble breathing, her fear squeezed the air from her lungs. She forced herself to stare at the tomb until her fear dissipated. She was not looking at a body dead these two hundred years. The Knight was carved of stone.

Her breathing coming easier, Kit walked boldly over to the tomb. Her mistake was a reasonable one. The helm was the same: old-fashioned, made of one piece just like the helm worn by the Knight. The armor was the same down to the last detail.

The tomb was open. The marble lid had been shoved aside.

"So that's how it got out," she muttered. "I wonder what happened to the body?"

Kit peered inside the tomb, searched the shadows. Solamnic Knights often buried weapons with their dead. She thought it possible that she might find a sword or at the very least a ceremonial dagger. Possible, but not probable. The tomb was stripped bare. Not so much as a leg bone, not so much as a finger left behind. Probably the body had crumbled to dust.

Kit shivered. "The sooner I get back to sunlight and fresh air the better. Now for the gate. Let's hope this leads me to where I want to go. . . ."

"You need go no farther," said a voice. "The treasure of which I spoke is here for you to find."

"Where are you?" Kitiara demanded. "Let me see you!"

She heard a whispered cry, caught a glimpse of movement out of the corner of her eye. Her hand reached instinctively for her sword and she muttered a curse as her fingers closed over air. Placing her back against the sarcophagus, she turned to confront whatever was in the mausoleum, ready to fight with fists, feet, and teeth, if necessary.

Nothing attacked her. Nothing threatened her. The movement came from a part of the circular room near the second door, the door leading out of the mausoleum. On the floor lay what appeared to be a body. Just when Kitiara had decided it was a dead body, it stirred, moaned in pain.

"Sir Nigel?" Kitiara hissed.

No answer.

Kit was exasperated. Just when it seemed she must be nearing the end of her search, she'd run into yet another obstacle.

"Look, I'm sorry," she advised the person, "but there's nothing I can do for you. I'm on an urgent errand and I don't have much time. I'll send someone back for you. . . ."

The person moaned again.

Kitiara headed resolutely toward the door. Halfway there, she recalled the Knight's words. The treasure was here. Perhaps this person had found it first. Kit veered from her path. Keeping a sharp lookout for attackers lurking in the shadows, thinking that this might be a trap, she moved swiftly to where the body lay huddled on the floor and knelt down beside it.

The body was that of a woman, Kit saw in astonishment. A woman dressed in black, skintight clothing, clothing meant to be worn beneath metal armor. She lay on her stomach, her face pressed against the stone floor. She had been in a horrific fight, by the look of her. Long bloody gashes had torn her clothes. Her black curly hair was matted with blood. A large pool of blood had formed beneath her stomach. Judging by that and the victim's ashen skin, Kit guessed that the woman was near death. Kit searched, but found no treasure. Disappointed, she started to rise to her feet, then paused, looked more closely at the dying woman.

Something about her seemed familiar.

Kit reached out her hand to brush aside the woman's hair, get a better look at the face. Her fingers touched . . .

Black curly hair cut short. The hair Kit was touching she'd touched many, many times before. The hair was her own.

Kitiara snatched her hand back. Her mouth went dry, breathing ceased. Terror stole her reason. She couldn't think, she couldn't move.

The hair was her own. The face was her own.

"I have always loved you, half-elf," the dying woman whispered.

The voice was her own. Kitiara looked upon herself, wounded, dying.

Kit jumped to her feet and fled. She hit the iron gate running, flung her weight against it, beat on it with her fists when it wouldn't open. Pain from bruised flesh brought her to her senses. The darkness that had blinded her cleared from her eyes. She saw that the gate had a handle and, with a sob of relief, she grabbed it and turned.

The catch clicked. She shoved open the gate, raced through it, slammed the gate shut behind her with all her strength. She leaned against the gate, too weak from fear to keep moving. Panting for air, she waited for her heartbeat to slow, the sweat to dry on her palms, her legs to stop shaking.

"That was me!" she gasped, shuddering. "That was me back there. And I was dying. Dying horribly, painfully . . . 'I have always loved you . . .' My voice! My words!" Kitiara buried her face in her hands, prey to such terror as she had never before known. "No! Please, no! I . . . I . . ."

Kit drew in a breath. "I am a fool!" She slumped against the door, shivering, a reaction to her fear. She gave herself a mental slap, intended to clear her mind of what had to be visions, fancies, a waking dream. . . .

"It wasn't real. It couldn't have been real." She sighed and swallowed, swallowed again. The moisture had returned to her mouth and with it the bitter aftertaste of terror. "I'm tired. I haven't slept well. When a person doesn't sleep, he starts to see things. Remember Harwood in the Plains of Dust, fighting goblins? Stayed awake three nights running, then went rampaging through the camp, screaming that snakes were crawling on his head."

Kitiara stood leaning against the gate, hugging her chill body, trying to banish the memory of the dream.

It had to be a dream. No other explanation.

"If I walked back in there," she told herself, "I'd find nothing. No body. Nothing. That's what I'd find. Nothing."

But she didn't walk back in there.

Kitiara drew a deep breath and, feeling the horror start to fade, she shook off the unreasoning fear and looked at her surroundings.

She stood inside a large cavern, an enormous cavern. A glow came from the far end of the cavern, a glow that might have been created by torchlight shining on mounds of silver and of gold.

"Come now, this is better," said Kitiara, cheering up immensely. "I think I may be getting somewhere."

She hurried in the direction of the shining light, glad to have a purpose, extremely glad to leave the ill-fated chamber behind her.

The cavern floor was smooth, the cavern itself commodious. Immolatus in dragon form could have fit himself in here and still accommodated two or three large red friends. If ever there was an ideal location for dragons to hide their eggs, this was it. Excited at the prospect, Kitiara broke into a run. The blood pumped through her body, brought warmth back to numb feet and hands.

She reached her destination, breathing hard, but feeling refreshed and renewed. And triumphant.

Nestled in an alcove in the cavern were hundreds of eggs. Enormous eggs. One egg was as tall as Kitiara or taller and so wide around that she might extend her arms and only embrace a small portion of the shell. Each egg radiated with a soft light. Some of the eggs shone with a golden light, some gleamed silver. There were a great many. Kitiara couldn't begin to count them, but counting them was what she was going to have to do. A task that would be tedious and boring. Still, she found herself looking forward to it.

Cataloging eggs and mapping their location for future reference would be drudge work, guaranteed to brush away the last vestiges of horror that webbed her mind. Just as she reached this satisfying conclusion, she felt a breath of air, fresh air, touch her cheek. She inhaled deeply.

A large tunnel, large enough for a dragon's body, led to the secret entrance for which Immolatus had been searching. An enormous hole in the side of the mountain, a hole completely hidden from the outside by a stand of fir trees. Pushing her way past the trees, Kitiara stepped out onto a large rock ledge. She looked up into the night sky, hazy with smoke, looked down on the doomed city of Hope's End. It must be about midnight. Time enough to complete her work and make her way down the mountainside to the camp of Commander Kholos.

Kitiara returned to the chamber of the eggs, which gave off light enough for her to see by, and went to work, thankful to have something to occupy her thoughts. Taking out the small leather-bound book Immolatus had given her, Kit searched until she found a bit of sandstone, which she could use like chalk.

First she drew a map of the location of the hidden entrance, making careful calculation of where it stood in relation to the city walls and landmarks, so that Commander Kholos could find this cavern without going through the temple. She had to wonder how he was going to cart the eggs down the mountainside, for the way was steep. But that wasn't her concern, thank the Dark Queen. Her task was finished.

Map completed, she stood up and walked into the chamber of the eggs, a chamber suffused in golden and silver light, the light of unborn dragons, whose souls played among the star fields and danced on the ethers.

What would happen to those souls who would never be born into this life? Kit shrugged. That was not her concern either.

She eyed the eggs, decided that it would be best to count them by rows in order not to lose track. Clambering onto a rock ledge that overlooked the chamber, Kitiara spread the book out on her lap.

"You discovered the treasure," said a voice behind her.

Kitiara closed the book hastily, covered it with her hand, and turned around. "Sir Nigel," she said. "So this is where you flitted off to. As for treasure, hah! I didn't find anything except these things, whatever they are. Eggs, I guess. Big, aren't they? Make a whopping big omelet. Big enough to feed an army. What sort of creature do you suppose laid them?"

"This is not the treasure," said the Knight. "The treasure was inside the mausoleum, a treasure left there by Paladine."

Kitiara managed a shaky grin. "Tell this Paladine that I prefer my treasure in rubies and emeralds."

"You have seen your death. A horrible one. You can yet change your fate, however," Sir Nigel continued. "That is why the future was revealed to you. You have the power to alter it. Leave your task here unfinished. Do so, and you will take the first step to stop what otherwise must be."

Kitiara was tired and she was hungry. The burn on her hand hurt, she didn't like being reminded of the horrible sight in that mausoleum. She had work to do and this blasted spirit was interrupting her.

She turned her back on him, hunkered over her book. "Hey, I thought I heard your god calling you. Maybe you better go answer."

Sir Nigel made no response. Kit looked over her shoulder, was relieved to find that he had gone.

Putting the ghost and his "treasure" out of her mind, she settled down to count eggs.

7

"RED! PASS THE WORD FOR RED!"

Raistlin was in his tent, taking advantage of a few quiet moments in the late evening to continue his study of the book about Magius. Raistlin had read the book through once, but parts remained unclear—the handwriting of the chronicler was almost unreadable in places—and Raistlin was now going through the book line by line, making his own copy for future reference.

"Horkin wants you," said one of the soldiers, poking his head inside. "He's in the wizard tent."

"You sent for me, sir?" Raistlin said.

"That you, Red?" Horkin did not look up. He was engrossed in his work, heating a concoction in a small pot hung on a tripod over a charcoal brazier. He took a sniff, frowned, and stuck the tip of his little finger into the pot. Shaking his head, he stirred the mixture. "Not hot enough." He glared impatiently at the pot.

"You sent for me, sir," Raistlin said again.

Horkin nodded, still not looking at him. "I know it's late, Red, but I've a job for you. I think this one you might even like. More interesting than my socks."

He cast a sidelong glance at Raistlin, who flushed in embarrassment. True, he had been frustrated beyond measure at being made to perform menial tasks about camp, tasks that wouldn't have challenged a gully dwarf: washing linens to be used for bandages, cutting those same linens, sorting through bags of herbs and flowers, watching some foul brew simmer over the brazier. The last tug of the dwarf's beard had been darning Horkin's socks.

Horkin was no seamstress and when he discovered that Raistlin had a certain talent in this field—a talent gained during the lean days when he and his twin were orphaned, forced to live on their own—Horkin had given Raistlin the chore. Raistlin imagined that he had handled the onerous tasks with good grace. Apparently not.

"Commander Morgon tells me that there's a red-robed mage marching with the army of our allies. Morgon says he caught a glimpse of him walking through camp."

"Indeed, sir?" Raistlin was definitely interested.

"I thought you might enjoy going on a trading expedition, if you're not too tired."

"I'm not tired at all, sir." Raistlin accepted the assignment with far more enthusiasm than any he'd received thus far. "What do you want me to take to trade?"

Horkin rubbed his chin. "I've been considering. We've got those scrolls neither of us can read. Perhaps this mage can make something of them. Don't let on you don't know what's in 'em, though. If he thinks you can't read them, he'll pass them off as trash and we won't get a cracked amulet for them."

"I understand, sir," said Raistlin. His chagrin at being unable to read the scrolls ran deep.

"Speaking of amulets, I brought that box of stuff you sorted and labeled. Anything in there you think might be worth something?"

"You never know, sir," Raistlin replied. "Just because we don't consider an artifact valuable doesn't mean another wizard might not find a use for it. At any rate," he added with a sly smile, "I can hint to him that they're more than they are. I am your apprentice, after all. It's not likely you would trust me to handle such magical objects if I understood their true power."

"I knew you were the right man for the job," Horkin said, greatly delighted. "Throw in a couple of our healing ointments for good measure. And, don't show this around"—Horkin handed over a bag of coins—"but if he has something really valuable and he won't trade for it, you can pay in steel. Now, what are we in the market for?"

The two went over what magic they already possessed, determined what they lacked, debated over what might be useful and how much Raistlin would be willing to pay.

"Five steel for a scroll, ten for a potion, twenty for a spellbook, and twenty-five for an artifact. That's my limit," Horkin stated.

Raistlin argued that his master was out of touch with current market prices, but Horkin refused to budge. Raistlin could do nothing but agree, though he privately resolved to take along some of his own money, do his own bargaining if he found something of value priced beyond what Horkin was willing to give.

"Ah, it's done!" Horkin said, looking with satisfaction into the pot, whose contents were now bubbling. He wrapped the handle in cloth, lifted the pot from the heat and carefully poured the contents into a large crock. Stopping the crock with a cork, he wiped off the sides and placed the crock into a basket. He handed the basket to Raistlin. "There, take that to the Red Robe. It's a deal clincher if there ever was one."

"What is it, sir?" Raistlin asked, mystified. He had caught only a glimpse of the brew—some sort of cloudy liquid filled with whitish lumps. "A potion?"

"Chicken and dumplings for his dinner," said Horkin. "My own recipe. Give him a taste and he'll hand over his smalls if that's what you want." He gave the crock a fond pat. "There's not a wizard alive who won't succumb to my chicken and dumplings."

✪

Loaded down with artifacts, scroll cases, and the crock of chicken and dumplings, along with numerous jars of ointments and unguents and a flask of honey wine to smooth the wizard's throat into saying "yes," Raistlin left the baron's camp and walked toward the camp of their ally. Horkin did not think to provide the young mage with an armed escort, although if he had heard Commander Morgan's full report about what he and the baron had seen and heard in the ally's camp that afternoon, he might have done so. As it was, Raistlin took only the Staff of Magius for light and his small, hidden knife for protection. After all, he thought, he was among friends.

His first encounter was with the line of pickets of the allied force. The soldiers regarded him with considerable suspicion, but by now Raistlin was accustomed to dark looks and knew how to handle the situation. He stated his errand truthfully, said he was visiting a fellow wizard interested in doing a little trading. At first the soldiers had no idea what he was talking about. A Red Robe? They didn't think so.

Then one recalled that a Red Robe had arrived in camp earlier that evening, appearing out of nowhere. A slimy fellow, no one liked him, the soldier said. They'd thought of slitting his throat, but there was something about him . . . The Red Robe insisted on meeting with Kholos and, such was the unease the wizard inspired, he'd been taken immediately to the commander. The next thing the soldiers knew, they were pitching a tent for the Red Robe and treating him as if he were the commander's long-lost brother-in-law. The soldiers passed Raistlin on through the lines, with only a cursory examination of what he carried—no one wanted to investigate a wizard's wares too closely. Several hinted broadly that if Raistlin would like to leave his basket and take the Red Robe back with him, it would be much appreciated.

Apparently, unlike the popular Horkin, this war wizard was not held in high regard by his fellow soldiers.

"But then, neither am I," Raistlin said to himself and continued on through the lines into the allied camp.

He saw the punishment detail, but he did not understand what was transpiring. Seeing men lying comatose on the ground, he assumed this was merely some sort of strange practice common among soldiers and walked by without a second glance. He did not see the corpses dangling from the gibbets, but, from what he'd seen of harsh military discipline, even that might not have surprised him.

He asked around for the tent of the war wizard. It was pointed out to him with reluctance and one man asked him outright if he was certain he wanted to have dealings with the wizard. All who spoke of him did so with surly looks behind which was a hint of fear. Raistlin's estimation of this Red Robe rose accordingly.

Raistlin eventually found the wizard's tent, positioned at a distance from all the other tents in the encampment. The tent was large and commodious.

Raistlin paused outside the tent, drew in a deep breath to calm his excitement and anticipation. He was about to meet a true war wizard, a fellow Red Robe, perhaps of high ranking. A wizard who might be in the market for an apprentice. Raistlin would not leave Horkin, not yet. He was bound by contract and honor to serve out his term with the baron. But here was a chance to make himself known and, perhaps, favorably impress the wizard. Who knew? This Red Robe might be so impressed that he would be willing to buy out Raistlin's contract, take him on immediately.

The young are made of dreams.

Peering through the slight part in the tent flap opening, Raistlin could catch just a glimpse of red by the light of a dip set in a bowl of perfumed oil. He heard the sound of what seemed hissing breath. He had regained his composure, was prepared to represent himself as cool and competent and professional. Raistlin shifted the basket with the chicken and dumplings onto the arm that was also holding the Staff of Magius and knocked on the tent post with his free hand.

"Is that you, worm?" came a deep voice from within the tent. "If so, quit shaking the tent and come inside and make your report. What did you find in that damn temple?"

Raistlin was in an extremely awkward situation. He had to admit that he was not the expected "worm" and, from that unpropitious start, go on to introduce himself. Worse, he felt his lungs starting to clog. He made a desperate attempt to clear his throat with a single, harsh cough, and decided to pretend he hadn't heard.

"Excuse me for disturbing you, Master," he called, thankful to feel the smothering sensation in his lungs recede. "My name is Raistlin Majere. I am a red-robed wizard connected with the army of Baron Ivor Langtree. I have with me various scrolls, magical artifacts, and potions. I've come to see if you might be interested in making a trade."

"Go to the Abyss."

Considerably taken aback by the rude remark, Raistlin stared at the tent post in speechless amazement. Whatever he had expected, it wasn't this.

He had never met the wizard, not even the powerful and puissant Par-Salian himself, who would pass up an opportunity to acquire new magic. Curiosity alone would have had any wizard of Raistlin's acquaintance barging out of that tent to rummage through the scroll cases and bag of artifacts. Perhaps the Red Robe wasn't in the market for trading. But, damn it, at the very least, the man should be interested to see what Raistlin had brought with him.

Raistlin risked peeping inside the tent, hoping to see the wizard. The Red Robe was leaning back in his chair, apparently, for he was lost in the shadows.

"Perhaps you did not understand me, Master," Raistlin said, speaking with the utmost respect. "I have brought with me many magical items, some of which are quite powerful, in hopes that you—"

He heard a sound as of a kettle boiling over, an angry rustling of robes and suddenly the tent flap jerked aside. A face—livid, with glaring red eyes—thrust out of the tent. Anger like a hot wind struck Raistlin, caused him to retreat a step.

"Leave me in peace," the Red Robe snarled, "or, by the Dark Queen, I'll send you to the Abyss myself—"

The Red Robe's glaring red eyes widened in shock. The furious oath died on his lips. The wizard glared, not at Raistlin, but at the staff in Raistlin's hands. As for Raistlin, he gazed intently at the wizard. Neither spoke a word, both were struck dumb, each seeing something he had not expected.

"Why are you staring at me!" the wizard demanded.

"I might ask the same question, sir!" Raistlin countered, shaken.

"I'm not staring at *you*, worm," Immolatus growled, and that was true enough. He had barely glanced at the human. The dragon's gaze was riveted upon the staff.

Immolatus's first dragonish impulse was simply to snatch the staff and incinerate the human. His fingers twitched, the words of the spell flared in his throat, burned on his tongue. He resisted the impulse, after a struggle. Killing the human would invite unwanted attention, require tedious explanations, and leave a blackened, greasy mark on the ground outside his tent. Most important in his decision to allow the human to live—at least temporarily—was the dragon's curiosity about the staff. One could not gain information from a greasy spot on the grass.

Immolatus realized, much to his ire, that in order to find out the answers to the questions boiling in his mind he would actually have to be—what was the word uth Matar was always using? "Diplomatic." He would have to be diplomatic in his dealings with the human. Difficult to manage when what Immolatus really wanted to do was to rip open the creature, yank out its brain, and pick through it with a sharpened foreclaw.

"You had better come inside," Immolatus muttered and he actually considered that a gracious invitation.

Raistlin remained where he was standing, outside the tent. He had grown accustomed to his accursed eyesight, to looking at the world through the spell-laden eyes, which saw all things as they were affected by time, saw youth wither, saw beauty brought to dust. Looking at this man, who was, perhaps, in his early forties, Raistlin should have seen the Red Robe wrinkled and elderly. What Raistlin saw was a blurred portrait, two faces instead of one, two faces in a botched painting, as if the artist had allowed all the colors to run together.

One face was the face of a human wizard. The other face was more difficult to see, but Raistlin had a fleeting impression of red, vibrant red, glittering red. There was something reptilian about the man, something reptilian about his second face.

Raistlin had the feeling that if he could just focus on that second face, he would see it clearly and understand what he saw. But every time he tried to concentrate, the second face flowed into the lines of the first.

Two faces, he noticed, yet both regarded him with a single pair of red-flame eyes. The man was dangerous, but then all wizards are dangerous.

Wary, cautious, Raistlin accepted the invitation to enter the tent for exactly the same reason that he'd been invited. Curiosity.

The Red Robe was tall and thin, his clothes rich and expensive. He walked to a small camp table, sat down in a folding chair and made an abrupt gesture at the table. His movements were both graceful and awkward at the same time, rather like the blurred double image of the face. Small movements—the flutter of the long fingers, for example, or the slight inclination of the head—were performed easily and with fluid motion. Larger movements—seating himself in the chair—were clumsy, as if he were unaccustomed to such motions and had to stop to think about what he was doing.

"Let's see what you've brought," Immolatus said.

Absorbed in trying to sort out this mystery, Raistlin did not respond. He stood and stared, clutching the basket and the scroll cases and the staff.

"Why in the Abyss do you look at me with those freakish eyes of yours?" Immolatus demanded irritably. "Have you come to deal or not? Let us see what you have." He tapped impatiently on the table with the long, sharp nail of a forefinger.

Actually there was only one artifact in the tent in which Immolatus was truly interested and that was the staff. But he needed to find out a few things about it first, most especially—how much did the human know about what he held? To look at him, not much. Certainly not like the first human Immolatus had met who had wielded that staff. Immolatus ground his teeth at the memory.

Raistlin lowered his gaze, ignored the insult about his eyes. He could have made a few choice remarks about this man's appearance had he chosen. He refrained. The wizard was his elder and his better, no question about that. Raistlin felt himself standing in the center of a veritable vortex of magical power. The magic whirled and crackled and sparked around him and all of that power emanated from this man. Raistlin had experienced nothing like this magical storm before, not even in the presence of the Head of the Conclave. He was humbled and consumed with envy and resolved to learn from this man or perish in the attempt.

In order to have both hands free to divest himself of the trade goods, Raistlin leaned the Staff of Magius against the small camp table.

Immolatus's hand snaked across the table toward it.

Raistlin saw the move and dropped the basket. He caught hold of the staff, stood clutching it close to his body.

"A fine walking staff," said Immolatus, baring his teeth in what he meant for a friendly, disarming smile. "How did you come by it?"

Raistlin had no intention of discussing the staff and so he pretended he had not heard. Keeping fast hold of the staff in one hand, he spread out the scrolls, the artifacts, unpacked the jars of potions, much like a peddler at a fair.

"We have several very interesting items, sir. Here is a scroll captured from a Black Robe whom we have reason to believe was of extremely high rank and here is—"

Immolatus thrust out his arm and swept all the objects—scrolls, potions, basket, and crock—off the table. "There is only one magical item I am interested in obtaining," he said, and his gaze went to the staff.

The scroll cases rolled under the table, the artifacts scattered in every direction. The crock crashed to the hard-packed ground and broke, splashing chicken broth on the hem of Raistlin's robes.

"This is one magical artifact which I have no intention of trading, sir," Raistlin said, holding on to the staff so tightly that the muscles of his hand and forearm began to ache with the strain. "Some of the rest of these are quite powerful—"

"Bah!" Immolatus seethed. He rose to his feet with a twist of his body, uncoiling, not standing. "I have more power in my little finger than is contained in any one of the paltry trinkets you have the temerity to try to palm off on me. Except the staff. I might possibly be interested in that staff. How did you come by it?"

It was on the tip of Raistlin's tongue to tell the truth, to say—with some pride—that the staff had been a gift from the great Par-Salian. His natural proclivity to secrecy stopped the words in his throat. Describing the staff as a gift from the Head of the Conclave would only invite more discussion, more questions, perhaps increase the value of the staff in this wizard's eyes. Raistlin wanted nothing more to do with this wizard, wanted to leave this strange man's presence as soon as possible.

"The staff has been in my family for generations," he said, edging backward toward the tent flap. "Thus, you see, sir, I am constrained by family tradition and honor not to part with it. Since it seems we cannot do business, sir, I bid you good day."

By accident, Raistlin said the right words, words that probably saved his life. Immolatus immediately jumped to the conclusion that Raistlin was a descendant of the powerful wizard Magius. Magius must have left a written account of the powers of the staff with his relations or at least handed down such an account by word of mouth. Now that Immolatus looked at the young man, he did seem to bear a certain family resemblance to Magius of accursed memory.

For it was Magius who had defeated the red dragon Immolatus. Magius and the magical power of that very staff had come very near slaying Immolatus, had wounded him grievously, wounds that, though healed, still pained him. Immolatus dreamed of that staff, its magic flaring, blinding, searing, killing, for long centuries. He would have traded all his lost treasure for that staff, to seize it, hold it, dote on it, use it to strike back at his enemies, use it to slay them as it had very nearly slain him. Use it to slay the descendant of Magius.

Immolatus could not battle the heir to the staff in this puny, human body. He considered changing back to his dragon form, decided against it. He would have his revenge upon all those who had wronged him—the gold dragons and the silver, his duplicitous queen, and now Magius. The dragon had waited years upon years for his revenge, a few more days were drops of water in the ocean of his waiting.

"You forget your wares, Peddler," Immolatus said, casting a scathing glance at the magical paraphernalia that lay scattered at his feet.

Raistlin was not about to start crawling on the ground, gathering up the scrolls and jars and rings, leaving himself vulnerable to attack.

"Keep them, sir. As you have said, they are of little value."

Raistlin made a slight bow to the wizard, a bow that was more than mere politeness, for he was able to use the bow as an excuse to depart the tent gracefully, without turning his back on the wizard.

Immolatus made no response, but watched Raistlin leave—or rather watched the staff leave—with red eyes whose gaze, like that of a crystal absorbing and focusing the energy of sun upon a straw, might have set the staff ablaze.

Raistlin walked from the tent and kept walking with a rapid pace, seeing nothing in his path and not even very certain of the direction he was taking. His one thought was to put as much distance as possible between himself and the fey man with the blurred face and lethal eyes.

Only when he was safely in sight of the bonfires of his own camp, the comforting sight of hundreds of well-armed soldiers, did Raistlin slow his pace. As thankful as he was to be back among friends, Raistlin pulled his hood over his head and took a circuitous route back to his tent. He did not want to talk to anyone, especially not Horkin.

Once safely hidden from view, Raistlin sank, exhausted, upon his bed. Sweat bathed his body, he felt dizzy and light-headed and sick to his stomach. Holding on to the staff, still afraid to let go, he stared down at his boots, wet with chicken broth.

The smell sickened him, brought back to Raistlin the terror of the encounter in the tent, the memory of the red-fire eyes of the wizard, the horror-filled, helpless knowledge that if the Red Robe had chosen, he could have taken the precious staff and Raistlin would have been powerless to prevent him.

Raistlin choked and retched. Months after, the very sight of a stewed chicken would fail to render him so nauseous that he would be forced to leave the table, making Caramon the one clear winner in the encounter.

Once the sickness passed and he felt more equal to the task, Raistlin went to make his report to Horkin. Raistlin pondered long over what to say. His first impulse was to lie about the incident, which made him appear a fool at best.

In the end, Raistlin decided to tell Horkin the truth, not from any noble aspirations, but because he could not think of a lie that would adequately explain the loss of their magewares. Where were kender when you needed them?

Horkin was astonished to see Raistlin return empty-handed. Astonishment gave way to glowering anger when Raistlin admitted calmly and steadily that he had fled the tent of the Red Robe, leaving the magewares behind.

"I think you better explain yourself, Red," Horkin said grimly.

Raistlin did explain, portraying the meeting in vivid detail. He described the Red Robe, described his own fear and the almost blind panic that had overtaken him when he was certain that the Red Robe was going to attack him to gain the staff. Raistlin kept to himself only one thing and that was the appearance of the two faces, merging and separating and merging again. He could never explain that, not even to himself.

Horkin listened to the tale with suspicion at first. He was truly disappointed in his apprentice, suspected that the young mage had sold the goods himself and was intent on keeping what he had earned, though—Horkin admitted—he found such a deed difficult to believe of a young man he'd come to grudgingly respect and even like a little. Horkin eyed Raistlin closely, well aware that this young man would have no compunction about lying if he thought a lie might be to his gain. But Horkin saw no lie here. Raistlin's complexion paled when he spoke of the encounter, a shudder shook the frail body, the shadow of remembered fear haunted his eyes.

The longer Raistlin talked—and once he had overcome his reluctance to speak of the matter, he talked with an almost feverish compulsion—the more Horkin came to believe the young man was telling the truth, strange as that truth might be.

"This wizard is powerful, you say." Horkin rubbed his chin, an action that apparently aided him in thinking, for he often resorted to it when puzzled.

Raistlin halted his pacing of the wizard tent. Though he was dead tired, he could not sit still, but walked the length and breadth of the small tent restlessly, leaning upon the staff, which he had resolved not to let out of his sight or his grasp.

"Powerful!" Raistlin exclaimed. "I have stood in the presence of the Head of the Conclave himself, the great Par-Salian, purportedly one of the most powerful archmages ever to have lived, and the magic I felt emanate from him was as a summer shower compared to a cyclone in the presence of this man!"

"And a Red Robe, for all that."

Raistlin hesitated before replying. "Let me say, sir, that although this wizard wore red robes, I had the distinct impression that they were not worn out of allegiance to one of the gods of magic so much as they were . . . well"—he shrugged helplessly—"like his skin."

"Red eyes and orange-colored skin. He's an albino, maybe. I knew an albino once. A soldier when I first joined up with the baron. In C Company, I think it was. He—"

"Begging your pardon, sir." Raistlin cut off Horkin's reminiscences impatiently. "But what should we do?"

"Do? About what? The wizard?" Horkin shook his head. "Leave him alone, I should say. Sure, he stole our stuff, but, let's face it, Red, there was nothing there of any value except your staff, which he spotted right off, small blame to him. If you don't mind, though, I think I will mention the incident to the baron."

"Tell the baron that I ran away in a panic, sir?" Raistlin asked bitterly.

"Of course not, Red," Horkin replied gently. "Given the circumstances, it seems to me that you acted with good, plain common sense. No, I'll just mention to the baron that we think there's something a bit sinister about this wizard. Judging by what else I've heard of our allies, I doubt if his lordship will be much surprised," Horkin added dryly.

"There's a possibility that this wizard is a renegade, sir," Raistlin said.

"Aye, Red, there is," Horkin returned.

Renegade wizards did not follow the laws laid down by the Conclave of Wizards, laws designed to assure that powerful magicks would not be used recklessly or with abandon. Such laws were meant to protect not only the general populace but wizards themselves. A renegade wizard was a danger to every other wizard, and it was the avowed duty and responsibility of every wizard, who was a member of the Conclave to seek out renegades and either attempt to persuade them to join the Conclave or to destroy them if they refused.

"What do you intend to do about it, Red?" Horkin continued. "Challenge him? Call him out?"

"In other days I might have," Raistlin said with a slight smile, remembering the time he had challenged another renegade wizard, with almost disastrous results. "I have since learned my lesson. I am not such a fool as to go up against this man, who—as he said—has more magic in his little finger than I do in my entire body."

"Don't sell yourself short, Red," Horkin said. "You've got potential. You're young yet, that's all. Someday, you'll be a match for the best of them."

Raistlin regarded the master with astonishment. This was the first compliment Horkin had ever paid him and the chill of the young man's fear warmed with pleasure.

"Thank you, sir."

"Likely that day will be long in coming," Horkin continued cheerfully. "Seeing that you can't even cast a burning-hands spell now without setting your own clothes afire."

"I told you, sir, I was not feeling well that day—" Raistlin began.

Horkin grinned. "Just teasing, Red. Just teasing."

Raistlin was in no mood for Horkin's jollity. "If you will excuse me, sir, I am very tired. It must be well past midnight and from what I understand there is a battle to be fought tomorrow morning. With your permission, I will go to bed."

"It's all very strange," muttered Horkin to himself after his apprentice had departed. "This albino wizard. Like nothing I've encountered before and I've been pretty well all over this continent. But then it seems to me that Krynn itself is becoming a very strange place. A very strange place indeed."

Shaking his head, Horkin went off to drink a late night's toast to the world's strangeness with the baron.

8

THE BARON HAD SAID NOTHING TO HIS TROOPS ABOUT COMMANDER Kholos and his insulting remarks. But the baron had not forbidden his bodyguards to talk of what they had seen and heard in the ally's camp. The commander's words about "yelping curs" spread among the mercenaries like a forest fire during the night, jumping from one knot of angry men to the next, starting blazes all over camp. The men began to say that they'd take the west wall, damn the commander's eyes, and not only that, they'd take the whole blasted city, too, before he'd finished his breakfast.

When word came that the flank company, under command of Master Senej, would have the honor of attacking in the morning, the rest of the soldiers regarded them with raw envy, while members of the lucky company busily polished their armor and tried to look nonchalant, as if this were all in a day's work.

"Raist!" Caramon burst like a gust of wind into his brother's tent. "Did you hear—"

"I am trying to sleep, Caramon," Raistlin said caustically. "Go away."

"But this is important. Raist, it's our squad that's—"

"You knocked over my staff," Raistlin observed.

"Sorry. I'll pick it—"

"Don't touch it!" Raistlin ordered. Rising from his bed, he retrieved the staff, moved it to stand by the head of his cot. "Now, what is it you want?" he asked wearily. "Make it quick. I am extremely tired."

Not even his brother's ill temper could destroy Caramon's pride and excitement. He seemed to fill the entire tent as he spoke, his good health and his powerful body swelling in the darkness, expanding to take up all the space, sucking away all the air, leaving his twin crushed and smothered.

"Our squad's been chosen to lead the assault tomorrow morning. 'First to fight,' that's what the master said. Are you coming with us, Raist? This'll be our first battle!"

Raistlin stared into the darkness. "If so, I have not yet received any orders."

"Oh, uh, that's too bad." Caramon was momentarily deflated. But excitement soon returned, swelling him again. "You will. I'm sure of it. Just think! Our first battle!"

Raistlin turned his head on the pillow, away from his brother.

Caramon felt suddenly that it was time to leave. "I got to sharpen my sword. I'll see you in the morning, Raist. G'night." He departed with as much noise and clamor as he had entered.

☥

"Excuse me, sir," said Raistlin, standing outside Horkin's tent. "Are you asleep?"

There came a grumbling growl in response. "Yes."

"I'm sorry to wake you, sir." Raistlin slipped inside the tent where his master lay on a cot, blankets pulled up to his chin. "But I have just heard that my brother's company has been ordered to attack the west wall tomorrow morning. I thought perhaps you would like me to prepare some magicks—"

Horkin sat up, his eyes squinched shut against the light of the Staff of Magius. The mage did not sleep in his robes, which were folded neatly on top of his pack at the side of cot. He slept in what he termed his "altogether."

"Shut off that damn light, Red! What are you trying to do? Blind me? There, that's better. Now, what is this folderol you're singing me?"

Patiently Raistlin repeated himself. Quenching the light of his staff, he stood in the darkness of the tent, a darkness that smelled of stale sweat and crushed flowers.

"You woke me up to tell me that?" Horkin grumbled. Lying back down, he grabbed hold of the blanket, twitched it up over his shoulders. "We'll both need our sleep, Red. We'll have wounded tomorrow."

"Yes, sir," Raistlin said. "But about the battle—"

"The baron hasn't given me any orders about the battle tomorrow, Red. But then"—Horkin tended to be sarcastic when he was sleepy—"perhaps he gave them to you."

"No, sir," Raistlin said. "I just thought—"

"There you go, thinking again!" Horkin snorted. "Listen to me, Red. Tomorrow's fight is a feint, a skirmish. We're testing the city's defenses. And the last thing you want to do when you're testing the enemy is to show them everything you've got! We're the big finish, you and I, Red. The baron brings us mages in at the last act to the dismay and wonderment of all. Now go and let me get some sleep!"

Horkin pulled the blankets up over his head.

❸

No one wanted to settle down to sleep that night. Everyone wanted to stay up and talk and boast of what deeds he would do tomorrow or complain bitterly that he was being left out or go offer advice and well-wishes to those fortunate enough to be in on the first assault. The sergeants let them talk it out, then went through the camp, ordering everyone to hit the hay, they'd need their rest for the morrow. Eventually, the camp quieted, though few actually slept.

Raistlin returned to his tent, where he was seized with an unusually severe fit of coughing. He spent most of the night attempting to breathe.

The baron lay in his tent thinking regretfully of all the things he might have said to flatten Commander Kholos.

Horkin, having been awakened by Raistlin, could not go back to sleep. He lay awake in bed, muttering imprecations on the head of his assistant and thinking about the upcoming assault. Horkin's usually cheerful face was grave. He sighed and with a muttered prayer to his drinking buddy, dear Luni, he fell asleep.

Scrounger lay awake staring into the darkness in fear and trembling because someone had told him that he was going to be left behind during the assault due to the fact that he was too short.

After Caramon had polished his armor until it was a wonder he didn't wear a hole in it, he rolled himself in his blanket, lay down, and thought, "You know, I might die tomorrow." He was pondering this eventuality and wondering how he felt about it when he woke to find it was morning.

❸

The sky was pearl gray, covered with low-hanging clouds. And though it was not yet raining, everything in camp was wet. The air itself was damp and soggy, hot without the hint of a breeze. The company flag hung limp and listless on its standard. All sounds were muted in the thick air. The blacksmith's usually ringing blows sounded discordant and tinny.

Master Senej's company was up early. They fell into line in front of the mess tent.

"First to fight, first to breakfast!" Caramon said, grinning as he clapped Scrounger on the back. "I like this arrangement!"

During the nights leading up to the attack, the flank company had been out scouting, which meant that they were the last ones into camp and the last to line up for breakfast or what was left of breakfast after the rest of the troops had descended on it like gully dwarves. Caramon, who had been subsisting on cold oatmeal for the past few days, eyed the rashers of sizzling bacon and fresh hot bread with immense satisfaction.

"Aren't you eating?" he asked Scrounger.

"No, Caramon, I'm not hungry. Do you really think what Damark said was true? Do you really think the sergeant won't let me—"

"Go on, fill your plate!" Caramon urged. "I'll eat what you don't want. He'll have some of those wheat cakes, too," Caramon told the cook.

Caramon settled down at the long plank table with two loaded plates. Scrounger sat beside him, chewing on his nails and casting pleading glances at the sergeant every time she walked past.

"Oh, hullo, Raist," Caramon said, looking up from his food to find his brother standing over him.

Raistlin was pale and wan, with dark smudges beneath his eyes. His robes were soaked with rain and his own sweat. The hand holding the staff trembled.

"You don't look good, Raist," Caramon said worriedly, rising to his feet, breakfast forgotten. "Do you feel all right?"

"No," Raistlin returned in a rasping voice. "I don't feel 'all right.' I never feel 'all right.' If you must know, I have been up all night. No, don't fuss over me! I am better now. I cannot stay long. I have my duties to attend to. Rolling bandages in the healing tent." He sounded bitter. "I just came by to wish you well."

Raistlin's thin fingers touched Caramon's forearm, startling him.

"Take care of yourself, my brother," Raistlin said quietly.

"Uh, sure. I will. Thanks, Raist," Caramon said, touched.

He started to add that his twin should also take care of himself, but by the time the words were out, Raistlin was gone.

"Gee, that was odd," said Scrounger as Caramon resumed his seat and his breakfast.

"Not really," Caramon said, smiling, elated. "We're brothers."

"I know. It's just that I . . ."

"You what?" Caramon looked up.

Scrounger had been about to say that he had never before known Raistlin to do or say anything the least bit brotherly and that it was odd for him to start now. But seeing Caramon's open face and his honest pleasure, the half-kender changed his mind.

"You want my eggs?"

Caramon grinned. "Hand 'em over."

He had no chance to finish his own eggs, however. The attack was set for early morning and before he was halfway through breakfast, the drums began to beat, calling the men of Flank Company to arms. As the soldiers were putting on their gear, a light rain began to fall. Water dribbled down metal helms into their eyes and seeped into their leather padding, causing it to chafe the skin. Beads of water formed in the men's beards, droplets hung off the men's noses. The soldiers wiped their eyes to see. Their hands fumbled on the wet metal of buckles. Leather straps proved recalcitrant in the damp. No amount of tugging would cause them to cinch properly. Swords slipped from wet hands.

Most strange and ominous, the rain caused the city walls to change color. The walls were formed of rock that was a light brown in color. The rain brought out a red tint in the rock, made the walls look as if they had been washed with a thin coating of blood. The soldiers cast dour glances at the west wall that was their objective and then looked glumly at the sky, hoping the sun would reappear.

Scrounger assisted Caramon to put on the leather armor, which was different from the armor the Flank Company usually wore. This armor was padded along the arms and the torso, then covered with strips of metal. The armor was heavy but provided much better protection than the light-weight leather armor the men wore during scouting missions. The men had borrowed the armor from A Company, along with the large shields they would be carrying into battle this day.

Scrounger was glum, kept blinking his eyes. The rumor he'd heard had proven true. He'd been ordered to stay behind while the rest of the company advanced for the attack. Scrounger had pleaded and even argued until Sergeant Nemiss lost patience with him. She brought forth one of the huge shields the soldiers would be carrying and tossed it to the half-kender. The shield knocked him flat.

"See there," she said. "You can't even lift it!"

The men laughed. Scrounger struggled out from under the heavy shield, still arguing. Sergeant Nemiss clapped him on the shoulder and told him he "was a game little fighting cock" and that "if he could find a big shield he could carry, he could come along." Then she ordered Scrounger to help the other soldiers with their armor.

He did as he was ordered, complaining and protesting the entire time that it wasn't fair. He had as much training as anyone. The others would think he was a coward. He didn't see why he couldn't use his old shield and so on. Suddenly, however, Scrounger's complaints ended.

Caramon felt badly for his friend, but he thought that the whining had really gone on long enough. He breathed a sigh of relief, thinking that Scrounger had finally accepted his cruel fate. "I'll see you after we take that wall," said Caramon, putting on his helm.

"Good luck, Caramon," said Scrounger, holding out his hand with a smile.

Caramon stared hard at his friend. He'd seen that same sweet and inno-cent smile before on the face of another good friend, Tasslehoff Burrfoot. Caramon knew kender well enough to be highly suspicious. He couldn't imagine what Scrounger might be up to and before he could give the matter serious thought, Sergeant Nemiss called the company to attention.

Master Senej rode his horse to the front of the ranks. Dismounting, he made a quick but thorough inspection, tugging on armor to make sure it wasn't going to come loose, examining the points of the spears to make certain they were sharp. Inspection completed, he faced his troops. The entire camp had gathered to listen and to watch.

"We're going to test the western defenses today, men. We want to see if there are any surprises waiting for us in that city. The drill is simple. Close ranks as tight as possible, hold your shields high, and march in formation toward the wall. We'll take a hell of a beating from their archers, but most of the arrows will hit our shields.

"Our own archers will try to clear the wall as best they can, but don't think they're going to solve our problems. Having seen our archers at practice, I'm more worried about them hitting us than I am about them clearing the wall."

Archer Company began to jeer and boo. The Flank Company laughed. Tension eased, which was what the master intended. He knew that unless the enemy was completely incompetent, his men would be facing overwhelming odds. How overwhelming the odds and how skilled the enemy were two questions he was about to have answered. He did not mention the army of their allies, who had gathered to watch the assault. The hulking figure of their commander could be seen mounted on his battle horse a safe distance from the firing.

"Enough talk then!" Master Senej shouted. "As soon as we get the signal that the Archer Company is in place, we'll do our duty and be back in time for lunch." His gaze roamed the lines, fixed on Caramon. The master smiled and added, "We're first in line for lunch, too, Majere."

Caramon felt his face redden, but he was always ready to laugh at himself and he joined good-naturedly in the ribbing.

C Company marched to the front of the camp and assembled in tight formation, three ranks deep. Caramon stood in the last rank. Master Senej took his place in the front of the ranks. An aide led his horse away. The master was going to walk with his men. As the master raised his sword, Caramon felt a hand tugging the back of his armor. Twisting his head, he looked around and saw Scrounger crowding close behind him, nearly stepping on the big man's heels.

"The sergeant said I could come if I found a shield," Scrounger said. "I guess you're it, Caramon. I hope you don't mind."

Caramon didn't know whether he minded or not. He didn't have time to consider. Off to the right, a flag dipped and raised again. Archer Company was in place. The master raised his sword.

"Forward! Flank Company—first to fight!"

The company gave a cheer and began to march forward at a slow but steady pace, their flag bearer proudly taking the lead behind the master.

Back in camp, the trumpets and drums of the baron's signalers began to play a marching tune with a pounding beat making it easier for the men to keep in step. Left feet came down with the beat of the bass drum. The soldiers moved forward in unison, locked together with their shields and spears at the ready.

The music heightened Caramon's excitement. He looked at the men next to him, his comrades, and his heart swelled with pride. He had never felt so close to anyone before, not even to his twin, as to these men moving forward to face death together. The little flutter of fear that had bothered his stomach and gripped his bowels disappeared. He was invincible, nothing could harm him. Not this day.

A small creek crossed the field between the camp and the city wall that was their objective. The creek bed was dry in the summer, but the sides were fairly steep and it would take time to cross, particularly as the grass that covered the bank was slippery wet with the light rain. The company met the creek bed at an angle, the right flank of the company crossing before the left. Small gaps appeared in the line while the soldiers slowed to watch their footing, then the line reformed on the other side.

"Why haven't they fired at us?" Scrounger wondered. "Why are they waiting?"

Sergeant Nemiss, off to Caramon's left, barked, "Shut up and keep tight. They'll fire soon enough. Sooner than you're ready!"

A soft sibilant sound, unlike any sound Caramon had ever heard in his life—a hissing and a whirring and a swishing sound all combined—caused the hair to rise on the back of his neck.

The line's advance faltered. Everyone heard the ominous noise. Caramon looked up over his shield to see. The sky above him was dark with what he realized in astonishment was a deadly flight of hundreds of arrows.

"Keep your damned shield up!" the sergeant yelled.

Remembering his training, Caramon hastily lifted his shield over his head. Less than a second later, the shield vibrated and shook with the impact of arrows. Caramon was amazed at the force of the blows, as if someone were pounding on his shield with a war hammer.

And then it was over.

Caramon hesitated, cringing, waiting for another attack. When none came, he ventured to look at the front of his shield. Four arrows stuck out of it, their feathered shafts lodged solidly in the metal. Caramon gulped, thinking what those arrows would have done if they had struck him instead of the shield. Some of the soldiers were yanking the arrows from their shields, tossing them aside. Caramon twisted around to see how Scrounger had fared.

Scrounger looked up with a tremulous smile. "Whoo, boy!" was all he said.

Caramon glanced on either side, couldn't see anyone down. There were no holes in the line. The master looked back with a quick glance to see that the company was still with him.

"Forward, men!" he yelled.

The sibilant hissing came again, but this time, from their right flank. Archer Company was firing back. Arrows sped toward the city walls, flying over the heads of the Flank Company as they moved forward. Another flight of arrows launched from the city.

Caramon raised his shield. Arrows thunked home. He staggered from the impact, but continued moving forward. A ragged cry nearby caused him to jerk his head. A man in Caramon's line dropped to the ground, rocking back and forth in agony, screaming. An arrow had shattered his shinbone. A hole gaped in the line. The man behind the wounded man jumped over him and plugged the hole.

C Company continued to move. Caramon was angry and frustrated. He wanted to lash out, to attack something, but there was nothing to attack. He couldn't do a damn thing but walk forward and get shot at.

Archer Company's return fire didn't seem to be having any effect. Yet another volley of arrows rained down from the sky.

The third volley struck. A man in front of Caramon fell backward, landed at Caramon's feet. The man didn't scream. He couldn't scream, Caramon saw, horrified. The man had taken an arrow through the throat. He clasped his hand over the terrible wound. Gurgling sounds came from his gaping mouth.

"Don't stop! Close up the line, damn you!" a veteran yelled and thwacked Caramon on the arm with his shield.

Caramon hopped sideways to avoid stepping on the wounded man. Slipping on the wet, bloody grass, he nearly lost his balance. Hands behind him grasped hold of his belt, helped him keep his feet. When the whirring sound came again, Caramon scrunched down to try to make himself as small as he could behind his shield.

And then, inexplicably, the arrows stopped. The company closed within a hundred and fifty yards of the objective. Perhaps Archer Company had cleared the wall. Perhaps the enemy had turned tail and fled. Caramon lifted his head cautiously to see. Then came a thud that Caramon felt more than heard, as of something heavy hitting the sodden ground. The thud was followed by a crack. Caramon looked around to see the nature of the odd sounds, watched two files of men cease to exist. One second there were six men to his right. The next, no one.

A large boulder rolled and bounded across the bloodstained grass, finally came to a halt. Fired from a catapult atop the city wall, the boulder had plowed into the line of men, and they were no longer men. They were nothing but blood and mangled flesh and splintered bone.

The screams of the wounded, the stench of blood and urine and excrement, for many of the dying soldiers could no longer control their bowels, caused Caramon to lose the breakfast he'd been so pleased to eat. Bending over, he purged his stomach. The sound of another volley was almost too much for him. He longed to run away, to flee this dreadful killing field. His training held him in place, training and the thought that if he ran he would be branded a coward, forever disgraced.

He crouched behind his shield. Twisting his head, he looked behind him, worried for Scrounger, but couldn't find his friend. Three men went down to his left, including the company standard-bearer. The company flag dropped forward into the grass. The entire line had stopped moving. Both the master and the sergeant were still advancing.

Suddenly there was Scrounger. Hopping over bodies of the dead and dying, he reached the standard-bearer and, braving a flight of arrows from the city walls, he picked up the flag and waved it proudly over his head with a defiant yell.

The rest of C Company joined the yell, but it was ragged. Both the sergeant and master turned their heads and saw the terrible destruction. Another volley of arrows and the thud of another boulder—this time falling short of the mark—spurred the master to action. His men had taken enough punishment.

"Fall back! Fall back in ranks! Keep your shields up!" the master yelled.

Caramon dashed over to protect Scrounger, covering his back with his shield. The half-kender paid no attention to the arrows that darted around him, but marched proudly, waving the flag in his hands. The company moved in orderly retreat, no panic, no breaking and running. If a man fell, the others moved in to close the line. Some stopped to help the wounded back to the camp. Archer Company sent volley after volley into the city walls, covering the retreat.

Scrounger carried the flag, Caramon held his shield so that it protected both of them. Fifty more paces, and the men began to relax. No more arrows came from the walls. The soldiers were finally out of range.

A hundred more paces and the master halted the company. He lowered his shield to the ground. The rest of the company did the same. Caramon felt the shield's weight fall from his arm. It must have weighed a hundred pounds, or so he felt. His arm trembled from the strain.

Scrounger, his face dead white, continued to hold the flag.

"You can put it down now," Caramon said to his friend.

"I can't let go," Scrounger said, his voice quivering. He stared at his hand as if it were a hand belonging to someone else. "I can't let go, Caramon!" He burst into tears.

Caramon reached out his hand to help loosen Scrounger's grasp. The big man saw his own hand covered with blood. Glancing down, he saw his breastplate smeared with blood and spatters of gore. He lowered his hand, did not touch Scrounger.

"All right. Listen here!" the master yelled. "The baron knows what he wanted to know. The city's defenses are more than adequate."

The men said nothing. They were exhausted, the spirit drained from them.

"You fought well. I'm proud of you. We lost good men out there today," Master Senej continued, "and I intend to go out there and bring back the bodies. We'll wait for nightfall."

A murmur of agreement came from the men.

Sergeant Nemiss dismissed the company. The men wandered back to their tents or went to the tents of the healers, to see how wounded comrades fared. Some of the new recruits, Caramon and Scrounger among them, remained standing in line, too dazed and shocked to leave.

The sergeant approached Scrounger. Reaching out her hand, she took the company standard from the half-kender's deathlike grip.

"You disobeyed orders, soldier," Sergeant Nemiss said, her voice stern.

"No, I didn't, sir," Scrounger said. "I found a shield." He pointed at Caramon. "One I could use."

Sergeant Nemiss grinned, shook her head. "If we measured men by their spirit, you'd be a giant. Speaking of giants, you did well yourself out there, Majere. I thought you'd be the first man hit. You make a great target."

"I don't remember much, sir," Caramon replied, bound to be honest, though it might lower him in her estimation. "If you want to know the truth, I was scared spitless." He hung his head. "I spent most of the battle hiding behind my shield."

"That's what kept you alive today, Majere," said the sergeant. "Looks like I might have taught you something after all."

The sergeant walked away, handing the standard to one of the veterans as she passed.

"You go on to lunch," Caramon said to his friend. "I'm not very hungry. I think I'm going to go lie down."

"Lunch?" Scrounger stared at him. "It's not near time for lunch. It's only been half an hour since we ate breakfast."

Half an hour. It might have been half a year. Half a lifetime. A whole lifetime for some.

Tears welled up in Caramon's eyes. He turned his head quickly, so no one would notice.

9

FLANK COMPANY RECOVERED ITS DEAD UNDER COVER OF DARKNESS, buried them in darkness in a single grave so that the enemy would not be able to calculate how many men were lost. The baron spoke at the simple ceremony, citing each man by name and recounting some tale of his heroism, past and present. The common grave was covered with dirt and an honor guard was posted to keep off roving wolves. The baron gave C Company a barrel of dwarf spirits and bid them drink to the memory of their fallen comrades.

Caramon drank not only to their memory but also to the memories of those who had fallen since time began, or so it seemed to Scrounger, who had to practically drag the big man back to the tent. Caramon collapsed in a drunken stupor, falling face first into his cot with a thud that smashed the cot and caused the men in the tents on either side to wonder if the enemy was hurling more boulders at them.

Raistlin spent the night in the tent with the wounded, assisting Horkin with bandages and ointment. Most of the wounds were minor flesh wounds, with the exception of the soldier with the shattered leg. His comrades had carried him under a rain of arrows to the healing tent. Raistlin was privileged to witness his first battlefield amputation. He mixed a potion of mandrake root to be used to render the patient unconscious, added to that a sleep spell. The man's friends held his arms and shoulders to halt any involuntary movement.

Raistlin had spent hours with Weird Meggin, dissecting corpses under her tutelage to learn more about the marvels of the human body, and had not felt the least squeamish. He had practiced his healing skills among the plague-ravaged populace of Solace without blenching. He had volunteered to assist at the operation, had assured the leech that he was impervious to the sight of blood and would not fail at his post.

The blood—and there was an enormous quantity of it, Raistlin could not imagine that one body could hold so much—did not shake him. It was the sound of the saw blade, rasping and hacking through the bone just below the knee, that caused Raistlin to clench his teeth against the bile surging up from his stomach, caused him to close his eyes more than once to prevent himself from fainting.

He managed to make it through the operation, but when the leg was removed and carried off to be buried in the grave with the dead, Raistlin asked permission to leave the tent for a moment. The surgeon, looking at his assistant's deathly pale face, nodded his head curtly and told Raistlin to go get some sleep. The patient would manage well enough until morning.

Between mandrake and magic and loss of blood, the amputee was quiet. The other wounded were asleep. Raistlin returned to his tent, his body bathed in sweat, and sank down into his cot, an object of scorn and derision to one person at least. Himself.

☻

The allies met again at noon, the baron once again riding over to confer with Commander Kholos. The commander was more respectful, if not more cordial. He permitted the baron to retain his sword and actually invited him to sit down while they discussed plans for the coming battle that would bring Hope's End to its knees.

Both men agreed that the city's defenses, as demonstrated yesterday, were formidable. A direct assault, even by the combined strength of both their armies, would most likely fail. Their forces would be decimated by the time they reached the walls. Kholos proposed settling in for a prolonged siege. Give the people of Hope's End a few months to deplete their food stores, a few more months of eating rats and watching their children die of starvation, and their enthusiasm for this rebellion would wane.

This plan was not acceptable to the baron, who had no intention of remaining in the commander's company for any longer than was absolutely necessary. The baron offered an alternative.

"I propose that we end this war quickly. Send a force inside the city, attack them from behind, and open the gate before they know what's hit them."

"Defeat them by treachery?" Kholos grinned. "I like it!"

"Yes, I thought you would," the baron said dryly.

"Whose force would we use to infiltrate behind enemy lines?" Kholos asked, frowning.

"I offer my men," the baron replied with dignity, having known that this question would be asked. "You have seen them in action. You cannot question their valor."

"Wait outside," said Kholos. "I have to think about this, discuss it with my officers."

Pacing outside the commander's tent, the baron overheard much of the conversation within. He flushed in anger and ground his teeth at Kholos's loud statement, "If the mercenaries are killed, we've lost nothing. We can always starve out the town later. If they succeed, we save ourselves a lot of time and trouble."

When he was invited back inside the commander's tent, the baron voluntarily handed over his sword to Kholos's aide, so as to not be tempted to use it.

"Very well, Baron," said Kholos. "We have decided to follow your plan. Your men will enter the city, attack from behind. At your signal, we will attack the gates from the front."

"I trust I may count upon you to storm the walls," the baron said, regarding the commander intently. "If your men do not draw off resistance, my people will be slaughtered."

"Yes, I'm aware of that," Kholos replied, picking his teeth with a bird bone. He grinned and winked. "I give you my word."

"Do you trust him, sir?" Commander Morgon asked, as they left Kholos's tent.

"Not as far as I can smell him," said the baron grimly.

"That would imply a considerable amount of trust, sir," said Morgon with a straight face.

"Ha! Ha!" The baron laughed boisterously and slapped his commander on the back. "A good one, Morgon. A very good one." He chuckled all the way back to camp.

❸

"Sir," said Master Senej, "C Company volunteers for this duty. You owe us, sir," he added loudly. Every other company commander was making the same offer.

The baron cut them off, turned to Senej. "Explain yourself, Master."

"The men went out on a hopeless mission, sir," he said. "They were whipped. They had to turn tail in the face of the enemy and run for it."

"They knew there was that possibility when they went into battle," said the baron, frowning.

"Yes, sir." Master Senej stood his ground. "But they feel it, sir. Their heads are down, their rear ends dragging. That was the first time C Company has ever been defeated—"

"But, for the love of Kiri-Jolith, Master—" the baron began, exasperated.

"My lord, that was the first time anyone in this army has been defeated," Master Senej said, standing stiffly at attention. "The men want a chance to redeem their honor, sir."

The other commanders were silent. Though all were itching to take part in the action, they accepted the right of Major Senej to put forth his cause.

"Very well," the baron said. "Major Senej, C Company will enter the city. But this time I'm sending along a wizard. Master Horkin!"

"My lord!"

"You will go along on this mission."

"Begging your pardon, my lord, but I suggest that you send my assistant."

"Is the young man ready for an assignment this important, Horkin?" the baron asked gravely. "Majere seems awfully weak and sickly to me. I was going to suggest that he be mustered out."

"Red's stronger than he appears, my lord," said Horkin. "Stronger than he knows himself or such is my opinion. He's a better mage than I am." Horkin said this without rancor, simply stating a fact. "Where the lives of the men are at stake, I think you should use the best."

"Well, of course," said the baron, taken aback. "But you've had experience—"

"And how did I get that experience, my lord, if it wasn't for the experience," Horkin returned triumphantly. "Which he'll never get if you don't let him."

"I suppose that's true," the baron replied, though he still looked dubious. "You're in command of the wizardry. What I know about magic you could put in a rat's teacup. Major Senej, find Majere and tell him that he's now attached to your company. Report back to me for your orders."

"Yes, sir!" Major Senej said, saluting. "And thank you, my lord!"

☻

"Raist, did you hear the news?" Caramon stood meekly outside the entrance to Raistlin's tent. The big man had a terrible headache, felt like gnomes were using his stomach for a boiler. What with the horror of the battle, the solemnity of the funeral, and the aftereffects of the wake, he was beginning to rethink his commitment to a life in the military. He tried to appear excited, however. For his brother's sake. "We're infiltrating the city and you're coming with us!"

"Yes, I heard," Raistlin called irritably, not looking up from the spellbook he had balanced on his knees. "Now go away and leave me alone, Caramon. I have all these spells to memorize before nightfall."

"This is what we always wanted, Raist," Caramon said, sounding wistful. "Isn't it?"

"Yes, Caramon, I suppose it is," Raistlin replied.

Caramon stood a moment longer, hoping to be asked inside, hoping to have a chance to talk about his fear, his shame, his longing to go back home. But Raistlin said nothing, gave no indication that he was aware of his twin's continued existence. Eventually, Caramon left.

After his brother had gone, Raistlin sat and stared at the spellbook. The letters ran higgledy-piggledy across the pages, the words slid from his brain as if they were greased. His brother and the others were going to be dependent on him to keep them alive. What a joke! But then, the gods were always playing jokes on him.

Raistlin went back despairingly to his studies, a coward so cowardly he dared not admit he was one.

10

Kitiara arrived in Kholos's camp the afternoon following the failed attack by the mercenaries on the city's wall. She was later than she'd thought she would be, knew that Immolatus would be seething with impatience. The secret opening in the mountain proved to be farther from camp than she had guessed, the way more difficult to travel.

She found the dragon sleeping soundly in his tent, heedless of the furious hammerings of the blacksmith, whose portable forge was nearby.

Kit could hear Immolatus's snore over the pounding of the smith's hammer. She barged into the dragon's tent without bothering to announce herself, tripped on something that rolled out from under her foot. Swearing roundly, she caught her balance, peered down at the object closely in the dim light.

A map case? She was about to pick it up when she saw that it was a scroll case, such as wizards use to carry their magic spells. Kit let the case lie. No telling what spells of protection might be laid upon it. Several other scroll cases lay scattered about, as well as numerous rings that had spilled out of a pouch and a broken crock of what had been, by the smell, chicken broth.

Here was a mystery. The scroll cases did not belong to Immolatus, nor did he appear to have any interest in them, since he left them lying on the ground. Kit guessed that some sort of meeting had occurred in her absence, though with whom she could not fathom. The scroll cases bespoke a wizard, the chicken broth a cook. Perhaps the camp cook was also a dabbler in magic. Kit hoped to the heavens that Immolatus had not insulted the cook. The food was bad enough as it was.

She stood glaring down at him, resenting the fact that he was here snug and cozy in his tent, taking a nap while she'd been out doing his dirty work. She took grim delight in waking him.

"Eminence." Kit shook him by the shoulder. "Immolatus."

He woke swiftly, eyes open, fully conscious, staring up at her with a fury and a loathing that was not directed so much at her but at the daily realization and bitter disappointment he experienced on waking to find himself imprisoned in human flesh. He glared up at her, his red eyes cold, hating her, despising her as he despised all her kind, regarding her as she herself might regard a bloated, swollen tick.

She moved her hand from his shoulder swiftly, took a step back. She had never known anyone rise from the depths of slumber to this level of awareness so quickly. There was something unnatural about it.

"I'm sorry to wake you, Eminence," she said, and that much was true. "But I thought you would like to know that I succeeded in completing our assignment." She really could not help adding a slight ironic emphasis to the plural. "I thought you might want to hear what I found."

Glancing about, she added offhandedly, "What happened, Eminence? What is all this stuff?"

Immolatus sat up on the bed. He slept in his red robes, never removed them, never washed them, never bathed. He gave off a disgusting odor, a musty smell of death and decay that reminded Kitiara of the dragon's dank lair.

"I had a most interesting encounter with a young mage," Immolatus replied.

Kitiara kicked aside a scroll case that was in her way and sat down. "He must have left in a hurry."

"Yes, he did not care to linger." Immolatus smiled unpleasantly, muttered, "He has something I want."

"Why didn't you just take it from him?" Kit asked impatiently.

She was truly not the least bit interested. The journey had been long. She was tired and irritable. She had important information to convey, if only the dragon would shut up long enough to hear it.

"A typical human response." Immolatus glowered. "There are subtleties involved that you would not understand. I will have the item, but in my own way and my own time. You will find a note on the table. I want you to take it to the young mage. He serves, I believe, with those we so quaintly term our allies."

Immolatus gestured to a scroll case lying on the table. The scroll had been removed. Apparently the message was inside.

Kit started to angrily retort that she was not Immolatus's errand boy.

Fearing that this would provoke an argument, when all she wanted to do was to relay her information and go to bed, she swallowed the words.

"What is the mage's name, my lord?" Kitiara asked.

"Magius," returned Immolatus.

"Magius." She left the tent, hailed a passing soldier, and handed over the scroll case with orders to see that it was delivered.

"Well, uth Matar?" Immolatus said, on her return, "what of your mission? Was it successful? I gather it was not, since you are stalling, refusing to tell me."

In answer, Kitiara pulled the book from her belt and handed in to the dragon. "See for yourself, Eminence."

He accepted the proffered book eagerly, almost snatching it from her hand. "So you did find the eggs of the metallic dragons."

A low chuckle of malicious joy gurgled deep in his throat. He scanned the numbers covetously, as she explained her notation.

"I counted them by rows; there are quite a number of them. 'G' stands for 'gold' and 's' for silver, so that '11/34 eggs s' means that there are thirty-four silver dragon eggs in row number eleven."

"I am quite capable of understanding your scrawls, despite the fact that they look as if a hen has walked over the pages."

"I am glad my work pleases you, my lord," Kitiara said, too tired to care if he heard the sarcasm or not.

He did not hear her. He was intent upon studying her notes, muttering to himself, performing calculations, nodding, pleased, and emitting that sinister chuckle. When he turned the page and saw the map, a smirk contorted his features. He very nearly purred with delight.

"So this . . . this is the route to the secret entrance in the mountain." He eyed it, frowning. "It seems clear enough."

"It will be quite clear to Commander Kholos," Kitiara said, yawning. She held out her hand. "I'll take it to him now, Eminence, if you're finished with it."

Immolatus did not hand it back. He stared with intense concentration at the map. Kitiara had the impression that he was committing the map to memory.

"Are you going to the cave, Eminence?" Kitiara asked, startled and uneasy. "There's no reason for you to do so. I assure you that my figures are accurate. If you doubt me—"

"I do not doubt you, uth Matar," said the dragon pleasantly. He was in an extremely good humor. "At least not more than I would doubt any worm such as yourself."

"Then, Eminence," said Kitiara, giving him one of her most charming smiles, "you should not waste your time traveling to this cave. Our work is finished. Now would be an excellent time for us to depart. General Ariakas gave orders that we were to return to him with this information as quickly as possible."

"You are right, uth Matar," said Immolatus. "You should return to General Ariakas immediately."

"Eminence—"

The dragon was laughing at her. "I have no further need of your services, uth Matar. Go back to Ariakas and claim your reward. I am certain he will be most happy to provide it."

Immolatus rose from his bed, brushed past her, heading out of the tent. Kitiara caught hold of his arm.

"What are you going to do?" she demanded.

He gazed balefully at her. "Release your hold of me, worm."

"What are you going to do?" Kitiara knew the answer. What she didn't know was what in the name of all that was holy she was going to do about it.

"That is my business, uth Matar," he said. "Not yours. You have nothing to say in the matter."

"You're going to destroy the eggs."

He shrugged off her grasp, again started to leave the tent.

"Damn it!" Kitiara pursued him, seized hold of his arm, digging her nails into his flesh. "You know your orders—"

"My orders!" He rounded on her, furious, savage. "I do not take orders! Certainly not from some piddling human who sticks a horned helm on his head and calls himself a 'dragonlord'!

"Oh, yes." Immolatus bared his teeth in a scornful grin. "I have heard Ariakas term himself this. 'Dragonlord!' As if he or any other human had the right to link his puny might and his pitiful mortality with us! Not that I blame him. He thinks that by emulating us in this pathetic fashion, he can garner for himself some small portion of the respect and fear that all species on Krynn grant to us."

The dragon snorted, a gout of flame flickered in his nostrils. He hissed his words. "Like a child parading around in his father's armor, he will find the weight too heavy to bear, and he will fall, a victim to his own self-delusion!

"I am going to destroy the eggs," the dragon said with soft fury. "Do you dare to try to stop me?"

Kitiara was in dire peril, but, as she saw it, she didn't have much to lose.

"General Ariakas gave the order, that is true, Eminence," she said, boldly meeting the dragon's glaring eyes. "But we both know who it is who gives him his orders. Will you disobey your Queen?"

"In a heartbeat," said Immolatus with a snap of his teeth. "You think I fear her? Perhaps I would, if Takhisis were in this world. She isn't, you know. She's trapped in the Abyss. Oh, she can rant and rave and stamp her pretty little foot but she can't touch me. And therefore I will have my revenge. I will avenge myself on the foul golds and silvers who slaughtered my comrades and drove us into isolation and oblivion. I will destroy their young as they destroyed ours. I will destroy the evil temple of an accursed god. I will destroy the city in which the temple stands and then"—his tongue flicked, a flame licking blood—"I will destroy the descendant of Magius. My revenge on them all will be complete."

The red eyes flickered. "You should leave while you can, uth Matar. If I find that Kholos and his rabble stand in my way, I will destroy them, as well."

"Lord," Kit argued desperately, "Her Dark Majesty has plans for these eggs."

"So do I," said Immolatus. "Soon Krynn and its people will see the true might of dragons. They will know that we have returned to take up our proper sphere—rulership of the world."

Kitiara could not allow him to ruin Ariakas's plans, could not allow the dragon to flout the orders of the Dark Queen. Above all, she could not allow Immolatus to wreck her plans and hopes and ambitions.

She drew her sword as he talked, her motion swift and fluid. Had Immolatus been human, he would have found a foot of steel in his gut before he could draw his next breath.

He was not human. He was a dragon, a red dragon, one of the most powerful beings on Krynn. Flame enveloped Kitiara. The air sizzled and crackled around her, burned her lungs when she tried to draw breath enough to scream, searing her flesh. She fell to her knees and waited to die.

The flames abated suddenly. She was not hurt, she realized after a moment, except for the horrible memory of being burned alive. For the moment, that's all it was, a memory. A memory and a threat. She remained where she had fallen, dejected, defeated.

"Farewell, uth Matar," said Immolatus pleasantly. "Thank you for your help." He left with a smile, a mocking bow, and a snap of his teeth.

Kitiara watched him walk out of the tent, watched her career walk out the tent with him.

She remained in her crouched and fallen position until she was certain that he would not return. Painfully, stiffly, she leveraged herself to her feet, using the cot to assist her. Once up and moving about, Kitiara felt better.

She walked outside, drew in a deep breath. Smoke-polluted air was better than the fetid, dragon-tinged air inside that tent. She sought a secluded part of the camp, found it behind the gallows. No one came here if he could help it. The only drawback was the flies. Kit ignored them. Alone, unseen, Kitiara mulled over her predicament.

She could not—*must* not—allow Immolatus to proceed with his intentions. Kit cared nothing for the dragon eggs. She cared nothing for the city or its inhabitants. As for the temple, after her unpleasant experience, she would have gleefully helped Immolatus destroy it herself. But she could not indulge in personal revenge, nor could the dragon. There was too much at stake here, the prize for which they gambled was enormous. And now, instead of placing what they'd won on the final bet, the dragon was going to spend their winnings on dinner and a show. And what a show it would be! Kitiara stomped the ground in anger and frustration.

Soon everyone in Ansalon would know that dragons had returned. Ariakas's army was not yet ready to launch a full-scale assault. That much was obvious by simply looking around this camp. Kholos and his raw recruits would be dog's meat for Solamnic Knights or any other well-trained force. They would lose the war before it had even started, all because one arrogant and egotistical monster decided to spit in his Queen's eye.

"I cannot best him in a fight," Kitiara muttered, walking ten paces one direction, turning and walking ten paces back. "His magic is too powerful. He's proven that. But even the most powerful mage has a weak spot—right between the shoulder blades."

She drew her dagger from her boot, stood turning the blade in her hand, watching the sunlight glint off the sharp steel. Though "Sir Nigel" might have been a phony Knight, he was true to his promise. She had recovered both her sword and her knife from the cavern.

"Even dragons don't have eyes in the backs of their heads. And Immolatus thinks himself invincible, always a mistake."

Locating a knot on a tree about twenty paces from where she stood, Kit held the dagger by the blade, aimed, and threw. The blade flashed through the air, buried itself about a handsbreadth from the knothole.

Kit grimaced. "Always did pull to the right." Going to the tree, she yanked out the dagger, which was buried in the wood almost to the hilt. "That would have killed him," she reflected. "At least when he's in human form. It wouldn't have done much to a dragon."

The thought was daunting. If he changed form, she didn't stand a chance. A horrible qualm seized her—suppose he had changed form already! He might, since he obviously didn't give a damn about anyone seeing him. He might have decided to fly to the cavern. . . .

No, Kit reflected. Immolatus would remain in his disguise, at least until he reached the cave. For all he knew, the eggs might have a guardian. He had been in such a hurry, he never asked her about that. A guardian who wouldn't be concerned at the coming of a red-robed mage, but who would sound the alarm at the advent of a red dragon.

Immolatus would use his human form to sneak inside the cave. At least that's what she hoped he had the good sense to do. And at the thought of relying on the dragon's good sense, Kitiara shook her head and sighed.

But whether he did or he didn't, she didn't have much choice. She had to find a way to stop him or she would be nothing but an itinerant sell-sword for the rest of her days.

Like your father, said an unbidden voice inside her.

Ignoring the voice, angry with it, Kitiara replaced the dagger in her boot and set off on the trail of the dragon.

11

MASTER SENEJ WAS RIGHT. His company's morale lifted considerably on being told they had been chosen to infiltrate the city and undermine its defenses from the inside. The mission was dangerous, but after having been forced to endure the deadly fire from the walls without being able to strike back, the men welcomed the opportunity.

"This is what we've been trained for," Sergeant Nemiss told her assembled troops. "Secrecy, stealth. Right up our alley. Here's the plan.

"We scale the cliffs to the south of the city, cross over a ridge, and climb down the mountain. We enter the city on the side of the wall that butts up against the mountain. No one will be looking for us to come that way, so it should be minimally guarded.

"The baron's map shows that there is a warehouse district located near an old abandoned temple close to where we go over the wall. From what we hear, no one has goods to sell, so we should find the warehouse empty. The plan is to reach the city before dawn tomorrow, hole up in the warehouse during the day. Late the next night we launch our attack."

Sergeant Nemiss jerked a thumb in the direction of Raistlin, who stood on the outskirts of the crowd.

"The wizard Raistlin Majere will be marching with us."

"Hurrah!" yelled Caramon from his place in the ranks.

Raistlin flushed deeply and cast his brother an annoyed glance. He noted that the rest of the members of C Company were not nearly so enthusiastic at the idea. Horkin's long years of service had endeared him to the men, who tended to regard his being a mage as a minor personality flaw that they, as friends, were more than willing to overlook. Raistlin's odd appearance, his sickly demeanor, and his tendency to remain aloof from the other soldiers combined to make them chary of his company.

The men muttered into their beards, but no one said anything aloud. Caramon was watching them and those few who had come into contact with his fists had a healthy respect for his ability to punish any insult, real or imagined, to his twin. Sergeant Nemiss was also watching them. She would not tolerate any "bellyaching" about orders. Thus Raistlin was accepted into Flank Company without a word of complaint. One man even offered to carry his gear for him, but Caramon took that upon himself.

Raistlin would carry his scrolls, his staff, and his magical components himself. He would have liked to have taken along a spellbook, for though he had finally been able to memorize the spells Horkin considered necessary to an operation of this kind, Raistlin would have felt more confident with several more hours of study. But Horkin said that the risk of the precious spellbook falling into enemy hands was too great.

"I can replace you, Red," he added jovially. "I can't replace that spellbook."

"As soon as night falls, we'll begin the march," Sergeant Nemiss continued. "We hope to be through the mountains, ready to enter the city around dawn. Our allies are supposed to mount a diversion to keep the eyes of the rebels fixed on the front of the wall, not the back."

Someone in line made a rude sound.

Sergeant Nemiss nodded. "Yeah, I know what you're thinking. I think the same, but there's not much we can do about it. Any questions?"

Someone wondered what happened if anyone was separated from the group.

"Right, that's a good one," the sergeant answered. "If any of you get separated, return to camp. Don't try to sneak into the city on your own. You could put the entire plan at risk. No more questions? You're dismissed. Meet back here at sunset."

The men returned to their tents to pack up their gear. They left their tents in place so that the enemy would think they were still sleeping in them. They took with them only short swords, dirks and knives. No shields, no mail, no long swords or spears. Two men skilled in archery carried two of the valued elven longbows and quivers of arrows. All wore leather armor, no mail or plate, deemed too heavy and cumbersome for mountain climbing and too noisy for stealth. Each man carried a coil of rope over his shoulder. They would find water on the trail and march with short rations.

The prospect dismayed Caramon, but he bore up under the blow by reminding himself of the hardships of war. Caramon was feeling much better at the prospect of action. Caught up in the excitement of the moment, he was able to banish the terrible memories of the attack on the wall. Never one to dwell on the past, Caramon looked forward confidently to the future. He accepted whatever came, did not waste time worrying over what might have been or what might be coming.

By contrast, Raistlin worried over what he considered his failure when confronting the renegade wizard, fretted that he did not have his spells letter-perfect, imagined every dire event that might occur to him, from tumbling down the side of the mountain to being captured and tortured by the enemy. By the time the company was ready to move out, he had worked himself into such a fever of dread that he feared he was too weak to make the trip. He considered pleading illness and was on his feet to report to Horkin when he heard a name being shouted through the camp.

"Magius! Pass the word for Magius."

Magius! A name that might have rung through Huma's camp hundreds of years ago, but had no place in this day and age. Then Raistlin remembered. He had given the name Magius to the wizard Immolatus. Ducking out of his tent, Raistlin called, "What do you want with Magius?"

"Why, do you know him?" a soldier asked. "I have a message for him."

"I know *of* him," Raistlin said. "Give me the message. I will see to it that it is delivered."

The soldier did not hesitate. The scroll case he was supposed to deliver was covered with strange-looking symbols that appeared to be magical. The sooner he was free of the thing, the better. He handed it over.

"Who sent this?" Raistlin asked.

"The wizard in the other camp," the soldier replied and left quickly, not anxious to stay around to see what the case contained.

Retreating to his tent, Raistlin shut the flap and tied it tightly. He inspected the scroll case with the greatest care, alive to the possibility that it might be rigged for his destruction. He sensed an aura of magic about the case, but that was only natural. The magic did not appear to be very strong, however. Still, it was wise not to take a chance.

Raistlin placed the scroll case on the ground, facing away from him. Drawing his small knife, he positioned the tip of the blade on the lid of the case. He worked the tip in between the lid and the case itself and slowly, carefully began to prize off the lid.

The tent was hot from the afternoon sun. His tension increased the heat tenfold. Sweat bathed his neck and breast. He continued grimly with his task. He almost had it, the lid was close to coming off, when the knife slipped from his wet hand, jarred the case. The lid suddenly popped loose, rolled away.

Raistlin scrambled backward, nearly overturning his cot, his heart lurching in fright.

Nothing happened. The lid wobbled over the uneven ground, came to rest at the edge of the tent.

Raistlin paused to wipe his forehead and calm his heartbeat, then reached out and gingerly lifted the scroll case. He peered cautiously inside.

A bit of parchment paper had been stuffed into the case. He could make out handwriting. He held the case to the light, tried to see if the words were ordinary or the words of a magical spell. He couldn't tell and finally, impatient and no longer mindful of the consequences, he snatched the paper from the case.

Magius the Younger. I truly enjoyed our conversation. I was sorry to see you leave. Perhaps I said something to offend you. If so, I want to apologize and also to return your things you inadvertently left behind. When the city falls to our might, I look forward to renewing our acquaintance. We can have a pleasant chat.

The message was signed, *Immolatus.*

"So this is what he thinks of me," Raistlin said bitterly. "He takes me for a simple-minded fool who would walk into a trap so blatantly obvious that a blind, deaf, and dumb gully dwarf would avoid it. No, my two-faced friend, as interesting as you are, I have no intention of remaking your acquaintance."

He crumpled the missive in his hand. On his way to join C Company, he flung it contemptuously into a campfire. All thoughts of refusing to go on this mission evaporated in the heat of the insult. He was so fired up for action now that if had he not been assigned to this mission, he would have volunteered for it. He took his place beside Caramon.

"Move out!" The word passed quietly down the line from man to man. "Move out!"

❽

The sky was overcast. A light rain continued to fall. The damp soaked into everything—the bread was soggy, firewood wouldn't light. The soldiers complained of the wet. Sergeant Nemiss and Master Senej were both in good humor. Heavy clouds meant no moonlight or starlight this night.

C Company marched for three hours before they reached the cliffs that rose up behind the city of Hope's End. The distance was not that great—a good brisk walk of less than an hour would have taken them to the same place had they traveled in a straight line. Master Senej wanted to make certain that no one in the city gained an inkling of their plan and, though it was not likely that even the sharpest-eyed scout on the wall could have seen them, C Company took a circuitous route, marching directly away from the city and then doubling back.

Advance scouts had been sent ahead to search for a suitable location for the company to begin their ascent. At first, the scouts couldn't find any place. They began to fear that they would have to report to Major Senej that he better think of a new plan. The problem was fording the Hope River, for which the city had been named, a deep, swift-flowing river that cut through a canyon at the bottom of the mountain. The river was dotted with mills, whose wheels still turned, creaking and groaning, though the mills themselves were abandoned, their contents looted. The scouts began to worry.

The sun had set and C Company was on its way by the time the scouts found a place to ford the river. Flowing down out of the mountain, the river split around an island of rock, forming two relatively shallow streams that merged together farther down and tumbled headlong into the canyon. Pleased and relieved, the scouts hastened back to the assigned meeting place to serve as guides to the ford.

The soldiers waded into the rushing water, holding their weapons high. Though the air was warm, the water, coming down out of the mountains, was frigid. Caramon offered to carry his twin, but Raistlin gave him a look that might have turned butter rancid. He girded his robes up around his waist and entered the stream.

He crossed slowly, testing each step, terrified of plunging into the icy current. He was not concerned so much with himself as with his magical scrolls. Though they were safely secured in scroll cases, which were tightly sealed, he could not afford to take the chance that even the tiniest drop of water should seep in, set the ink to running, spoil the magic. When at last he was safely across, he was chilled to the bone, shivering so with the cold that his teeth chattered in his head.

The rocks that formed the island also formed a natural bridge across the second stream. Raistlin would be spared having to enter the water again. His relief was short-lived. The climb over the rock bridge proved as difficult as wading through the water, if not quite as uncomfortable. Raistlin's legs and feet were numb from the cold. He couldn't feel his toes, the rock was slippery from the constant rain. Even the veterans lost their footing, muttering soft curses as they slipped and slithered in the darkness. More than one came perilously close to falling into the water below. Between Caramon and Scrounger, who proved extremely adept at rock climbing, they managed to assist Raistlin over the most difficult parts.

C Company finally reached the bottom of the cliffs, where the real work would begin. Breathing heavily, nursing cuts and bruises, the men eyed the dark immensity of the mountain in silence. The scouts pointed out a ledge far above. Beyond that ledge, they could see the top of the cliff.

Cross that ridge, said the scouts, and beyond lies the city wall.

"Majere, you're the strongest," said Sergeant Nemiss, handing him an iron grappling hook. "Throw that as high above the ledge as you can throw."

Caramon swung the heavy grappling hook twice round and then released, his powerful arms heaving the hook straight up. The hook made a graceful arc and came crashing back down a few seconds later, nearly smashing in the sergeant's skull. Sergeant Nemiss had to make a quick scramble to save herself.

"Sorry, sir," Caramon mumbled.

"Try it again, Majere," the sergeant ordered, this time from a safe distance.

Caramon threw again, this time taking care to launch the grappling hook at the mountain. The hook and rope sailed up at an angle. The hook clanged off a rock at the top and began to slide down the rock. At the last moment, it caught on a rock outcropping and snagged. Caramon pulled with all his might on the rope. The rope held.

"Tumbler, you're up first," the sergeant said. "Take more rope with you."

No one knew Tumbler's real name, including himself, for, he said, he had been called that as a child and now it came natural to him. He was from a family of circus folk, who had performed in fairs throughout Solamnia, including the royal circus in the lordcity of Palanthas. No one knew why he'd left the circus. He never spoke of it, though it was whispered that he'd lost his wife and partner in an accident during their rope-walking act and that he'd left the circus life, vowing never to return.

If this was true, his loss hadn't soured his disposition. He was jovial and friendly and was always willing to show off his skills in camp, to the admiration of his comrades. He could walk on his hands as easily as most men did on their feet. He could bend and twist his body into knots, cause his double-jointed fingers to stick out in strange directions, and climb any tree or wall in existence.

Reaching the ledge, Tumbler secured several more ropes and tossed them down to the waiting soldiers below. The men formed lines and, one by one, began the climb.

Raistlin watched and pondered. He had barely enough strength in his thin arms to lift a full wine cup, let alone pull himself bodily up a rope.

Caramon recognized this fact, as well. "How're you going to manage, Raist?" he asked in a whisper.

"You will carry me," Raistlin said matter-of-factly.

"Hunh?" Caramon eyed the rope, the distance he would have to climb, and looked at his twin in some dismay.

Though Raistlin was thin, he was a full-grown man and, in addition, he had with him his staff, his scroll cases, and his spell components.

"You will never notice my weight, Caramon," Raistlin said smoothly. "I will cast a spell on myself that will make me light as a chicken feather."

"Oh? Will you? That's fine then," Caramon said with unquestioning trust. He bent his back so that Raistlin could climb on. "Lock your hands around my neck. Is your staff secure?"

The Staff of Magius was secure, as were the scroll cases, fastened by leather thongs that ran around Raistlin's shoulders. Caramon began to climb the rope, pulling himself up hand over hand.

"Did you cast the spell, Raist?" he asked. "I didn't hear any magic words."

"I know my business, Caramon," Raistlin returned.

Caramon continued to climb, adrenaline pumping. He noticed very little extra weight.

"Raist! Your spell's working!!" he said over his shoulder. "I can barely feel you!"

"Shut up and pay attention to where you're going!" Raistlin returned, trying not to let his cursed imagination think of what would happen if Caramon lost his grip on the rope.

When they reached the ledge, Raistlin slid off his brother's back and sank down on the rock ledge, pressing his back against the cliff. He drew in a deep breath and almost immediately began to cough. Removing a small flask that hung from his belt, he sipped the special concoction that eased his breathing. His cough abated. He was already exhausted and the most difficult and dangerous part of the journey was yet to come.

"One more climb, men," said the sergeant, handing Caramon the grappling hook.

The top of the cliff was not as high above them as the ledge had been from the ground. Caramon threw the hook and secured the rope on the first try. Tumbler scrambled up the rope with ease, secured his ropes, sent them spiraling back down.

Raistlin once more climbed onto Caramon's back. This time, Caramon could definitely feel his brother's extra weight. The big man's arms began to ache with the strain. He barely had strength enough to pull them both up the cliff. Fortunately the distance they had to cover was shorter or he would have never made it.

"I don't think your spell was working that time, Raist," Caramon said, panting, wiping sweat and rainwater from his face. "Are you sure you cast it? I still didn't hear you say anything."

"You were fatigued, that's all," said Raistlin shortly.

The captain ordered a rest, and then they began marching toward the city. The terrain was rough, the going slow. The men labored up steep rock outcroppings, slid down into boulder-strewn depressions. The time was well past midnight, and the watch fires burning on the city walls did not seem to be appreciably closer. Master Senej was looking grim, when the scouts returned with welcome news.

"Sir, we found a path that runs right down into the city. Probably an old goatherd's trail."

The path cut through the rocks. It was well worn, but narrow. The men were forced to walk single file and even then some, like Caramon, had to edge along parts of it sideways in order to fit. They came to a halt in a rocky clearing to see the city directly below them. Enemy soldiers stood guard on the walls or gathered around the watch fires, talking in low voices, occasionally glancing out to where the bonfires of the besieging armies burned brightly.

The watch fires lit parts of the cliff face as bright as day. The men felt exposed on the rock ledge, even though they knew that someone standing down below would have to look very hard to see them. Moving quietly, keeping to the shadows, the soldiers continued to follow the path leading down into the city. They were within spitting distance of the walls, when Raistlin's worst fears were realized. He drew in a breath to find his air passages blocked. He struggled, trying to stifle his cough, but failed.

Master Senej halted, turned to glare.

"Stop that racket!" the sergeant hissed from her place in the front of the line.

"Stop that racket!" The word whispered from man to man, all of them looking angrily at Raistlin.

"He can't help it!" Caramon growled back, standing in front of his twin.

Raistlin fumbled at the flask, brought it to his mouth, gulped down the ill-tasting liquid. Sometimes the herbal concoction didn't work right away. Sometimes these coughing spells could last for hours. If so, he was certain the men would toss him off the cliff. Either the herbal tea helped him this time or his sheer force of will dampened the smothering ash that seemed to fill his lungs.

C Company continued on until the city's wall was almost directly beneath them. Master Senej sent the scouts ahead to reconnoiter. The soldiers flattened themselves against the cliff face, waited for the scouts to return. Raistlin took sips of his tea at intervals, was careful to keep his throat from drying out.

The scouts came back and this time their news was disappointing. The path led to a stream that entered the city through an aperture in the wall. The scouts had investigated the opening, hoping to be able to use it to enter themselves, but reported that it was so small not even Scrounger could squeak through. The only way into the city was over the wall. The men were almost level with a guard tower. A light burned brightly inside and they could see the silhouettes of at least three men moving back and forth in front of the arrow slits that served as windows.

"We'll have to jump for it, I guess," Master Senej said, eyeing the wall and the guard tower with a frown.

"We're likely going to have every guard in that tower on top of us, sir," said Sergeant Nemiss. "But I don't see any other way in."

Master Senej passed the word for the archers. Hearing the command, Raistlin left his position at the rear of the line.

"I need to reach the master," he said, and the men assisted him, hanging on to him as he edged his way along the narrow ledge.

"Cover us from up here until we can get down off the wall, then follow us in." The master was giving his orders to the bowmen. "Be accurate, that's all I have to say. Shoot to kill. The first scream and we're done for."

"No matter how accurate they are, their officers will find the bodies filled with arrows, sir," Raistlin said, climbing down to stand beside the archers. "They'll know we're in the city."

"Yes, but they won't know where we're hiding," the master argued.

"They'll start searching for us, sir. They'll have all day to find us."

"Do you have a better way, Wizard?" The master glowered.

"Yes, sir. My own way. I will see to it that we enter the city safely and secretly. No one will be the wiser."

The master and the sergeant were dubious. The only mage they trusted was Horkin and that was because he was more soldier than wizard. Neither of them liked Raistlin, they considered him weak and undisciplined. The coughing incident had only bolstered their bad opinion. But they had been ordered to take him and ordered to make use of him. The master and the sergeant exchanged glances.

"Well, I don't suppose we've got much to lose," Master Senej said ungraciously.

"Go ahead, Majere. You men"—Sergeant Nemiss glanced back at the archers—"keep your arrows nocked, just in case." She did not add that the first person they should shoot if the mage betrayed them was the mage himself, but that pretty much went without saying.

"How will you climb down there, Majere?" the sergeant asked.

A good question. The Staff of Magius possessed a spell that would allow the caster to float through the air light as a feather. Raistlin had read about the spell in the book on Magius he'd discovered in the Tower of High Sorcery. He'd tried practicing it a couple of times. The first resulted in a nasty fall from a rooftop. The second had been a success. He had never jumped from such a height, however. He was not certain how far the spell would carry him. This did not appear to be the time to experiment.

"I will climb down the same way I climbed up," he said, and the word was passed for Caramon.

Caramon secured a length of rope to a rock and tossed it over the edge.

"Wait!" Sergeant Nemiss held them.

One of the guards walking his beat on the wall passed right below them. They waited until he turned and began walking away.

Raistlin climbed onto his twin's broad back. Caramon grasped the rope with both hands, slid over the side, and began to rappel down the cliff face. They began their descent in shadow but soon passed into the light of the watch fires, reflecting off the cliff face.

The soldiers on the ledge held their collective breath. All it would take was one guard in the tower to look casually out of the arrow slits that served as windows and they would be discovered.

Raistlin looked over his shoulder at the wall and the tower. A guard's bulk blotted out the light in the narrow opening.

"Caramon, stop!" Raistlin breathed.

Caramon held in his position. He could not remain here long, supporting himself and his twin. His arms were already tired. They quivered from the strain. He and Raistlin would be ideal targets dangling helplessly from the rope. Raistlin waited for the man to cry out, but he left the window. No alarm followed. He had not seen them.

"Now!" Raistlin gasped.

Caramon began his descent again. The last few feet, his arms gave out. He slid down the rope, peeling most of the skin from his palms, and landed heavily on the wall. Raistlin slid from his back and scrambled for cover. He and Caramon ducked into the shadow of the wall, waited, cringing, certain that someone must have heard them.

The men inside the tower were talking loudly, arguing about something from the sound of it. They had not heard a thing. Raistlin peered down the length of the wall. The next guard tower was a good fifty yards distant. Nothing to worry about there.

"What do you want me to do?" Caramon whispered.

"Hand over your flask," Raistlin said softly.

"Flask?" Caramon tried to look innocent. "I don't—"

"Damn it, Caramon! Give me the flask of dwarf spirits you have stashed away in your pants. I know you carry it!"

Wordlessly, chagrined, Caramon dug the small pewter flask from beneath his armor and handed it to his twin.

"Wait for me here," Raistlin ordered.

"But, Raist, I—"

"Hush!" Raistlin hissed. "Do as I say!"

He left without further argument.

Not knowing what his brother intended and fearing to imperil him by disobeying, Caramon remained crouched in the shadows, his hand on the hilt of his short sword.

Raistlin crept silently along the wall until he reached the window of the guard tower. Inside, he could hear the guards talking. Raistlin paid no attention to anything they said. His entire concentration was focused on his spells. Kneeling beneath the slit in the wall, he drew forth a small box and slid open the lid. He called the words of the spell to mind, was gratified to note that the magic came to him immediately. His fear gone, he was amazed at his own calmness. He drew out a pinch of sand and tossed it in through the opening, spoke the words of magic.

The voices slid into incoherence, then silence. Something fell to the floor and broke with a loud crash. Raistlin cringed, waited a moment, just to make certain that the noise had not attracted attention. No one came to investigate. These guards were probably the only people in the tower. Cautiously Raistlin rose to his feet and looked inside.

Three men sprawled on a wooden table, deep in a magical slumber. The crash he'd heard was a mug, fallen from a nerveless hand. The arrow slit was too narrow for a man to enter. Raistlin uncorked the flask, tossed it into the room. The flask landed square on the table. The potent liquor sloshed over the table, dripped onto the floor. The place soon reeked of dwarf spirits.

Raistlin paused a moment to admire his handiwork. When the officer of the watch arrived, he would find three guards who had hoped to ease the monotony of their watch by a taste of spirits, only to imbibe a bit too much. Preferable to the officer finding three of his men had suddenly fallen sound asleep while on guard duty. Much preferable to the officer finding three guards with arrows sticking out of their backs.

When they wakened, the three would deny they had been drinking. No one will believe them. They would be punished for their dereliction in duty, perhaps even executed. Raistlin looked at them. One of the men was quite young, maybe not even seventeen. The other two were older, family men, perhaps, with wives at home, waiting, worrying . . .

Raistlin lowered himself from the window. These men were the enemy. He could not allow them to become people.

These three guards were settled for the night. The other guard had vanished into the shadows. Running soft-footed, Raistlin returned to his brother.

"All is well," he reported.

"What happened to the guards?" Caramon asked.

"No time for explanations!" Raistlin said. "Hurry! Bring the men down."

Caramon tugged three times on the rope.

A few moments later, the Tumbler shimmied down the rope, followed by the sergeant.

"The tower?" she asked.

"All is well, sir," Raistlin reported.

Sergeant Nemiss twitched an eyebrow. "Tumbler, go look," she said.

Angry words came to Raistlin's lips. He had sense enough to eat them, choke them back down. He stood in silence while the sergeant checked up on him.

"They're all taking a snooze, sir," Tumbler reported, grinning. He winked at Raistlin.

"Good," was all Sergeant Nemiss said, but she granted Raistlin a look of approval, then tugged on the rope. Scrounger slid down next, his grin wide and excited. The sergeant issued orders.

"Tumbler, find a good place to send the men over the wall. Scrounger, keep watch on that other tower."

The first signs of gray sky hinted that morning was very close. Tumbler peered over the edge of the far side of the wall. He returned to report that below them was an alleyway behind a large building, perhaps the very warehouse they were hoping to use for a hiding place.

"No one about, sir," he stated.

"There soon will be," the sergeant muttered. Her troops were still in shadows, but day was dawning with what seemed cruel rapidity. "Get the men down there fast." She glanced out in the direction of the besieging armies. "Where's that damn diversion we were promised?"

The men slid along the rope swiftly. Caramon remained at the wall, ready to assist the soldiers to make a silent landfall. He sent them across the ramparts. Tumbler tied a length of rope around one of the wall's crenellations, held the rope fast while the men slithered down the wall and ran down the alley. One of the men waved his arm and pointed at the building. Apparently they had found a way to enter.

"Sir!" Scrounger reported. "Someone's coming from the other tower! Walking this way!"

The sergeant swore. Most of the men had descended, but five still remained on the rock ledge, including Master Senej. And there was still no sound or sign of the promised attack from their allies.

"It's probably an officer," the sergeant said, "making his rounds. I'll go—" She drew her knife.

"I'll handle him, sir," Raistlin offered.

"Wizard! No—" the sergeant began.

But Raistlin was gone, keeping to the shadows, moving so silently he melded with the darkness.

The sergeant started to go after him.

"Begging your pardon, sir," Caramon said with dignity, laying a hand on the sergeant's arm, restraining her, "but Raist said he'd deal with the guard. He hasn't let you down yet."

A large wooden water barrel banded by rings of iron stood on the wall, kept there to put out fires should the enemy hurl flaming missiles. Raistlin crouched behind the water barrel, watched as the officer approached. He walked with his head down, deep in thought. He had only to lift his head and, if his eyesight was quite good, he would see the thin length of rope descending from the rock. All would be over.

"Master! Come quickly!"

The man's head snapped up. He did not look in front of him. He looked behind him, in the direction of the sound of the voice.

"Master! Make haste! The enemy!"

The officer hesitated, staring back at the tower he'd just left. Then, with perfect timing, the diversion came. Trumpets sounded, off-key and tinny, the sweetest music Raistlin had ever heard. The master-at-arms, now convinced of an imminent attack, turned and dashed back along the ramparts.

Raistlin smiled, pleased with himself. He hadn't used his ventriloquism skills in a long time, not since his days of working the local fairs. Good to know that he hadn't lost his talent.

By the time he returned, most of the company was over the wall and into the city. The sergeant had gone with them, along with Master Senej, leaving only Caramon and Tumbler.

A thought occurred to Caramon. "How will you get down?" he asked Tumbler.

"Same as you. The rope," Tumbler replied.

"But then, who's going to stay up here and untie the other end?" Caramon argued. "Someone has to, otherwise they'll know we're here!"

"A good point," said Tumbler solemnly. "Why don't you stay up here and untie the rope after I'm down."

"Sure, I'll do that," Caramon said, then he frowned. "But how will I get down if I untie the rope?"

"That's a problem," said Tumbler, appearing concerned. "I don't suppose you can fly? No? Then I guess you'll have to let me worry about it."

Shaking his head, still concerned, Caramon climbed down the rope, his brother clinging to his twin's broad back. Tumbler waited until they were down, then he followed, shinnying down the rope with ease. Arriving at the bottom, he looked back up at the rope, which was tied firmly to the crenellation. Tumbler gave the rope a jerk. The knot came loose. The rope slithered down the wall and landed at his feet. Tumbler looked over at the two and winked.

"He said that knot was tight!" Caramon cried, aghast. "We could have been killed!"

"Come along, Caramon," Raistlin ordered irritably. His exhilaration was fading. The weakness that set in after his use of magic was starting to affect him. "You've wasted enough time proving to the world that you're a fool."

"But, Raist, I don't understand . . ."

Still talking, Caramon trailed after his twin.

Tumbler coiled the rope over his shoulder and hurried after them. He ducked into the warehouse just as the city woke in an uproar to prepare for the coming assault.

12

Once the warehouse was taken, secured, searched, and deemed as safe a hiding place as could possibly be found inside an enemy city under siege, the sergeant of C Company set the watch and told the rest to get some sleep. Raistlin was already deep in an exhausted slumber, worn out from the physical exertion and the rigors of his spell-casting.

Those keeping lookout tried hard to ignore the snoring of their comrades. The guards walked off their tiredness, pacing the length of the empty warehouse floor, pausing now and then to glance out the windows or exchange soft snatches of conversation. By the end of the watch, they were nodding at their posts, eyes closing and heads falling forward only to snap awake in sudden alertness at the sound of a footstep in the street or a rat in the rafters.

The morning passed without incident. Few people walked the streets in this part of town. The gate tax had shut down the markets, emptied the warehouses of their goods. The only civilians who ventured past were apparently on their way somewhere else, for they looked neither to the left nor to the right but continued on, their heads bowed with trouble. Once four guards marched into view, causing those on watch to lay their hands on their swords and prepare to wake their comrades. But the guards kept on going and the watch looked at each other, nodded, and grinned. The mage's tactics had apparently been successful. No one knew that the town's defense had been breached. No one knew they were here.

The rain ceased with the dawn. The midday sun rose high overhead. Raistlin slept as though he might never waken, his twin keeping watch over his brother. The rest of the men either continued their slumbers or lounged on the floor, glad of the chance to do nothing for a change, resting up for what was likely going to be a long and dangerous night.

Except Scrounger.

Scrounger was much more human than kender. The kender blood in him ran thin, but there were times when it would bubble up to the surface and break out all over him like a bad rash. The particular itch tormenting him at the moment was boredom. A bored kender is a dangerous kender, as anyone on Ansalon will tell you. A bored half-kender might be said to be only half as dangerous. However, those in the presence of a bored half-kender would do well to loosen their swords in their sheaths and be ready for trouble.

Scrounger'd had his fill of sleep; he needed little sleep as it was, and after four hours he was up and ready for action.

Action was a long way off, unfortunately. Scrounger whiled away an hour searching the warehouse from ceiling to cellar in hopes of finding something that might come in handy for bartering. Judging by the dust and chaff on the floor, the warehouse had been used as a granary. All Scrounger came across were some empty bags, the rats having done their own scrounging.

Returning empty-handed from his foraging, Scrounger attempted to engage Caramon in conversation, but was sharply and angrily "shushed!," told to keep his mouth shut so that he wouldn't wake Raistlin. It appeared to Scrounger that nothing short of a gnomic Steam-powered Screaming Window Washing device, such as he had seen once, when younger, would wake the mage.

Reminded of the device, Scrounger had been going to relate the interesting story to Caramon, all about how the device had not only failed to clean the windowpanes but had broken every one of them in the process. The owners of the windows had been furious and were about to set upon the gnomes, who, however, pointed out that the paneless windows now provided a perfectly clear and unobstructed view of the outdoors, which was all that the contract required. Proclaiming their machine a success, the gnomes left town. Another group of gnomes from the GlaziersGlassSpunandBlownMirrors-aSpecialtySevenYearsBadLuck Committee had arrived shortly after (they made it a policy to follow the windowwashers), but had been turned away at the border.

Caramon shushed Scrounger again, right at the interesting part where the gnomes set off their machine and the mayor's ears had started to bleed. The half-kender wandered off.

Scrounger made another desultory round of the warehouse, occasionally falling over a slumbering body lying unseen in the shadows, to be kicked and damned to the Abyss. In a sunlit corner, Master Senej and Sergeant Nemiss were hunched over a map, plotting the night's attack. Here, at least, was something interesting. Scrounger stood near, peering down at the map.

"This is the main street leading to the north gate. According to this map," the master was saying, "this building standing right here will provide excellent cover for the men right up until the time they have to break out into the open to attack."

"And I'm saying, sir, that one of our spies told us this building burned down a month ago," Sergeant Nemiss argued. "You can't count on it being there. And if it's not there, we're in the open all the way from this block to the gate."

"There are trees here. . . ."

"They've been cut down, sir."

"According to your spy."

"I know you don't think much of him, sir, and I admit that he failed to warn us about the catapults, but—"

"Wait a minute, Sergeant." Aware of a shadow falling over the map, Master Senej looked up. "Can we help you, soldier?"

"I can go," Scrounger offered, ignoring the sarcasm. "I can go see if the house is still there and if the trees have been cut down. Please, sir. I really need to be doing something. I have this itching in my hands and my feet."

"Trenchfoot," the master said, frowning.

"Not trenchfoot, sir," said Sergeant Nemiss. "Kender. Half-kender, that is."

The master's frown darkened.

"I could be there and back in two shakes of a griffon's tail, sir," Scrounger pleaded.

"Out of the question," Master Senej said shortly. "The risk that you'd be noticed and caught is too great."

"But, sir—" Scrounger begged.

The master glowered. "Perhaps we should tie him up."

"You know, sir," Sergeant Nemiss said, "that's really not a bad idea."

"Tying him up?"

"No, sir. Sending him out to reconnoiter. The lives of the men might depend on whether that house is there or not. Scrounger's proven himself valuable before now."

The master eyed Scrounger, who, in order to inspire confidence, tried to look more human and less kender.

"I agree. It would help to know about that house. Very well," the master said, making up his mind. "But you're on your own, Scrounger. If you're caught, we can't imperil the mission to come rescue you."

"I fully understand that, sir," said Scrounger. "I won't be caught. I have a sort of way of blending in so that people never notice me or if they do they think that I'm—"

The master glared at him. "Shouldn't you be gone by now?"

"Yes, sir. Going now, sir."

Scrounger crept back to where Raistlin lay sleeping and Caramon lay watching his brother sleep.

"Caramon," Scrounger whispered, "I need to borrow that pouch."

"That's got our rations in it," Caramon protested. "What's left of 'em," he added gloomily.

"I know. I'll bring the food back. I promise. I might even bring you more."

"But you've got a pouch!" Caramon protested.

"Staff . . ." Raistlin murmured in his sleep. "The staff is . . . mine . . . No!" He shouted the word, began to thrash about, arms flailing.

"Hush! Raist! Hush! It's all right," Caramon whispered. Holding his brother by the shoulders, he cast a sidelong glance in the direction of Sergeant Nemiss, who had looked over, glowering, at the commotion. "Your staff is here, Raist. Right here."

Caramon placed the staff beneath his brother's frantic hand. Raistlin grasped hold of the staff protectively, sighed, and sank back into sleep.

"He's going to get in trouble with the sergeant if he keeps yelling like that," Scrounger observed.

"I know. That's why I'm with him. He's quieter if I'm here." Caramon shook his head. "I don't know what's wrong. I've never seen him like this. He keeps thinking someone's trying to take the staff away from him."

Scrounger shrugged. Nothing Raistlin did or thought was of much interest to him. "C'mon. Hand over the pouch."

Caramon handed it over, watched as Scrounger looped Caramon's pouch over one shoulder, his own pouch over the other shoulder. "I really could use a couple more, but I guess this will have to do. Too bad they cut my hair. How does this look?"

Running his hands through his short hair, Scrounger caused it to stand on end, stick out every which way. He assumed a cheery, carefree smile.

"Say," said Caramon, astonished. "You look just like a kender. No offense," he added, knowing how sensitive his friend was on that point.

"None taken," said Scrounger, grinning. "That's what I wanted to hear, in fact. Be seein' you."

"Where are you going?" Caramon demanded.

"To reconnoiter," Scrounger said proudly.

In a walled human city where everyone knows everyone else and has known them for probably as long as they've been alive, any stranger entering town is certain to stand out, under the best of conditions. Now, with the city surrounded by enemy troops, everyone was on edge. Citizens went about their daily business armed to the teeth and ready for attack. Any stranger was set upon immediately, trussed up, and hauled off for interrogation. With the exception of kender.

The problem is not that kender all look alike to humans, but that the same kender never looks the same two times running. He has either switched clothes with a friend or snitched clothes from a friend or borrowed interesting-looking clothes left out to dry. He might have flowers in his hair one day and maple syrup in his hair the next. He might be wearing his shoes or your shoes or no shoes at all. Small wonder that most humans— especially upset, fearful, and worried humans—did not know whether they were seeing the same kender over a period of several days or several kender all attired in more or less the same outfit.

Thus, no one in Hope's End paid the slightest attention to Scrounger, beyond the instinctive reaction of clapping a protective hand over a purse.

Scrounger strolled down the main street of the walled city, admiring the tall houses crowded together side by side, houses made of plaster with dark wood supports. Lead-paned glass sparkled in the second-floor bay windows that bowed out over the street. Some of the buildings needed painting, however. Others were in a state of disrepair, which would not have been permitted had the owners had the means to fix the sagging eaves or replace the broken window.

The merchant shops he passed were boarded up, market stalls empty and falling down. Only the taverns were busy, that was where everyone went to hear the news. News that was, for the most part, not good.

The people Scrounger encountered were pale and downcast. If they paused to speak, their conversations were held in low and anxious voices. He loudly bid people a good day, but no one responded. Most just shook their heads and hurried on. The only cheerful people he saw in the entire city were two small boys, dirty and ragged, running through the streets, bashing each other with wooden swords.

"So these are the rebels," Scrounger said.

He passed by an open window where a thin young woman, who looked half-starved herself, was trying to nurse a fretful baby.

Scrounger brought to mind the sight of Borar taking the arrow in his throat. He pictured the smashed and battered bodies lying underneath the huge boulders and he was able to summon up a fair amount of hatred for these people. But since it was only the human part of Scrounger that could hate and that human part constituted only half of him, his hatred was considerably diluted. What hatred there was carried him up to the city gate, which was closed, barred and barricaded.

The spy had been partially right. The house in question had burned down, but the stands of tall trees beneath the wall, trees that were part of the city's defenses, would unwittingly help the city's attackers by supplying adequate cover for their assault.

Scrounger lingered near the wall, absorbing details of his surroundings, trying to anticipate the questions the master and sergeant were bound to put to him. This didn't take long. He supposed he should go back to the warehouse, but the thought of being cooped up in that building, watching Raistlin sleep, was too much for him to bear.

"The master would really like it if I could bring back some information on the enemy," Scrounger said to himself. "The enemy's all around me. Somewhere someone must be talking about what they plan to do."

A brief search produced a likely looking source. A group of people, a mix of soldiers and civilians, to judge by their dress, had gathered atop the city wall near a guard tower. One of the men, a large man, corpulent and well dressed, wore a heavy chain of gold around his neck. Such a chain as might denote a man of important standing.

Scrounger was just wishing most earnestly that he could be a mouse, skittering about their feet, when the sight of the trees against the wall gave him a better idea. He would not be a mouse, but a bird.

Selecting the tree that was tallest and nearest the group, Scrounger waited at the bottom, in the shadows, until he was quite certain the few passersby hadn't noticed him. He divested himself of his pouches, deposited them at the tree's base, and began climbing. Nimble and deft, he moved carefully from limb to limb, taking his time, studying out each hand- and foothold with care so as not to rustle the branches. So quiet was he that he startled a squirrel in her nest.

She scolded him roundly and flitted out of the hole in the tree, her young following her, tails twitching and voices raised in shrill alarm. The squirrels' turmoil provided excellent cover, permitting Scrounger to climb much closer than he'd hoped. He settled himself on a branch directly below the wall and concentrated on listening. A thrill went over him from head to toe when he heard one of the men refer to the man with the golden chain as "lord mayor."

"A council of war!" said Scrounger excitedly. "I've stumbled on a council of war!"

That was not precisely true, as he was soon to discover. The mayor had come up to view the results of the enemy's latest attack, an attack that had halted about mid-morning with the enemy retreating back to camp.

"That's two assaults we've driven off now," the mayor was saying in hopeful tones. "I think we stand a good chance of winning this war."

"Bah! Both of those were feints." The speaker was a elderly man, rough and grizzled. "Just drawing us out, testing our strength. They have a fair notion of it now, thanks to the numskull who gave the order to loose the catapult yesterday morning."

The lord mayor gave a deprecating cough, which was followed by silence. Then the elderly man spoke.

"You should face the facts, Lord mayor, Your Honor. We don't have a prayer of winning this fight."

More silence.

"Not a prayer," he continued after a moment. "I'm leading untrained men, for the most part. Oh, I've a few archers who can hit their mark but not many and they'll be cut down in the first major assault. Do you know what happened this morning, sir? I found three of my guard dead drunk on duty. Small blame to 'em. I'da been dead drunk myself last night if I could have laid hands on the wherewithall."

"What would you have us do?" the mayor asked, his voice breaking. He sounded on the verge of hysteria. "We tried to surrender! You heard what that . . . that fiend said!"

"Yeah, I heard him. And that's the one reason I wasn't dead drunk last night." The commander's voice tightened. "I'm hoping to live long enough to have my chance at him."

"It seems incredible to me," said the mayor, "but I could well believe that King Wilhelm wants us all dead. He had to know that imposing that outrageous tax on us would lead to open rebellion. He forced us to take this position, then he sent in his army to teach us a lesson. When we tried to make peace, his general gave us terms so impossible that no rational person could agree to them."

"You won't get any arguments from me on that, Your Honor."

"But why?" the mayor demanded helplessly. "Why is he doing this to us?"

"If the gods were around, they'd know. Since they're not, I have to assume that only King Wilhelm knows and he's gone potty, if what we hear is true.

Perhaps he has new tenants for our homes. I'll tell you one thing, though. That's not the army of Blödehelm out there."

"It's not?" The mayor sounded astonished. "Then . . . what army is it?"

"I dunno. But I served a number of years in the army of Blödehelm and that ain't it. We were a homegrown army. We left our plows to pick up our swords, did a few hours march, fought our battle, and were back in our homes in time for supper. This army, now. This army's a fighting man's army. A professional army, not a bunch of farmers wearing their grandpappy's armor."

"But then . . . what does that mean?" The mayor sounded dazed, as if someone had struck him with a rock.

"It means that you're right, Your Honor," said the commander laconically. "The king—or someone—wants us all dead."

The commander bowed to the mayor, then walked away. The mayor muttered to himself, heaved a vast sigh, stood a moment or two longer on the wall, then descended.

Scrounger sat in his tree awhile longer himself, going over the conversation so that he could repeat it accurately. Once he had it memorized, he scrambled down out of the tree, retrieved his pouches, and emerged from the grove right under the nose of the lord mayor.

The lord mayor jumped and made a reflexive grab for his purse. "Get away!"

Scrounger was only too happy to take him up on his suggestion.

The mayor took a second look, shifted his bulk, and planted his substantial body squarely in front of the half-kender.

"Wait a minute! Do I know you?" The mayor regarded Scrounger intently.

"Oh, yes," Scrounger said cheerfully.

"How?" The mayor frowned.

"I've had the honor of appearing before you many times, Your mayorship." Scrounger gave a polite bow.

"Indeed?" The mayor was dubious.

"At the morning assize. You know. When they let us out of jail after we've all been arrested the night before and they take us before you and you make those really fine speeches—very affecting—about law and order and honesty being the best policy and all that."

"I see." The mayor still appeared puzzled.

"I've cut my hair," Scrounger offered. "Maybe that's why you don't recognize me. And I haven't been in jail in a long time. Your speeches," he swore solemnly, "helped me turn my life around."

"Well, I'm happy about that," the mayor said. "See that it continues. Good day to you."

He walked down the street, and mounted the steps of a very fine house, the finest house on the block.

"Whew!" Scrounger said, making certain he took a different street himself, not intending to give the mayor another look at him. "That was close. I can't believe he got down off the wall that fast! He moves pretty quick for a fat man, I'll say that for him."

❂

"They tried to surrender?" Master Senej stared in blank astonishment. "You mean to tell me that we lost good men to a city that doesn't want to fight?"

"He must have heard wrong. You must have heard wrong," Sergeant Nemiss said to Scrounger. "What were the exact words?"

"'We tried to surrender,'" said Scrounger. "And there's more, sirs. Listen." He went on to relate the entire conversation verbatim.

"You know," said Master Senej, his brow furrowed, "I had the same thought about that army myself. I never fought with or for the army of Blödehelm, but I'd heard of them and they were just as that old man described—drop the plow to pick up the sword, drop the sword to go back to the plow."

"But if that's true, what does it all mean, sir?" Sergeant Nemiss asked, unconsciously echoing the lord mayor.

"It means that the enemy's raised his hand in surrender and we're about to lop off his head," said the master. "The baron won't like this, not one bit."

"What do we do, sir? The assault's set for tomorrow morning. Our orders are to attack the gates from behind. We can't go against orders."

The master pondered a moment, then made up his mind. "The baron should know what's going on. He has the reputation for being a just and honorable man. Think how his reputation and ours will suffer if it turns out that we're taking part in a cold-blooded butchery! No one would ever hire us again. He should at least have a chance to remand his orders or change them."

"I doubt we have time to send back a messenger, sir."

"It's only a little after midday now, sergeant. A man alone can move faster than an entire troop. If he cuts straight across country, he can be there in three hours. An hour to explain things to the baron. Three hours back. Allow an hour or two for mischance and he should be back here by sunset at the latest. The attack isn't scheduled until dawn. Who's your best man?"

"Tumbler," Sergeant Nemiss said. "Pass the word for Tumbler."

Tumbler appeared, disheveled from sleep and still yawning.

"We need you to take a message to the baron," said the master, and the tense tone of his voice jolted Tumbler to full wakefulness.

"Yes, sir," he said, straightening.

"You can't wait for darkness. You'll have to go now. The best route is probably back over the wall. We're dealing with a bunch of citizen soldiers, but take care all the same. No matter whether a trained man or an untrained one kills you, you're just as dead."

"I know the drill, sir. I'll get across," Tumbler said confidently.

"Take the most direct route to the camp. Report to the baron. This is what I want you to tell him. How's your memory?"

"Excellent, sir."

"Scrounger, tell him what you told us."

Scrounger repeated his story. Tumbler listened carefully, nodded once, said he had it. He was offered equipment, but he said all he needed was a rope and a knife, which were already in his possession. When the watch reported the street empty, Tumbler ducked out the door and vanished around the side of the warehouse.

"Nothing to do now but wait," said the master.

❂

The hours of the afternoon crawled. The men passed the time playing at knight's jump, a game in which the player presses on the edges of a small metal counter with a larger counter, causing the smaller counter to "jump" into a cup. The person with the highest number of counters in the cup at the end of the game is the winner.

A very old game—it was said to have been a favorite of the legendary Knight, Huma—knight's jump was popular among the baron's men, who valued their hand-made counters as highly as coins of the realm. Each soldier's counters were commissioned from the blacksmith, who made them from leftover scraps of metal; each was marked with his or her own special design. Variations of the game had developed. Sometimes the player was required not only to "jump" the counter into the cup but also to stack his counter neatly on top of the counter already in the cup.

The baron was a terror at knight's jump and it also proved to be a game at which Raistlin—with his highly developed manual dexterity—excelled. One of the few "frivolous" pursuits the usually serious-minded young man enjoyed, he played with a single-minded intensity and skill that casual players found extremely daunting, but which the experts were quick to recognize and approve. One poor sport insisted sourly that the mage must be using his magic to win, but Raistlin easily proved his detractor wrong to the satisfaction of his supporters, of which he had many. Not because they liked him, but because he made them money.

Raistlin's natural thrift and disinclination to wager his own hard-earned money kept him from joining in on the high-stakes games, but he soon found those who were glad to stake him for a share in the profits.

Caramon, with his big and clumsy hands, was a mediocre player at best. He enjoyed watching his twin, though he often annoyed Raistlin beyond measure with his well-meaning but ill-judged advice.

The only sound that could be heard all through the afternoon was the chink of counters rattling in the metal drinking cups and the occasional soft groan or muffled curse from the losers, murmured praise for the winner. The game ended with the setting of the sun and then only when it became too dark to adequately judge the distance needed for the jump. The men dispersed to eat their supper, munching on cold meat and hard bread, washed down with water. After that some slept, knowing that they had an early rising ahead of them. Others passed the time in storytelling or word games. Raistlin handed over his share of the winnings to Caramon for safekeeping, sipped cold tea, and slept peacefully, dreaming of counters and cups instead of sinister wizards.

Everyone knew of Tumbler's assignment by now, they knew the danger he ran. They followed him along his route in their minds, making calculations on the length of time it would take him to reach camp, arguing about whether he would stick to the main road or take a shortcut, speculating and even wagering money on the baron's answer.

As darkness neared, the soldiers looked at the door, peered out the windows, appeared hopeful when a footstep was heard in the otherwise deserted street, were downcast when the footsteps continued on. The time came and went by which Tumbler could have reasonably been expected to return. Master Senej and Sergeant Nemiss continued with their plans for the dawn attack.

And then one of the sentries called out softly and tensely, "Who goes there?"

"Kiri-Jolith and the kingfisher," was the password, correctly given, and a tired but grinning Tumbler slipped past the sentry.

"What did the baron say?" Major Senej demanded.

"Ask him yourself, sir," said Tumbler. With a jerk of his thumb, he indicated the baron, standing behind him.

The men stared, astonished.

"Attention!" Sergeant Nemiss called out, jumping to her feet. The men scrambed to obey. The baron waved his hand, ordered them to remain where they were.

"I'm going to get to the bottom of this barrel," he stated. "It may be clear water at the top but I've got the feeling there's sludge beneath. I don't like what I'm hearing about our so-called allies. I certainly didn't like what I saw of them."

"Yes, sir. What are your orders, sir?"

"I want to talk to someone in authority in this city. Maybe that commander—"

"That will be dangerous, sir."

"Damn it, I know it will be dangerous. I—"

"Begging your pardon, my lord." Scrounger popped up from beneath the baron's elbow. "But I know the house where the lord mayor lives. At least, I think it must be his house. It's the biggest and the finest on the block."

"Who are you?" the baron asked, unable to see the shadowy figure in the darkness.

"Scrounger, sir. I was the one who overhead the mayor talking and I watched him as he went down a street and turned into a house."

"Can you find your way back there?"

"Yes, sir," Scrounger replied.

"Good, let's go, then. It's not long until morning. Master Senej, you and Sergeant Nemiss stay with the troops. If we're not back by sunrise, go forward with the attack."

"Yes, my lord. Might I suggest, sir, that you take along a couple more men in case you run into trouble?"

"If I do run into trouble, Master, it won't much matter whether there are two of us or four of us, will it? Not if we're facing fifty angry citizens. And I don't want to go marching around town with an army rattling and clanking behind me."

"You don't need the army, sir," said the master stubbornly. "You should at least take the wizard Majere. He proved himself a real asset to us last night, my lord. Take him and his brother. Caramon Majere's a good fighter and big as a house. The two of them can't hurt, sir, and they could be a real help."

"Very well, Master. I like your suggestion. Pass the word for the Majeres."

"And, my lord," said Master Senej quietly, drawing the baron to one side, "if you don't like what His Honor the mayor has to say, he would always make a valuable hostage."

"My thoughts exactly, Master," the baron replied.

13

T HOUGH IT WAS ONLY A FEW HOURS AFTER DARK, THE STREETS OF HOPE'S End were deserted. Even the taverns had closed. People were in their homes, either finding refuge from their trouble in sleep or lying awake, staring into the darkness, awaiting the dawn with dread. Those who heard footsteps and who were actually curious enough or frightened enough to look out their windows saw only what appeared to be a patrol marching down the street.

"If we tiptoe and hug the shadows and look the part of spies sneaking around the city, we'll be taken for spies sneaking around the city. If we march straight down the middle of the road, not flaunting our presence but not hiding it either, chances are that in the darkness we'll be taken for the local militia making its rounds. We just have to hope," the baron added with characteristic calm, "that we don't run into the local militia making its rounds. Then there'll be trouble. Our cause is just. Kiri-Jolith will keep us out of harm's way."

Kiri-Jolith probably had little to do in those days, few prayers to answer. Perhaps he was as bored as the men forced to lie in wait in the warehouse, without even the mild distraction of a game of knight's jump to cheer their dull eternity. The baron's prayer, falling on his ears, might have come as a welcome change, an opportunity to be up and doing. The baron and his party encountered no living being on their swift march from the warehouse, not even a stray cat.

"That's the house I saw him enter, my lord," Scrounger whispered, pointing.

"Are you quite sure?" the baron asked. "You're looking at it from a different direction."

"Yes, I'm sure, sir. As you can see, it's the biggest house in the block and I remember that there was a stork's nest atop the chimney."

Solinari was almost full this night, shed his silver light down upon the city streets. The tall chimneys of the row of houses were lined up like soldiers. A stork's nest atop one was like a bristly hat.

"What if this isn't his house? It could be he was just visiting a friend," the baron suggested.

"He didn't knock on the door," Scrounger offered. "He just went right in as if he owned the place."

"And if it is not his house, my lord," Raistlin added, "then we will capture and interrogate some other prominent citizen. Whoever lives in this house is a person of wealth."

The baron agreed that this would suit him just as well. The small band left the street, circled around to an alley, which ran behind the row of houses. The houses looked much different from the back, but the house they wanted was easy to locate, due mainly to the nest on the chimney.

"I've heard that a stork's nest brings good luck to the house," Scrounger whispered.

"Let us hope that you're right in this instance, young man," the baron replied. "No lights in the house. The family must be in bed. I doubt they're out socializing. Who can pick this lock?" The baron looked at Scrounger, who shook his head.

"Sorry, sir. My mother tried to teach me. I just never took to it."

"I believe that I might be able to deal with the lock, my lord," Raistlin said quietly.

"You have a spell?"

"No, my lord," Raistlin returned. "In my school days, my master kept all his spellbooks in a locked case. Caramon, I'll need to borrow your knife."

Wooden stairs led to the back door. Raistlin glided up the stairs, taking care to keep from tripping on his robes. The others stood watch in the alley, looking in all directions, their hands on their weapons. The baron hadn't even begun to grow impatient when Raistlin motioned with his hand, pale white in the moonlight. The door stood open.

They entered the house quietly, or as quietly as possible with Caramon among them. His heavy footfalls caused the floorboards to creak ominously as he entered the kitchen and set the pots, hanging on hooks on a wall, to rattling.

"Quiet, Majere!" the baron whispered urgently. "You'll wake the whole house!"

"Sorry, my lord," Caramon returned in a smothered breath.

"You stay here to guard the exit," the baron ordered. "If someone comes, bash 'em on the head and tie 'em up. No killing if you can help it. But don't let anyone cry out, either. Scrounger, you stay with him. If there's trouble, don't shout. Come fetch me."

Caramon nodded and took up his post at the door. Scrounger settled himself on a stool nearby.

"Wizard, you're with me." The baron padded through the kitchen. Finding a door, he opened it, peered inside. "Unless I miss my guess, these stairs are the stairs the servants use to gain access to the upper levels. That's where we'll find the bedrooms. Do you see a candle anywhere?"

"We have no need, my lord. If you want light, I can provide it. *Shirak*," Raistlin said and the crystal atop his staff began to glow with a soft white radiance.

The servants' staircase was narrow and winding. Raistlin and the baron crept up the stairs single file, the baron leading the way, moving with feline stealth. Raistlin followed as best he could, terrified of accidentally treading on a squeaky stair or knocking his staff against the wall.

"The master bedroom will be on the second floor," the baron whispered, pausing before a door leading off the spiraling staircase, which continued upward. "Douse that light!"

"*Dulak!*" Raistlin said softly, and the light went out, leaving them in darkness.

He waited on the stairs as the baron opened the door slowly and cautiously. From his vantage point, Raistlin could see a moonlit hallway hung with tapestries. A heavy wooden door, ornately carved, stood directly across from them. The sounds of snoring, loud and sonorous, came from behind the door.

"I have a sleep spell ready to cast on him, my lord," Raistlin said.

"He's already asleep. We want him awake," the baron returned. "We can't question him if he's asleep."

"True, my lord," Raistlin conceded, chagrined.

"You have that spell of yours ready to cast on his wife," the baron continued. "Women are screamers and there's nothing rouses the household faster than a woman's scream. Enchant her before she has a chance to wake up. I'll deal with the mayor."

The baron left the doorway, crossed the hall. Raistlin came after him, the words to the spell burning on his tongue. The thought came to him that he had not coughed once on the entire journey and, of course, now that he had thought of it, a cough began to tickle his throat. Desperately he forced the cough down.

The baron placed his hand on the door handle, turned it softly, and pushed on the door. The mayor must employ good help, for the door hinges opened without a creak. Moonlight illuminated the room through a mullioned window. The baron soft-footed into the room, Raistlin keeping close behind.

A large bed, with bed curtains pulled closed, stood in the center of the room. The sound of snoring came from behind the curtains. The baron tiptoed across the floor, peeped through a crack in the bed curtain.

Fortunately for them, perhaps unfortunately for the lord mayor, he slept alone. One look convinced the baron that the man in the bed was the mayor. He fit Scrounger's description of a rotund, cheerful-faced man, now clad in a sleeping gown and a nightcap instead of his rich robes.

Flinging aside the curtains, the baron was on the slumbering man in a bound, clapped his hand over the snoring man's open mouth.

The mayor woke with a gasp muffled by the baron's hand. The mayor blinked at his captor with sleep-fuddled eyes.

"Make no sound!" the baron hissed. "We mean you no harm. Wizard, shut the door!"

Raistlin did as he was told, easing shut the door. He returned quickly, crossed over to the opposite side of the bed to be ready if needed.

The mayor stared at his captor in terror, shaking in fear so that the bed curtains swayed on their golden rings.

"Light," the baron ordered.

Raistlin spoke, and the crystal on the Staff of Magius gleamed brightly, revealing the baron's face.

"My name is Baron Ivor of Langtree," said the baron, still keeping his hand fast over the mayor's mouth. "Perhaps you've heard of me. That's my army out there, ready to attack your city the moment I give the order. I was hired by King Wilhelm to overthrow rebels who are said to be in control of the city. Are you understanding me?"

The mayor nodded his head. He still looked frightened half out of his wits, but he had stopped shaking.

"Good. I'll let you go in a moment, if you promise you won't yell for help. Are there servants in the house?"

The mayor shook his head. The baron snorted, obviously aware the man was lying. No one lived in a house this large without servants. He wondered whether to continue to press the issue or to carry on. He made a compromise.

"Wizard, watch the door. If anyone enters, cast your spell."

Raistlin opened the door a crack, placed himself so as to command a view of the hallway and also be able to see and hear what was transpiring in the bedroom.

The baron continued his one-way conversation. "I've seen some things and heard some things that have led me to question my reason for taking this assignment. I'm hoping you can help me. I want straight answers from you, Your Honor. That's all. I don't intend to harm you. Give me them and I'll leave as quickly as I've come. Do you agree?"

The mayor nodded his head tentatively. The tassel on his nightcap quivered.

"Play me false," said the baron, still not releasing the grip, "and I'll order my wizard to change you into a slug!"

Raistlin glowered at the mayor, looked stern and threatening, though he could no more have done the baron's bidding than he could have flown around the room. Thanks to the peculiar tint of his skin and the strange appearance of his eyes, he did look extremely intimidating, especially to a man who has just been violently roused from a sound sleep.

The mayor cast Raistlin a terrified glance and this time his nod was more emphatic.

Slowly, the baron moved his hand.

The mayor gulped and licked his lips, drew the bedclothes up to his chin as if they might protect him. His eyes went from the baron to Raistlin and back again. He was in a pitiable state and Raistlin wondered how they would ever get anything intelligent out of him.

"Good," said the baron. Looking around, he drew up a chair and, placing it beside the bed, sat down and faced the mayor, who appeared considerably astonished at this proceeding. "Now, tell me your story. From the beginning. Keep it short, though. We don't have much time. The attack is slated to start at dawn."

This news was not exactly conducive to putting the mayor at his ease. After many fits and false starts and beginning in the middle and having to backtrack, His Honor became immersed in the story of the wrongs inflicted on them by Good King Wilhelm. Forgetting his fear, he spoke passionately.

"We sent an ambassador to the king. He had the man disemboweled! We tried to surrender. The commander of the king's army said that 'we should line up our women' for him to take his pick!"

"You believed him?" the baron said, his dark brows drawn together in a heavy frown.

"Of course we believed him, my lord!" The mayor mopped his sweating forehead with the tassel of his nightcap. "What choice did we have? Besides"—he shuddered—"we heard the screams of those they took prisoner. We saw their homes and barns burning. Yes, we believed him."

Having met Kholos, the baron believed as well. He thought over all he'd heard, tugging on his black beard.

"Do *you* know what's going on, my lord?" the mayor asked meekly.

"No," the baron answered bluntly. "But I have the feeling that I have been duped. If you have heard of me, then you know that I am a man of honor. My ancestors were Knights of Solamnia and, though I am not, I still hold by the precepts of that noble order."

"You will call off the attack then?" the mayor asked with pathetic hopefulness.

"I don't know," said the baron, his head sunk in thought. "I signed a contract. I gave my word I would attack on the morrow. If I refuse and turn and flee the battle, I will be taken for an oath-breaker, probably a coward. No prospective employer will ask the circumstances. He will conclude that I am untrustworthy and refuse to work with me. If I attack, I will be taken for a man who slaughters innocents attempting to surrender! A fine spot I'm in!" he added angrily, rising to his feet. "Goblins to the left of me and ogres on the right."

"There aren't goblins and ogres out there, too, are there?" the mayor gasped, clutching at the blanket.

"A figure of speech," the baron muttered, pacing the room. "What is the hour, Wizard?"

Raistlin went to look out the window, saw the moon starting to wane. "Near midnight, my lord."

"I must make up my mind one way or the other and soon."

The baron marched the length of the bedroom one direction. Turning tightly on his heel in military fashion, as if he were on guard duty, he marched back the other, fighting his mental battle against the ogres of foul scheming on one flank and the goblins of dishonor on the other. To Raistlin the decision was an easy one—call off the attack and go home. He was not a Knight, however, with knightly notions of honor, however misguided. Nor was he responsible for an army, whose soldiers would expect to be paid as promised. Payment would not be forthcoming if the baron went back on the terms of the contract. A pretty dilemma and one Raistlin was thankful was not his own.

For the first time, he saw the burden of command, the isolation of the person in authority, the terrible loneliness of the commander. The lives of thousands of people hung in the balance of this decision. The lives of his men, for whom the baron was responsible, and now the lives of the people of this doomed city. The baron was the only one who could make this decision and he must make it immediately. Worse, he had to make it without being in full possession of the facts.

What had happened to King Wilhelm? Why was he intent on destroying this city and its inhabitants? Was it possible that the king had a good reason? Was this mayor telling the truth or, finding his city in a now untenable position, was this all a complete fabrication? The baron marched and Raistlin watched in silence, curious as to the outcome.

In the end, he was not to know it. The baron halted at a midpoint.

"I have made my decision," he said, his tone heavy. "Now tell me the truth, Your Honor. How many servants do you have in the house and where are they?"

"Two, my lord," the mayor said meekly. "A married couple, who have been with me a long, long time. You need fear nothing from them, sir. They both sleep soundly and would not waken if the city wall fell on them."

"Let's hope it doesn't come to that," the baron said gravely. "Wizard, find these servants and see to it that they continue to slumber."

"Yes, my lord," Raistlin said, as he was bound to say, though he was extremely loath to leave.

"After that, go tell my guards that I will be ready to depart shortly."

"He won't hurt them?" the mayor asked anxiously, referring to the servants.

"He won't hurt them," the baron replied.

The mayor was pale and unhappy, dismayed by the baron's dark and frowning expression and his ominous words. He supplied directions on where to find the servants. Raistlin lingered a moment longer, hoping the baron would give some hint as to his intentions. He waited so long that the baron glanced his way, frowning. Raistlin had no choice but to carry out the order or face an angry reprimand.

"These servants are probably fast asleep," Raistlin fumed as he ascended the stairs to the servants' quarters, a small room with a single gabled window located in the top part of the house, not far below the stork's nest. "Sending me to deal with them was just an excuse. The baron doesn't trust me, that's what it is. He has manufactured this fool's errand in order to get rid of me. He would have allowed Horkin to remain."

As it turned out, the baron's instincts were accurate. Perhaps he had heard some sound that had indicated the servants might be stirring. Raistlin opened the door to the bedroom to find the middle-aged retainer seated on the edge of the bed, tugging on his boots while his wife poked him in the back, saying frantically that she was certain someone was in the house.

Raistlin cast his spell just as the wife caught sight of him in the moonlight. Sleep closed her mouth over her scream. The husband dropped the other boot with a clunk and fell back on the bed. The spell would last a long time. Just to be safe, however, Raistlin locked the door and carried away the key, which he would afterward deposit on the kitchen table.

Somewhat mollified by the fact that there had indeed been danger of discovery, Raistlin returned to the kitchen, where he found Caramon keeping watch out the back window.

"Where's Scrounger?"

"He went to the front to make sure no one came in that way."

"I'll go fetch him. The baron says that he will be ready to leave shortly. You are to make certain the way is secure."

"Sure, Raist. What did he decide to do? Are we going to attack?"

"Does it matter one way or the other to us, my brother?" Raistlin asked indifferently. "We are being paid to obey orders, not question them."

"Yeah, I guess you're right," said Caramon. "Still, aren't you curious to know?"

"Not in the least," Raistlin said and left to retrieve Scrounger.

☻

The baron gave no hint as to his intentions on their way back. The streets were empty. They took no chances but kept close to buildings, paused to look searchingly down side streets and alleyways before they passed them. They were about to cross the last street, the warehouse directly ahead of them, when Caramon, who had been walking in the lead, caught a glow of light from the corner of his eye and fell back against the side of an abandoned house.

"What is it?" the baron whispered.

"Light. Down at the end of the street," Caramon whispered. "It wasn't there when we left."

Motioning the others to remain in the shadows, the baron looked around the corner in the direction Caramon had indicated.

"I'll be blessed," he said softly, awed. "You have to come see this!"

The others stepped around him into the street. They halted, stared, struck by the sight, even to the point of forgetting that they were standing out in the open.

At the end of the street stood a building, a decaying, tumbledown building, that must have, at one time, been lovely. The remnants of graceful columns supported a roof decorated with carvings, whose images had been obliterated, either by time's blows or man's. The building was surrounded by a courtyard, its flagstones broken and overrun with weeds. Caramon would have walked right past this relic, taken no notice of it at all, had it not been for the moonlight.

Either by design or by accident, the building captured Solinari's moonbeams and held them within the stone, as a child captures fireflies in a jar, causing the building to shimmer with an argent radiance.

"I've never seen the like," said the baron in a voice that was hushed and reverent.

"Me neither," said Scrounger. "It's so beautiful it makes me hurt, right here." He laid his hand over his heart.

"Is it magic, Raist?" Caramon asked.

"Enchantment, surely." Raistlin spoke in a whisper, fearful that the sound of his voice might break the spell. "Enchantment," he repeated, "yet not magic."

"Huh?" Caramon was confused. "What other kind of magic is there?"

"Once there was the magic of the gods," Raistlin said.

"Of course!" the baron exclaimed. "That must be the Temple of Paladine. I saw it marked on the map. Probably one of the few temples to the old god left standing in all of Ansalon."

"The Temple of Paladine," Raistlin repeated. He glanced at Solinari, the silver moon. According to legend, the son of Paladine. "Yes, that would explain it."

"I must pay my respects before we depart," the baron said.

Recalling that they had urgent matters to decide before morning, he continued on his way to the warehouse. Caramon and Scrounger followed. Raistlin trailed behind them all. When they came to the warehouse, he paused at the door for a last look at the wondrous sight. His gaze left the temple, again drawn to the silver moon, to Solinari.

The god of the silver moon had appeared to Raistlin before now; all three of the gods, Solinari, Lunitari, and Nuitari had honored the young mage with their attention. It was to Lunitari that Raistlin owed his primary allegiance, but a wizard who chooses to worship one of the siblings must in some part of his soul worship the other two.

Raistlin had always honored Solinari, though the young mage had the idea that the god of White Magic did not entirely approve of him. Gazing at the temple shining in the silver moonlight, Raistlin had the sudden impression that Solinari had lit the temple purposely, to call their attention to it as one might light a beacon fire. If that was true, did the light burn to warn them away from a perilous lee shore or was the light placed there to guide them through the storm?

"Raist?" Caramon's voice shattered his brother's reverie. "Say, guys, have you see my brother? He was right behind me . . . Oh, there you are. I was worried. Where have you been? Still looking at that old temple, huh? Gives you a kind of strange feeling inside, doesn't it?

"You know, Raist," Caramon added impulsively, "I'd like to go inside there, walk around. I know it's a temple to an old god who's not with us anymore, but I think if I went inside, I'd find the answer to my most important questions."

"I doubt seriously if the temple could tell you when your next meal is going to be," Raistlin said.

He did not know why, but he was always provoked beyond reason when Caramon spoke aloud what Raistlin had been thinking.

A cloud drifted across the moon, a piece of black cloth dropped over the silver orb. The temple disappeared, lost in the darkness. If it had ever known the answers to life's mysteries, the temple had long ago forgotten them.

"Hunh." Caramon grunted. "You better come inside, Raist. We're not supposed to be out here. Against orders."

"Thank you, Caramon, for reminding me of my duty," Raistlin returned, pushing past his twin.

"Sure, Raist," Caramon said cheerfully. "Any time."

In a corner of the warehouse, Master Senej and Sergeant Nemiss were meeting with the baron. They spoke in low tones. No one could hear what they said, not even Scrounger, who'd been caught lurking behind a barrel by an irritated Sergeant Nemiss and sent off to stand watch as punishment. The soldiers studied the faces of the three, searching in the shifting expressions for some sign of the baron's intentions.

"Whatever it is the baron's saying," Caramon said softly, "Master Senej doesn't look happy about it."

Master Senej was frowning and shaking his head. He was overheard to say, "don't trust" in loud and stern tones. Sergeant Nemiss was apparently not pleased, either, for she made an emphatic gesture with her hand, as if throwing away something. The baron listened to their arguments, appeared to consider them. Eventually, however, he shook his head. A slicing motion of his hand ended the debate.

"You have your orders, master," he said, for everyone in the warehouse to hear.

"Yes, sir," Master Senej replied.

"Tumbler," the sergeant called. "The baron's ready to leave now. You'll escort the baron back to camp."

"Yes, sir. Do I come back here, sir?"

"There won't be time before the attack," the sergeant said, her voice deliberately calm and even.

The men glanced at each other. The attack was going forward. Few said anything, either in pleasure or disappointment. They had come to fight, and fight was what they would do.

Tumbler saluted and gathered up his coil of rope.

He and the baron departed. Sergeant Nemiss and Major Senej conferred for a few moments longer, then the sergeant went to check the watch. The master lay down on the floor, pulled his hat over his face.

The men followed his example. Caramon was soon snoring loudly, so loudly that Sergeant Nemiss kicked him, told him to roll over and quit making such a racket; they could probably hear him in Solamnia.

Scrounger slept curled up in a tight, compact ball, rather like a dormouse, even to putting his hands over his eyes.

Raistlin, who had slept most of the day, was not tired. He sat with his back against the wall and recited his spells, over and over, until he had them fixed firmly in his mind.

The words of magic were still on his lips when sleep stole upon him, bringing him dreams of a temple bathed in silver moonlight.

14

"PUNY HUMAN BODY, MY ASS!" KIT MUTTERED, ON THE TRAIL OF the dragon.

Having heard Immolatus complain bitterly about having to walk half a block from the inn to the tavern, Kitiara had figured she would catch up with him at the first creek where he'd stop to soak his aching feet. His track was easy to find—branches broken, bushes hacked to shreds, weeds trampled. The dragon was traveling at a pace that astonished Kit, left her far behind at the outset of the chase. Concentrating intently on his goal, Immolatus appeared to have forgotten he had taken human form. In his mind, he was barreling through the forest with lashing tail and crushing claws.

Already tired, Kit had to push herself to try to overtake him, for she wanted to catch him in the wilderness, before he reached the cavern where he could safely transform back to his old dragony self. And she had to catch him before night fell, for he could see in the dark and she could not.

Once Kit made up her mind to action, she set about her task resolutely, swiftly, with no second thoughts or hesitation. Self-doubt was a weakness, tiny cracks in the foundation that would someday bring down the wall; faulty links in the chain mail would allow the arrow to penetrate. Tanis had been afflicted with this weakness. He constantly questioned, constantly analyzed his own actions and reactions. Kit had found this habit of his particularly annoying, and had tried constantly to break him of it.

"When you decide to do a thing, do it!" she had scolded him. "Don't dither and blather and mull over it. Don't dive into the river and then flounder about wondering if you're going to sink. You *will* sink if you do that. Jump in and start swimming. And never look back to shore."

"I suppose it's the elf blood in me," Tanis had replied. "Elves never make any major decisions until they have thought the matter over for at least a year or two, gone round to all their friends and relatives and discussed the problem, done research, read tomes, consulted the sages."

"And what happens then?" Kit had demanded, still irritated.

"By then they've usually forgotten what it was they meant to do in the first place," he had replied, smiling.

She had laughed; he could always tease her out of a bad humor. She did not laugh now and she was sorry she'd thought about him again. The one time Tanis had made up his mind to act was the decision he'd made to leave her. Taking her own advice, she put him out of her mind and continued on.

Kit had one advantage over the dragon in that she knew where she was going. With her usual thoroughness and attention to detail, she'd drawn an excellent map, using landmarks as guideposts and keeping track of the distance by counting her paces. "Seventy paces from the lightning-struck oak to the bear's-head rock. Turn left on the deer path, cross the stream, travel up the cliff to the high ledge." Immolatus had studied the map, but he hadn't taken it with him. Probably because the dragon was not accustomed to using a map. You have little need to know trails over streams if you're flying far above those streams. Her thinking proved correct. She'd been following his trail for about three hours when she came across a place where had deviated from her directions. He had realized his mistake and doubled back, but he'd lost a considerable amount of time and Kit had gained it.

She traveled swiftly, but not carelessly. She kept silent as possible, watched her footing so that she did not step on a dry stick or crash noisily through the underbrush. She would see him long before he heard or saw her. She had transferred the knife from her boot to her belt, within easy reach. He would never know what hit him.

As for the dragon, he left a trail a blind gully dwarf could have followed: footprints in the mud, broken tree limbs, and once even a bit of red cloth, torn from his robes, caught in a bramble bush. Drawing near the mountains, entering the foothills, she found fewer signs of the dragon's passing, but that was to be expected on the hard, rock-strewn ground. Here were no twigs to bend, no mud in which to heedlessly place a booted foot. Still, she was certain she was on the right track. Immolatus was, after all, following her directions.

Shadows lengthened. Kit was footsore and tired, hungry and frustrated.

She had only another hour of daylight left. The thought of giving up, of calling it quits, came to mind. Ambition dug his spurs into her flanks and drove her on.

The sun was setting. She followed the sheepherder's trail she had marked on her map, a trail that meandered up and down the rolling foothills. The sheep and their herders had fled to the safety of the city with the coming of war, but they had left their marks on the mountainside. She paused to rest from the heat in a small hut made snug with hay, drank from a water-skin dropped in the mad scramble to seek the shelter of the city walls. She was negotiating her way across a small, swift-rushing stream, taking care not to lose her footing. Instinct, or perhaps a smell or a sound, caused her to pause where she was, steady herself on the slippery rocks, look ahead instead of at her feet.

Immolatus stood not twenty paces from her, farther up the path that wound along the side of a steep cliff. His back was turned. Kit recalled the map, remembered that at this point, one had to leave the path behind, begin the ascent into the mountains. The trail would look tempting, compared to climbing up into rough and rocky terrain. The path was deceptive, looked as if it would lead the way the dragon wanted to go. Kit had seen from her vantage point atop the mountain that the sheep trail led, as one might expect, to a small grassy valley. Immolatus was trying to decide which route to take, trying to call the map to memory.

Caught out in the open, inwardly cursing, Kitiara clasped the knife's hilt and prepared a charming smile, ready to greet the dragon joyfully when he turned around to find her stalking him. She had her excuse prepared—urgent information from Commander Kholos about the disposition of the troops. She'd heard from the soldiers in camp that a mercenary force had sneaked into the city during the previous night, was planning to attack the city from the inside at dawn, while Kholos and his troops attacked from the outside. She thought the dragon should be informed of this important development, and so forth and so on.

Immolatus did not turn around.

Kitiara watched him warily, wondering if this was a trick. He must have heard her splashing through the creek; she did not see how he could have missed hearing her. She had been proceeding carefully, but her attention had of necessity been concentrated more on not falling in the water than on moving with silent stealth.

Immolatus remained standing with his head bowed, his back turned, studying his shoes or the trail or perhaps even taking a piss.

This was a lucky break obviously. Kit did not question her luck, prepared to take advantage of it. Queen Takhisis was going to go into battle minus one red dragon. Kit took hold of the knife's blade, balanced, aimed, and threw.

She was dead on her target. The knife passed right between Immolatus's shoulder blades. Passed through the shoulder blades and kept going, its steel blade catching the sunlight as its flight carried it beyond her sight. She heard steel hit rock with a small metallic clang, a scraping sound, and then nothing.

Kitiara stared, astounded, her brain scrabbling for purchase, trying to make sense of the senseless. She wasn't certain what had happened, but she knew she was in danger. She drew her sword, splashed through the creek, prepared to face Immolatus's fury. The damn dragon still didn't turn around, didn't move, didn't stir. Only when she came close to him, close enough to slice off his head, did Kit understand.

The moment she understood, the illusion of Immolatus standing on the trail disappeared.

A grating sound above her drew her attention. She looked up in time to see a boulder thundering down the hillside.

Kitiara fell to her stomach, pressing her body against the sun-warmed rock and covered her head with her hands. The boulder sailed past her, struck an outcropping of rock right below her and bounded into the creek with a splash. Another boulder followed. This one came closer. Immolatus missed again, but he could keep throwing rocks at her all day long. She had no where to go and sooner or later he'd hit his mark.

"Let him hit it then," Kit muttered.

Swiftly, she undid the straps holding the steel breastplate she wore, avoiding yet another boulder.

Craning her neck, she peered upward. The next boulder came thundering down. Kitiara drew in a deep breath and let it out in a scream, threw her breastplate directly into the boulder's path. The boulder caught the breastplate a glancing blow, sending it spinning into the creek, the steel flashing red by the light of the setting sun.

Dropping to her hands and knees, making herself as small as possible, Kit took advantage of the twilight, which would make it difficult for even the dragon to see if he had truly killed her. She used the noise of the falling boulder to cover the sound of her movements, scrambled into the brush alongside the path. She located a small crevice in the cliff face and wormed her way inside, scraping most of the skin off her thighs and her knees and her elbows, but safe for the moment from the dragon. Provided he had fallen for her ruse.

Kitiara waited, her cheek pressed against the rock, panting for breath. No more boulders came hurtling down the mountainside, but that meant nothing. If he did not believe he'd killed her, he might very well come back to hunt her down. She listened for the sound of his pursuit, cursed her heart for beating so loudly.

She heard nothing and she began to breathe a bit easier. Yet she did not move. She remained hidden, just in case he was hanging about to watch. Time passed and Kitiara became convinced. The dragon must believe her to be dead. She would have been nothing more to him than a bright flash of armor on the mountain and he had seen that bright flash fall, heard her death cry. Arrogant as he was, Immolatus would easily convince himself that his clever little ruse had worked. He would wait a few moments to make certain, but, sure of himself and eager for his vengeance, he would not linger long, not with the smell of eggs in his nostrils.

"Still," Kitiara reminded herself ruefully, "I underestimated him once and nearly died for my mistake."

She would not do the same again.

Kitiara waited another few moments then, impatient, cramped and uncomfortable, she made up her mind that a fight would be preferable to being wedged between two slabs of rock. She slid cautiously out from her hiding place. Crouched on the trail, she peered upward, searching the shadows for a bit of red robe or a red wing tip or the glitter of a red scale.

Nothing. The mountainside was desolate, as far as she could see.

Seating herself on the trail, Kitiara examined her sword to make certain it had suffered no damage. Satisfied as to her weapon, she next looked for damage to herself. Cuts and bruises, that was about the extent of it. She dug a few sharp pieces of rock out of the palms of her hands, sucked blood from a deep cut on her knee, and wondered gloomily what to do next.

Give up, return to camp. That was the sensible course of action. To do so was to admit defeat and Kitiara had been defeated only once in her life and that was in love, not battle. Her own thoughts were bloody with vengeance. Up to now, she would have been content to merely stop Immolatus from destroying the eggs. Now she wanted him dead. She would make him pay for those few horrible moments she'd spent cowering in terror on the mountainside. She'd track the damn dragon through the mountains all night, if that was what it took to catch him.

Fortunately, Solinari would shine brightly tonight. And if Kit was very lucky or if Queen Takhisis was inclined to lend her aid, the dragon would manage to lose himself in the mountains during the night. He'd already started up the mountains the wrong way, to judge by the direction of the boulders.

If you make up your mind to do a thing, do it. Don't bother with the how and the why. Just do it.

Grimly, resolutely, Kitiara began her climb up the mountainside.

15

THE NIGHT WAS A LONG ONE FOR KITIARA, SLOGGING THROUGH THE mountains. The night was also long for Immolatus. Kit's prayers were answered, he did manage to lose his way. Immolatus was tempted more than once to return to his dragon body with its glorious wings, wings that would carry him off this damnable mountain, wings that would carry him into the skies.

But Immolatus had the impression that the sneaky god Paladine had set spies on him, was watching for him. Immolatus imagined golden dragons lurking on the mountaintop, just waiting for him to change form to pounce upon him. Little as he liked to admit it, this human body was a useful disguise. If only it wasn't so weak. The dragon sat down for just a few moments to rest and woke later from a nap he'd never meant to take, to find that it was almost dawn.

The night was long for the men in the warehouse, who had finally been given their orders for the predawn attack and who, while not looking forward to the morning, would just as soon have it over.

The night was a short one for the lord mayor, who faced the coming dawn with extreme apprehension. The night was short for the people of Hope's End, well aware that this night might be their last. The night was extremely short for the baron, who had to reach his camp before the dawn.

The night was just another night for Commander Kholos, who snored all the way through it.

"You wanted to be wakened early, sir." Master Vardash entered the commander's tent, stood respectfully beside the bed, another prize from one of the manor houses, lugged along at considerable cost and inconvenience.

"What? What is it? What's going on?" Kholos blinked at his officer, who was lighting a lamp on the desk.

"It is nearly dawn, sir. You wanted me to waken you early. The city comes under assault today."

"Oh, yes." The commander yawned, scratched himself. "I suppose I had better get up then."

"Here is your ale, sir. The venison steaks are coming. The cook wants to know if you'll have potatoes or bread this morning."

"Both. And tell him to put some onions in those potatoes. I had an idea last night," Kholos added, seating himself on the bed and pulling on his boots. "Is that wizard Immolatus still around?"

"I suppose so, sir," Vardash answered slowly, trying to remember. "I haven't seen him recently, but then he keeps to himself."

"Eating our rations and not doing a damn thing to earn it. Well, I have work for him this morning. I was thinking that when the baron's men reach the wall—what's left of them after our archers are finished—the wizard could work some sort of magic, drop the wall on them. What do you think?"

"It's an awfully big wall, sir," suggested Vardash hesitantly.

"I know it's a big wall," Kholos returned peevishly, "but these wizards must have spells to handle that sort of thing. Or what use are they? Have the blasted wizard report to me. I'll ask him myself."

Kholos rose to his feet, naked except for his boots. Long, thick hair covered most of his body, except where his battle scars roped and slashed through the thick pelt. As he spoke, he scratched at himself again, captured a flea and crushed it between his thumb and forefinger.

Vardash dispatched a soldier to find the wizard. Breakfast arrived. The general devoured the still-bloody steaks, a loaf of bread, and quantities of potatoes and onions, all the while issuing orders in preparation for the day's battle. Though the sky was still dark, with dawn presaged by only a hint of pink along the horizon, the camp was up and doing. The men were eating breakfast, to judge by the noise coming from the mess tent.

The sky grew perceptibly brighter. A bird practiced a tentative call or two. His aide assisted Commander Kholos to dress and helped him on with his armor, which was heavy and massive. The aide had to ask Vardash for assistance with the commander's breastplate, which required two men to lift it. An ordinary human would have sunk to the ground beneath it. Commander Kholos gave a grunt, banged himself on the chest a few times to position the breastplate, adjusted his bracers, and pronounced himself ready.

A soldier arrived to say that the wizard was not in his tent, neither was

Commander uth Matar. No one had seen either of them for some time now. One soldier said he had overheard uth Matar saying something to the wizard about the job being finished and returning to Sanction.

"Who gave them permission to return to Sanction?" Kholos demanded angrily. "They were supposed to bring me a map showing me where to find those blasted dragon eggs!"

"They were acting under Lord Ariakas's direct orders, sir," Vardash reminded him respectfully. "Perhaps the general changed his mind. Perhaps he intends to search for the eggs himself. To be honest, Commander, I think we are well rid of the wizard. I did not altogether trust him."

"I didn't plan on trusting him," Kholos returned irritably. "I just wanted him to knock down a single goddam wall. How hard can that be? Still and all, I guess you're right. Hand me my sword. And I'll take the battle-axe as well. We'll count on the archers to dispose of the baron's men. Do they have their orders, master? They know what to do?"

"Yes, sir. Their orders are to shoot them in the back, sir, the minute they've captured the gate. A far better plan than trusting to magic, if I may say so, sir."

"Perhaps you're right, Vardash. Between our archers and those in the city, the baron's army should be wiped out by—what time would you say, Vardash?"

"Noon, I should think, sir."

"Really? That late? I was thinking midmorning myself. A wager?"

"I would be delighted, sir," Vardash said without enthusiasm.

He never won a wager with Kholos, who, no matter what the outcome, conveniently remembered the terms of the bet as being favorable to himself. If the baron's men were still alive and kicking by noon, the commander would recall that he'd said noon himself and that it was Vardash who'd been overly optimistic and said midmorning.

Kholos was in a good humor. The city would most certainly fall into his hands this day. Tonight, he'd be sleeping in the lord mayor's bed, perhaps with the lord mayor's wife, if she wasn't a cow. If she was, he'd have his pick of the rest of the women of the town. He'd spend a day or two mopping up any resistance, selecting the choicest slaves, putting to death those who didn't make the cut, loading the wagons with loot, and then he'd set fire to the city. Once Hope's End was in ashes, he would start on the long, but triumphant road back to Sanction.

✷

The mercenary camp was also up and at 'em this morning.

"Sir, you asked to be wakened before sunup," Commander Morgon started to say, then saw it wasn't necessary.

The baron was already awake. He had arrived back in camp just an hour earlier, lain down for a brief rest, and was now lying on his cot, mulling over his plans for the day. Swinging his legs over the side of the cot, he pulled on his tall leather boots. He was already wearing his breeches and shirt.

"Breakfast, sir?" Morgon asked.

The baron nodded. "Yes, have all the officers meet me in my command tent and have breakfast served there."

"Venison steaks and potatoes with onions, sir?" Morgon suggested with a grin.

The baron looked up, eyes narrowed. "What are you trying to do, Morgon, kill me before the enemy has a crack at me?"

"No, sir." Morgon laughed. "I've just returned from the camp of our gallant allies. That is Commander Kholos's favorite meal before a battle."

"I hope it gives him heartburn," said the baron grumpily. "I'll have the usual. Toast strips soaked in honey wine. And tell cook to mix up an egg in that. What did our gallant allies have to say for themselves?"

"The commander wishes us luck with our attack, and promises to support us on the way in."

The two exchanged glances.

"Very good, Morgon," the baron replied. "You have your orders. You know what to do."

"Yes, sir." Morgon saluted and departed.

The baron met with his officers, went over the plans for the assault on the gate.

"I'm not asking for questions, gentlemen," he said at the conclusion of the meeting. "I don't have the answers. Good luck to us all."

Four buglers, four drummers, a standard-bearer, several staff officers, five runners, and ten bodyguards formed the command group in the center of the infantry line.

"Uncase the standard," the baron ordered.

The standard-bearer pulled a lanyard attached to the top of the standard, caused the rolled flag to unfurl. The symbol of the bison fluttered above the army.

"Buglers—sound the call to arms!"

The four buglers blasted out notes in unison, repeating the short call three times. Morgon touched the baron's arm, pointed. Across the field, the first companies of Kholos's army were moving into position on the right flank.

When Kholos's heavy infantry had formed in the center of his line, the commander's standard went up, indicating he was in position.

The baron nodded. "Very well, lads. This is the big finish. Time to earn our pay. Or not," he muttered into his beard. He paused a moment, wondering if he'd made the right decision. Too late now if he hadn't. Shrugging, he sat up straight on his horse. "Buglers!" he shouted. "Sound Advance!"

A single note, held long and wailing, echoed back from the mountains. The note's end was punctuated by a boom from the four drummers, beating in unison, pounding out a continuous and slow cadence. The companies moved forward in battle line.

The baron looked down the left of the line. The polished breastplates shone in the newly risen morning sun. Sunlight glinted off spearpoints. The men carried spears and shields with short swords sheathed. The archers had taken up their positions to the far left of the line. They wore no breastplates, but carried large wooden shields that had spikes at the bottom tips. When the archers stopped to fire, they would plant the shields in the ground and fire from behind.

To the baron's right, a company of eight men carried a huge battering ram made of solid oak tipped with iron. Each man held a shield he would use to cover his head and body from attack while the ram battered the gates. More men marched alongside, ready to run in and take over a position if a man fell.

The men moved forward, rank upon rank. They could see soldiers crowding the top of the city's wall, but there was no answering fire. Not yet. The attackers were still out of range. The regiment neared the creek bed. The baron watched the tops of the battlements closely.

"Wait for it, wait for it." He issued the order to himself.

A flag flew up the flag post atop the wall, accompanied by the deadly hum of hundreds of loosed arrows.

"Now!" the baron yelled.

The buglers blew Charge, the drummers pounded a furious rhythm.

The men ran forward, fast enough to evade the first volley. Arrows thunked into the ground behind them. No one fell.

The men hauling the battering ram came within a hundred yards of the wall, heading straight for the gate.

The city loosed a second volley. Every man in the regiment ran harder, faster, trying to get ahead of the deadly rain of arrows. Again they outran them. None of the arrows hit, all fell behind the regiment's lines. The men cheered and jeered at the enemy.

The last hundred yards were a sprint. The line lost cohesion as everyone dashed toward the objective. The battering ram crew closed on the gate, came to a stop.

The men swung back once, then let the weight of the ram smack into the gate. The giant wooden structure resounded with a hollow boom. The gates flew open.

☻

Across the field, Commander Kholos turned to his archers.

"Now! Now! They've breached the gates! Fire!"

A hundred archers fired into the mercenary's rear ranks. Before the first volley had hit home, a second was in the air.

The baron's troops had converged on the open gate, pushing to get through. A few soldiers fell, but not nearly as many as Kholos had hoped. Fuming, he turned to glare at his archers.

"Punishment detail for any man who misses a shot!" he yelled.

The archers reloaded, and fired two more volleys. But they were fast running out of targets.

"The fighting must have moved inside, sir," Vardash said. "The baron's men have breached the city's defenses. Should I send the archers forward? Apparently the fools haven't figured out that we're firing on them."

Kholos frowned. Something was wrong. He called for his spyglass, raised it to his eye, stared intently at the city gate. Snapping the glass shut, his goblinish face livid with fury, he turned to his signal drummers.

"Quickly! Sound Attack!"

Vardash turned. "Attack, sir? Now? I thought we were going to let the baron's men do the brunt of the fighting?"

Kholos struck Vardash a blow that crushed his jaw, sent him sprawling backward into the mud.

"You idiot!" Kholos howled, jumping over Vardash's unmoving body, racing forward to take his place at the head of the troops. "The bastards have tricked us! There *is* no fighting at the gate."

16

KITIARA PULLED HERSELF CAUTIOUSLY UP THE LAST ROCK LEDGE LEADING to the cavern's hidden entrance. She moved slowly, testing every hand- and foothold, taking care not to dislodge any rocks whose clattering fall might alert the dragon. Reaching the top, she crouched, sword in hand, looking and listening, thinking he might be lying in wait for her, to ambush her.

"The way is clear!" called a voice. "Come quickly. We don't have much time."

"Who is that?" Kit demanded, peering through the shadows cast by the tall pine trees that screened the entrance. The sun had just risen. Trumpet calls bounced off the rocks around her, the attack on the city of Hope's End had begun. "Sir Nigel? Or whatever the hell it is you're calling yourself?"

She found the spirit standing where she'd left it, inside the entrance to the cavern.

"I've been waiting for you," said Sir Nigel. "Hurry. We don't have much time."

"I take that to mean that you encountered the wizard." Kit entered the cavern. The dark cool shadows of the rock washed over her, chilling after the heat of her pursuit. Her skin prickled, she rubbed her arms.

"Yes, he passed by some time ago. You told him where to find the eggs," Sir Nigel said accusingly.

"Those were my orders," Kit returned. "I suppose even spirit-knights obey orders."

"But now you're here to stop him from destroying them."

"Those are my orders, too," Kit stated coldly and, walking past the ghost, she entered the cave, leaving the ghost to come or go as it chose.

The ghost entered with her and, once again, as when she had first entered the tunnel from the other direction, she found her way lighted.

No, she thought, it was not so much that her way was lighted, but that the darkness receded. When the spirit raised its hand, the darkness flowed away from it like the tide from the shoreline. Gold and silver scales, shed long ago, gleamed on the path, glittered on the walls. As long as Kitiara kept close to the ghostly Knight, she could find her way. Darkness flowed in behind them after the Knight had passed. If she lagged behind, even a pace or two, the darkness engulfed her.

"This spirit is just full of tricks," Kit muttered. She hurried to keep up. "Tell me how you knew I was coming back," she challenged him. "Or do all ghosts read minds."

"There is nothing very mystical in my knowledge," the Knight said, with a slight smile. "When Immolatus arrived in the cavern, he did not proceed straight to his goal, but stopped and waited, looking behind him, back the way he'd come. He waited until he caught sight of something and then he nodded to himself as if he'd expected to see what he saw. Following his line of sight, I observed you farther down the mountainside.

"Immolatus was not pleased," the Knight continued. "He growled and muttered, called you a nuisance, said he should have finished you when he had the chance. He hesitated and I thought he planned to stay and wait for you. He thought so himself, I believe, but then he glanced down the corridor, into the darkness, and his red eyes glowed.

" 'First I'll have my revenge,' he said and left."

Sir Nigel looked back at her, a measuring gaze.

"He is in dragon form now, Kitiara uth Matar."

Kit drew in a breath, tightened her grip on her sword. Logic dictated that Immolatus would change back. She'd expected nothing else, yet the knowledge that he'd actually done so was a blow to the pit of the stomach. Now that the ghost had mentioned it, she could feel the onset of the terrible debilitating fear that had come near to crippling her the first time she'd seen the dragon. The fear caused her palms to sweat and her mouth to go dry. She was angry at the Knight, angry at herself.

"Do you mean to tell me that you were lurking in that cavern all the time?" Kit demanded. "Why didn't you strike him? Stab him from behind before he had a chance to change his form! He obviously had no idea you were there!"

"Useless," Sir Nigel replied. "My sword has no bite."

Kit swore, beside herself with rage. "A fine guardian you make!" she sneered.

"I am the guardian of the eggs," the Knight replied. "Those are *my* orders."

"And how do you propose to guard them, Sir Undead? Say, 'Please, Master Dragon, go away and don't break the pretty eggs'?"

The Knight's face darkened or perhaps the light that flowed from him dimmed, because it seemed that the shadows closed in on them. "This is my geas," he said in a low voice. "I chose it myself, none laid it on me. But sometimes it is hard to bear. Soon, however, my watch will be over, for good or ill, and I will continue on my long-delayed journey. As for my plan, I will distract the dragon from the front. When his attention is concentrated on me, you will strike."

"Distract? What are you going to do? A little song and dance—"

"Hush!" Sir Nigel lifted his hand in warning. "We are close to the chamber!"

Kit knew well enough where she was. The corridor in which they stood made a turn. A short distance beyond, it opened into the huge chamber where the eggs were hidden. Kitiara stood just before that turn. Walk around the jutting rock wall to the right and she would walk into the chamber.

Walk into Immolatus.

Kitiara heard the dragon, heard his massive tail scraping over the rock, heard his stentorian breathing and the rumbling of the fire burning in his belly. She could smell him, smell the sulfur and the stench of reptile. The smell sickened her, her fear sickened her. She heard the dragon lash his tail against the rock. The corridor in which they stood shuddered. Her body went hot and then cold. Her palms were slippery, she had to continually adjust her grasp on the sword's hilt.

Immolatus was talking to the unborn of his enemies, haranguing them in the language of dragons, presumably. Kitiara couldn't understand a word.

"I must go now," Sir Nigel said and she felt his words as a breath on her cheek. She could hear nothing over the dragon's howls and grunts and taunting words that were like the cracking of bones. "Await my signal."

"Don't bother!" Kitiara snapped, angry, afraid. "Go back to your tomb. Maybe I'll join you."

Sir Nigel looked at her long and searchingly. "You truly do not understand anything you have seen or heard since you entered this temple?"

"I understand that I have to do this myself," Kit retorted. "That I can count on no one but myself! The way it's always been."

"Ah, that explains it." Sir Nigel raised his hand in salute. "Farewell, Kitiara uth Matar."

The light vanished and Kit was alone, alone in a darkness that was not as dark as she could have wished it, a darkness that was tinged with red, the fire of the dragon.

"He left me!" Kitiara said to herself, amazed. She had trusted she would be able to shame him into staying. "That bastard ghost really left me here to die! A pox on him, then. His soul to the Abyss."

Aware that she had to act now, while she was more angry than she was frightened, Kitiara wiped the wet palm of her sword hand upon her leather tunic, clenched her hand around the hilt, and strode through the fire-singed darkness.

❂

Immolatus was enjoying himself. He had a right to indulge. He'd earned this moment, paid for it in blood, and he meant to make it last. Besides, he needed time to accustom himself to his dragon form again, revel in the return of his strength and power. He raked his front claws against the ceiling of the cavern, leaving great gouges in the stone. His hind claws dug into the rock, breaking it and tearing it. He would have liked to spread his wings, to stretch the muscles. Unfortunately the chamber, though large enough to accommodate him, was not large enough to accommodate his full wingspan. He made do with lashing his tail, feeling in satisfaction the very bones of the mountain tremble at his might.

Immolatus spoke to the unborn of his enemies, knowing that somewhere his enemies could hear him. They would sense his presence in the nest of their young. They would know what he intended and they would be powerless to stop him. He felt the parents' anguish, their helpless dread, and he laughed at them and mocked them and made ready to destroy their children.

He had planned to incinerate the unborn dragons; indeed, that is what he'd intended to do. The fire in his belly had very nearly gone out, having been nothing but a measly spark in his human form, a spark he had to constantly nurse to maintain. Needing time to stoke the fire, he determined that, in the beginning at least, he would crack the eggs with his claws and maybe even suck out the yokes of a dozen or so.

Anticipating the pleasure, he recited the catalog of his wrongs and gloated over his revenge, savoring every moment in order to relive it later in his hundred-year-long dreams.

Immolatus was enjoying himself so much that he paid little attention to the speck of light shining silver-white at his feet. He thought the light nothing more than one of the myriad silver scales left scattered about by his enemies. He shifted his head slightly, hoping the light would go away, for he found that it irritated him, like a bit of chaff caught in his eye.

The light remained. He could not rid himself of it and he was forced to pause in his recitative to deal with it. He looked at the light closely, though it hurt him to do so, and as he looked he saw it take form and shape. He recognized it.

One of Paladine's flunkies.

"A Solamnic Knight for me to kill!" Immolatus chuckled. "What joy! I could have wished for nothing more to increase my pleasure. Who says my Queen has abandoned me? No, she has given me this gift."

The Knight said no word. He drew his sword from its antique scabbard.

The dragon blinked, half-blinded. The silver light was a silver lance, stabbing through his eye. The pain was excruciating and growing worse.

"I would play with you longer, worm," Immolatus growled, "but I find that you begin to annoy me."

He made a swipe at the Knight with a slashing claw, intending to rip through the armor, impale him.

The Knight did not attack. Seeing certain death descending on him, he raised his sword, hilt-first, to heaven.

"Paladine, god of my order and of my soul," the Knight called out. "Witness that I have been faithful to my vow!"

Ridiculous Knights, Immolatus thought, his claw stabbing downward. Vowing, praying—even after their fickle god had abandoned them. Just as my Queen abandoned me, then returned to demand homage and service and worship, as if she deserved it!

Searing pain pierced the dragon's insides. His slashing blow went wild, missed its target. Furious, Immolatus turned to see what had hit him.

The worm. Uth Matar. That annoying, bloodsucking worm inflicted on him by that human excrement, Ariakas.

☉

Kitiara had been both pleased and astonished to see the ghost reappear. The sight of the Knight lent her courage. Creeping around the dragon's left hind leg, she struck the dragon from behind, driving her sword with both hands deep into the dragon's flank. She aimed for a vital organ. Uncertain of dragon anatomy, she hoped to hit the heart, hoped for a quick kill. Her sword glanced off a scale. Her stab struck deep, but it struck a rib, nothing vital.

"Damn!" Kitiara yanked free the bloody sword and, guessing that her time was limited, made a desperate attempt to stab again.

Attacked from the front and on his flank, Immolatus returned his gaze to what he deemed the more dangerous foe, the accursed Solamnic. His lashing tail would deal with the worm. Quick as a whip snap, the dragon's tail curled and released. The tail hit Kitiara full in the chest, a blow that sent her tumbling, rolling head over heels back down the corridor. Her sword flew from her hand.

Immolatus would finish off this Knight, then he would finish off the worm.

"Requite my faith, my god," the Knight was yelling at the empty heavens. "Grant that I may fulfill my vow."

The Knight flung his sword into the air.

A stupid move, but one that was a popular among Knights. They were always hoping to poke out an eye. The blade blazed with silver fire. Immolatus made the standard defense, jerked his head up and back.

Sir Nigel had not aimed for the dragon's eye. The blade, blazing silver, soared high into the air, struck the ceiling of the cavern.

The sword that had no bite plunged deep into the rock.

The dragon laughed. He lowered his head, jaws snapping, intending to seize the Knight in his crushing jaws. His fangs opened and closed over nothing but air.

The Knight remained standing calmly, gazing upward, his hands raised in a salute or perhaps in prayer. Behind him, the eggs of gold and silver dragons lay nestled in a chamber of rock. Above him, the ceiling started to crack.

A large chunk of rock fell, struck Immolatus on the head. Another followed and another, and then a veritable cascade of rocks plunged down, threatening to bury the dragon. Sharp stones hit his body, wounding him, bruising him. One tore through a wing. Another crushed a toe.

Stunned by the blows raining down on him, Immolatus sought shelter. He retreated back down the corridor, trusting that its ceiling would hold, would not collapse around him. He crouched there as the ground shook beneath his feet. Dust and sharp shards filled the air, ricocheted off the cavern's wall. He couldn't see, could barely breathe.

And then the shaking ended. The avalanche ceased. The dust cleared.

Immolatus opened an eyelid cautiously, peered around. He was afraid to move, afraid that he would bring down the entire mountain.

The Solamnic Knight was gone, buried under a massive rockslide. Gone, too, were the eggs, their chamber sealed closed by tons of rocks and boulders. The unborn dragons were safely beyond Immolatus's reach.

Roaring his disappointment and outrage, he belched a blast of fire from his belly against the newly formed rock wall, but all that did was to superheat the granite, cause it to fuse together in a solid mass, impossible to shift. He scrabbled at the wall with a claw and, after much work, managed to dislodge a single small boulder, which rolled down the hill of rock and landed on the dragon's foot, hurting him.

He glared at the wall. Revenge might be sweet, but it was an awful lot of work. And then there was Her Dark Majesty. She would not be pleased at this turn of events, and though Immolatus might sneer at his goddess and dismiss her as fickle and capricious, deep inside him, he feared her wrath. If he had destroyed the eggs, he might have talked his way around her. No use crying over spilt yolks. Having disobeyed her orders and in so doing inadvertently sealed up the eggs where they would be safe until the day came when they hatched and their parents could come to free them. Immolatus had the feeling Her Majesty might be difficult.

He had a moment's fleeting hope that the eggs had all been smashed by the fall of the ceiling, but he knew Paladine well of old, knew that the Knight's prayer had been heard. The blow that had brought the ceiling down around the dragon's ears had not been struck by any mortal hand.

By some fluke, Immolatus himself had escaped the god's anger. He might not be so lucky the next time. As it was, he could feel the mountain continue to shake. It was time to go, before Paladine tried again. Immolatus turned to leave by the same way he had entered, only to find the corridor blocked, choked up with debris.

The dragon snarled in irritation. He was more annoyed than frightened. Dragons are accustomed to dwelling underground, their eyes can penetrate the darkness, their nostrils sniff out the tiniest whiff of air.

Immolatus smelled fresh air. He knew there was another opening somewhere. He recalled the map of the temple the worm had drawn for him, recalled another corridor leading up and out. A corridor that led into the accursed Temple of Paladine.

"If I do nothing else, I'll level that foul blot upon the landscape," Immolatus muttered, flame hissing through his teeth. "I'll burn it and then I'll burn this city. They'll smell the smoke of death in the Abyss and let my Queen or any other god try to touch me then! Just let them!"

Mumbling and grumbling his defiance, he sniffed the fresh air, located its source. Thrusting a clawed hand into the rubble blocking the way, rubble that was not very thick at this point, the dragon cleared it easily.

He found the corridor he'd remembered from the map. The corridor was open and clear, remained unaffected by the landslide. But it was a small corridor. A narrow corridor. A man-sized corridor.

Immolatus groaned and came near sinking under the weight of his severe disappointment. He would have to take that form again, that hated, heinous form, that weak and puny form, that human form. Fortunately, he would not have to traipse about in the flesh-bag too long, only long enough to traverse this corridor, which, if memory of the map served him correctly, was not very long.

He pronounced the words of magic, grinding them with his teeth, detesting every one of them, and the transfiguration occurred, painful and humiliating as usual. Immolatus the red-robed wizard stood in the midst of the ruin of the corridor. The fabric of his robe immediately stuck to a wound in his side, a wound that his dragon self had barely noticed, but a wound his human self was concerned to see was deep and bleeding freely.

Cursing the worm who had inflicted it, Immolatus wondered what had become of her. He glanced around the wreckage, saw no sign of her. He listened, but heard no sound, no moaning, no cries for help, and he assumed that she must be lying under half the mountain by now.

Good riddance, he thought and, pressing his hand against his side, each breath coming in a pain-filled gasp, he entered the corridor, cursing his weak human flesh with every step.

❂

Kitiara waited until she no longer heard his footfalls and then waited to the count of a hundred after that. Certain that he had gone far enough that he would not hear her, she crawled out from beneath the rubble that had saved her life, protected her from the dragon's huge body.

Bruised, bleeding from countless cuts, covered with rock dust, exhausted by her fear and her exertions, Kit was fed up with this job. Her ambition was at the ebb. She would have traded the generalship of the dragonarmies for a mug of dwarf spirits and a hot bath. She would have walked away from this wretched place here and now, leaving the dragon to do his damnedest, had there been anywhere to walk. Unfortunately, the only way out was the dragon's way out. The path he walked was the path she would have to walk. Unless she wanted to remain down here in the dark, trapped inside an unstable mountain, she would have to deal with him.

"Sir Nigel?" she risked calling.

There was no answer. No help from that quarter. She had seen him buried beneath the mountain of rock. But his vow was fulfilled. He'd found a way to protect the eggs. A pity he hadn't killed the dragon in the process. It was up to her now. She was on her own. As usual.

She found her sword, partially buried in rubble. And she still had her knife. Immolatus had his magic—powerful, deadly magic. He was in his vulnerable human form, the path he walked was dark, his back was to her. His real back this time, not an illusion.

Kitiara drew her knife from the top of her boot, rubbed the grit from her eyes, spit the dust from her mouth. Entering the corridor, she padded soft-footed after the dragon.

17

BREAKING RANKS, THE SOLDIERS SURGED THROUGH THE OPEN CITY GATES, carrying the battering ram with them. Once inside, temporarily out of danger, they came to a halt, breathless and seething with anger as word spread like flaming dwarf spirits that men in the rear ranks had dropped down dead, with black-fletched arrows in their backs. Some in the forward companies actually turned around, headed out the gate, prepared to go back to the field and claim vengeance.

Officers shouted, bullied, and tried to restore order, as the citizens of Hope's End watched warily from the walls. They had been told these hardened mercenaries brought salvation, but the first sight of them—howling for blood—left the civilians pale and shaking. The lord mayor was put in mind of the old saying—better the kender in front of you than the kender with his hand in your back pocket. He was clearly regretting that he'd ever opened the gates to these cold-eyed professionals, swearing terrible oaths of death on those who had betrayed them.

"Shut those gates!" the baron shouted from the back of his war-horse. The horse plunged and danced with excitement, nostrils flared, ears laid back, nipping at anyone who came too close. "Haul those wagons back in place! Archers, to the wall!

"Those bastards!" he yelled to Commander Morgon, who—greatly daring—had caught hold of the horse's bridle. "Did you see what they did? Fired at us when our backs were turned! By heavens, I'll find that Commander Kholos and cut out his liver! I'll have *it* with potatoes and onions!"

"Yes, my lord. I saw, sir." Commander Morgon calmed the horse, calmed the master at the same time. "You were right, Baron! I was wrong. I admit it freely."

"And don't think I'm ever going to let you forget it! Ha, ha, ha!" The baron roared his manic laugh, which just about finished the terror-stricken citizens. "By Kiri-Jolith," he added, glowering around him at the stamping, sword-clashing, swearing soldiers of his command, "these fools have gone berserk! I'll have order restored, Commander Morgon! Now!"

C Company had been responsible for clearing the barricades from the gates. The battering ram, pounding once on the gate, had been the signal for C Company to swing the gates wide open. Their two bowmen provided covering fire for their comrades, before retreating back inside the city in good order. C Company stood ready, poised for action, keeping themselves free of the tumult.

"Shut the gates!" Master Senej commanded, hearing the baron's order. "Keep everyone inside the city walls!"

The men of C Company acted swiftly to obey. Some sprang to the gates. Others shoved or struck with the flat of their blades those soldiers who had lost all reason and were trying to leave the city in order to revenge their fallen comrades.

"Stand there, Majere!" Sergeant Nemiss ordered, posting Caramon in the very center of the road, as the men worked to push the heavy wooden gates shut behind him. "Don't let anyone past!"

"Yes, sir." Caramon took up his position, unmindful of enemy arrows, which were flying through the slowly closing gate. His massive legs spread to maintain his balance, his arm muscles flexed. Those who tried to get past him were either hurled backward, plucked off their feet, or—as a last extremity—given a gentle buffet on the head intended to restore them to their senses.

The gates slammed shut. The flights of arrows ceased as the enemy paused to consider the unlooked-for situation and regroup.

"What now, sir?" Commander Morgon asked. "Do we stay here under siege?"

"That depends entirely on Kholos," said the baron. "If you were him, what would you do, Morgon?"

"I'd pull back my troops, establish my supply lines, and wait until everyone in the city starved to death, my lord," Morgon replied.

"Very good, Commander Morgon," said the baron. "What do you think Kholos will do?"

"Well, my lord, I think he's going to be madder than a wet wyvern. My guess is that he will throw everything he's got at us, try to breach the gates and cut us down where we stand."

"My thoughts precisely. I'm going up on the wall to take a look. Have the officers arrange their companies into column, center company leading, line companies to follow. You've got ten minutes and no more!"

Commander Morgon ran off, shouting for his officers. He issued orders quickly. Soon the drums were beating, the trumpets braying. Sergeants yelled, kicked, and shoved the men into position. Reassured by the familiar sounds that promised discipline and order, the soldiers settled down and reformed into ranks with alacrity.

"Do we put the barricades back in place, sir?" Master Senej asked.

Commander Morgon glanced up at the wall where the baron stood in conference with the lord mayor and the city's officers. Morgon shook his head. "No, Senej. I think I know what the baron has planned. Keep them ready just in case, though."

During the height of the confusion, Raistlin searched for Horkin. At first Raistlin was unable to find the master in the midst of the tumult and he began to be worried, especially when he heard of the casualties. The gates were swinging shut and Raistlin had begun to think that "dear Luni" had abandoned her drinking buddy, when he saw Horkin come lurching through the gate, lending an arm to a fellow soldier with an arrow shaft stuck clean through his leg. The man's pain must have been intense, he could not put his foot to the ground without gasping and shuddering.

"I'm glad to find you, sir!" Raistlin said earnestly. He had not known until that moment how much he valued the bluff and gruff Horkin.

Raistlin added his arm to help share the burden of the wounded man. Between the two of them, they carried him to a quiet place beneath the trees, where more wounded had congregated. "I feared you were among the fallen. What happened out there?"

"Treachery, Red," said Horkin with a dark glance back out the gate. "Treachery and murder. We've been betrayed, there's no doubt about it. As to the why and wherefore, I know nothing." He cast Raistlin a shrewd glance. "It seems you might know more than I do, Red. The baron told me that you accompanied him to the mayor's dwelling last night. He said you proved quite useful."

"I gave an old couple probably the best night's rest they've had in years," Raistlin returned dryly, "and that was the extent of my service. As to what the baron and the mayor discussed, I have no more knowledge than yourself. He sent me from the room."

"Don't take it to heart, Red. That's the baron all over. The fewer who know a secret, the more likely to keep a secret, that's his motto. One reason he's lived so long. And now"—Horkin looked about him—"what are we to do with the wounded?"

"I was about to tell you, sir. I believe that I have found a place to shelter the wounded. Did you know that there is an old temple to Paladine in the city, sir?"

"A temple to Paladine? Here?" Horkin rubbed his chin.

"Yes, sir. It's a safe distance from the fighting. If we could commandeer a wagon, we could transport the wounded in that."

"And why do you think this old temple would be a good place to house our wounded?" Horkin asked.

"I saw the temple last night, sir. It seems, well . . ." Raistlin hesitated. "It seems a blessed place, sir."

"It might have been blessed once, Red," said Horkin with a sigh. "But not anymore."

"Who can tell, sir?" Raistlin said in a low voice. "You and I both know that one goddess has not left Krynn."

Horkin considered. "You say it's a safe distance from the fighting?"

"As safe as anything can be, sir," Raistlin replied.

"It must be old. Is it in ruins?"

"It has certainly been neglected, sir. We would need to investigate further, of course, but the building seems to be in fairly good shape."

"I suppose it can't hurt to go look at it," said Horkin. "And who knows? Even if Paladine is long gone, perhaps there's some residual holiness still hanging about. I just hope the roof is sound," he added, glancing skyward. "There'll be rain before nightfall. If the roof leaks, we'll find someplace else, blessing or no blessing. Go check your temple out, Red. I'll round up a wagon. Tell Sergeant Nemiss to give you an escort."

"I really don't need anyone, sir," Raistlin said.

After spending the night dreaming of the temple bathed in silver moonlight, Raistlin was now more convinced than ever that Solinari had drawn the mage's attention to the temple for a reason. Raistlin had no idea what that reason might be. He wanted to enter the temple alone, wanted to open himself to the will of the god. To do that, he needed to be attuned to whatever voice might choose to speak to him. He did not want some loud-mouthed clod stomping about, making crude remarks and offending whatever spirits might linger in the holy place.

"You'll probably want to take your brother with you," said Horkin.

"No, sir," Raistlin returned emphatically, this being the clod he'd had in mind. The temple was his discovery, belonged to him. He conveniently forgot the fact that it was Caramon who had first seen the temple. "I really don't need anyone—"

"You'll need a good fighter, Red," Horkin said crisply. "Never know what you might find lurking about in an old temple. I'll speak to Sergeant Nemiss. Perhaps she'll even let you have Scrounger."

Raistlin gave an inward groan.

❂

The gray and lowering clouds, which had blanketed the city almost since the day the army had arrived, were blown to rags by a strong chill wind coming down from out of the mountain. The air temperature dropped precipitously, changing from early summer to late fall in a breath. Rain might fall tonight, as Horkin anticipated, but for now bright sunshine—so bright that it seemed newly minted—and crisp, fresh air lifted the hearts of those in the besieged city, although that hope dimmed somewhat when they looked over the walls to see the immense army of Commander Kholos marching to attack.

The baron laid out his plan. It was met by dismay from the lord mayor and his officers at first, but they were soon persuaded that this was Hope's End's last hope. The baron left to put his plan into action, as the first black-fletched arrows launched over the walls.

The refreshing wind dried the sweat on Caramon's body, and he filled his lungs with it, expanding his muscular chest with each huge breath, much to the admiration of several housewives, who peeped at him from behind closed shutters. Caramon had at first been devastated at having to miss the fighting, but the thought of finding shelter for his wounded comrades somewhat mollified him.

Scrounger was pleased with the assignment, figuring he would have been of little use in the upcoming battle anyway. He looked forward to investigating the temple and regaled them with stories of lost and forgotten treasure well known to lie hidden in such places.

"You don't suppose that someone might have thought to look for treasure in the last three hundred years or so," Raistlin said sarcastically.

He was in a bad mood. Everything irritated him, from the change in the weather to the company he was forced to keep. The wind caught at his robes, blew them around his ankles, nearly tripping him. The breeze was chill, set him shivering, and something in the air took him by the throat, made him cough so hard he had to lean against a building until he regained his strength.

"If there's treasure, there's bound to be a guard on the treasure," Scrounger said in a thrilled whisper. "You know what inhabits old temples, don't you? The undead! Skeletal warriors. Ghouls. Maybe even a demon or two . . ."

Caramon was starting to look uneasy. "Raist, maybe this isn't such a—"

"I promise to deal with any ghouls we meet, Caramon," Raistlin said in a croaking voice.

Behind them, they could hear the trumpets and the drums and a great shout, given by the men of the baron's army.

"That's the signal to attack!" Caramon said, halting and looking back over his shoulder.

"Which means that there will be more wounded," said Raistlin, with a jab of conscience.

Recalling the gravity of their mission, the three increased their pace. There was no further talk of undead or of treasure.

Arriving back at the warehouse, they followed the street that led to the temple and easily found the building.

"Is that the right place?" Caramon said, his brow wrinkled.

"It has to be!" Raistlin began to cough.

Last night, surrounded by darkness, the temple had seemed a place of awe and mystery. Viewed in the bright light of day, the temple was a disappointment. The columns supporting the roof were cracked. The roof itself sagged. The walls were stained and discolored, the courtyard drowning in weeds.

Worn out and aching from his coughing fit, chilled to the bone, Raistlin was beginning to regret ever having seen the temple, much less suggesting it as a refuge for the wounded. The building was far more shabby and decrepit than he had imagined. Recalling Horkin's injunction about the leaky roof, Raistlin doubted if there was a roof to the place at all. He could imagine this raw wind blowing a gale through the drafty ruins.

"It was a mistake to come here," he said.

"No, it wasn't, Raist," Caramon said stoutly. "There's a good feeling about this place. I like it. We'll have to make sure it's safe first, secure the perimeter." He'd heard Sergeant Nemiss use that expression and had been waiting for an opportunity to use it himself. "Secure the perimeter," he repeated with a relish.

"What perimeter? There is no perimeter!" Raistlin returned crossly. "There is nothing but a dilapidated old building and a weed-covered courtyard."

He was extremely disappointed and he couldn't understand why. What had he expected to find here? The gods?

"The building looks to be sturdy enough. Solid architecture. I think it must have been built by dwarves," Caramon stated with all the authority of one who knows absolutely nothing about the matter.

"It must be solid, to stand all these centuries." Scrounger added the voice of practicality.

"We should at least go check it out," Caramon urged.

Raistlin hesitated. Last night, Solinari had seemed to point the way, had urged his disciple to come to this once-holy place. But that had been at night, in the moonlight, a time when the mind—so stolid and trustworthy during the daylight hours—gives way to its dream-side and twists the dark shadows into all varieties of fanciful, frightful forms. Last night, the building had seemed so beautiful, safe, blessed. Today, there was something sinister about it.

He felt very strongly that he should turn away, leave in haste, and never come back.

"You can stay here in the street where it's safe, Raist," Caramon said with well-meaning solicitude. "Scrounger and I'll go take a look."

Raistlin shot his brother a glance that might have been one of the black-fletched arrows.

"Did I say 'safe'?" Caramon went red in the face, as red as if the arrow had pierced his forehead and drawn blood. "I meant 'warm.' That's what I meant to say, Raist. I didn't mean—"

"Come along, the two of you," Raistlin snapped. "I will take the lead."

Caramon opened his mouth to suggest that this was a rash course of action, that he—as the stronger and larger and better armed—should take the lead. At the sight of his brother's tightly drawn lips and glittering eyes, Caramon thought better of the notion and fell meekly into step behind.

The courtyard provided no cover. They would be in sight and range of anyone hiding inside the temple. Raistlin was disturbed to see that some of the chickweed growing up through the flagstones was trampled and broken. Someone else had walked across this courtyard and recently at that. The broken stems were still green, the leaves only starting to wither.

Raistlin pointed silently to the evidence that they might not be alone. Caramon put his hand to the hilt of his sword. Scrounger drew his knife. The three proceeded across the courtyard, eyes searching, ears pricked to catch the least sound. They heard nothing but the wind sweeping dead leaves into corners, saw nothing but the shadows of high, white clouds scuttle across the cracked flagstone. Drawing near the golden doors, Raistlin began to relax. If others had been here, they were gone now. The temple was deserted, he was certain.

But on reaching the steps leading up to the temple, Raistlin noted that the golden doors, which he had thought were closed, actually stood slightly ajar, as if someone inside had opened the doors a crack to peep out at them.

Seeing this, Caramon boldly took the lead, placing his body in front of his brother's. "Let us look inside, Raist."

Drawing his sword, he ran up the stairs, flattened himself with his back against the wall near the door. Scrounger dashed after him, took his place on the opposite side of the door, his knife in his hand.

"I don't hear anything," he said in a whisper.

"I don't see anything," Caramon returned. "It's dark as the Abyss in there."

He reached out his hand to press on the door, let in more light. As he did, the sun lifted above the city walls, a beam of sunshine struck the doors at the same time as did Caramon's fingers, making it seem as if his touch was the sun's touch. He burnished the gold, set it shining.

In that instant Raistlin, saw the temple not as it was, but as it had been. He gazed in wonder, awed and captivated. The cracks in the marble vanished. The patina of grime and dirt burned away in the light. The temple walls gleamed white. The frieze on the portico, obliterated in anger, was restored. In that frieze was a message, an answer, a solution. Raistlin stared at it. He needed only a few seconds to puzzle it out and he would understand. . . .

The world turned on its axis, the sun's dazzling rays were blocked by a guard tower on the wall. The tower's shadow fell across the golden doors. The vision vanished, the temple was as it had been—shabby, neglected, forgotten. Raistlin stared hard at the broken frieze, trying to fill in the missing pieces with the remnants of the vision, but he found he could not remember it, like a dream one loses on waking.

"I'm going inside," Caramon said. He returned his sword to its sheath.

"Unarmed?" Scrounger asked, amazed.

"It's not proper, taking a weapon in there," Caramon replied, his voice deep and solemn. "It's not . . ." He fumbled for a word. "Respectful."

"But there's nobody left to respect!" Scrounger argued.

"Caramon is right," Raistlin said firmly, to his brother's great astonishment. "We don't need weapons here. Put your sword away."

" 'Crazy as a kender,' they say," Scrounger muttered to himself. "Hah! Kender have nothing on these two!"

Having no desire to argue with the mage, however, Scrounger slid his knife back into his belt (though he kept his hand on the hilt) and accompanied the brothers inside.

Contrasted with the brightness of the reflected sunlight beating on the gold, the interior of the temple was so dark that for a few moments they could see nothing at all. But as their eyes became accustomed to the change, the darkness receded. The temple's interior seemed brighter than the bright day outside.

Fear vanished. No harm could come to them in this place. Raistlin felt the tightness in his chest ease, he breathed more deeply, less painfully. Solinari's promise held true, and Raistlin was more than a little ashamed of having doubted. The wounded could be made quite comfortable here. There was a purity to the air, a softness to the light that had healing qualities, of that he was convinced. The blessings of the old gods still lingered here, if the gods themselves were gone.

"This was a really good idea of yours, Raist," said Caramon.

"Thank you, my brother," Raistlin returned and, after a pause, he added, "I am sorry I was angry with you back there. I know you didn't mean it."

Caramon regarded his twin with amazed, marveling awe. He could not recall ever having heard his brother apologize to anyone for anything. He was about to reply when Scrounger motioned him to be quiet.

Scrounger pointed to a door, a silver door. "I think I heard something!" he whispered. "Behind that door!"

"Mice," said Caramon and, putting his hand on the door, he gave it a shove.

The door swung open silently, smoothly.

Fear flowed from the opening, a black, foul river of dread so strong, so palpable that Caramon felt it wash over him, try to drown him. He staggered backward, raising his hands as if he were sinking beneath turgid waves.

Raistlin tried to call out, tried to warn his brother to shut the door, but fear seized him by the throat and squeezed off his voice.

The dread rushed into the temple in a dark, crashing wave, submerging the kender part of Scrounger, leaving him a prey to human terror. "I . . . I never felt like this!" He whimpered, crouching back against the wall. "What's happening? I don't understand!"

Raistlin did not understand either. He had known fear. Any who take the deadly Test in the Tower of High Sorcery know fear. He had known the fear of pain, the fear of death, the fear of failure. He had never felt fear like this.

This was a fear that came from far away, a fear borne in the distant past, a fear felt by those very first people to walk upon this world. A primeval fear that looked up into the heavens and saw the fiery stars wheeling overhead, saw the sun, a bright and terrible orb of flame, hurtling down upon them. It was the fear of the noisome darkness, when neither stars nor moons were visible and the wood was wet and would not light and growls and snarls of unsatiated hunger came from the wilderness.

Raistlin wanted to flee, but the fear sucked the strength from his bones, left them soft and pliable as the bones of a newborn child. His brain shot jolts of fire to his muscles. His limbs trembled and jerked in panicked response. He clutched at his staff, and was astonished to see the crystal atop the staff—the crystal held by the dragon's claw—glowing with a strange light.

Raistlin had seen the staff glow before. He had only to say, "*Shirak*," and the crystal would light the darkness. But he had never seen it glow like this; a light that flared in anger, red around the edges, white at its heart, like the flame of the forge fire.

A Knight, clad in silver armor of ornate design appeared in the doorway. The Knight wore the symbol of a rose upon his tabard. He held his sword in his gloved hand. He removed the helm he wore and his eyes looked straight into Raistlin's heart and beyond that, into his soul.

"Magius," the Knight said, "I require your help to save that which must not perish from the world."

"I am not Magius," Raistlin answered, constrained by the Knight's noble aspect and mien to tell the truth.

"You bear his staff," said the Knight. "The fabled Staff of Magius."

"A gift," Raistlin said, lowering his head. Yet he could still feel the eyes of the Knight delving the depths of his being.

"Truly a valuable gift," said the Knight. "Are you worthy of it?"

"I . . . don't know," Raistlin replied in confusion.

"An honest answer," said the Knight, and he smiled. "Find out. Aid me in my cause."

"I am afraid!" Raistlin gasped, holding up his hand to ward off the terror. "I cannot do anything to help you or anyone!"

"Overcome your fear," said the Knight. "If you do not, you will walk in fear the rest of your life."

The light from the crystal blazed brilliant as a lightning bolt. Raistlin was forced to shut his eyes against the painful glare, lest it blind him. When he opened his eyes, the Knight was gone, as if he had never been.

The silver doors stood open and death lay beyond.

You had courage enough to pass the Test, said an inner voice.

"Courage enough to kill my own brother!" Raistlin answered.

Par-Salian and Antimodes and all the rest might view Raistlin with contempt, but they could never match the contempt with which he viewed himself. Bitter self-recrimination tagged always at his heels. Self-loathing was his constant shadow.

"Courage enough to kill Caramon when he came to rescue me, kill him as he stood before me, helpless, unarmed, disarmed by his love for me. That is my sort of courage," Raistlin said.

You will walk in fear the rest of your life.

"No," said Raistlin. "I won't."

Refusing to allow himself to think what he was doing, he lifted the Staff of Magius and, holding its shining light above him, he walked through the silver doors into darkness.

18

CARAMON HAD NEVER EXPERIENCED SUCH FEAR. Not during that terrible and hopeless attack on the city, not when the arrows thudded into his shield, not when the boulders smashed into his comrades, changing them from living men into bloody pulp and bone slivers. His fear then had been gut-wrenching, but not debilitating. His training and his discipline had carried him through.

This fear was different. It didn't wrench the gut, it reduced the gut to water. It didn't galvanize the body to action, it wrung the body, left it limp as a bar rag. Caramon had one thought in his mind and that was to run as fast as he could away from this place, away from the unknown evil that flowed out of the silver door in a chill and sickening wave. He didn't know what was down there, he didn't want to know what was down there. Whatever it was, it was not meant for mortals to encounter.

Caramon watched with a horror that left him breathless and gasping, watched his brother cross that awful threshold.

"Raist, don't!" Caramon cried, but the cry came out a pitiful wail, like that of a frightened child.

If Raistlin heard him, he did not turn back.

Caramon wondered what dark force had seized hold of his brother, caused him to enter that place of certain death. In answer Caramon heard a voice, faint and distant, calling for aid. An armored Knight stood in the doorway. Reminded fondly of Sturm, Caramon would have been glad to go with the Knight but for this strange and horrible fear that had him groveling on the floor of the temple in a panic.

But that changed when Raistlin entered the darkness. Caramon had no choice but to go after him. Fear for his brother's life was like a fire in his brain and blood, burned away the sickening, unnameable fear. Sword drawn, he ran through the silver door into the corridor after his brother.

Left behind, Scrounger stared, disbelieving. His friend, his best friend, and his friend's twin, had just walked into death.

"Fools!" Scrounger pronounced them. "You're both crazy!"

His teeth chattered, he could barely speak. Pressed flat against the wall by his own terror, he tried to take a step toward that dark entrance, but his feet wouldn't obey what was admittedly a feeble command.

Where, oh, where was the kender side of him now that he needed it! All his life he had fought against that part of himself—slapped back the fingers that itched to touch, to handle, to take; fought against the wanderlust that tempted him to leave his honest work and go skipping down an untraveled road. Now, when his mother's kender fearlessness—a fearlessness that had nothing to do with courage and everything to do with curiosity—might have stood him in good stead, he searched for it and found it wanting.

His mother would have said it served him right.

Scrounger wasn't in the temple any longer. He was a little child standing with his mother outside a cave they'd stumbled across during one of their many rambles.

"Aren't you curious to know what's in there?" she asked him. "Don't you wonder what's inside? Maybe a dragon's treasure hoard. Maybe a sorcerer's workshop. Maybe a princess who needs rescuing. Don't you want to find out?"

"No," Scrounger wailed. "I don't want to go in! It's dark and horrible and it smells bad!"

"You're no child of mine," his mother said, not angrily, but fondly. She patted his head. She went into the cave, came dashing out about three minutes later with a giant bugbear in hot pursuit.

Scrounger remembered that moment, remembered the bugbear—the first one he'd ever seen and the last he ever wanted to see—remembered his mother haring out of that cave, her clothes in wild disorder, her pouches flapping open, spilling their contents, her face red with exertion, her grin wide. She caught Scrounger by the hand. They ran for their lives.

Fortunately the bugbear didn't have any staying power. It soon given up the chase. But Scrounger had determined in that moment that his mother was right. He was no child of hers and he didn't want to be.

"I know what I'll do," said Scrounger to himself, "I'll go back to the army. I'll get reinforcements!"

At that moment, a large hand reached out from the silver door, grabbed hold of Scrounger's shoulder, yanked him off his feet, and pulled him inside.

"Cripes, Caramon, you scared m-me half to death! What did you do that for?" Scrounger demanded when he could feel his heart start to beat again.

"Because I need your help to find Raist," Caramon said grimly. "You were running away!"

"I was g-going to g-get help," Scrounger said through the chattering of his teeth.

"You're not supposed to be scared." Caramon glared at the trembling Scrounger. "What kind of kender are you?"

"Half-kender," Scrounger retorted. "The smart half."

Now that he was here, he supposed he had to make the best of it. Anyway, he was too scared to go back alone.

"Is it all right with you if I draw my sword now? Or would that be disrespectful to whatever's down here that's going to murder us and chop up our bodies into little pieces and suck out our souls."

"I think drawing your sword would be a wise move," Caramon replied gravely.

They stood inside a tunnel that had been carved through the rock. The tunnel walls were smooth and formed an arch above them, the floor sloped slightly downward. The tunnel did not appear as dark once they'd entered it as it had seemed from outside. Sunlight reflecting off the silver door lit their way for a considerable distance, far longer than either would have imagined was possible. But there was no sign of Raistlin.

They kept going. The tunnel made a sharp curve. Coming around the corner, they saw, ahead of them, a shining light, brilliant as a star.

"Raist!" Caramon called softly.

The light wavered, halted. Raistlin turned and they could see his face, the skin glistening faintly gold in the light cast by the Staff of Magius. He beckoned. Caramon hurried ahead, Scrounger at his heels—close at his heels.

Raistlin's hand closed over his brother's arm, clasped Caramon warmly. "I'm glad you are here, my brother," he said earnestly.

"Well, I'm not glad to be here!" Caramon said in a low voice. He looked nervously to the left, to the right, ahead and behind. "I don't like this place and I think we should leave. Something down here doesn't want us down here. Remember what Scrounger said about ghouls? I tell you, Raist, I've never been so scared in my life. I only came to find you and the Knight."

"What Knight?" Scrounger demanded.

"So you saw him, too," Raistlin murmured.

"What Knight?" Scrounger persisted.

Raistlin did not answer immediately. When he did reply, he said only, "Come with me, both of you. There's something I want to show you."

"Raist, I don't think—" Caramon began.

The mountain shook. The tunnel shuddered, the floor trembled.

The three fell back against the tunnel walls, almost too startled to be frightened. Rock dust sifted down on their heads, but before the realization came to them that they were in danger of being buried beneath the mountain, the shaking ceased.

"That does it," Caramon said. "We're getting out of here."

"A minor tremor. These mountains are subject to them, I believe. Did the Knight say anything to you?"

"He said he needed help. Look, Raist, I—" Caramon paused, regarded his brother anxiously. "Are you all right?"

Raistlin was choking on the rock dust, which had flown down his throat. He shook his head at the inanity of the question. "No, I'm not all right," he gasped when he could speak. "But I will be better in a moment."

"Let's leave," Caramon said. "You shouldn't be down here. The dust is bad for you."

"It's bad for me, too," said Scrounger.

They both stood there, waiting for Raistlin. When he could breathe, he looked back toward the silver door, then ahead. "Do what you want. But I am going to go on. We could not bring wounded into the temple without knowing that it is completely safe. Besides, I'm curious to know what lies ahead."

"Probably my poor mother's last words," Scrounger said gloomily.

Caramon shook his head, but he followed after his twin. Scrounger waited, still thinking he would take the mage up on his offer and run away. He waited until the comforting light of the mage's staff had almost vanished. Only when the darkness started to close over him did he race to catch up with the light.

The smooth tunnel walls gave way to natural rock. The path was uneven, more difficult to follow. It wound about among the stalagmites, led them from one cavern room into another and always down, down deep into the mountain. And then it ended, abruptly, in a cul-de-sac.

A wall of rock blocked their way.

"All this for nothing," said Caramon. "Well, at least we know it's safe. Let's go back."

Raistlin shone the light on the wall, soon discovered the alcove with the gate made of silver and gold. He looked through the gate into a small round chamber. Caramon peered over his shoulder. The chamber was empty except for a sarcophagus located in the very center of the oval room.

"Raist, this is a tomb," Caramon said uneasily.

"How very observant of you, Caramon," Raistlin returned.

Ignoring his brother's pleas, he pushed open the gate.

The light of the Staff of Magius shone with a bright silver radiance as he entered the chamber. He raised the staff so that the light fell on the sarcophagus, illuminated the stone figure carved on the top. Raistlin stood staring in silence.

"Look at this, my brother," he said at last, his voice soft, awed. "What do you see?"

"A tomb," said Caramon nervously.

He came to a standstill under the arch, his big body blocking the way. Behind him, Scrounger had no intention of being left alone in the tunnel. He shoved his way past the big man, wormed his way inside.

"Look at the tomb, Caramon," Raistlin persisted. "What do you see?"

"A Knight, I guess. It's hard to tell. There's so much dust." Caramon averted his eyes. He had just noticed that the lid of the sarcophagus was open. "Raist, we shouldn't be here! It's not right!"

Raistlin paid no heed to his brother. Approaching the sarcophagus, he peered inside the open lid. He stopped, stared, drew back slightly.

"I knew it!" Caramon gripped his sword so hard his hand ached.

Raistlin beckoned. "Come here, my brother. You should see this."

"No, I shouldn't," Caramon said firmly, shaking his head.

"I said come look at this, Caramon!" Raistlin's voice rasped.

Shambling, reluctant, Caramon edged his way forward. Scrounger came with him, holding on to his sword with one hand and Caramon's belt loop with the other.

Caramon sneaked a quick look inside the tomb, looked quickly away before he had a chance to see anything horrible, like a moldy skeleton with bits of flesh hanging off the bones. Startled by what he saw, he looked back.

"The Knight!" Caramon breathed. "The Knight who called to me!"

A body lay in the tomb, a body clad in ancient armor that gleamed in the light of the Staff of Magius, a soft light shed down upon the Knight with loving grace. The Knight wore a helm made in a style that had been popular before the Cataclysm. He wore a tabard over his armor. The tabard's fabric was old, yellowed; the embroidered satin rose that adorned it was worn and faded. The Knight clasped the hilt of a sword in his hands. Dried rose petals surrounded the Knight's body, lay scattered over the tabard and the shining sword. A sweet fragrance of roses lingered in the air.

"I thought I recognized the carven figure on the tomb," Raistlin said thoughtfully. "The armor, the tabard, the helm—all exactly like those worn by the Knight who came to ask us to aid him. A Knight who has been dead perhaps hundreds of years!"

"Don't say things like that," Scrounger pleaded, his voice a squeak. "This place is spooky enough as it is! Wouldn't this be a good time to go?"

Looking at the Knight lying in his tomb, Caramon was again reminded of his friend Sturm. The reminder was not a happy one. Caramon hoped it wasn't an omen.

He began to brush away some of the dust from the still, stone figure carved upon the lid.

Raistlin stood gazing upon the Knight, resting in a peace and tranquillity that the young mage, who suffered the constant burning in his lungs and the more painful burning of his own ambitions, momentarily envied.

"Look at this, Raist!" Caramon marveled. "There's an inscription."

Brushing aside the dust, he uncovered a small plaque made of bronze that had been set into the stone above the knight's heart.

"I can't read it," Caramon said, twisting his head at an odd angle to see.

"It's in Solamnic," Raistlin said, recognizing immediately the language he'd been wrestling for months, ever since receiving the book describing the Staff of Magius. "It says—" He brushed aside more dust and read aloud.

" 'Here lies one who died defending the Temple of Paladine and its servants from the faithless and the forlorn. By the Knight's last request, made with his dying breath, we bury him in this chamber so that he may continue to stand watch over the precious treasure, which it is our duty and our privilege to guard. Paladine grant him rest when his duty is fulfilled.' "

All three looked at one another. All three repeated the same word at the same time.

"Treasure!"

Caramon looked about the chamber as if he expected to see chests spilling out coins and jewels. "Scrounger was right! Does it say where the treasure is, Raist?"

Raistlin continued to brush away dust, but there was nothing more to be read.

"It's funny, but I'm not the least bit scared anymore," Scrounger announced. "I wouldn't mind exploring."

"It wouldn't hurt to look around," said Caramon, bending down to try to peer underneath the tomb. He was disappointed to find it set solidly into the cavern floor. "What do you say, Raist?"

Raistlin was sorely tempted. The strange and unreasoning fear he'd experienced was gone. He had a responsibility to the wounded, but as he had said before, he had a responsibility to make certain that the temple was safe. If he happened to come across a treasure chest while doing so, no one could fault him.

"What would you do if you found a treasure, Caramon?" Scrounger asked.

"I'd buy an inn," Caramon said.

"You'd be your own best customer." Scrounger laughed.

I would do only good, if a treasure came into my possession, Raistlin thought. I would move to Palanthas and purchase the largest house in the city. I would have servants to wait on me and to work in my laboratory, which would be the largest and finest money could buy. I would purchase every spellbook in every mageware shop from here to Northern Ergoth. I would start a library that would rival the library in the Tower of High Sorcery. I would buy magical artifacts and magical gems and wands and potions and scrolls.

He saw himself rich, powerful, beloved, feared. Saw himself quite clearly. He stood in a tower, dark, foreboding, surrounded by death. He wore black robes, around his neck, a pendant of green stone streaked with blood. . . .

"Look what I found!" Scrounger called out excitedly, pointing. "Another gate!"

Raistlin only half-heard him. The image of himself was slow to dissolve. When it finally faded away, it left a disquieting feeling behind.

Scrounger stood beside a wrought iron gate, his face pressed against the bars, staring into the darkness beyond.

"It leads into another tunnel," he reported. "Maybe it's the tunnel where the treasure is!"

"We've found it, Raist!" Caramon said exultantly, crowding behind Scrounger, looking out over his head. "I know we've found it! Bring your light over here!"

"I don't suppose it would hurt to take a look," Raistlin said. "Move away from there. Give me room to see what I'm doing. Don't touch the gate, Caramon! It might be magically trapped. Let me look at it."

Caramon and Scrounger dutifully stepped back.

Raistlin approached the gate. He could sense magical power, immense magical power. But not from the gate. The power lay beyond. Magical artifacts, perhaps. Artifacts from hundreds of years ago, before the Cataclysm. Lying undisturbed all this time, waiting . . . waiting . . .

He turned the handle. The iron gate creaked open. Raistlin took one step into the darkness beyond only to find a shadowy form blocking his way.

"*Shirak*." He lifted the staff to see what it was.

The staff's white light gleamed red in the burning eyes of Immolatus.

19

THE WIZARD'S EYES BURNED RED, FED FROM THE FIRE OF HATRED AND frustration that still roared in his belly and that could find no outlet in this accursed body. The heat of the flames radiated from his flesh. He had lost considerable blood from the wound in his side. Each breath he drew was agony. His head ached and throbbed. These weaknesses, a plague to his weak human form, would disappear once he regained his splendid, strong, and powerful dragon form. Once he was out of this accursed building. He would make them pay, make them all pay. . . .

Finding his way blocked, Immolatus lifted his gaze and focused on a bright light, which pierced his aching eyes like a steel lance. He glared at the light, furious, and then he saw its source.

"The Staff of Magius!" Immolatus cried with a grinding glee. "I'll have something from this misadventure, after all."

Reaching out his hand, the dragon plucked the staff from Raistlin's grasp, and with the other hand, he struck the young man a blow that sent him sprawling to the stone floor.

❂

Kitiara had trailed Immolatus through the cavern's corridors. When he stopped at the entrance to the burial chamber, Kitiara crept forward, sword drawn, planning to attack the wizard in the burial chamber, where she had room to swing her sword.

Unexpectedly, Immolatus stopped before entering the gate, shouting something about a staff. He sounded pleased, exultant, as if he'd just stumbled across a long-lost companion. Fearful that the dragon had found a friend and that he might yet escape her, Kitiara looked past Immolatus's shoulder to see what new foe she might face.

Caramon!

Paralyzed with amazement, Kitiara at first doubted her senses. Caramon was safely back in Solace, not wandering about caverns in Hope's End. But there was no mistaking those massive shoulders, the ham-fisted hands, the curly hair, and that gaping expression of dumbfounded astonishment.

Caramon! Here! She was so lost in startlement that she barely paid attention to his companions—a red-robed wizard and a kenderish-looking fellow. Kit paid little attention to them. The sight of her brother, wearing the armor of the baron—the enemy no less—brought such confused thoughts to her that she lowered her sword and retreated a safe distance back down the corridor to consider how to deal with this bizarre situation.

One thought was uppermost in her mind: now was *not* the time for a family reunion.

❽

The blow of the wizard's hand struck Raistlin squarely on the breastbone. Stunned at the sight of Immolatus springing up out of the darkness, Raistlin could not react fast enough to save himself. He went down as if felled by a thunderbolt, struck his head when he landed—sprawled and gasping for breath—on the cavern floor. Pain lanced through his skull. He came near to blacking out.

Looking up blearily from the floor, Raistlin saw Immolatus holding the Staff of Magius, gloating over his prize. Raistlin's most precious possession, his most valued treasure, the symbol of his achievement, his triumph over sickness and suffering, his reward for long and torturous hours of study, his victory over himself—this was the prize Immolatus had taken from him.

The loss of the staff banished pain, banished amazement, banished any fear he held for his life, any value placed on that life.

With a snarl of fury, Raistlin leapt to his feet, heedless of the pain and the blue and yellow stars that shot through his vision, half-blinding him. He attacked Immolatus with a courage and strength and ferocity that astounded his brother, already astounded by the sight of the strange Red Robe who had burst upon them so suddenly.

Raistlin did not fight his desperate battle alone. The Staff of Magius aided him. Created by an archmage of immense power, brought into being with one intent—to aid in the fight against Queen Takhisis—the staff and its master had fought her evil wyrms during the last Dragon War.

The staff had never known its master's fate. The staff knew that Magius was dead only when they came to bring the staff to be laid to rest on his funeral pyre. History never recorded the name of the White Robe who saved the staff. Some say that it was Solinari himself, come down from the heavens, who plucked the staff from the flames. Certainly it was someone who had the foresight and the wisdom to know that although the Queen might be defeated now, dark wings would once again blot out Krynn's sun.

The Staff of Magius penetrated Immolatus's disguise. The staff knew that a dragon, a red dragon, a minion of Queen Takhisis, had laid covetous hands upon it. The staff unleashed its anger, an anger pent up for hundreds of years. The staff waited until Immolatus had a good, solid grip on it, then let loose its magic.

An explosion of white light erupted from the staff. A blast rocked the burial chamber. Caramon was staring directly at the staff when its anger flared. The light seared his eyes. He fell back in agony, clapping his hands over his face. A black hole ringed round with purple fire obscured his vision, left him blind as a child in the womb. Warm blood splattered his face and hands. He heard a horrible, rising scream.

"Raist!" he cried, ragged and fearful, trying desperately to see. "Raist!"

The blast knocked Scrounger to the cavern floor, rattled his wits in his head. He lay staring up dazedly at the ceiling, wondering how a lightning bolt had managed to strike this far underground.

Raistlin had sensed the staff's fury, realized it was about to unleash its magical rage. Averting his eyes, he flung up his arm to protect his face. The force of the explosion sent him staggering back against the tomb, where, it seemed, he felt a firm hand support and steady him, keep him from falling. Raistlin thought the comforting touch belonged to his twin. Raistlin would later come to realize that Caramon, blind and helpless, was halfway across the burial chamber at the time.

Immolatus screamed. Pain such as he had known only once before—pain inflicted by the magical dragonlance—flared up his arm, spread like searing flame throughout his body. The dragon let go of the staff. He had no choice. He no longer had a hand.

Drenched with his own blood, cut by the shards of his own broken bones, Immolatus had never been so furious in his life. Though grievous, the dragon's wounds were not mortal. He had one desire and that was to kill these wretched beings who had inflicted such horrible damage on him. He released himself from the spell that bound him to human form. When he had regained his own body, he would incinerate these gnats, these worms with their infernal stinging bite.

Raistlin's enchanted gaze saw the dragon in midtransformation, he saw the wizard's human body shriveling, saw something red, glittering, monstrously evil rising from it. What that being was, he had no idea. Raistlin had one thought now and that was to retrieve his staff, which lay on the floor, its crystal blazing fiercely. He knelt, seized the staff. Using all his strength, strength he did not know he possessed, drawing on his fear and his terror and his pain, he swung the staff at Immolatus, smote him on the chest.

The staff's own magical fury added impetus to Raistlin's strike. Their combined force was like a lightning strike.

The blow lifted Immolatus, propelled him backward through the iron gate, flung him, half in and half out of his dragon form, clear of the burial chamber into the narrow tunnel. Immolatus smashed up against the rock wall of the corridor. Bones cracked and snapped, but they were the bones of his feeble human form and he could knit them back together with a single word of magic.

Immolatus lay a moment in the tunnel, in the darkness, reveling in the sensation of his strength, his power, his immenseness returning. His jaws grew and elongated, his teeth snapped with anticipation of crunching human bone, the muscles of his body rippled pleasantly beneath the newly forming scales that were soft now but would soon be hard as diamond. The fire burned in his belly, gurgled in his throat. He was growing too big for the corridor, but that didn't matter. He would rise up, cleave through the rock, raise the mountain, and drop it on the bodies of those who had dared insult him. He needed only a few more moments. . . .

A voice, a woman's voice, cold and biting as steel, pierced his head. "You have disobeyed me for the last time."

Kitiara's sword caught the light of the Staff of Magius and shone silver in that light.

Wounded, weakened by loss of blood and his spellcasting, dazzled by the flaring light, Immolatus looked into that light and thought he saw his Queen.

Furious, vengeful, implacable. She stood over him and pronounced his doom.

The sword drove into his back, severed his spine.

Immolatus gave a horrific cry of anger and malice, he jerked and twitched spasmodically, no longer in control of his own body. He glared at his destroyer and though he saw her through a blood-dimmed mist, he recognized Kitiara.

"I will not die . . . a human!" Immolatus hissed. "This will be my tomb. But I will see to it that it is yours, as well, worm!"

Kitiara wrenched her sword free of the body, stumbled backward. In his death throes, the dying dragon was continuing to revert to his original form. The transformation was almost complete, his body—a body far too big for the narrow cavern corridor in which she stood—continued to expand.

Immolatus twisted and writhed, his massive tail thrashed about, struck the rock wall, time and again. Wings flapped wildly, his clawed feet scrabbled and scraped against the tunnel walls. The ceiling cracked, supporting timbers creaked and sagged. The mountain shuddered, the floor shook.

"Raist!" Caramon's frantic voice. "Where are you? I . . . I can't see! What's happening?"

"I am here, my brother. Here. I have hold of you! Stop flailing about! Take my hand! Scrounger, help me with him! Back out the way we came! Quickly!"

Kitiara made a convulsive leap for the wrought iron gate. She stumbled into the burial chamber in time to see a flutter of red robe, a flickering light that came from a crystal atop a staff. The iron gate swung shut. The tunnel behind her gave way with a crash. Kitiara staggered toward the tomb of the Knight, hoping against hope that the burial chamber was strong enough to withstand the fury of a vindictive goddess.

Rocks fell down around her. She grabbed hold of the tomb, clung to it as the floor shook.

"I helped you, Sir Phantom!" she cried. "Now it's your turn!"

She crouched by the tomb, keeping her hand on the marble. Rocks fell, but not near her. They fell on the place where she'd seen the body, the body of herself. Nothing there now but crumbled stone. Kitiara shut her eyes against the grit and the dust and pressed herself close against the tomb with more fondness than she had ever pressed against the body of any lover.

Eventually the rumbling ceased, the dust settled.

Kitiara stirred, opened her eyes, blinked away the grime, and dared to draw a breath. Dust flew into her mouth, she began to cough. The darkness was absolute. She could see nothing, not even her hand in front of her face. Hands outstretched, she grabbed hold of the top of the tomb, felt the marble, smooth and cold. She pulled herself to her feet and stood leaning against the sarcophagus for support.

A faint light, softly gleaming, began to shine. Kit looked for the source, saw that the light came from the tomb. The sarcophogus was no longer empty, as it had been when she'd first seen it. It held a corpse. Kitiara looked on face of the corpse, a face at peace, a face victorious.

"Thanks, Sir Nigel," said Kit. "I guess we're even."

She looked around, took stock of her situation. The cavern was filled with fallen rock, but she could see no cracks in the ceiling or the floor, no holes in the walls. She looked back at the iron gate that led to the tunnel into the mountains. Beyond the iron gate was a wall of rock. The dragon's body lay buried beneath a cairn, flung down on him by his Queen. That way was blocked. But the way in, through the other silver and gold gate, was open and relatively clear of debris.

"Be seeing you," she said to the Knight and started to leave.

A force held her, a force not of this world.

Kitiara's hand, her sword hand, froze to the marble as if she had placed wet fingers on a block of ice. Fear twisted her stomach. She might wrench her hand free, but she would leave her flesh and her blood behind. For one horrible moment she thought that was to be the price she would have to pay, and then she realized, suddenly, that she might escape with a lesser cost.

She reached for her belt with her other hand, fumbled with numb fingers until she located the book containing the map that led to the egg chamber. She shook so she could barely hold the small volume. Wanting only to be rid of it, she flung the book into the open tomb.

"There!" she said bitterly. "Satisfied?"

The force released her. She snatched her hand from the tomb, rubbed her chill fingers, massaged life into them.

The burial chamber might be a safe haven, but Kitiara had seen all of it she wanted. She left by the silver and gold gate, taking the same route her brothers had taken, and kept walking until she had left the burial chamber and Sir Nigel far behind.

The sound of voices brought her to a halt. Up ahead, she could hear her brothers' voices and their footfalls echoing along the corridor. She could have caught up with them, but Kit decided she didn't want to see them. She didn't want to have to answer their questions, didn't want to have to make up a story to explain why she was here and what she was doing. Above all, she didn't want to join them in reminiscences about the days gone by, past times, old friends—especially old friends. She would wait here in the corridor until she was certain they were long gone, then she would sneak out.

Kitiara leaned back against the rocks, made herself as comfortable as she could. She wasn't bothered by the darkness. She found it soothing after that eerie and unnatural light in the Knight's tomb. Resting, she considered her future. She would return to Lord Ariakas. True, she had failed in her mission to steal the dragon eggs, but she could lay the fault for that failure squarely on the dragon. Since sending the dragon to find the eggs had been Lord Ariakas's idea, he had no one but himself to blame. She would be the one who had salvaged this mission, had seen to it that the dragon paid for his crime of disobedience, had taken care that the body of the slain beast was buried where no one would ever be the wiser.

"I'll have my promotion," Kitiara reflected, stretching out her legs. "And this will be just the beginning. I'll make myself indispensable to Ariakas, in more ways than one." She smiled to herself in the darkness. "The two of us will have the power to rule Krynn. In Her Majesty's name, of course," Kit added with an apprehensive glance into the darkness around her. She had witnessed the Queen's wrath, had come to respect it.

She had witnessed another power that day, the power of love, of self-sacrifice, of honor and resolve. She made nothing of that, however. Any feeling of respect she might have held for the Knight had vanished in resentment that he had bested her at the tomb. Her hand still hurt.

Exhausted by her efforts, Kitiara rested, half-dozed. She could no longer hear her brothers' voices. They had probably reached the entrance by now. She'd give them time enough to completely vacate the premises, then she would follow and leave this ill-fated temple.

She found herself thinking of her brothers. She had been disturbed at seeing them, at first. The twins brought back memories of a life and time she'd outgrown, memories of people she didn't want to remember. But now that they were gone and she was not ever likely to see them again, Kit was glad she'd had this opportunity to see how they had turned out.

Caramon was a warrior now, it seemed, and though he had not accorded himself with any particular distinction in this magical fight, Kitiara could well believe that in ordinary battles, he would prove himself a good and effective soldier. As for Raistlin, she didn't know what to make of him. She would never have recognized him had it not been for his voice, and even that had grown weaker than she remembered. But he was a wizard now, apparently, and he had fought Immolatus with a ferocity and courage she found extremely gratifying.

"Just as I planned," she said to herself. "They've both turned out just as I hoped."

Kitiara felt an almost maternal pride in her boys as she sat in the darkness, cleaning the dragon's blood from her sword, waiting for an opportunity to escape this accursed temple, leave the unlucky city of Hope's End.

✴

"Raist! There's light ahead, isn't there?" Caramon said hoarsely, his voice raw with fear. "I think I can see it, though it's awfully dim."

"Yes, Caramon, there is light," Raistlin replied. "We are back in the temple. The light you see is sunlight." He did not add that it was bright sunlight.

"I'll be able to see again, won't I, Raist?" Caramon asked anxiously. "You'll be able to heal me, won't you?"

Raistlin didn't answer immediately and Caramon turned his sightless eyes in the direction of his brother. Scrounger, staggering beneath Caramon's weight, looked hopefully at Raistlin, as well.

"He *will* be all right, won't he?" the half-kender asked in trepidation.

"Certainly," Raistlin said. "The condition is only a temporary one."

He hoped to heaven that his diagnosis was true. If the damage was permanent, it was beyond his ability to heal, beyond anyone's ability to heal in this day and age when no clerics walked the land.

Raistlin recalled one of Weird Meggin's patients, a man who had stared too long into the sun during a solar eclipse. She had tried treating him with poultices and salves to no avail. His sight had been irrevocably lost. Raistlin did not mention this to Caramon, however.

"Raist," Caramon persisted anxiously. "*When* do you think this will go away. When do you think I'll be able to see—"

"Raistlin," Scrounger said at the same time. "Who was that ugly old wizard? It seemed like he knew you."

Raistlin did not want to tell Caramon the truth, did not want to say the words, "Maybe never." Raistlin feared that even the blind Caramon must eventually see through a comforting lie. Raistlin was thankful to Scrounger for changing the subject and answered the half-kender with a cordiality that both astonished and pleased him.

"His name was Immolatus. I met him in the enemy's camp," Raistlin replied. "Master Horkin sent me there to trade magical goods, but the wizard wanted none of what we had to offer. He wanted only. thing—my staff."

He paused a moment, thinking how to phrase the next question, wondering even if he should ask it. His need to know was strong, overcame his natural reticence.

"Scrounger, Caramon, I want to ask you both something." He hesitated another moment, then said, "What did you see when you looked at the wizard?"

"A wizard?" said Caramon cautiously, afraid that this might be a trick question.

"I saw a wizard," said Scrounger. "A wizard in red robes like yours, only they were more of a fiery red now that I think about it."

"Why, Raist?" Caramon asked with disquieting astuteness. "What did *you* see when you looked at him?"

Raistlin thought back to the red-scaled monstrosity that for an instant had shimmered in his cursed vision. He tried to put shape and form to it, but nothing emerged. The Staff of Magius had struck at that moment, cast the wizard into darkness, a darkness that had come crashing down on top of him.

"I saw a wizard, Caramon," he said. His voice hardened. "A wizard who wanted to steal my staff from me."

"Then why did you ask the question?" Scrounger started to ask, but was silenced by a baleful glance.

"That magic spell you cast was really something, Raist," Caramon said, after a moment. "How did you do it?"

"You would not understand if I told you, Caramon," Raisltin said irritably. "Now, no more talking. It's bad for you."

Scrounger demanded to know how talking could be bad for Caramon's eyesight, but Raistlin didn't hear him or, if he did, he pretended that he didn't. He was thinking about the magic.

Ever since he had been given the Staff of Magius, Raistlin had been acutely aware of the life within the staff, magical sentience given to it by its creator. He had experienced a vague feeling of inadequacy, as if the staff were comparing him to its creator and finding him lacking. He remembered the terrible fear when Immolatus took the staff from him, the fear that the staff had left Raistlin of its own accord, leapt gladly into the hand of a wizard of more skill and power.

Raistlin had been overjoyed and relieved when the staff joined him in the battle. After the initial shock of the explosion, which he had sensed coming, but which he had not commanded, he and the staff had acted as a team. He had the feeling that the staff was pleased with itself and that it was also pleased with him. Odd to think, but he felt that he had earned the staff's respect.

His hand tightened lovingly on the staff as he emerged from the silver doors into the welcome light of the sun streaming in through the windows of the abandoned temple.

The sun shone warm on Caramon's face and he smiled. His vision was returning. He was certain of it, he said. He could see the sunlight and he swore he could see shadowy images of his brother and Scrounger.

"That is well, my brother," Raistlin said. "Keep your eyes closed, however. The sunlight is too strong and might do them more injury. Sit down here for a moment while I make a bandage."

He cut a strip of cloth from the hem of his robe and tied it gently around it Caramon's eyes. Caramon protested at first, but Raistlin was firm and, accustomed to obeying his brother, Caramon submitted to being blind-folded. He trusted his brother's diagnosis, accepted that his vision would return. Fretting and worrying would do him no good, and so he sat with his back against the sun-warmed stone, basked in the light shining on his face, and wondered how the attack was proceeding and if they'd set up the mess tent.

"Can you walk, Caramon?" Raistlin asked.

There had been no more tremors, but he had no idea if the temple had suffered any structural damage. Until someone who knew something about such matters came to look at it, he did not trust to its safety.

This holy place does appear to exert a healthful influence, Raistlin thought, watching color return to his brother's wan face. His pulse was strong and he stated stoutly that he was well enough to run up good old Heave-Gut hill. He gave it as his opinion that he was completely cured and if Raistlin would just take off this damn rag . . .

Raistlin said firmly that the rag must stay. He and Scrounger assisted Caramon to stand. Caramon walked under his own power, accepting his brother's hand on his arm to guide him.

The three left the temple to the sunshine and the silver moonlight, to the dead and to the living and the dragons, sleeping safely in their leathery shells, their spirits roaming the stars, waiting to be born.

20

"Here they come!" the sergeant of the archers of Hope's End yelled from the wall. As if in witness to the truth of his words, the man standing next to him dropped down dead, an arrow through his helmet.

The baron's men stood at the ready behind the gates. One moment there had been confusion, yelling and shouting. The next, disciplined silence. All eyes were on the officers, whose eyes were on the baron, standing atop the wall, looking out at the enemy, an enemy whose numbers seemed to grow alarmingly. Even counting the forces of the city, the baron was outnumbered almost two to one. And these were fresh troops, well armed, with an able, if loathsome, commander.

Under heavy covering fire, the enemy's engineers were running across the ground, hauling siege ladders and battering rams. The ranks of the infantry were four deep and marched to the sound of booming drums. Even as he watched death flow toward him across the bloody ground, the baron admired the precise discipline, the men keeping their formation even when arrows from the wall hit their first ranks.

Looking at the size and might of the forces arrayed against him, the baron was confirmed in his thinking. No matter what others might say, the action he intended was not the rash act of a madman. It was the only way to save this city, save his own forces. If they remained here, hiding behind the walls, the great numbers of the enemy would swarm over them like ants on a carcass.

The baron turned to look to his own men. They were lined up by company along the road. Each company was eight men across and as many as twenty men deep. There was no talking in the ranks, no foolery. The men were in grim and deadly earnest. The baron looked down at them, and he was proud of them.

"Soldiers of the Army of the Mad Baron!" he yelled from the wall. The men looked up at him, answered with a cheer. "This is the end!" he continued. "We are victorious this day or we are dead." He pointed a jabbing finger out over the wall. "When you set eyes upon the enemy, remember that they *shot our dead in the back!*"

A roar of anger rumbled through the troops.

"It is time to take our revenge!"

The roar of anger swelled to a cheer for the baron.

"Good luck to us," he said to the city's commander and to the lord mayor, shaking each by the hand.

The lord mayor was ashen in color. Sweat rolled down his face, despite the cool wind that had recently surged out of the mountains. He was a political figure, he could have sought refuge in his own home, and few would have thought worse of him. But he was grimly determined to stick to his post, though he cringed and shook at every trumpet blast.

"Good luck to you, Mad Lad," said the elderly commander to the baron and ducked just in time to avoid an arrow. "Confound it," the old man muttered, with a sour look for the arrow that lay spent at his feet. "Let me at least live long enough to see this sight. Win or lose, it's going to be glorious."

The baron left the wall, ran nimbly down the stairs and back to street level. He took his place on foot at the front of his army, drew his sword, and raised it high. The sun's bright rays flashed along the blade. He held the sword poised, waiting.

The gate boomed and shuddered. The first of the battering rams had arrived. Before the enemy could hit the gate a second time, the baron gave the signal.

The gates to the city of Hope's End swung open. The attackers cheered, thinking they had breached the defenses.

The baron let fall his sword. Trumpets sounded, drums rolled. "Attack!" the baron yelled and ran forward through the open gates, straight into the ranks of the enemy. Behind him came Center Company, the most experienced veterans in the army, the most heavily armored and armed. With a savage yell, they thundered through the gates, wielding swords and battle-axes.

Caught completely by surprise, the soldiers manning the battering ram dropped the oak log, fumbled for their swords. The baron hit their leader squarely in the chest with his sword, drove the weapon clean through the man's body so that it emerged covered with blood from his back. The baron yanked free his weapon, parried a vicious chop from another of the enemy, who was attacking him on his flank, thrust the sword into the man's rib cage.

He tried to recover the sword, only to find his weapon fouled in the man's ribs. He couldn't pull the sword free. Fighting and death were all around him. His men were shouting and screaming with rage, blood spattered on them all like rain. The baron placed his foot on the body, held it down and yanked free his sword. He was ready to face the next enemy soldier, only to find there were none. The battering ram lay in front of the gates, surrounded by the dead bodies of those who had wielded it.

Now began the real battle.

The baron looked for his standard-bearer, found the man right beside him.

"Forward!" he yelled and began the advance, his standard snapping in the cold wind.

Center Company continued their advance on the run, yelling their battle cries, brandishing weapons stained with blood. Arrows from Archer Company, manning the walls, buzzed over their heads and fell among the enemy like vicious wasps, decimating the enemy's front ranks. For many of the enemy soldiers, this was their first combat. And this was nothing like training. Their comrades were dying around them. An army of savage, screaming monsters hurtled toward them. The front ranks of the enemy halted, the soldiers wavered. Officers plied their whips, shouted for the lines to hold.

Center Company, led by the baron, hit the front ranks of the enemy with an armor-plated crash that could be heard on the walls. They stabbed and sliced and chopped, showing no mercy, giving no quarter. They had seen the bodies of their comrades lying before the gate, the black-feathered arrows in their backs. They had one thought and that was to kill those who had used them so treacherously.

The front ranks of the enemy collapsed under the fury of the charge. Those who stood their ground paid for their courage with their lives. A few fell back fighting. Many more flung down their shields and, heedless of the whips, broke and ran.

Center Company kept going, plowing through the enemy's lines, leaving a bloody furrow behind. Other companies came behind Center Company, fighting those of the enemy who, driven by the whips of their officers, came surging in to fill the great gaping hole left by the onslaught of the baron and his company.

"There's our objective!" the baron shouted and pointed to a small rise, where stood Commander Kholos.

Kholos had laughed loudly and derisively at the sight of the baron's men pouring out of the gate, leaving the safety of the city behind in a mad charge. He waited confidently for his men to overwhelm the baron's forces, crush them, annihilate them. He heard the crash as the two armies came together, he waited for the baron's standard to fall.

The standard did not fall. The standard advanced. It was Kholos's men who were running now, running in the wrong direction.

"Shoot those cowards!" Kholos roared in fury to his archers. Foam flecked his mouth. He pointed at his own fleeing troops.

"Commander!" Master Vardash, his face swollen from his commander's blow, came running up to report. "The enemy has broken through the lines!"

"My horse!" Kholos yelled.

Other officers were shouting for their horses, but before the squires could bring forward the horses, Center Company and the baron smashed into the knot of men and their bodyguards. Master Vardash fell in the first onslaught, his face now a mask of blood.

"Kholos is mine!" the baron yelled and pushed and shoved his way through the press of heaving, struggling bodies to reach the commander who had insulted him and murdered his men.

Kholos held his ground and it seemed that he alone might yet turn the tide of battle. Heavily armored, he scorned to use a shield, fought with two weapons, a longsword in one hand and a dirk in the other. He thrust and slashed, seeming to use very little effort. Three men fell to the ground before him, one with his skull cleaved in two, another decapitated, the third from a dirk stab to the heart.

So formidable was Kholos that Center Company's advance faltered. The most experienced of the veterans fell back before him. The baron halted, shocked at the sight of that goblinish face twisted into a horrible smile, a smile made hideous with battle-lust and the delight in killing.

"You betrayed us!" the baron roared. "By Kiri-Jolith, I swear that I'll nail your head to my tent post this night! And spit on it in the morning!"

"Mercenary scum." Trampling bodies beneath his feet, Kholos strode forward. "I challenge you to single combat! A fight to the death! If you've the stomach for it, you cheap sell-sword."

The baron's face split into a grin. "I accept!" he yelled. Glancing behind him, he shouted, "You men know what to do!"

"Yes, sir," Commander Morgon bellowed.

The baron marched forward to meet his foe. His men held back, watching grimly.

Kholos swung a vicious blow with his longsword, but he was used to fighting taller enemies. The sword whistled clean over the head of the baron, who crouched low and made a running dive for Kholos's knees. The move took Kholos completely by surprise. The baron barreled into Kholos, took him down to the ground.

"Now!" shouted Commander Morgon.

The soldiers of Center Company rushed forward, leapt on top of the fallen commander, swords slashing and stabbing.

The baron crawled out from under the crush.

"Are you hurt, my lord?" Commander Morgon asked, assisting the baron to stand.

"I don't think so," said the baron. "I think this is mostly his blood. I can't believe that bastard thought I'd actually fight him in honorable combat! Ha, ha, ha!"

Morgon waded back into the fray, grabbed hold of his soldiers, pulled them back.

"All right, boys! Fun's over. I think the bastard's dead."

The men gradually fell back, breathing hard, bloody but grinning. The baron walked over to look at the body of the commander, weltering in his own blood, his eyes staring skyward, a look of utter surprise on his yellow, goblin face.

The baron nodded in grim satisfaction, then turned, his sword in his hand. "Our work's not done yet, men—" he began.

"I'm not so sure of that, my lord," said Commander Morgon. "Look at that, will you, sir?"

The baron looked around the field. The officers of Kholos's command staff who were not dead or wounded were on their knees, hands raised in surrender. The rest of the enemy was fleeing the field, running for the shelter of the woods, the baron's men in pursuit.

"It's a rout, sir!" said Morgon.

The baron frowned. Caught up in their own battle-lust, his troops had broken ranks, were scattered all over the field. The enemy was on the run now, but it would take only one courageous and level-headed officer to halt the rout, regroup his men, and turn defeat into victory.

"The bugler?" The baron looked around. "Where in the name of Kiri-Jolith is my goddamned bugler?"

"I think he was killed, my lord," said Morgon.

The sight of sunshine gleaming off brass caught the baron's eye. Among the enemy officers stood a boy, shivering and frightened, a bugle clutched in his white-knuckled hand.

"Bring me that boy!" the baron commanded.

Commander Morgon grabbed hold of the boy, dragged him forward. The boy fell to his knees in abject terror.

"Stand up and look at me, blast you. Do you know 'A Posey from Abanasinia'?" the baron demanded.

The boy slowly and fearfully regained his feet, stared at the baron in blank astonishment.

"Do you know it, boy?" the baron roared. "Or don't you?"

The boy gave a trembling nod. The tune was a common one.

"Good!" The baron smiled. "Sound the first chorus, and I'll let you go."

The boy shivered, panicked, confused.

"It's all right, son," the baron said, his voice softening. He placed his hand on the boy's shoulder. "My regiment uses that tune as Recall. Go ahead and blow it."

Reassured, the boy brought his instrument to his lips. The first note was a failure. The baron winced. Gamely, the boy licked his lips and tried again. The clear sounds of the call cut across the sounds of battle and pursuit.

"Good, boy, good!" the baron said with approval. "Repeat it, and keep repeating it!"

The boy did as he was told. The familiar call brought the men to their senses. They broke off the attack, looked around for their officers, began to reform into ranks.

"March them back to the city, Morgon," the baron ordered. "Pick up any of our wounded on the way." He cast a grim glance in the direction of the enemy encampment. "We may have to do this all over again tomorrow."

"I doubt it, my lord," said Morgon. "Their officers are either dead or our prisoners. The soldiers will wait for nightfall, then break camp and head for home. There won't be a tent standing there by morning."

"A wager on that, Morgon?"

"A wager, my lord."

The two clasped hands. "This is one bet I hope I lose," said the baron.

Morgon ran off to organize the withdrawal. The baron was about to follow, realized that the trumpet was still blowing raucously and desperately.

"Very good, son," the baron said. "You can stop blowing now."

The boy lowered his trumpet hesitantly to his side.

The baron nodded, waved his hand. "Run along, lad. I said I'd let you go. You're free. No one will hurt you."

The boy didn't move. He stood staring at the baron, wide-eyed.

The baron, shrugging, started to walk away.

"Sir, sir!" the boy called. "Can I join *your* army?"

The baron stopped, looked back. "How old are you, boy?"

"Eighteen, sir," he answered.

"You mean thirteen, don't you?"

The boy hung his head.

"You're too young for a life like this, son. You've seen too much death already. Go home to your ma. Likely she's worried sick about you."

The boy didn't budge.

The baron shook his head, resumed walking. He heard footsteps patter along behind him. He sighed again, but did not turn around.

"My lord, are you all right?" Master Senej asked.

"Dead tired," the baron answered. "And I hurt all over. But otherwise unharmed, praise be to my god." He glanced behind him, motioned the officer to come near. "Can you use some help, Senej?"

The master nodded. "Yes, my lord. We've got a lot of wounded, not to mention all these prisoners. I could definitely use another hand."

The baron jerked his thumb back at the boy. "You've got one. Go with Master Senej, boy. Do as you're told."

"Yes, my lord!" The boy smiled tremulously. "Thank you, my lord."

Shaking his head, the baron trudged across the field, heading back to the city of Hope's End, whose bells were ringing in wild triumph.

21

A GLORIOUS FIGHT, RED!" HORKIN SAID, GLEEFULLY RUBBING HIS HANDS, which were black with flash powder. He came through the gates with the first of the wounded, to find his apprentice waiting for him. "You should have been there."

Horkin gazed intently at Raistlin. "I take that back. Looks like you saw some action yourself, Red. What happened?"

"Do we really have time to waste on this, sir?" Raistlin asked. "With all these wounded to care for? I found the temple. I think it would be an excellent shelter, but I'd like you to take a look at it."

"Perhaps you're right," said Horkin, giving Raistlin a searching glance.

"This way, sir," said Raistlin and turned away.

Raistlin explained that the temple had been shaken by tremors, nothing unusual for this region, according to the citizens. Horkin examined the temple, studied the pillars and the walls and finally deemed it sound. All that was needed now was a source for water. A search revealed a well of clear, cold springwater at the rear of the temple. Horkin gave orders that the wounded should be brought to this restful place.

The wagons bearing the wounded trundled through the streets. The grateful citizens crowded around with offers of blankets, food, bedding, medicines, Soon blankets covered the temple floor in neat and even rows. The surgeon plied his tools. Raistlin and Horkin and skilled healers from the city worked among the men, doing what they could to ease their pain and make them comfortable.

No miracles of healing occurred in the temple. Some of the soldiers died, others lived, but it did seem to Horkin's mind that those who died were more at peace and that the wounded who survived healed much more rapidly and completely than could have been expected.

The first order of business for the baron was to visit the wounded. He came as he was, fresh from the battlefield—grimy, bloody, some of the blood his own, most of it his enemy's. Though he was near to falling with exhaustion, he did not show it. He did not rush his visit, but took time to say a few words to each one of the casualties. He called all the soldiers by name, recalled his courage in the field. He seemed to have personally witnessed each valorous act. He promised the dying he would support their families. Raistlin would afterward learn that this was a vow the baron held sacred.

His visit to the wounded concluded, the baron paused to chat with Horkin and Raistlin about the temple they had discovered. The baron was intrigued to hear that a tomb of a Solamnic Knight lay in a burial chamber beneath the cavern. Raistlin described most of their experience in detail, keeping to himself certain facts that were really no one else's business. The baron listened attentively, frowned when he heard that the lid of the Knight's sarcophagus had been opened.

"That must be attended to," he said. "Robbers may have already tried to loot the tomb. This gallant Knight should be allowed to continue his slumber in peace. You have no notion of what this treasure is, do you, Majere?"

"The inscription made no mention of it, sir," Raistlin answered. "My guess is that whatever it was, it now lies beneath tons of rock. The tunnel that leads out from the burial chamber is completely impassable."

"I see." The baron eyed Raistlin closely.

Raistlin returned the baron's gaze steadily and it was the baron who shifted his eyes away from the stare of the strange hourglass pupils. Continuing his rounds of the wounded, the baron came to the cot where Caramon fretted and fidgeted, an extremely uncooperative patient. He wasn't hurt, he maintained. Nothing wrong with him. He wanted to be up and around and doing. He wanted a proper meal, not some water they'd dragged a chicken through and called it soup. His vision was fine, or rather it would be if they'd just take off this confounded rag. Scrounger remained with the patient, trying to distract him with stories and reminding him twenty times a half-hour not to rub his eyes.

Though busy with his other patients, Raistlin kept watch on the baron's movements through the temple and when the baron came to his twin, Raistlin hastened over to be present during this conversation.

"Caramon Majere!" the baron said, shaking his hand. "What happened to you? I don't recall seeing you in the battle."

"Baron?" Caramon brightened. "Hullo, sir! I'm sorry I missed the fighting. I heard it was a glorious victory. I was here, sir. We—"

Raistlin laid a hand on his brother's shoulder and, when the baron wasn't looking, gave Caramon a hard pinch with his fingers.

"Ouch!" Caramon yelped. "What—"

"There, there," said Raistlin soothingly, adding in an undertone, "He has these momentary flashes of pain, my lord. As for what happened to him, he was with me, exploring the temple. We were caught in the tunnels when the quake hit. Rock dust flew in Caramon's eyes, blinding him. The blindness is temporary. He needs rest, that is all."

Raistlin's fingers, digging into Caramon's flesh, warned him to keep silent. A piercing glance at Scrounger caused the half-kender, who had opened his mouth, to shut it again.

"Excellent! Glad to hear it!" the baron said heartily. "You're a good soldier, Majere. I'd hate to lose you."

"Really, sir?" Caramon asked. "Thank you, sir."

"You rest like they tell you," the baron added. "You're under the healer's orders now. I want you back on the line as soon as you're fit."

"I will, sir. Thank you, sir," Caramon said again, smiling proudly. "Raist," he whispered, when he heard the baron's heavy boots move away, "why didn't you tell him what really happened? Why didn't you tell him you fought the enemy wizard and beat him?"

"Yes, why?" Scrounger asked eagerly, leaning across Caramon.

The answer: because it was in Raistlin's nature to be secretive, because he didn't want Horkin asking prying questions, because he didn't want Horkin or anyone else finding out about the amazing power of the staff, a power Raistlin had no idea how to use himself at the moment. All these reasons he could have given his brother and the half-kender, but he knew they wouldn't understand.

Sitting down by his brother's side, Raistlin motioned Scrounger to come close. "We didn't exactly cover ourselves in glory," Raistlin told them dryly. "Our orders were to inspect the temple and return to report. Instead, we were about to set off in search of treasure."

"That's true," said Caramon, his face flushing.

"You wouldn't want the baron to be disappointed in you," Raistlin continued.

"No, of course not," Caramon said.

"Me neither," Scrounger said, chagrined.

"Then we will keep the truth to ourselves. We hurt no one by doing so." Raistlin rose to his feet, prepared to return to his duties.

Scrounger plucked the sleeve of Raistlin's robe.

"Yes, what do you want?" Raistlin glowered.

"What's the real reason you don't want us to tell?" Scrounger asked in an undertone.

Raistlin made a show of glancing about to see if anyone was listening. He bent down, whispered in Scrounger's ear. "The treasure."

Scrounger's eyes opened wide. "I knew it! We're going back for it!"

"Someday, perhaps," Raistlin said softly. "Don't tell a soul!"

"I won't! I promise! This is so exciting," Scrounger said and winked several times in a manner calculated to arouse instant suspicion in anyone who happened to be watching.

Raistlin went about his duties, satisfied that his brother would keep silent out of shame and that Scrounger would keep silent out of hope. Raistlin would have never trusted a true kender with this secret, but in Scrounger's case, the mage guessed that the human side would see to it that the kender side kept its mouth shut.

Someday, Raistlin did intend to return. Perhaps the treasure was buried. Perhaps it was not.

"If I could find out what the treasure was," Raistlin said to himself, deftly wrapping a bandage around a soldier's lacerated leg, "I might have some idea of where to start looking for it."

He spoke with several of the city's inhabitants, asked subtle questions concerning the possibility of a treasure buried in the mountains.

The residents smiled, shook their heads, and said that he must have been taken in by some traveling peddler. Hope's End was a prosperous town, but certainly not a wealthy one. They knew of no treasure.

Raistlin could almost believe that the people of Hope's End were conspiring to keep the treasure from him, except that they were so damn complacent about it, so smiling in their denials, so amused by the entire notion. He began to think that perhaps they were right, that this was all a kender tale.

He went to his bed that night in an extremely bad mood, a mood not helped by the fact that he was troubled by fearful dreams in which he was being attacked by some immense, awful creature, a creature he could not see because a bright silver light had struck him blind.

❂

The next day, the baron held a ceremony to clean the tomb of the fallen rocks and dust, replace the lid of the sarcophagus over the dead

Knight. The baron's commanders accompanied him and, because they had discovered the Knight's tomb, Raistlin and Caramon and Scrounger were invited to be part of the honor guard.

Caramon wanted to remove the bandage. He could see fine, he said, except for a little blurriness. Raistlin was adamant. The bandage must stay. Caramon would have continued the argument, but the baron himself offered Caramon an arm in support, a great honor for the young soldier. Flushed with pleasure and embarrassment, Caramon accepted the baron's guidance, walked proudly if haltingly at the baron's side.

The baron and the honor guard, carrying torches, entered the burial chamber with grave and solemn aspect, silent and respectful. The baron took his place at the head of the carved Knight. The company commanders ranged themselves around the tomb. They stood with hands clasped before them, heads bowed, some praying to Kiri-Jolith, others thinking somber thoughts, reflecting on their own mortality. Raistlin took his place at the head of the sarcophagus, keeping close to his brother. Glancing inside the tomb, Raistlin was momentarily paralyzed with astonishment.

Inside the tomb was a leather-bound book.

Raistlin thought back to yesterday, tried to recall if the book had been there or not. He didn't remember seeing it, but the chamber had been dark yesterday, with only his staff for light. The book was pressed against the side of the marble casket. He might have easily overlooked the book in the shadows.

The thought came to Raistlin that this book contained information about the treasure, perhaps revealed its hiding place. He trembled with desire. He needed that book and, even as he stood gazing at it, the baron had ceased his prayers, was ordering his commanders to prepare to slide the lid of the sarcophagus back in place.

"I beg one moment, sir," Raistlin said, his voice half-stifled by his excitement and his fear that someone else would see the book and announce the fact. "I would do honor to the Knight."

The baron raised his eyebrows, probably wondering why a wizard should honor a Solamnic Knight, but he nodded that Raistlin was to proceed.

Reaching into one of his pouches, Raistlin drew out a handful of rose petals. He opened his palm, so that all could see what he held. The baron smiled and nodded.

"Most appropriate," he said, and looked upon Raistlin with approval and new respect.

Raistlin lowered his hand into the tomb, to scatter the rose petals over the body of the Knight. When he withdrew his arm, he managed that the capacious sleeve of his red robe covered his hand, concealed his fingers, which had deftly taken hold of the slim leather volume. Keeping the precious book hidden in his sleeve, Raistlin stepped back from the tomb and stood with his head bowed.

The baron looked to Commander Morgon, who ordered the officers to place their hands on the tomb's covering. At a second command, the officers lifted the heavy lid. The baron came to attention, raised his hand in the Solamnic Knight's salute.

"Kiri-Jolith be with him," the baron said.

At another command from Morgon, the officers slid the marble top into place. The lid settled upon the sarcophagus with a soft sigh that bore with it the fragrance of dried rose petals.

22

RAISTLIN HAD HIS DUTIES TO ATTEND TO BEFORE HE COULD TAKE TIME to examine his prize. He secreted the book beneath Caramon's mattress, not telling him of it, returning at every opportunity to make certain the book was still there, had not been discovered. Caramon was touched to find his brother so unusually attentive.

Raistlin or Horkin usually sat up during the night with the patients, not keeping broad awake, like those on guard duty, but dozing in a chair, starting up at the sound of a moan of pain, assisting a patient to answer nature's call. That night, Raistlin volunteered to take the first watch. The weary Horkin didn't argue, but lay down on his own cot and was soon adding his snores to the cacophony of snores, grunts, groans, coughs, and wheezes of the rest.

Raistlin made his rounds, dispensing doses of poppy syrup to those who were in pain, bathing the foreheads of the feverish, adding more blankets to those who chilled. His touch was gentle and his voice held a sympathy in which the wounded could believe. Not like the sympathy of the healthy, the robust, however well meaning.

"I know what it is to suffer," Raistlin seemed to say. "I know what it is to feel pain."

His fellow soldiers, who had never had much use for him, who had called him names behind his back and occasionally to his face (if his brother weren't around), now begged him to stay by their beds "just a moment more," gripped his arm when the pain was the worst, asked him to write letters to wives and loved ones. Raistlin would sit and he would write and he would tell stories to take their minds off their pain. After they were healed, those who had never liked him before he nursed them found that they didn't like him any better afterward, the difference being that now they would knock the head off anyone who said a bad word against him.

When the last patient had finally succumbed to the poppy juice and drifted off to sleep, Raistlin was free to examine his book. He slid it out from its hiding place carefully, although he did not particularly fear waking Caramon, who generally slept the deep sleep ascribed to dogs and the virtuous. Book in hand, concealed in the folds of his sleeves, Raistlin cast a sharp glance at Horkin. The mage slept lightly when he had wounded to tend, the slightest moan or restless tossing would wake him. As it was, he did open one eye, peered sleepily at Raistlin.

"All is well, Master," Raistlin said softly. "Go back to sleep."

Horkin smiled, rolled over, and was soon snoring lustily. Raistlin watched his superior a moment longer, determined at last that the man must be asleep. No one could fake such obstreperous snores, not without half-strangling himself.

Horkin had built a fire in a brazier placed at the front of the temple where an altar might be found. He had not done so out of reverence, although he had taken care to be extremely respectful, but to warm the building against the night's chill. Raistlin drew his chair close to the brazier of charcoal, which burned with a yellow-blue light. He'd added some sage and dried lavender to the fire to try to mask the smell of blood, urine, and vomit that was all-pervasive in the sick chamber, a smell he himself no longer noticed. Settling by the blaze, he cast a sharp look around the room. Everyone was asleep.

Raistlin breathed in a deep sigh, leaned the Staff of Magius against the wall, and examined his prize.

The book was made of sheets of parchment bound and stitched together. A leather cover shielded it from the elements. He found no markings on the outside, it was unlike a spellbook in that regard. It was an ordinary book of the type used by the quartermaster to mark down how many barrels of ale were drunk, how many casks of salt pork were left, how many baskets of apples he had remaining. Raistlin frowned, this was not a propitious omen.

His spirits improved immensely when he opened the book to find a hand-drawn map on one page and some scrawled letters and numbers on another. This looked much more promising. He glanced hurriedly at the numerals, saw only that they were probably keeping count of something. Jewels? Money? Almost certainly. Now he was getting somewhere! He left the notation, went back to the map.

The map had been drawn in haste, with the book resting on an uneven surface—as if the mapper had steadied it on a rock or perhaps his knee. Raistlin spent several moments puzzling out the crude drawings and the even cruder notations. At last he determined that he held in his hands a map showing a path that led to a hidden entrance into a mountain.

Raistlin pored over the map, studying every detail, and came at last to the unwanted and frustrated conclusion that the map was worthless to him. The mapper had drawn a clear trail that would be easy to follow once one found the trail's starting point. The mapper had marked the trail's starting point—a stand of three pines—but had not given any indication of where these pines might be found in relation to the mountain. Were they on the north, the south? Were they halfway up the mountainside, in the foothills?

One could presumably search the entire mountain for a stand of three pine trees, but that might take a lifetime. The mapper knew where to find the stand of pines. The mapper could return to the stand without difficulty, therefore the mapper had seen no need to add the route to the stands. A wise precaution in case the map fell into the wrong hands. The map was intended to refresh the mapper's memory when he came to claim the treasure.

Raistlin stared at the map gloomily, willing it to tell him something more, stared at it until the red lines began to swim in his vision. Irritably he flipped the page, returned to the notations, hoping that perhaps they would provide some clue.

He studied them, intrigued, baffled, so intent upon his work that he did not hear footsteps approaching. He did not know someone was standing behind him until the person's shadow fell across the book.

Raistlin started, covered the book with the sleeve of his robe, and sprang to his feet.

Caramon backed up a step, raised his hands as if to ward off a blow. "Uh, sorry, Raist! I didn't mean to startle you."

"What are you doing sneaking up on me like that!" Raistlin demanded.

"I thought you might be asleep," Caramon replied meekly. "I didn't want to wake you."

"I wasn't asleep," Raistlin retorted. He sat back down, calmed his racing heart, half dizzy with the sudden rush of blood and adrenaline.

"You're studying your spells. I'll leave you alone." Caramon started to tiptoe away.

"No, wait," Raistlin said. "Come here. I want you to look at something. By the way, who told you you could take off the bandage?"

"No one. But I can see fine, Raist. Even the blurriness is gone. And I'm sick of broth. That's all they feed a guy around here. There's nothing wrong with my stomach."

"That much is obvious," Raistlin said with a disparaging glance at his twin's rotund belly.

Caramon sat down on the floor beside his brother. "What have you got there?" he asked, eyeing the book with suspicion. He knew from sad experience that books his brother read were likely to be incomprehensible at best, downright dangerous at worst.

"I found this book in the Knight's tomb today," Raistlin said in a smothered whisper.

Caramon's eyes widened, rounded. "You took it? From a tomb?"

"Don't look at me like that, Caramon," Raistlin snapped. "I am not a grave robber! I think it was placed there on purpose. For me to find."

"The Knight wanted us to have it," Caramon said in excitement. "It's about the treasure, isn't it! He wants us to find it—"

"If he does, he's making it damn difficult," Raistlin remarked coldly. "Here, I want you to look at this word. Tell me what it says."

Raistlin opened the book to the page of notations. Caramon looked obediently at the word. There wasn't much doubt.

"Eggs," he said promptly.

"Are you certain?" Raistlin persisted.

"*E-g-g-s.* Eggs. Yep, I'm sure."

Raistlin sighed deeply.

Caramon gazed at him in sudden, stunned comprehension. "You're not saying that the treasure is . . . is . . ."

"I don't know what the treasure is," Raistlin said gloomily. "Nor, I'm thinking, did the person who wrote this down in the book. It appears that the Knight has given us his grocery list!"

"Let me see that!" Caramon took the book from his twin, stared at it, pondered it, even tried turning it upside down. "These figures—where it says, '25 g. and 50 s.' That could be twenty-five gold and fifty silver," he argued hopefully.

"Or twenty-five grapes and fifty sausages," Raistlin returned sarcastically.

"But there's a map—"

"—which is completely useless. Even if we knew where to find the starting point, which we don't, the trail leads into tunnels in the mountain, tunnels we saw collapse."

He held out his hand for the book.

Caramon was still staring at it. "You know, Raist, this handwriting looks familiar."

Raistlin snorted. "Give me back the book."

"It does, Raist! I swear!" Caramon's brow furrowed, an aid to his mental process. "I've seen this writing before."

"And you said your eyesight was improved. Go back to bed. And put that bandage on."

"But, Raist—"

"Go to bed, Caramon," Raistlin ordered irritably. "I'm tired and my head aches. I'll wake you in time to breakfast in the mess tent."

"Will you? That'll be great, Raist, thanks." Caramon cast one last lingering and puzzled glance at the book, then handed it back to his brother. His twin knew best, after all.

Raistlin made his rounds. Finding that everyone was slumbering more or less peacefully, he left to use the privies that were located in a small outbuilding behind the temple. On his return, he tossed the leather book onto the rubbish heap, set for tomorrow's burning.

Entering the temple, Raistlin found Horkin wide awake, warming his hands by the glowing fire. The elder mage's eyes were bright, quizzical in the firelight.

"You know, Red," Horkin said companionably, rubbing his hands in the comfortable warmth, "that red-robed wizard you talked about wasn't in the battle. I know because I was on the watch for him. A powerful war wizard, from what you said. He might have made a difference in that fight. We might not have won if he'd been there, and that's a fact. Strange, that Commander Kholos had a powerful war wizard on his side and didn't use him in the final conflict. Very strange, that, Red."

Horkin shook his head. He shifted his eyes from the blaze to look directly at Raistlin. "You wouldn't happen to know why that wizard wasn't there, would you, Red?"

He wasn't there because I was fighting him, Raistlin could have said with blushing modesty. I defeated him. I don't consider myself a hero. But if you insist on presenting me with that medal . . .

The Staff of Magius stood against the altar. Raistlin reached out his hand to touch the staff, to feel the life inside the wood, magical life, warm and responsive to him now.

"I have no idea what could have happened to the wizard, Master Horkin," Raistlin said.

"You weren't in the battle, Red," said Horkin. "And that wizard wasn't in the battle. Seems odd, that it does."

"A coincidence, nothing more, sir," Raistlin replied.

"Humpf." Horkin shook his head. Shrugging away his questions, he changed the subject. "Well, Red, you survived your first battle and I don't mind telling you that you handled yourself well. For one, you didn't get yourself killed, and that's a plus. For two, you kept me from getting myself killed, and that's a bigger plus. You're a skilled healer, and who knows but that someday, with the proper training, you'll be a skilled mage."

Horkin winked and Raistlin wisely chose not to be offended.

"Thank you, sir," he said, with a smile. "Your praise means a great deal to me."

"You deserve it, Red. What I guess I'm saying in my clumsy way is that I'm going to put you up for promotion. I'm going to recommend that you be made Master's Assistant. With an increase in pay, of course. That is, if you intend to stick with us."

Promotion! Raistlin was amazed. Horkin rarely had a good word to say to him. Raistlin would not have been surprised to have been paid off and dismissed. He was beginning to understand his superior officer a bit better now, however. Quick to tell him what he was doing wrong, Horkin would never praise him for doing right. But he wouldn't forget what Raistlin had done either.

"Thank you for your faith in me, Master," Raistlin said. "I was thinking of leaving the army. I have been thinking lately that it is wrong for one man to be paid for killing another, for taking another's life."

"We did some good here, Red," Horkin said. "We saved the people in this city from slavery and death. We were on the side of right."

"But we started out on the side of wrong," Raistlin countered.

"We switched to the correct side in time, though," Horkin said comfortably.

"By chance, by happenstance!" Raistlin shook his head.

"Nothing ever happens by chance, Raistlin," Horkin said quietly. "Everything happens for a reason. Your brain may not know the reason. Your brain may never figure it out. But your heart knows. Your heart always knows.

"Now," he added kindly, "go get some sleep."

Raistlin went to his bed, but not to sleep. He thought about Horkin's words, thought about all that had happened to him. And then it occurred to him, hearing Horkin's words again in his head, that the mage had called him by name. Raistlin. Not Red.

Rising from his bed, Raistlin walked back outside. Solinari was full and bright, shining on the town as if he were pleased with the outcome. Raistlin searched the rubbish heap in the moonlight, found the book lying where he had tossed it.

"*Everything happens for a reason,*" Raistlin repeated, opening the book. He looked at the worthless map, its red lines stark and clear in the silver moonlight. *Perhaps I'll never know what that reason is. But if I can make nothing out of this book, maybe others can.*

Returning to his bed, he did not lie down, but sat up the rest of the night, writing a letter detailing his encounters—both encounters—with Immolatus. When the missive was complete, he folded the letter over the small book, recited an incantation over both book and letter, and wrapped it up in a parcel addressed to *Par-Salian, Head of the Conclave, Tower of High Sorcery, Wayreth.*

The next morning, he would ask if the baron had any messengers riding in the direction of Flotsam. He placed another spell upon the package, to keep it safe from prying eyes, then wrote on the outside, "Antimodes of Flotsam" along with the name of the street where his mentor resided. By the time Raistlin was finished, night had departed. The sun's rays crept softly into the temple to gently waken the sleeping.

Caramon was the first one up.

"Come with me, Raist," he said. "You should eat something."

Raistlin was surprised to find that he was hungry, unusually hungry. He and his twin left the temple, were on their way to the mess tent, when they were joined by Horkin.

"You don't mind if I tag along, do you, Red?" Horkin asked. "The wounded are getting along so well I figured I'd have a proper breakfast this morning myself. I hear cook's preparing a special treat. Besides, we have something to celebrate. Your brother's been promoted, Majere."

"Have you? That's great!" Caramon paused, the implication of this suddenly occurring to him. "Does this mean that we're staying with the baron's army?"

"We're staying," Raistlin said.

"Hurrah!" Caramon gave a shout that woke up half the town. "There goes Scrounger. Wait till he hears. Scrounger!" Caramon bellowed, waking the other half of the town. "Scrounger, hey! Come here!"

Scrounger was pleased to hear of Raistlin's promotion, especially pleased when he heard this meant that the twins would be staying with the army.

"What *are* we having for breakfast?" Caramon asked. "You said it was special, sir?"

"A gift from the grateful people of Hope's End," said Horkin, adding, with a suspicious quiver in his voice, "a real treasure, you might say."

"What do you mean, sir?" Raistlin asked, casting the mage a sharp glance.

"Eggs," said Horkin with a grin and a wink.

23

FOR YOU, ARCHMAGUS," SAID AN APPRENTICE, STANDING DEFERENTIALLY in the door leading to Par-Salian's study. "Just arrived by messenger from Flotsam." He placed a parcel on the table and departed with a bow.

Par-Salian picked up the parcel, studied it curiously. It was addressed to Antimodes, he had apparently forwarded it on. Par-Salian examined the handwriting on the address: quick, eager, impatient strokes, overlarge capital letters—flaunting creativity, a nervous curl to the tail of an *s*. A leftward slant and sharpness to the letters that was like a line of a lance. An image formed in his mind of the writer and he was not surprised to find, on opening the letter inside, that it had been written by young Raistlin Majere.

Par-Salian sat down and read with interest, astonishment, and wonder the forthright, bald, and unimpassioned account of the meetings between Raistlin and a wizard described as a renegade, a wizard who called himself Immolatus.

Immolatus. The name was familiar. Par-Salian finished his perusal of the missive, read it over twice more, then turned his attention to the small leather-bound book. He understood its secrets immediately. Not surprising. The mages who resided in the Tower often saw Par-Salian standing in the window, bathed in silver moonlight, his lips moving in a one-sided conversation. All knew he communed directly with Solinari.

Par-Salian's heart lurched, his hands chilled and trembled as he realized the terrible danger, the awful tragedy that had very nearly occurred, a tragedy they had escaped through the valor of a dead Knight, the inadvertent courage of a young wizard, and the long-nurtured vengeance of a stick of wood.

Par-Salian believed, as did Horkin and with perhaps better cause, that everything happens for a reason. Still, he found this account amazing, astounding, terrifying.

There was no doubt in his mind that whoever had ordered that attack on the city of Hope's End had known about the treasure beneath the mountain, had chosen that city to attack in order to win the treasure. But for what reason, what dark purpose, Par-Salian could not guess. Destruction of the eggs was the most likely, but there were arguments against that. Why go to the trouble to attack and take a walled city with an army when a few hardened men with pickaxes could do the job just as well?

A month had passed since young Majere had written this letter and it had reached Wayreth. In that time, word had come to Par-Salian that the king of Blödehelm, King Wilhelm, had been discovered in his own dungeon, having been made prisoner by strange and sinister people, who had run the business of the kingdom in his name. Par-Salian heard the story of how these same people had fled on the arrival of Baron Ivor of Langtree and his army, who marched into Vantal and laid siege to the castle. It was the baron himself who had freed the unfortunate king. Par-Salian had not given much thought to the story then. Now he viewed it with alarm.

Forces were at work in the world, dark forces. They had no face yet, but he could give them a name. Which reminded him. Immolatus. That name was undoubtedly familiar. Opening a secret compartment in a secret drawer, he drew forth the book he had been reading when Raistlin Majere left these very walls.

When Par-Salian read a book, he did not simply remember the gist of its contents, he remembered each and every page, the written text lithographed onto the stone tablet of his mind. He had only to turn through the pages of a thousand, thousand texts cataloged in his brain until he found the one he wanted. He turned immediately to the page he recalled and there it was.

The lists of the enemy arrayed against Huma were formidable, comprised of Her Dark Majesty's strongest, most powerful, cruel, and terrible dragons. Included in their ranks were Thunderstrike the Great Blue, Werewrym the Black, Icekill the White, and Her Majesty's favorite, the red known as Immolatus. . . . "

"Immolatus," said Par-Salian and he sighed and shuddered. "So it has started. Thus we begin the long journey into darkness."

He looked back at the letter written in that quick, nervous, bold, and hungry hand, signed at the bottom:

Raistlin Majere, Magus.

Par-Salian picked up the letter. Speaking a word of magic, he caused it to be consumed by fire.

"At least," he said, "we do not walk alone."

DUNGEONS & DRAGONS®

FROM THE RUINS OF FALLEN EMPIRES, A NEW AGE OF HEROES ARISES

It is a time of magic and monsters, a time when the world struggles against a rising tide of shadow. Only a few scattered points of light glow with stubborn determination in the deepening darkness.

It is a time where everything is new in an ancient and mysterious world.

BE THERE AS THE FIRST ADVENTURES UNFOLD.

THE MARK OF NERATH
Bill Slavicsek
August 2010

THE SEAL OF KARGA KUL
Alex Irvine
December 2010

The first two novels in a new line set in the evolving world of the DUNGEONS & DRAGONS® game setting. If you haven't played . . . or read D&D® in a while, your reintroduction starts in August!

ALSO AVAILABLE AS E-BOOKS!